THE COLLECTE
OSCAR WILDE

ARNES
NOBLE
LASSICS

Introduction and Notes by Angus Fletcher

oughs Adam Smith John Adams Voltaire Booker T. Washington Sinclair Lewis L. Frank Baum Jane Austen H. G. Wells Jules Verne James Joyce Wilhe

More Thomas Hardy Henry James Sir Arthur Conan Doyle Theodore Dreiser Owen Wister Virgil Joseph Conrad Karl Marx Anne Brontë Dante

Washington Irving W. Somerset Maugham T. S. Eliot Thomas Jefferson O. Henry Nikolai Gogol Emily Brontë Barnes & Noble Classics Sophocles

James Weldon Johnson Bram Stoker Miguel de Cervantes Pierre Choderlos de Laclos Henry David Thoreau Giovanni Boccaccio John Bunyan Elizabeth G

Gaston Leroux Emily Dickinson Robert Louis Stevenson Niccolò Machiavelli Henrik Ibsen Hermann Hesse Geoffrey Chaucer Saint Augustine Sa

Swift Jacob Grimm Richard Henry Dana Friedrich Nietzsche Wilkie Collins Barnes & Noble Classics Alexander Hamilton Louisa May Alcott James

. M. Forster Guy de Maupassant Rafael Sabatini Edith Wharton Edith Nesbit Sir Walter Scott Hans Christian Andersen Ivan Turgenev Edgar Allan Poe

adison Harriet Jacobs Euripides Barnes & Noble Classics Benjamin Franklin Marcel Proust Sigmund Freud Aristotle William Makepeace Thackeray B

Melville Victor Hugo Thomas Bulfinch H. Rider Haggard George Bernard Shaw Sojourner Truth Henry Fielding William James John Jay Honoré

Dumas Barnes & Noble Classics Kenneth Grahame Ford Madox Ford Anthony Trollope Edmond Rostand George Eliot Ralph Waldo Emerson A.

rroll Barnes & Noble Classics Walt Whitman F. Scott Fitzgerald Herodotus Barnes & Noble Classics Plato Mark Twain William Dean Howe

Charles Darwin John Milton Frances Hodgson Burnett Baroness Orczy Robert Frost Homer Kate Chopin Émile Zola Fyodor Dostoevsky Nathan

efoe Jack London Upton Sinclair Charlotte Brontë Joshua Slocum Stephen Crane W. E. B. Du Bois Willa Cather Barnes & Noble Classics Oscar

D. H. Lawrence Thomas Paine Thucydides Franz Kafka Virginia Woolf J. M. Barrie Leo Tolstoy Lao Tzu Harriet Beecher Stowe Anton Chekhov

oughs Adam Smith John Adams Voltaire Booker T. Washington Sinclair Lewis L. Frank Baum Barnes & Noble Classics Jane Austen H. G. Wells Ju

helm Grimm Thomas More Thomas Hardy Henry James Sir Arthur Conan Doyle Theodore Dreiser Owen Wister Virgil Joseph Conrad Karl Marx

ghieri Rudyard Kipling Washington Irving W. Somerset Maugham T. S. Eliot Thomas Jefferson O. Henry Nikolai Gogol Barnes & Noble Classics E

Frederick Douglass James Weldon Johnson Bram Stoker Miguel de Cervantes Pierre Choderlos de Laclos Henry David Thoreau Giovanni Boccaccio John

Gaskell Gustave Flaubert Gaston Leroux Emily Dickinson Robert Louis Stevenson Niccolò Machiavelli Barnes & Noble Classics Henrik Ibsen Hern

& Noble Classics Geoffrey Chaucer Saint Augustine Sarah Orne Jewett Jonathan Swift Jacob Grimm Richard Henry Dana Friedrich Nietzsche

Hamilton Louisa May Alcott James Fenimore Cooper E. M. Forster Guy de Maupassant Rafael Sabatini Edith Wharton Edith Nesbit Sir Walter

Classics Hans Christian Andersen Ivan Turgenev Edgar Allan Poe Aesop James Madison Harriet Jacobs Euripides Benjamin Franklin Marcel Proust Sig

William Makepeace Thackeray Booth Tarkington Herman Melville Victor Hugo Thomas Bulfinch H. Rider Haggard George Bernard Shaw Sojourner Truth

Barnes & Noble Classics William James John Jay Honoré de Balzac Alexandre Dumas Kenneth Grahame Ford Madox Ford Anthony Trollope Edmon

liot Ralph Waldo Emerson A. E. W. Mason Lewis Carroll Barnes & Noble Classics Walt Whitman F. Scott Fitzgerald Herodotus Plato Ma

Dean Howells Barnes & Noble Classics Charles Dickens Charles Darwin John Milton Frances Hodgson Burnett Baroness Orczy Robert Frost Homer

la Fyodor Dostoevsky Nathaniel Hawthorne Barnes & Noble Classics Daniel Defoe Jack London Upton Sinclair Charlotte Brontë Joshua Slocum Ste

Bois Willa Cather Oscar Wilde Sun Tzu Stendhal D. H. Lawrence Thomas Paine Thucydides Franz Kafka Virginia Woolf J. M. Barrie Leo Tolstoy Lao

towe Anton Chekhov Ovid Edgar Rice Burroughs Adam Smith John Adams Voltaire Booker T. Washington Barnes & Noble Classics Sinclair

m Jane Austen H. G. Wells Barnes & Noble Classics Jules Verne James Joyce Wilhelm Grimm Thomas More Thomas Hardy Henry James Sir Arth

eodore Dreiser Owen Wister Virgil Joseph Conrad Karl Marx Anne Brontë Dante Alighieri Rudyard Kipling Washington Irving W. Somerset Maugham T. S

efferson O. Henry Nikolai Gogol Emily Brontë Sophocles Frederick Douglass James Weldon Johnson Bram Barnes & Noble Classics Stoker Miguel de

oderlos de Laclos Henry David Thoreau Giovanni Boccaccio John Bunyan Elizabeth Gaskell Gustave Flaubert Gaston Leroux Emily Dickinson Robert Loui

lachiavelli Henrik Ibsen Hermann Hesse Geoffrey Chaucer Saint Augustine Sarah Orne Jewett Jonathan Swift Jacob Grimm Richard Henry Dana

Wilkie Collins Alexander Hamilton Louisa May Alcott James Fenimore Cooper E. M. Forster Guy de Maupassant Rafael Sabatini Edith Wharton Edith N

ott Barnes & Noble Classics Hans Christian Andersen Ivan Turgenev Edgar Allan Poe Aesop James Madison Harriet Jacobs Euripides Benjamin Fran

From the Pages of

THE COLLECTED OSCAR WILDE

"What would you say about a young man who had a strange theory about a certain work of art, believed in his theory, and committed a forgery in order to prove it?"

(from *The Portrait of Mr. W. H.*, page 5)

Romance is the privilege of the rich, not the profession of the unemployed. The poor should be practical and prosaic. It is better to have a permanent income than to be fascinating. These are the great truths of modern life which Hughie Erskine never realised.

(from "The Model Millionaire," page 113)

Then, turning to my love, I said,
"The dead are dancing with the dead,
The dust is whirling with the dust."

(from "The Harlot's House," page 243)

Yet each man kills the thing he loves,
  By each let this be heard,
Some do it with a bitter look,
  Some with a flattering word.
The coward does it with a kiss,
  The brave man with a sword!

(from *The Ballad of Reading Gaol*, page 249)

All the cities that have beautiful names derive them from the Spanish or the French. The English people give intensely ugly names to places. One place had such an ugly name that I refused to lecture there. It was called Grigsville. Supposing I had founded a school of Art there—fancy "Early Grigsville." Imagine a School of Art teaching "Grigsville Renaissance."

(from "Impressions of America," pages 299–300)

"Where we differ from each other is purely in accidentals: in dress, manner, tone of voice, religious opinions, personal appearance, tricks of habit, and the like. The more one analyses people, the more all reasons for analysis disappear. Sooner or later one comes to that dreadful universal thing called human nature. Indeed, as any one who has ever worked among the poor knows only too well, the brotherhood of man is no mere poet's dream, it is a most depressing and humiliating reality."

(from "The Decay of Lying," page 368)

You have told me many strange things tonight, Gilbert. You have told me that it is more difficult to talk about a thing than to do it, and that to do nothing at all is the most difficult thing in the world; you have told me that all Art is immoral, and all thought dangerous; that criticism is more creative than creation, and that the highest criticism is that which reveals in the work of Art what the artist had not put there; that it is exactly because a man cannot do a thing that he is the proper judge of it; and that the true critic is unfair, insincere, not rational. My friend, you are a dreamer.

(from "The Critic as Artist, Part II," pages 462–463)

Disobedience, in the eyes of any one who has read history, is man's original virtue. It is through disobedience that progress has been made, through disobedience and through rebellion.

(from "The Soul of Man under Socialism," page 494)

To love oneself is the beginning of a life-long romance.

(from "Phrases and Philosophies for the Use of the Young," page 533)

I am sick to death of cleverness. Everybody is clever now-a-days. You can't go anywhere without meeting clever people. The thing has become an absolute public nuisance.

(from *The Importance of Being Earnest*, page 558)

In matters of grave importance, style, not sincerity, is the vital thing.

(from *The Importance of Being Earnest*, page 591)

THE COLLECTED
OSCAR WILDE

With an Introduction and Notes
by Angus Fletcher

George Stade
Consulting Editorial Director

Barnes & Noble Classics
New York

Barnes & Noble Classics
New York

Published by Barnes & Noble Books
122 Fifth Avenue
New York, NY 10011

www.barnesandnoble.com/classics

See Original Publication Information in the back of the book for original publication dates and venues.

Published in 2007 by Barnes & Noble Classics with new Introduction, Notes, Biography, Chronology, Original Publication Information, Inspired By, Comments & Questions, and For Further Reading.

The Collected Oscar Wilde
ISBN 978-1-59308-310-6
LC Control Number 2007925228

Produced and published in conjunction with:
Fine Creative Media, Inc.
322 Eighth Avenue
New York, NY 10001

Michael J. Fine, President and Publisher

Printed in the United States of America

QM

7 9 11 13 15 17 16 14 12 10 8 6

OSCAR WILDE

Oscar Fingal O'Flahertie Wills Wilde was born on October 16, 1854, to an intellectually prominent Dublin family. His father, Sir William Wilde, was a renowned physician who was knighted for his work as medical adviser to the 1841 and 1851 Irish censuses; his mother, Lady Jane Francesca Elgee, was a poet and journalist. Wilde showed himself to be an exceptional student. While at the Portora Royal School in Enniskillen, he took First Prize in classics. He continued his studies at Trinity College, Dublin, on scholarship, where he won high honors, including the Demyship Scholarship to Magdalen College, Oxford.

At Oxford, Wilde engaged in self-discovery, through both intellectual and personal pursuits. He fell under the influence of the Aesthetic philosophy of Walter Pater, a tutor and author who inspired Wilde to create art for the sake of art alone. It was during these years that Wilde developed a reputation as an eccentric and a foppish dresser who always had a flower in his lapel. Wilde won his first recognition as a writer when the university awarded him the Newdigate Prize for his poem "Ravenna" (1878).

Wilde went from Oxford to London, where he published his first volume of verse, *Poems*, in 1881. From 1882 to 1884, he toured the United States, Ireland, and England, giving a series of lectures on Aestheticism. In America, between speaking engagements, he met some of the great literary minds of the day, including Henry Wadsworth Longfellow, Oliver Wendell Holmes, and Walt Whitman. His first play, *Vera*, was staged in New York but did poorly. After his marriage to Constance Lloyd in 1884 and the birth of his two sons, Wilde began to make his way into the London theater, literary, and homosexual scenes. He published *Intentions*, a collection of dialogues on Aesthetic philosophy, in 1891, the year he met Lord Alfred

Douglas, who became his lover and his ultimate downfall. Wilde soon produced several successful plays, including *Lady Windermere's Fan* (1892) and *A Woman of No Importance* (1893).

Wilde's popularity was short-lived, however. In 1895, during the concurrent runs of his plays *An Ideal Husband* and *The Importance of Being Earnest*, he became the subject of a homosexual scandal that led him to withdraw all theater engagements and declare bankruptcy. Urged by many to flee the country rather than face a trial in which he would surely be found guilty, Wilde chose instead to remain in England. Arrested and found guilty of "homosexual offenses," Wilde was sentenced to two years' hard labor and began serving time in Wandsworth prison. He was later transferred to Reading Gaol, where he composed *De Profundis*, a dramatic monologue written as a letter to Lord Alfred Douglas that was published in 1905. Upon his release in 1897, Wilde retreated to the Continent, where he lived out the rest of his life under a pseudonym. He published his last work, *The Ballad of Reading Gaol*, in 1898 while living in exile.

During his lifetime, Wilde was most often the center of controversy. *The Picture of Dorian Gray*, which appeared as the lead story in *Lippincott's Monthly Magazine* on June 20, 1890, and was published in book form the next year, is considered to be Wilde's most personal work. Scrutinized by critics who questioned its morality, the novel portrays the author's internal battles and arrives at the disturbing possibility that "ugliness is the only reality." Oscar Wilde died penniless of cerebral meningitis in Paris on November 30, 1900. He is buried in Père Lachaise Cemetery, Paris.

TABLE OF CONTENTS

JOURNALISM

– On America –

– On Art –

– On Literature –

ESSAYS

APHORISMS

THE IMPORTANCE OF BEING EARNEST

THE WORLD OF OSCAR WILDE

1854 Oscar Fingal O'Flahertie Wills Wilde is born on October 16 in Dublin to William Wilde, a prominent ophthalmologist, and Jane Francesca Elgee, a renowned poet and journalist.

1864 Wilde enters the Portora Royal School in Enniskillen, where he excels, and subsequently takes First Prize in classics and Second Prize in drawing.

1867 On February 23 Wilde's sister, Isola, dies of a sudden fever. Profoundly affected by the death, Wilde keeps a lock of her hair until the end of his life.

1871 Wilde enrolls as a Royal School Scholar at Trinity College, Dublin, where he earns the Foundation Scholarship (the highest honor bestowed on an undergraduate) as well as the Berkeley Gold Medal for Greek and the Demyship Scholarship to Magdalen College, Oxford.

1874 As a student at Magdalen College, Wilde finds a mentor in Walter Pater, a tutor and writer whose works, along with those of the Pre-Raphaelites, inspire Wilde to subscribe to the Aesthetic movement, which promotes "art for art's sake." Wilde develops a reputation for his flamboyant mannerisms, including his dandyism and long hair.

1876 Wilde's father dies.

1878 Wilde wins the Newdigate Prize for his poem "Ravenna," as well as "First in Greats" by his examiners. Wilde's eldest brother, Henry Wilson, dies.

1879 Upon graduation, Wilde moves to London with Frank Miles, a friend and portrait painter, and begins his writing career.

1881 Wilde publishes his first volume of verse, *Poems*, which is well received by critics. He becomes the subject of the Gilbert and Sullivan comic operetta *Patience*, which satirizes the Aesthetic movement. He embarks upon a series of lectures in the United States; originally scheduled to last only four months, the tour is extended to fifty lectures and lasts nearly a year.

1882 Wilde meets Henry Wadsworth Longfellow, Oliver Wendell Holmes, Walt Whitman, and Henry James. He also arranges for his first play, *Vera*, to be staged in New York; it is a commercial flop.

1883 Wilde lectures throughout the United Kingdom.

1884 On May 29 Wilde marries Constance Lloyd, the heiress of a Dublin barrister. The couple resides in Chelsea, a London neighborhood popular with artists, writers, and intellectuals. Wilde writes his second play, *The Duchess of Padua*.

1885 Wilde's first son, Cyril, is born. The Criminal Law Amendment Act, under which Wilde would later be prosecuted for engaging in "gross indecency," is passed.

1886 Another son, Vyvyan, is born.

1887 Wilde accepts an editor's position with *Woman's World*, a popular magazine, where he remains for two years.

1888 A collection of fairy tales, *The Happy Prince and Other Tales*, is published.

1889 Wilde's story "The Portrait of Mr. W. H." appears in *Blackwood's Magazine*; it asserts that Shakespeare's sonnets have a homoerotic subtext. "The Decay of Lying," a dialogue on Aesthetics and other subjects, is published in *The Nineteenth Century*, a literary review.

1890 *The Picture of Dorian Gray* appears in *Lippincott's Monthly Magazine*, published in Philadelphia.

1891 The publication of *The Picture of Dorian Gray*, an extended version of the magazine piece and Wilde's only novel, arouses controversy over the work's morality but makes little money. Wilde also produces several works that reflect his varied interests: *Intentions*, a collection of dialogues on Wilde's Aesthetic philosophy, *Lord Arthur Savile's Crime and Other Stories*, a volume of short fiction, and *The House of Pomegranates*, a collection of short stories. He meets Lord Alfred Douglas, an undergraduate at Oxford, and they become lovers. Wilde also befriends André Gide, the French writer and spokesman for homosexual rights.

1892 In February the first of Wilde's domestic comedies, *Lady Windermere's Fan*, opens at the St. James's Theatre to accolades. The financial success enables him to continue writing plays, and he completes *Salomé*, a reinterpretation in French of John the Baptist's martyrdom; he is unable to produce the play because of a law prohibiting theatrical depictions of biblical characters.

1893 Wilde again enjoys theatrical success with his second domestic comedy, *A Woman of No Importance*. He becomes friendly with Max Beerbohm, a fledgling writer at Oxford who soon becomes Britain's foremost caricaturist; his first subject is Wilde.

1894 In Paris, Sarah Bernhardt gives a performance of *Salomé*. In April "A Defence of Cosmetics," Beerbohm's parody of Wildean Aestheticism, appears in *The Yellow Book*, an avant-garde literary journal.

1895 Wilde is immensely popular on the London theater circuit: *An Ideal Husband* is performed at the Haymarket Theatre, and *The Importance of Being Earnest* debuts at the St. James's. Wilde becomes involved in three trials: In the first he sues the Marquess of Queensberry, the father of his lover Lord Alfred Douglas, for libel after the Marquess refers to him in a note as a sodomite. The defense counsel denounces *Dorian Gray* as an immoral book, and enough evidence is presented to try Wilde for engaging in homosexual activity. After two trials he is sentenced to Wandsworth prison for two years' hard labor. Wilde's wife and sons relocate to Italy and adopt an old family name, Holland.

1897 Wilde is transferred from Wandsworth to Reading Gaol. While detained, he writes *De Profundis*, a dramatic monologue and biography addressed to Alfred Douglas that will be published in part in 1905. Upon his release from prison, Wilde goes into exile to the Continent, where he lives under the alias Sebastian Melmoth.

1898 *The Ballad of Reading Gaol*, Wilde's final work, is published. Wilde also publishes two letters on prison reform. Constance dies. Wilde briefly reunites with Douglas but spends most of his time traveling throughout Europe, occasionally writing for Parisian journals.

1900 Wilde is said to convert to Roman Catholicism on his deathbed, after a lifelong flirtation with the religion. He dies of cerebral meningitis at the Hotel D'Alsace in Paris on November 30. He is buried at Père Lachaise Cemetery, Paris.

1905 Wilde's play *Salomé* inspires German composer Richard Strauss to write a one-act opera of the same name.

INTRODUCTION

The life of Oscar Wilde is a parable of creative genius, unsung generosity, lonely pride, triumphant success, uneven fame, obsessive addiction, and ultimate personal catastrophe. Yet beneath the glamorous celebrity heralded by one romantic Irish name—born in Dublin on October 16, 1854, he was christened Oscar Fingal O'Flahertie Wills Wilde—there resides a deeper secret: how, within one mind and one tall, massive, almost elephantine body, there might be exercised the most remarkable powers of social perception and expressive skill.

The public always simplified Wilde the man, reducing his character to costume and his manner to the extravagant public gestures of a dandy, but inwardly and dominantly his life was intellectually subtle—at the depth of his downfall and his degrading imprisonment for homosexual offenses the Warden of Reading Gaol called him "all brains." At heart this most entertaining master of one-liner paradoxes burned with a luminous instinct for contradiction, much as another, later Irish author, Samuel Beckett, would chase humorous absurdities in order to unweave the mysterious ligatures of soul and body, much as earlier poets like Shakespeare attempted pictures of the "marriage of true minds," or as another Elizabethan poet, the dazzling John Donne, wrote that life demands a probing soul-search, "else a great prince in prison lies."

It was no accident that Oscar Wilde was the martyr of wit and wit's excess. His delight in the contradictions of human existence inevitably threatened unreflecting Victorian custom, as he unmasked the righteous appearances of piety. Good poetry is usually at war with the conformist, while the poet's vocation becomes even more hazardous when wit and charm attempt examination of façade and at last the amusing author is blamed for his skepticism. Society hates to see its contradictions exposed.

When young Cecil Graham in *Lady Windermere's Fan* (1892) wonders aloud what the definition of a cynic might be, Lord Darlington replies with a joke that has entered the language: "A man who knows the price of everything and the value of nothing." This war between cynical pricing and thoughtful evaluation, between calculating numbered surface and immeasurable depth, resonates throughout Wilde's plays, stories, poems, maxims, and essays. Immediately following Lord Darlington's aphorism, Cecil adds that even cynicism has its opposite, namely sentimentality. With Faustian intensity, the charm of such clever talk turns into a search for deeper meanings, and in Cecil's case, price and value are contrasted, to show that neither term is significant unless it is analyzed into its depth, into its psychology, into its social function as virtually a piece of secular religion. Victorian hypocrisy may be an ethical issue, as Lytton Strachey suggested throughout his *Eminent Victorians* (1918), but it could be so only if tested by irony, a modern irony dedicated to exposing the typical marriage of sentimentality and cynicism. With such a complex modern society to deal with, it would be the work of a lifetime, however short, to produce a relevant, penetrating critique.

For Wilde, the quest of his own critique, finding beauty amidst dross, finding truth amidst lies, yields a drama that may conveniently be divided into five acts.

Act I is the story of a rich, classical schooling in Dublin and Oxford, where Wilde wins the notable Newdigate Prize for his poem "Ravenna" (1878). Already he has visited Italy and Greece, traveling with his Dublin tutor, the Rev. Dr. John P. Mahaffy. From his father Wilde learned habits of hard intellectual work. From his mother he acquired higher, more dangerous gifts. Lady Jane Francesca Wilde—she called herself "Speranza" (or Hope) when she published—enjoyed star billing in Dublin cultural circles. Her weekly salon was attended by the most distinguished intellectual and artistic company, and given that her husband was writing important scientific treatises besides endowing a clinic for medical research, we are not surprised that they had sent their younger son, Oscar, to the well-established Portora Royal School, where his linguistic skill was matched by his prize-winning work in art and drawing. Between

1871 and 1874 he attended Trinity College in Dublin, winning highest honors for Greek and a scholarship to Oxford. The consequence of this increasing literary recognition was an effective advancement, since later in 1874 he matriculated at Magdalen College, Oxford, where his knowledge of ancient literature could flower in full. Soon he joined forces with other young collegians whose creed was fashionable Aestheticism, a philosophy of life judged by the standards of harmony, beauty, and sensitive artistic taste developed to the highest degree. Aestheticism could lead in different directions, but for a poet it meant that literary achievement was to be valued for its formal skill, chiefly by undermining the usual preachments of Polonius—that is, by resisting standard middle-class values, which young men could interpret as repressive, middle-aged Puritanism.

The slogan "Art for Art's Sake" opposes aesthetic values—the esteem of artistic creations, for example—to all kinds of political correctness. Primarily Wilde and his fellow aesthetes aspired to an ethical philosophy based on sensitive perceptions. At Oxford, rhetorical prowess was also prized, verbal virtuosity appearing a magical gift. The tall, powerfully built, elegantly attired, six foot three Oscar Wilde was by all accounts his college's most dazzling student of classical Latin and Greek, from which all later Western thought and literature derive. In the first act of his drama Wilde was getting ready to launch forth into all the favored literary forms of his day: novel, short story, lyric poetry, critical journalism, cultural essay, and play—especially the comedy of manners. Graduating with highest honors, Wilde was poised to move very fast into the limelight.

Act II traces the fortunes of a rapidly rising literary and cultural presence, including the publication of Wilde's *Poems* (1881), a notorious lecture tour in America and Canada, and the composition of two plays, one of which, *Vera; or, The Nihilists* (1882), while unsuccessful on the American stage, indicates Wilde's not always overt political concerns. Later he will be the author of a long essay, "The Soul of Man under Socialism" (1891).

Act III begins in 1884 with the poet's marriage to Constance Lloyd, their settling into a house in London—on Tite Street in Chelsea—followed soon by the birth of two boys, Cyril and Vyvyan.

During the next five years Wilde divides his time between journalism, writing on cultural happenings, and writing short fiction; he publishes *The Happy Prince and Other Tales* in 1888. Journalism pays the bills for the family and prepares Wilde for his remarkable next five years of literary production.

Act IV begins with a unique set of essays in critical theory, written as dialogues, including "The Decay of Lying" (1889), "The Critic as Artist" (1890), and "The Truth of Masks" (1891). In 1891 *The Duchess of Padua* is produced on the New York stage under the title *Guido Ferranti*; two books of short stories appear: *Lord Arthur Savile's Crime and Other Stories* and *A House of Pomegranates*; he publishes a revised and expanded version of the scandalous *Picture of Dorian Gray*, first published a year earlier in *Lippincott's Monthly Magazine*; and he begins work on his drama of morbid aestheticism, *Salomé*, initially writing its script in French. Also in 1891 another very different event occurs, one that will shape the whole of the poet's remaining life: He meets a fatal friend, the superficially refined, primping, poetizing doll Lord Alfred Douglas. By 1895 he has created and produced four new plays, works of such ironic perfection and verve that they remain in the repertory to this day.

Act V comprises the last five years of his life. In 1895 he scores simultaneous hits on the London stage with *An Ideal Husband* and *The Importance of Being Earnest* (this intellectual farce was chosen to replace Henry James's memorable fiasco *Guy Domville*). But in April 1895 Wilde makes a tragic error. He sues the Marquess of Queensberry—the insanely belligerent father of Lord Alfred Douglas—for libelous allegations that he is a sodomite. Queensberry had left a calling card at Wilde's club, scribbled on it the words "To Oscar Wilde posing Somdomite" (his Lordship was a poor speller). But, although few could see it, perhaps not even the poet himself, what enrages and maddens Queensberry is the thought that Wilde could succeed in life by "posing"—pose and posing are the crux. For Wilde has already shown that by attacking the pose, like a scoundrel finally adopting the shield of patriotism, Queensberry is confessing himself the worst sort of poseur, the hypocritical proponent of the plain truth. Wilde grasps the social importance of a principle later enunciated by a famed Hollywood producer—that sincerity is the main trick for the actor: "Once you learn how to fake sincerity, you've got it made!" The real poser's game is to attack a man who has deliberately, even humorously, adopted the art of the aesthetic stance. Of course, that is a game full of hazard. Wilde wants to expose his enemy's perverse, shallow vulgarity, but foolishly he also fails to heed the counsel of his closest friends: do not get tangled up in a law case against Douglas's father. Rhetorical power, unfortunately, is not always its own best judge. Rhetorically perhaps, Wilde "wins" a first trial, accusing Queensberry of slanderous libel, but after a second and third trial, society takes its revenge, and he is convicted of "gross indecency" and sentenced to two years of hard labor in prison. He is declared bankrupt by the end of the year, and his belongings are sold off and dispersed. In the following year Wilde's mother dies.

Probably the worst prison to which Wilde was committed was the ruinous Pentonville, where all sewer pipes and latrines had simply been removed, to keep prisoners from tapping messages. This improvement left only a tin pot each prisoner could empty three times by day, or forcibly leave unemptied during the night, with excrement running out over the floor. Wilde, who had always been a strong if not always healthy man, suffered dangerously untreated diarrhea. Like other prisoners condemned to hard manual labor, he passed his days outdoors in all weathers, pulling oakum tar from the twists of old ropes. He lived in virtual isolation. Until 1896, by which time he was in Reading Gaol, he was denied books for reading and paper for writing, and he suffered an atmosphere of callous indifference difficult to describe with appropriate force. None of this treatment would differ from that of other common prisoners, but the poet was not exactly accustomed to a workingman's life or a soldier's.

Commenting on his own not unrelated imprisonment for pacifist resistance, the philosopher Bertrand Russell later said that during his jail sentence he had the time, means, and leisure to read and to write one whole book on mathematics and to begin another book, on the nature of mind. But Russell, later Lord Russell, was a member of the highest aristocracy, and he was permitted to do his time in a "level one" institution. He comments: "For anybody not in the first division, especially for a person accustomed to reading and writing, prison is a severe and terrible punishment."

Another torture ensued: Wilde began to see the folly of his own infatuation: Lord Alfred Douglas began to seem to him a demon of superficial narcissism. True affection could only wither and turn to rage—understandably, since Lord Alfred had egged him on to an ultimately unnecessary fight with his mad father.

After his release from prison in 1897, Wilde went over to the Continent, where he said to a fellow artist, "the intense energy of creation has been kicked out of me." He could hardly be expected to invent major works, though he wrote letters to newspapers condemning the mistreatment of common prisoners. He increasingly fell into dissipation, drifting from one casual sexual or social encounter to another; he passed his afternoons and evenings drinking absinthe, cognac, or his favored liqueurs, green and yellow chartreuse. He could no longer work. He was chronically without money, which he would beg from almost anyone who visited or to whom he could write. Soon, at war with himself and against the advice of his other friends, he began to see Lord Alfred again. From prison he had brought his copy of a long, rambling, self-justifying, and self-accusing letter to Lord Alfred, later known as *De Profundis* (it was published in part in 1905). He managed now to compose only the tragic *Ballad of Reading Gaol* (1898), despite dreams of writing new plays.

Wilde was never to return home; he was destined to die miserably ill, penniless, and finally deprived of what he most craved, his adoring audience. Public and private rejection became his fate. Increasingly, he suffered acute physical pain, presumably from meningitis, although our diagnosis must be merely conjectural. Always the unrepentant humorist, as he lay dying in what was then a cheap Left Bank *pension*, the Hotel d'Alsace, he reportedly said to a friend, "In this room I am fighting a duel to the death with the wallpaper. One of us must go."

What persistently permeates the complex, five-act drama that was Wilde's life is a battle between a relentless critical intelligence and an almost absurd craving for aesthetic perfection in affairs of the heart.

He could never quite understand and accept that Lord Alfred Douglas—young "Bosie," as his friends called him—was ignorantly cruel and relentlessly superficial, and was soon to metamorphose into the exact image of his brutal father. Wilde was indeed "all brains." Unfortunately, throughout history the *common* attitude toward the arts has fostered a failure to grasp that the better artists are always thinking, criticizing, and exercising their artistic intelligence. Serious artists are better thinkers than is usually understood. Artists do not need to be sincere, but they do need to know what they are doing as artists. For Wilde this meant fanciful invention under the command of criticism, a self-conscious, highly trained grasp of what medium and dream may accomplish. The term "criticism" was central for authors like Walter Pater, John Ruskin, and, towering even more impressively among Victorians, Matthew Arnold, author of an inaugural university lecture, "The Function of Criticism at the Present Time" (1864). For these Victorian thinkers, however little they were understood by a complacent middle class, the duties of a critical perspective on life assumed paramount importance, and Wilde the storyteller shared their critically oriented sense of literary value. He mastered different forms of critical composition, while his fictions assume a double purpose—entertainment on the one hand, critical enlightenment on the other. Starting from ancient Hellenic literature, moving through his favorite Renaissance authors and artists, assimilating the cosmopolitan Hegelian philosophy promulgated by the celebrated Oxford classicist Benjamin Jowett, and above all drawing inspiration from the English Romantics, Wilde greatly broadened the role of the critic. Born on an island, he was never insular.

A late enlightenment figure, Wilde became what he himself called "the critic as artist"; he is reserved and dignified even when he adopts the pose of an elegant aesthetic arbiter of taste. The darker side of his nature enticed him to veil his critical intensity, as he went about explaining the wedding of surface and depth, a marriage manifest in all truly beautiful works of art. He saw that average Victorians were conditioned to distrust the ambiguous claims of art, fearing the play of natural language. It is as if he instantly recognized his enemies to be the enemies of art and saw they were allies and agents of an imperial mechanism, the greatest empire the world had ever seen, centering authority and power in London, cloaked in the royal mantle of the "Widow of Windsor," Queen Victoria, whose empire stretched forth its grasping fingers of cultural, military, and commercial dominance across every continent of the terrestrial globe. This was the same British Empire that Joseph Conrad, an aristocratic exile from his native Poland, would always consider the noblest state known to the modern world. In Britain the principles of Common Law had discovered their origins, evolved their principles, such as the writ of habeas corpus, and thence had ventured forth on a worldwide mission. For good or ill, Great Britain brought railroads and industrial progress to the modern world. Politically and in the theory of representative parliamentary government, Britain had long before founded the most serious modern ideas of freedom, while British politicians—influenced by the rhetoric and thought of another Anglo-Irishman, Edmund Burke—generally rejected all extremist principles of revolution. Above all, there was Shakespeare and the other great English poets.

This England, "this royal throne of kings," was to be both kind and killing to the author of *Lady Windermere's Fan* and *An Ideal Husband*. *The Ballad of Reading Gaol* ends on the tragic note that "each man kills the thing he loves," a principle applying on all social levels, and not only for the romantic lover. Britain was for Wilde both his betrayer and his fervent admirer, creating for him an adopted cultural family, whose mastery of the English language nourished his mind, as he often observed. But this imperial brood was a society he could only attack with acerbically pointed rhetorical barbs. Wedded to London's literary life, he showed toward its higher social circles a marked ambivalence, while simultaneously refusing to pander to the masses.

In essence, Wilde perceived that the middle classes were coming to resemble the lower classes, culturally and psychologically. In the aristocracy he found an unpalatable tribal society, quipping once that its landed, fox-hunting members were "the unspeakable in pursuit of the inedible." Like other celebrity-seekers, he trod a dangerous path. In the end, Britain—he would probably have said England—could not tolerate his flamboyant Irish charm and oddly bardic manner, whose mysterious tone complemented his critical instincts. A widespread middle-class mediocrity could only silence such a charmingly dissident visitor, albeit with his own dark connivance.

When Wilde fell for Lord Alfred Douglas, he had ventured upon a hate-driven affray between a poetizing son and a pugilistic, athletic father, the two of them as disturbed a pair as ever lived to wreak destruction on the congenitally unwary. Lord Alfred clearly needed Wilde to stand in for him in this obsessed familial conflict, nor can we avoid overstatement when we describe this tangled relationship. Yet the poet and aesthetic mentor was in no position to be Lord Alfred's champion. The Marquess, for example, was the codifier and promulgator of the Marquess of Queensberry Rules, the rules of modern boxing. Languid, elegant verses could be no match for such bellicose accomplishments. This was to be no medieval joust; there would be no ribbons and favors in this contest. To defend the arts of gentleness, so important to Wilde's infatuation, rhetoric could find no adequate weapon. We ask, therefore, how such a shrewd observer of human society would fail to perceive his own error before it was too late. This was not a matter of the level playing field—there was no playing field at all, as it turned out. In one of his own plays Wilde himself would have cheerfully demonstrated such a failure, suggesting that it issued from some inner flaw of character and circumstance. But in life he could not manage this proof.

His attraction toward Douglas was in fact a travesty, a weird exaggeration of his aesthetic theory that somehow Life imitates Art. The passion had pride in it, too, for if he could rise above allegations of deviance, and hence rise above scandal, Victorian society would be revealed as beneath him. As an actor on his life's stage, he moves as if danger was an aphrodisiac. Later, in North Africa, where he participated casually in André Gide's coming out as a homosexual, it was the cautious and puritanical Gide who warned him against bearding the establishment in a court trial. "Do you realize the risk?" Gide asked. Richard Ellmann, Wilde's biographer, notes of this interchange that Wilde shared an obsession Henry James once called "the imagination of disaster." Another linked pattern was Wilde's increased consumption of alcohol; a friend called him "thirsty Oscar." He was always the gambler; life itself was a gamble, like a play that might or might not succeed.

Not surprisingly, the master of a repartee that sparkles in the plays was noted for his eloquence in conversation, whose richly varied intonation carried the weight of penetrating analysis. On one occasion he started the evening's conversation by boldly silencing his sophisticated Parisian hosts, only to find that such oppressively grand manners failed to impress them. Instantly he reversed direction, unobtrusively changing his style before dessert. With one dramatic turn he won his listeners completely. They later confessed they had never heard such quiet eloquence, not realizing that as a playwright he knew all about the need to vary the pace.

Conversation and improvising over port and brandy is one thing, pleading in a criminal court another, and Wilde was wrong to believe that he could win any legal struggle by mere eloquence of speech. The law always spoke a duller language, except in fictions where the *agon* of drama omits the tedious circumstantial testimony. The poet assumed that paradoxes occupy a higher ground than law, or rather that its laws were of a nobler kind, subject to no common social constraint. At his second trial he fell victim to an insidiously clever compatriot, Edward Carson. Learning of Carson's appointment, Wilde ominously joked: "No doubt he will pursue his case with the added bitterness of an old friend." Carson was no common attorney, but as a prosecutor he breathed the air and manipulated the mildest breezes of dangerous innuendo. Under cross-examination Wilde finally succumbed to a lower realism, against which, as critic, he had often railed.

The law, he now learned, would not allow him to act as if private sexual behavior were a metaphorical activity. Sex was denied its rights as a figure of thought. Yet from his early education and above the teaching of the magisterial Plato, sex and love are nothing if not metaphors and symbolic actions. Plato had taught a principle of inner freedom, but society wanted external conformity and discretion. Right-thinking Victorians read such freedom as incipient social anarchy, and they got into the habit of denying their secrets, including illegitimate births, which they politely called "indiscretions." Monogamy and the difficulty of divorce for women were part of this dark equation. Among Victorians there developed the ancient (biblical) fascination with what is forbidden, a reverse Puritanism, so that a limited mental and social space opened out to accommodate improper secret lives. In this context, another deeper question now arises regarding Wilde's personal and professional life: is wit a mechanism of uncovering secrecy, is humor the true enemy of deceit, is paradox the true challenger of the lie? For him the seemingly unrealistic practice of paradox is in fact the prime mechanism for telling truth. As psychoanalysis later proved, the dream, driven by *eros*, speaks a language of double meanings. If the aim of art is then to encourage self-awareness, this means we need a language of complex words. In any case, a liberating paradoxical vision became Wilde's main poetic theme, as it was his favorite device.

For a materialist age, the emphasis on fiction as truth, or minimally a path toward truth, was bound to smack of decadence. How, a Victorian might ask, can fables tell us what we want to know about hard facts? This is a wrong-headed question, tending to support earnest complacency. Among other things, it fails to see that Art is a hypothetical exercise. Trained by poetry, we begin to perceive the deeper complexities of life; we become philosophers of appearance. An eerie sensual melodrama like *Salomé*, which was to become the basis of Richard Strauss's overwrought 1905 opera, inevitably seemed to solid English citizens to be dangerously intellectual, more frivolously French than solidly British. But to deny the weird sexual impulses of humans is to lose all understanding of their middle ground as well. Poetry and its metaphors are exercises in crossing mental boundaries, thus blocking the human tendency toward prejudice. Metaphors do for human experience what exact measured descriptions do for scientific fact. Along with the tag of "decadence" went another slur, that Wilde was just another brilliant Irish word spinner, as if that eloquence had not been the goal of Shakespeare himself. The irony here is that Wilde might early achieve celebrity and notoriety for his posing in excessively refined costume, he might affect a languid manner of speaking, he might disreputably seek the company of good-looking adolescent males, but, we may say, he was not the only aesthete in the land, and London society knew that. When Reginald Bunthorne, the aesthete in Gilbert and Sullivan's *Patience* (1881), "walks down Piccadilly / With a tulip or a lily / In his medieval hand," the lines flattered an audience that wanted applause for seeking the social graces, especially since most found these graces hard to acquire without upsetting the program of greedy capitalist tedium.

The audience therefore craved an elite status that Wilde skillfully wove into his plays without descending to cynical disapproval. *Patience* and the other Gilbert and Sullivan operas never really rejected the clichés and habits they satirized, whether poking fun at the Royal Navy in *H.M.S. Pinafore* (1878), or self-improvement societies in *Ruddigore* (1887), or the police in *The Pirates of Penzance* (1879), or pretentious parvenu office holders in *The Gondoliers* (1889), or Shakespearean bardolatry in *The Yeoman of the Guard* (1888), or even the Queen and her royal household in *The Mikado* (1885). Music domesticates satire, and we are still delighted by the good-natured charm of *Patience*. G and S, as they were called, nudged social uncertainty toward a wry acceptance and affectionate critique, all of it sung, with often hilarious incongruity between word and melody, to Sir Arthur Sullivan's charming melodies. As a rule, a musical setting will disguise political messages, which we find even in operas like Mozart's *Don Giovanni* (1787) and *The Marriage of Figaro* (1786), or Verdi's *Nabucco* (1842) and *Don Carlos* (1867). When it came to promoting *Patience* for American audiences, librettist and composer encouraged their manager, Richard D'Oyly Carte, to send the young aesthete on a lecture tour to the United States. They were dispatching "the real thing" to the provinces, to create interest in the new sensation, the Aesthete as Eloquent Giant. At home in London, the real star of each comedy was the poet's sparkling language itself, a loosely musical orchestration of voices very close in effect to the blank verse drama of Elizabethan and Jacobean dramatists. By an excessive reliance upon ornamental devices, evidenced in his first book of *Poems* (1881), Wilde acquired great fluency, and at first, we admit, a slavish use of earlier conventions. Such florid, conventional poetic styles fundamentally show a love of classic form, fueled by a master text, Walter Pater's *Studies in the History of the Renaissance* (1873; later called simply *The Renaissance*), with its vastly influential conclusion. This allegiance in turn harks back to ancient literature, which for Wilde participated in the late Romantic renaissance of wonder.

What is odd about Wilde is that to this preference for classic elegance he added a desire to know the roughest sides of late-nineteenth-century life. The American lecture tour was just such an experiment, a marathon taking him east and west, north and south, crisscrossing the United States, lecturing in more than sixty different towns and cities. Typically, he dined at the bottom of a mine in Leadville, Colorado, where he took particular note of a sign decorating a miner's saloon, "Don't Shoot the Piano Player—He Is Doing His Best." Maybe he thought the words were referring to his own efforts. Wilde was fascinated by the unfinished, unapologetically crude aspirations of the Americans, and an essay like "The American Invasion" shows he was a discerning critic of American life. The public role of arbiter came naturally to the poet. Nor was the field of criticism alien to writers in the age of Arnold, Pater, and Ruskin, but initially for Wilde it represented simply an interesting way to make a living, to support his family and his own lavish life. Wilde never stinted on his tailor or wine merchant, or the costs of dining out. Such expenses he handled by writing feverishly, first as a contributing journalist of culture and fashion, producing more than seventy reviews for the *Pall Mall Gazette* (an evening daily paper costing one penny), with numerous occasionally long articles for the *Dramatic Review* and the *Court and Society Review* and then by reviewing for two more years as editor of *Woman's World*, a monthly magazine. Wilde's journalistic output was thus extensive and steady, but finally he tired of its deadlines and its triviality. Nevertheless, during the 1880s he was tracking and tracing many of the most important social and cultural phenomena of his time, a training that later he would deploy with effortless ease, on a more general plane, as he created his famous social comedies for the stage.

At the same time the poet in him needed a stronger claim upon public attention. He showed an insatiable need for immediate, live, wide response. To this end "bad publicity" was necessarily not all bad. Cartoons and operettas would force the public to notice him. Competing for command of the great ship, Aesthetics, he might challenge the bitter, if brilliant American painter and wit, his rival in the celebrity stakes, James McNeill Whistler. When he admitted to Whistler that he wished he had made a particularly brilliant Whistler remark, the painter replied: "You will, Oscar, you will."

The American tour was an early source of independent perspective. Stepping off the SS *Arizona* in New York, he announced to the customs official, for all to hear, "I have nothing to declare but my genius." From this journey to the New World he emerged a full-fledged celebrity, hardened to opprobrium leveled by reviewers and gossip columnists, amused and doubtless refreshed by a sense of American absurdity when it came to cultural pretensions. Occasionally, as when he visited Walt Whitman, he would be moved by an experience of rare intimacy, of entering the inner circle of the great poets. Doubtless, had his later years taken a happier turn, one imagines he would have returned to America with wry enthusiasm, for although, as he once said, the United States may have moved from barbarism to decadence without experiencing civilization in between, Americans still epitomized Walt Whitman's much vaunted difference and diversity. This was also the America that accepted so many immigrants, among them the refugees from the terrible Irish potato famine.

Travel is a young man's avenue to imaginative growth, and we are not therefore startled by the almost unprecedented variety of literary output marking the evolution of the poet's art during the 1880s. With speed of production came serious critical thought, and with that came an increasingly reflective literary vision. The year 1889 saw the publication of a fantastic but no less important critical essay dealing with Shakespeare's imagined Platonic love life, "The Portrait of Mr. W. H.," while in 1890 he published the initial magazine version of *The Picture of Dorian Gray*, an elegant work instantly classified as a decadent tract, whose narrative traces the Gothic destiny of the handsome, idealized youth Dorian. The novel intensifies the reader's sense of aesthetic powers and suggests French literature, with its overtones of J.-K. Huysmans's classically decadent novel *À Rebours*

(1884: translated as *Against the Grain* or *Against Nature*), by representing Dorian's decay through the gradual metamorphosis of his representation in art, through a magic transformation of his artistic likeness. This fiction exploits the most primitive "magic of similarity," as anthropologists would call it. Dorian's image decays as its lines and colors distort, while his actual body and actual physical appearance appear to remain forever young. Thus an ancient myth is brought up to date, with no loss of metaphysical import. By antithetically reversing our "normal" expectations, the story manages to suggest that Art is magically prior to Life. The portrait of Dorian represents what is "real," while the natural body is a mere shadow, leaving the reader with an old religious question: wherein resides young Dorian's soul? (A similar interest in the soul animates the virtuoso fantasy-essay about Shakespeare, and a certain Willie Hughes—supposedly the beloved recipient of the Sonnets, the "Mr. W. H.," named in the mysterious dedication of the first 1609 edition—flies off the printed page into the clear space of dreams and wish-fulfillments. Mr. W. H. is said to be a beautiful boy actor in the playwright's theatrical company, the King's Men.) In literary terms, the *Portrait* is an odd combination of wild imagining and genuine historical knowledge, in which once again Wilde explores the metaphysical authority of the work of art, especially the shifting image; thus an otherwise slender fable carries the weight of serious interpretation. By dramatizing the fate of an image and our minds responding to it, Wilde catches the tyrannical religious power of love's perceptions, leading so often (with both men and women, it must be said) to the aesthetic ecstasy and spiritualized passion of Platonic love, a theme studied in so many ways by many of the Sonnets.

Wilde devises criticism that reads like a purely fictional invention, as if to say that aesthetic taste can never be nailed down to a platform of academic positivism. The jeweler's brooch is not assessed with regard to the specific gravity of gold bullion. "The Portrait of Mr. W. H." imagines magic as a fantastic mode of truth, while the purpose underlying *The Picture of Dorian Gray* is similarly intertwined with a vision that life should never be subjected to material success, as neutered and measured by money or technology, but should be experienced with joy and a sense of the beautiful—something young lovers know only too much about. Art shares in a purifying aesthetic interest, so easy to lose, and to address this threat of loss, Wilde later wrote one of his essays, "The Soul of Man under Socialism," a work of primitive Christian piety that could only infuriate complacent Victorian proponents of industrial capitalism with its material expectations. Wilde identifies the more generous life with a primitive notion of socialist sharing. Hence his stories frequently allude to the Gospel plea that we give to those less fortunate than ourselves. Clearly Wilde was caught up in the mysteries of sacrifice.

The conditions of rural and urban poverty were also pragmatically evident to the author of "The Soul of Man." Londoners lived, consciously or not, in the world of Mrs. Elizabeth Gaskell's study of industrial strife and suffering, *North and South* (1854); of the relentless "facts" Charles Dickens would satirize in *Hard Times* (1854); and equally in the world of waste described in Dickens's last completed novel, *Our Mutual Friend* (1865); or considering literature as analyzed by George Gissing's novel about hack writing, *New Grub Street* (1891). Wilde in his exploration of the city's sexual underworld was always skirting the seedier, harder side of existence, from which he sought not to be sheltered, which indeed he wished to embrace, despite the risks. As an artist he imagined he would be seen to "rise above" behavior officially denounced as immoral and indecent. Meanwhile, like his great Irish predecessor, Jonathan Swift, he understood the need for genuine material equity.

To promote such thoughts he would write fables like "The Happy Prince," which adopt the teaching role of traditional fables and biblical parables. Wilde was fond of parables. No doubt he first acquired this taste from reading and hearing the Bible read out loud, though his parents were both hardly model Christians. Parable and fable are also very close to the traditional folktale, which both his parents were studying in virtually professional ways, as part of the Celtic Revival. Underneath the myriad purposes to which parable may be put, there is, however, one determining interest of the genre. It will always be a slender allegory, conveying hidden senses by decorative means. Wilde costumes the truth in what he took to be its most seductive apparel, by emulating old masters, especially perhaps Italian Renaissance author, sculptor, and jeweler Benvenuto Cellini.

The magic of the representing image may take many forms, stretching beyond Cellini's refinement. For one so viciously persecuted in the name of public morals, it is ironic that Wilde's literary work is always moral in purport, often inspired by the theme of the double. This romantic motif was best known from Robert Louis Stevenson's *Dr. Jekyll and Mr. Hyde* (1886). Doubles imply secret lives and revealing depths; hence the fable of the *doppelgänger* perfectly suits the Victorian (or, in France, a late Symbolist, Baudelairean) temperament. The aim of such literary inventions is to show that underneath the fixed, "correct" social value there always lives a double, its moral opposite. This thought in turn leads the reader to question all unexamined ideas of personal or social identity, for if we are really doubles of ourselves, we have no guarantee of any single fixed political identity. In this skeptical quest Wilde was a true modern. His journalism brought him face to face with the passing social world, and it trained him to question endemic public illusions, including the unquestioned "democratic" overvaluation of journalism itself. That trade, he thought, may become a method of spreading ignorance by promoting the opinions of the uneducated. In America, he wrote, "the President reigns for four years, and Journalism reigns forever." He was a skeptic about much of what he himself had written in order to make a decent living, as well as being skeptical about the truthfulness of image-making and hence of the use of magic imagery.

In such circumstances, it is crucial for the serious student of Oscar Wilde to distinguish his hackwork from essays concerned with his doctrines of art and aesthetics. In the remarkable essays "The Decay of Lying" and "The Critic as Artist," he turns to the genre of the imaginary conversation, whose original is the greatest of philosophical models, the dialogues of Plato. The dialectic method supports an obvious educational purpose, since one of two interlocutors seeks agreement from the other. Vivian and Gilbert, leading the conversation, are both professors of aesthetics. Their arguments betray Wilde's classical training; he rethinks Horace's ancient Latin *Art of Poetry*, with its principle that the purpose of art is to teach by delighting us. The English inheritance from Horace is handed down by Sir Philip Sidney's Elizabethan *Defence of Poesie* (1595), which states the principle that since "the poet nothing affirmeth," because he actively encourages hypothetical use of fictions, he cannot be accused of deliberate untruth. "The Decay of Lying" makes this same point with greater focus and philosophical rigor. Wilde takes the case for the imaginative, hypothetical fictional patterning the whole way, till he reaches the conclusion that Life imitates Art, to block our yearning for fixed meanings. This was John Keats's principle of negative capability, couched in different terms. For Art cannot fixate a picture of life if it "nothing affirmeth."

Wilde and Sidney reverse the usual assumption, memorably spoken by Hamlet to the Players, that Art is supposed to "hold . . . the mirror up to nature," an assumption based on belief in a correspondence between reality and picture—but it will not hold true, given any complex rendering of human experience and consciousness. Exact correspondence of object and picture must be the aim of descriptive science, but Art and Life both make a mess of that paradigm, since there is nothing fixed or pragmatically stable about our world or its image, so that for Wilde it follows that "illusion is the first of all pleasures." Wilde is saying that for human significance to be generated, pleasure and humor give the truest mirror. The paradox on which this view hinges is that in literature Realism is deceptive; it fails to tell "beautiful untrue things" which in turn imply the life of the imagination, a rather more dreamlike mode of representation. The hypothetical "lying" that literature has lost, driven out by the technologically driven "realism" of many modern novels, is virtually another term for "imagination." If we are attracted by realism, that sordid "truthfulness" finally destroys spiritual flexibility, whereby our human aim reaches toward an ideal, universal vision of life. We are not to descend, in art, to voyeuristic fascination with grubby reality, with what in the novel of the period is often called "naturalism." How, we may ask, does Wilde avoid aligning his argument with the very philistinism he so sharply mocks? If Art is aimed toward "higher things," if it eschews the vulgar naturalistic exposures of seamy reality, then how can it possibly stay in touch with "real life," with the lives we all actually live, in all our imperfection? Surely a serious realism is preferable to a cloudy piety toward higher laws. Surely Wilde himself is on the road toward a fatal sentimentality, thence to be drawn toward his own version of cynicism.

But such, finally, is not the case. Philistine attitudes are a duplicitous veil cast over "the cynicism of the real," the low cunning of those who pretend to have a passion for the facts. By rejecting all average clichés, the aesthetic experimenter seeks instead an oblique but powerful renovation of values, the values of potential harmony linked to Aristotelian, balanced ethical judgments. As in mathematics, formal refinement and beauty of expression imply an underlying truth, the sort of order that inspires us to take good actions, even when life is too complicated. Paradox, riddle, the joke, and humor at many levels will enter the picture here, because these cognitive devices are the mind's mechanism for simultaneously seeing more than one side to any question. A joke is an instantaneous perception of the doubleness, the doubling, involved in all perceptions that rise to the level of those complex conditions life actually presents to the thinking mind.

Paradoxes reveal the need for deliberation and dialogue—not mindless, sound-bitten, television backchat, but real debate. Quite simply, jokes train the mind to think about life. Paradoxes attack our complacent assumption that "*We* know X or Y," whereas in fact we do not know, we have only been told X or Y by some self-appointed authority. Finally, the mode of paradox is a method of language referring to itself and to its own entrapments. The most succinct of all paradoxes is one we have already mentioned, called "the liar's paradox," which logically contradicts its own claim to truth. Such tangled, self-reflexive inversions of logic are precisely what Plato's dialectic was intended to clarify, and this was the function of Wildean comedy, no less than formal logic. The game seems arcane, but it simply means that surfaces imply depths, and their interaction must be studied. Surfaces are precisely where deceptions arise and where we most need illumination. Paradox therefore trains us to investigate what we carelessly assume to be "obvious," so that modern art, for example, has to question the curious "honesty" of "honest" journalism and advertising, which are intended to sell something, not to show its truth or falsity. In this quest the artist may go a long way to reaching into a philosophy of life. He knows better, when the cunning advertiser says: "It only looks that way; don't worry . . . down is up."

George Orwell would have said that in strong fiction the analytic paradoxes attack an official doublethink mediated by power-driven, bureaucratic, inert language. To break the lock of such newspeak, the truth-loving speaker may have to exaggerate; in dialogue Vivian says, "As a method, realism is a complete failure." This comically exaggerated dismissal might trouble some very serious novelists, notably Henry James (he perhaps defensively did not care for Wilde the man or author) and Émile Zola, but from Vivian's tone we get a momentary shock. We wake to a question.

Drama carries "the realism question" even further, while critical interests drove Wilde to dramatic composition, every bit as much as knowing that successful plays could bring material monetary rewards. He was always working on a play or thinking about a new one, and he had plans far beyond his drawing room comedies. He regarded theater as "the greatest of all art forms," because on stage the character of a human being is revealed; as he put it, the play gives us "a sense of what it is to be a human being." This lofty vision of drama goes back at least to Aristotle's *Poetics,* in which the philosopher observes that drama is "more philosophic" than history, because history deals only in particulars, whereas drama treats universal principles.

Wilde's Act V had centered upon the poet's passion and expert theatrical concern for all the details of dramatic production. Wilde always passed beyond the glamour of theatrical show, however, seeking the intellectual purpose—Aristotle's *Poetics* called it the "thought"—of dramatic action. He generally followed the great English classics, beginning with his early efforts such as *The Duchess of Padua* (never produced in Great Britain), or French tradition, with the political drama *Vera*, which did not fare well in its American debut, mainly because it was miscast. His first great success, however, was bound to appeal to an established middle class. Comedy of manners, of course, had a long history; its English classics belong to the late seventeenth century. Starting memorably (and very profitably) with *Lady Windermere's Fan*, Wilde followed up with the more serious drama *A Woman of No Importance* (1893), and then *An Ideal Husband*, topping these successes with the most brilliantly curious comedy of all, *The Importance of Being Earnest*. The genre had been perfected by Restoration authors such as George Farquhar (1678–1707) and the subtle William Congreve (1670–1729) and then by Oliver Goldsmith's *She Stoops to Conquer* (1773) or another comic masterpiece, still eminently playable, Richard Brinsley Sheridan's *The School for Scandal* (1777). The immediate charm of such works always belies a thoughtful, critical, underlying sense that life is very much a gamble, in love as much as anywhere.

Drama, by giving a central place to figures of speech and thought, is designed to reach recognition scenes, where secrets are revealed, facts and actual feelings "made known." In farce these revelations are merely embarrassing; in tragedy they embody the most fearful counterturns of destiny. After his release from prison Wilde wrote the despairing *Ballad of Reading Gaol*, a frightening poem attacking the horrors of England's "level two" prisons, where once again we find the poet expressing inconvenient truths. In complex societies such truths can rarely be approached directly; they need the play of wit and double senses. Ambiguity is not a perversion poets maliciously practice; it is the heart of their method. Their fascination with doubleness turns on the use of irony, to show that wrong is mostly done through a combination of bad desires and plain ignorance. The aim of irony is a larger and wiser veracity, which in turn saves poetic and dramatic irony from the charge of duplicity.

The poetic manner of Wilde's comedies relies on his unfailingly light humor—for humor, as Freud observed in a late and important essay, expresses a censorship and puritanical conscience that "gives in," forgiving our human folly. The plays explore a vein of idealized religious contrition and comfort, the very state of kindness that comedies ideally seek to produce by their resolving powers. In the event, though the poet craved personally experimental freedom, he also wanted a forgiving version of the "real world." To hope that in these respects the artist, like his work, is unique is a desperate gamble. Wilde grew up amidst high standards of middle class comfort, and in his last years, if not before, he was perpetually short of cash. Perhaps, as Wilde thought, personal charm and intellectual sparkle guaranteed belonging to the higher circles of mind, but short of a large marital settlement or a run of successful dramas, it did not guarantee a good income. The sad fact, then, is that wit became an almost fatal end in itself, as the playwright attempted to endow language with enviable elegance, energy, and hope, his comedies obeying a symphonic law, with all their separate voices speaking, at last, in the voice of the playwright.

Wilde was a proud man, author of "The Decay of Lying," but he would soon be forced to accommodate to the narrower aims of society. Though "The Decay of Lying" had shown that Life indeed does imitate Art—we are creatures of our myths, in short—it was still perilous to relish this view. Like a hallucination, the verbal universe might acquire a shamanistic dream function, but when Wilde was brought to trial the second time as a result of collateral revelations about his sex life, he had entered upon a new, and quite different, dramatic career. He was soon obliged to abandon rhetoric and to answer, not Queensberry the man and father, but the newly enacted statute law of the land. Now the antagonist was Victorian society at large, speaking the major role in the drama of a court case brought against the poet under the authority of the Criminal Law Amendment Act, passed ten years earlier and widely known as the "Blackmailer's Charter." Ironies abound in the affair, beginning, as we said, with the fact that Wilde was prosecuted by his former schoolmate, Edward Carson, who happened to be a Unionist Irish politician. Carson did indeed press his case with "all the bitterness of an old friend," as Wilde ominously said he would. Significantly, since it reveals the sexual politics of Wilde's position, this same Carson later defended "the Winslow boy" (his real name: George Archer-Shee), the young protagonist in Terence Rattigan's famous play of that name (1946), later made into more than one successful film. Accusations of theft are one thing, sexual deviance another. Theft is never perceived as undermining empire; it is a favored imperial mode.

On the day Wilde was found guilty, harlots danced before the doors of the criminal court. Accused of consorting with male prostitutes, he was mocked by women engaged in the oldest profession who were, as such, Members of the Establishment. They were the unlicensed poor of sexual free enterprise. Historians have long known, if others have not, that illegal heterosexual sex for hire has a close connection to urban poverty, and Wilde understood this only too well. His most famous lyric poem is "The Harlot's House," an impressionistic lament for the child prostitute's lost innocence. Eros should rather have implied equity, he thought. Perhaps only a deliberate pre-Freudian dreamer could think this way, as we find if we look beneath the surface of "The Soul of Man under Socialism." An essay on that theme speaks to questions of friendship indirectly, without the sinister overtones of a work such as Henry James's *The Turn of the Screw*, published in a volume entitled *The Two Magics*, the one involving a governess, the other involving real estate. Unlike James, Wilde always radiates a somewhat forlorn belief in human kindness as a permanent value. He seems linked to a utopian Catholic worldview, while, with virtually opposed vision, he thrusts a paradox-based theory of art into the twentieth century.

With *The Importance of Being Earnest* this theory had fully passed beyond treating the supposedly "real" events that occupy the first three plays. The secrets revealed in those comedies had been quite simply "real secrets," secrets about real things and real events. The dramatic appearance and disappearance of Lady Windermere's fan are as real as the fan itself, a thing in itself. In *Lady Windermere's Fan*, a secret affair has had real consequences—indeed a child is born, from whose birth the whole plot derives. A parallel situation drives the action in *A Woman of No Importance*, where Mrs. Arbuthnot's illegitimate and "concealed" son by Lord Illingworth is a very real "Gerald" in the story. Sir Robert Chiltern's crime against his government in *An Ideal Husband* is a real crime, again with material results, including his acquiring great wealth, as well as a brilliant position in politics. In the same play Mrs. Cheveley is privy to this dangerously real secret, and she blackmails Sir Robert. He must pay in real currency for a real misdeed, for which she possesses documentary proof. These are of course perceived or imagined realities, however much their intrigues engage our intelligence. They are close to our human involvements with each other. What makes Mrs. Cheveley's mischievous game of power intriguing is that Life has entangled it with sex.

Generally the playwright exploits a vaguely metaphysical aspect of all these real events surrounded by secrecy, which for the most part he attaches to the power games of aristocracy, with various hungers for property, marriage, and unexpected love leading somewhere or nowhere. The charm of the plays comes mainly from an acute sense of the style and stylized life occurring in Chelsea or Belgrave Square. Standards of behavior are controlled in these plays by good manners, by social norms, but the dramatic plots are inspired "lying" from one end to the other, expressing the poet's irresistible flow of epigram, ironies, and jokes, which are as varied and amusing for us today as they ever were. Our minds take wing with delight in verbal wit, to be sure, but we always refer the action to real-world standards.

By contrast, with its strong impulse toward idle and ideal conjecture, *The Importance of Being Ernest* was intended to escape those middle- and upper-class social practices. The author said it was to be "about nothing at all," its chief interest being, like something Hamlet would conjure, a mere word—the word "earnest," albeit a term covering all Victorian piety like an umbrella, capacious enough to include earnest hypocrisy, self-improvement programs, patriotism, and the like. For the second time the word "importance" appears in a Wilde play title, marking his skepticism. Many in the early audiences found this last play a mere farce, a set of raveling, unraveling, manifestly trivial loves, all their disconcerting tangles untied at the end through the most hackneyed of all theatrical devices, the discovery of a true paternity, the revelation of the truth about that stock type, the changeling. This favorite farcical device suggests a generalized social anxiety about illegitimacy and about the illegitimate children born into the Victorian shadow-world. Despite these deeper worries, the play sports a splendidly theatrical plot, full of perfect timing and farcical compressions of the action, so that as one door opens, another closes, until all is revealed and concluded in a ridiculously comic triple wedding.

Literary experience determines the driving conceptual pace of the play. Everything now revolves around a semantic question Romeo had long before posed to his beloved Juliet, "What's in a name?" There is an intellectual humor in the fact that *The Importance of Being Earnest* is a sharp anticipation of modern linguistic philosophy, for its plot continuously questions the naming of its two heroes, with their aliases, not to mention providing an ecclesiastical, even hermeneutic satire implicit in the names of Miss Prism and Mr. Chasuble. The fearsome Lady Bracknell is no less a name, for she is brackish, but once was a Nell Gwyn. The use of comic names is old, as old as Jonsonian urban comedy in the 1600s, and it had featured in the Restoration comedy of manners, where stereotypes are labeled and packaged as sets of comical cognomens—familiarly, many of these devices later animate the pages of Dickens's novels. Each name denotes a commending attitude or humor, as the Elizabethans would have said. Novels had made the humor comedies a familiar type; names like Henry James's Fanny Assingham occur as counterpoint in *The Golden Bowl*—a most serious novel. But names can also mean destiny, arising from what anthropologists were learning to call "the magic of names." For Wilde, as we saw, "The Decay of Lying" and "The Truth of Masks" are precisely intended to show that when language notably names its objects, something almost supernatural is bound to be involved.

If names have magic power to fix and fixate meaning, this raises the question, does not Wildean paradox undo this dream of fixity? Is that not what happens with puns, jokes, double meanings, and the like? His final comedy sets out to explore, if not resolve, such questions. With *The Importance of Being Earnest* the entire plot hinges upon the merest fragment of a word—not even a whole name, as it were, but only a bit of it: in short, a single letter, where the presence or absence of an "a" in the word or name "Earnest/Ernest" creates a different magic and a different world, depending on what is there or not there. Like the deconstructive philosopher Jacques Derrida, with his famed word *difference*—you cannot *hear*, in French, if this is difference with an "a" or an "e"—Wilde sets up the naming-game so that you cannot hear the shift between a present or an absent "a." Is one Earnest or Ernest? Which of the two does the play reveal Jack Worthing to be? You can only imagine the inscribed shift, because you cannot exactly hear it, and thus you are forced to exercise the free play of imagination. Picking up the naming-games of Laurence Sterne, anticipating Joyce's fiction, the turn of the century becomes quite an Irish literary affair for those who write in English.

This naming-game might suggest an impoverished play on words, were it not that Wilde had already established his authorial principle that critical intelligence, not sincerity and emotion, nor sentimental pressure and cynical cunning, should be the key to literary power in the modern world, since only by such sleights of ear and eye can we the readers learn to look deeper beneath surfaces. If we are creatures of the names we are "given," it follows that life does imitate art. The audience is being led to question the reigning fashions of earnest plodders. We must therefore try to question all blindly ritualistic sanctions of moral pretense. Above all, the medium we most trust and least examine, our wondrous natural language, constitutes the critical field of required self-examination, not something to be abused by oppressive journalistic iteration or governmental and commercial censorship. The truth about Jack Worthing is shown to issue from his birth into language, which is a naming day, an identity made "real" by a proper name. The changeling is the child with no fixed term, while to be named is to enter upon a radically uncertain mode of existence. Under such circumstances theory becomes a fact of life, and since it implies an art, we again can see how life imitates art.

When in his appended preface to *The Picture of Dorian Gray*, Wilde says that all art is "quite [that is, perfectly] useless," he did not mean trivial or without value; he meant without materialistic advantage. When he said, "all bad poetry springs from genuine feeling," he cast his ironic gaze upon spurious displays of emotion, upon the ungrounded stock responses generated by melodrama. He might have been thinking of *Romeo and Juliet*. Without Mercutio's sardonic wit, there would be no effective truth contraposing the adolescent effusions of Romeo and Juliet, while as Robert Penn Warren showed long ago, next door to Mercutio's irony the passion of Romeo and Juliet—young love itself—gains poignant, memorable, critical value.

The sophisticated farce of Algernon and Jack in *The Importance of*

Being Earnest depends entirely upon serious feelings filtered through the whirling turns and counterturns of language itself, and this game in its turn gives drama its power in the human world, where, as Wilde once remarked, "the truth is rarely pure and never simple." The lesson seems clear enough: only a verbal technique of high polish and classic form will catch patterns within the impurity and complexity of life, which itself is almost too serious to be announced, except indirectly, through artistic illusions. At the end of *The Importance of Being Earnest* we believe fully in the triumph of romance, partly because the story is too fantastic for words, but more deeply because our minds are carried beyond boring daily existence, on the wings of wit and paradox and wordplay. We leave behind all vulgar realism, and in this way we experience civility in a drama of forgiveness. We certainly get a refresher course in dealing with hypocrisy. From that perspective Wilde appears a generous critic of his period, whose studied hypocrisy he had so often deplored and reduced to paradoxical exposure. He produces an atmosphere of humor that transcends all the jokes made at the expense of social norms, and that humor is what he seems to have most admired, as much almost as personal loyalty. He deserved better of his society in England, even if he should have known better than to rely so entirely upon its willingness to be entertained. Charles Laughton once said to an actor friend, "To be a good actor, you need the hide of an elephant, and the soul of an angel." Perhaps, in spite of other gifts, Wilde could not be so divided against himself.

He at last became, if he had not planned to be, an unwilling rebel. One question remains about his life and work: why is it necessary for nations and religions to suppress individual differences, as with the law that sent Wilde to Reading Gaol? There is a clue in the fact that Wilde's aesthetic philosophy threatened fixed systems. He championed humor, eloquence, and wit, following Baldassare Castiglione, author of the great Renaissance *Book of the Courtier* (1528)—perhaps a destabilizing vaunt. He promoted and yet questioned his claims for Art. Was it not dangerous for him to be "all brains?" In his essays and plays there lurks always a suggestion, a suspicion, that outsiders will not be tolerated for long. In Wilde's day the power of the rich and the great to control what was considered "right thinking" far outweighed individual talent, especially when the individual in question was sexually different from the supposed mass.

Finally, however, to focus on Wilde the social and political phenomenon, while interesting and important in itself and moving as a dramatic subject, is to neglect what gives him his lasting importance, namely his uncanny command of lighthearted paradox and his gift for unmasking the secrets of our hearts and desires. In that pursuit of human relativity he is an absolute master.

ANGUS FLETCHER is Distinguished Professor Emeritus of English and Comparative Literature at the Graduate School of the City University of New York. Recipient of a 2004 Guggenheim Fellowship, he is the author of books on allegory, prophecy, court masque, and the philosophy of literature, specializing in the theory of literature and in the symbolic connections between literature and the other arts. His interdisciplinary concerns are reflected in *A New Theory for American Poetry: Democracy, the Environment, and the Future of Imagination* (2004) and in *Time, Space, and Motion in the Age of Shakespeare* (2007; published in England as *Time, Space, and Motion in English Renaissance Poetry*). In 1995 he was awarded a Senior Fellowship from the National Endowment for the Humanities to support research into ecology and the literary imagination, particularly as these relate to the English poet John Clare. In 1992 he received the Harold D. Vursell Memorial Award from the American Academy and Institute of Arts and Letters for *Colors of the Mind: Conjectures on Thinking in Literature* (1991). He has lectured widely on many questions of literary history and theory. In 1982 he presented the Christian Gauss Lectures at Princeton University on the topic "Mazes and Thresholds: The Theory of Liminal Poetics." In 1981 he was North American Delegate to the Milan Conference on "The Labyrinth." In the mid-1970s he served on the Supervising Committee of the English Institute, for whom he edited *The Literature of Fact* (1976). In 1979 he held a Senior Fellowship from the National Endowment for the Humanities, which led primarily to the publication of *Colors of the Mind*. Mr. Fletcher did his graduate work at Yale and Harvard, and has taught at Cornell University, Columbia University, the University of California at Los Angeles, the State University of New York–Buffalo, the California Institute of Technology, the University of California at Santa Cruz, the University of California at Berkeley, and the City University of New York. Currently he lives with his wife, Michelle, in Albuquerque, New Mexico.

THE COLLECTED
OSCAR WILDE

FICTION

THE PORTRAIT OF MR. W. H.

– 1 –

I HAD BEEN DINING with Erskine in his pretty little house in Birdcage Walk,* and we were sitting in the library over our coffee and cigarettes, when the question of literary forgeries happened to turn up in conversation. I cannot at present remember how it was that we struck upon this somewhat curious topic, as it was at that time, but I know we had a long discussion about Macpherson, Ireland, and Chatterton,[1] and that with regard to the last I insisted that his so-called forgeries were merely the result of an artistic desire for perfect representation; that we had no right to quarrel with an artist for the conditions under which he chooses to present his work; and that all Art being to a certain degree a mode of acting, an attempt to realise one's own personality on some imaginative plane out of reach of the trammelling accidents and limitations of real life, to censure an artist for a forgery was to confuse an ethical with an æsthetical problem.

Erskine, who was a good deal older than I was, and had been listening to me with the amused deference of a man of forty, suddenly put his hand upon my shoulder and said to me, "What would you say about a young man who had a strange theory about a certain work of art, believed in his theory, and committed a forgery in order to prove it?"

"Ah! that is quite a different matter," I answered.

Erskine remained silent for a few moments, looking at the thin grey threads of smoke that were rising from his cigarette. "Yes," he said, after a pause, "quite different."

* Fashionable promenade close to St. James's Palace; named for a royal aviary located there during the time of James I, who ruled England and Ireland from 1603 to 1625.

There was something in the tone of his voice, a slight touch of bitterness perhaps, that excited my curiosity. "Did you ever know anybody who did that?" I cried.

"Yes," he answered, throwing his cigarette into the fire—"a great friend of mine, Cyril Graham. He was very fascinating, and very foolish, and very heartless. However, he left me the only legacy I ever received in my life."

"What was that?" I exclaimed laughing. Erskine rose from his seat, and going over to a tall inlaid cabinet that stood between the two windows, unlocked it, and came back to where I was sitting, carrying a small panel picture set in an old and somewhat tarnished Elizabethan frame.

It was a full-length portrait of a young man in late sixteenth-century costume, standing by a table, with his right hand resting on an open book. He seemed about seventeen years of age, and was of quite extraordinary personal beauty, though evidently somewhat effeminate. Indeed, had it not been for the dress and the closely cropped hair, one would have said that the face, with its dreamy, wistful eyes and its delicate scarlet lips, was the face of a girl. In manner, and especially in the treatment of the hands, the picture reminded one of François Clouet's* later work. The black velvet doublet with its fantastically gilded points, and the peacock-blue background against which it showed up so pleasantly, and from which it gained such luminous value of colour, were quite in Clouet's style; and the two masks of Tragedy and Comedy that hung somewhat formally from the marble pedestal had that hard severity of touch—so different from the facile grace of the Italians—which even at the Court of France the great Flemish master never completely lost, and which in itself has always been a characteristic of the northern temper.

"It is a charming thing," I cried, "but who is this wonderful young man whose beauty Art has so happily preserved for us?"

"This is the portrait of Mr. W. H.," said Erskine, with a sad smile.

* Sixteenth-century portrait painter at the French court.

It might have been a chance effect of light, but it seemed to me that his eyes were swimming with tears.

"Mr. W. H.!" I repeated; "who was Mr. W. H.?"

"Don't you remember?" he answered; "look at the book on which his hand is resting."

"I see there is some writing there, but I cannot make it out," I replied.

"Take this magnifying-glass and try," said Erskine, with the same sad smile still playing about his mouth.

I took the glass, and moving the lamp a little nearer, I began to spell out the crabbed sixteenth-century handwriting. "To The Onlie Begetter Of These Insuing Sonnets."* . . . "Good heavens!" I cried, "is this Shakespeare's Mr. W. H.?"

"Cyril Graham used to say so," muttered Erskine.

"But it is not a bit like Lord Pembroke," I rejoined. "I know the Wilton portraits very well. I was staying near there a few weeks ago."

"Do you really believe then that the Sonnets are addressed to Lord Pembroke?"† he asked.

"I am sure of it," I answered. "Pembroke, Shakespeare, and Mrs. Mary Fitton‡ are the three personages of the Sonnets; there is no doubt at all about it."

"Well, I agree with you," said Erskine, "but I did not always think so. I used to believe—well, I suppose I used to believe in Cyril Graham and his theory."

"And what was that?" I asked, looking at the wonderful portrait, which had already begun to have a strange fascination for me.

"It is a long story," he murmured, taking the picture away from me—rather abruptly I thought at the time—"a very long story; but if you care to hear it, I will tell it to you."

---

* From the dedication of Shakespeare's *Sonnets*. Wilde gives the complete text of the dedication below, on pages 25–26.

† William Herbert, third earl of Pembroke (1580–1630), a notable patron of poets, including Shakespeare.

‡ Pembroke's mistress, lady-in-waiting to Queen Elizabeth I; often thought to be the "Dark Lady" of the Sonnets.

"I love theories about the Sonnets," I cried; "but I don't think I am likely to be converted to any new idea. The matter has ceased to be a mystery to any one. Indeed, I wonder that it ever was a mystery."

"As I don't believe in the theory, I am not likely to convert you to it," said Erskine, laughing; "but it may interest you."

"Tell it to me, of course," I answered. "If it is half as delightful as the picture, I shall be more than satisfied."

"Well," said Erskine, lighting a cigarette, "I must begin by telling you about Cyril Graham himself. He and I were at the same house at Eton. I was a year or two older than he was, but we were immense friends, and did all our work and all our play together. There was, of course, a good deal more play than work, but I cannot say that I am sorry for that. It is always an advantage not to have received a sound commercial education, and what I learned in the playing fields at Eton has been quite as useful to me as anything I was taught at Cambridge. I should tell you that Cyril's father and mother were both dead. They had been drowned in a horrible yachting accident off the Isle of Wight. His father had been in the diplomatic service, and had married a daughter, the only daughter, in fact, of old Lord Crediton, who became Cyril's guardian after the death of his parents. I don't think that Lord Crediton cared very much for Cyril. He had never really forgiven his daughter for marrying a man who had no title. He was an extraordinary old aristocrat, who swore like a costermonger, and had the manners of a farmer. I remember seeing him once on Speech-day. He growled at me, gave me a sovereign, and told me not to grow up a 'damned Radical' like my father. Cyril had very little affection for him, and was only too glad to spend most of his holidays with us in Scotland. They never really got on together at all. Cyril thought him a bear, and he thought Cyril effeminate. He was effeminate, I suppose, in some things, though he was a capital rider and a capital fencer. In fact he got the foils before he left Eton. But he was very languid in his manner, and not a little vain of his good looks, and had a strong objection to football, which he used to say was a game only suitable for the sons of the middle classes. The two things that really gave him pleasure were poetry and acting. At Eton he was always dressing up and reciting Shakespeare, and when we went up to Trinity he became a member of the A.D.C.* in his first term. I remember I was always very jealous of his acting. I was absurdly devoted to him; I suppose because we were so different in most things. I was a rather awkward, weakly lad, with huge feet, and horribly freckled. Freckles run in Scotch families just as gout does in English families. Cyril used to say that of the two he preferred the gout; but he always set an absurdly high value on personal appearance, and once read a paper before our Debating Society to prove that it was better to be good-looking than to be good. He certainly was wonderfully handsome. People who did not like him, philistines and college tutors, and young men reading for the Church, used to say that he was merely pretty; but there was a great deal more in his face than mere prettiness. I think he was the most splendid creature I ever saw, and nothing could exceed the grace of his movements, the charm of his manner. He fascinated everybody who was worth fascinating, and a great many people who were not. He was often wilful and petulant, and I used to think him dreadfully insincere. It was due, I think, chiefly to his inordinate desire to please. Poor Cyril! I told him once that he was contented with very cheap triumphs, but he only tossed his head, and smiled. He was horribly spoiled. All charming people, I fancy, are spoiled. It is the secret of their attraction.

"However, I must tell you about Cyril's acting. You know that no women are allowed to play at the A.D.C. At least they were not in my time. I don't know how it is now. Well, of course Cyril was always cast for the girls' parts, and when 'As You Like It' was produced he played Rosalind. It was a marvellous performance. You will laugh at me, but I assure you that Cyril Graham was the only perfect Rosalind I have ever seen. It would be impossible to describe to you the beauty, the delicacy, the refinement of the whole thing. It made an immense sensation, and the horrid little theatre, as it was then, was crowded every night. Even now when I read the play I can't help thinking of

* From the famed preparatory school Eton College, Cyril went up to Trinity College, Cambridge, where he joined the Amateur Dramatic Company.

Cyril; the part might have been written for him, he played it with such extraordinary grace and distinction. The next term he took his degree, and came to London to read for the Diplomatic.* But he never did any work. He spent his days in reading Shakespeare's Sonnets, and his evenings at the theatre. He was, of course, wild to go on the stage. It was all that Lord Crediton and I could do to prevent him. Perhaps, if he had gone on the stage he would be alive now. It is always a silly thing to give advice, but to give good advice is absolutely fatal. I hope you will never fall into that error. If you do, you will be sorry for it.

"Well, to come to the real point of the story, one afternoon I got a letter from Cyril asking me to come round to his rooms that evening. He had charming chambers in Piccadilly overlooking the Green Park, and as I used to go to see him almost every day, I was rather surprised at his taking the trouble to write. Of course I went, and when I arrived I found him in a state of great excitement. He told me that he had at last discovered the true secret of Shakespeare's Sonnets; that all the scholars and critics had been entirely on the wrong track; and that he was the first who, working purely by internal evidence, had found out who Mr. W. H. really was. He was perfectly wild with delight, and for a long time would not tell me his theory. Finally, he produced a bundle of notes, took his copy of the Sonnets off the mantelpiece, and sat down and gave me a long lecture on the whole subject.

"He began by pointing out that the young man to whom Shakespeare addressed these strangely passionate poems must have been somebody who was a really vital factor in the development of his dramatic art, and that this could not be said of either Lord Pembroke or Lord Southampton.† Indeed, whoever he was, he could not have been anybody of high birth, as was shown very clearly by Sonnet xxv,

---

* That is, to study to take exams for an official foreign service position.

† To yet another Mr. W. H. (this one with the initials reversed), Henry Wriothesley, third earl of Southampton (1573–1624), Shakespeare dedicated his poems *Venus and Adonis* (1593) and *The Rape of Lucrece* (1594).

in which Shakespeare contrasts himself with men who are 'great princes' favourites'; says quite frankly—

> Let those who are in favour with their stars
> Of public honour and proud titles boast,
> Whilst I, whom fortune of such triumph bars,
> Unlooked for joy in that I honour most;

and ends the sonnet by congratulating himself on the mean state of him he so adored:

> Then happy I, that love and am beloved
> Where I may not remove nor be removed

This sonnet Cyril declared would be quite unintelligible if we fancied that it was addressed to either the Earl of Pembroke or the Earl of Southampton, both of whom were men of the highest position in England and fully entitled to be called 'great princes'; and he in corroboration of his view read me Sonnets CXXIV and CXXV, in which Shakespeare tells us that his love is not 'the child of state,' that it 'suffers not in smiling pomp,' but is 'builded far from accident.' I listened with a good deal of interest, for I don't think the point had ever been made before; but what followed was still more curious, and seemed to me at the time to dispose entirely of Pembroke's claim. We know from Meres* that the Sonnets had been written before 1598, and Sonnet CIV informs us that Shakespeare's friendship for Mr. W. H. had been already in existence for three years. Now Lord Pembroke, who was born in 1580, did not come to London till he was eighteen years of age, that is to say till 1598, and Shakespeare's acquaintance with Mr. W. H. must have begun in 1594, or at the latest in 1595. Shakespeare, accordingly, could not have known Lord Pembroke until after the Sonnets had been written.

* In a 1598 account of Elizabethan verse, Francis Meres spoke of Shakespeare's "sugared sonnets" being known privately to an inner circle of friends.

"Cyril pointed out also that Pembroke's father did not die until 1601; whereas it was evident from the line,

You had a father, let your son say so,

that the father of Mr. W. H. was dead in 1598; and laid great stress on the evidence afforded by the Wilton portraits which represent Lord Pembroke as a swarthy dark-haired man, while Mr. W. H. was one whose hair was like spun gold, and whose face the meeting-place for the 'lily's white' and the 'deep vermilion in the rose'; being himself 'fair,' and 'red,' and 'white and red,' and of beautiful aspect. Besides it was absurd to imagine that any publisher of the time,[2] and the preface is from the publisher's hand, would have dreamed of addressing William Herbert, Earl of Pembroke, as Mr. W. H.; the case of Lord Buckhurst being spoken of as Mr. Sackville being not really a parallel instance, as Lord Buckhurst, the first of that title, was plain Mr. Sackville when he contributed to the 'Mirror for Magistrates,' while Pembroke, during his father's lifetime, was always known as Lord Herbert. So far for Lord Pembroke, whose supposed claims Cyril easily demolished while I sat by in wonder. With Lord Southampton Cyril had even less difficulty. Southampton became at a very early age the lover of Elizabeth Vernon, so he needed no entreaties to marry; he was not beautiful; he did not resemble his mother, as Mr. W. H. did—

Thou art thy mother's glass, and she in thee
Calls back the lovely April of her prime;

and, above all, his Christian name was Henry, whereas the punning sonnets (CXXXV and CXLIII) show that the Christian name of Shakespeare's friend was the same as his own—*Will*.

"As for the other suggestions of unfortunate commentators, that Mr. W. H. is a misprint for Mr. W. S., meaning Mr. William Shakespeare; that 'Mr. W. H. all' should be read 'Mr. W. Hall'; that Mr. W. H. is Mr. William Hathaway; that Mr. W. H. stands for Mr. Henry Willobie, the young Oxford poet, with the initials of his name reversed; and that a full stop should be placed after 'wisheth,' making Mr. W. H. the writer and not the subject of the dedication,—Cyril got rid of them in a very short time; and it is not worth while to mention his reasons, though I remember he sent me off into a fit of laughter by reading to me, I am glad to say not in the original, some extracts from a German commentator called Barnstorff, who insisted that Mr. W. H. was no less a person than 'Mr. William Himself.' Nor would he allow for a moment that the Sonnets are mere satires on the work of Drayton and John Davies of Hereford. To him, as indeed to me, they were poems of serious and tragic import, wrung out of the bitterness of Shakespeare's heart, and made sweet by the honey of his lips. Still less would he admit that they were merely a philosophical allegory, and that in them Shakespeare is addressing his Ideal Self, or Ideal Manhood, or the Spirit of Beauty, or the Reason, or the Divine Logos, or the Catholic Church. He felt, as indeed I think we all must feel, that the Sonnets are addressed to an individual,—to a particular young man whose personality for some reason seems to have filled the soul of Shakespeare with terrible joy and no less terrible despair.

"Having in this manner cleared the way, as it were, Cyril asked me to dismiss from my mind any preconceived ideas I might have formed on the subject, and to give a fair and unbiased hearing to his own theory. The problem he pointed out was this: Who was that young man of Shakespeare's day who, without being of noble birth or even of noble nature, was addressed by him in terms of such passionate adoration that we can but wonder at the strange worship, and are almost afraid to turn the key that unlocks the mystery of the poet's heart? Who was he whose physical beauty was such that it became the very corner-stone of Shakespeare's art; the very source of Shakespeare's inspiration; the very incarnation of Shakespeare's dreams? To look upon him as simply the object of certain love-poems was to miss the whole meaning of the poems: for the art of which Shakespeare talks in the Sonnets is not the art of the Sonnets themselves, which indeed were to him but slight and secret things—it is the art of the dramatist to which he is always alluding; and he to whom Shakespeare said—

Thou art all my art, and dost advance
As high as learning my rude ignorance,—

he to whom he promised immortality,

Where breath most breathes, even in the mouths of men,—

he who was to him the tenth 'muse' and

Ten times more in worth
Than those old nine which rhymers invocate,

was surely none other than the boy-actor for whom he created Viola and Imogen, Juliet and Rosalind, Portia and Desdemona, and Cleopatra herself."

"The boy-actor of Shakespeare's plays?" I cried.

"Yes," said Erskine. "This was Cyril Graham's theory, evolved as you see purely from the Sonnets themselves, and depending for its acceptance not so much on demonstrable proof of formal evidence, but on a kind of spiritual and artistic sense, by which alone he claimed could the true meaning of the poems be discerned. I remember his reading to me that fine sonnet—

How can my Muse want subject to invent,
While thou dost breathe, that pour'st into my verse
Thine own sweet argument, too excellent
For every vulgar paper to rehearse
O give thyself the thanks, if aught in me
Worthy perusal stand against thy sight;
For who's so dumb that cannot write to thee,
When thou thyself dost give invention light?

—and pointing out how completely it corroborated his view; and indeed he went through all the Sonnets carefully, and showed, or fancied that he showed, that, according to his new explanation of their meaning, things that had seemed obscure, or evil, or exaggerated, became clear and rational, and of high artistic import, illustrating Shakespeare's conception of the true relations between the art of the actor and the art of the dramatist.

"It is of course evident that there must have been in Shakespeare's company some wonderful boy-actor of great beauty, to whom he intrusted the presentation of his noble heroines; for Shakespeare was a practical theatrical manager as well as an imaginative poet; and Cyril Graham had actually discovered the boy-actor's name. He was Will, or, as he preferred to call him, Willie Hughes. The Christian name he found of course in the punning sonnets, CXXXV and CXLIII; the surname was, according to him, hidden in the seventh line of Sonnet XX, where Mr. W. H. is described as—

A man in hew, all *Hews* in his controwling.

"In the original edition of the Sonnets 'Hews' is printed with a capital letter and in italics, and this, he claimed, showed clearly that a play on words was intended, his view receiving a good deal of corroboration from those sonnets in which curious puns are made on the words 'use' and 'usury,' and from such lines as—

Thou art as fair in knowledge as in hew.

Of course I was converted at once, and Willie Hughes became to me as real a person as Shakespeare. The only objection I made to the theory was that the name of Willie Hughes does not occur in the list of the actors of Shakespeare's company as it is printed in the first folio. Cyril, however, pointed out that the absence of Willie Hughes' name from this list really corroborated the theory, as it was evident from Sonnet LXXXVI, that he had abandoned Shakespeare's company to play at a rival theatre, probably in some of Chapman's* plays. It was

* George Chapman (1559–1634)—poet, playwright, and translator of Homer's *Odyssey* and *Iliad*—is here identified as a rival for Willie Hughes's affection.

in reference to this that in the great sonnet on Chapman Shakespeare said to Willie Hughes—

> But when your countenance filled up his line,
> Then lacked I matter; that enfeebled mine—

the expression 'when your countenance filled up his line' referring clearly to the beauty of the young actor giving life and reality and added charm to Chapman's verse, the same idea being also put forward in Sonnet LXXIX:

> Whilst I alone did call upon thy aid,
> My verse alone had all thy gentle grace,
> But now my gracious numbers are decayed,
> And my sick Muse doth give another place;

and in the immediately preceding sonnet, where Shakespeare says,

> Every alien pen hath got my *use*
> And under thee their poesy disperse,

the play upon words (use = Hughes) being of course obvious and the phrase, 'under thee their poesy disperse,' meaning 'by your assistance as an actor bring their plays before the people.'

"It was a wonderful evening, and we sat up almost til dawn reading and re-reading the Sonnets. After some time however, I began to see that before the theory could be placed before the world in a really perfected form, it was necessary to get some independent evidence about the existence of this young actor, Willie Hughes. If this could be once established, there could be no possible doubt about his identity with Mr. W. H.; but otherwise the theory would fall to the ground. I put this forward very strongly to Cyril, who was a good deal annoyed at what he called my philistine tone of mind, and indeed was rather bitter upon the subject. However, I made him promise that in his own interest he would not publish his discovery till he had put the whole matter beyond the reach of doubt; and for weeks and weeks we searched the registers of City churches, the Alleyn MSS.* at Dulwich, the Record Office, the books of the Lord Chamberlain†—everything, in fact, that we thought might contain some allusion to Willie Hughes. We discovered nothing, of course, and each day the existence of Willie Hughes seemed to me to become more problematical. Cyril was in a dreadful state, and used to go over the whole question again and again, entreating me to believe; but I saw the one flaw in the theory, and I refused to be convinced till the actual existence of Willie Hughes, a boy-actor of the Elizabethan stage, had been placed beyond the reach of doubt or cavil.

"One day Cyril left town to stay with his grandfather, I thought at the time, but I afterwards heard from Lord Crediton that this was not the case; and about a fortnight afterwards I received a telegram from him, handed in at Warwick, asking me to be sure to come and dine with him in his chambers, that evening at eight o'clock. When I arrived, he said to me, 'The only apostle who did not deserve proof was St. Thomas, and St. Thomas was the only apostle who got it.' I asked him what he meant. He answered that he had been able not merely to establish the existence in the sixteenth century of a boy-actor of the name of Willie Hughes, but to prove by the most conclusive evidence that he was the Mr. W. H. of the Sonnets. He would not tell me anything more at the time; but after dinner he solemnly produced the picture I showed you, and told me that he had discovered it by the merest chance nailed to the side of an old chest that he had bought at a farmhouse in Warwickshire.‡ The chest itself, which was a very fine example of Elizabethan work, and thoroughly authentic, he had, of course, brought with him, and in the centre of the front panel the initials W. H. were undoubtedly carved. It was this monogram that had attracted his attention, and he told me that it was not till he had had the chest in his possession for several days that he had thought of making any careful examination of the inside. One morning, however, he

* Collection of private papers left by wealthy actor Edward Alleyn (1566–1626).

† The Lord Chamberlain's Office granted or refused licenses for the public performance of plays; two hundred years later this office rejected Wilde's *Salomé*.

‡ County where Shakespeare was born and died, at Stratford-upon-Avon.

saw that the right-hand side of the chest was much thicker than the other, and looking more closely, he discovered that a framed panel was clamped against it. On taking it out, he found it was the picture that is now lying on the sofa. It was very dirty, and covered with mould, but he managed to clean it, and, to his great joy, saw that he had fallen by mere chance on the one thing for which he had been looking. Here was an authentic portrait of Mr. W. H. with his hand resting on the dedicatory page of the Sonnets, and on the corner of the picture could be faintly seen the name of the young man himself written in gold uncial letters on the faded *bleu de paon** ground, 'Master Will Hews.'

"Well, what was I to say? It is quite clear from Sonnet XLVII that Shakespeare had a portrait of Mr. W. H. in his possession, and it seemed to me more than probable that here we had the very 'painted banquet' on which he invited his eye to feast; the actual picture that awoke his heart 'to heart's and eye's delight.' It never occurred to me for a moment that Cyril Graham was playing a trick on me, or that he was trying to prove his theory by means of a forgery."

"But is it a forgery?" I asked.

"Of course it is," said Erskine. "It is a very good forgery but it is a forgery none the less. I thought at the time that Cyril was rather calm about the whole matter; but I remember he kept telling me that he himself required no proof of this kind, and that he thought the theory complete without it. I laughed at him, and told him that without it the entire theory would fall to the ground, and I warmly congratulated him on his marvellous discovery. We then arranged that the picture should be etched or facsimiled, and placed as the frontispiece to Cyril's edition of the Sonnets; and for three months we did nothing but go over each poem line by line, till we had settled every difficulty of text or meaning. One unlucky day I was in a print-shop in Holborn, when I saw upon the counter some extremely beautiful drawings in silver-point. I was so attracted by them that I bought

* Peacock blue (French); on the blue background was displayed the name, written in gold capitals, or uncials.

them; and the proprietor of the place, a man called Rawlings, told me that they were done by a young painter of the name of Edward Merton, who was very clever, but as poor as a church mouse. I went to see Merton some days afterwards, having got his address from the print-seller, and found a pale, interesting young man, with a rather common-looking wife,—his model, as I subsequently learned. I told him how much I admired his drawings, at which he seemed very pleased, and I asked him if he would show me some of his other work. As we were looking over a portfolio, full of really very lovely things,—for Merton had a most delicate and delightful touch,—I suddenly caught sight of a drawing of the picture of Mr. W. H. There was no doubt whatever about it. It was almost a facsimile,—the only difference being that the two masks of Tragedy and Comedy were not suspended from the marble table as they are in the picture but were lying on the floor at the young man's feet. 'Where on earth did you get that?' I asked. He grew rather confused, and said,—'Oh, that is nothing. I did not know it was in this portfolio. It is not a thing of any value.' 'It is what you did for Mr. Cyril Graham,' exclaimed his wife; 'and if this gentleman wishes to buy it, let him have it.' 'For Mr. Cyril Graham?' I repeated. 'Did you paint the picture of Mr. W. H.?' 'I don't understand what you mean,' he answered growing very red. Well, the whole thing was quite dreadful. The wife let it all out. I gave her five pounds when I was going away. I can't bear to think of it, now; but of course I was furious. I went off at once to Cyril's chambers, waited there for three hours before he came in, with that horrid lie staring me in the face, and told him I had discovered his forgery. He grew very pale, and said,—'I did it purely for your sake. You would not be convinced in any other way. It does not affect the truth of the theory.' 'The truth of the theory!' I exclaimed; 'the less we talk about that the better. You never even believed in it yourself. If you had, you would not have committed a forgery to prove it.' High words passed between us; we had a fearful quarrel. I daresay I was unjust, and the next morning he was dead."

"Dead!" I cried.

"Yes, he shot himself with a revolver. By the time I arrived,—his servant had sent for me at once,—the police were already there. He had left a letter for me, evidently written in the greatest agitation and distress of mind."

"What was in it?" I asked.

"Oh, that he believed absolutely in Willie Hughes; that the forgery of the picture had been done simply as a concession to me, and did not in the slightest degree invalidate the truth of the theory; and that in order to show me how firm and flawless his faith in the whole thing was, he was going to offer his life as a sacrifice to the secret of the Sonnets. It was a foolish, mad letter. I remember he ended by saying that he intrusted to me the Willie Hughes theory, and that it was for me to present it to the world, and to unlock the secret of Shakespeare's heart."

"It is a most tragic story," I cried, "but why have you not carried out his wishes?"

Erskine shrugged his shoulders. "Because it is a perfectly unsound theory from beginning to end," he answered.

"My dear Erskine," I exclaimed, getting up from my seat, "you are entirely wrong about the whole matter. It is the only perfect key to Shakespeare's Sonnets that has ever been made. It is complete in every detail. I believe in Willie Hughes."

"Don't say that," said Erskine, gravely; "I believe there is something fatal about the idea, and intellectually there is nothing to be said for it. I have gone into the whole matter, and I assure you the theory is entirely fallacious. It is plausible up to a certain point. Then it stops. For heaven's sake, my dear boy, don't take up the subject of Willie Hughes. You will break your heart over it."

"Erskine," I answered, "it is your duty to give this theory to the world. If you will not do it, I will. By keeping it back you wrong the memory of Cyril Graham, the youngest and the most splendid of all the martyrs of literature. I entreat you to do him this bare act of justice. He died for this thing,—don't let his death be in vain."

Erskine looked at me in amazement. "You are carried away by the sentiment of the whole story," he said. "You forget that a thing is not necessarily true because a man dies for it. I was devoted to Cyril Graham. His death was a horrible blow to me. I did not recover from it for years. I don't think I have ever recovered from it. But Willie Hughes!

There is nothing in the idea of Willie Hughes. No such person ever existed. As for bringing the matter before the world,—the world thinks that Cyril Graham shot himself by accident. The only proof of his suicide was contained in the letter to me, and of this letter the public never heard anything. To the present day Lord Crediton is under the impression that the whole thing was accidental."

"Cyril Graham sacrificed his life to a great idea," I answered; "and if you will not tell of his martyrdom, tell at least of his faith."

"His faith," said Erskine, "was fixed in a thing that was false, in a thing that was unsound, in a thing that no Shakespearian scholar would accept for a moment. The theory would be laughed at. Don't make a fool of yourself, and don't follow a trail that leads nowhere. You start by assuming the existence of the very person whose existence is the thing to be proved. Besides, everybody knows that the Sonnets were addressed to Lord Pembroke. The matter is settled once for all."

"The matter is not settled," I exclaimed. "I will take up the theory where Cyril Graham left it, and I will prove to the world that he was right."

"Silly boy!" said Erskine. "Go home, it is after three, and don't think about Willie Hughes any more. I am sorry I told you anything about it, and very sorry indeed that I should have converted you to a thing in which I don't believe."

"You have given me the key to the greatest mystery of modern literature," I answered; "and I will not rest till I have made you recognise, till I have made everybody recognise, that Cyril Graham was the most subtle Shakespearian critic of our day."

I was about to leave the room when Erskine called me back. "My dear fellow," he said, "let me advise you not to waste your time over the Sonnets. I am quite serious. After all, what do they tell us about Shakespeare? Simply that he was the slave of beauty."

"Well, that is the condition of being an artist!" I replied.

There was a strange silence for a few moments. Then Erskine got up, and looking at me with half closed eyes, said, "Ah! how you remind me of Cyril! He used to say just that sort of thing to me." He tried to smile, but there was a note of poignant pathos in his voice that I remember to the present day, as one remembers the tone of a particular violin that has charmed one, the touch of a particular woman's hand. The great events of life often leave one unmoved; they pass out of consciousness, and, when one thinks of them, become unreal. Even the scarlet flowers of passion seem to grow in the same meadow as the poppies of oblivion. We reject the burden of their memory, and have anodynes against them. But the little things, the things of no moment, remain with us. In some tiny ivory cell the brain stores the most delicate, and the most fleeting impressions.

As I walked home through St. James's Park, the dawn was just breaking over London. The swans were lying asleep on the smooth surface of the polished lake, like white feathers fallen upon a mirror of black steel. The gaunt Palace looked purple against the pale green sky, and in the garden of Stafford House the birds were just beginning to sing. I thought of Cyril Graham, and my eyes filled with tears.

– 2 –

It was past twelve o'clock when I awoke, and the sun was streaming in through the curtains of my room in long dusty beams of tremulous gold. I told my servant that I would not be at home to any one, and after I had discussed a cup of chocolate and a *petit-pain,** I took out of the library my copy of Shakespeare's Sonnets, and Mr. Tyler's facsimile edition† of the Quarto, and began to go carefully through them. Each poem seemed to me to corroborate Cyril Graham's theory. I felt as if I had my hand upon Shakespeare's heart, and was counting each separate throb and pulse of passion. I thought of the wonderful boy-actor, and saw his face in every line.

Previous to this, in my Lord Pembroke days, if I may so term them, I must admit that it had always seemed to me very difficult to understand how the creator of Hamlet and Lear and Othello could have addressed in such extravagant terms of praise and passion one who was merely an ordinary young nobleman of the day.

---

* Roll (French).

† In 1886 Thomas Tyler published a facsimile replica of the original 1609 edition; in that volume he advanced his theory that Mary Fitton was the "Dark Lady" of the *Sonnets*.

Along with most students of Shakespeare, I had found myself compelled to set the Sonnets apart as things quite alien to Shakespeare's development as a dramatist, as things possibly unworthy of the intellectual side of his nature. But now that I began to realise the truth of Cyril Graham's theory, I saw that the moods and passions they mirrored were absolutely essential to Shakespeare's perfection as an artist writing for the Elizabethan stage, and that it was in the curious theatre conditions of that stage that the poems themselves had their origin. I remember what joy I had in feeling that these wonderful Sonnets,

> Subtle as Sphinx; as sweet and musical
> As bright Apollo's lute, strung with his hair,

were no longer isolated from the great æsthetic energies of Shakespeare's life, but were an essential part of his dramatic activity, and revealed to us something of the secret of his method. To have discovered the true name of Mr. W. H. was comparatively nothing: others might have done that, had perhaps done it: but to have discovered his profession was a revolution in criticism.

Two sonnets, I remember, struck me particularly. In the first of these (LIII) Shakespeare, complimenting Willie Hughes on the versatility of his acting, on his wide range of parts, a range extending, as we know, from Rosalind to Juliet, and from Beatrice to Ophelia, says to him:—

> What is your substance, whereof are you made?
> That millions of strange shadows on you tend?
> Since everyone hath, every one, one shade,
> And you, but one, can every shadow lend—

lines that would be unintelligible if they were not addressed to an actor, for the word "shadow" had in Shakespeare's day a technical meaning connected with the stage. "The best in this kind are but shadows," says Theseus of the actors in the "Midsummer Night's Dream";

Life's but a walking shadow, and poor player
That struts and frets his hour upon the stage,

cries Macbeth in the moment of his despair, and there are many similar allusions in the literature of the day. This sonnet evidently belonged to the series in which Shakespeare discusses the nature of the actor's art, and of the strange and rare temperament that is essential to the perfect stage-player. "How is it," says Shakespeare to Willie Hughes, "that you have so many personalities?" and then he goes on to point out that his beauty is such that it seems to realise every form and phase of fancy, to embody each dream of the creative imagination,—an idea that is still further expanded in the sonnet that immediately follows, where, beginning with the fine thought,

O, how much more doth beauty beauteous seem
By that sweet ornament which *truth* doth give!

Shakespeare invites us to notice how the truth of acting, the truth of visible presentation on the stage, adds to the wonder of poetry, giving life to its loveliness, and actual reality to its ideal form. And yet, in Sonnet LXVII, Shakespeare calls upon Willie Hughes to abandon the stage with its artificiality, its unreal life of painted face and mimic costume, its immoral influences and suggestions, its remoteness from the true world of noble action and sincere utterance.

Ah, wherefore with infection should he live,
And with his presence grace impiety,
That sin by him advantage should receive,
And lace itself with his society?
Why should false painting imitate his cheek,
And steal dead seeing of his living hue?
Why should poor beauty indirectly seek
Roses of shadow, since his rose is true?

It may seem strange that so great a dramatist as Shakespeare, who realised his own perfection as an artist and his full humanity as a man on the ideal plane of stage-writing and stage-playing, should have written in these terms about the theatre; but we must remember that in Sonnets CX and CXI, Shakespeare shows us that he too was wearied of the world of puppets, and full of shame at having made himself "a motley to the view." Sonnet CXI is especially bitter:—

> O, for my sake do you with Fortune chide,
> The guilty goddess of my harmful deeds,
> That did not better for my life provide
> Than public means which public manners breeds.
> Thence comes it that my name receives a brand,
> And almost thence my nature is subdued
> To what it works in, like the dyer's hand:
> Pity me, then, and wish I were renewed—

and there are many signs of the same feeling elsewhere, signs familiar to all real students of Shakespeare.

One point puzzled me immensely as I read the Sonnets, and it was days before I struck on the true interpretation, which indeed Cyril Graham himself seemed to have missed. I could not understand how it was that Shakespeare set so high a value on his young friend marrying. He himself had married young and the result had been unhappiness, and it was not likely that he would have asked Willie Hughes to commit the same error. The boy-player of Rosalind had nothing to gain from marriage, or from the passions of real life. The early sonnets with their strange entreaties to love children seemed to be a jarring note.

The explanation of the mystery came on me quite suddenly and I found it in the curious dedication. It will be remembered that this dedication was as follows:—

"TO.THE.ONLIE.BEGETTER.OF.

THESE.INSUING.SONNETS.

MR.W.H.ALL.HAPPINESSE.

AND.THAT.ETERNITIE.

PROMISED.BY.

OUR. EVER-LIVING. POET.

WISHETH.

THE. WELL-WISHING.

ADVENTURER. IN.

SETTING.

FORTH

T. T."

Some scholars have supposed that the word "begetter" here means simply the procurer of the Sonnets for Thomas Thorpe the publisher; but this view is now generally abandoned, and the highest authorities are quite agreed that it is to be taken in the sense of inspirer, the metaphor being drawn from the analogy of physical life. Now I saw that the same metaphor was used by Shakespeare himself all through the poems, and this set me on the right track. Finally I made my great discovery. The marriage that Shakespeare proposes for Willie Hughes is the "marriage with his Muse," an expression which is definitely put forward in Sonnet LXXXII where, in the bitterness of his heart at the defection of the boy-actor for whom he had written his greatest parts, and whose beauty had indeed suggested them, he opens his complaint by saying—

I grant thou wert not married to my Muse.

The children he begs him to beget are no children of flesh and blood, but more immortal children of undying fame. The whole cycle of the early sonnets is simply Shakespeare's invitations to Willie Hughes to go upon the stage and become a player. How barren and profitless a thing, he says, is this beauty of yours if it be not used:

When forty winters shall besiege thy brow,
And dig deep trenches in thy beauty's field,
Thy youth's proud livery, so gazed on now,
Will be a tattered weed, of small worth held:
Then being asked where all thy beauty lies,
Where all the treasure of thy lusty days,

To say, within thine own deep-sunken eyes,
Were an all-eating shame and thriftless praise.

You must create something in art: my verse "is thine and *born* of thee"; only listen to me, and I will

bring forth eternal numbers to outlive long date,

and you shall people with forms of your own image the imaginary world of the stage. These children that you beget, he continues, will not wither away, as mortal children do, but you shall live in them and in my plays: do but—

Make thee another self, for love of me,
That beauty still may live in thine or thee!

Be not afraid to surrender your personality, to give your "semblance to some other":

To give away yourself keeps yourself still,
And you must live, drawn by your own sweet skill.

I may not be learned in astrology, and yet, in those "constant stars" your eyes,

I read such art
As truth and beauty shall together thrive,
If from thyself to store thou wouldst convert.

What does it matter about others?

Let those whom Nature hath not made for store,
Harsh, featureless, and rude, barrenly perish:

With you it is different, Nature—

carv'd thee for her seal, and meant thereby
Thou shouldst print more, nor let that copy die.

Remember, too, how soon Beauty forsakes itself. Its action is no stronger than a flower, and like a flower it lives and dies. Think of "the stormy gusts of winter's day," of the "barren edge of Death's eternal cold," and—

ere thou be distilled,
Make sweet some vial; treasure thou some place
With beauty's treasure, ere it be self-killed.

Why, even flowers do not altogether die. When roses wither,

Of their sweet deaths are sweetest odours made:

and you who are "my rose" should not pass away without leaving your form in Art. For Art has the very secret of joy.

Ten times thyself were happier than thou art,
If ten of thine ten times refigur'd thee.

You do not require the "bastard signs of fair," the painted face, the fantastic disguises of other actors:

. . . the golden tresses of the dead,
The right of sepulchres,

need not be shorn away for you. In you—

. . those holy antique hours are seen,
Without all ornament, itself and true,
Making no summer of another's green.

All that is necessary is to "copy what in you is writ"; to place you on the stage as you are in actual life. All those ancient poets who have written of "ladies dead and lovely knights"* have been dreaming of such a one as you, and:

> All their praises are but prophecies
> Of this our time, all you prefiguring.

For your beauty seems to belong to all ages and to all lands. Your shade comes to visit me at night, but, I want to look upon your "shadow" in the living day, I want to see you upon the stage. Mere description of you will not suffice:

> If I could write the beauty of your eyes,
> And in fresh numbers number all your graces,
> The age to come would say, "This poet lies;
> Such heavenly touches ne'er touched earthly faces."

It is necessary that "some child of yours," some artistic creation that embodies you, and to which your imagination gives life, shall present you to the world's wondering eyes. Your own thoughts are your children, offspring of sense and spirit; give some expression to them, and you shall find—

> Those children nursed, delivered from thy brain.

My thoughts, also, are my "children." They are of your begetting and my brain is:

> the womb wherein they grew.

For this great friendship of ours is indeed a marriage, it is the "marriage of true minds."

I collected together all the passages that seemed to me to

* This phrase and the following two lines are from Sonnet 106, not from an ancient poet.

corroborate this view, and they produced a strong impression on me, and showed me how complete Cyril Graham's theory really was. I also saw that it was quite easy to separate those lines in which Shakespeare speaks of the Sonnets themselves, from those in which he speaks of his great dramatic work. This was a point that had been entirely overlooked by all critics up to Cyril Graham's day. And yet it was one of the most important in the whole series of poems. To the Sonnets Shakespeare was more or less indifferent. He did not wish to rest his fame on them. They were to him his "slight Muse," as he calls them, and intended, as Meres tells us, for private circulation only among a few, a very few, friends. Upon the other hand he was extremely conscious of the high artistic value of his plays, and shows a noble self-reliance upon his dramatic genius. When he says to Willie Hughes:

> But thy eternal summer shall not fade,
> Nor lose possession of that fair thou owest;
> Nor shall Death brag thou wander'st in his shade,
> When in *eternal lines* to time thou growest:
> So long as men can breathe or eyes can see,
> So long lives this and this gives life to thee;—

the expression "eternal lines" clearly alludes to one of his plays that he was sending him at the time, just as the concluding couplet points to his confidence in the probability of his plays being always acted. In his address to the Dramatic Muse (Sonnets C and CI) we find the same feeling:

> Where art thou, Muse, that thou forget'st so long
> To speak of that which gives thee all thy might?
> Spend'st thou thy fury on some worthless song,
> Darkening thy power to lend base subjects light?

he cries, and he then proceeds to reproach the mistress of Tragedy and Comedy for her "neglect of truth in beauty dyed," and says:

Because he needs no praise, wilt thou be dumb?
Excuse not silence so; for 't lies in thee
To make him much outlive a gilded tomb,
And to be praised of ages yet to be.
Then do thy office, Muse, I teach thee how,
To make him seem long hence as he shows now.

It is, however, perhaps in Sonnet LV that Shakespeare gives to this idea its fullest expression. To imagine that the "powerful rhyme" of the second line refers to the sonnet itself was entirely to mistake Shakespeare's meaning. It seemed to me that it was extremely likely, from the general character of the sonnet, that a particular play was meant, and that the play was none other but "Romeo and Juliet."

Not marble, nor the gilded monuments
Of princes shall outlive this powerful rhyme;
But you shall shine more bright in these contents
Than unswept stone besmeared with sluttish time.
When wasteful war shall statues overturn,
And broils root out the work of masonry,
Not Mars his sword nor war's quick fire shall burn
The living record of your memory
'Gainst death and all-oblivious enmity
Shall you pace forth; your praise shall still find room
Even in the eyes of all posterity
That wear this world out to the ending doom.
So, till the judgment that yourself arise,
You live in this, and dwell in lovers' eyes.

It was also very suggestive to note how here as elsewhere Shakespeare promised Willie Hughes immortality in a form that appealed to men's eyes—that is to say, in a spectacular form, in a play that is to be looked at.

For two weeks I worked hard at the Sonnets, hardly ever going out, and refusing all invitations. Every day I seemed to be discovering something new, and Willie Hughes became to me a kind of spiritual presence, an ever-dominant personality. I could almost fancy that I saw him standing in the shadow of my room, so well had Shakespeare drawn him, with his golden hair, his tender flower-like grace, his dreamy deep-sunken eyes, his delicate mobile limbs, and his white lily hands. His very name fascinated me. Willie Hughes! Willie Hughes! How musically it sounded! Yes; who else but he could have been the master-mistress of Shakespeare's passion,* the lord of his love to whom he was bound in vassalage,† the delicate minion of pleasure,‡ the rose of the whole world,§ the herald of the spring,¶ decked in the proud livery of youth,** the lovely boy whom it was sweet music to hear,†† and whose beauty was the very raiment of Shakespeare's heart,‡‡ as it was the keystone of his dramatic power? How bitter now seemed the whole tragedy of his desertion and his shame!—shame that he made sweet and lovely§§ by the mere magic of his personality, but that was none the less shame. Yet as Shakespeare forgave him, should not we forgive him also? I did not care to pry into the mystery of his sin or of the sin, if such it was, of the great poet who had so dearly loved him. "I am that I am," said Shakespeare in a sonnet of noble scorn,—

> I am that I am, and they that level
> At my abuses reckon up their own;
> I may be straight, though they themselves be bevel;
> By their rank thoughts my deeds must not be shown.

---

* Sonnet XX.2. [Wilde's note. This footnote and the ones below epitomize Wilde's persistent scholarly tone.]

† Sonnet XXVI.1. [Wilde's note]

‡ Sonnet CXXVI.9. [Wilde's note]

§ Sonnet CIX.14. [Wilde's note]

¶ Sonnet I.10. [Wilde's note]

** Sonnet II.3. [Wilde's note]

†† Sonnet VIII.1. [Wilde's note]

‡‡ Sonnet XXII.6. [Wilde's note]

§§ Sonnet XCV.1. [Wilde's note]

Willie Hughes's abandonment of Shakespeare's theatre was a different matter, and I investigated it at great length. Finally I came to the conclusion that Cyril Graham had been wrong in regarding the rival dramatist of Sonnet LXXX as Chapman. It was obviously Marlowe* who was alluded to. At the time the Sonnets were written, which must have been between 1590 and 1595, such an expression as "the proud full sail of his great verse" could not possibly have been used of Chapman's work, however applicable it might have been to the style of his later Jacobean plays. No; Marlowe was clearly the rival poet of whom Shakespeare spoke in such laudatory terms; the hymn he wrote in Willie Hughes' honour was the unfinished "Hero and Leander," and that

Affable familiar ghost
Which nightly gulls him with intelligence,

was the Mephistopheles of his Doctor Faustus. No doubt, Marlowe was fascinated by the beauty and grace of the boy-actor and lured him away from the Blackfriars Theatre, that he might play the Gaveston of his "Edward II." That Shakespeare had some legal right to retain Willie Hughes in his own company seems evident from Sonnet LXXXVII, where he says:

Farewell! thou art too dear for my possessing,
And like enough thou know'st thy estimate:
The *charter of thy worth* gives thee releasing;
My *bonds* in thee are all determinate.
For how do I hold thee but by thy granting?
And for that riches where is my deserving?
The cause of this fair gift in me is wanting,
And so my patent back again is swerving.

---

* Christopher Marlowe (1564–1593), the founding genius of Elizabethan drama; he wrote the plays *Tamburlaine*, *Doctor Faustus*, and *Edward II*, and the erotic poem *Hero and Leander*.

Thyself thou gav'st, thy own worth then not knowing,
Or me, to whom thou gav'st it, else mistaking;
So thy great gift, upon misprision growing,
Comes home again, on better judgment making.
Thus have I had thee, as a dream doth flatter,
In sleep a king, but waking no such matter.

But him whom he could not hold by love, he would not hold by force. Willie Hughes became a member of Lord Pembroke's company, and perhaps in the open yard of the Red Bull Tavern, played the part of King Edward's delicate minion. On Marlowe's death, he seems to have returned to Shakespeare, who, whatever his fellow-partners may have thought of the matter, was not slow to forgive the wilfulness and treachery of the young actor.

How well, too, had Shakespeare drawn the temperament of the stage-player! Willie Hughes was one of those—

That do not do the thing they most do show,
Who, moving others, are themselves as stone.

He could act love, but could not feel it, could mimic passion without realising it.

In many's looks the false heart's history
Is writ in moods and frowns and wrinkles strange,

but with Willie Hughes it was not so. "Heaven," says Shakepeare, in a sonnet of mad idolatry—

Heaven in thy creation did decree
That in thy face sweet love should ever dwell;
Whate'er thy thoughts or thy heart's workings be,
Thy looks should nothing thence but sweetness tell.

In his "inconstant mind" and his "false heart" it was easy to recognise the insincerity that somehow seems inseparable from the artistic nature, as in his love of praise, that desire for immediate recognition that characterises all actors. And yet, more fortunate in this than other actors, Willie Hughes was to know something of immortality. Intimately connected with Shakespeare's plays, he was to live in them, and by their production.

> Your name from hence immortal life shall have,
> Though I, once gone, to all the world must die:
> The earth can yield me but a common grave,
> When you entombed in men's eyes shall lie.
> Your monument shall be my gentle verse,
> Which eyes not yet created shall o'er-read,
> And tongues to be your being shall rehearse,
> When all the breathers of this world are dead.

Nash with his venomous tongue had railed against Shakespeare for "reposing eternity in the mouth of a player," the reference being obviously to the Sonnets.

But to Shakespeare, the actor was a deliberate and self-conscious fellow worker who gave form and substance to a poet's fancy, and brought into Drama the elements of a noble realism. His silence could be as eloquent as words, and his gesture as expressive, and in those terrible moments of Titan agony or of god-like pain, when thought outstrips utterance, when the soul sick with excess of anguish stammers or is dumb, and the very raiment of speech is rent and torn by passion in its storm, then the actor could become, though it were but for a moment, a creative artist, and touch by his mere presence and personality those springs of terror and of pity to which tragedy appeals. This full recognition of the actor's art, and of the actor's power, was one of the things that distinguished the Romantic from the Classical Drama, and one of the things, consequently, that we owed to Shakespeare, who, fortunate in much, was fortunate also in this, that he was able to find Richard Burbage* and to fashion Willie Hughes.

---

* Richard Burbage (c.1567–1619) was a theater owner and the greatest tragic actor of his time.

With what pleasure he dwelt upon Willie Hughes' influence over his audience—the "gazers" as he calls them; with what charm of fancy did he analyse the whole art! Even in the "Lover's Complaint" he speaks of his acting, and tells us that he was a nature so impressionable to the quality of dramatic situations that he could assume all "strange forms"—

> Of burning blushes, or of weeping water,
> Or swooning paleness:

explaining his meaning more fully later on where he tells us how Willie Hughes was able to deceive others by his wonderful power to—

> Blush at speeches rank, to weep at woes,
> Or to turn white and swoon at tragic shows.

It had never been pointed out before that the shepherd of this lovely pastoral, whose "youth in art and art in youth" are described with such subtlety of phrase and passion, was none other than the Mr. W. H. of the Sonnets. And yet there was no doubt that he was so. Not merely in personal appearance are the two lads the same, but their natures and temperaments are identical. When the false shepherd whispers to the fickle maid—

> All my offences that abroad you see
> Are errors of the blood, none of mind;
> Love made them not:

when he says of his lovers,

> Harm have I done to them, but ne'er was harmed;
> Kept hearts in liveries, but mine own was free,
> And reigned, commanding in his monarchy:

when he tells us of the "deep-brained sonnets" that one of them had sent him, and cries out in boyish pride—

The broken bosoms that to me belong
Have emptied all their fountains in my well:

it is impossible not to feel that it is Willie Hughes who is speaking to us. "Deep-brained sonnets," indeed, had Shakespeare brought him, "jewels" that to his careless eyes were but as "trifles," though—

each several stone,
With wit well blazoned, smiled or made some moan;

and into the well of beauty he had emptied the sweet fountain of his song. That in both places it was an actor who was alluded to, was also clear. The betrayed nymph tells us of the "false fire" in her lover's cheek, of the "forced thunder" of his sighs, and of his "borrowed motion": of whom, indeed, but of an actor could it be said that to him "thought, characters, and words" were "merely Art," or that—

To make the weeper laugh, the laugher weep,
He had the dialect and different skill,
Catching all passions in his craft of will?

The play on words in the last line is the same as that used in the punning sonnets, and is continued in the following stanza of the poem, where we are told of the youth who—

did in the general bosom reign
Of young, of old; and sexes both enchanted,

that there were those who—

. . dialogued for him what he would say,
Asked their own wills, and made their Wills obey.

Yes: the "rose-cheeked Adonis" of the Venus poem, the false shepherd of the "Lover's Complaint," the "tender churl," the "beauteous niggard" of the Sonnets, was none other but a young actor; and as I read through the various descriptions given of him, I saw that the love that Shakespeare bore him was as the love of a musician for some delicate instrument on which he delights to play, as a sculptor's love for some rare and exquisite material that suggests a new form of plastic beauty, a new mode of plastic expression. For all Art has its medium, its material, be it that of rhythmical words, or of pleasurable colour, or of sweet and subtly-divided sound; and, as one of the most fascinating critics of our day has pointed out, it is to the qualities inherent in each material, and special to it, that we owe the sensuous element in Art, and with all that in Art is essentially artistic. What then shall we say of the material that the Drama requires for its perfect presentation? What of the Actor, who is the medium through which alone the Drama can truly reveal itself? Surely, in that strange mimicry of life by the living which is the mode and method of theatric art, there are sensuous elements of beauty that none of the other arts possess. Looked at from one point of view, the common players of the saffron-strewn stage are Art's most complete, most satisfying instruments. There is no passion in bronze, nor motion in marble. The sculptor must surrender colour, and the painter fullness of form. The epos changes acts into words, and music changes words into tones. It is the Drama only that, to quote the fine saying of Gervinus,* uses all means at once, and, appealing both to eye and ear, has at its disposal, and in its service, form and colour, tone, look, and word, the swiftness of motion, the intense realism of visible action.

It may be that in this very completeness of the instrument lies the secret of some weakness in the art. Those arts are happiest that employ a material remote from reality, and there is a danger in the absolute identity of medium and matter, the danger of ignoble realism and unimaginative imitation. Yet Shakespeare himself was a player, and wrote for players. He saw the possibilities that lay hidden in an art that up to his time had expressed itself but in bombast or in clowning. He has left us the most perfect rules for acting that have ever been written. He created parts that can be only truly revealed to us on the

* Wilde owned *Shakespeare Commentaries* (translated from the original German in 1863), by G. G. Gervinus, who is quoted here.

stage, wrote plays that need the theatre for their full realisation, and we cannot marvel that he so worshipped one who was the interpreter of his vision, as he was the incarnation of his dreams.

There was, however, more in his friendship than the mere delight of a dramatist in one who helps him to achieve his end. This was indeed a subtle element of pleasure, if not of passion, and a noble basis for an artistic comradeship. But it was not all that the Sonnets revealed to us. There was something beyond. There was the soul, as well as the language, of neo-Platonism.

"The fear of the Lord is the beginning of wisdom," said the stern Hebrew prophet: "The beginning of wisdom is Love," was the gracious message of the Greek. And the spirit of the Renaissance, which already touched Hellenism at so many points, catching the inner meaning of this phrase and divining its secret, sought to elevate friendship to the high dignity of the antique ideal, to make it a vital factor in the new culture, and a mode of self-conscious intellectual development. In 1492 appeared Marsilio Ficino's translation of the "Symposium" of Plato,* and this wonderful dialogue, of all the Platonic dialogues perhaps the most perfect, as it is the most poetical, began to exercise a strange influence over men, and to colour their words and thoughts, and manner of living. In its subtle suggestions of sex in soul, in the curious analogies it draws between intellectual enthusiasm and the physical passion of love, in its dream of the incarnation of the Idea in a beautiful and living form, and of a real spiritual conception with a travail and a bringing to birth, there was something that fascinated the poets and scholars of the sixteenth century. Shakespeare, certainly, was fascinated by it, and had read the dialogue, if not in Ficino's translation, of which many copies found their way to England, perhaps in that French translation by Leroy to which Joachim du Bellay contributed so many graceful metrical versions. When he says to Willie Hughes,

---

* In the late 1400s, Ficino translated the *Symposium* and other works by Plato from Greek to Latin, and thus fueled a Renaissance interest in the Platonic theory of ideal love.

he that calls on thee, let him bring forth
Eternal numbers to outlive long date,

he is thinking of Diotima's theory* that Beauty is the goddess who presides over birth, and draws into the light of day the dim conceptions of the soul: when he tells us of the "marriage of true minds," and exhorts his friend to beget children that time cannot destroy, he is but repeating the words in which the prophetess tells us that "friends are married by a far nearer tie than those who beget mortal children, for fairer and more immortal are the children who are their common offspring." So, also, Edward Blount in his dedication of "Hero and Leander" talks of Marlowe's works as his "right children," being the "issue of his brain"; and when Bacon claims that "the best works and of greatest merit for the public have proceeded from the unmarried and childless men, which both in affection and means have married and endowed the public," he is paraphrasing a passage in the "Symposium."

Friendship, indeed, could have desired no better warrant for its permanence or its ardours than the Platonic theory, or creed, as we might better call it, that the true world was the world of ideas, and that these ideas took visible form and became incarnate in man, and it is only when we realise the influence of neo-Platonism on the Renaissance that we can understand the true meaning of the amatory phrases and words with which friends were wont, at this time, to address each other. There was a kind of mystic transference of the expressions of the physical sphere to a sphere that was spiritual, that was removed from gross bodily appetite, and in which the soul was Lord. Love had, indeed, entered the olive garden of the new Academe,† but he wore the same flame-coloured raiment, and had the same words of passion on his lips.

Michael Angelo, the "haughtiest spirit in Italy" as he has been

---

* Diotima is the Platonic priestess of ultimate wisdom, who in the *Symposium* reveals the true secret of pure aesthetic attraction.

† Plato's school of philosophy was called the Academy.

called, addresses the young Tommaso Cavalieri* in such fervent and passionate terms that some have thought that the sonnets in question must have been intended for that noble lady, the widow of the Marchese di Pescara, whose white hand, when she was dying, the great sculptor's lips had stooped to kiss. But that it was to Cavalieri that they were written, and that the literal interpretation is the right one, is evident not merely from the fact that Michael Angelo plays with his name, as Shakespeare plays with the name of Willie Hughes, but from the direct evidence of Varchi, who was well acquainted with the young man, and who, indeed, tells us that he possessed "besides imcomparable personal beauty, so much charm of nature, such excellent abilities, and such a graceful manner, that he deserved, and still deserves, to be the better loved the more he is known." Strange as these sonnets may seem to us now, when rightly interpreted they merely serve to show with what intense and religious fervour Michael Angelo addressed himself to the worship of intellectual beauty, and how, to borrow a fine phrase from Mr. Symonds,† he pierced through the veil of flesh and sought the divine idea it imprisoned. In the sonnet written for Luigi del Riccio on the death of his friend, Cecchino Bracci, we can also trace, as Mr. Symonds points out, the Platonic conception of love as nothing if not spiritual, and of beauty as a form that finds its immortality within the lover's soul. Cecchino was a lad who died at the age of seventeen, and when Luigi asked Michael Angelo to make a portrait of him, Michael Angelo answered, "I can only do so by drawing you in whom he still lives."

> If the beloved in the lover shine,
> Since Art without him cannot work alone,
> Thee must I carve, to tell the world of him.

---

* Handsome and accomplished young Roman aristocrat to whom Michelangelo addressed many of his most powerful and thoughtful poems.

† English poet and literary critic John Addington Symonds (1840–1893) had sent Wilde his translation of Michelangelo's poems; he later discussed their homoerotic aspect in his multivolume *The Renaissance in Italy* (1875–1886).

The same idea is also put forward in Montaigne's noble essay* on Friendship, a passion which he ranks higher than the love of brother for brother, or the love of man for woman. He tells us—I quote from Florio's translation, one of the books with which Shakespeare was familiar—how "perfect amitie" is indivisible, how it "possesseth the soule, and swaies it in all soveraigntie," and how "by the interposition of a spiritual beauty the desire of a spiritual conception is engendered in the beloved." He writes of an "internall beauty, of difficile knowledge, and abtruse discovery" that is revealed unto friends, and unto friends only. He mourns for the dead Etienne de la Boëtie,† in accents of wild grief and inconsolable love. The learned Hubert Languet, the friend of Melanchthon and of the leaders of the reformed church, tells the young Philip Sidney how he kept his portrait by him some hours to feast his eyes upon it, and how his appetite was "rather increased than diminished by the sight," and Sidney writes to him, "the chief hope of my life, next to the everlasting blessedness of heaven, will always be the enjoyment of true friendship, and there you shall have the chiefest place." Later on there came to Sidney's house in London, one—some day to be burned at Rome, for the sin of seeing God in all things—Giordano Bruno, just fresh from his triumph before the University of Paris. "A filosofia è necessario amore"‡ were the words ever upon his lips, and there was something in his strange ardent personality that made men feel that he had discovered the new secret of life. Ben Jonson writing to one of his friends subscribes himself "your true lover," and dedicates his noble eulogy on Shakespeare "To the memory of my Beloved." Richard Barnfield in his "Affectionate Shepherd" flutes on soft Virgilian reed the story of his attachment to some young Elizabethan of the day. Out of all the Eclogues, Abraham Fraunce selects the second for translation, and

* The *Essays* of French writer Michel de Montaigne (1533–1592) explore ideas (for example, of friendship) in relation to experience. In 1603 John Florio translated the *Essays* into English.

† In this paragraph Wilde lists distinguished poets, scholars, and philosophers who expressed idealized versions of homoerotic love during the Renaissance.

‡ Philosophy requires love (Italian).

Fletcher's lines to Master W. C. show what fascination was hidden in the mere name of Alexis.

It was no wonder then that Shakespeare had been stirred by a spirit that so stirred his age. There had been critics, like Hallam, who had regretted that the Sonnets had ever been written, who had seen in them something dangerous, something unlawful even. To them it would have been sufficient to answer in Chapman's noble words:

> There is no danger to a man that knows
> What Life and Death is: there's not any law
> Exceeds his knowledge: neither is it lawful
> That he should stoop to any other law.

But it was evident that the Sonnets needed no such defence as this, and that those who had talked of "the folly of excessive and misplaced affection" had not been able to interpret either language or the spirit of these great poems, so intimately connected with the philosophy and the art of their time. It is no doubt true that to be filled with an absorbing passion is to surrender the security of one's lover life, and yet in such surrender there may be gain, certainly there was for Shakespeare. When Pico della Mirandola* crossed the threshold of the villa of Careggi, and stood before Marsilio Ficino in all the grace and comeliness of his wonderful youth, the aged scholar seemed to see in him the realisation of the Greek ideal, and determined to devote his remaining years to the translation of Plotinus, that new Plato, in whom, as Mr. Pater reminds us, "the mystical element in the Platonic philosophy had been worked out to the utmost limit of vision and ecstasy." A romantic friendship with a young Roman of his day initiated Winckelmann into the secret of Greek art, taught him the mystery of its beauty and the meaning of its form. In Willie Hughes, Shakespeare found not merely a most delicate instrument for the presentation of his art, but

---

* Giovanni Pico della Mirandola (1463–1494), an astonishingly brilliant philosopher, admired Marsilio Ficino (see footnote on page 39), as essayist Walter Pater once observed.

the visible incarnation of his idea of beauty, and it is not too much to say that to this young actor, whose very name the dull writers of his age forgot to chronicle, the Romantic Movement of English Literature is largely indebted.

– 3 –

One evening I thought that I had really discovered Willie Hughes in Elizabethan literature. In a wonderfully graphic account of the last days of the great Earl of Essex,* his chaplain, Thomas Knell, tells us that the night before the Earl died, "he called William Hewes, which was his musician, to play upon the virginals and to sing. 'Play,' said he, 'my song, Will Hewes, and I will sing it myself.' So he did it most joyfully, not as the howling swan, which, still looking down, waileth her end, but as a sweet lark, lifting up his hands and casting up his eyes to his God, with this mounted the crystal skies, and reached with his unwearied tongue the top of highest heavens." Surely the boy who played on the virginals to the dying father of Sidney's Stella was none other than the Will Hewes to whom Shakespeare dedicated the Sonnets, and who he tells us was himself sweet "music to hear." Yet Lord Essex died in 1576, when Shakespeare was but twelve years of age. It was impossible that his musician could have been the Mr. W. H. of the Sonnets. Perhaps Shakespeare's young friend was the son of the player upon the virginals? It was at least something to have discovered that Will Hewes was an Elizabethan name. Indeed the name Hews seemed to have been closely connected with music and the stage. The first English actress was the lovely Margaret Hews, whom Prince Rupert so madly adored. What more probable than that between her and Lord Essex' musician had come the boy-actor of Shakespeare's plays? In 1587 a certain Thomas Hews brought out at Gray's Inn a Euripidean tragedy entitled "The Misfortunes of Arthur," receiving much assistance in the arrangement of the dumb shows from one Francis

* Wilde inserts this anecdote despite its avowed irrelevance to his purpose, offering it as evidence that the name "Hews" was linked to theater.

Bacon,* then a student of law. Surely he was some near kinsman of the lad to whom Shakespeare said—

> Take all my loves, my love, yea, take them all;

the "profitless usurer" of "unused beauty," as he describes him. But the proofs, the links—where were they? Alas! I could not find them. It seemed to me that I was always on the brink of absolute verification, but that I could never really attain to it. I thought it strange that no one had ever written a history of the English boy-actors of the sixteenth and seventeenth centuries, and determined to undertake the task myself, and to try to ascertain their true relations to the drama. The subject was, certainly, full of artistic interest. These lads had been the delicate reeds through which our poets had sounded their sweetest strains, the gracious vessels of honour into which they had poured the purple wine of their song. Foremost, naturally, among them all had been the youth to whom Shakespeare had intrusted the realisation of his most exquisite creations. Beauty had been his, such as our age has never, or but rarely seen, a beauty that seemed to combine the charm of both sexes, and to have wedded, as the Sonnets tell us, the grace of Adonis and the loveliness of Helen. He had been quick-witted, too, and eloquent, and from those finely curved lips that the satirist had mocked at had come the passionate cry of Juliet, and the bright laughter of Beatrice, Perdita's flower-like words, and Ophelia's wandering songs. Yet as Shakespeare himself had been but as a god among giants, so Willie Hughes had only been one out of many marvellous lads to whom our English Renaissance owed something of the secret of its joy, and it appeared to me that they also were worthy of some study and record.

In a little book with fine vellum leaves and damask silk cover—a fancy of mine in those fanciful days—I accordingly collected such

---

* A philosopher and a brilliant, devious lawyer, Bacon (1561–1626) wrote important essays and major treatises on the aims of science; he was lord chancellor under James I.

information as I could about them, and even now there is something in the scanty record of their lives, in the mere mention of their names, that attracts me. I seemed to know them all: Robin Armin,[3] the goldsmith's lad who was lured by Tarlton to go on the stage: Sandford, whose performance of the courtezan Flamantia Lord Burleigh witnessed at Gray's Inn: Cooke, who played Agrippina in the tragedy of "Sejanus": Nat. Field, whose young and beardless portrait is still preserved for us at Dulwich, and who in "Cynthia's Revels" played the "Queen and Huntress chaste and fair": Gil. Carie, who, attired as a mountain nymph, sang in the same lovely masque Echo's song of mourning for Narcissus: Parsons, the Salmacis of the strange pageant of "Tamburlaine": Will. Ostler, who was one of "The Children of the Queen's Chapel," and accompanied King James to Scotland: George Vernon, to whom the King sent a cloak of scarlet cloth, and a cape of crimson velvet: Alick Gough, who performed the part of Cænis, Vespasian's concubine, in Massingers' "Roman Actor," and three years later that of Acanthe, in the same dramatist's "Picture": Barrett, the heroine of Richards' tragedy of "Messalina": Dicky Robinson, "a very pretty fellow," Ben Jonson tells us, who was a member of Shakespeare's company, and was known for his exquisite taste in costume, as well as for his love of woman's apparel: Salathiel Pavy, whose early and tragic death Jonson mourned in one of the sweetest threnodies of our literature: Arthur Savile, who was one of "the players of Prince Charles," and took a girl's part in a comedy by Marmion: Stephen Hammerton, "a most noted and beautiful woman actor," whose pale oval face with its heavy-lidded eyes and somewhat sensuous mouth looks out at us from a curious miniature of the time: Hart, who made his first success by playing the Duchess in the tragedy of "The Cardinal," and who in a poem that is clearly modelled upon some of Shakespeare's Sonnets is described by one who had seen him as "beauty to the eye, and music to the ear": and Kynaston, of whom Betterton said that "it has been disputed among the judicious, whether any woman could have more sensibly touched the passions," and whose white hands and amber-coloured hair seem to have retarded by some years the introduction of actresses upon our stage.

The Puritans, with their uncouth morals and ignoble minds, had of course railed against them, and dwelt on the impropriety of boys disguising as women, and learning to affect the manners and passions of the female sex. Gosson, with his shrill voice, and Prynne, soon to be made earless for many shameful slanders, and others to whom the rare and subtle sense of abstract beauty was denied, had from pulpit and through pamphlet said foul or foolish things to their dishonour. To Francis Lenton, writing in 1629, what he speaks of as—

loose action, mimic gesture
By a poor boy clad in a princely vesture,

is but one of the many—

tempting baits of hell
Which draw more youth unto the damned cell
Of furious lust, than all the devil could do
Since he obtained his first overthrow.

Deuteronomy was quoted and the ill-digested learning of the period laid under contribution. Even our own time had not appreciated the artistic conditions of the Elizabethan and Jacobean drama. One of the most brilliant and intellectual actresses of this century had laughed at the idea of a lad of seventeen or eighteen playing Imogen, or Miranda, or Rosalind. "How could any youth, however gifted and specially trained, even faintly suggest these fair and noble women to an audience? . . . One quite pities Shakespeare, who had to put up with seeing his brightest creations marred, misrepresented, and spoiled." In his book on "Shakespeare's Predecessors" Mr. John Addington Symonds also had talked of "hobbledehoys" trying to represent the pathos of Desdemona and Juliet's passion. Were they right? Are they right? I did not think so then. I do not think so now. Those who remember the Oxford production of the "Agamemnon," the fine utterance and marble dignity of the Clytemnestra, the romantic and imaginative rendering of the prophetic madness of Cassandra, will not agree with Lady Martin* or Mr. Symonds in their strictures on the conditions of the Elizabethan stage.

Of all the motives of dramatic curiosity used by our great playwrights, there is none more subtle or more fascinating than the ambiguity of the sexes. This idea, invented, as far as an artistic idea can be said to be invented, by Lyly,† perfected and made exquisite for us by Shakespeare, seems to me to owe its origin, as it certainly owes its possibility of life-like presentation, to the circumstance that the Elizabethan stage, like the stage of the Greeks, admitted the appearance of no female performers. It is because Lyly was writing for the boy-actors of St. Paul's that we have the confused sexes and complicated loves of Phillida and Gallathea: it is because Shakespeare was writing for Willie Hughes that Rosalind dons doublet and hose, and calls herself Ganymede, that Viola and Julia put on pages' dress, that Imogen steals away in male attire. To say that only a woman can portray the passions of a woman, and that therefore no boy can play Rosalind, is to rob the art of acting of all claim to objectivity, and to assign to the mere accident of sex what properly belongs to imaginative insight and creative energy. Indeed, if sex be an element in artistic creation, it might rather be urged that the delightful combination of wit and romance which characterises so many of Shakespeare's heroines was at least occasioned if it was not actually caused by the fact that the players of these parts were lads and young men, whose passionate purity, quick mobile fancy, and healthy freedom from sentimentality can hardly fail to have suggested a new and delightful type of girlhood or of womanhood. The very difference of sex between the player and the part he represented must also, as Professor Ward points out, have constituted "one more demand upon the imaginative capacities of the spectators,"

---

* Helena Faucit was a nineteenth-century actress who worked with actor and theater manager William Charles Macready and wrote a book on Shakespearean female roles. She married poet and translator Theodore Martin, who was later knighted.

† Elizabethan dramatists John Lyly (1555–1606) and Thomas Dekker (1569–1632), following custom, assumed that adolescent males would play women's parts.

and must have kept them from that over-realistic identification of the actor with his *rôle*, which is one of the weak points in modern theatrical criticism.

This, too, must be granted, that it was to these boy-actors that we owe the introduction of those lovely lyrics that star the plays of Shakespeare, Dekker, and so many of the dramatists of the period, those "snatches of bird-like or god-like song," as Mr. Swinburne calls them. For it was out of the choirs of the cathedrals and royal chapels of England that most of these lads came, and from their earliest years they had been trained in the singing of anthems and madrigals, and in all that concerns the subtle art of music. Chosen at first for the beauty of their voices, as well as for a certain comeliness and freshness of appearance, they were then instructed in gesture, dancing, and elocution, and taught to play both tragedies and comedies in the English as well as in the Latin language. Indeed, acting seems to have formed part of the ordinary education of the time, and to have been much studied not merely by the scholars of Eton and Westminster, but also by the students at the Universities of Oxford and Cambridge, some of whom went afterwards upon the public stage, as is becoming not uncommon in our own day. The great actors, too, had their pupils and apprentices, who were formally bound over to them by legal warrant, to whom they imparted the secrets of their craft, and who were so much valued that we read of Henslowe, one of the managers of the Rose Theatre, buying a trained boy of the name of James Bristowe for eight pieces of gold. The relations that existed between the masters and their pupils seem to have been of the most cordial and affectionate character.* Robin Armin was looked upon by Tarlton as his adopted son, and in a will dated "the fourth daie of Maie, anno Domini 1605," Augustine Phillips, Shakespeare's dear friend and fellow-actor, bequeathed to one of his apprentices his "purple cloke, sword, and dagger," his "base viall," and much rich apparel,

* The ensuing account—partly cobbled from volumes of J. A. Symonds's *The Renaissance in Italy* (1875–1886) and A. W. Ward's *History of English Dramatic Literature to the Death of Queen Anne* (1875)—is perhaps more expressive than exact, but no less telling.

and to another a sum of money and many beautiful instruments of music, "to be delivered unto him at the expiration of his terme of yeres in his indenture of apprenticehood." Now and then, when some daring actor kidnapped a boy for the stage, there was an outcry or an investigation. In 1600, for instance, a certain Norfolk gentleman of the name of Henry Clifton came to live in London in order that his son, then about thirteen years of age, might have the opportunity of attending the Bluecoat School, and from a petition which he presented to the Star Chamber, and which has been recently brought to light by Mr. Greenstreet, we learn that as the boy was walking quietly to Christ Church cloister one winter morning he was waylaid by James Robinson, Henry Evans, and Nathaniel Giles, and carried off to the Blackfriars Theatre, "amongste a companie of lewde and dissolute mercenarie players," as his father calls them, in order that he might be trained "in acting of parts in base playes and enterludes." Hearing of his son's misadventure, Mr. Clifton went down at once to the theatre, and demanded his surrender, but "the sayd Nathaniel Giles, James Robinson and Henry Evans most arrogantlie then and there answered that they had authoritie sufficient soe to take any noble man's sonne in this land," and handing the young schoolboy "a scrolle of paper, conteyning parte of one of their said playes and enterludes," commanded him to learn it by heart. Through a warrant issued by Sir John Fortescue, however, the boy was restored to his father the next day, and the Court of Star Chamber seems to have suspended or cancelled Evans' privileges.

The fact is that, following a precedent set by Richard III, Elizabeth had issued a commission authorising certain persons to impress into her service all boys who had beautiful voices that they might sing for her in her Chapel Royal, and Nathaniel Giles, her Chief Commissioner, finding that he could deal profitably with the managers of the Globe Theatre, agreed to supply them with personable and graceful lads for the playing of female parts, under colour of taking them for the Queen's service. The actors, accordingly, had a certain amount of legal warrant on their side, and it is interesting to note that many of the boys whom they carried off from their schools or homes, such as Salathiel Pavy, Nat. Field, and Alvery Trussell, became so fascinated by their new art that they attached themselves permanently to the theatre, and would not leave it.

Once it seemed as if girls were to take the place of boys upon the stage, and among the christenings chronicled in the registers of St. Giles', Cripplegate, occurs the following strange and suggestive entry: "Comedia, base-born, daughter of Alice Bowker and William Johnson, one of the Queen's plaiers, 10 Feb. 1589." But the child upon whom such high hopes had been built died at six years of age, and when, later on, some French actresses came over and played at Blackfriars, we learn that they were "hissed, hooted, and pippin-pelted from the stage." I think that, from what I have said above, we need not regret this in any way. The essentially male culture of the English Renaissance found its fullest and most perfect expression by its own method, and in its own manner.

I remember I used to wonder, at this time, what had been the social position and early life of Willie Hughes before Shakespeare had met with him. My investigations into the history of the boy-actors had made me curious of every detail about him. Had he stood in the carved stall of some gilded choir, reading out of a great book painted with square scarlet notes and long black key-lines? We know from the Sonnets how clear and pure his voice was, and what skill he had in the art of music. Noble gentlemen, such as the Earl of Leicester and Lord Oxford, had companies of boy-players in their service as part of their household. When Leicester went to the Netherlands in 1585 he brought with him a certain "Will" described as a "plaier." Was this Willie Hughes? Had he acted for Leicester at Kenilworth, and was it there that Shakespeare had first known him? Or was he, like Robin Armin, simply a lad of low degree, but possessing some strange beauty and marvellous fascination? It was evident from the early sonnets that when Shakespeare first came across him he had no connection whatsoever with the stage, and that he was not of high birth has already been shewn. I began to think of him not as the delicate chorister of a Royal Chapel, not as a petted minion trained to sing and dance in Leicester's stately masque, but as some fair-haired English lad whom in one of London's hurrying streets, or on Windsor's green silent meadows, Shakespeare had seen and followed, recognising the artistic possibilities that lay hidden in so comely and gracious a form, and divining by a quick and subtle instinct what an actor the lad would make could he be induced to go upon the stage. At this time Willie Hughes' father was dead, as we learn from Sonnet XIII, and his mother, whose remarkable beauty he is said to have inherited, may have been induced to allow him to become Shakespeare's apprentice by the fact that boys who played female characters were paid extremely large salaries, larger salaries, indeed, than were given to grown-up actors. Shakespeare's apprentice, at any rate, we know that he became, and we know what a vital factor he was in the development of Shakespeare's art. As a rule, a boy-actor's capacity for representing girlish parts on the stage lasted but for a few years at most. Such characters as Lady Macbeth, Queen Constance and Volumnia, remained of course always within the reach of those who had true dramatic genius and noble presence. Absolute youth was not necessary here, not desirable even. But with Imogen, and Perdita, and Juliet, it was different. "Your beard has begun to grow, and I pray God your voice be not cracked," says Hamlet mockingly to the boy-actor of the strolling company that came to visit him at Elsinore; and certainly when chins grew rough and voices harsh much of the charm and grace of the performance must have gone. Hence comes Shakespeare's passionate preoccupation with the youth of Willie Hughes, his terror of old age and wasting years, his wild appeal to time to spare the beauty of his friend:

> Make glad and sorry seasons as thou fleet'st,
> And do whate'er thou wilt, swift-footed time,
> To the wide world and all her fading sweets;
> But I forbid thee one most heinous crime:
> O carve not with thy hours my Love's fair brow
> Nor draw no lines there with thine antique pen;
> Him in thy course untainted do allow
> For beauty's pattern to succeeding men.

Time seems to have listened to Shakespeare's prayers, or perhaps Willie Hughes had the secret of perpetual youth. After three years he is quite unchanged:

To me, fair friend, you never can be old,
For as you were when first your eye I eyed,
Such seems your beauty still. Three winters' cold
Have from the forests shook three summers' pride,
Three beauteous springs to yellow autumn turned,
In process of the seasons have I seen,
Three April perfumes in three hot Junes burned,
Since first I saw you fresh which yet are green.

More years pass over, and the bloom of his boyhood seems to be still with him. When, in "The Tempest," Shakespeare, through the lips of Prospero, flung away the wand of his imagination and gave his poetic sovereignty into the weak, graceful hands of Fletcher, it may be that the Miranda who stood wondering by was none other than Willie Hughes himself, and in the last sonnet that his friend addressed to him, the enemy that is feared is not Time but Death.

O thou, my lovely boy, who in thy power
Dost hold time's fickle glass, his sickle hour;
Who hast by waning grown, and therein show'st
Thy lovers withering as thy sweet self grow'st;
If Nature, sovereign mistress over wrack,
As thou goest onwards, still will pluck thee back,
She keeps thee to this purpose, that her skill
May Time disgrace and wretched minutes kill.
Yet fear her, O thou minion of her pleasure!
She may detain, but not still keep, her treasure.
Her audit, though delay'd, answer'd must be,
And her quietus is to render thee.

– 4 –

It was not for some weeks after I had begun my study of the subject that I ventured to approach the curious group of Sonnets (CXXVII–CLII) that deal with the dark woman who, like a shadow or thing of evil omen, came across Shakespeare's great romance, and for a season stood between him and Willie Hughes. They were obviously printed out of their proper place and should have been inserted between Sonnets XXXIII and XL. Psychological and artistic reasons necessitated this change, a change which I hope will be adopted by all future editors, as without it an entirely false impression is conveyed of the nature and final issue of this noble friendship.

Who was she, this black-browed, olive-skinned woman, with her amorous mouth "that Love's own hand did make," her "cruel eye," and her "foul pride," her strange skill on the virginals and her false, fascinating nature? An over-curious scholar of our day had seen in her a symbol of the Catholic Church, of that Bride of Christ who is "black but comely." Professor Minto,* following in the footsteps of Henry Brown, had regarded the whole group of Sonnets as simply "exercises of skill undertaken in a spirit of wanton defiance and derision of the commonplace." Mr. Gerald Massey, without any historical proof or probability, had insisted that they were addressed to the celebrated Lady Rich, the Stella of Sir Philip Sidney's sonnets, the Philoclea of his "Arcadia," and that they contained no personal revelation of Shakespeare's life and love, having been written in Lord Pembroke's name and at his request. Mr. Tyler had suggested that they referred to one of Queen Elizabeth's maids-of-honour, by name Mary Fitton. But none of these explanations satisfied the conditions of the problem. The woman that came between Shakespeare and Willie Hughes was a real woman, black-haired, and married, and of evil repute. Lady Rich's fame was evil enough, it is true, but her hair was of—

fine threads of finest gold,
In curled knots man's thought to hold,

and her shoulders like "white doves perching." She was, as King James said to her lover, Lord Mountjoy, "a fair woman with a black soul." As for Mary Fitton, we know that she was unmarried in 1601, the time when her amour with Lord Pembroke was discovered, and besides,

* William Minto (1845–1893), Charles Armitage Brown (1786–1842), Gerald Massey (1828–1907), and Thomas Tyler (1826–1902) were fascinated by questions of hidden meanings in Shakespeare.

any theories that connected Lord Pembroke with the Sonnets were, as Cyril Graham had shewn, put entirely out of court by the fact that Lord Pembroke did not come to London till they had been actually written and read by Shakespeare to his friends.

It was not, however, her name that interested me. I was content to hold with Professor Dowden* that "To the eyes of no diver among the wrecks of time will that curious talisman gleam." What I wanted to discover was the nature of her influence over Shakespeare, as well as the characteristics of her personality. Two things were certain: she was much older than the poet, and the fascination that she exercised over him was at first purely intellectual. He began by feeling no physical passion for her. "I do not love thee with mine eyes," he says:

> Nor are mine ears with thy tongue's tune delighted;
> Nor tender feeling to base touches prone,
> Nor taste, nor smell, desire to be invited
> To any sensual feast with thee alone.

He did not even think her beautiful:

> My mistress' eyes are nothing like the sun;
> Coral is far more red than her lips' red:
> If snow be white, why then her breasts are dun;
> If hairs be wires, black wires grow on her head.

He had his moments of loathing for her, for, not content with enslaving the soul of Shakespeare, she seems to have sought to snare the senses of Willie Hughes. Then Shakespeare cries aloud,—

> Two loves I have of comfort and despair,
> Which like two spirits do suggest me still:
> The better angel is a man right fair,

---

* Edward Dowden (1843–1913), a distinguished Irish literary historian, helped Wilde to think spiritually, not allegorically, about his love story.

The worser spirit a woman colour'd ill.
To win me soon to hell, my female evil
Tempteth my better angel from my side,
And would corrupt my saint to be a devil,
Wooing his purity with her foul pride.

Then he sees her as she really is, the "bay where all men ride," the "wide world's common place," the woman who is in the "very refuse" of her evil deeds, and who is "as black as hell, as dark as night." Then it is that he pens that great sonnet upon Lust ("Th' expense of spirit in a waste of shame"), of which Mr. Theodore Watts* says rightly that it is the greatest sonnet ever written. And it is then, also, that he offers to mortgage his very life and genius to her if she will but restore to him that "sweetest friend" of whom she had robbed him.

To compass this end he abandons himself to her, feigns to be full of an absorbing and sensuous passion of possession, forges false words of love, lies to her, and tells her that he lies.

My thoughts and my discourse as madmen's are,
At random from the truth vainly express'd;
For I have sworn thee fair, and thought thee bright,
Who art as black as hell, as dark as night.

Rather than suffer his friend to be treacherous to him, he will himself be treacherous to his friend. To shield his purity, he will himself be vile. He knew the weakness of the boy-actor's nature, his susceptibility to praise, his inordinate love of admiration, and deliberately set himself to fascinate the woman who had come between them.

It is never with impunity that one's lips say Love's Litany. Words have their mystical power over the soul, and form can create the feeling from which it should have sprung. Sincerity itself, the ardent,

---

* Critic and poet Theodore Watts-Dunton (1832–1914) saved the poet Algernon Charles Swinburne (1837–1909) from his alcoholism. His praise of the ominous Sonnet 129 marks a turn to higher intensity in Wilde's fable.

momentary sincerity of the artist, is often the unconscious result of style, and in the case of those rare temperaments that are exquisitely susceptible to the influences of language, the use of certain phrases and modes of expression can stir the very pulse of passion, can send the red blood coursing through the veins, and can transform into a strange sensuous energy what in its origin had been mere æsthetic impulse, and desire of art. So, at least, it seems to have been with Shakespeare. He begins by pretending to love, wears a lover's apparel and has a lover's words upon his lips. What does it matter? It is only acting, only a comedy in real life. Suddenly he finds that what his tongue had spoken his soul had listened to, and that the raiment that he had put on for disguise is a plague-stricken and poisonous thing that eats into his flesh, and that he cannot throw away. Then comes Desire, with its many maladies, and Lust that makes one love all that one loathes, and Shame, with its ashen face and secret smile. He is enthralled by this dark woman, is for a season separated from his friend, and becomes the "vassal-wretch" of one whom he knows to be evil and perverse and unworthy of his love, as of the love of Willie Hughes. "O, from what power," he says,—

hast thou this powerful might,
With insufficiency my heart to sway?
To make me give the lie to my true sight,
And swear that brightness does not grace the day?
Whence hast thou this becoming of things ill,
That in the very refuse of thy deeds
There is such strength and warranties of skill
That, in my mind, thy worst all best exceeds?

He is keenly conscious of his own degradation, and finally, realising that his genius is nothing to her compared to the physical beauty of the young actor, he cuts with a quick knife the bond that binds him to her, and in this bitter sonnet bids her farewell:—

In loving thee thou know'st I am forsworn,
But thou art twice forsworn, to me love swearing;

In act thy bed-vow broke, and new faith torn,
In vowing new hate after new love bearing.
But why of two oaths' breach do I accuse thee,
When I break twenty? I am perjur'd most;
For all my vows are oaths but to misuse thee,
And all my honest faith in thee is lost:
For I have sworn deep oaths of thy deep kindness,
Oaths of thy love, thy truth, thy constancy;
And, to enlighten thee, gave eyes to blindness,
Or made them swear against the thing they see;
For I have sworn thee fair; more perjur'd I,
To swear against the truth so foul a lie!

His attitude towards Willie Hughes in the whole matter shews at once the fervour and the self-abnegation of the great love he bore him. There is a poignant touch of pathos in the close of this sonnet:

Those pretty wrongs that liberty commits,
When I am sometime absent from thy heart,
Thy beauty and thy years full well befits,
For still temptation follows where thou art.
Gentle thou art, and therefore to be won,
Beauteous thou art, therefore to be assailed;
And when a woman woos, what woman's son
Will sourly leave her till she have prevailed?
Ay me! but yet thou mightst my seat forbear,
And chide thy beauty and thy straying youth,
Who lead thee in their riot even there
Where thou art forc'd to break a two-fold truth,—
Hers, by thy beauty tempting her to thee,
Thine, by thy beauty being false to me.

But here he makes it manifest that his forgiveness was full and complete:

No more be griev'd at that which thou hast done:
Roses have thorns, and silver fountains mud;
Clouds and eclipses stain both moon and sun,
And loathsome canker lives in sweetest bud.
All men make faults, and even I in this,
Authorising thy trespass with compare,
Myself corrupting, salving thy amiss,
Excusing thy sins more than thy sins are;
For to thy sensual fault I bring in sense,—
Thy adverse party is thy advocate,—
And 'gainst myself a lawful plea commence:
Such civil war is in my love and hate,
That I an accessary needs must be
To that sweet thief which sourly robs from me.

Shortly afterwards Shakespeare left London for Stratford (Sonnets XLIII–LII), and when he returned Willie Hughes seems to have grown tired of the woman who for a little time had fascinated him. Her name is never mentioned again in the Sonnets, nor is there any allusion made to her. She had passed out of their lives.

But who was she? And, even if her name has not come down to us, were there any allusions to her in contemporary literature? It seems to me that although better educated than most of the women of her time, she was not nobly born, but was probably the profligate wife of some old and wealthy citizen. We know that women of this class, which was then first rising into social prominence, were strangely fascinated by the new art of stage playing. They were to be found almost every afternoon at the theatre, when dramatic performances were being given, and "The Actors' Remonstrance"* is eloquent on the subject of their amours with the young actors.

* English poet and literary critic John Addington Symonds (1840–1893) had found this 1643 tract, which complained that women were attracted to the young male actors, partly by their gorgeous costumes, it seems.

Cranley* in his "Amanda" tells us of one who loved to mimic the actor's disguises, appearing one day "embroidered, laced, perfumed, in glittering show . . . as brave as any Countess," and the next day, "all in mourning, black and sad," now in the grey cloak of a country wench, and now "in the neat habit of a citizen." She was a curious woman, "more changeable and wavering than the moon," and the books that she loved to read were Shakespeare's "Venus and Adonis," Beaumont's "Salmacis and Hermaphroditus," amorous pamphlets, and "songs of love and sonnets exquisite." These sonnets, that were to her the "bookes of her devotion," were surely none other but Shakespeare's own, for the whole description reads like the portrait of the woman who fell in love with Willie Hughes, and, lest we should have any doubt on the subject, Cranley, borrowing Shakespeare's play on words, tells us that, in her "proteus-like strange shapes," she is one who—

Changes hews with the chameleon.

Manningham's Table-book,† also, contains a clear allusion to the same story. Manningham was a student at the Middle Temple with Sir Thomas Overbury and Edmund Curle, whose chambers he seems to have shared; and his Diary is still preserved among the Harleian MSS. at the British Museum, a small duodecimo book written in a fair and tolerably legible hand, and containing many unpublished anecdotes about Shakespeare, Sir Walter Raleigh, Spenser, Ben Jonson and others. The dates, which are inserted with much care, extend from January 1600–1 to April 1603, and under the heading "March 13, 1601," Manningham tells us that he heard from a member of Shakespeare's company that a certain citizen's wife being at the Globe Theatre one afternoon, fell in love with one of the actors, and "grew so

* In Symonds's *Shakespere's* [sic] *Predecessors in the English Drama* (1884) Wilde read about Thomas Cranley's *Amanda; or, The Reformed Whore* (1635).

† *Diary of John Manningham*, a London lawyer; entries for 1602–1603 gossip about notable authors, including Overbury, who wrote an important book, *Characters*.

farre in liking with him, that before shee went from the play shee appointed him to come that night unto hir," but that Shakespeare "overhearing their conclusion" anticipated his friend and came first to the lady's house, "went before and was entertained," as Manningham puts it, with some added looseness of speech which it is unnecessary to quote.

It seemed to me that we had here a common and distorted version of the story that is revealed to us in the Sonnets, the story of the dark woman's love for Willie Hughes, and Shakespeare's mad attempt to make her love him in his friend's stead. It was not, of course, necessary to accept it as absolutely true in every detail. According to Manningham's informant, for instance, the name of the actor in question was not Willie Hughes, but Richard Burbage. Tavern gossip, however, is proverbially inaccurate, and Burbage was, no doubt, dragged into the story to give point to the foolish jest about William the Conqueror and Richard the Third, with which the entry in Manningham's Diary ends. Burbage was our first great tragic actor, but it needed all his genius to counterbalance the physical defects of low stature and corpulent figure under which he laboured, and he was not the sort of man who would have fascinated the dark woman of the Sonnets, or would have cared to be fascinated by her. There was no doubt that Willie Hughes was referred to, and the private diary of a young law student of the time thus curiously corroborated Cyril Graham's wonderful guess at the secret of Shakespeare's great romance. Indeed, when taken in conjunction with "Amanda," Manningham's Tablebook seemed to me to be an extremely strong link in the chain of evidence, and to place the new interpretation of the Sonnets on something like a secure historic basis, the fact that Cranley's poem was not published till after Shakespeare's death being really rather in favour of this view, as it was not likely that he would have ventured during the lifetime of the great dramatist to revive the memory of this tragic and bitter story.

This passion for the dark lady also enabled me to fix with still greater certainty the date of the Sonnets. From internal evidence, from the characteristics of language, style, and the like, it was evident that they belonged to Shakespeare's early period, the period of "Love's

Labour's Lost" and "Venus and Adonis." With the play, indeed, they are intimately connected. They display the same delicate euphuism,* the same delight in fanciful phrase and curious expression, the artistic wilfulness and studied graces of the same "fair tongue, conceit's expositor," Rosaline, the—

> whitely wanton with a velvet brow,
> With two pitch-balls stuck in her face for eyes,

who is born "to make black fair," and whose "favour turns the fashion of the days," is the dark lady of the Sonnets who makes black "beauty's successive heir." In the comedy as well as in the poems we have that half-sensuous philosophy that exalts the judgment of the senses "above all slower, more toilsome means of knowledge," and Berowne is perhaps, as Walter Pater suggests, a reflex of Shakespeare himself "when he has just become able to stand aside from and estimate the first period of his poetry."

Now though "Love's Labour's Lost" was not published till 1598, when it was brought out "newlie corrected and augmented" by Cuthbert Burby, there is no doubt that it was written and produced on the stage at a much earlier date, probably, as Professor Dowden points out, in 1588–9. If this be so, it is clear that Shakespeare's first meeting with Willie Hughes must have been in 1585, and it is just possible that this young actor may, after all, have been in his boyhood the musician of Lord Essex.

It is clear, at any rate, that Shakespeare's love for the dark lady must have passed away before 1594. In this year there appeared, under the editorship of Hadrian Dorell, that fascinating poem, or series of poems, "Willobie his Avisa," which is described by Mr. Swinburne as the one contemporary book which has been supposed to throw any direct or indirect light on the mystic matter of the Sonnets. In it we learn how a young gentleman of St. John's College, Oxford, by name

---

* As Pater remarks, this artificial style of balanced sentences marks Shakespeare's early work, from which he quite soon learned "to stand aside."

Henry Willobie, fell in love with a woman so "fair and chaste" that he called her Avisa, either because such beauty as hers had never been seen, or because she fled like a bird from the snare of his passion, and spread her wings for flight when he ventured but to touch her hand. Anxious to win his mistress, he consults his familiar friend W. S., "who not long before had tried the curtesy of the like passion, and was now newly recovered of the like infection." Shakespeare encouraged him in the siege that he is laying to the Castle of Beauty, telling him that every woman is to be wooed, and every woman to be won; views this "loving comedy" from far off, in order to see "whether it would sort to a happier end for this new actor than it did for the old player," and "enlargeth the wound with the sharpe razor of a willing conceit," feeling the purely æsthetic interest of the artist in the moods and emotions of others. It is unnecessary, however, to enter more fully into this curious passage in Shakespeare's life, as all that I wanted to point out was that in 1594 he had been cured of his infatuation for the dark lady, and had already been acquainted for at least three years with Willie Hughes.

My whole scheme of the Sonnets was now complete, and, by placing those that refer to the dark lady in their proper order and position, I saw the perfect unity and completeness of the whole. The drama—for indeed they formed a drama and a soul's tragedy of fiery passion and of noble thought—is divided into four scenes or acts. In the first of these (Sonnets I–XXXII) Shakespeare invites Willie Hughes to go upon the stage as an actor, and to put to the service of Art his wonderful physical beauty, and his exquisite grace of youth, before passion has robbed him of the one, and time taken from him the other. Willie Hughes, after a time, consents to be a player in Shakespeare's company, and soon becomes the very centre and keynote of his inspiration. Suddenly, in one red-rose July (Sonnets XXXIII–LII, LXI, and CXXVII–CLII) there comes to the Globe Theatre a dark woman with wonderful eyes, who falls passionately in love with Willie Hughes. Shakespeare, sick with the malady of jealousy, and made mad by many doubts and fears, tries to fascinate the woman who had come between him and his friend. The love, that is at first feigned, becomes real, and he finds himself enthralled and dominated by a woman whom he knows to be evil and unworthy. To her the genius of a man is as nothing compared to a boy's beauty. Willie Hughes becomes for a time her slave and the toy of her fancy, and the second act ends with Shakespeare's departure from London. In the third act her influence has passed away. Shakespeare returns to London, and renews his friendship with Willie Hughes, to whom he promises immortality in his plays. Marlowe, hearing of the wonder and grace of the young actor, lures him away from the Globe Theatre to play Gaveston in the tragedy of "Edward II," and for the second time Shakespeare is separated from his friend. The last act (Sonnets C–CXXVI) tells us of the return of Willie Hughes to Shakespeare's company. Evil rumour has now stained the white purity of his name, but Shakespeare's love still endures and is perfect. Of the mystery of this love, and of the mystery of passion, we are told strange and marvellous things, and the Sonnets conclude with an envoi of twelve lines, whose motive is the triumph of Beauty over Time, and of Death over Beauty.

And what had been the end of him who had been so dear to the soul of Shakespeare, and who by his presence and passion had given reality to Shakespeare's art? When the Civil War broke out, the English actors took the side of their king, and many of them, like Robinson foully slain by Major Harrison at the taking of Basing House, laid down their lives in the king's service. Perhaps on the trampled heath of Marston, or on the bleak hills of Naseby,* the dead body of Willie Hughes had been found by some of the rough peasants of the district, his gold hair "dabbled with blood," and his breast pierced with many wounds. Or it may be that the Plague, which was very frequent in London at the beginning of the seventeenth century, and was indeed regarded by many of the Christians as a judgment sent on the city for its love of "vaine plaies and idolatrous shewes," had touched the lad while he was acting, and he had crept home to his lodging to die there alone, Shakespeare being far away at Stratford, and those who had

* Marston Moor (1644) and Naseby (1645) were battles in which the Parliamentary Army defeated the Royalists, to clinch the Puritan victory in the English Civil War.

flocked in such numbers to see him, the "gazers" whom, as the Sonnets tell us, he had "led astray," being too much afraid of contagion to come near him. A story of this kind was current at the time about a young actor, and was made much use of by the Puritans in their attempts to stifle the free development of the English Renaissance. Yet, surely, had this actor been Willie Hughes, tidings of his tragic death would have been speedily brought to Shakespeare as he lay dreaming under the mulberry tree in his garden at New Place, and in an elegy as sweet* as that written by Milton on Edward King, he would have mourned for the lad who had brought such joy and sorrow into his life, and whose connection with his art had been of so vital and intimate a character. Something made me feel certain that Willie Hughes had survived Shakespeare, and had fulfilled in some measure the high prophecies the poet had made about him, and one evening the true secret of his end flashed across me.

He had been one of those English actors who in 1611, the year of Shakespeare's retirement from the stage, went across sea to Germany and played before the great Duke Henry Julius of Brunswick, himself a dramatist of no mean order, and at the Court of that strange Elector of Brandenburg, who was so enamoured of beauty that he was said to have bought for his weight in amber the young son of a travelling Greek merchant, and to have given pageants in honour of his slave, all through that dreadful famine year of 1606–7, when the people died of hunger in the very streets of the town, and for the space of seven months there was no rain. The Library at Cassel contains to the present day a copy of the first edition of Marlowe's "Edward II," the only copy in existence, Mr. Bullen tells us. Who could have brought it to that town, but he who had created the part of the king's minion,† and for whom indeed it had been written? Those stained and yellow pages had once been touched by his white hands. We also know that "Romeo and Juliet," a play specially connected with Willie Hughes, was brought out at Dresden, in 1613, along with "Hamlet" and "King

* *Lycidas*, perhaps the greatest English elegy, was written for King in 1637.

† Piers Gaveston, the aesthete and courtier in Marlowe's tragedy *Edward II* (1592).

Lear," and certain of Marlowe's plays, and it was surely to none other than Willie Hughes himself that in 1617 the death-mask of Shakespeare was brought by one of the suite of the English ambassador, pale token of the passing away of the great poet who had so dearly loved him. Indeed there was something peculiarly fitting in the idea that the boy-actor, whose beauty had been so vital an element in the realism and romance of Shakespeare's art, had been the first to have brought to Germany the seed of the new culture, and was in his way the precursor of the *Aufklärung* or Illumination of the eighteenth century, that splendid movement which, though begun by Lessing and Herder, and brought to its full and perfect issue by Goethe was in no small part helped on by a young actor—Friedrich Schroeder—who awoke the popular consciousness, and by means of the feigned passions and mimetic methods of the stage showed the intimate, the vital, connection between life and literature. If this was so,—and there was certainly no evidence against it,—it was not improbable that Willie Hughes was one of those English comedians (*mimi quidam ex Britannia*,* as the old chronicle calls them), who were slain at Nuremberg in a sudden uprising of the people, and were secretly buried in a little vineyard outside the city by some young men "who had found pleasure in their performances, and of whom some had sought to be instructed in the mysteries of the new art." Certainly no more fitting place could there be for him to whom Shakespeare said "thou art all my art," than this little vineyard outside the city walls. For was it not from the sorrows of Dionysos that Tragedy sprang? Was not the light laughter of Comedy, with its careless merriment and quick replies, first heard on the lips of the Sicilian vine-dressers? Nay, did not the purple and red stain of the wine-froth on face and limbs give the first suggestion of the charm and fascination of disguise?—the desire for self-concealment, the sense of the value of objectivity, thus showing itself in the rude beginnings of the art. At any rate, wherever he lay—whether in the little vineyard at the gate of the Gothic town, or in some dim London churchyard amidst the roar and bustle of our great

---

* Certain actors from Britain (Latin).

city—no gorgeous monument marked his resting place. His true tomb, as Shakespeare saw, was the poet's verse, his true monument the permanence of the drama. So had it been with others whose beauty had given a new creative impulse to their age. The ivory body of the Bithynian slave rots in the green ooze of the Nile, and on the yellow hills of the Cerameicus is strewn the dust of the young Athenian; but Antinous lives in sculpture, and Charmides* in philosophy.

– 5 –

A young Elizabethan, who was enamoured of a girl so white that he named her Alba, has left on record the impression produced on him by one of the first performances of "Love's Labour's Lost." Admirable though the actors were, and they played "in cunning wise," he tells us, especially those who took the lover's parts, he was conscious that everything was "feigned," that nothing came "from the heart," that though they appeared to grieve they "felt no care," and were merely presenting "a show in jest." Yet, suddenly, this fanciful comedy of unreal romance became to him, as he sat in the audience, the real tragedy of his life. The moods of his own soul seemed to have taken shape and substance, and to be moving before him. His grief had a mask that smiled, and his sorrow wore gay raiment. Behind the bright and quickly-changing pageant of the stage, he saw himself, as one sees one's image in a fantastic glass. The very words that came to the actors' lips were wrung out of his pain. Their false tears were of his shedding.

There are few of us who have not felt something akin to this. We become lovers when we see Romeo and Juliet, and Hamlet makes us students. The blood of Duncan is upon our hands, with Timon we rage against the world, and when Lear wanders out upon the heath the terror of madness touches us. Ours is the white sinlessness of Desdemona, and ours, also, the sin of Iago. Art, even the art of fullest

* Antinous, a Bithynian youth beloved of the Emperor Hadrian (76–138 C.E.), represents Wilde's ideal of beauty, as does Charmides, chief speaker in Plato's dialogue *Charmides*.

scope and widest vision, can never really show us the external world. All that it shows us is our own soul, the one world of which we have any real cognizance. And the soul itself, the soul of each one of us, is to each one of us a mystery. It hides in the dark and broods, and consciousness cannot tell us of its workings. Consciousness, indeed, is quite inadequate to explain the contents of personality. It is Art, and Art only, that reveals us to ourselves.

We sit at the play with the woman we love, or listen to the music in some Oxford garden, or stroll with our friend through the cool galleries of the Pope's house at Rome, and suddenly we become aware that we have passions of which we have never dreamed, thoughts that make us afraid, pleasures whose secret has been denied to us, sorrows that have been hidden from our tears. The actor is unconscious of our presence: the musician is thinking of the subtlety of the fugue, of the tone of his instrument; the marble gods that smile so curiously at us are made of insensate stone. But they have given form and substance to what was within us; they have enabled us to realise our personality; and a sense of perilous joy, or some touch or thrill of pain, or that strange self-pity that man so often feels for himself, comes over us and leaves us different.

Some such impression the Sonnets of Shakespeare had certainly produced on me. As from opal dawns to sunsets of withered rose I read and re-read them in garden or chamber, it seemed to me that I was deciphering the story of a life that had once been mine, unrolling the record of a romance that, without my knowing it, had coloured the very texture of my nature, had dyed it with strange and subtle dyes. Art, as so often happens, had taken the place of personal experience. I felt as if I had been initiated into the secret of that passionate friendship, that love of beauty and beauty of love, of which Marsilio Ficino tells us, and of which the Sonnets, in their noblest and purest significance, may be held to be the perfect expression.

Yes: I had lived it all. I had stood in the round theatre with its open roof and fluttering banners, had seen the stage draped with black for a tragedy, or set with gay garlands for some brighter show. The young gallants came out with their pages, and took their seats in front of the tawny curtain that hung from the satyr-carved pillars of the inner scene. They were insolent and debonair in their fantastic dresses. Some of them wore French lovelocks, and white doublets stiff with Italian embroidery of gold thread, and long hose of blue or pale yellow silk. Others were all in black, and carried huge plumed hats. These affected the Spanish fashion. As they played at cards, and blew thin wreaths of smoke from the tiny pipes that the pages lit for them, the truant prentices and idle schoolboys that thronged the yard mocked them. But they only smiled at each other. In the side boxes some masked women were sitting. One of them was waiting with hungry eyes and bitten lips for the drawing back of the curtain. As the trumpet sounded for the third time she leant forward, and I saw her olive skin and raven's-wing hair. I knew her. She had marred for a season the great friendship of my life. Yet there was something about her that fascinated me.

The play changed according to my mood. Sometimes it was "Hamlet." Taylor acted the Prince, and there were many who wept when Ophelia went mad. Sometimes it was "Romeo and Juliet." Burbage was Romeo. He hardly looked the part of the young Italian, but there was a rich music in his voice, and passionate beauty in every gesture. I saw "As You Like It," and "Cymbeline," and "Twelfth Night," and in each play there was some one whose life was bound up into mine, who realised for me every dream, and gave shape to every fancy. How gracefully he moved! The eyes of the audience were fixed on him.

And yet it was in this century that it had all happened. I had never seen my friend, but he had been with me for many years, and it was to his influence that I had owed my passion for Greek thought and art, and indeed all my sympathy with the Hellenic spirit. (*Φιλοσοφεῖν μὲτ' ἐρῶτος*!)* How that phrase had stirred me in my Oxford days! I did not understand then why it was so. But I knew now. There had been a presence beside me always. Its silver feet had trod night's shadowy

---

* To philosophize through love (Greek); quoted from Plato's *Republic*, book 6; the phrase means to approach transcendent truths by starting first on the lower levels of physical desire.

meadows, and the white hands had moved aside the trembling curtains of the dawn. It had walked with me through the grey cloisters, and when I sat reading in my room, it was there also. What though I had been unconscious of it? The soul had a life of its own, and the brain its own sphere of action. There was something within us that knew nothing of sequence or extension, and yet, like the philosopher of the Ideal City, was the spectator of all time and of all existence. It had senses that quickened, passions that came to birth, spiritual ecstasies of contemplation, ardours of fiery-coloured love. It was we who were unreal, and our conscious life was the least important part of our development. The soul, the secret soul, was the only reality.

How curiously it had all been revealed to me! A book of Sonnets, published nearly three hundred years ago, written by a dead hand and in honour of a dead youth, had suddenly explained to me the whole story of my soul's romance. I remembered how once in Egypt I had been present at the opening of a frescoed coffin that had been found in one of the basalt tombs at Thebes. Inside there was the body of a young girl swathed in tight bands of linen, and with a gilt mask over her face. As I stooped down to look at it, I had seen that one of the little withered hands held a scroll of yellow papyrus covered with strange characters. How I wished now that I had had it read to me! It might have told me something more about the soul that hid within me, and had its mysteries of passion of which I was kept in ignorance. Strange, that we knew so little about ourselves, and that our most intimate personality was concealed from us! Were we to look in tombs for our real life, and in art for the legend of our days?

Week after week, I pored over these poems, and each new form of knowledge seemed to me a mode of reminiscence. Finally, after two months had elapsed, I determined to make a strong appeal to Erskine to do justice to the memory of Cyril Graham, and to give to the world his marvellous interpretation of the Sonnets—the only interpretation that thoroughly explained the problem. I have not any copy of my letter, I regret to say, nor have I been able to lay my hand upon the original; but I remember that I went over the whole ground, and covered sheets of paper with passionate reiteration of the arguments and proofs that my study had suggested to me.

It seemed to me that I was not merely restoring Cyril Graham to his proper place in literary history, but rescuing the honour of Shakespeare himself from the tedious memory of a commonplace intrigue. I put into the letter all my enthusiasm. I put into the letter all my faith.

No sooner, in fact, had I sent it off than a curious reaction came over me. It seemed to me that I had given away my capacity for belief in the Willie Hughes theory of the Sonnets, that something had gone out of me, as it were, and that I was perfectly indifferent to the whole subject. What was it that had happened? It is difficult to say. Perhaps, by finding perfect expression for a passion, I had exhausted the passion itself. Emotional forces, like the forces of physical life, have their positive limitations. Perhaps the mere effort to convert any one to a theory involves some form of renunciation of the power of credence. Influence is simply a transference of personality, a mode of giving away what is most precious to one's self, and its exercise produces a sense, and, it may be, a reality of loss. Every disciple takes away something from his master. Or perhaps I had become tired of the whole thing, wearied of its fascination, and, my enthusiasm having burnt out, my reason was left to its own unimpassioned judgment. However it came about, and I cannot pretend to explain it, there was no doubt that Willie Hughes suddenly became to me a mere myth, an idle dream, the boyish fancy of a young man who, like most ardent spirits, was more anxious to convince others than to be himself convinced.

I must admit that this was a bitter disappointment to me. I had gone through every phase of this great romance. I had lived with it, and it had become part of my nature. How was it that it had left me? Had I touched upon some secret that my soul desired to conceal? Or was there no permanence in personality? Did things come and go through the brain, silently, swiftly, and without footprints, like shadows through a mirror? Were we at the mercy of such impressions as Art or Life chose to give us? It seemed to me to be so.

It was at night-time that this feeling first came to me. I had sent my servant out to post the letter to Erskine, and was seated at the window looking out at the blue and gold city. The moon had not yet risen, and there was only one star in the sky, but the streets were full of quick-moving and flashing lights, and the windows of Devonshire House were illuminated for a great dinner to be given to some of the foreign princes then visiting London. I saw the scarlet liveries of the royal carriages, and the crowd hustling about the sombre gates of the courtyard.

Suddenly, I said to myself: "I have been dreaming, and all my life for these two months has been unreal. There was no such person as Willie Hughes." Something like a faint cry of pain came to my lips as I began to realise how I had deceived myself, and I buried my face in my hands, struck with a sorrow greater than any I had felt since boyhood. After a few moments I rose, and going into the library took up the Sonnets, and began to read them. But it was all to no avail. They gave me back nothing of the feeling that I had brought to them; they revealed to me nothing of what I had found hidden in their lines. Had I merely been influenced by the beauty of the forged portrait, charmed by that Shelley-like face into faith and credence? Or, as Erskine had suggested, was it the pathetic tragedy of Cyril Graham's death that had so deeply stirred me? I could not tell. To the present day I cannot understand the beginning or the end of this strange passage in my life.

However, as I had said some very unjust and bitter things to Erskine in my letter, I determined to go and see him as soon as possible, and make my apologies to him for my behaviour. Accordingly, the next morning I drove down to Birdcage Walk, where I found him sitting in his library, with the forged picture of Willie Hughes in front of him.

"My dear Erskine!" I cried, "I have come to apologise to you."

"To apologise to me?" he said. "What for?"

"For my letter," I answered.

"You have nothing to regret in your letter," he said. "On the contrary, you have done me the greatest service in your power. You have shown me that Cyril Graham's theory is perfectly sound."

I stared at him in blank wonder.

"You don't mean to say that you believe in Willie Hughes?" I exclaimed.

"Why not?" he rejoined. "You have proved the thing to me. Do you think I cannot estimate the value of evidence?"

"But there is no evidence at all," I groaned, sinking into a chair. "When I wrote to you I was under the influence of a perfectly silly enthusiasm. I had been touched by the story of Cyril Graham's death, fascinated by his artistic theory, enthralled by the wonder and novelty of the whole idea. I see now that the theory is based on a delusion. The only evidence for the existence of Willie Hughes is that picture in front of you, and that picture is a forgery. Don't be carried away by mere sentiment in this matter. Whatever romance may have to say about the Willie Hughes theory, reason is dead against it."

"I don't understand you," said Erskine, looking at me in amazement. "You have convinced me by your letter that Willie Hughes is an absolute reality. Why have you changed your mind? Or is all that you have been saying to me merely a joke?"

"I cannot explain it to you," I rejoined, "but I see now that there is really nothing to be said in favour of Cyril Graham's interpretation. The Sonnets may not be addressed to Lord Pembroke. They probably are not. But for heaven's sake don't waste your time in a foolish attempt to discover a young Elizabethan actor who never existed, and to make a phantom puppet the centre of the great cycle of Shakespeare's Sonnets."

"I see that you don't understand the theory," he replied.

"My dear Erskine," I cried, "not understand it! Why, I feel as if I had invented it. Surely my letter shows you that I not merely went into the whole matter, but that I contributed proofs of every kind. The one flaw in the theory is that it presupposes the existence of the person whose existence is the subject of dispute. If we grant that there was in Shakespeare's company a young actor of the name of Willie Hughes, it is not difficult to make him the object of the Sonnets. But as we know that there was no actor of this name in the company of the Globe Theatre, it is idle to pursue the investigation further."

"But that is exactly what we don't know," said Erskine. "It is quite true that his name does not occur in the list given in the first folio; but, as Cyril pointed out, that is rather a proof in favour of the existence of Willie Hughes than against it, if we remember his treacherous desertion of Shakespeare for a rival dramatist. Besides," and here I must admit that Erskine made what seems to me now a rather good point, though, at the time, I laughed at it, "there is no reason at all why Willie Hughes should not have gone upon the stage under an assumed name. In fact it is extremely probable that he did so. We know that there was a very strong prejudice against the theatre in his day, and nothing is more likely than that his family insisted upon his adopting some *nom de plume.** The editors of the first folio would naturally put him down under his stage name, the name by which he was best known to the public, but the Sonnets were of course an entirely different matter, and in the dedication to them the publisher very properly addresses him under his real initials. If this be so, and it seems to me the most simple and rational explanation of the matter, I regard Cyril Graham's theory as absolutely proved."

"But what evidence have you?" I exclaimed, laying my hand on his. "You have no evidence at all. It is a mere hypothesis. And which of Shakespeare's actors do you think that Willie Hughes was? The 'pretty fellow' Ben Jonson tells us of, who was so fond of dressing up in girls' clothes?"

"I don't know," he answered rather irritably. "I have not had time to investigate the point yet. But I feel quite sure that my theory is the true one. Of course it is a hypothesis, but then it is a hypothesis that explains everything, and if you had been sent to Cambridge to study science, instead of to Oxford to dawdle over literature, you would know that a hypothesis that explains everything is a certainty."

"Yes, I am aware that Cambridge is a sort of educational institute," I murmured. "I am glad I was not there."

"My dear fellow," said Erskine, suddenly turning his keen grey eyes on me, "you believe in Cyril Graham's theory, you believe in Willie Hughes, you know that the Sonnets are addressed to an actor, but for some reason or other you won't acknowledge it."

"I wish I could believe it," I rejoined. "I would give anything to be able to do so. But I can't. It is a sort of moonbeam theory, very lovely, very fascinating, but intangible. When one thinks that one has got hold of it, it escapes one. No: Shakespeare's heart is still to us 'a closet never pierc'd with crystal eyes,' as he calls it in one of the sonnets. We shall never know the true secret of the passion of his life."

---

* Pen name (French).

Erskine sprang from the sofa, and paced up and down the room. "We know it already," he cried, "and the world shall know it some day."

I had never seen him so excited. He would not hear of my leaving him, and insisted on my stopping for the rest of the day.

We argued the matter over for hours, but nothing that I could say could make him surrender his faith in Cyril Graham's interpretation. He told me that he intended to devote his life to proving the theory, and that he was determined to do justice to Cyril Graham's memory. I entreated him, laughed at him, begged of him, but it was to no use. Finally we parted, not exactly in anger, but certainly with a shadow between us. He thought me shallow, I thought him foolish. When I called on him again, his servant told me that he had gone to Germany. The letters that I wrote to him remained unanswered.

Two years afterwards, as I was going into my club, the hall porter handed me a letter with a foreign postmark. It was from Erskine, and written at the Hôtel d'Angleterre, Cannes. When I had read it, I was filled with horror, though I did not quite believe that he would be so mad as to carry his resolve into execution. The gist of the letter was that he had tried in every way to verify the Willie Hughes theory, and had failed, and that as Cyril Graham had given his life for this theory, he himself had determined to give his own life also to the same cause. The concluding words of the letter were these: "I still believe in Willie Hughes; and by the time you receive this I shall have died by my own hand for Willie Hughes' sake: for his sake, and for the sake of Cyril Graham, whom I drove to his death by my shallow scepticism and ignorant lack of faith. The truth was once revealed to you, and you rejected it. It comes to you now, stained with the blood of two lives.—do not turn away from it."

It was a horrible moment. I felt sick with misery, and yet I could not believe that he would really carry out his intention. To die for one's theological opinions is the worst use a man can make of his life; but to die for a literary theory! It seemed impossible.

I looked at the date. The letter was a week old. Some unfortunate chance had prevented my going to the club for several days, or I might have got it in time to save him. Perhaps it was not too late. I drove off to my rooms, packed up my things, and started by the night mail from

Charing Cross. The journey was intolerable. I thought I would never arrive.

As soon as I did, I drove to the Hôtel d'Angleterre. It was quite true. Erskine was dead. They told me that he had been buried two days before in the English cemetery. There was something horribly grotesque about the whole tragedy. I said all kinds of wild things, and the people in the hall looked curiously at me.

Suddenly Lady Erskine, in deep mourning, passed across the vestibule. When she saw me she came up to me, murmured something about her poor son, and burst into tears. I led her into her sitting room. An elderly gentleman was there, reading a newspaper. It was the English doctor.

We talked a great deal about Erskine, but I said nothing about his motive for committing suicide. It was evident that he had not told his mother anything about the reason that had driven him to so fatal, so mad an act. Finally Lady Erskine rose and said, "George left you something as a memento. It was a thing he prized very much. I will get it for you."

As soon as she had left the room I turned to the doctor and said, "What a dreadful shock it must have been for Lady Erskine! I wonder that she bears it as well as she does."

"Oh, she knew for months past that it was coming," he answered.

"Knew it for months past!" I cried. "But why didn't she stop him? Why didn't she have him watched? He must have been out of his mind."

The doctor stared at me. "I don't know what you mean," he said.

"Well," I cried, "if a mother knows that her son is going to commit suicide—"

"Suicide!" he answered. "Poor Erskine did not commit suicide. He died of consumption.* He came here to die. The moment I saw him I knew that there was no chance. One lung was almost gone, and the other was very much affected. Three days before he died he asked me was there any hope. I told him frankly that there was none, and that

* The common nineteenth-century name for tuberculosis.

he had only a few days to live. He wrote some letters, and was quite resigned, retaining his senses to the last."

I got up from my seat, and going over to the open window I looked out on the crowded promenade. I remember that the brightly-coloured umbrellas and gay parasols seemed to me like huge fantastic butterflies fluttering by the shore of a blue-metal sea, and that the heavy odour of violets that came across the garden made me think of that wonderful sonnet in which Shakespeare tells us that the scent of these flowers always reminded him of his friend. What did it all mean? Why had Erskine written me that extraordinary letter? Why when standing at the very gate of death had he turned back to tell me what was not true? Was Hugo right?* Is affectation the only thing that accompanies a man up the steps of the scaffold? Did Erskine merely want to produce a dramatic effect? That was not like him. It was more like something I might have done myself. No: he was simply actuated by a desire to reconvert me to Cyril Graham's theory, and he thought that if I could be made to believe that he too had given his life for it, I would be deceived by the pathetic fallacy of martyrdom. Poor Erskine! I had grown wiser since I had seen him. Martyrdom was to me merely a tragic form of scepticism, an attempt to realise by fire what one had failed to do by faith. No man dies for what he knows to be true. Men die for what they want to be true, for what some terror in their hearts tells them is not true. The very uselessness of Erskine's letter made me doubly sorry for him. I watched the people strolling in and out of the cafés, and wondered if any of them had known him. The white dust blew down the scorched sunlit road, and the feathery palms moved restlessly in the shaken air.

At that moment Lady Erskine returned to the room carrying the fatal portrait of Willie Hughes. "When George was dying, he begged me to give you this," she said. As I took it from her, her tears fell on my hand.

---

* In *Les Miserables* (1862) Victor Hugo says that because sublime or noble actions are commonly misunderstood, people often claim them to be "mere affectation."

This curious work of art hangs now in my library, where it is very much admired by my artistic friends, one of whom has etched it for me. They have decided that it is not a Clouet but an Ouvry.* I have never cared to tell them its true history but sometimes, when I look at it, I think there is really a great deal to be said for the Willie Hughes theory of Shakespeare's Sonnets.

* An unknown painter; Wilde may have wished to suggest a rival of Jean Clouet, a lesser member of his courtly circle of artists.

LORD ARTHUR SAVILE'S CRIME

A Study of Duty

– 1 –

It was Lady Windermere's last reception before Easter, and Bentinck House was even more crowded than usual. Six Cabinet Ministers had come on from the Speaker's Levée* in their stars and ribands, all the pretty women wore their smartest dresses, and at the end of the picture-gallery stood the Princess Sophia of Carlsrühe, a heavy Tartar-looking lady, with tiny black eyes and wonderful emeralds, talking bad French at the top of her voice, and laughing immoderately at everything that was said to her. It was certainly a wonderful medley of people. Gorgeous peeresses chatted affably to violent Radicals, popular preachers brushed coat-tails with eminent sceptics, a perfect bevy of bishops kept following a stout prima-donna from room to room, on the staircase stood several Royal Academicians,† disguised as artists, and it was said that at one time the supper-room was absolutely crammed with geniuses. In fact, it was one of Lady Windermere's best nights, and the Princess stayed till nearly half-past eleven.

As soon as she had gone, Lady Windermere returned to the picture-gallery, where a celebrated political economist was solemnly explaining the scientific theory of music to an indignant virtuoso

---

* At the fashionable reception called the levée, the Speaker of the House of Commons was waited on by ministers and other dignitaries in full ceremonial dress.

† Members of the Royal Academy of Art, hence officially recognized painters and sculptors.

from Hungary, and began to talk to the Duchess of Paisley. She looked wonderfully beautiful with her grand ivory throat, her large blue forget-me-not eyes, and her heavy coils of golden hair. *Or pur** they were—not that pale straw colour that nowadays usurps the gracious name of gold, but such gold as is woven into sunbeams or hidden in strange amber; and they gave to her face something of the frame of a saint, with not a little of the fascination of a sinner. She was a curious psychological study. Early in life she had discovered the important truth that nothing looks so like innocence as an indiscretion; and by a series of reckless escapades, half of them quite harmless, she had acquired all the privileges of a personality. She had more than once changed her husband; indeed, Debrett† credits her with three marriages; but as she had never changed her lover, the world had long ago ceased to talk scandal about her. She was now forty years of age, childless, and with that inordinate passion for pleasure which is the secret of remaining young.

Suddenly she looked eagerly round the room, and said, in her clear contralto voice, "Where is my chiromantist?"

"Your what, Gladys?" exclaimed the Duchess, giving an involuntary start.

"My chiromantist, Duchess; I can't live without him at present."

"Dear Gladys! you are always so original," murmured the Duchess, trying to remember what a chiromantist really was, and hoping it was not the same as a chiropodist.

"He comes to see my hand twice a week regularly," continued Lady Windermere, "and is most interesting about it."

"Good heavens!" said the Duchess to herself, "he is a sort of chiropodist after all. How very dreadful. I hope he is a foreigner at any rate. It wouldn't be quite so bad then."

"I must certainly introduce him to you."

"Introduce him!" cried the Duchess; "you don't mean to say he is here?" and she began looking about for a small tortoise-shell fan

---

* Pure gold (French).

† *Debrett's Peerage*, first published in London in 1802 by John Debrett, is a genealogical guide to the titled British aristocracy.

and a very tattered lace shawl, so as to be ready to go at a moment's notice.

"Of course he is here; I would not dream of giving a party without him. He tells me I have a pure psychic hand, and that if my thumb had been the least little bit shorter, I should have been a confirmed pessimist, and gone into a convent."

"Oh, I see!" said the Duchess, feeling very much relieved; "he tells fortunes, I suppose?"

"And misfortunes, too," answered Lady Windermere, "any amount of them. Next year, for instance, I am in great danger, both by land and sea, so I am going to live in a balloon, and draw up my dinner in a basket every evening. It is all written down on my little finger, or on the palm of my hand, I forget which."

"But surely that is tempting Providence, Gladys."

"My dear Duchess, surely Providence can resist temptation by this time. I think every one should have their hands told once a month so as to know what not to do. Of course, one does it all the same, but it is so pleasant to be warned. Now if some one doesn't go and fetch Mr. Podgers at once, I shall have to go myself."

"Let me go, Lady Windermere," said a tall handsome young man, who was standing by, listening to the conversation with an amused smile.

"Thanks so much, Lord Arthur; but I am afraid you wouldn't recognise him."

"If he is as wonderful as you say, Lady Windermere, I couldn't well miss him. Tell me what he is like, and I'll bring him to you at once."

"Well, he is not a bit like a chiromantist. I mean he is not mysterious, or esoteric, or romantic-looking. He is a little, stout man, with a funny, bald head, and great gold-rimmed spectacles; something between a family doctor and a country attorney. I'm really very sorry, but it is not my fault. People are so annoying. All my pianists look exactly like poets; and all my poets look exactly like pianists; and I remember last season asking a most dreadful conspirator to dinner, a man who had blown up ever so many people, and always wore a coat of mail, and carried a dagger up his shirt-sleeve; and do you know that when he came he looked just like a nice old clergyman, and cracked jokes all the evening? Of course, he was very amusing, and all that, but I was awfully disappointed; and when I asked him about the coat of mail, he only laughed, and said it was far too cold to wear in England. Ah, here is Mr. Podgers! Now, Mr. Podgers, I want you to tell the Duchess of Paisley's hand. Duchess, you must take your glove off. No, not the left hand, the other."

"Dear Gladys, I really don't think it is quite right," said the Duchess, feebly unbuttoning a rather soiled kid glove.

"Nothing interesting ever is," said Lady Windermere: "*on a fait le monde ainsi.** But I must introduce you. Duchess, this is Mr. Podgers, my pet chiromantist. Mr. Podgers, this is the Duchess of Paisley, and if you say that she has a larger mountain of the moon than I have, I will never believe in you again."

"I am sure, Gladys, there is nothing of the kind in my hand," said the Duchess gravely.

"Your Grace is quite right," said Mr. Podgers, glancing at the little fat hand with its short square fingers, "the mountain of the moon is not developed. The line of life, however, is excellent. Kindly bend the wrist. Thank you. Three distinct lines on the *rascette*![†] You will live to a great age, Duchess, and be extremely happy. Ambition—very moderate, line of intellect not exaggerated, line of heart——"

"Now, do be indiscreet, Mr. Podgers," cried Lady Windermere.

"Nothing would give me greater pleasure," said Mr. Podgers, bowing, "if the Duchess ever had been, but I am sorry to say that I see great permanence of affection, combined with a strong sense of duty."

"Pray go on, Mr. Podgers," said the Duchess, looking quite pleased.

"Economy is not the least of your Grace's virtues," continued Mr. Podgers, and Lady Windermere went off into fits of laughter.

---

* That's the way things are (French).

† In palm reading, or chiromancy, the rascettes are lines where the wrist joins the hand (from French).

"Economy is a very good thing," remarked the Duchess complacently; "when I married Paisley he had eleven castles, and not a single house fit to live in."

"And now he has twelve houses, and not a single castle," cried Lady Windermere.

"Well, my dear," said the Duchess, "I like——"

"Comfort," said Mr. Podgers, "and modern improvements, and hot water laid on in every bedroom. Your Grace is quite right. Comfort is the only thing our civilisation can give us."

"You have told the Duchess's character admirably, Mr. Podgers, and now you must tell Lady Flora's"; and in answer to a nod from the smiling hostess, a tall girl, with sandy Scotch hair, and high shoulder-blades, stepped awkwardly from behind the sofa, and held out a long, bony hand with spatulate fingers.

"Ah, a pianist! I see," said Mr. Podgers, "an excellent pianist, but perhaps hardly a musician. Very reserved, very honest, and with a great love of animals."

"Quite true!" exclaimed the Duchess, turning to Lady Windermere, "absolutely true! Flora keeps two dozen collie dogs at Macloskie, and would turn our town house into a menagerie if her father would let her."

"Well, that is just what I do with my house every Thursday evening," cried Lady Windermere, laughing, "only I like lions better than collie dogs."

"Your one mistake, Lady Windermere," said Mr. Podgers, with a pompous bow.

"If a woman can't make her mistakes charming, she is only a female," was the answer. "But you must read some more hands for us. Come, Sir Thomas, show Mr. Podgers yours;" and a genial-looking old gentleman, in a white waistcoat, came forward, and held out a thick rugged hand, with a very long third finger.

"An adventurous nature; four long voyages in the past, and one to come. Been shipwrecked three times. No, only twice, but in danger of a shipwreck your next journey. A strong Conservative, very punctual and with a passion for collecting curiosities. Had a severe illness between the ages of sixteen and eighteen. Was left a fortune when about thirty. Great aversion to cats and Radicals."

"Extraordinary!" exclaimed Sir Thomas: "you must really tell my wife's hand, too."

"Your second wife's," said Mr. Podgers quietly, still keeping Sir Thomas's hand in his. "Your second wife's. I shall be charmed"; but Lady Marvel, a melancholy-looking woman, with brown hair and sentimental eyelashes, entirely declined to have her past or her future exposed; and nothing that Lady Windermere could do would induce Monsieur de Koloff, the Russian Ambassador, even to take his gloves off. In fact, many people seemed afraid to face the odd little man with his stereotyped smile, his gold spectacles, and his bright, beady eyes; and when he told poor Lady Fermor right out before every one, that she did not care a bit for music, but was extremely fond of musicians, it was generally felt that chiromancy was a most dangerous science, and one that ought not to be encouraged, except in a *tête-à-tête*.*

Lord Arthur Savile, however, who did not know anything about Lady Fermor's unfortunate story, and who had been watching Mr. Podgers with a great deal of interest, was filled with an immense curiosity to have his own hand read, and feeling somewhat shy about putting himself forward, crossed over the room to where Lady Windermere was sitting, and, with a charming blush, asked her if she thought Mr. Podgers would mind.

"Of course he won't mind," said Lady Windermere, "that is what he is here for. All my lions, Lord Arthur, are performing lions, and jump through hoops whenever I ask them. But I must warn you beforehand that I shall tell Sybil everything. She is coming to lunch with me to-morrow, to talk about bonnets, and if Mr. Podgers finds out that you have a bad temper, or a tendency to gout, or a wife living in Bayswater, I shall certainly let her know all about it."

Lord Arthur smiled, and shook his head. "I am not afraid," he answered. "Sybil knows me as well as I know her."

"Ah! I am a little sorry to hear you say that. The proper basis for

---

* Private conversation (French).

marriage is a mutual misunderstanding. No, I am not at all cynical, I have merely got experience, which, however, is very much the same thing. Mr. Podgers, Lord Arthur Savile is dying to have his hand read. Don't tell him that he is engaged to one of the most beautiful girls in London, because that appeared in the *Morning Post* a month ago."

"Dear Lady Windermere," cried the Marchioness of Jedburgh, "do let Mr. Podgers stay here a little longer. He has just told me I should go on the stage, and I am so interested."

"If he has told you that, Lady Jedburgh, I shall certainly take him away. Come over at once, Mr. Podgers, and read Lord Arthur's hand."

"Well," said Lady Jedburgh, making a little *moue** as she rose from the sofa, "if I am not to be allowed to go on the stage, I must be allowed to be part of the audience at any rate."

"Of course; we are all going to be part of the audience," said Lady Windermere; "and now, Mr. Podgers, be sure and tell us something nice. Lord Arthur is one of my special favourites."

But when Mr. Podgers saw Lord Arthur's hand he grew curiously pale, and said nothing. A shudder seemed to pass through him, and his great bushy eyebrows twitched convulsively, in an odd, irritating way they had when he was puzzled. Then some huge beads of perspiration broke out on his yellow forehead, like a poisonous dew, and his fat fingers grew cold and clammy.

Lord Arthur did not fail to notice these strange signs of agitation, and, for the first time in his life, he himself felt fear. His impulse was to rush from the room, but he restrained himself. It was better to know the worst, whatever it was, than to be left in this hideous uncertainty.

"I am waiting, Mr. Podgers," he said.

"We are all waiting," cried Lady Windermere, in her quick, impatient manner, but the chiromantist made no reply.

"I believe Arthur is going on the stage," said Lady Jedburgh, "and that, after your scolding, Mr. Podgers is afraid to tell him so."

Suddenly Mr. Podgers dropped Lord Arthur's right hand, and seized hold of his left, bending down so low to examine it that the

---

* Making a little face; pouting (French).

gold rims of his spectacles seemed almost to touch the palm. For a moment his face became a white mask of horror, but he soon recovered his *sang-froid*,* and looking up at Lady Windermere, said with a forced smile, "It is the hand of a charming young man."

"Of course it is!" answered Lady Windermere, "but will he be a charming husband? That is what I want to know."

"All charming young men are," said Mr. Podgers.

"I don't think a husband should be too fascinating," murmured Lady Jedburgh pensively, "it is so dangerous."

"My dear child, they never are too fascinating," cried Lady Windermere. "But what I want are details. Details are the only things that interest. What is going to happen to Lord Arthur?"

"Well, within the next few months Lord Arthur will go on a voyage——"

"Oh yes, his honeymoon, of course!"

"And lose a relative."

"Not his sister, I hope?" said Lady Jedburgh, in a piteous tone of voice.

"Certainly not his sister," answered Mr. Podgers, with a deprecating wave of the hand, "a distant relative merely."

"Well, I am dreadfully disappointed," said Lady Windermere. "I have absolutely nothing to tell Sybil to-morrow. No one cares about distant relatives nowadays. They went out of fashion years ago. However, I suppose she had better have a black silk by her; it always does for church, you know. And now let us go to supper. They are sure to have eaten everything up, but we may find some hot soup. François used to make excellent soup once, but he is so agitated about politics at present, that I never feel quite certain about him. I do wish General Boulanger† would keep quiet. Duchess, I am sure you are tired?"

"Not at all, dear Gladys," answered the Duchess, waddling towards the door. "I have enjoyed myself immensely, and the chiropodist, I

* Cold-blooded self-possession (French).

† General Georges Boulanger (1837–1891) was the French minister of war. He became an arch conservative who attacked the Republic and later fled Paris to escape warrants for his arrest.

mean the chiromantist, is most interesting. Flora, where can my tortoise-shell fan be? Oh, thank you, Sir Thomas, so much. And my lace shawl, Flora? Oh, thank you, Sir Thomas, very kind, I'm sure"; and the worthy creature finally managed to get downstairs without dropping her scent-bottle more than twice.

All this time Lord Arthur Savile had remained standing by the fireplace, with the same feeling of dread over him, the same sickening sense of coming evil. He smiled sadly at his sister, as she swept past him on Lord Plymdale's arm, looking lovely in her pink brocade and pearls, and he hardly heard Lady Windermere when she called to him to follow her. He thought of Sybil Merton, and the idea that anything could come between them made his eyes dim with tears.

Looking at him, one would have said that Nemesis had stolen the shield of Pallas, and shown him the Gorgon's head.* He seemed turned to stone, and his face was like marble in its melancholy. He had lived the delicate and luxurious life of a young man of birth and fortune, a life exquisite in its freedom from sordid care, its beautiful boyish insouciance; and now for the first time he had become conscious of the terrible mystery of Destiny, of the awful meaning of Doom.

How mad and monstrous it all seemed! Could it be that written on his hand, in characters that he could not read himself, but that another could decipher, was some fearful secret of sin, some blood-red sign of crime? Was there no escape possible? Were we no better than chessmen, moved by an unseen power, vessels the potter fashions at his fancy, for honour or for shame? His reason revolted against it, and yet he felt that some tragedy was hanging over him, and that he had been suddenly called upon to bear an intolerable burden. Actors are so fortunate. They can choose whether they will appear in tragedy or in comedy, whether they will suffer or make merry, laugh or shed

* In ancient Greek mythology, a Gorgon was a vicious female monster with living, poisonous snakes in place of hair; anyone looking at a Gorgon's head turned to stone. Perseus, a son of Zeus, used a mirror when he killed a Gorgon, attaching her head to the shield of Pallas Athena, goddess of wisdom.

tears. But in real life it is different. Most men and women are forced to perform parts for which they have no qualifications. Our Guildensterns play Hamlet for us, and our Hamlets have to jest like Prince Hal. The world is a stage, but the play is badly cast.

Suddenly Mr. Podgers entered the room. When he saw Lord Arthur he started, and his coarse, fat face became a sort of greenish-yellow colour. The two men's eyes met, and for a moment there was silence.

"The Duchess has left one of her gloves here, Lord Arthur, and has asked me to bring it to her," said Mr. Podgers finally. "Ah, I see it on the sofa! Good evening."

"Mr. Podgers, I must insist on your giving me a straightforward answer to a question I am going to put to you."

"Another time, Lord Arthur, but the Duchess is anxious. I am afraid I must go."

"You shall not go. The Duchess is in no hurry."

"Ladies should not be kept waiting, Lord Arthur," said Mr. Podgers, with his sickly smile. "The fair sex is apt to be impatient."

Lord Arthur's finely-chiselled lips curled in petulant disdain. The poor Duchess seemed to him of very little importance at that moment. He walked across the room to where Mr. Podgers was standing, and held his hand out.

"Tell me what you saw there," he said. "Tell me the truth. I must know it. I am not a child."

Mr. Podger's eyes blinked behind his gold-rimmed spectacles, and he moved uneasily from one foot to the other, while his fingers played nervously with a flash watch-chain.

"What makes you think that I saw anything in your hand, Lord Arthur, more than I told you?"

"I know you did, and I insist on your telling me what it was. I will pay you. I will give you a cheque for a hundred pounds."

The green eyes flashed for a moment, and then became dull again.

"Guineas?" said Mr. Podgers at last, in a low voice.

"Certainly. I will send you a cheque to-morrow. What is your club?"

"I have no club. That is to say, not just at present. My address is——, but allow me to give you my card"; and producing a bit of gilt-edge pasteboard from his waistcoat pocket, Mr. Podgers handed it, with a low bow, to Lord Arthur, who read on it, "*Mr. Septimus R. Podgers, Professional Chiromantist, 1030 West Moon Street.*"

"My hours are from ten to four," murmured Mr. Podgers mechanically, "and I make a reduction for families."

"Be quick," cried Lord Arthur, looking very pale, and holding his hand out.

Mr. Podgers glanced nervously round, and drew the heavy *portière** across the door.

"It will take a little time, Lord Arthur, you had better sit down."

"Be quick, sir," cried Lord Arthur again, stamping his foot angrily on the polished floor.

Mr. Podgers smiled, drew from his breast-pocket a small magnifying glass, and wiped it carefully with his handkerchief.

"I am quite ready," he said.

– 2 –

Ten minutes later, with face blanched by terror, and eyes wild with grief, Lord Arthur Savile rushed from Bentinck House, crushing his way through the crowd of fur-coated footmen that stood round the large striped awning, and seeming not to see or hear anything. The night was bitter cold, and the gas-lamps round the square flared and flickered in the keen wind; but his hands were hot with fever, and his forehead burned like fire. On and on he went, almost with the gait of a drunken man. A policeman looked curiously at him as he passed, and a beggar, who slouched from an archway to ask for alms, grew frightened, seeing misery greater than his own. Once he stopped under a lamp, and looked at his hands. He thought he could detect the stain of blood already upon them, and a faint cry broke from his trembling lips.

* Curtain (from French).

Murder! that is what the chiromantist had seen there. Murder! The very night seemed to know it, and the desolate wind to howl it in his ear. The dark corners of the streets were full of it. It grinned at him from the roofs of the houses.

First he came to the Park, whose sombre woodland seemed to fascinate him. He leaned wearily up against the railings, cooling his brow against the wet metal, and listening to the tremulous silence of the trees. "Murder! murder!" he kept repeating, as though iteration could dim the horror of the word. The sound of his own voice made him shudder, yet he almost hoped that Echo might hear him, and wake the slumbering city from its dreams. He felt a mad desire to stop the casual passer-by, and tell him everything.

Then he wandered across Oxford Street into narrow, shameful alleys. Two women with painted faces mocked at him as he went by. From a dark courtyard came a sound of oaths and blows, followed by shrill screams, and, huddled upon a damp door-step, he saw the crooked-back forms of poverty and eld. A strange pity came over him. Were these children of sin and misery predestined to their end, as he to his? Were they, like him, merely the puppets of a monstrous show?

And yet it was not the mystery, but the comedy of suffering that struck him; its absolute uselessness, its grotesque want of meaning. How incoherent everything seemed! How lacking in all harmony! He was amazed at the discord between the shallow optimism of the day, and the real facts of existence. He was still very young.

After a time he found himself in front of Marylebone Church. The silent roadway looked like a long riband of polished silver, flecked here and there by the dark arabesques of waving shadows. Far into the distance curved the line of flickering gas-lamps, and outside a little walled-in house stood a solitary hansom, the driver asleep inside. He walked hastily in the direction of Portland Place, now and then looking round, as though he feared that he was being followed. At the corner of Rich Street stood two men, reading a small bill upon a hoarding. An odd feeling of curiosity stirred him, and he crossed over. As he came near, the word 'Murder,' printed in black letters, met his eye. He started, and a deep flush came into his cheek. It was an advertisement offering a reward for any information leading to the arrest of a man of medium height, between thirty and forty years of age, wearing a billy-cock hat, a black coat, and check trousers, and with a scar upon his right cheek. He read it over and over again, and wondered if the wretched man would be caught, and how he had been scarred. Perhaps, some day, his own name might be placarded on the walls of London. Some day, perhaps, a price would be set on his head also.

The thought made him sick with horror. He turned on his heel, and hurried into the night.

Where he went he hardly knew. He had a dim memory of wandering through a labyrinth of sordid houses, and it was bright dawn when he found himself at last in Piccadilly Circus. As he strolled home towards Belgrave Square, he met the great waggons on their way to Covent Garden. The white-smocked carters, with their pleasant sunburnt faces and coarse curly hair, strode sturdily on, cracking their whips, and calling out now and then to each other; on the back of a huge grey horse, the leader of a jangling team, sat a chubby boy, with a bunch of primroses in his battered hat, keeping tight hold of the mane with his little hands, and laughing; and the great piles of vegetables looked like masses of jade against the morning sky, like masses of green jade against the pink petals of some marvellous rose. Lord Arthur felt curiously affected, he could not tell why. There was something in the dawn's delicate loveliness that seemed to him inexpressibly pathetic, and he thought of all the days that break in beauty, and that set in storm. These rustics, too, with their rough, good-humoured voices, and their nonchalant ways, what a strange London they saw! A London free from the sin of night and the smoke of day, a pallid, ghost-like city, a desolate town of tombs! He wondered what they thought of it, and whether they knew anything of its splendour and its shame, of its fierce, fiery-coloured joys, and its horrible hunger, of all it makes and mars from morn to eve. Probably it was to them merely a mart where they brought their fruit to sell, and where they tarried for a few hours at most, leaving the streets still silent, the houses still asleep. It gave him pleasure to watch them as they went by. Rude as they were, with their heavy, hob-nailed shoes, and their awkward gait, they brought a little of Arcady with them. He felt that they had lived with Nature, and that she had taught them peace. He envied them all that they did not know.

By the time he had reached Belgrave Square the sky was a faint blue, and the birds were beginning to twitter in the gardens.

– 3 –

When Lord Arthur woke it was twelve o'clock, and the midday sun was streaming through the ivory-silk curtains of his room. He got up and looked out of the window. A dim haze of heat was hanging over the great city, and the roofs of the houses were like dull silver. In the flickering green of the square below some children were flitting about like white butterflies, and the pavement was crowded with people on their way to the Park. Never had life seemed lovelier to him, never had the things of evil seemed more remote.

Then his valet brought him a cup of chocolate on a tray. After he had drunk it, he drew aside a heavy *portière* of peach-coloured plush, and passed into the bathroom. The light stole softly from above, through thin slabs of transparent onyx, and the water in the marble tank glimmered like a moonstone. He plunged hastily in, till the cool ripples touched throat and hair, and then dipped his head right under, as though he would have wiped away the stain of some shameful memory. When he stepped out he felt almost at peace. The exquisite physical conditions of the moment had dominated him, as indeed often happens in the case of very finely-wrought natures, for the senses, like fire, can purify as well as destroy.

After breakfast, he flung himself down on a divan and lit a cigarette. On the mantel-shelf, framed in dainty old brocade, stood a large photograph of Sybil Merton, as he had seen her first at Lady Noel's ball. The small, exquisitely-shaped head drooped slightly to one side, as though the thin, reed-like throat could hardly bear the burden of so much beauty; the lips were slightly parted, and seemed made for sweet music; and all the tender purity of girlhood looked out in wonder from the dreaming eyes. With her soft, clinging dress of *crêpe de chine*,* and her large leaf-shaped fan, she looked like one of those delicate little figures men find in the olive-woods near Tana-

* Soft fine or sheer fabric, especially of silk.

gra; and there was a touch of Greek grace in her pose and attitude. Yet she was not *petite.** She was simply perfectly proportioned—a rare thing in an age when so many women are either over life-size or insignificant.

Now as Lord Arthur looked at her, he was filled with the terrible pity that is born of love. He felt that to marry her, with the doom of murder hanging over his head, would be a betrayal like that of Judas, a sin worse than any the Borgia† had ever dreamed of. What happiness could there be for them, when at any moment he might be called upon to carry out the awful prophecy written in his hand? What manner of life would be theirs while Fate still held this fearful fortune in the scales? The marriage must be postponed, at all costs. Of this he was quite resolved. Ardently though he loved the girl, and the mere touch of her fingers, when they sat together, made each nerve of his body thrill with exquisite joy, he recognised none the less clearly where his duty lay, and was fully conscious of the fact that he had no right to marry until he had committed the murder. This done, he could stand before the altar with Sybil Merton, and give his life into her hands without terror of wrong-doing. This done, he could take her to his arms, knowing that she would never have to blush for him, never have to hang her head in shame. But done it must be first; and the sooner the better for both.

Many men in his position would have preferred the primrose path of dalliance to the steep heights of duty; but Lord Arthur was too conscientious to set pleasure above principle. There was more than mere passion in his love; and Sybil was to him a symbol of all that is good and noble. For a moment he had a natural repugnance against what he was asked to do, but it soon passed away. His heart told him that it was not a sin, but a sacrifice; his reason reminded him that there was no other course open. He had to choose between living for himself and living for others, and terrible though the task laid upon him undoubtedly was, yet he knew that he must not suffer selfishness

---

* Small (French).

† The Borgias were a family of Renaissance Italian princes notorious for their violence, including the liberal use of poisons.

to triumph over love. Sooner or later we are all called upon to decide on the same issue—of us all the same question is asked. To Lord Arthur it came early in life—before his nature had been spoiled by the calculating cynicism of middle-age, or his heart corroded by the shallow, fashionable egotism of our day, and he felt no hesitation about doing his duty. Fortunately also, for him, he was no mere dreamer, or idle dilettante. Had he been so, he would have hesitated, like Hamlet, and let irresolution mar his purpose. But he was essentially practical. Life to him meant action, rather than thought. He had that rarest of all things, common sense.

The wild, turbid feelings of the previous night had by this time completely passed away, and it was almost with a sense of shame that he looked back upon his mad wanderings from street to street, his fierce emotional agony. The very sincerity of his sufferings made them seem unreal to him now. He wondered how he could have been so foolish as to rant and rave about the inevitable. The only question that seemed to trouble him was, whom to make away with; for he was not blind to the fact that murder, like the religions of the Pagan world, requires a victim as well as a priest. Not being a genius, he had no enemies, and indeed he felt that this was not the time for the gratification of any personal pique or dislike, the mission in which he was engaged being one of great and grave solemnity. He accordingly made out a list of his friends and relatives on a sheet of notepaper, and after careful consideration, decided in favour of Lady Clementina Beauchamp, a dear old lady who lived in Curzon Street, and was his own second cousin by his mother's side. He had always been very fond of Lady Clem, as every one called her, and as he was very wealthy himself, having come into all Lord Rugby's property when he came of age, there was no possibility of his deriving any vulgar monetary advantage by her death. In fact, the more he thought over the matter, the more she seemed to him to be just the right person, and, feeling that any delay would be unfair to Sybil, he determined to make his arrangements at once.

The first thing to be done was, of course, to settle with the chiromantist; so he sat down at a small Sheraton writing-table that stood near the window, drew a cheque for £105, payable to the order of

Mr. Septimus Podgers, and, enclosing it in an envelope, told his valet to take it to West Moon Street. He then telephoned to the stables for his hansom, and dressed to go out. As he was leaving the room he looked back at Sybil Merton's photograph, and swore that, come what may, he would never let her know what he was doing for her sake, but would keep the secret of his self-sacrifice hidden always in his heart.

On his way to the Buckingham, he stopped at a florist's, and sent Sybil a beautiful basket of narcissi, with lovely white petals and staring pheasants' eyes, and on arriving at the club went straight to the library, rang the bell, and ordered the waiter to bring him a lemon-and-soda, and a book on Toxicology. He had fully decided that poison was the best means to adopt in this troublesome business. Anything like personal violence was extremely distasteful to him, and besides, he was very anxious not to murder Lady Clementina in any way that might attract public attention, as he hated the idea of being lionised at Lady Windermere's, or seeing his name figuring in the paragraphs of vulgar society-newspapers. He had also to think of Sybil's father and mother, who were rather old-fashioned people, and might possibly object to the marriage if there was anything like a scandal, though he felt certain that if he told them the whole facts of the case they would be the very first to appreciate the motives that had actuated him. He had every reason, then, to decide in favour of poison. It was safe, sure, and quiet, and did away with any necessity for painful scenes, to which, like most Englishmen, he had a rooted objection.

Of the science of poisons, however, he knew absolutely nothing, and as the waiter seemed quite unable to find anything in the library but *Ruff's Guide* and *Bailey's Magazine* he examined the book-shelves himself, and finally came across a handsomely-bound edition of the *Pharmacopœia*, and a copy of Erskine's *Toxicology*, edited by Sir Mathew Reid, the President of the Royal College of Physicians, and one of the oldest members of the Buckingham, having been elected in mistake for somebody else; a *contretemps** that so enraged the Committee, that

* Embarrassing event (French).

when the real man came up they black-balled him unanimously. Lord Arthur was a good deal puzzled at the technical terms used in both books, and had begun to regret that he had not paid more attention to his classics at Oxford, when in the second volume of Erskine, he found a very interesting and complete account of the properties of aconitine, written in fairly clear English. It seemed to him to be exactly the poison he wanted. It was swift—indeed, almost immediate, in its effect—perfectly painless, and when taken in the form of a gelatine capsule, the mode recommended by Sir Mathew, not by any means unpalatable. He accordingly made a note, upon his shirt-cuff, of the amount necessary for a fatal dose, put the books back in their places, and strolled up St. James's Street, to Pestle and Humbey's, the great chemists. Mr. Pestle, who always attended personally on the aristocracy, was a good deal surprised at the order, and in a very deferential manner murmured something about a medical certificate being necessary. However, as soon as Lord Arthur explained to him that it was for a large Norwegian mastiff that he was obliged to get rid of, as it showed signs of incipient rabies, and had already bitten the coachman twice in the calf of the leg, he expressed himself as being perfectly satisfied, complimented Lord Arthur on his wonderful knowledge of Toxicology, and had the prescription made up immediately.

Lord Arthur put the capsule into a pretty little silver *bonbonnière** that he saw in a shop window in Bond Street, threw away Pestle and Humbey's ugly pill-box, and drove off at once to Lady Clementina's.

"Well, *monsieur le mauvais sujet*,"† cried the old lady, as he entered the room, "why haven't you been to see me all this time?"

"My dear Lady Clem, I never have a moment to myself," said Lord Arthur, smiling.

"I suppose you mean that you go about all day long with Miss Sybil Merton, buying *chiffons* and talking nonsense? I cannot understand why people make such a fuss about being married. In my day we never dreamed of billing and cooing in public, or in private for that matter."

---

* Candy box (French).

† You naughty fellow (French).

"I assure you I have not seen Sybil for twenty-four hours, Lady Clem. As far as I can make out, she belongs entirely to her milliners."

"Of course; that is the only reason you come to see an ugly old woman like myself. I wonder you men don't take warning. *On a fait des folies pour moi*,* and here I am, a poor rheumatic creature, with a false front and a bad temper. Why, if it were not for dear Lady Jansen, who sends me all the worst French novels she can find, I don't think I could get through the day. Doctors are no use at all, except to get fees out of one. They can't even cure my heartburn."

"I have brought you a cure for that, Lady Clem," said Lord Arthur gravely. "It is a wonderful thing, invented by an American."

"I don't think I like American inventions, Arthur. I am quite sure I don't. I read some American novels lately, and they were quite nonsensical."

"Oh, but there is no nonsense at all about this, Lady Clem! I assure you it is a perfect cure. You must promise to try it"; and Lord Arthur brought the little box out of his pocket, and handed it to her.

"Well, the box is charming, Arthur. Is it really a present? That is very sweet of you. And is this the wonderful medicine? It looks like a *bonbon*.† I'll take it at once."

"Good heavens! Lady Clem," cried Lord Arthur, catching hold of her hand, "you mustn't do anything of the kind. It is a homœopathic medicine, and if you take it without having heartburn, it might do you no end of harm. Wait till you have an attack, and take it then. You will be astonished at the result."

"I should like to take it now," said Lady Clementina, holding up to the light the little transparent capsule, with its floating bubble of liquid aconitine. "I am sure it is delicious. The fact is that, though I hate doctors, I love medicines. However, I'll keep it till my next attack."

"And when will that be?" asked Lord Arthur eagerly. "Will it be soon?"

---

* People have done foolish things for me (French).

† Piece of candy (French).

"I hope not for a week. I had a very bad time yesterday morning with it. But one never knows."

"You are sure to have one before the end of the month then, Lady Clem?"

"I am afraid so. But how sympathetic you are to-day, Arthur! Really, Sybil has done you a great deal of good. And now you must run away, for I am dining with some very dull people, who won't talk scandal, and I know that if I don't get my sleep now I shall never be able to keep awake during dinner. Good-bye, Arthur, give my love to Sybil, and thank you so much for the American medicine."

"You won't forget to take it, Lady Clem, will you?" said Lord Arthur, rising from his seat.

"Of course I won't, you silly boy. I think it is most kind of you to think of me, and I shall write and tell you if I want any more."

Lord Arthur left the house in high spirits, and with a feeling of immense relief.

That night he had an interview with Sybil Merton. He told her how he had been suddenly placed in a position of terrible difficulty, from which neither honour nor duty would allow him to recede. He told her that the marriage must be put off for the present, as until he had got rid of his fearful entanglements, he was not a free man. He implored her to trust him, and not to have any doubts about the future. Everything would come right, but patience was necessary.

The scene took place in the conservatory of Mr. Merton's house, in Park Lane, where Lord Arthur had dined as usual. Sybil had never seemed more happy, and for a moment Lord Arthur had been tempted to play the coward's part, to write to Lady Clementina for the pill, and to let the marriage go on as if there was no such person as Mr. Podgers in the world. His better nature, however, soon asserted itself, and even when Sybil flung herself weeping into his arms, he did not falter. The beauty that stirred his senses had touched his conscience also. He felt that to wreck so fair a life for the sake of a few months' pleasure would be a wrong thing to do.

He stayed with Sibyl till nearly midnight, comforting her and being comforted in turn, and early the next morning he left for Venice, after writing a manly, firm letter to Mr. Merton about the necessary postponement of the marriage.

– 4 –

In Venice he met his brother, Lord Surbiton, who happened to have come over from Corfu in his yacht. The two young men spent a delightful fortnight together. In the morning they rode on the Lido, or glided up and down the green canal in their long black gondola; in the afternoon they usually entertained visitors on the yacht; and in the evening they dined at Florian's,* and smoked innumerable cigarettes on the Piazza. Yet somehow Lord Arthur was not happy. Every day he studied the obituary column in the *Times*, expecting to see a notice of Lady Clementina's death, but every day he was disappointed. He began to be afraid that some accident had happened to her, and often regretted that he had prevented her taking the aconitine when she had been so anxious to try its effect. Sybil's letters, too, though full of love, and trust, and tenderness, were often very sad in their tone, and sometimes he used to think that he was parted from her for ever.

After a fortnight Lord Surbiton got bored with Venice, and determined to run down the coast to Ravenna, as he heard that there was some capital cock-shooting in the Pinetum. Lord Arthur at first refused absolutely to come, but Surbiton, of whom he was extremely fond, finally persuaded him that if he stayed at Danielli's by himself he would be moped to death, and on the morning of the 15th they started, with a strong nor'east wind blowing, and a rather choppy sea. The sport was excellent, and the free, open-air life brought the colour back to Lord Arthur's cheek, but about the 22nd he became anxious about Lady Clementina, and, in spite of Surbiton's remonstrances, came back to Venice by train.

As he stepped out of his gondola on to the hotel steps, the proprietor came forward to meet him with a sheaf of telegrams. Lord Arthur snatched them out of his hand, and tore them open. Everything had

* Café in Venice, on the Piazza San Marco, across the lagoon from the Lido.

been quite successful. Lady Clementina had died quite suddenly on the night of the 17th!

His first thought was for Sybil, and he sent her off a telegram announcing his immediate return to London. He then ordered his valet to pack his things for the night mail, sent his gondoliers about five times their proper fare, and ran up to his sitting-room with a light step and a buoyant heart. There he found three letters waiting for him. One was from Sybil herself, full of sympathy and condolence. The others were from his mother, and from Lady Clementina's solicitor. It seemed that the old lady had dined with the Duchess that very night, had delighted every one by her wit and *esprit*,* but had gone home somewhat early, complaining of heartburn. In the morning she was found dead in her bed, having apparently suffered no pain. Sir Mathew Reid had been sent for at once, but, of course, there was nothing to be done, and she was to be buried on the 22nd at Beauchamp Chalcote. A few days before she died she had made her will, and left Lord Arthur her little house in Curzon Street, and all her furniture, personal effects, and pictures, with the exception of her collection of miniatures, which was to go to her sister, Lady Margaret Rufford, and her amethyst necklace, which Sybil Merton was to have. The property was not of much value; but Mr. Mansfield, the solicitor, was extremely anxious for Lord Arthur to return at once, if possible, as there were a great many bills to be paid, and Lady Clementina had never kept any regular accounts.

Lord Arthur was very much touched by Lady Clementina's kind remembrance of him, and felt that Mr. Podgers had a great deal to answer for. His love of Sybil, however, dominated every other emotion, and the consciousness that he had done his duty gave him peace and comfort. When he arrived at Charing Cross, he felt perfectly happy.

The Mertons received him very kindly. Sybil made him promise that he would never again allow anything to come between them, and the marriage was fixed for the 7th June. Life seemed to him once more bright and beautiful, and all his old gladness came back to him again.

---

* Spirit (French).

One day, however, as he was going over the house in Curzon Street, in company with Lady Clementina's solicitor and Sybil herself, burning packages of faded letters and turning out drawers of odd rubbish, the young girl suddenly gave a cry of delight.

"What have you found, Sybil?" said Lord Arthur, looking up from his work, and smiling.

"This lovely little silver *bonbonnière*, Arthur. Isn't it quaint and Dutch? Do give it to me! I know amethysts won't become me till I am over eighty."

It was the box that had held the aconitine.

Lord Arthur started, and a faint blush came into his cheek. He had almost entirely forgotten what he had done, and it seemed to him a curious coincidence that Sybil, for whose sake he had gone through all that terrible anxiety, should have been the first to remind him of it.

"Of course you can have it, Sybil. I gave it to poor Lady Clem myself."

"Oh! thank you, Arthur; and may I have the *bonbon* too? I had no notion that Lady Clementina liked sweets. I thought she was far too intellectual."

Lord Arthur grew deadly pale, and a horrible idea crossed his mind.

"*Bonbon*, Sybil? What do you mean?" he said in a slow, hoarse voice.

"There is one in it, that is all. It looks quite old and dusty, and I have not the slightest intention of eating it. What is the matter, Arthur? How white you look!"

Lord Arthur rushed across the room, and seized the box. Inside it was the amber-coloured capsule, with its poison-bubble. Lady Clementina had died a natural death after all!

The shock of the discovery was almost too much for him. He flung the capsule into the fire, and sank on the sofa with a cry of despair.

– 5 –

Mr. Merton was a good deal distressed at the second postponement of the marriage, and Lady Julia, who had already ordered her dress for the wedding, did all in her power to make Sybil break off the match. Dearly, however, as Sybil loved her mother, she had given her whole life into Lord Arthur's hands, and nothing that Lady Julia could say could make her waver in her faith. As for Lord Arthur himself, it took him days to get over his terrible disappointment, and for a time his nerves were completely unstrung. His excellent common sense, however, soon asserted itself, and his sound, practical mind did not leave him long in doubt about what to do. Poison having proved a complete failure, dynamite, or some other form of explosive, was obviously the proper thing to try.

He accordingly looked again over the list of his friends and relatives, and, after careful consideration, determined to blow up his uncle, the Dean of Chichester. The Dean, who was a man of great culture and learning, was extremely fond of clocks, and had a wonderful collection of timepieces, ranging from the fifteenth century to the present day, and it seemed to Lord Arthur that this hobby of the good Dean's offered him an excellent opportunity for carrying out his scheme. Where to procure an explosive machine was, of course, quite another matter. The London Directory gave him no information on the point, and he felt that there was very little use in going to Scotland Yard about it, as they never seemed to know anything about the movements of the dynamite faction till after an explosion had taken place, and not much even then.

Suddenly he thought of his friend Rouvaloff, a young Russian of very revolutionary tendencies, whom he had met at Lady Windermere's in the winter. Count Rouvaloff was supposed to be writing a life of Peter the Great, and to have come over to England for the purpose of studying the documents relating to that Tsar's residence in this country as a ship carpenter; but it was generally suspected that he was a Nihilist agent, and there was no doubt that the Russian Embassy did not look with any favour upon his presence in London. Lord Arthur felt that he was just the man for his purpose, and drove down one morning to his lodgings in Bloomsbury, to ask his advice and assistance.

"So you are taking up politics seriously?" said Count Rouvaloff, when Lord Arthur had told him the object of his mission; but Lord Arthur, who hated swagger of any kind, felt bound to admit to him that he had not the slightest interest in social questions, and simply wanted the explosive machine for a purely family matter, in which no one was concerned but himself.

Count Rouvaloff looked at him for some moments in amazement, and then seeing that he was quite serious, wrote an address on a piece of paper, initialled it, and handed it to him across the table.

"Scotland Yard would give a good deal to know this address, my dear fellow."

"They shan't have it," cried Lord Arthur, laughing; and after shaking the young Russian warmly by the hand he ran downstairs, examined the paper, and told the coachman to drive to Soho Square.

There he dismissed him, and strolled down Greek Street, till he came to a place called Bayle's Court. He passed under the archway, and found himself in a curious *cul-de-sac*,* that was apparently occupied by a French laundry, as a perfect network of clothes-lines was stretched across from house to house, and there was a flutter of white linen in the morning air. He walked right to the end, and knocked at a little green house. After some delay, during which every window became a blurred mass of peering faces, the door was opened by a rather rough-looking foreigner, who asked him in very bad English what his business was. Lord Arthur handed him the paper Count Rouvaloff had given him. When the man saw it he bowed, and invited Lord Arthur into a very shabby front parlour on the ground floor, and in a few moments Herr Winckelkopf, as he was called in England, bustled into the room, with a very wine-stained napkin round his neck, and a fork in his left hand.

"Count Rouvaloff has given me an introduction to you," said Lord Arthur, bowing, "and I am anxious to have a short interview with you on a matter of business. My name is Smith, Mr. Robert Smith, and I want you to supply me with an explosive clock."

"Charmed to meet you, Lord Arthur," said the genial little German, laughing. "Don't look so alarmed, it is my duty to know everybody, and I remember seeing you one evening at Lady Windermere's. I hope her ladyship is quite well. Do you mind sitting with me while I finish my breakfast? There is an excellent *paté*, and my friends are kind enough to say that my Rhine wine is better than any they get at the German Embassy," and before Lord Arthur had got over his surprise at being

* Dead end (French).

recognised, he found himself seated in the back-room, sipping the most delicious Marcobrünner out of a pale yellow hock-glass marked with the Imperial monogram, and chatting in the friendliest manner possible to the famous conspirator.

"Explosive clocks," said Herr Winckelkopf, "are not very good things for foreign exportation, as, even if they succeed in passing the Custom House, the train service is so irregular, that they usually go off before they have reached their proper destination. If, however, you want one for home use, I can supply you with an excellent article, and guarantee that you will be satisfied with the result. May I ask for whom it is intended? If it is for the police, or for any one connected with Scotland Yard, I am afraid I cannot do anything for you. The English detectives are really our best friends, and I have always found that by relying on their stupidity, we can do exactly what we like. I could not spare one of them."

"I assure you," said Lord Arthur, "that it has nothing to do with the police at all. In fact, the clock is intended for the Dean of Chichester."

"Dear me! I had no idea that you felt so strongly about religion, Lord Arthur. Few young men do nowadays."

"I am afraid you overrate me, Herr Winckelkopf," said Lord Arthur, blushing. "The fact is, I really know nothing about theology."

"It is a purely private matter then?"

"Purely private."

Herr Winckelkopf shrugged his shoulders, and left the room, returning in a few minutes with a round cake of dynamite about the size of a penny, and a pretty little French clock, surmounted by an ormolu figure of Liberty trampling on the hydra of Despotism.

Lord Arthur's face brightened up when he saw it. "That is just what I want," he cried, "and now tell me how it goes off."

"Ah! there is my secret," answered Herr Winckelkopf, contemplating his invention with a justifiable look of pride; "let me know when you wish it to explode, and I will set the machine to the moment."

"Well, to-day is Tuesday, and if you could send it off at once——"

"That is impossible; I have a great deal of important work on hand for some friends of mine in Moscow. Still, I might send it off to-morrow."

"Oh, it will be quite time enough!" said Lord Arthur politely, "if it is delivered to-morrow night or Thursday morning. For the moment of the explosion, say Friday at noon exactly. The Dean is always at home at that hour."

"Friday, at noon," repeated Herr Winckelkopf, and he made a note to that effect in a large ledger that was lying on a bureau near the fireplace.

"And now," said Lord Arthur, rising from his seat, "pray let me know how much I am in your debt."

"It is such a small matter, Lord Arthur, that I do not care to make any charge. The dynamite comes to seven and sixpence, the clock will be three pounds ten, and the carriage about five shillings. I am only too pleased to oblige any friend of Count Rouvaloff's."

"But your trouble, Herr Winckelkopf?"

"Oh, that is nothing! It is a pleasure to me. I do not work for money; I live entirely for my art."

Lord Arthur laid down £4 2s. 6d. on the table, thanked the little German for his kindness, and, having succeeded in declining an invitation to meet some Anarchists at a meat-tea on the following Saturday, left the house and went off to the Park.

For the next two days he was in a state of the greatest excitement, and on Friday at twelve o'clock he drove down to the Buckingham to wait for news. All the afternoon the stolid hall-porter kept posting up telegrams from various parts of the country giving the results of horse-races, the verdicts in divorce suits, the state of the weather, and the like, while the tape ticked out wearisome details about an all-night sitting in the House of Commons, and a small panic on the Stock Exchange. At four o'clock the evening papers came in, and Lord Arthur disappeared into the library with the *Pall Mall*, the *St. James's*, the *Globe*, and the *Echo*, to the immense indignation of Colonel Goodchild, who wanted to read the reports of a speech he had delivered that morning at the Mansion House, on the subject of South African Missions, and the advisability of having black Bishops in every province, and for some reason or other had a strong prejudice against the *Evening News*. None of the papers, however, contained even the slightest allusion to Chichester, and Lord Arthur felt that the attempt must have failed. It was a terrible blow to him, and for a time he was quite unnerved. Herr Winckelkopf, whom he went to see the next day, was full of elaborate apologies, and offered to supply him with another clock free of charge, or with a case of nitro-glycerine bombs at cost price. But he had lost all faith in explosives, and Herr Winckelkopf himself acknowledged that everything is so adulterated nowadays, that even dynamite can hardly be got in a pure condition. The little German, however, while admitting that something must have gone wrong with the machinery, was not without hope that the clock might still go off, and instanced the case of a barometer that he had once sent to the military Governor at Odessa, which, though timed to explode in ten days, had not done so for something like three months. It was quite true that when it did go off, it merely succeeded in blowing a housemaid to atoms, the Governor having gone out of town six weeks before, but at least it showed that dynamite, as a destructive force, was, when under the control of machinery, a powerful, though somewhat unpunctual agent. Lord Arthur was a little consoled by this reflection, but even here he was destined to disappointment, for two days afterwards, as he was going upstairs, the Duchess called him into her boudoir, and showed him a letter she had just received from the Deanery.

"Jane writes charming letters," said the Duchess; "you must really read her last. It is quite as good as the novels Mudie sends us."

Lord Arthur seized the letter from her hand. It ran as follows:—

The Deanery, Chichester,
27th May.

My dearest Aunt,

Thank you so much for the flannel for the Dorcas Society, and also for the gingham. I quite agree with you that it is nonsense their wanting to wear pretty things, but everybody is so Radical and irreligious nowadays, that it is difficult to make them see that they should not try and dress like the upper classes. I am sure I don't know what we are coming to. As papa has often said in his sermons, we live in an age of unbelief.

We have had great fun over a clock that an unknown admirer sent papa last Thursday. It arrived in a wooden box from London, carriage paid; and papa feels it must have been sent by some one who had read his remarkable sermon, "Is Licence Liberty?" for on the top of the clock was a figure of a woman, with what papa said was the cap of Liberty on her head. I don't think it very becoming myself, but papa said it was historical, so I suppose it is all right. Parker unpacked it, and papa put it on the mantelpiece in the library, and we were all sitting there on Friday morning, when just as the clock struck twelve, we heard a whirring noise, a little puff of smoke came from the pedestal of the figure, and the goddess of Liberty fell off, and broke her nose on the fender! Maria was quite alarmed, but it looked so ridiculous, that James and I went off into fits of laughter, and even papa was amused. When we examined it, we found it was a sort of alarm clock, and that, if you set it to a particular hour, and put some gunpowder and a cap under a little hammer, it went off whenever you wanted. Papa said it must not remain in the library, as it made a noise, so Reggie carried it away to the schoolroom, and does nothing but have small explosions all day long. Do you think Arthur would like one for a wedding present? I suppose they are quite fashionable in London. Papa says they should do a great deal of good, as they show that Liberty can't last, but must fall down. Papa says Liberty was invented at the time of the French Revolution. How awful it seems!

I have now to go to the Dorcas, where I will read your most instructive letter. How true, dear aunt, your idea is, that in their rank of life they should wear what is unbecoming. I must say it is absurd, their anxiety about dress, when there are so many more important things in this world, and in the next. I am so glad your flowered poplin turned out so well, and that your lace was not torn. I am wearing my yellow satin, that you so kindly gave me, at the Bishop's on Wednesday, and think it will look all right. Would you have bows or not? Jennings says that every one wears bows now, and that the underskirt should be frilled. Reggie has just had another explosion, and papa has ordered the clock to be sent to the stables. I don't think papa likes it so much as he did at first, though he is very flattered at being sent such a pretty and ingenious toy. It shows that people read his sermons, and profit by them.

Papa sends his love, in which James, and Reggie, and Maria all unite, and, hoping that Uncle Cecil's gout is better, believe me, dear aunt, ever your affectionate niece,

Jane Percy.

PS.—Do tell me about the bows. Jennings insists they are the fashion.

Lord Arthur looked so serious and unhappy over the letter, that the Duchess went into fits of laughter.

"My dear Arthur," she cried, "I shall never show you a young lady's letter again! But what shall I say about the clock? I think it is a capital invention, and I should like to have one myself."

"I don't think much of them," said Lord Arthur, with a sad smile, and, after kissing his mother, he left the room.

When he got upstairs, he flung himself on a sofa, and his eyes filled with tears. He had done his best to commit this murder, but on both occasions he had failed, and through no fault of his own. He had tried to do his duty, but it seemed as if Destiny herself had turned traitor. He was oppressed with the sense of the barrenness of good intentions, of the futility of trying to be fine. Perhaps it would be better to break off the marriage altogether. Sybil would suffer, it is true, but suffering could not really mar a nature so noble as hers. As for himself, what did it matter? There is always some war in which a man can die, some cause to which a man can give his life, and as life had no pleasure for him, so death had no terror. Let Destiny work out his doom. He would not stir to help her.

At half-past seven he dressed, and went down to the club. Surbiton was there with a party of young men, and he was obliged to dine with them. Their trivial conversation and idle jests did not interest him, and as soon as coffee was brought he left them, inventing some engagement in order to get away. As he was going out of the club, the hall-porter handed him a letter. It was from Herr Winckelkopf, asking him to call down the next evening, and look at an explosive umbrella, that went off as soon as it was opened. It was the very latest invention, and had just arrived from Geneva. He tore the letter up into fragments. He had made up his mind not to try any more experiments. Then he wandered down to the Thames Embankment, and sat for hours by the river. The moon peered through a mane of tawny clouds, as if it were a lion's eye, and innumerable stars spangled the hollow vault, like gold dust powdered on a purple dome. Now and then a barge swung out into the turbid stream, and floated away with the tide, and the railway signals changed from green to scarlet as the trains ran shrieking across the bridge. After some time, twelve o'clock boomed from the tall tower at Westminster, and at each stroke of the sonorous bell the night seemed to tremble. Then the railway lights went out, one solitary lamp left gleaming like a large ruby on a giant mast, and the roar of the city became fainter.

At two o'clock he got up, and strolled towards Blackfriars. How unreal everything looked! How like a strange dream! The houses on the other side of the river seemed built out of darkness. One would have said that silver and shadow had fashioned the world anew. The huge dome of St. Paul's loomed like a bubble through the dusky air.

As he approached Cleopatra's Needle* he saw a man leaning over the parapet, and as he came nearer the man looked up, the gas-light falling full upon his face.

It was Mr. Podgers, the chiromantist! No one could mistake the fat, flabby face, the gold-rimmed spectacles, the sickly feeble smile, the sensual mouth.

Lord Arthur stopped. A brilliant idea flashed across him, and he stole softly up behind. In a moment he had seized Mr. Podgers by the legs, and flung him into the Thames. There was a coarse oath, a heavy splash, and all was still. Lord Arthur looked anxiously over, but could see nothing of the chiromantist but a tall hat, pirouetting in an eddy of moonlit water. After a time it also sank, and no trace of Mr. Podgers was visible. Once he thought that he caught sight of the bulky misshapen figure striking out for the staircase by the bridge, and a horrible feeling of failure came over him but it turned out to be merely a

---

* Ancient Egyptian obelisk that stands in the City of Westminster. Given to Britain in the early nineteenth century by the viceroy of Egypt to commemorate the victories over the French of Lord Nelson at the Battle of the Nile (1798) and Sir Ralph Abercromby at the Battle of Alexandria (1801), it was brought to London in the late nineteenth century.

reflection, and when the moon shone out from behind a cloud it passed away. At last he seemed to have realised the decree of Destiny. He heaved a deep sigh of relief, and Sybil's name came to his lips.

"Have you dropped anything, sir?" said a voice behind him suddenly.

He turned round, and saw a policeman with a bull's-eye lantern.

"Nothing of importance, sergeant," he answered, smiling, and hailing a passing hansom, he jumped in, and told the man to drive to Belgrave Square.

For the next few days he alternated between hope and fear. There were moments when he almost expected Mr. Podgers to walk into the room, and yet at other times he felt that Fate could not be so unjust to him. Twice he went to the chiromantist's address in West Moon Street, but he could not bring himself to ring the bell. He longed for certainty, and was afraid of it.

Finally it came. He was sitting in the smoking-room of the club having tea, and listening rather wearily to Surbiton's account of the last comic song at the Gaiety, when the waiter came in with the evening papers. He took up the *St. James's*, and was listlessly turning over its pages, when this strange heading caught his eye:

"SUICIDE OF A CHIROMANTIST."

He turned pale with excitement, and began to read. The paragraph ran as follows:

> "Yesterday morning, at seven o'clock, the body of Mr. Septimus R. Podgers, the eminent chiromantist, was washed on shore at Greenwich, just in front of the Ship Hotel. The unfortunate gentleman had been missing for some days, and considerable anxiety for his safety had been felt in chiromantic circles. It is supposed that he committed suicide under the influence of a temporary mental derangement, caused by overwork, and a verdict to that effect was returned this afternoon by the coroner's jury. Mr. Podgers had just completed an elaborate treatise on the subject of the Human Hand, that will shortly be published, when it will no doubt attract much

attention. The deceased was sixty-five years of age, and does not seem to have left any relations."

Lord Arthur rushed out of the club with the paper still in his hand, to the immense amazement of the hall-porter, who tried in vain to stop him, and drove at once to Park Lane. Sybil saw him from the window, and something told her that he was the bearer of good news. She ran down to meet him, and, when she saw his face, she knew that all was well.

"My dear Sybil," cried Lord Arthur, "let us be married to-morrow!"

"You foolish boy! Why, the cake is not even ordered!" said Sybil, laughing through her tears.

– 6 –

When the wedding took place, some three weeks later, St. Peter's was crowded with a perfect mob of smart people. The service was read in the most impressive manner by the Dean of Chichester, and everybody agreed that they had never seen a handsomer couple than the bride and bridegroom. They were more than handsome, however—they were happy. Never for a single moment did Lord Arthur regret all that he had suffered for Sybil's sake, while she, on her side, gave him the best things a woman can give to any man—worship, tenderness, and love. For them romance was not killed by reality. They always felt young.

Some years afterwards, when two beautiful children had been born to them, Lady Windermere came down on a visit to Alton Priory, a lovely old place, that had been the Duke's wedding present to his son; and one afternoon as she was sitting with Lady Arthur under a lime-tree in the garden, watching the little boy and girl as they played up and down the rose-walk, like fitful sunbeams, she suddenly took her hostess's hand in hers, and said, "Are you happy, Sybil?"

"Dear Lady Windermere, of course I am happy. Aren't you?"

"I have no time to be happy, Sybil. I always like the last person who is introduced to me; but, as a rule, as soon as I know people I get tired of them."

"Don't your lions satisfy you, Lady Windermere?"

"Oh dear, no! lions are only good for one season. As soon as their manes are cut, they are the dullest creatures going. Besides, they behave very badly, if you are really nice to them. Do you remember that horrid Mr. Podgers? He was a dreadful impostor. Of course, I didn't mind that at all, and even when he wanted to borrow money I forgave him, but I could not stand his making love to me. He has really made me hate chiromancy. I go in for telepathy now. It is much more amusing."

"You mustn't say anything against chiromancy here, Lady Windermere; it is the only subject that Arthur does not like people to chaff about. I assure you he is quite serious over it."

"You don't mean to say that he believes in it, Sybil?"

"Ask him, Lady Windermere, here he is"; and Lord Arthur came up the garden with a large bunch of yellow roses in his hand, and his two children dancing round him.

"Lord Arthur?"

"Yes, Lady Windermere."

"You don't mean to say that you believe in chiromancy?"

"Of course I do," said the young man, smiling.

"But why?"

"Because I owe to it all the happiness of my life," he murmured, throwing himself into a wicker chair.

"My dear Lord Arthur, what do you owe to it?"

"Sybil," he answered, handing his wife the roses, and looking into her violet eyes.

"What nonsense!" cried Lady Windermere. "I never heard such nonsense in all my life."

THE MODEL MILLIONAIRE

A Note of Admiration

UNLESS ONE IS WEALTHY there is no use in being a charming fellow. Romance is the privilege of the rich, not the profession of the unemployed. The poor should be practical and prosaic. It is better to have a permanent income than to be fascinating. These are the great truths of modern life which Hughie Erskine never realised. Poor Hughie! Intellectually, we must admit, he was not of much importance. He never said a brilliant or even an ill-natured thing in his life. But then he was wonderfully good-looking, with his crisp, brown hair, his clear-cut profile, and his grey eyes. He was as popular with men as he was with women, and he had every accomplishment except that of making money. His father had bequeathed him his cavalry sword and a *History of the Peninsular War** in fifteen volumes. Hughie hung the first over his looking-glass, put the second on a shelf between *Ruff's Guide*† and *Bailey's Magazine*, and lived on two hundred a year that an old aunt allowed him. He had tried everything. He had gone on the Stock Exchange for six months; but what was a butterfly to do among bulls and bears? He had been a tea-merchant for a little longer, but had soon tired of pekoe and souchong. Then he had tried selling dry sherry. That did not answer; the sherry was a little too dry. Ultimately he became nothing, a delightful, ineffectual young man with a perfect profile and no profession.

To make matters worse, he was in love. The girl he loved was Laura Merton, the daughter of a retired Colonel who had lost his temper

---

* Between 1808 and 1814, Spain, Portugal, and Britain resisted the Napoleonic invasion of the Iberian Peninsula, fighting many battles.

† A horse-racing magazine.

and his digestion in India, and had never found either of them again. Laura adored him, and he was ready to kiss her shoe-strings. They were the handsomest couple in London, and had not a penny-piece between them. The Colonel was very fond of Hughie, but would not hear of any engagement.

"Come to me, my boy, when you have got ten thousand pounds of your own, and we will see about it," he used to say; and Hughie looked very glum in those days, and had to go to Laura for consolation.

One morning, as he was on his way to Holland Park, where the Mertons lived, he dropped in to see a great friend of his, Alan Trevor. Trevor was a painter. Indeed, few people escape that nowadays. But he was also an artist, and artists are rather rare. Personally he was a strange rough fellow, with a freckled face and a red, ragged beard. However, when he took up the brush he was a real master, and his pictures were eagerly sought after. He had been very much attracted by Hughie at first, it must be acknowledged, entirely on account of his personal charm. "The only people a painter should know," he used to say, "are people who are *bête** and beautiful, people who are an artistic pleasure to look at and an intellectual repose to talk to. Men who are dandies and women who are darlings rule the world, at least they should do so." However, after he got to know Hughie better, he liked him quite as much for his bright, buoyant spirits and his generous, reckless nature, and had given him the permanent *entrée*† to his studio.

When Hughie came in he found Trevor putting the finishing touches to a wonderful life-size picture of a beggar-man. The beggar himself was standing on a raised platform in a corner of the studio. He was a wizened old man, with a face like wrinkled parchment, and a most piteous expression. Over his shoulder was flung a coarse brown cloak, all tears and tatters; his thick boots were patched and cobbled, and with one hand he leant on a rough stick, while with the other he held out his battered hat for alms.

---

* Stupid (French).

† Access (French).

"What an amazing model!" whispered Hughie, as he shook hands with his friend.

"An amazing model?" shouted Trevor at the top of his voice; "I should think so! Such beggars as he are not to be met with every day. A *trouvaille, mon cher*;* a living Velasquez!† My stars! what an etching Rembrandt would have made of him!"

"Poor old chap!" said Hughie, "how miserable he looks! But I suppose, to you painters, his face is his fortune?"

"Certainly," replied Trevor, "you don't want a beggar to look happy, do you?"

"How much does a model get for sitting?" asked Hughie, as he found himself a comfortable seat on a divan.

"A shilling an hour."

"And how much do you get for your picture, Alan?"

"Oh, for this I get two thousand!"

"Pounds?"

"Guineas. Painters, poets, and physicians always get guineas."

"Well, I think the model should have a percentage," cried Hughie, laughing; "they work quite as hard as you do."

"Nonsense, nonsense! Why, look at the trouble of laying on the paint alone, and standing all day long at one's easel! It's all very well, Hughie, for you to talk, but I assure you that there are moments when Art almost attains to the dignity of manual labour. But you mustn't chatter; I'm very busy. Smoke a cigarette, and keep quiet."

After some time the servant came in, and told Trevor that the framemaker wanted to speak to him.

"Don't run away, Hughie," he said, as he went out, "I will be back in a moment."

The old beggar man took advantage of Trevor's absence to rest for a moment on a wooden bench that was behind him. He looked so forlorn and wretched that Hughie could not help pitying him, and felt in his pockets to see what money he had. All he could find was a sovereign and

---

* A discovery, my dear friend (French).

† The early work of Diego Velázquez (1599–1660), perhaps the greatest Spanish painter of his time, focused on realistic scenes from the lives of common people.

some coppers. “Poor old fellow,” he thought to himself, “he wants it more than I do, but it means no hansoms for a fortnight”; and he walked across the studio and slipped the sovereign into the beggar’s hand.

The old man started, and a faint smile flitted across his withered lips. “Thank you, sir,” he said, “thank you.”

Then Trevor arrived, and Hughie took his leave, blushing a little at what he had done. He spent the day with Laura, got a charming scolding for his extravagance, and had to walk home.

That night he strolled into the Palette Club about eleven o’clock, and found Trevor sitting by himself in the smoking-room drinking hock and seltzer.

“Well, Alan, did you get the picture finished all right?” he said, as he lit his cigarette.

“Finished and framed, my boy!” answered Trevor; “and, by the bye, you have made a conquest. That old model you saw is quite devoted to you. I had to tell him all about you—who you are, where you live. What your income is, what prospects you have——”

“My dear Alan,” cried Hughie, “I shall probably find him waiting for me when I go home. But, of course, you are only joking. Poor old wretch! I wish I could do something for him. I think it is dreadful that any one should be so miserable. I have got heaps of old clothes at home—do you think he would care for any of them? Why, his rags were falling to bits.”

“But he looks splendid in them,” said Trevor. “I wouldn’t paint him in a frock coat for anything. What you call rags I call romance. What seems poverty to you is picturesqueness to me. However, I’ll tell him of your offer.”

“Alan,” said Hughie seriously, “you painters are a heartless lot.”

“An artist’s heart is his head,” replied Trevor; “and besides, our business is to realise the world as we see it, not to reform it as we know it. *A chacun son métier.** And now tell me how Laura is. The old model was quite interested in her.”

“You don’t mean to say you talked to him about her?” said Hughie.

---

* Everyone to his own trade (French).

"Certainly I did. He knows all about the relentless Colonel, the lovely Laura, and the £10,000."

"You told that old beggar all my private affairs?" cried Hughie, looking very red and angry.

"My dear boy," said Trevor, smiling, "that old beggar, as you call him, is one of the richest men in Europe. He could buy all London to-morrow without overdrawing his account. He has a house in every capital, dines off gold plate, and can prevent Russia going to war when he chooses."

"What on earth do you mean?" exclaimed Hughie.

"What I say," said Trevor. "The old man you saw to-day in the studio was Baron Hausberg. He is a great friend of mine, buys all my pictures and that sort of thing, and gave me a commission a month ago to paint him as a beggar. *Que voulez-vous? La fantaisie d'un millionnaire!** And I must say he made a magnificent figure in his rags, or perhaps I should say in my rags; they are an old suit I got in Spain."

"Baron Hausberg!" cried Hughie. "Good heavens! I gave him a sovereign!" and he sank into an arm-chair the picture of dismay.

"Gave him a sovereign!" shouted Trevor, and he burst into a roar of laughter. "My dear boy, you'll never see it again. *Son affaire c'est l'argent des autres.*"†

"I think you might have told me, Alan," said Hughie sulkily, "and not have let me make such a fool of myself."

"Well, to begin with, Hughie," said Trevor, "it never entered my mind that you went about distributing alms in that reckless way. I can understand your kissing a pretty model, but your giving a sovereign to an ugly one—by Jove, no! Besides, the fact is that I really was not at home to-day to any one; and when you came in I didn't know whether Hausberg would like his name mentioned. You know he wasn't in full dress."

"What a duffer he must think me!" said Hughie.

"Not at all. He was in the highest spirits after you left; kept

---

* What do you expect? It's a millionaire's whim! (French).

† His business is other people's money (French).

chuckling to himself and rubbing his old wrinkled hands together. I couldn't make out why he was so interested to know all about you; but I see it all now. He'll invest your sovereign for you, Hughie, pay you the interest every six months, and have a capital story to tell after dinner."

"I am an unlucky devil," growled Hughie. "The best thing I can do is to go to bed; and, my dear Alan, you mustn't tell any one. I shouldn't dare show my face in the Row."

"Nonsense! It reflects the highest credit on your philanthropic spirit, Hughie. And don't run away. Have another cigarette, and you can talk about Laura as much as you like."

However, Hughie wouldn't stop, but walked home, feeling very unhappy, and leaving Alan Trevor in fits of laughter.

The next morning, as he was at breakfast, the servant brought him up a card on which was written, "Monsieur Gustave Naudin, *de la part de** M. le Baron Hausberg." "I suppose he has come for an apology," said Hughie to himself; and he told the servant to show the visitor up.

An old gentleman with gold spectacles and grey hair came into the room, and said, in a slight French accent, "Have I the honour of addressing Monsieur Erskine?"

Hughie bowed.

"I have come from Baron Hausberg," he continued. "The Baron ——"

"I beg, sir, that you will offer him my sincerest apologies," stammered Hughie.

"The Baron," said the old gentleman with a smile, "has commissioned me to bring you this letter"; and he extended a sealed envelope.

On the outside was written, "A wedding present to Hugh Erskine and Laura Merton, from an old beggar," and inside was a cheque for £10,000.

When they were married Alan Trevor was the best man, and the Baron made a speech at the wedding breakfast.

"Millionaire models," remarked Alan, "are rare enough; but, by Jove, model millionaires are rarer still!"

---

* On behalf of (French).

THE CANTERVILLE GHOST

*A Hylo-Idealistic Romance**

– 1 –

WHEN MR. HIRAM B. OTIS, the American minister, bought Canterville Chase, every one told him he was doing a very foolish thing, as there was no doubt at all that the place was haunted. Indeed, Lord Canterville himself, who was a man of the most punctilious honour, had felt it his duty to mention the fact to Mr. Otis, when they came to discuss terms.

"We have not cared to live in the place ourselves," said Lord Canterville, "since my grand-aunt, the Dowager Duchess of Bolton, was frightened into a fit, from which she never really recovered, by two skeleton hands being placed on her shoulders as she was dressing for dinner, and I feel bound to tell you, Mr. Otis, that the ghost has been seen by several living members of my family, as well as by the rector of the parish, the Rev. Augustus Dampier, who is a fellow of King's College, Cambridge. After the unfortunate accident to the Duchess, none of our younger servants would stay with us, and Lady Canterville often got very little sleep at night, in consequence of the mysterious noises that came from the corridor and the library."

"My lord," answered the Minister, "I will take the furniture and the ghost at a valuation. I come from a modern country, where we have everything that money can buy; and with all our spry young fellows painting the Old World red, and carrying off your best actresses and prima-donnas, I reckon that if there were such a thing as a ghost

* In ancient Greek philosophy, the transcendent world of ideas is opposed to the material, hylozoic world. The story is partly a satire upon American materialism.

in Europe, we'd have it at home in a very short time in one of our public museums, or on the road as a show."

"I fear that the ghost exists," said Lord Canterville, smiling, "though it may have resisted the overtures of your enterprising impresarios. It has been well known for three centuries, since 1584 in fact, and always makes its appearance before the death of any member of our family.

"Well, so does the family doctor for that matter, Lord Canterville. But there is no such thing, sir, as a ghost, and I guess the laws of nature are not going to be suspended for the British aristocracy."

"You are certainly very natural in America," answered Lord Canterville, who did not quite understand Mr. Otis's last observation, "and if you don't mind a ghost in the house, it is all right. Only you must remember I warned you."

A few weeks after this, the purchase was completed, and at the close of the season the Minister and his family went down to Canterville Chase. Mrs. Otis, who, as Miss Lucretia R. Tappan, of West 53rd Street, had been a celebrated New York belle, was now a very handsome middle-aged woman, with fine eyes, and a superb profile. Many American ladies on leaving their native land adopt an appearance of chronic ill-health, under the impression that it is a form of European refinement, but Mrs. Otis had never fallen into this error. She had a magnificent constitution, and a really wonderful amount of animal spirits. Indeed, in many respects, she was quite English, and was an excellent example of the fact that we have really everything in common with America nowadays, except, of course, language. Her eldest son, christened Washington by his parents in a moment of patriotism, which he never ceased to regret, was a fair-haired, rather good-looking young man, who had qualified himself for American diplomacy by leading the German at the Newport Casino for three successive seasons, and even in London was well known as an excellent dancer. Gardenias and the peerage were his only weaknesses. Otherwise he was extremely sensible. Miss Virginia E. Otis was a little girl of fifteen, lithe and lovely as a fawn, and with a fine freedom in her large blue eyes. She was a wonderful amazon, and had once raced old Lord Bilton on her pony twice round the park, winning by a length and a half, just in front of Achilles statue, to the huge delight of the young Duke of Cheshire, who proposed to her on the spot, and was sent back to Eton that very night by his guardians, in floods of tears. After Virginia came the twins, who were usually called "The Stars and Stripes" as they were always getting swished. They were delightful boys, and with the exception of the worthy Minister the only true republicans of the family.

As Canterville Chase is seven miles from Ascot, the nearest railway station, Mr. Otis had telegraphed for a waggonette to meet them, and they started on their drive in high spirits. It was a lovely July evening, and the air was delicate with the scent of the pinewoods. Now and then they heard a wood pigeon brooding over its own sweet voice, or saw, deep in the rustling fern, the burnished breast of the pheasant. Little squirrels peered at them from the beech-trees as they went by, and the rabbits scudded away through the brushwood and over the mossy knolls, with their white tails in the air. As they entered the avenue of Canterville Chase, however, the sky became suddenly overcast with clouds, a curious stillness seemed to hold the atmosphere, a great flight of rooks passed silently over their heads, and, before they reached the house, some big drops of rain had fallen.

Standing on the steps to receive them was an old woman, neatly dressed in black silk, with a white cap and apron. This was Mrs. Umney, the housekeeper, whom Mrs. Otis, at Lady Canterville's earnest request, had consented to keep on in her former position. She made them each a low curtsey as they alighted, and said in a quaint, old-fashioned manner, "I bid you welcome to Canterville Chase." Following her, they passed through the fine Tudor hall into the library, a long, low room, panelled in black oak, at the end of which was a large stained-glass window. Here they found tea laid out for them, and, after taking off their wraps, they sat down and began to look round, while Mrs. Umney waited on them.

Suddenly Mrs. Otis caught sight of a dull red stain on the floor just by the fireplace and, quite unconscious of what it really signified, said to Mrs. Umney, "I am afraid something has been spilt there."

"Yes, madam," replied the old housekeeper in a low voice, "blood has been spilt on that spot."

"How horrid," cried Mrs. Otis; "I don't at all care for blood-stains in a sitting-room. It must be removed at once."

The old woman smiled, and answered in the same low, mysterious voice, "It is the blood of Lady Eleanore de Canterville, who was murdered on that very spot by her own husband, Sir Simon de Canterville, in 1575. Sir Simon survived her nine years, and disappeared suddenly under very mysterious circumstances. His body has never been discovered, but his guilty spirit still haunts the Chase. The blood-stain has been much admired by tourists and others, and cannot be removed."

"That is all nonsense," cried Washington Otis; "Pinkerton's Champion Stain Remover and Paragon Detergent will clean it up in no time," and before the terrified housekeeper could interfere he had fallen upon his knees, and was rapidly scouring the floor with a small stick of what looked like a black cosmetic. In a few moments no trace of the blood-stain could be seen.

"I knew Pinkerton would do it," he exclaimed triumphantly, as he looked round at his admiring family; but no sooner had he said these words than a terrible flash of lightning lit up the sombre room, a fearful peal of thunder made them all start to their feet, and Mrs. Umney fainted.

"What a monstrous climate!" said the American Minister calmly, as he lit a long cheroot. "I guess the old country is so overpopulated that they have not enough decent weather for everybody. I have always been of opinion that emigration is the only thing for England."

"My dear Hiram," cried Mrs. Otis, "what can we do with a woman who faints?"

"Charge it to her like breakages," answered the Minister; "she won't faint after that"; and in a few moments Mrs. Umney certainly came to. There was no doubt, however, that she was extremely upset, and she sternly warned Mr. Otis to beware of some trouble coming to the house.

"I have seen things with my own eyes, sir," she said, "that would make any Christian's hair stand on end, and many and many a night I have not closed my eyes in sleep for the awful things that are done here." Mr. Otis, however, and his wife warmly assured the honest soul that they were not afraid of ghosts, and, after invoking the blessings of Providence on her new master and mistress, and making arrangements for an increase of salary, the old housekeeper tottered off to her own room.

– 2 –

The storm raged fiercely all that night, but nothing of particular note occurred. The next morning, however, when they came down to breakfast, they found the terrible stain of blood once again on the floor. "I don't think it can be the fault of the Paragon Detergent," said Washington, "for I have tried it with everything. It must be the ghost." He accordingly rubbed out the stain a second time, but the second morning it appeared again. The third morning also it was there, though the library had been locked up at night by Mr. Otis himself, and the key carried upstairs. The whole family were now quite interested; Mr. Otis began to suspect that he had been too dogmatic in his denial of the existence of ghosts, Mrs. Otis expressed her intention of joining the Psychical Society, and Washington prepared a long letter to Messrs. Myers and Podmore on the subject of the Permanence of Sanguineous Stains when connected with crime. That night all doubts about the objective existence of phantasmata were removed for ever.

The day had been warm and sunny; and, in the cool of the evening, the whole family went out for a drive. They did not return home till nine o'clock, when they had a light supper. The conversation in no way turned upon ghosts, so there were not even those primary conditions of receptive expectation which so often precede the presentation of psychical phenomena. The subjects discussed, as I have since learned from Mr. Otis, were merely such as form the ordinary conversation of cultured Americans of the better class, such as the immense superiority of Miss Fanny Davenport over Sarah Bernhardt as an actress; the difficulty of obtaining green corn, buckwheat cakes, and hominy, even in the best English houses; the importance of Boston in the development of the world-soul; the advantages of the baggage check system in railway travelling; and the sweetness of the New York accent as compared to the London drawl. No mention at all was made of the supernatural, nor was Sir Simon de Canterville alluded to in any way. At eleven o'clock the family retired and by half-past all the lights were out. Some time after, Mr. Otis was awakened by a curious noise in the corridor, outside his room. It sounded like the clank of metal, and seemed to be coming nearer every moment. He got up at once, struck a match, and looked at the time. It was exactly one o'clock. He was quite calm, and felt his pulse, which was not at all feverish. The strange noise still continued, and with it he heard distinctly the sound of footsteps. He put on his slippers, took a small oblong phial out of his dressing-case, and opened the door. Right in front of him he saw, in the wan moonlight, an old man of terrible aspect. His eyes were as red as burning coals; long grey hair fell over his shoulders in matted coils; his garments, which were of antique cut, were soiled and ragged, and from his wrists and ankles hung heavy manacles and rusty gyves.

"My dear sir," said Mr. Otis, "I really must insist on your oiling those chains, and have brought you for that purpose a small bottle of the Tammany Rising Sun Lubricator. It is said to be completely efficacious upon one application, and there are several testimonials to that effect on the wrapper from some of our most eminent native divines. I shall leave it here for you by the bedroom candles, and will be happy to supply you with more should you require it." With these words the United States Minister laid the bottle down on a marble table, and, closing his door, retired to rest.

For a moment the Canterville ghost stood quite motionless in natural indignation; then, dashing the bottle violently upon the polished floor, he fled down the corridor, uttering hollow groans, and emitting a ghastly green light. Just, however, as he reached the top of the great oak staircase, a door was flung open, two little white-robed figures appeared, and a large pillow whizzed past his head! There was evidently no time to be lost, so, hastily adopting the Fourth Dimension of Space as a means of escape, he vanished through the wainscoting, and the house bcame quite quiet.

On reaching a small secret chamber in the left wing, he leaned up against a moonbeam to recover his breath, and began to try and realise his position. Never, in a brilliant and uninterrupted career of three hundred years, had he been so grossly insulted. He thought of the Dowager Duchess, whom he had frightened into a fit as she stood before the glass in her lace and diamonds; of the four housemaids, who had gone off into hysterics when he merely grinned at them through the curtains of one of the spare bedrooms; of the rector of the parish, whose candle he had blown out as he was coming late one night from the library, and who had been under the care of Sir William Gull ever since, a perfect martyr to nervous disorders; and of old Madame de Tremouillac, who, having wakened up one morning early and seen a skeleton seated in an arm-chair by the fire reading her diary had been confined to her bed for six weeks with an attack of brain fever, and, on her recovery, had become reconciled to the Church, and had broken off her connection with that notorious sceptic Monsieur de Voltaire. He remembered the terrible night when the wicked Lord Canterville was found choking in his dressing-room, with the knave of diamonds half-way down his throat, and confessed, just before he died, that he had cheated Charles James Fox* out of £50,000 at Crockford's by means of that very card, and swore that the ghost had made him swallow it. All his great achievements came back to him again, from the butler who had shot himself in the pantry because he had seen a green hand tapping at the window pane, to the beautiful Lady Stutfield, who was always obliged to wear a black velvet band round her throat to hide the mark of five fingers burnt upon her white skin, and who drowned herself at last in the carp-pond at the end of the King's Walk. With the enthusiastic egotism of the true artist he went over his most celebrated performances, and smiled bitterly to himself as he recalled to mind his last appearance as "Red Ruben, or the Strangled Babe," his *début* as "Gaunt Gibeon, the Blood-sucker of Bexley Moor," and the *furore* he had excited one lonely June evening by merely playing ninepins with his own bones upon the lawn-tennis ground. And after all this, some wretched modern Americans were to come and offer him the Rising Sun Lubricator, and throw pillows at his head! It was quite unbearable. Besides, no ghosts in history had ever been treated in this manner. Accordingly, he determined to have vengeance, and remained till daylight in an attitude of deep thought.

* Fox (1749–1806), a British politician, supported the American and French Revolutions, and opposed slavery. He was often in debt.

– 3 –

The next morning when the Otis family met at breakfast, they discussed the ghost at some length. The United States Minister was naturally a little annoyed to find that his present had not been accepted. "I have no wish," he said, "to do the ghost any personal injury, and I must say that, considering the length of time he has been in the house, I don't think it is at all polite to throw pillows at him"—a very just remark, at which, I am sorry to say, the twins burst into shouts of laughter. "Upon the other hand," he continued, "if he really declines to use the Rising Sun Lubricator, we shall have to take his chains from him. It would be quite impossible to sleep, with such a noise going on outside the bedrooms."

For the rest of the week, however, they were undisturbed, the only thing that excited any attention being the continual renewal of the blood-stain on the library floor. This certainly was very strange, as the door was always locked at night by Mr. Otis, and the windows kept closely barred. The chameleon-like colour, also, of the stain excited a good deal of comment. Some mornings it was a dull (almost Indian) red, then it would be vermilion, then a rich purple, and once when they came down for family prayers, according to the simple rites of the Free American Reformed Episcopalian Church, they found it a bright emerald-green. These kaleidoscopic changes naturally amused the party very much, and bets on the subject were freely made every evening. The only person who did not enter into the joke was little Virginia, who, for some unexplained reason, was always a good deal distressed at the sight of the blood-stain, and very nearly cried the morning it was emerald-green.

The second appearance of the ghost was on Sunday night. Shortly after they had gone to bed they were suddenly alarmed by a fearful crash in the hall. Rushing downstairs, they found that a large suit of old armour had become detached from its stand, and had fallen on the stone floor, while, seated in a high-backed chair, was the Canterville ghost, rubbing his knees with an expression of acute agony on his face. The twins, having brought their peashooters with them, at once discharged two pellets on him, with that accuracy of aim which can only be attained by long and careful practice on a writing-master, while the United States Minister covered him with his revolver, and called upon him, in accordance with Californian etiquette, to hold up his hands! The ghost started up with a wild shriek of rage, and swept through them like a mist, extinguishing Washington Otis's candle as he passed, and so leaving them all in total darkness. On reaching the top of the staircase he recovered himself, and determined to give his celebrated peal of demoniac laughter. This he had on more than one occasion found extremely useful. It was said to have turned Lord Raker's wig grey in a single night, and had certainly made three of Lady Canterville's French governesses give warning before their month was up. He accordingly laughed his most horrible laugh, till the old vaulted roof rang and rang again, but hardly had the fearful echo died away when a door opened, and Mrs. Otis came out in a light blue dressing-gown. "I am afraid you are far from well," she said, "and have brought you a bottle of Dr. Dobell's tincture. If it is indigestion, you will find it a most excellent remedy." The ghost glared at her in fury, and began at once to make preparations for turning himself into a large black dog, an accomplishment for which he was justly renowned, and to which the family doctor always attributed the permanent idiocy of Lord Canterville's uncle, the Hon. Thomas Horton. The sound of approaching footsteps, however, made him hesitate in his fell purpose, so he contented himself with becoming faintly phosphorescent, and vanished with a deep churchyard groan, just as the twins had come up to him.

On reaching his room he entirely broke down, and became a prey to the most violent agitation. The vulgarity of the twins, and the gross materialism of Mrs. Otis, were naturally extremely annoying, but what really distressed him most was, that he had been unable to wear the suit of mail. He had hoped that even modern Americans would be thrilled by the sight of a Spectre In Armour, if for no more sensible reason, at least out of respect for their national poet Longfellow, over whose graceful and attractive poetry he himself had whiled away many a weary hour when the Cantervilles were up in town. Besides, it was his own suit. He had worn it with success at the Kenilworth tournament, and had been highly complimented on it by no less a person than the Virgin Queen herself.* Yet when he had put it on, he had been completely overpowered by the weight of the huge breastplate and steel casque, and had fallen heavily on the stone pavement, barking both his knees severely, and bruising the knuckles of his right hand.

For some days after this he was extremely ill, and hardly stirred out of his room at all, except to keep the blood-stain in proper repair. However, by taking great care of himself, he recovered, and resolved to make a third attempt to frighten the United States Minister and his family. He selected Friday, the 17th of August, for his appearance, and spent most of that day in looking over his wardrobe, ultimately deciding in favour of a large slouched hat with a red feather, a winding-sheet frilled at the wrists and neck, and a rusty dagger. Towards evening a violent storm of rain came on, and the wind was so high that all the windows and doors in the old house shook and rattled. In fact, it was just such weather as he loved. His plan of action was this. He was to make his way quietly to Washington Otis's room, gibber at him from the foot of the bed, and stab himself three times in the throat to the sound of slow music. He bore Washington a special grudge, being quite aware that it was he who was in the habit of removing the famous Canterville blood-stain, by means of Pinkerton's Paragon Detergent. Having reduced the reckless and foolhardy youth to a condition of abject terror, he was then to proceed to the room occupied by the United States Minister and his wife, and there to place a clammy hand on Mrs. Otis's forehead, while he hissed into her trembling husband's ear the awful secrets of the charnel-house. With regard to little Virginia, he had not quite made up his mind. She had never insulted him in any way, and was pretty and gentle. A few hollow groans from the wardrobe, he thought, would be more than sufficient, or, if that failed to wake her, he might grabble at the counterpane with palsy-twitching fingers. As for the twins, he was quite determined to teach them a lesson. The

* Queen Elizabeth I (1533–1603); she never married.

first thing to be done was, of course, to sit upon their chests, so as to produce the stifling sensation of nightmare. Then, as their beds were quite close to each other, to stand between them in the form of a green, icy-cold corpse, till they became paralysed with fear, and finally, to throw off the winding-sheet, and crawl round the room, with white bleached bones and one rolling eyeball, in the character of "Dumb Daniel, or the Suicide's Skeleton," a *rôle* in which he had on more than one occasion produced a great effect, and which he considered quite equal to his famous part of "Martin the Maniac, or the Masked Mystery."

At half-past ten he heard the family going to bed. For some time he was disturbed by wild shrieks of laughter from the twins, who, with the light-hearted gaiety of schoolboys, were evidently amusing themselves before they retired to rest, but at a quarter-past eleven all was still, and, as midnight sounded, he sallied forth. The owl beat against the window panes, the raven croaked from the old yew-tree, and the wind wandered moaning round the house like a lost soul; but the Otis family slept unconscious of their doom, and high above the rain and storm he could hear the steady snoring of the Minister for the United States. He stepped stealthily out of the wainscoting, with an evil smile on his cruel, wrinkled mouth, and the moon hid her face in a cloud as he stole past the great oriel window, where his own arms and those of his murdered wife were blazoned in azure and gold. On and on he glided, like an evil shadow, the very darkness seeming to loathe him as he passed. Once he thought he heard something call, and stopped; but it was only the baying of a dog from the Red Farm, and he went on, muttering strange sixteenth-century curses, and ever and anon brandishing the rusty dagger in the midnight air. Finally he reached the corner of the passage that led to luckless Washington's room. For a moment he paused there, the wind blowing his long grey locks about his head, and twisting into grotesque and fantastic folds the nameless horror of the dead man's shroud. Then the clock struck the quarter, and he felt the time was come. He chuckled to himself, and turned the corner; but no sooner had he done so, than, with a piteous wail of terror, he fell back, and hid his blanched face in his long, bony hands. Right in front of him was standing a horrible spectre, motionless as a carven image, and monstrous as a madman's dream! Its head was bald and burnished; its face round, and fat, and white; and hideous laughter seemed to have writhed its features into an eternal grin. From the eyes streamed rays of scarlet light, the mouth was a wide well of fire, and a hideous garment, like to his own, swathed with its silent snows the Titan form. On its breast was a placard with strange writing in antique characters, some scroll of shame it seemed, some record of wild sins, some awful calendar of crime, and, with its right hand, it bore aloft a falchion of gleaming steel.

Never having seen a ghost before, he naturally was terribly frightened, and, after a second hasty glance at the awful phantom, he fled back to his room, tripping up in his long winding-sheet as he sped down the corridor, and finally dropping the rusty dagger into the Minister's jack-boots, where it was found in the morning by the butler. Once in the privacy of his own apartment, he flung himself down on a small pallet-bed and hid his face under the clothes. After a time, however, the brave old Canterville spirit asserted itself, and he determined to go and speak to the other ghost as soon as it was daylight. Accordingly, just as the dawn was touching the hills with silver, he returned towards the spot where he had first laid eyes on the grisly phantom, feeling that, after all, two ghosts were better than one, and that, by the aid of his new friend, he might safely grapple with the twins. On reaching the spot, however, a terrible sight met his gaze. Something had evidently happened to the spectre, for the light had entirely faded from its hollow eyes, the gleaming falchion had fallen from its hand, and it was leaning up against the wall in a strained and uncomfortable attitude. He rushed forward and seized it in his arms, when, to his horror, the head slipped off and rolled on the floor, the body assumed a recumbent posture, and he found himself clasping a white dimity bed-curtain, with a sweeping-brush, a kitchen cleaver, and a hollow turnip lying at his feet! Unable to understand this curious transformation, he clutched the placard with feverish haste, and there, in the grey morning light, he read these fearful words:—

YE OTES GHOSTE,
Ye Onlie True and Originale Spook.
Beware of Ye Imitationes.
All others are Counterfeite.

The whole thing flashed across him. He had been tricked, foiled, and outwitted! The old Canterville look came into his eyes; he ground his toothless gums together; and, raising his withered hands high above his head, swore, according to the picturesque phraseology of the antique school, that when Chanticleer had sounded twice his merry horn, deeds of blood would be wrought, and Murder walk abroad with silent feet.

Hardly had he finished this awful oath when, from the red-tiled roof of a distant homestead, a cock crew. He laughed a long, low, bitter laugh, and waited. Hour after hour he waited, but the cock, for some strange reason, did not crow again. Finally, at half-past seven, the arrival of the housemaids made him give up his fearful vigil, and he stalked back to his room, thinking of his vain hope and baffled purpose. There he consulted several books of ancient chivalry, of which he was exceedingly fond, and found that, on every occasion on which his oath had been used, Chanticleer had always crowed a second time. "Perdition seize the naughty fowl," he muttered, "I have seen the day when, with my stout spear, I would have run him through the gorge, and made him crow for me an 'twere in death!" He then retired to a comfortable lead coffin, and stayed there till evening.

– 4 –

The next day the ghost was very weak and tired. The terrible excitement of the last four weeks was beginning to have its effect. His nerves were completely shattered, and he started at the slightest noise. For five days he kept his room, and at last made up his mind to give up the point of the blood-stain on the library floor. If the Otis family did not want it, they clearly did not deserve it. They were evidently people on a low, material plane of existence, and quite incapable of appreciating the symbolic value of sensuous phenomena. The question of phantasmic apparitions, and the development of astral bodies, was of course quite a different matter, and really not under his control. It was his solemn duty to appear in the corridor once a week, and to gibber from the large oriel window on the first and third Wednesday in every month, and he did not see how he could honourably escape from his obligations. It is quite true that his life had been very evil, but, upon the other hand, he was most conscientious in all things connected with the supernatural. For the next three Saturdays, accordingly, he traversed the corridor as usual between midnight and three o'clock, taking every possible precaution against being either heard or seen. He removed his boots, trod as lightly as possible on the old worm-eaten boards, wore a large black velvet cloak, and was careful to use the Rising Sun Lubricator for oiling his chains. I am bound to acknowledge that it was with a good deal of difficulty that he brought himself to adopt this last mode of protection. However, one night, while the family were at dinner, he slipped into Mr. Otis's bedroom and carried off the bottle. He felt a little humiliated at first, but afterwards was sensible enough to see that there was a great deal to be said for the invention, and, to a certain degree, it served his purpose. Still, in spite of everything, he was not left unmolested. Strings were continually being stretched across the corridor, over which he tripped in the dark, and on one occasion, while dressed for the part of "Black Isaac, or the Huntsman of Hogley Woods," he met with a severe fall, through treading on a butter-slide, which the twins had constructed from the entrance of the Tapestry Chamber to the top of the oak staircase. This last insult so enraged him, that he resolved to make one final effort to assert his dignity and social position, and determined to visit the insolent young Etonians the next night in his celebrated character of "Reckless Rupert, or the Headless Earl."

He had not appeared in this disguise for more than seventy years; in fact, not since he had so frightened pretty Lady Barbara Modish by means of it, that she suddenly broke off her engagement with the present Lord Canterville's grandfather, and ran away to Gretna Green with handsome Jack Castleton, declaring that nothing in the world would induce her to marry into a family that allowed such a horrible phantom to walk up and down the terrace at twilight. Poor Jack was afterwards shot in a duel by Lord Canterville on Wandsworth Common, and Lady Barbara died of a broken heart at Tunbridge Wells before the year was out, so, in every way, it had been a great success. It was, however, an extremely difficult "make-up," if I may use such a theatrical expression in connection with one of the greatest mysteries of the supernatural, or, to employ a more scientific term, the higher-natural world, and it took him fully three hours to make his preparations. At last everything was ready, and he was very pleased with his appearance. The big leather riding-boots that went with the dress were just a little too large for him, and he could only find one of the two horse-pistols, but, on the whole, he was quite satisfied, and at a quarter-past one he glided out of the wainscoting and crept down the corridor. On reaching the room occupied by the twins, which I should mention was called the Blue Bed Chamber, on account of the colour of its hangings, he found the door just ajar. Wishing to make an effective entrance, he flung it wide open, when a heavy jug of water fell right down on him, wetting him to the skin, and just missing his left shoulder by a couple of inches. At the same moment he heard stifled shrieks of laughter proceeding from the four-post bed. The shock to his nervous system was so great that he fled back to his room as hard as he could go, and the next day he was laid up with a severe cold. The only thing that at all consoled him in the whole affair was the fact that he had not brought his head with him, for, had he done so, the consequences might have been very serious.

He now gave up all hope of ever frightening this rude American family, and contented himself, as a rule, with creeping about the passages in list slippers, with a thick red muffler round his throat for fear of draughts, and a small arquebuse, in case he should be attacked by the twins. The final blow he received occurred on the 19th of September. He had gone downstairs to the great entrance-hall, feeling sure that there, at any rate, he would be quite unmolested, and was amusing himself by making satirical remarks on the large Saroni photographs of the United States Minister and his wife, which had now taken the place of the Canterville family pictures. He was simply but neatly clad in a long shroud, spotted with churchyard mould, had tied up his jaw with a strip of yellow linen, and carried a small lantern and a sexton's spade. In fact, he was dressed for the character of "Jonas the Graveless, or the Corpse-Snatcher of Chertsey Barn," one of his most remarkable impersonations, and one which the Cantervilles had every reason to remember, as it was the real origin of their quarrel with their neighbour, Lord Rufford. It was about a quarter past two o'clock in the morning, and, as far as he could ascertain, no one was stirring. As he was strolling towards the library, however, to see if there were any traces left of the blood-stain, suddenly there leaped out on him from a dark corner two figures, who waved their arms wildly above their heads, and shrieked out "BOO!" in his ear.

Seized with a panic, which, under the circumstances, was only natural, he rushed for the staircase, but found Washington Otis waiting for him there with the big garden-syringe; and being thus hemmed in by his enemies on every side, and driven almost to bay, he vanished into the great iron stove, which, fortunately for him, was not lit, and had to make his way home through the flues and chimneys, arriving at his own room in a terrible state of dirt, disorder, and despair.

After this he was not seen again on any nocturnal expedition. The twins lay in wait for him on several occasions, and strewed the passages with nutshells every night to the great annoyance of their parents and the servants, but it was of no avail. It was quite evident that his feelings were so wounded that he would not appear. Mr. Otis consequently resumed his great work on the history of the Democratic Party, on which he had been engaged for some years; Mrs. Otis organised a wonderful clambake, which amazed the whole county; the boys took to lacrosse, euchre, poker, and other American national games; and Virginia rode about the lanes on her pony, accompanied by the young Duke of Cheshire, who had come to spend the last week of his holidays at Canterville Chase. It was generally assumed that the ghost had gone away, and, in fact, Mr. Otis wrote a letter to that effect to Lord Canterville, who, in reply, expressed his great pleasure at the news, and sent his best congratulations to the Minister's worthy wife.

The Otises, however, were deceived, for the ghost was still in the house, and though now almost an invalid, was by no means ready to let matters rest, particularly as he heard that among the guests was the young Duke of Cheshire, whose grand-uncle, Lord Francis Stilton, had once bet a hundred guineas with Colonel Carbury that he would play dice with the Canterville ghost, and was found the next morning lying on the floor of the card-room in such a helpless paralytic state, that though he lived on to a great age, he was never able to say anything again but "Double Sixes." The story was well known at the time, though, of course, out of respect to the feelings of the two noble families, every attempt was made to hush it up; and a full account of all the circumstances connected with it will be found in the third volume of Lord Tattle's *Recollections of the Prince Regent and his Friends.* The ghost, then, was naturally very anxious to show that he had not lost his influence over the Stiltons, with whom indeed, he was distantly connected, his own first cousin having been married *en secondes noces** to the Sieur de Bulkeley, from whom, as every one knows, the Dukes of Cheshire are lineally descended. Accordingly, he made arrangements for appearing to Virginia's little lover in his celebrated impersonation of "The Vampire Monk, or, the Bloodless Benedictine," a performance so horrible that when old Lady Startup saw it, which she did on one fatal New Year's Eve, in the year 1764, she went off into the most piercing shrieks, which culminated in violent apoplexy, and died in three days, after disinheriting the Cantervilles, who were her nearest relations, and leaving all her money to her London apothecary. At the last moment, however, his terror of the twins prevented his leaving his room, and the little Duke slept in peace under the great feathered canopy in the Royal Bedchamber, and dreamed of Virginia.

– 5 –

A few days after this, Virginia and her curly-haired cavalier went out riding on Brockley meadows, where she tore her habit so badly in getting through a hedge, that, on her return home, she made up her mind to go up by the back staircase so as not to be seen. As she was

* For the second time (French).

running past the Tapestry Chamber, the door of which happened to be opened, she fancied she saw some one inside, and thinking it was her mother's maid, who sometimes used to bring her work there, looked in to ask her to mend her habit. To her immense surprise, however, it was the Canterville Ghost himself! He was sitting by the window, watching the ruined gold of the yellow trees fly through the air, and the red leaves dancing madly down the long avenue. His head was leaning on his hand, and his whole attitude was one of extreme depression. Indeed, so forlorn, and so much out of repair did he look, that little Virginia, whose first idea had been to run away and lock herself in her room, was filled with pity, and determined to try and comfort him. So light was her footfall, and so deep his melancholy, that he was not aware of her presence till she spoke to him.

"I am so sorry for you," she said, "but my brothers are going back to Eton to-morrow, and then, if you behave yourself, no one will annoy you."

"It is absurd asking me to behave myself," he answered, looking round in astonishment at the pretty little girl who had ventured to address him, "quite absurd. I must rattle my chains, and groan through keyholes, and walk about at night, if that is what you mean. It is my only reason for existing."

"It is no reason at all for existing, and you know you have been very wicked. Mrs. Umney told us, the first day we arrived here, that you had killed your wife."

"Well, I quite admit it," said the Ghost petulantly, "but it was a purely family matter, and concerned no one else."

"It is very wrong to kill any one," said Virginia, who at times had a sweet Puritan gravity, caught from some old New England ancestor.

"Oh, I hate the cheap severity of abstract ethics! My wife was very plain, never had my ruffs properly starched, and knew nothing about cookery. Why, there was a buck I had shot in Hogley Woods, a magnificent pricket, and do you know how she had it sent up to table? However, it is no matter now, for it is all over, and I don't think it was very nice of her brothers to starve me to death, though I did kill her."

"Starve you to death? Oh, Mr. Ghost, I mean Sir Simon, are you hungry? I have a sandwich in my case. Would you like it?"

"No, thank you, I never eat anything now; but it is very kind of you, all the same, and you are much nicer than the rest of your horrid, rude, vulgar, dishonest family."

"Stop!" cried Virginia, stamping her foot, "it is you who are rude, and horrid, and vulgar; and as for dishonesty, you know you stole the paints out of my box to try and furbish up that ridiculous blood-stain in the library. First you took all my reds, including the vermilion, and I couldn't do any more sunsets, then you took the emerald-green and the chrome-yellow, and finally I had nothing left but indigo and Chinese white, and could only do moonlight scenes, which are always depressing to look at, and not at all easy to paint. I never told on you, though I was very much annoyed, and it was most ridiculous, the whole thing; for who ever heard of emerald-green blood?"

"Well, really," said the Ghost, rather meekly, "what was I to do? It is a very difficult thing to get real blood nowadays, and, as your brother began it all with his Paragon Detergent, I certainly saw no reason why I should not have your paints. As for colour, that is always a matter of taste: the Cantervilles have blue blood, for instance, the very bluest in England; but I know you Americans don't care for things of this kind."

"You know nothing about it, and the best thing you can do is to emigrate and improve your mind. My father will be only too happy to give you a free passage, and though there is a heavy duty on spirits of every kind, there will be no difficulty about the Custom House, as the officers are all Democrats. Once in New York, you are sure to be a great success. I know lots of people there who would give a hundred thousand dollars to have a grandfather, and much more than that to have a family Ghost."

"I don't think I should like America."

"I suppose because we have no ruins and no curiosities," said Virginia satirically.

"No ruins! no curiosities!" answered the Ghost; "you have your navy and your manners."

"Good evening; I will go and ask papa to get the twins an extra week's holiday."

"Please don't go, Miss Virginia," he cried; "I am so lonely and so unhappy, and I really don't know what to do. I want to go to sleep and I cannot."

"That's quite absurd! You have merely to go to bed and blow out the candle. It is very difficult sometimes to keep awake, especially at church, but there is no difficulty at all about sleeping. Why, even babies know how to do that, and they are not very clever."

"I have not slept for three hundred years," he said sadly, and Virginia's beautiful blue eyes opened in wonder; "for three hundred years I have not slept, and I am so tired."

Virginia grew quite grave, and her little lips trembled like rose-leaves. She came towards him, and kneeling down at his side, looked up into his old withered face.

"Poor, poor Ghost," she murmured; "have you no place where you can sleep?"

"Far away beyond the pine-woods," he answered, in a low dreamy voice, "there is a little garden. There the grass grows long and deep, there are the great white stars of the hemlock flower, there the nightingale sings all night long. All night long he sings, and the cold, crystal moon looks down, and the yew-tree spreads out its giant arms over the sleepers."

Virginia's eyes grew dim with tears, and she hid her face in her hands.

"You mean the Garden of Death," she whispered.

"Yes, Death. Death must be so beautiful. To lie in the soft brown earth, with the grasses waving above one's head, and listen to silence. To have no yesterday, and no to-morrow. To forget time, to forgive life, to be at peace. You can help me. You can open for me the portals of Death's house, for Love is always with you, and Love is stronger than Death is."

Virginia trembled, a cold shudder ran through her, and for a few moments there was silence. She felt as if she was in a terrible dream.

Then the Ghost spoke again, and his voice sounded like the sighing of the wind.

"Have you ever read the old prophecy on the library window?"

"Oh, often," cried the little girl, looking up; "I know it quite well.

It is painted in curious black letters, and it is difficult to read. There are only six lines:

> When a golden girl can win
> Prayer from out the lips of sin,
> When the barren almond bears,
> And a little child gives away its tears,
> Then shall all the house be still
> And peace come to Canterville.

But I don't know what they mean."

"They mean," he said sadly, "that you must weep for me for my sins, because I have no tears, and pray with me for my soul, because I have no faith, and then, if you have always been sweet, and good, and gentle, the Angel of Death will have mercy on me. You will see fearful shapes in darkness, and wicked voices will whisper in your ear, but they will not harm you, for against the purity of a little child the powers of Hell cannot prevail."

Virginia made no answer, and the Ghost wrung his hands in wild despair as he looked down at her bowed golden head. Suddenly she stood up, very pale, and with a strange light in her eyes. "I am not afraid," she said firmly, "and I will ask the Angel to have mercy on you."

He rose from his seat with a faint cry of joy, and taking her hand bent over it with old-fashioned grace and kissed it. His fingers were as cold as ice, and his lips burned like fire, but Virginia did not falter, as he led her across the dusky room. On the faded green tapestry were broidered little huntsmen. They blew their tasselled horns and with their tiny hands waved to her to go back. "Go back! little Virginia," they cried, "go back!" but the Ghost clutched her hand more tightly, and she shut her eyes against them. Horrible animals with lizard tails, and goggle eyes, blinked at her from the carven chimney-piece, and murmured "Beware! little Virginia, beware! we may never see you again," but the Ghost glided on more swiftly, and Virginia did not listen. When they reached the end of the room he stopped, and muttered some words she could not understand. She opened her eyes, and saw the wall slowly fading away like a mist, and a great black cavern in front of her. A bitter cold wind swept round them, and she felt something pulling at her dress. "Quick, quick," cried the Ghost, "or it will be too late," and, in a moment, the wainscoting had closed behind them, and the Tapestry Chamber was empty.

– 6 –

About ten minutes later, the bell rang for tea, and, as Virginia did not come down, Mrs. Otis sent up one of the footmen to tell her. After a little time he returned and said that he could not find Miss Virginia anywhere. As she was in the habit of going out to the garden every evening to get flowers for the dinner-table, Mrs. Otis was not at all alarmed at first, but when six o'clock struck, and Virginia did not appear, she became really agitated, and sent the boys out to look for her, while she herself and Mr. Otis searched every room in the house. At half-past six the boys came back and said that they could find no trace of their sister anywhere. They were all now in the greatest state of excitement, and did not know what to do, when Mr. Otis suddenly remembered that, some few days before, he had given a band of gypsies permission to camp in the park. He accordingly at once set off for Blackfell Hollow, where he knew they were, accompanied by his eldest son and two of the farm-servants. The little Duke of Cheshire, who was perfectly frantic with anxiety, begged hard to be allowed to go too, but Mr. Otis would not allow him, as he was afraid there might be a scuffle. On arriving at the spot, however, he found that the gypsies had gone, and it was evident that their departure had been rather sudden, as the fire was still burning, and some plates were lying on the grass. Having sent off Washington and the two men to scour the district, he ran home, and despatched telegrams to all the police inspectors in the county, telling them to look out for a little girl who had been kidnapped by tramps or gypsies. He then ordered his horse to be brought round, and, after insisting on his wife and the three boys sitting down to dinner, rode off down the Ascot Road with a groom. He had hardly, however, gone a couple of miles when he heard somebody galloping after him, and, looking round, saw the little Duke coming up on his pony, with his face very flushed and no hat. "I'm awfully sorry, Mr. Otis," gasped out the boy, "but I can't eat any dinner as long as Virginia is lost. Please, don't be angry with me; if you had let us be engaged last year, there would never have been all this trouble. You won't send me back, will you? I can't go! I won't go!"

The Minister could not help smiling at the handsome young scapegrace, and was a good deal touched at his devotion to Virginia, so leaning down from his horse, he patted him kindly on the shoulders, and said, "Well, Cecil, if you won't go back I suppose you must come with me, but I must get you a hat at Ascot."

"Oh, bother my hat! I want Virginia!" cried the little Duke, laughing, and they galloped on to the railway station. There Mr. Otis inquired of the station-master if any one answering the description of Virginia had been seen on the platform, but could get no news of her. The station-master, however, wired up and down the line, and assured him that a strict watch would be kept for her, and, after having bought a hat for the little Duke from a linen-draper, who was just putting up his shutters, Mr. Otis rode off to Bexley, a village about four miles away, which he was told was a well-known haunt of the gypsies, as there was a large common next to it. Here they roused up the rural policeman, but could get no information from him, and, after riding all over the common, they turned their horses' heads homewards, and reached the Chase about eleven o'clock, dead-tired and almost heartbroken. They found Washington and the twins waiting for them at the gate-house with lanterns, as the avenue was very dark. Not the slightest trace of Virginia had been discovered. The gypsies had been caught on Broxley meadows, but she was not with them, and they had explained their sudden departure by saying that they had mistaken the date of Chorton Fair, and had gone off in a hurry for fear they might be late. Indeed, they had been quite distressed at hearing of Virginia's disappearance, as they were very grateful to Mr. Otis for having allowed them to camp in his park, and four of their number had stayed behind to help in the search. The carp-pond had been dragged, and the whole Chase thoroughly gone over, but without any result. It was evident that, for that night at any rate, Virginia was lost to them; and it was in a state of the deepest depression that Mr. Otis and the boys walked up to the house, the groom following behind with the two horses and the pony. In the hall they found a group of frightened servants, and lying on a sofa in the library was poor Mrs. Otis, almost out of her mind with terror and anxiety, and having her forehead bathed with eau-de-Cologne by the old housekeeper. Mr. Otis at once insisted on her having something to eat, and ordered up supper for the whole party. It was a melancholy meal, as hardly any one spoke, and even the twins were awestruck and subdued, as they were very fond of their sister. When they had finished, Mr. Otis, in spite of the entreaties of the little Duke, ordered them all to bed, saying that nothing more could be done that night, and that he would telegraph in the morning to Scotland Yard for some detectives to be sent down immediately. Just as they were passing out of the dining-room, midnight began to boom from the clock tower, and when the last stroke sounded they heard a crash and a sudden shrill cry; a dreadful peal of thunder shook the house, a strain of unearthly music floated through the air, a panel at the top of the staircase flew back with a loud noise, and out on the landing, looking very pale and white, with a little casket in her hand, stepped Virginia. In a moment they had all rushed up to her. Mrs. Otis clasped her passionately in her arms, the Duke smothered her with violent kisses, and the twins executed a wild war-dance round the group.

"Good heavens! child, where have you been?" said Mr. Otis, rather angrily, thinking that she had been playing some foolish trick on them. "Cecil and I have been riding all over the country looking for you, and your mother has been frightened to death. You must never play these practical jokes any more."

"Except on the Ghost! except on the Ghost!" shrieked the twins, as they capered about.

"My own darling, thank God you are found; you must never leave my side again," murmured Mrs. Otis, as she kissed the trembling child, and smoothed the tangled gold of her hair.

"Papa," said Virginia quietly, "I have been with the Ghost. He is dead, and you must come and see him. He had been very wicked, but he was really sorry for all that he had done, and he gave me this box of beautiful jewels before he died."

The whole family gazed at her in mute astonishment, but she was quite grave and serious; and, turning round, she led them through the opening in the wainscoting down a narrow secret corridor, Washington following with a lighted candle, which he had caught up from the table. Finally, they came to a great oak door, studded with rusty nails. When Virginia touched it, it swung back on its heavy hinges, and they found themselves in a little low room, with a vaulted ceiling, and one tiny grated window. Imbedded in the wall was a huge iron ring, and chained to it was a gaunt skeleton, that was stretched out at full length on the stone floor, and seemed to be trying to grasp with its long fleshless fingers an old-fashioned trencher and ewer, that were placed just out of its reach. The jug had evidently been once filled with water, as it was covered inside with green mould. There was nothing on the trencher but a pile of dust. Virginia knelt down beside the skeleton, and, folding her little hands together, began to pray silently, while the rest of the party looked on in wonder at the terrible tragedy whose secret was now disclosed to them.

"Hallo!" suddenly exclaimed one of the twins, who had been looking out of the window to try and discover in what wing of the house the room was situated. "Hallo! the old withered almond-tree has blossomed. I can see the flowers quite plainly in the moonlight."

"God has forgiven him," said Virginia gravely, as she rose to her feet, and a beautiful light seemed to illumine her face.

"What an angel you are!" cried the young Duke, and he put his arm round her neck and kissed her.

– 7 –

Four days after these curious incidents a funeral started from Canterville Chase at about eleven o'clock at night. The hearse was drawn by eight black horses, each of which carried on its head a great tuft of nodding ostrich-plumes, and the leaden coffin was covered by a rich purple pall, on which was embroidered in gold the Canterville coat-of-arms. By the side of the hearse and the coaches walked the servants with lighted torches, and the whole procession was wonderfully impressive. Lord Canterville was the chief mourner, having come up specially from Wales to attend the funeral, and sat in the first carriage along with little Virginia. Then came the United States Minister and his wife, then Washington and the three boys, and in the last carriage was Mrs. Umney. It was generally felt that, as she had been frightened by the ghost for more than fifty years of her life, she had a right to see the last of him. A deep grave had been dug in the corner of the churchyard, just under the old yew-tree, and the service was read in the most impressive manner by the Rev. Augustus Dampier. When the ceremony was over the servants according to an old custom observed in the Canterville family, extinguished their torches, and, as the coffin was being lowered into the grave, Virginia stepped forward and laid on it a large cross made of white and pink almond-blossoms. As she did so, the moon came out from behind a cloud, and flooded with its silent silver the little churchyard, and from a distant copse a nightingale began to sing. She thought of the ghost's description of the Garden of Death, her eyes became dim with tears, and she hardly spoke a word during the drive home.

The next morning, before Lord Canterville went up to town, Mr. Otis had an interview with him on the subject of the jewels the ghost had given to Virginia. They were perfectly magnificent, especially a certain ruby necklace with old Venetian setting, which was really a superb specimen of sixteenth-century work, and their value was so great that Mr. Otis felt considerable scruples about allowing his daughter to accept them.

"My Lord," he said, "I know that in this country mortmain is held to apply to trinkets as well as to land, and it is quite clear to me that these jewels are, or should be, heirlooms in your family. I must beg you, accordingly, to take them to London with you, and to regard them simply as a portion of your property which has been restored to you under certain strange conditions. As for my daughter, she is merely a child, and has as yet, I am glad to say, but little interest in such appurtenances of idle luxury. I am also informed by Mrs. Otis, who, I may say, is no mean authority upon Art—having had the privilege of spending several winters in Boston when she was a girl—that these gems are of great monetary worth, and if offered for sale would fetch a tall price. Under these circumstances, Lord Canterville, I feel sure that you will recognise how impossible it would be for me to allow them to remain in the possession of any member of my family; and, indeed, all such vain gauds and toys, however suitable or necessary to the dignity of the British aristocracy, would be completely out of place among those who have been brought up on the severe, and I believe immortal, principles of republican simplicity. Perhaps I should mention that Virginia is very anxious that you should allow her to retain the box as a memento of your unfortunate but misguided ancestor. As it is extremely old, and consequently a good deal out of repair, you may perhaps think fit to comply with her request. For my own part, I confess I am a good deal surprised to find a child of mine expressing sympathy with mediævalism in any form, and can only account for it by the fact that Virginia was born in one of your London suburbs shortly after Mrs. Otis had returned from a trip to Athens."

Lord Canterville listened very gravely to the worthy Minister's speech, pulling his grey moustache now and then to hide an involuntary smile, and when Mr. Otis had ended, he shook him cordially by the hand, and said, "My dear sir, your charming little daughter rendered my unlucky ancestor, Sir Simon, a very important service, and I and my family are much indebted to her for her marvellous courage and pluck. The jewels are clearly hers, and, egad, I believe that if I were heartless enough to take them from her, the wicked old fellow would be out of his grave in a fortnight, leading me the devil of a life. As for their being heirlooms, nothing is an heirloom that is not so mentioned in a will or legal document, and the existence of these jewels has been quite unknown. I assure you I have no more claim on them than your butler, and when Miss Virginia grows up I daresay she will be pleased to have pretty things to wear. Besides, you forget, Mr. Otis, that you took the furniture and the ghost at a valuation, and anything that belonged to the ghost passed at once into your possession, as, whatever activity Sir Simon may have shown in the corridor at night, in point of law he was really dead, and you acquired his property by purchase."

Mr. Otis was a good deal distressed at Lord Canterville's refusal, and begged him to reconsider his decision, but the good-natured peer was quite firm, and finally induced the Minister to allow his daughter to retain the present the ghost had given her, and when, in the spring of 1890, the young Duchess of Cheshire was presented at the Queen's first drawing-room on the occasion of her marriage, her jewels were the universal theme of admiration. For Virginia received the coronet, which is the reward of all good little American girls, and was married to her boy-lover as soon as he came of age. They were both so charming, and they loved each other so much, that every one was delighted at the match, except the old Marchioness of Dumbleton, who had tried to catch the Duke for one of her seven unmarried daughters, and had given no less than three expensive dinner-parties for that purpose, and, strange to say, Mr. Otis himself. Mr. Otis was extremely fond of the young Duke personally, but, theoretically, he objected to titles, and, to use his own words, "was not without apprehension lest, amid the enervating influences of a pleasure-loving aristocracy, the true principles of republican simplicity should be forgotten." His objections, however, were completely overruled, and I believe that when he walked up the aisle of St. George's, Hanover Square, with his daughter leaning on his arm, there was not a prouder man in the whole length and breadth of England.

The Duke and Duchess, after the honeymoon was over, went down to Canterville Chase, and on the day after their arrival they walked over in the afternoon to the lonely churchyard by the pine-woods. There had been a great deal of difficulty at first about the inscription on Sir Simon's tombstone, but finally it had been decided to engrave on it simply the initials of the old gentleman's name, and the verse from the library window. The Duchess had brought with her some lovely roses, which she strewed upon the grave, and after they had stood by it for some time they strolled into the ruined chancel of the old abbey. There the Duchess sat down on a fallen pillar, while her husband lay at her feet smoking a cigarette and looking up at her beautiful eyes. Suddenly he threw his cigarette away, took hold of her hand, and said to her, "Virginia, a wife should have no secrets from her husband."

"Dear Cecil! I have no secrets from you."

"Yes, you have," he answered, smiling, "you have never told me what happened to you when you were locked up with the ghost."

"I have never told any one, Cecil," said Virginia gravely.

"I know that, but you might tell me."

"Please don't ask me, Cecil, I cannot tell you. Poor Sir Simon! I owe him a great deal. Yes, don't laugh, Cecil, I really do. He made me see what Life is, and what Death signifies, and why Love is stronger than both."

The Duke rose and kissed his wife lovingly.

"You can have your secret as long as I have your heart," he murmured.

"You have always had that, Cecil."

"And you will tell our children some day, won't you?"

Virginia blushed.

THE YOUNG KING

It was the night before the day fixed for his coronation, and the young King was sitting alone in his beautiful chamber. His courtiers had all taken their leave of him, bowing their heads to the ground, according to the ceremonious usage of the day, and had retired to the Great Hall of the Palace, to receive a few last lessons from the Professor of Etiquette; there being some of them who had still quite natural manners, which in a courtier is, I need hardly say, a very grave offence.

The lad—for he was only a lad, being but sixteen years of age—was not sorry at their departure, and had flung himself back with a deep sigh of relief on the soft cushions of his embroidered couch, lying there, wild-eyed and open-mouthed, like a brown woodland Faun, or some young animal of the forest newly snared by the hunters.

And, indeed, it was the hunters who had found him, coming upon him almost by chance as, bare-limbed and pipe in hand, he was following the flock of the poor goatherd who had brought him up, and whose son he had always fancied himself to be. The child of the old King's only daughter by a secret marriage with one much beneath her in station—a stranger, some said, who, by the wonderful magic of his lute-playing, had made the young Princess love him; while others spoke of an artist from Rimini,* to whom the Princess had shown much, perhaps too much honour, and who had suddenly disappeared from the city, leaving his work in the Cathedral unfinished—he had been, when but a week old, stolen away from his mother's side, as she slept, and given into the charge of a common peasant and his wife, who were without children of their own, and lived in a remote part

* Ancient Italian city on the Adriatic Coast.

of the forest, more than a day's ride from the town. Grief, or the plague, as the court physician stated, or, as some suggested, a swift Italian poison administered in a cup of spiced wine, slew, within an hour of her wakening, the white girl who had given him birth, and as the trusty messenger who bare the child across his saddle-bow stooped from his weary horse and knocked at the rude door of the goatherd's hut, the body of the Princess was being lowered into an open grave that had been dug in a deserted churchyard, beyond the city gates, a grave where it was said that another body was also lying, that of a young man of marvellous and foreign beauty, whose hands were tied behind him with a knotted cord, and whose breast was stabbed with many red wounds.

Such, at least, was the story that men whispered to each other. Certain it was that the old King, when on his death-bed, whether moved by remorse for his great sin, or merely desiring that the kingdom should not pass away from his line, had had the lad sent for, and, in the presence of the Council, had acknowledged him as his heir.

And it seems that from the very first moment of his recognition he had shown signs of that strange passion for beauty that was destined to have so great an influence over his life. Those who accompanied him to the suite of rooms set apart for his service, often spoke of the cry of pleasure that broke from his lips when he saw the delicate raiment and rich jewels that had been prepared for him, and of the almost fierce joy with which he flung aside his rough leathern tunic and coarse sheepskin cloak. He missed, indeed, at times the freedom of the forest life, and was always apt to chafe at the tedious Court ceremonies that occupied so much of each day, but the wonderful palace—*Joyeuse*,* as they called it—of which he now found himself lord, seemed to him to be a new world fresh-fashioned for his delight; and as soon as he could escape from the council-board or audience-chamber, he would run down the great staircase, with its lions of gilt bronze and its steps of bright porphyry, and wander from room to room, and from corridor to corridor, like one who was

---

* Joyful (French).

seeking to find in beauty an anodyne from pain, a sort of restoration from sickness.

Upon these journeys of discovery, as he would call them—and, indeed, they were to him real voyages through a marvellous land, he would sometimes be accompanied by the slim, fair-haired Court pages, with their floating mantles, and gay fluttering ribands; but more often he would be alone, feeling through a certain quick instinct, which was almost a divination, that the secrets of art are best learned in secret, and that Beauty, like Wisdom, loves the lonely worshipper.

Many curious stories were related about him at this period. It was said that a stout Burgomaster, who had come to deliver a florid oratorical address on behalf of the citizens of the town, had caught sight of him kneeling in real adoration before a great picture that had just been brought from Venice, and that seemed to herald the worship of some new gods. On another occasion he had been missed for several hours, and after a lengthened search had been discovered in a little chamber in one of the northern turrets of the palace gazing, as one in a trance, at a Greek gem carved with the figure of Adonis. He had been seen, so the tale ran, pressing his warm lips to the marble brow of an antique statue that had been discovered in the bed of the river on the occasion of the building of the stone bridge, and was inscribed with the name of the Bithynian slave of Hadrian.* He had passed a whole night in noting the effect of the moonlight on a silver image of Endymion.

All rare and costly materials had certainly a great fascination for him, and in his eagerness to procure them he had sent away many merchants, some to traffic for amber with the rough fisher-folk of the north seas, some to Egypt to look for that curious green turquoise which is found only in the tombs of kings, and is said to possess magical properties, some to Persia for silken carpets and painted pottery, and others to India to buy gauze and stained ivory moonstones and bracelets of jade, sandal-wood and blue enamel and shawls of fine wool.

* Roman emperor (ruled 117–138 C.E.), who fell in love with the beautiful youth Antinous, the slave whose statue the young King kisses.

But what had occupied him most was the robe he was to wear at his coronation, the robe of tissued gold, and the ruby-studded crown, and the sceptre with its rows and rings of pearls. Indeed, it was of this that he was thinking to-night, as he lay back on his luxurious couch, watching the great pinewood log that was burning itself out on the open hearth. The designs, which were from the hands of the most famous artists of the time, had been submitted to him many months before, and he had given orders that the artificers were to toil night and day to carry them out, and that the whole world was to be searched for jewels that would be worthy of their work. He saw himself in fancy standing at the high altar of the cathedral in the fair raiment of a King, and a smile played and lingered about his boyish lips, and lit up with a bright lustre his dark woodland eyes.

After some time he rose from his seat, and leaning against the carved penthouse of the chimney, looked round at the dimly-lit room. The walls were hung with rich tapestries representing the Triumph of Beauty. A large press, inlaid with agate and lapis lazuli, filled one corner, and facing the window stood a curiously wrought cabinet with lacquer panels of powdered and mosaiced gold, on which were placed some delicate goblets of Venetian glass, and a cup of dark-veined onyx. Pale poppies were broidered on the silk coverlet of the bed, as though they had fallen from the tired hands of sleep, and tall reeds of fluted ivory bare up the velvet canopy, from which great tufts of ostrich plumes sprang, like white foam, to the pallid silver of the fretted ceiling. A laughing Narcissus in green bronze held a polished mirror above its head. On the table stood a flat bowl of amethyst.

Outside he could see the huge dome of the cathedral, looming like a bubble over the shadowy houses, and the weary sentinels pacing up and down on the misty terrace by the river. Far away, in an orchard, a nightingale was singing. A faint perfume of jasmine came through the open window. He brushed his brown curls back from his forehead, and taking up a lute, let his fingers stray across the cords. His heavy eyelids drooped, and a strange languor came over him. Never before had he felt so keenly, or with such exquisite joy, the magic and mystery of beautiful things.

When midnight sounded from the clock-tower he touched a

bell, and his pages entered and disrobed him with much ceremony, pouring rose-water over his hands, and strewing flowers on his pillow. A few moments after that they had left the room, he fell asleep.

And as he slept he dreamed a dream, and this was his dream.

He thought that he was standing in a long, low attic, amidst the whir and clatter of many looms. The meagre daylight peered in through the grated windows, and showed him the gaunt figures of the weavers bending over their cases. Pale, sickly-looking children were crouched on the huge crossbeams. As the shuttles dashed through the warp they lifted up the heavy battens, and when the shuttles stopped they let the battens fall and pressed the threads together. Their faces were pinched with famine, and their thin hands shook and trembled. Some haggard women were seated at a table sewing. A horrible odour filled the place. The air was foul and heavy, and the walls dripped and streamed with damp.

The young King went over to one of the weavers, and stood by him and watched him.

And the weaver looked at him angrily and said, "Why art thou watching me? Art thou a spy set on us by our master?"

"Who is thy master?" asked the young King.

"Our master!" cried the weaver, bitterly. "He is a man like myself. Indeed, there is but this difference between us—that he wears fine clothes while I go in rags, and that while I am weak from hunger he suffers not a little from overfeeding."

"The land is free," said the young King, "and thou art no man's slave."

"In war," answered the weaver, "the strong make slaves of the weak, and in peace the rich make slaves of the poor. We must work to live, and they give us such mean wages that we die. We toil for them all day long, and they heap up gold in their coffers, and our children fade away before their time, and the faces of those we love become hard and evil. We tread out the grapes, and another drinks the wine. We sow the corn, and our own board is empty. We have chains, though no eye beholds them; and we are slaves, though men call us free."

"Is it so with all?" he asked.

"It is so with all," answered the weaver, "with the young as well as with the old, with the women as well as with the men, with the little children as well as with those who are stricken in years. The merchants grind us down, and we must needs do their bidding. The priest rides by and tells his beads, and no man has care of us. Through our sunless lanes creeps Poverty with her hungry eyes, and Sin with his sodden face follows close behind her. Misery wakes us in the morning, and Shame sits with us at night. But what are these things to thee? Thou art not one of us. Thy face is too happy." And he turned away scowling, and threw the shuttle across the loom, and the young King saw that it was threaded with a thread of gold.

And a great terror seized upon him, and he said to the weaver, "What robe is this that thou art weaving?"

"It is the robe for the coronation of the young King," he answered; "what is that to thee?"

And the young King gave a loud cry and woke, and lo! he was in his own chamber, and through the window he saw the great honey-coloured moon hanging in the dusky air.

And he fell asleep again and dreamed, and this was his dream.

He thought that he was lying on the deck of a huge galley that was being rowed by a hundred slaves. On a carpet by his side the master of the galley was seated. He was black as ebony, and his turban was of crimson silk. Great ear-rings of silver dragged down the thick lobes of his ears, and in his hands he had a pair of ivory scales.

The slaves were naked, but for a ragged loincloth, and each man was chained to his neighbour. The hot sun beat brightly upon them, and the negroes ran up and down the gangway and lashed them with whips of hide. They stretched out their lean arms and pulled the heavy oars through the water. The salt spray flew from the blades.

At last they reached a little bay, and began to take soundings. A light wind blew from the shore, and covered the deck and the great lateen sail with a fine red dust. Three Arabs mounted on wild asses rode out and threw spears at them. The master of the galley took a painted bow in his hand and shot one of them in the throat. He fell heavily into the surf, and his companions galloped away. A woman wrapped in a yellow veil followed slowly on a camel, looking back now and then at the dead body.

As soon as they had cast anchor and hauled down the sail, the negroes went into the hold and brought up a long rope-ladder, heavily weighted with lead. The master of the galley threw it over the side, making the ends fast to two iron stanchions. Then the negroes seized the youngest of the slaves and knocked his gyves off, and filled his nostrils and his ears with wax, and tied a big stone round his waist. He crept wearily down the ladder, and disappeared into the sea. A few bubbles rose where he sank. Some of the other slaves peered curiously over the side. At the prow of the galley sat a shark-charmer, beating monotonously upon a drum.

After some time the diver rose up out of the water, and clung panting to the ladder with a pearl in his right hand. The negroes seized it from him, and thrust him back. The slaves fell asleep over their oars.

Again and again he came up, and each time that he did so he brought with him a beautiful pearl. The master of the galley weighed them, and put them into a little bag of green leather.

The young King tried to speak, but his tongue seemed to cleave to the roof of his mouth, and his lips refused to move. The negroes chattered to each other, and began to quarrel over a string of bright beads. Two cranes flew round and round the vessel.

Then the diver came up for the last time, and the pearl that he brought with him was fairer than all the pearls of Ormuz, for it was shaped like the full moon, and whiter than the morning star. But his face was strangely pale, and as he fell upon the deck the blood gushed from his ears and nostrils. He quivered for a little, and then he was still. The negroes shrugged their shoulders, and threw the body overboard.

And the master of the galley laughed, and, reaching out, he took the pearl, and when he saw it he pressed it to his forehead and bowed. “It shall be,” he said, “for the sceptre of the young King,” and he made a sign to the negroes to draw up the anchor.

And when the young King heard this he gave a great cry and woke, and through the window he saw the long grey fingers of the dawn clutching at the fading stars.

And he fell asleep again, and dreamed, and this was his dream.

He thought that he was wandering through a dim wood, hung with strange fruits and with beautiful poisonous flowers. The adders hissed at him as he went by, and the bright parrots flew screaming from branch to branch. Huge tortoises lay asleep upon the hot mud. The trees were full of apes and peacocks.

On and on he went, till he reached the outskirts of the wood, and there he saw an immense multitude of men toiling in the bed of a dried-up river. They swarmed up the crag like ants. They dug deep pits in the ground and went down into them. Some of them cleft the rocks with great axes; others grabbled in the sand. They tore up the cactus by its roots, and trampled on the scarlet blossoms. They hurried about, calling to each other, and no man was idle.

From the darkness of a cavern Death and Avarice watched them, and Death said, "I am weary; give me a third of them and let me go."

But Avarice shook her head. "They are my servants," she answered.

And Death said to her, "What hast thou in thy hand?"

"I have three grains of corn," she answered; "what is that to thee?"

"Give me one of them," cried Death, "to plant in my garden; only one of them, and I will go away."

"I will not give thee anything," said Avarice, and she hid her hand in the fold of her raiment.

And Death laughed, and took a cup, and dipped it into a pool of water, and out of the cup rose Ague. She passed through the great multitude, and a third of them lay dead. A cold mist followed her, and the water-snakes ran by her side.

And when Avarice saw that a third of the multitude was dead she beat her breast and wept. She beat her barren bosom, and cried aloud. "Thou hast slain a third of my servants," she cried, "get thee gone. There is war in the mountains of Tartary, and the kings of each side are calling to thee. The Afghans have slain the black ox, and are marching to battle. They have beaten upon their shields with their spears, and have put on their helmets of iron. What is my valley to thee, that thou shouldst tarry in it? Get thee gone, and come here no more."

"Nay," answered Death, "but till thou hast given me a grain of corn I will not go."

But Avarice shut her hand, and clenched her teeth. "I will not give thee anything," she muttered.

And Death laughed, and took up a black stone, and threw it into the forest, and out of a thicket of wild hemlock came Fever in a robe of flame. She passed through the multitude, and touched them, and each man that she touched died. The grass withered beneath her feet as she walked.

And Avarice shuddered, and put ashes on her head. "Thou art cruel," she cried; "thou art cruel. There is famine in the walled cities of India, and the cisterns of Samarcand have run dry. There is famine in the walled cities of Egypt, and the locusts have come up from the desert. The Nile has not overflowed its banks, and the priests have nursed Isis and Osiris.* Get thee gone to those who need thee, and leave me my servants."

"Nay," answered Death, "but till thou hast given me a grain of corn I will not go."

"I will not give thee anything," said Avarice.

And Death laughed again, and he whistled through his fingers, and a woman came flying through the air. Plague was written upon her forehead, and a crowd of lean vultures wheeled round her. She covered the valley with her wings, and no man was left alive.

And Avarice fled shrieking through the forest, and Death leaped upon his red horse and galloped away, and his galloping was faster than the wind. And out of the slime at the bottom of the valley crept dragons and horrible things with scales, and the jackals came trotting along the sand, sniffing up the air with their nostrils.

And the young King wept, and said: "Who were these men, and for what were they seeking?"

---

* Ancient goddess and god of fertility, both worshiped in Egypt. Wilde knew of them in part through his reading in Plutarch's *Moralia*.

"For rubies for a king's crown," answered one who stood behind him.

And the young King started, and, turning round, he saw a man habited as a pilgrim and holding in his hand a mirror of silver.

And he grew pale, and said: "For what king?"

And the pilgrim answered: "Look in this mirror, and thou shalt see him."

And he looked in the mirror, and, seeing his own face, he gave a great cry and woke, and the bright sunlight was streaming into the room, and from the trees of the garden and pleasaunce the birds were singing.

And the Chamberlain and the high officers of State came in and made obeisance to him, and the pages brought him the robe of tissued gold, and set the crown and the sceptre before him.

And the young King looked at them, and they were beautiful. More beautiful were they than aught that he had ever seen. But he remembered his dreams, and he said to his lords: "Take these things away, for I will not wear them."

And the courtiers were amazed, and some of them laughed, for they thought that he was jesting.

But he spake sternly to them again, and said: "Take these things away, and hide them from me. Though it be the day of my coronation, I will not wear them. For on the loom of sorrow, and by the white hands of Pain, has this my robe been woven. There is Blood in the heart of the ruby, and Death in the heart of the pearl." And he told them his three dreams.

And when the courtiers heard them they looked at each other and whispered, saying: "Surely he is mad; for what is a dream but a dream, and a vision but a vision? They are not real things that one should heed them. And what have we to do with the lives of those who toil for us? Shall a man not eat bread till he has seen the sower, nor drink wine till he has talked with the vinedresser?"

And the Chamberlain spake to the young King, and said, "My lord, I pray thee set aside these black thoughts of thine, and put on this fair robe, and set this crown upon thy head. For how shall the people know that thou art a king, if thou hast not a king's raiment?"

And the young King looked at him. "Is it so, indeed?" he questioned. "Will they not know me for a king if I have not a king's raiment?"

"They will not know thee, my lord," cried the Chamberlain.

"I had thought that there had been men who were kinglike," he answered, "but it may be as thou sayest. And yet I will not wear this robe, nor will I be crowned with this crown, but even as I came to the Palace so will I go forth from it."

And he bade them all leave him, save one page whom he kept as his companion, a lad a year younger than himself. Him he kept for his service, and when he had bathed himself in clear water, he opened a great painted chest, and from it he took the leathern tunic and rough sheepskin coat that he had worn when he had watched on the hillside the shaggy goats of the goatherd. These he put on, and in his hand he took his rude shepherd's staff.

And the little page opened his big blue eyes in wonder, and said smiling to him, "My lord, I see thy robe and thy sceptre, but where is thy crown?"

And the young King plucked a spray of wild briar that was climbing over the balcony, and bent it, and made a circlet of it, and set it on his own head.

"This shall be my crown," he answered.

And thus attired he passed out of his chamber into the Great Hall, where the nobles were waiting for him.

And the nobles made merry, and some of them cried out to him, "My lord, the people wait for their king, and thou showest them a beggar," and others were wroth and said, "He brings shame upon our state, and is unworthy to be our master." But he answered them not a word, but passed on, and went down the bright porphyry staircase, and out through the gates of bronze, and mounted upon his horse, and rode towards the cathedral, the little page running beside him.

And the people laughed and said, "It is the King's fool who is riding by," and they mocked him.

And he drew rein and said, "Nay, but I am the King." And he told them his three dreams.

And a man came out of the crowd and spake bitterly to him, and said, "Sir, knowest thou not that out of the luxury of the rich cometh the life of the poor? By your pomp we are nurtured, and your vices give us bread. To toil for a master is bitter, but to have no master to toil for is more bitter still. Thinkest thou that the ravens will feed us? And what cure hast thou for these things? Wilt thou say to the buyer, 'Thou shalt buy for so much,' and to the seller, 'Thou shalt sell at this price?' I trow not. Therefore go back to thy Palace and put on thy purple and fine linen. What hast thou to do with us, and what we suffer?'

"Are not the rich and the poor brothers?" asked the young King.

"Ay," answered the man, "and the name of the rich brother is Cain."

And the young King's eyes filled with tears, and he rode on through the murmurs of the people, and the little page grew afraid and left him.

And when he reached the great portal of the cathedral, the soldiers thrust their halberts out and said, "What does thou seek here? None enters by this door but the King."

And his face flushed with anger, and he said to them, "I am the King," and waved their halberts aside and passed in.

And when the old bishop saw him coming in his goatherd's dress, he rose up in wonder from his throne, and went to meet him, and said to him, "My son, is this a king's apparel? And with what crown shall I crown thee, and what sceptre shall I place in thy hand? Surely this should be to thee a day of joy, and not a day of abasement."

"Shall Joy wear what Grief has fashioned?" said the young King. And he told him his three dreams.

And when the Bishop had heard them he knit his brows, and said, "My son, I am an old man, and in the winter of my days, and I know that many evil things are done in the wide world. The fierce robbers come down from the mountains, and carry off the little children, and sell them to the Moors. The lions lie in wait for the caravans, and leap upon the camels. The wild boar roots up the corn in the valley, and the foxes gnaw the vines upon the hill. The pirates lay waste the sea-coast and burn the ships of the fishermen, and take their nets from them. In the salt-marshes live the lepers; they have houses of wattled reeds, and none may come nigh them. The beggars wander through the cities, and eat their food with the dogs. Canst thou make these things not to be? Will thou take the leper for thy bedfellow, and set the beggar at thy board? Shall the lion do thy bidding, and the wild boar obey thee? Is not He who made misery wiser than thou art? Wherefore I praise thee not for this that thou hast done, but I bid thee ride back to the Palace and make thy face glad, and put on the raiment that beseemeth a king, and with the crown of gold I will crown thee, and the sceptre of pearl will I place in thy hand. And as for thy dreams, think no more of them. The burden of this world is too great for one man to bear, and the world's sorrow too heavy for one heart to suffer."

"Sayest thou that in this house?" said the young King, and he strode past the Bishop, and climbed up the steps of the altar, and stood before the image of Christ.

He stood before the image of Christ, and on his right hand and on his left were the marvellous vessels of gold, the chalice with the yellow wine, and the vial with the holy oil. He knelt before the image of Christ, and the great candles burned brightly by the jewelled shrine, and the smoke of the incense curled in thin blue wreaths through the dome. He bowed his head in prayer, and the priests in their stiff copes crept away from the altar.

And suddenly a wild tumult came from the street outside, and in entered the nobles with drawn swords and nodding plumes, and shields of polished steel. "Where is this dreamer of dreams?" they cried. "Where is this King, who is apparelled like a beggar—this boy who brings shame upon our state? Surely we will slay him, for he is unworthy to rule over us."

And the young King bowed his head again, and prayed, and when he had finished his prayer he rose up, and turning round he looked at them sadly.

And lo! through the painted windows came the sunlight streaming upon him, and the sunbeams wove round him a tissued robe that was fairer than the robe that had been fashioned for his pleasure. The dead staff blossomed, and bare lilies that were whiter than pearls. The dry thorn blossomed, and bare roses that were redder than rubies. Whiter than fine pearls were the lilies, and their stems were of bright silver. Redder than male rubies were the roses, and their leaves were of beaten gold.

He stood there in the raiment of a king, and the gates of the jewelled shrine flew open and from the crystal of the many-rayed monstrance shone a marvellous and mystical light. He stood there in a king's raiment, and the Glory of God filled the place, and the saints in their carven niches seemed to move. In the fair raiment of a king he stood before them, and the organ pealed out its music, and the trumpeters blew upon their trumpets, and the singing boys sang.

And the people fell upon their knees in awe, and the nobles sheathed their swords and did homage, and the Bishop's face grew pale, and his hands trembled. "A greater than I hath crowned thee," he cried, and he knelt before him.

And the young King came down from the high altar, and passed home through the midst of the people. But no man dared look upon his face, for it was like the face of an angel.

THE BIRTHDAY OF THE INFANTA

It was the birthday of the Infanta.* She was just twelve years of age, and the sun was shining brightly in the gardens of the palace.

Although she was a real Princess and the Infanta of Spain, she had only one birthday every year, just like the children of quite poor people, so it was naturally a matter of great importance to the whole country that she should have a really fine day for the occasion. And a really fine day it certainly was. The tall striped tulips stood straight up upon their stalks, like long rows of soldiers, and looked defiantly across the grass at the roses, and said: "We are quite as splendid as you are now." The purple butterflies fluttered about with gold dust on their wings, visiting each flower in turn; the little lizards crept out of the crevices of the wall, and lay basking in the white glare; and the pomegranates split and cracked with the heat, and showed their bleeding red hearts. Even the pale yellow lemons, that hung in such profusion from the mouldering trellis and along the dim arcades, seemed to have caught a richer colour from the wonderful sunlight, and the magnolia trees opened their great glove-like blossoms of folded ivory, and filled the air with a sweet heavy perfume.

The little Princess herself walked up and down the terrace with her companions, and played at hide and seek round the stone vases and the old moss-grown statues. On ordinary days she was only allowed to play with children of her own rank, so she had always to play alone, but her birthday was an exception, and the King had given orders that she was to invite any of her young friends whom she liked

* The Infanta is next in line to assume the royal throne.

to come and amuse themselves with her. There was a stately grace about these slim Spanish children as they glided about, the boys with their large-plumed hats and short fluttering cloaks, the girls holding up the trains of their long brocade gowns, and shielding the sun from their eyes with huge fans of black and silver. But the Infanta was the most graceful of all, and the most tastefully attired, after the somewhat cumbrous fashion of the day. Her robe was of grey satin, the skirt and the wide puffed sleeves heavily embroidered with silver, and the stiff corset studded with rows of fine pearls. Two tiny slippers with big pink rosettes peeped out beneath her dress as she walked. Pink and pearl was her great gauze fan, and in her hair, which like an aureole of faded gold stood out stiffly round her pale little face, she had a beautiful white rose.

From a window in the palace the sad melancholy King watched them. Behind him stood his brother, Don Pedro of Aragon, whom he hated, and his confessor, the Grand Inquisitor of Granada, sat by his side. Sadder even than usual was the King, for as he looked at the Infanta bowing with childish gravity to the assembling courtiers, or laughing behind the fan at the grim Duchess of Albuquerque, who always accompanied her, he thought of the young Queen, her mother, who but a short time before—so it seemed to him—had come from the gay country of France, and had withered away in the sombre splendour of the Spanish court, dying just six months after the birth of her child, and before she had seen the almonds blossom twice in the orchard, or plucked the second year's fruit from the old gnarled fig-tree that stood in the centre of the now grass-grown courtyard. So great had been his love for her that he had not suffered even the grave to hide her from him. She had been embalmed by a Moorish physician, who in return for this service had been granted his life, which for heresy and suspicion of magical practices had been already forfeited, men said, to the Holy Office, and her body was still lying on its tapestried bier in the black marble chapel of the palace, just as the monks had borne her on that windy March day nearly twelve years before. Once every month the King, wrapped in a dark cloak and with a muffled lantern in his hand, went in and knelt by her side calling out, "*Mi reina! Mi reina!*"* and sometimes breaking through the formal etiquette that in Spain governs every separate action of life, and sets limits even to the sorrow of a King, he would clutch at the pale jewelled hands in a wild agony of grief, and try to wake by his mad kisses the cold painted face.

To-day he seemed to see her again, as he had seen her first at the Castle of Fontainebleau, when he was but fifteen years of age, and she still younger. They had been formally betrothed on that occasion by the Papal Nuncio in the presence of the French King and all the Court, and he had returned to the Escurial bearing with him a little ringlet of yellow hair, and the memory of two childish lips bending down to kiss his hand as he stepped into his carriage. Later on had followed the marriage, hastily performed at Burgos, a small town on the frontier between the two countries, and the grand public entry into Madrid with the customary celebration of high mass at the Church of La Atocha, and a more than usually solemn *auto-da-fé*, in which nearly three hundred heretics, amongst whom were many Englishmen,† had been delivered over to the secular arm to be burned.

Certainly he had loved her madly, and to the ruin, many thought, of his country, then at war with England for the possession of the empire of the New World. He had hardly ever permitted her to be out of his sight; for her, he had forgotten, or seemed to have forgotten, all grave affairs of State; and, with that terrible blindness that passion brings upon its servants, he had failed to notice that the elaborate ceremonies by which he sought to please her did but aggravate the strange malady from which she suffered. When she died he was, for a time, like one bereft of reason. Indeed, there is no doubt but that he would have formally abdicated and retired to the great Trappist monastery at Granada, of which he was already titular Prior, had he not been afraid to leave the little Infanta at the mercy of his brother, whose cruelty, even in Spain, was notorious, and who was suspected

---

* My queen! (Spanish).

† As Protestants, the English were condemned by the Spanish Inquisition to die by burning at an *auto-da-fé* (public penance; literally, act of the faith [Portuguese]. Wilde is getting at bad faith in religion driven by greed.

by many of having caused the Queen's death by means of a pair of poisoned gloves that he had presented to her on the occasion of her visiting his castle in Aragon. Even after the expiration of the three years of public mourning that he had ordained throughout his whole dominions by royal edict, he would never suffer his ministers to speak about any new alliance, and when the Emperor himself sent to him, and offered him the hand of the lovely Archduchess of Bohemia, his niece, in marriage, he bade the ambassadors tell their master that the King of Spain was already wedded to Sorrow, and that though she was but a barren bride he loved her better than Beauty; an answer that cost his crown the rich provinces of the Netherlands, which soon after, at the Emperor's instigation, revolted against him under the leadership of some fanatics of the Reformed Church.

His whole married life, with its fierce, fiery-coloured joys and the terrible agony of its sudden ending, seemed to come back to him today as he watched the Infanta playing on the terrace. She had all the Queen's pretty petulance of manner, the same wilful way of tossing her head, the same proud curved beautiful mouth, the same wonderful smile—*vrai sourire de France** indeed—as she glanced up now and then at the window, or stretched out her little hand for the stately Spanish gentlemen to kiss. But the shrill laughter of the children grated on his ears, and the bright pitiless sunlight mocked his sorrow, and a dull odour of strange spices such as embalmers use, seemed to taint—or was it fancy?—the clear morning air. He buried his face in his hands, and when the Infanta looked up again the curtains had been drawn, and the King had retired.

She made a little *moue*† of disappointment, and shrugged her shoulders. Surely he might have stayed with her on her birthday. What did the stupid State-affairs matter? Or had he gone to that gloomy chapel, where the candles were always burning, and where she was never allowed to enter? How silly of him, when the sun was shining so brightly, and everybody was so happy! Besides, he would miss the

---

* True smile of France (French).

† Pout (French).

sham bull-fight for which the trumpet was already sounding, to say nothing of the puppet-show and the other wonderful things. Her uncle and the Grand Inquisitor were much more sensible. They had come out on the terrace, and paid her nice compliments. So she tossed her pretty head, and taking Don Pedro by the hand, she walked slowly down the steps towards a long pavilion of purple silk that had been erected at the end of the garden, the other children following in strict order of precedence, those who had the longest names going first.

A procession of noble boys, fantastically dressed as *toreadors*, came out to meet her, and the young Count of Tierra-Nueva, a wonderfully handsome lad of about fourteen years of age, uncovering his head with all the grace of a born hidalgo and grandee of Spain, led her solemnly in to a little gilt and ivory chair that was placed on a raised dais above the arena. The children grouped themselves all round, fluttering their big fans and whispering to each other, and Don Pedro and the Grand Inquisitor stood laughing at the entrance. Even the Duchess—the Camerera-Mayor* as she was called—a thin, hard-featured woman with a yellow ruff, did not look quite so bad-tempered as usual, and something like a chill smile flitted across her wrinkled face and twitched her thin bloodless lips.

It certainly was a marvellous bull-fight, and much nicer, the Infanta thought, than the real bull-fight that she had been brought to see at Seville, on the occasion of the visit of the Duke of Parma to her father. Some of the boys pranced about on richly-caparisoned hobby-horses brandishing long javelins with gay streamers of bright ribands attached to them; others went on foot waving their scarlet cloaks before the bull, and vaulting lightly over the barrier when he charged them; and as for the bull himself, he was just like a live bull, though he was only made of wickerwork and stretched hide, and sometimes insisted on running round the arena on his hind legs, which no live bull ever dreams of doing. He made a splendid fight of it too, and the children got so excited that they stood up upon the benches, and

* Chief lady-in-waiting, sometimes called the lady of the royal bedchamber.

waved their lace handkerchiefs and cried out: *Bravo toro! Bravo toro!** just as sensibly as if they had been grown-up people. At last, however, after a prolonged combat, during which several of the hobby-horses were gored through and through, and their riders dismounted, the young Count of Tierra-Nueva brought the bull to his knees, and having obtained permission from the Infanta to give the *coup de grâce*,† he plunged his wooden sword into the neck of the animal with such violence that the head came right off, and disclosed the laughing face of little Monsieur de Lorraine, the son of the French Ambassador at Madrid.

The arena was then cleared amidst much applause, and the dead hobby-horses dragged solemnly away by two Moorish pages in yellow and black liveries, and after a short interlude, during which a French posture-master performed upon the tight-rope, some Italian puppets appeared in the semi-classical tragedy of *Sophonisba* on the stage of a small theatre that had been built up for the purpose. They acted so well, and their gestures were so extremely natural, that at the close of the play the eyes of the Infanta were quite dim with tears. Indeed some of the children really cried, and had to be comforted with sweetmeats, and the Grand Inquisitor himself was so affected that he could not help saying to Don Pedro that it seemed to him intolerable that things made simply out of wood and coloured wax, and worked mechanically by wires, should be so unhappy and meet with such terrible misfortunes.

An African juggler followed, who brought in a large flat basket covered with a red cloth, and having placed it in the centre of the arena, he took from his turban a curious reed pipe, and blew through it. In a few moments the cloth began to move, and as the pipe grew shriller and shriller two green and gold snakes put out their strange wedge-shaped heads and rose slowly up, swaying to and fro with the music as a plant sways in the water. The children, however, were rather frightened at their spotted hoods and quick darting tongues,

---

* Well done, bull! (Spanish).

† Finishing blow (French).

and were much more pleased when the juggler made a tiny orange-tree grow out of the sand and bear pretty white blossoms and clusters of real fruit; and when he took the fan of the little daughter of the Marquess de Las-Torres, and changed it into a blue bird that flew all round the pavilion and sang, their delight and amazement knew no bounds. The solemn minuet, too, performed by the dancing boys from the church of Nuestra Senora Del Pilar, was charming. The Infanta had never before seen this wonderful ceremony which takes place every year at Maytime in front of the high altar of the Virgin, and in her honour; and indeed none of the royal family of Spain had entered the great cathedral of Saragossa since a mad priest, supposed by many to have been in the pay of Elizabeth of England, had tried to administer a poisoned wafer to the Prince of the Asturias. So she had known only by hearsay of "Our Lady's Dance," as it was called, and it certainly was a beautiful sight. The boys wore old-fashioned court dresses of white velvet, and their curious three-cornered hats were fringed with silver and surmounted with huge plumes of ostrich feathers, the dazzling whiteness of their costumes, as they moved about in the sunlight, being still more accentuated by their swarthy faces and long black hair. Everybody was fascinated by the grave dignity with which they moved through the intricate figures of the dance, and by the elaborate grace of their slow gestures, and stately bows, and when they had finished their performance and doffed their great plumed hats to the Infanta, she acknowledged their reverence with much courtesy, and made a vow that she would send a large wax candle to the shrine of Our Lady of Pilar in return for the pleasure that she had given her.

A troop of handsome Egyptians—as the gipsies were termed in those days—then advanced into the arena, and sitting down cross-legs, in a circle, began to play softly upon their zithers, moving their bodies to the tune, and humming, almost below their breath, a low dreamy air. When they caught sight of Don Pedro they scowled at him, and some of them looked terrified, for only a few weeks before he had had two of their tribe hanged for sorcery in the market-place at Seville, but the pretty Infanta charmed them as she leaned back peeping over her fan with her great blue eyes, and they felt sure that one so lovely as she was could never be cruel to anybody. So they played on very gently and just touching the cords of the zithers with their long pointed nails, and their heads began to nod as though they were falling asleep. Suddenly, with a cry so shrill that all the children were startled, and Don Pedro's hand clutched at the agate pommel of his dagger, they leapt to their feet and whirled madly round the enclosure beating their tambourines, and chaunting some wild love-song in their strange guttural language. Then at another signal they all flung themselves again to the ground and lay there quite still, the dull strumming of the zithers being the only sound that broke the silence. After that they had done this several times, they disappeared for a moment and came back leading a brown shaggy bear by a chain, and carrying on their shoulders some little Barbary apes. The bear stood upon his head with the utmost gravity, and the wizened apes played all kinds of amusing tricks with two gipsy boys who seemed to be their masters, and fought with tiny swords, and fired off guns, and went through a regular soldier's drill just like the King's own bodyguard. In fact, the gipsies were a great success.

But the funniest part of the whole morning's entertainment, was undoubtedly the dancing of the little Dwarf. When he stumbled into the arena, waddling on his crooked legs and wagging his huge misshapen head from side to side, the children went off into a loud shout of delight, and the Infanta herself laughed so much that the Camerera was obliged to remind her that although there were many precedents in Spain for a King's daughter weeping before her equals, there were none for a Princess of the blood royal making so merry before those who were her inferiors in birth. The Dwarf, however, was really quite irresistible, and even at the Spanish Court, always noted for its cultivated passion for the horrible, so fantastic a little monster had never been seen. It was his first appearance, too. He had been discovered only the day before, running wild through the forest, by two of the nobles who happened to have been hunting in a remote part of the great cork-wood that surrounded the town, and had been carried off by them to the Palace as a surprise for the Infanta; his father, who was a poor charcoal-burner, being but too well pleased to get rid of so ugly and useless a child. Perhaps the most amusing thing about him was his complete unconsciousness of his own grotesque appearance. Indeed he seemed quite happy and full of the highest spirits. When the children laughed, he laughed as freely and as joyously as any of them, and at the close of each dance he made them each the funniest of bows, smiling and nodding at them just as if he was really one of themselves, and not a little misshapen thing that Nature, in some humorous mood, had fashioned for others to mock at. As for the Infanta, she absolutely fascinated him. He could not keep his eyes off her, and seemed to dance for her alone, and when at the close of the performance, remembering how she had seen the great ladies of the Court throw bouquets to Caffarelli, the famous Italian treble,* whom the Pope had sent from his own chapel to Madrid that he might cure the King's melancholy by the sweetness of his voice, she took out of her hair the beautiful white rose, and partly for a jest and partly to tease the Camerera, threw it to him across the arena with her sweetest smile. He took the whole matter quite seriously, and pressing the flower to his rough coarse lips he put his hand upon his heart, and sank on one knee before her, grinning from ear to ear, and with his little bright eyes sparkling with pleasure.

This so upset the gravity of the Infanta that she kept on laughing long after the little Dwarf had run out of the arena, and expressed a desire to her uncle that the dance should be immediately repeated. The Camerera, however, on the plea that the sun was too hot, decided that it would be better that her Highness should return without delay to the Palace, where a wonderful feast had been already prepared for her, including a real birthday cake with her own initials worked all over it in painted sugar and a lovely silver flag waving from the top. The Infanta accordingly rose up with much dignity, and having given orders that the little dwarf was to dance again for her after the hour of siesta, and conveyed her thanks to the young Count of Tierra-Nueva for his charming reception, she went back to

* Italian soprano.

her apartments, the children following in the same order in which they had entered.

Now when the little Dwarf heard that he was to dance a second time before the Infanta, and by her own express command, he was so proud that he ran out into the garden, kissing the white rose in an absurd ecstasy of pleasure, and making the most uncouth and clumsy gestures of delight.

The Flowers were quite indignant at his daring to intrude into their beautiful home, and when they saw him capering up and down the walks, and waving his arms above his head in such a ridiculous manner, they could not restrain their feelings any longer.

"He is really far too ugly to be allowed to play in any place where we are," cried the Tulips.

"He should drink poppy-juice, and go to sleep for a thousand years," said the great scarlet Lilies, and they grew quite hot and angry.

"He is a perfect horror!" screamed the Cactus. "Why, he is twisted and stumpy, and his head is completely out of proportion with his legs. Really he makes me feel prickly all over, and if he comes near me I will sting him with my thorns."

"And he has actually got one of my best blooms," exclaimed the White Rose-Tree. "I gave it to the Infanta this morning myself, as a birthday present, and he has stolen it from her." And she called out: "Thief, thief, thief!" at the top of her voice.

Even the red Geraniums, who did not usually give themselves airs, and were known to have a great many poor relations themselves, curled up in disgust when they saw him, and when the Violets meekly remarked that though he was certainly extremely plain, still he could not help it, they retorted with a good deal of justice that that was his chief defect, and that there was no reason why one should admire a person because he was incurable; and, indeed, some of the Violets themselves felt that the ugliness of the little Dwarf was almost ostentatious, and that he would have shown much better taste if he had looked sad, or at least pensive, instead of jumping about merrily, and throwing himself into such grotesque and silly attitudes.

As for the old Sundial, who was an extremely remarkable

individual, and had told the time of day to no less a person than the Emperor Charles V. himself, he was so taken aback by the little Dwarf 's appearance, that he almost forgot to mark two whole minutes with his long shadowy finger, and could not help saying to the great milk-white Peacock, who was sunning herself on the balustrade, that every one knew that the children of Kings were Kings, and that the children of charcoal-burners were charcoal-burners, and that it was absurd to pretend that it wasn't so; a statement with which the Peacock entirely agreed, and indeed screamed out, "Certainly, certainly," in such a loud, harsh voice, that the gold-fish who lived in the basin of the cool splashing fountain put their heads out of the water, and asked the huge stone Tritons what on earth was the matter.

But somehow the Birds liked him. They had seen him often in the forest, dancing about like an elf after the eddying leaves, or crouched up in the hollow of some old oak-tree, sharing his nuts with the squirrels. They did not mind his being ugly a bit. Why, even the nightingale herself, who sang so sweetly in the orange groves at night that sometimes the Moon leaned down to listen, was not much to look at after all; and, besides, he had been kind to them, and during that terribly bitter winter, when there were no berries on the trees, and the ground was as hard as iron, and the wolves had come down to the very gates of the city to look for food, he had never once forgotten them, but had always given them crumbs out of his little hunch of black bread, and divided with them whatever poor breakfast he had.

So they flew round and round him, just touching his cheek with their wings as they passed, and chattered to each other, and the little Dwarf was so pleased that he could not help showing them the beautiful white rose, and telling them that the Infanta herself had given it to him because she loved him.

They did not understand a single word of what he was saying, but that made no matter, for they put their heads on one side, and looked wise, which is quite as good as understanding a thing, and very much easier.

The Lizards also took an immense fancy to him, and when he grew tired of running about and flung himself down on the grass to rest, they played and romped all over him, and tried to amuse him in the best way they could. "Every one cannot be as beautiful as a lizard," they cried; "that would be too much to expect. And, though it sounds absurd to say so, he is really not so ugly after all, provided, of course, that one shuts one's eyes, and does not look at him." The Lizards were extremely philosophical by nature, and often sat thinking for hours and hours together, when there was nothing else to do, or when the weather was too rainy for them to go out.

The Flowers, however, were excessively annoyed at their behaviour, and at the behaviour of the birds. "It only shows," they said, "what a vulgarising effect this incessant rushing and flying about has. Well-bred people always stay exactly in the same place as we do. No one ever saw us hopping up and down the walks, or galloping madly through the grass after dragon-flies. When we do want change of air, we send for the gardener, and he carries us to another bed. This is dignified, and as it should be. But birds and lizards have no sense of repose, and indeed birds have not even a permanent address. They are mere vagrants like the gipsies, and should be treated in exactly the same manner." So they put their noses in the air, and looked very haughty, and were quite delighted when after some time they saw the little Dwarf scramble up from the grass, and make his way across the terrace to the Palace.

"He should certainly be kept indoors for the rest of his natural life," they said. "Look at his hunched back, and his crooked legs," and they began to titter.

But the little Dwarf knew nothing of all this. He liked the birds and the lizards immensely, and thought that the flowers were the most marvellous things in the whole world, except of course the Infanta, but then she had given him the beautiful white rose, and she loved him, and that made a great difference. How he wished that he had gone back with her! She would have put him on her right hand, and smiled at him, and he would have never left her side, but would have made her his playmate, and taught her all kinds of delightful tricks. For though he had never been in a palace before, he knew a great many wonderful things. He could make little cages out of rushes for the grasshoppers to sing in, and fashion the long-jointed bamboo into the pipe that Pan loves to hear. He knew the cry of every bird, and could call the starlings from the tree-top, or the heron from the mere. He knew the trail of every animal, and could track the hare by its delicate footprints, and the boar by the trampled leaves. All the wild-dances he knew, the mad dance in red raiment with the autumn, the light dance in blue sandals over the corn, the dance with white snow-wreaths in winter, and the blossom-dance, through the orchards in spring. He knew where the wood-pigeons built their nests, and once when a fowler had snared the parent birds, he had brought up the young ones himself, and had built a little dovecot for them in the cleft of a pollard elm. They were quite tame, and used to feed out of his hands every morning. She would like them, and the rabbits that scurried about in the long fern, and the jays with their steely feathers and black bills, and the hedgehogs that could curl themselves up into prickly balls, and the great wise tortoises that crawled slowly about, shaking their heads and nibbling at the young leaves. Yes, she must certainly come to the forest and play with him. He would give her his own little bed, and would watch outside the window till dawn, to see that the wild horned cattle did not harm her, nor the gaunt wolves creep too near the hut. And at dawn he would tap at the shutters and wake her, and they would go out and dance together all the day long. It was really not a bit lonely in the forest. Sometimes a Bishop rode through on his white mule, reading out of a painted book. Sometimes in their green velvet caps, and their jerkins of tanned deerskin, the falconers passed by, with hooded hawks on their wrists. At vintage-time came the grape-treaders, with purple hands and feet, wreathed with glossy ivy and carrying dripping skins of wine; and the charcoal burners sat round their huge braziers at night, watching the dry logs charring slowly in the fire, and roasting chestnuts in the ashes, and the robbers came out of their caves and made merry with them. Once, too, he had seen a beautiful procession winding up the long dusty road to Toledo. The monks went in front singing sweetly, and carrying bright banners and crosses of gold, and then, in silver armour, with matchlocks and pikes, came the soldiers, and in their midst walked three barefooted men, in strange yellow dresses painted all over with wonderful figures, and carrying lighted candles in their hands. Certainly there was a great deal to look at in the forest, and when she was tired he would find a soft bank of moss for her, or carry her in his arms, for he was very strong, though he knew that he was not tall. He would make her a necklace of red bryony berries, that would be quite as pretty as the white berries that she wore on her dress, and when she was tired of them, she could throw them away, and he would find her others. He would bring her acorn-cups and dew-drenched anemones, and tiny glow-worms to be stars in the pale gold of her hair.

But where was she? He asked the white rose, and it made him no answer. The whole palace seemed asleep, and even where the shutters had not been closed, heavy curtains had been drawn across the windows to keep out the glare. He wandered all round looking for some place through which he might gain an entrance, and at last he caught sight of a little private door that was lying open. He slipped through, and found himself in a splendid hall, far more splendid he feared, than the forest, for there was so much more gilding everywhere, and even the floor was made of great coloured stones, fitted together into a sort of geometrical pattern. But the little Infanta was not there, only some wonderful white statues that looked down on him from their jasper pedestals, with sad blank eyes and strangely smiling lips.

At the end of the hall hung a richly embroidered curtain of black velvet, powdered with suns and stars, the King's favourite devices, and broidered on the colour he loved best. Perhaps she was hiding behind that? He would try at any rate.

So he stole quietly across, and drew it aside. No; there was only another room, though a prettier room, he thought, than the one he had just left. The walls were hung with a many-figured green arras of needle-wrought tapestry representing a hunt, the work of some Flemish artists who had spent more than seven years in its composition. It had once been the chamber of *Jean le Fou*,* as he was called, that mad King who was so enamoured of the chase, that he had often tried in his delirium to mount the huge rearing horses, and to drag down the stag on which the great hounds were leaping, sounding his hunting horn, and stabbing with his dagger at the pale flying deer. It was now

* John the Mad (French).

used as the council-room, and on the centre table were lying the red portfolios of the ministers, stamped with the gold tulips of Spain, and with the arms and emblems of the house of Hapsburg.

The little Dwarf looked in wonder all round him, and was half-afraid to go on. The strange silent horsemen that galloped so swiftly through the long glades without making any noise, seemed to him like those terrible phantoms of whom he had heard the charcoal-burners speaking—the Comprachos, who hunt only at night, and if they meet a man, turn him into a hind, and chase him. But he thought of the pretty Infanta, and took courage. He wanted to find her alone, and to tell her that he too loved her. Perhaps she was in the room beyond.

He ran across the soft Moorish carpets, and opened the door. No! She was not here either. The room was quite empty.

It was a throne-room, used for the reception of foreign ambassadors, when the King, which of late had not been often, consented to give them a personal audience; the same room in which, many years before, envoys had appeared from England to make arrangements for the marriage of their Queen, then one of the Catholic sovereigns of Europe, with the Emperor's eldest son. The hangings were of gilt Cordovan leather, and a heavy gilt chandelier with branches for three hundred wax lights hung down from the black and white ceiling. Underneath a great canopy of gold cloth, on which the lions and towers of Castile were broidered in seed pearls, stood the throne itself, covered with a rich pall of black velvet studded with silver tulips and elaborately fringed with silver and pearls. On the second step of the throne was placed the kneeling-stool of the Infanta, with its cushion of cloth of silver tissue, and below that again, and beyond the limit of the canopy, stood the chair for the Papal Nuncio, who alone had the right to be seated in the King's presence on the occasion of any public ceremonial, and whose Cardinal's hat, with its tangled scarlet tassels, lay on a purple *tabouret** in front. On the wall, facing the throne, hung a life-sized portrait of Charles V. in hunting dress, with a great mastiff by his side, and a picture of Philip II. receiving the homage of

---

* Stool (French).

the Netherlands, occupied the centre of the other wall. Between the windows stood a black ebony cabinet, inlaid with plates of ivory, on which the figures from Holbein's Dance of Death had been graved—by the hand, some said, of that famous master himself.

But the little Dwarf cared nothing for all this magnificence. He would not have given his rose for all the pearls on the canopy, nor one white pearl of his rose for the throne itself. What he wanted was to see the Infanta before she went down to the pavilion, and to ask her to come away with him when he had finished his dance. Here, in the Palace, the air was close and heavy, but in the forest the wind blew free, and the sunlight with wandering hands of gold moved the tremulous leaves aside. There were flowers, too, in the forest, not so splendid, perhaps, as the flowers in the garden, but more sweetly scented for all that; hyacinths in early spring that flooded with waving purple the cool glens, and grassy knolls; yellow primroses that nestled in little clumps round the gnarled roots of the oak-trees; bright celandine, and blue speedwell, and irises lilac and gold. There were grey catkins on the hazels, and the foxgloves drooped with the weight of their dappled bee-haunted cells. The chestnut had its spires of white stars, and the hawthorn its pallid moons of beauty. Yes; surely she would come if he could only find her! She would come with him to the fair forest, and all day long he would dance for her delight. A smile lit up his eyes at the thought, and he passed into the next room.

Of all the rooms this was the brightest and the most beautiful. The walls were covered with a pink-flowered Lucca damask, patterned with birds and dotted with dainty blossoms of silver; the furniture was of massive silver, festooned with florid wreaths, and swinging Cupids; in front of the two large fireplaces stood great screens broidered with parrots and peacocks, and the floor, which was of sea-green oynx, seemed to stretch far away into the distance. Nor was he alone. Standing under the shadow of the doorway, at the extreme end of the room, he saw a little figure watching him. His heart trembled, a cry of joy broke from his lips, and he moved out into the sunlight. As he did so, the figure moved out also, and he saw it plainly.

The Infanta! It was a monster, the most grotesque monster he had ever beheld. Not properly shaped as all other people were, but hunchbacked, and crooked-limbed, with huge lolling head and mane of black hair. The little Dwarf frowned, and the monster frowned also. He laughed, and it laughed with him, and held its hands to its sides, just as he himself was doing. He made it a mocking bow, and it returned him a low reverence. He went towards it, and it came to meet him, copying each step that he made, and stopping when he stopped himself. He shouted with amusement, and ran forward, and reached out his hand, and the hand of the monster touched his, and it was as cold as ice. He grew afraid, and moved his hand across, and the monster's hand followed it quickly. He tried to press on, but something smooth and hard stopped him. The face of the monster was now close to his own, and seemed full of terror. He brushed his hair off his eyes. It imitated him. He struck at it, and it returned blow for blow. He loathed it, and it made hideous faces at him. He drew back, and it retreated.

What is it? He thought for a moment, and looked round at the rest of the room. It was strange, but everything seemed to have its double in this invisible wall of clear water. Yes, picture for picture was repeated, and couch for couch. The sleeping Faun that lay in the alcove by the doorway had its twin brother that slumbered, and the silver Venus that stood in the sunlight held out her arms to a Venus as lovely as herself.

Was it Echo? He had called to her once in the valley, and she had answered him word for word. Could she mock the eye, as she mocked the voice? Could she make a mimic world just like the real world? Could the shadows of things have colour and life and movement? Could it be that——?

He started, and taking from his breast the beautiful white rose, he turned round, and kissed it. The monster had a rose of its own, petal for petal the same! It kissed it with like kisses, and pressed it to its heart with horrible gestures.

When the truth dawned upon him, he gave a wild cry of despair, and fell sobbing to the ground. So it was he who was misshapen and hunchbacked, foul to look at and grotesque. He himself was the monster, and it was at him that all the children had been laughing, and the little Princess who he had thought loved him—she, too, had been merely mocking at his ugliness, and making merry over his twisted limbs. Why had they not left him in the forest, where there was no mirror to tell him how loathsome he was? Why had his father not killed him, rather than sell him to his shame? The hot tears poured down his cheeks, and he tore the white rose to pieces. The sprawling monster did the same, and scattered the faint petals in the air. It grovelled on the ground, and, when he looked at it, it watched him with a face drawn with pain. He crept away, lest he should see it, and covered his eyes with his hands. He crawled, like some wounded thing, into the shadow, and lay there moaning.

And at that moment the Infanta herself came in with her companions through the open window, and when they saw the ugly little Dwarf lying on the ground and beating the floor with his clenched hands, in the most fantastic and exaggerated manner, they went off into shouts of happy laughter, and stood all round him and watched him.

"His dancing was funny," said the Infanta; "but his acting is funnier still. Indeed, he is almost as good as the puppets, only, of course, not quite so natural." And she fluttered her big fan and applauded.

But the little Dwarf never looked up, and his sobs grew fainter and fainter, and suddenly he gave a curious gasp, and clutched his side. And then he fell back again, and lay quite still.

"That is capital," said the Infanta, after a pause; "but now you must dance for me."

"Yes," cried all the children, "you must get up and dance, for you are as clever as the Barbary apes, and much more ridiculous."

But the little Dwarf made no answer.

And the Infanta stamped her foot, and called out to her uncle, who was walking on the terrace with the Chamberlain, reading some despatches that had just arrived from Mexico, where the Holy Office had recently been established. "My funny little Dwarf is sulking," she cried, "you must wake him up, and tell him to dance for me."

They smiled at each other, and sauntered in, and Don Pedro stooped down, and slapped the Dwarf on the cheek with his embroidered glove. "You must dance," he said, "*petit monstre*.* You must dance. The Infanta of Spain and the Indies wishes to be amused."

But the little Dwarf never moved.

"A whipping master should be sent for," said Don Pedro wearily, and he went back to the terrace. But the Chamberlain looked grave, and he knelt beside the little Dwarf, and put his hand upon his heart. And after a few moments he shrugged his shoulders, and rose up, and having made a low bow to the Infanta, he said—

"*Mi bella Princesa,*† your funny little Dwarf will never dance again. It is a pity, for he is so ugly that he might have made the King smile."

"But why will he not dance again?" asked the Infanta, laughing.

"Because his heart is broken," answered the Chamberlain.

And the Infanta frowned, and her dainty rose-leaf lips curled in pretty disdain. "For the future let those who come to play with me have no hearts," she cried, and she ran out into the garden.

---

* Little monster (French).

† My beautiful Princess (Italian).

THE FISHERMAN AND HIS SOUL

Every evening the young Fisherman went out upon the sea, and threw his nets into the water.

When the wind blew from the land he caught nothing, or but little at best, for it was a bitter and black-winged wind, and rough waves rose up to meet it. But when the wind blew to the shore, the fish came in from the deep, and swam into the meshes of his nets, and he took them to the market-place and sold them.

Every evening he went out upon the sea, and one evening the net was so heavy that hardly could he draw it into the boat. And he laughed, and said to himself, "Surely I have caught all the fish that swim, or snared some dull monster that will be a marvel to men, or some thing of horror that the great Queen will desire," and putting forth all his strength, he tugged at the coarse ropes till, like lines of blue enamel round a vase of bronze, the long veins rose up on his arms. He tugged at the thin ropes, and nearer and nearer came the circle of flat corks, and the net rose at last to the top of the water.

But no fish at all was in it, nor any monster or thing of horror, but only a little Mermaid lying fast asleep.

Her hair was as a wet fleece of gold, and each separate hair as a thread of fine gold in a cup of glass. Her body was as white ivory, and her tail was of silver and pearl. Silver and pearl was her tail, and the green weeds of the sea coiled round it; and like sea-shells were her ears, and her lips were like sea-coral. The cold waves dashed over her cold breasts, and the salt glistened upon her eyelids.

So beautiful was she that when the young Fisherman saw her he was filled with wonder, and he put out his hand and drew the net close to him, and leaning over the side he clasped her in his arms. And when he touched her, she gave a cry like a startled sea-gull, and woke, and looked at him in terror with her mauve-amethyst eyes, and struggled that she might escape. But he held her tightly to him, and would not suffer her to depart.

And when she saw that she could in no way escape from him, she began to weep, and said, "I pray thee let me go, for I am the only daughter of a King, and my father is aged and alone."

But the young Fisherman answered, "I will not let thee go save thou makest me a promise that whenever I call thee, thou wilt come and sing to me, for the fish delight to listen to the song of the Sea-folk and so shall my nets be full."

"Wilt thou in very truth let me go, if I promise thee this?" cried the Mermaid.

"In very truth I will let thee go," said the young Fisherman.

So she made him the promise he desired, and sware it by the oath of the Sea-folk. And he loosened his arms from about her, and she sank down into the water, trembling with a strange fear.

Every evening the young Fisherman went out upon the sea, and called to the Mermaid, and she rose out of the water and sang to him. Round and round her swam the dolphins, and the wild gulls wheeled above her head.

And she sang a marvellous song. For she sang of the Sea-folk who drive their flocks from cave to cave, and carry the little calves on their shoulders; of the Tritons who have long green beards, and hairy breasts, and blow through twisted conchs when the King passes by; of the palace of the King which is all of amber, with a roof of clear emerald, and a pavement of bright pearl; and of the gardens of the sea where the great filigrane fans of coral wave all day long, and the fish dart about like silver birds, and the anemones cling to the rocks, and the pinks bourgeon in the ribbed yellow sand. She sang of the big whales that come down from the north seas and have sharp icicles hanging to their fins; of the Sirens who tell of such wonderful things that the merchants have to stop their ears with wax lest they should hear them, and leap into the water and be drowned; of the sunken galleys with their tall masts, and the frozen sailors clinging to the rigging, and the mackerel swimming in and out of the open portholes; of the little barnacles who are great travellers, and cling to the keels of the ships and go round and round the world; and of the cuttlefish who live in the sides of the cliffs and stretch out their long black arms, and can make night come when they will it. She sang of the nautilus who has a boat of her own that is carved out of an opal and steered with a silken sail; of the happy Mermen who play upon harps and can charm the great Kraken* to sleep; of the little children who catch hold of the slippery porpoises and ride laughing upon their backs; of the Mermaids who lie in the white foam and hold out their arms to the mariners; and of the sea-lions with their curved tusks, and the sea-horses with their floating manes.

And as she sang, all the tunny-fish came in from the deep to listen to her, and the young Fisherman threw his nets round them and caught them, and others he took with a spear. And when his boat was well-laden, the Mermaid would sink down into the sea, smiling at him.

Yet would she never come near him that he might touch her. Oftentimes he called to her and prayed of her, but she would not; and when he sought to seize her she dived into the water as a seal might dive, nor did he see her again that day. And each day the sound of her voice became sweeter to his ears. So sweet was her voice that he forgot his nets and his cunning, and had no care of his craft. Vermilion-finned and with eyes of bossy gold, the tunnies went by in shoals, but he heeded them not. His spear lay by his side unused, and his baskets of plaited osier were empty. With lips parted, and eyes dim with wonder, he sat idle in his boat and listened, listening till the sea-mists crept round him and the wandering moon stained his brown limbs with silver.

And one evening he called to her, and said: "Little Mermaid, little Mermaid, I love thee. Take me for thy bridegroom for I love thee."

But the Mermaid shook her head. "Thou hast a human Soul," she answered. "If only thou wouldst send away thy Soul, then could I love thee."

And the young Fisherman said to himself, "Of what use is my soul

---

* Huge legendary sea monsters with many tentacles, said to live off the coasts of Iceland and Norway.

to me? I cannot see it. I may not touch it. I do not know it. Surely I will send it away from me, and much gladness shall be mine." And a cry of joy broke from his lips, and standing up in the painted boat, he held out his arms to the Mermaid. "I will send my Soul away," he cried, "and you shall be my bride, and I will be thy bridegroom, and in the depth of the sea we will dwell together, and all that thou hast sung of thou shalt show me, and all that thou desirest I will do, nor shall our lives be divided."

And the little Mermaid laughed for pleasure and hid her face in her hands.

"But how shall I send my Soul from me?" cried the young Fisherman. "Tell me how I may do it, and lo! it shall be done."

"Alas! I know not," said the little Mermaid: "the Sea-folk have no souls." And she sank down into the deep, looking wistfully at him.

Now early on the next morning, before the sun was the span of a man's hand above the hill, the young Fisherman went to the house of the Priest and knocked three times at the door.

The novice looked out through the wicket, and when he saw who it was, he drew back the latch and said to him, "Enter."

And the young Fisherman passed in, and knelt down on the sweet-smelling rushes on the floor, and cried to the Priest who was reading out of the Holy Book and said to him, "Father, I am in love with one of the Sea-folk, and my Soul hindereth me from having my desire. Tell me how I can send my Soul away from me, for in truth I have no need of it. Of what value is my soul to me? I cannot see it. I may not touch it. I do not know it."

And the Priest beat his breast, and answered, "Alack, alack, thou art mad, or hast eaten of some poisonous herb, for the Soul is the noblest part of man, and was given to us by God that we should nobly use it. There is no thing more precious than a human soul, nor any earthly thing that can be weighed with it. It is worth all the gold that is in the world, and is more precious than the rubies of the kings. Therefore, my son, think not any more of this matter, for it is a sin that may not be forgiven. And as for the Sea-folk, they are lost, and they who would traffic with them are lost also. They are the beasts of the field that know not good from evil, and for them the Lord has not died."

The young Fisherman's eyes filled with tears when he heard the bitter words of the Priest, and he rose up from his knees and said to him, "Father, the Fauns live in the forest and are glad, and on the rocks sit the Mermen with their harps of red gold. Let me be as they are, I beseech thee, for their days are as the days of flowers. And as for my Soul, what doth my Soul profit me, if it stand between me and the thing that I love?"

"The love of the body is vile," cried the Priest, knitting his brows, "and vile and evil are the pagan things God suffers to wander through His world. Accursed be the Fauns of the woodland, and accursed be the singers of the sea! I have heard them at night-time, and they have sought to lure me from my beads. They tap at the window and laugh. They whisper into my ears the tale of their perilous joys. They tempt me with temptations, and when I would pray they make mouths at me. They are lost, I tell thee, they are lost. For them there is no heaven nor hell, and in neither shall they praise God's name."

"Father," cried the young Fisherman, "thou knowest not what thou sayest. Once in my net I snared the daughter of a King. She is fairer than the morning star, and whiter than the moon. For her body I would give my soul, and for her love I would surrender heaven. Tell me what I ask of thee, and let me go in peace."

"Away! Away!" cried the Priest: "thy leman is lost, and thou shalt be lost with her." And he gave him no blessing, but drove him from his door.

And the young Fisherman went down into the market-place, and he walked slowly, and with bowed head, as one who is in sorrow.

And when the merchants saw him coming, they began to whisper to each other, and one of them came forth to meet him, and called him by name, and said to him, "What hast thou to sell?"

"I will sell thee my Soul," he answered: "I pray thee buy it off me, for I am weary of it. Of what use is my Soul to me? I cannot see it. I may not touch it. I do not know it."

But the merchants mocked at him, and said, "Of what use is a man's soul to us? It is not worth a clipped piece of silver. Sell us thy body for a slave, and we will clothe thee in sea purple, and put a ring upon thy finger, and make thee the minion of the great Queen. But talk not of the Soul, for to us it is nought, nor has it any value for our service."

And the young Fisherman said to himself: "How strange a thing this is! The Priest telleth me that the Soul is worth all the gold in the world, and the merchants say that it is not worth a clipped piece of silver." And he passed out of the market-place, and went down to the shore of the sea, and began to ponder on what he should do.

And at noon he remembered how one of his companions, who was a gatherer of samphire, had told him of a certain young Witch who dwelt in a cave at the head of the bay and was very cunning in her witcheries. And he set to and ran, so eager was he to get rid of his soul, and a cloud of dust followed him as he sped round the sand of the shore. By the itching of her palm the young Witch knew his coming, and she laughed and let down her red hair. With her red hair falling around her, she stood at the opening of the cave, and in her hand she had a spray of wild hemlock that was blossoming.

"What d'ye lack? What d'ye lack?" she cried, as he came panting up the steep, and bent down before her. "Fish for thy net, when the wind is foul? I have a little reed-pipe, and when I blow on it the mullet come sailing into the bay. But it has a price, pretty boy, it has a price. What d'ye lack? What d'ye lack? A storm to wreck the ships, and wash the chests of rich treasure ashore? I have more storms than the wind has, for I serve one who is stronger than the wind, and with a sieve and a pail of water I can send the great galleys to the bottom of the sea. But I have a price, pretty boy, I have a price. What d'ye lack? What d'ye lack? I know a flower that grows in the valley, none knows it but I. It has purple leaves, and a star in its heart, and its juice is as white as milk. Shouldst thou touch with this flower the hard lips of the Queen, she would follow thee all over the world. Out of the bed of the King she would rise, and over the whole world she would follow thee. And it has a price, pretty boy, it has a price. What d'ye lack? What d'ye lack? I can pound a toad in a mortar, and make broth of it, and stir the broth with a dead man's hand. Sprinkle it on thine enemy while he sleeps, and he will turn into a black viper, and his own mother will slay him. With a wheel I can draw the Moon from heaven, and in a crystal I can show thee Death. What d'ye lack? What d'ye lack? Tell me thy desire, and I will give it thee, and thou shalt pay me a price, pretty boy, thou shalt pay me a price."

"My desire is but for a little thing," said the young Fisherman, "yet hath the Priest been wroth with me, and driven me forth. It is but for a little thing, and the merchants have mocked at me, and denied me. Therefore am I come to thee, though men call thee evil, and whatever be thy price I shall pay it."

"What wouldst thou?" asked the Witch, coming near to him.

"I would send my Soul away from me," answered the young Fisherman.

The Witch grew pale, and shuddered, and hid her face in her blue mantle. "Pretty boy, pretty boy," she muttered, "that is a terrible thing to do."

He tossed his brown curls and laughed. "My Soul is nought to me," he answered. "I cannot see it. I may not touch it. I do not know it."

"What wilt thou give me if I tell thee?" asked the Witch, looking down at him with her beautiful eyes.

"Five pieces of gold," he said, "and my nets, and the wattled house where I live, and the painted boat in which I sail. Only tell me how to get rid of my Soul, and I will give thee all that I possess."

She laughed mockingly at him, and struck him with the spray of hemlock. "I can turn the autumn leaves into gold," she answered, "and I can weave the pale moonbeams into silver if I will it. He whom I serve is richer than all the kings of this world, and has their dominions."

"What then shall I give thee," he cried, "if thy price be neither gold nor silver?"

The Witch stroked his hair with her thin white hand. "Thou must dance with me, pretty boy," she murmured, and she smiled at him as she spoke.

"Nought but that?" cried the young Fisherman in wonder, and he rose to his feet.

"Nought but that," she answered, and she smiled at him again.

"Then at sunset in some secret place we shall dance together," he said, "and after that we have danced thou shalt tell me the thing which I desire to know."

She shook her head. "When the moon is full, when the moon is full," she muttered. Then she peered all round, and listened. A blue bird rose screaming from its nest and circled over the dunes, and three spotted birds rustled through the coarse grey grass and whistled to each other. There was no other sound save the sound of a wave fretting the smooth pebbles below. So she reached out her hand, and drew him near to her and put her dry lips close to his ear.

"To-night thou must come to the top of the mountain," she whispered. "It is a Sabbath, and He will be there."

The young Fisherman started and looked at her, and she showed her white teeth and laughed. "Who is He of whom thou speakest?" he asked.

"It matters not," she answered. "Go thou to-night, and stand under the branches of the hornbeam, and wait for my coming. If a black dog run towards thee, strike it with a rod of willow, and it will go away. If an owl speak to thee, make it no answer. When the moon is full I shall be with thee, and we will dance together on the grass."

"But wilt thou swear to me to tell me how I may send my Soul from me?" he made question.

She moved out into the sunlight, and through her red hair rippled the wind. "By the hoofs of the goat I swear it," she made answer.

"Thou art the best of the witches," cried the young Fisherman, "and I will surely dance with thee to-night on the top of the mountain. I would indeed that thou hadst asked of me either gold or silver. But such as thy price is thou shalt have it, for it is but a little thing." And he doffed his cap to her, and bent his head low, and ran back to the town filled with a great joy.

And the Witch watched him as he went, and when he had passed from her sight she entered her cave, and having taken a mirror from a box of carved cedarwood, she set it up on a frame, and burned vervain on lighted charcoal before it, and peered through the coils of the smoke. And after a time she clenched her hands in anger. "He should have been mine," she muttered, "I am as fair as she is."

And that evening, when the moon had risen, the young Fisherman climbed up to the top of the mountain, and stood under the branches of the hornbeam. Like a targe of polished metal the round sea lay at his feet, and the shadows of the fishing-boats moved in the little bay. A great owl, with yellow sulphurous eyes, called to him by his name, but he made it no answer. A black dog ran towards him and snarled. He struck it with a rod of willow, and it went away whining.

At midnight the witches came flying through the air like bats. "Phew!" they cried, as they lit upon the ground, "there is some one here we know not!" and they sniffed about, and chattered to each other, and made signs. Last of all came the young Witch, with her red hair streaming in the wind. She wore a dress of gold tissue embroidered with peacocks' eyes, and a little cap of green velvet was on her head.

"Where is he, where is he?" shrieked the witches when they saw her, but she only laughed, and ran to the hornbeam, and taking the Fisherman by the hand she led him out into the moonlight and began to dance.

Round and round they whirled, and the young Witch jumped so high that he could see the scarlet heels of her shoes. Then right across the dancers came the sound of the galloping of a horse, but no horse was to be seen, and he felt afraid.

"Faster," cried the Witch, and she threw her arms about his neck, and her breath was hot upon his face. "Faster, faster!" she cried, and the earth seemed to spin beneath his feet, and his brain grew troubled, and a great terror fell on him, as of some evil thing that was watching him, and at last he became aware that under the shadow of a rock there was a figure that had not been there before.

It was a man dressed in a suit of black velvet, cut in the Spanish fashion. His face was strangely pale, but his lips were like a proud red flower. He seemed weary, and was leaning back toying in a listless manner with the pommel of his dagger. On the grass beside him lay a plumed hat, and a pair of riding-gloves gauntleted with gilt lace, and sewn with seed-pearls wrought into a curious device. A short cloak lined with sables hung from his shoulder, and his delicate white hands were gemmed with rings. Heavy eyelids drooped over his eyes.

The young Fisherman watched him, as one snared in a spell. At last their eyes met, and wherever he danced it seemed to him that the eyes of the man were upon him. He heard the Witch laugh, and caught her by the waist, and whirled her madly round and round.

Suddenly a dog bayed in the wood, and the dancers stopped, and going up two by two, knelt down, and kissed the man's hands. As they did so, a little smile touched his proud lips, as a bird's wing touches the water and makes it laugh. But there was disdain in it. He kept looking at the young Fisherman.

"Come! let us worship," whispered the Witch, and she led him up, and a great desire to do as she besought him seized on him, and he followed her. But when he came close, and without knowing why he did it, he made on his breast the sign of the Cross, and called upon the holy name.

No sooner had he done so than the witches screamed like hawks and flew away, and the pallid face that had been watching him twitched with a spasm of pain. The man went over to a little wood, and whistled. A jennet with silver trappings came running to meet him. As he leapt upon the saddle he turned round, and looked at the young Fisherman sadly.

And the Witch with the red hair tried to fly away also, but the Fisherman caught her by her wrists, and held her fast.

"Loose me," she cried, "and let me go. For thou hast named what should not be named, and shown the sign that may not be looked at."

"Nay," he answered, "but I will not let thee go till thou hast told me the secret."

"What secret?" said the Witch, wrestling with him like a wild cat, and biting her foam-flecked lips.

"Thou knowest," he made answer.

Her grass-green eyes grew dim with tears, and she said to the Fisherman, "Ask me anything but that!"

He laughed, and held her all the more tightly.

And when she saw that she could not free herself, she whispered to him, "Surely I am as fair as the daughter of the sea, and as comely as those that dwell in the blue waters," and she fawned on him and put her face close to his.

But he thrust her back frowning, and said to her, "If thou keepest not the promise that thou madest to me I will slay thee for a false witch."

She grew grey as a blossom of the Judas tree, and shuddered. "Be it so," she muttered. "It is thy Soul and not mine. Do with it as thou wilt." And she took from her girdle a little knife that had a handle of green viper's skin, and gave it to him.

"What shall this serve me?" he asked of her, wondering.

She was silent for a few moments, and a look of terror came over her face. Then she brushed her hair back from her forehead, and smiling strangely she said to him, "What men call the shadow of the body is not the shadow of the body, but is the body of the Soul. Stand on the sea-shore with thy back to the moon, and cut away from around thy feet thy shadow, which is thy Soul's body, and bid thy soul leave thee, and it will do so."

The young Fisherman trembled. "Is this true?" he murmured.

"It is true, and I would that I had not told thee of it," she cried, and she clung to his knees weeping.

He put her from him and left her in the rank grass, and going to the edge of the mountain he placed the knife in his belt and began to climb down.

And his Soul that was within him called out to him and said, "Lo! I have dwelt with thee for all these years, and have been thy servant. Send me not away from thee now, for what evil have I done thee?"

And the young Fisherman laughed. "Thou hast done me no evil, but I have no need of thee," he answered. "The world is wide, and there is Heaven also, and Hell, and that dim twilight house that lies between. Go wherever thou wilt, but trouble me not, for my love is calling to me."

And his Soul besought him piteously, but he heeded it not, but leapt from crag to crag, being surefooted as a wild goat, and at last he reached the level ground and the yellow shore of the sea.

Bronze-limbed and well-knit, like a statue wrought by a Grecian, he stood on the sand with his back to the moon, and out of the foam came white arms that beckoned to him, and out of the waves rose dim forms that did him homage. Before him lay his shadow, which was the body of his Soul, and behind him hung the moon in the honey-coloured air.

And his Soul said to him, "If indeed thou must drive me from thee, send me not forth without a heart. The world is cruel, give me thy heart to take with me."

He tossed his head and smiled. "With what should I love my love if I gave thee my heart?" he cried.

"Nay, but be merciful," said his Soul: "give me thy heart, for the world is very cruel, and I am afraid."

"My heart is my love's," he answered, "therefore tarry not, but get thee gone."

"Should I not love also?" asked his Soul.

"Get thee gone, for I have no need of thee," cried the young Fisherman, and he took the little knife with its handle of green viper's skin, and cut away his shadow from around his feet, and it rose up and stood before him, and looked at him, and it was even as himself.

He crept back, and thrust the knife into his belt, and a feeling of awe came over him. "Get thee gone," he murmured, "and let me see thy face no more."

"Nay, but we must meet again," said the Soul. Its voice was low and flute-like, and its lips hardly moved while it spake.

"How shall me meet?" cried the young Fisherman. "Thou wilt not follow me into the depths of the sea?"

"Once every year I will come to this place, and call to thee," said the Soul. "It may be that thou wilt have need of me."

"What need should I have of thee?" cried the young Fisherman, "but be it as thou wilt," and he plunged into the water, and the Tritons blew their horns, and the little Mermaid rose up to meet him, and put her arms around his neck and kissed him on the mouth.

And the Soul stood on the lonely beach and watched them. And when they had sunk down into the sea, it went weeping away over the marshes.

And after a year was over the Soul came down to the shore of the sea and called to the young Fisherman, and he rose out of the deep, and said, "Why dost thou call to me?"

And the Soul answered, "Come nearer, that I may speak with thee, for I have seen marvellous things."

So he came nearer, and couched in the shallow water, and leaned his head upon his hand and listened.

And the Soul said to him, "When I left thee I turned my face to the East and journeyed. From the East cometh everything that is wise. Six days I journeyed, and on the morning of the seventh day I came to a hill that is in the country of the Tartars. I sat down under the shade of a tamarisk tree to shelter myself from the sun. The land was dry and burnt up with the heat. The people went to and fro over the plain like flies crawling upon a disk of polished copper.

"When it was noon a cloud of red dust rose up from the flat rim of the land. When the Tartars saw it, they strung their painted bows, and having leapt upon their little horses they galloped to meet it. The women fled screaming to the waggons, and hid themselves behind the felt curtains.

"At twilight the Tartars returned, but five of them were missing, and of those that came back not a few had been wounded. They harnessed their horses to the waggons and drove hastily away. Three jackals came out of a cave and peered after them. Then they sniffed up the air with their nostrils, and trotted off in the opposite direction.

"When the moon rose I saw a camp-fire burning on the plain, and went towards it. A company of merchants were seated round it on carpets. Their camels were picketed behind them, and the negroes who were their servants were pitching tents of tanned skin upon the sand, and making a high wall of the prickly pear.

"As I came near them, the chief of the merchants rose up and drew his sword and asked me my business.

"I answered that I was a Prince in my own land, and that I had escaped from the Tartars, who had sought to make me their slave. The chief smiled, and showed me five heads fixed upon long reeds of bamboo.

"Then he asked me who was the prophet of God, and I answered him Mohammed.

"When he heard the name of the false prophet, he bowed and took me by the hand, and placed me by his side. A negro brought me some mare's milk in a wooden dish, and a piece of lamb's flesh roasted.

"At daybreak we started on our journey. I rode on a red-haired camel by the side of the chief, and a runner ran before us carrying a spear. The men of war were on either hand, and the mules followed with the merchandise. There were forty camels in the caravan, and the mules were twice forty in number.

"We went from the country of the Tartars into the country of those who curse the Moon. We saw the Gryphons* guarding their gold on the white rocks, and the scaled Dragons sleeping in their caves. As we passed over the mountains we held our breath lest the snows might fall on us, and each man tied a veil of gauze before his eyes. As we passed through the valleys the Pygmies shot arrows at us from the hollows of the trees, and at night-time we heard the wild men beating on their drums. When we came to the Tower of Apes we set fruits before them, and they did not harm us. When we came to the Tower of Serpents we gave them warm milk in bowls of brass, and they let us go by. Three times in our journey we came to the banks of the Oxus. We crossed it on rafts of wood with great bladders of blown hide. The river-horses raged against us and sought to slay us. When the camels saw them they trembled.

"The kings of each city levied tolls on us, but would not suffer us to enter their gates. They threw us bread over the walls, little maize-cakes baked in honey and cakes of fine flour filled with dates. For every hundred baskets we gave them a bead of amber.

"When the dwellers in the villages saw us coming, they poisoned the wells and fled to the hill-summits. We fought with the Magadae who are born old, and grow younger and younger every year, and die when they are little children; and with the Laktroi who say that they are the sons of tigers, and paint themselves yellow and black; and with the Aurantes who bury their dead on the tops of trees, and themselves live in dark caverns lest the Sun, who is their god, should slay them; and with the Krimnians who worship a crocodile, and give it ear-rings of green grass, and feed it with butter and fresh fowls; and with the Agazonbae, who are dog-faced; and with the Sibans, who have horses' feet, and run more swiftly than horses. A third of

---

* A gryphon (more commonly spelled griffin) is a powerful mythological monster with the body of a lion and the head and wings of an eagle. In the following pages, Wilde names various exotic figures and places to create an atmosphere of magic.

our company died in battle, and a third died of want. The rest murmured against me, and said that I had brought them an evil fortune. I took a horned adder from beneath a stone and let it sting me. When they saw that I did not sicken they grew afraid.

"In the fourth month we reached the city of Illel. It was nighttime when we came to the grove that is outside the walls, and the air was sultry, for the Moon was travelling in Scorpion. We took the ripe pomegranates from the trees, and brake them, and drank their sweet juices. Then we lay down on our carpets and waited for the dawn.

"And at dawn we rose and knocked at the gate of the city. It was wrought out of red bronze, and carved with sea-dragons and dragons that have wings. The guards looked down from the battlements and asked us our business. The interpreter of the caravan answered that we had come from the island of Syria with much merchandise. They took hostages, and told us that they would open the gate to us at noon, and bade us tarry till then.

"When it was noon they opened the gate, and as we entered in the people came crowding out of the houses to look at us, and a crier went round the city crying through a shell. We stood in the market-place, and the negroes uncorded the bales of figured cloths and opened the carved chests of sycamore. And when they had ended their task, the merchants set forth their strange wares, the waxed linen from Egypt, and the painted linen from the country of the Ethiops, the purple sponges from Tyre and the blue hangings from Sidon, the cups of cold amber and the fine vessels of glass and the curious vessels of burnt clay. From the roof of a house a company of women watched us. One of them wore a mask of gilded leather.

"And on the first day the priests came and bartered with us, and on the second day came the nobles, and on the third day came the craftsmen and the slaves. And this is their custom with all merchants as long as they tarry in the city.

"And we tarried for a moon, and when the moon was waning, I wearied and wandered away through the streets of the city and came to the garden of its god. The priests in their yellow robes moved silently through the green trees, and on a pavement of black marble stood the rose-red house in which the god had his dwelling. Its doors were of powdered lacquer, and bulls and peacocks were wrought on them in raised and polished gold. The tilted roof was of sea-green porcelain and the jutting eaves were festooned with little bells. When the white doves flew past, they struck the bells with their wings and made them tinkle.

"In front of the temple was a pool of clear water paved with veined onyx. I lay down beside it, and with my pale fingers I touched the broad leaves. One of the priests came towards me and stood behind me. He had sandals on his feet, one of soft serpent-skin and the other of birds' plumage. On his head was a mitre of black felt decorated with silver crescents. Seven yellows were woven into his robe, and his frizzed hair was stained with antimony.

"And after a little while he spake to me, and asked me my desire.

"I told him that my desire was to see the god.

" 'The god is hunting,' said the priest, looking strangely at me with his small slanting eyes.

" 'Tell me in what forest, and I will ride with him,' I answered.

"He combed out the soft fringes of his tunic with his long pointed nails. 'The god is asleep,' he murmured.

" 'Tell me on what couch, and I will watch by him,' I answered.

" 'The god is at the feast,' he cried.

" 'If the wine be sweet, I will drink it with him, and if it be bitter I will drink it with him also,' was my answer.

"He bowed his head in wonder, and, taking me by the hand, he raised me up, and led me into the temple.

"And in the first chamber I saw an idol seated on a throne of jasper bordered with great orient pearls. It was carved out of ebony, and in stature was of the stature of a man. On its forehead was a ruby, and thick oil dripped from its hair on to its thighs. Its feet were red with the blood of a newly-slain kid, and its loins girt with a copper belt that was studded with seven beryls.

"And I said to the priest, 'Is this the god?' And he answered me, 'This is the god.'

" 'Show me the god,' I cried, 'or I will surely slay thee.' And I touched his hand, and it became withered.

"And the priest besought me, saying, 'Let my lord heal his servant, and I will show him the god.'

"So I breathed with my breath upon his hand, and it became whole again, and he trembled and led me into the second chamber, and I saw an idol standing on a lotus of jade hung with great emeralds. It was carved out of ivory, and in stature was twice the stature of a man. On its forehead was a chrysolite, and its breasts were smeared with myrrh and cinnamon. In one hand it held a crooked sceptre of jade, and in the other a round crystal. It wore buskins of brass, and its thick neck was circled with a circle of selenites.

"And I said to the priest, 'Is this the god?' And he answered me, 'This is the god.'

" 'Show me the god,' I cried, 'or I will surely slay thee.' And I touched his eyes, and they became blind.

"And the priest besought me, saying, 'Let my lord heal his servant, and I will show him the god.'

"So I breathed with my breath upon his eyes, and the sight came back to them, and he trembled again, and led me into the third chamber, and lo! there was no idol in it, nor image of any kind, but only a mirror of round metal set on an altar of stone.

"And I said to the priest, 'Where is the god?'

"And he answered me: 'There is no god but this mirror that thou seest, for this is the Mirror of Wisdom. And it reflecteth all things that are in heaven and on earth, save only the face of him who looketh into it. This it reflecteth not, so that he who looketh into it may be wise. Many other mirrors are there, but they are mirrors of Opinion. This only is the Mirror of Wisdom. And they who possess this mirror know everything, nor is there anything hidden from them. And they who possess it not have not Wisdom. Therefore is it the god, and we worship it.' And I looked into the mirror, and it was even as he had said to me.

"And I did a strange thing, but what I did matters not, for in a valley that is but a day's journey from this place have I hidden the Mirror of Wisdom. Do but suffer me to enter into thee again and be thy servant, and thou shalt be wiser than all the wise men, and Wisdom shall be thine. Suffer me to enter into thee, and none will be as wise as thou."

But the young Fisherman laughed. "Love is better than Wisdom," he cried, "and the little Mermaid loves me."

"Nay, but there is nothing better than Wisdom," said the Soul.

"Love is better," answered the young Fisherman, and he plunged into the deep, and the Soul went weeping away over the marshes.

And after the second year was over, the Soul came down to the shore of the sea, and called to the young Fisherman and he rose out of the deep and said, "Why dost thou call to me?"

And the Soul answered, "Come nearer, that I may speak with thee, for I have seen marvellous things."

So he came nearer, and couched in the shallow water, and leaned his head upon his hand and listened.

And the Soul said to him, "When I left thee, I turned my face to the South and journeyed. From the South cometh everything that is precious. Six days I journeyed along the highways that lead to the city of Ashter, along the dusty red-dyed highways by which the pilgrims are wont to go did I journey, and on the morning of the seventh day I lifted up my eyes, and lo! the city lay at my feet, for it is in a valley.

"There are nine gates to this city, and in front of each gate stands a bronze horse that neighs when the Bedouins come down from the mountains. The walls are cased with copper, and the watch-towers on the wall are roofed with brass. In every tower stands an archer with a bow in his hand. At sunrise he strikes with an arrow on a gong, and at sunset he blows through a horn of horn.

"When I sought to enter, the guards stopped me and asked of me who I was. I made answer that I was a Dervish and on my way to the city of Mecca, where there was a green veil on which the Koran was embroidered in silver letters by the hands of the angels. They were filled with wonder, and entreated me to pass in.

"Inside it is even as a bazaar. Surely thou shouldst have been with me. Across the narrow streets the gay lanterns of paper flutter like large butterflies. When the wind blows over the roofs they rise and fall as painted bubbles do. In front of their booths sit the merchants on silken carpets. They have straight black beards, and their turbans are covered with golden sequins, and long strings of amber and carved peach-stones glide through their cool fingers. Some of them sell galbanum and nard, and curious perfumes from the islands of the

Indian Sea, and the thick oil of red roses, and myrrh and little nail-shaped cloves. When one stops to speak to them, they throw pinches of frankincense upon a charcoal brazier and make the air sweet. I saw a Syrian who held in his hands a thin rod like a reed. Grey threads of smoke came from it, and its odour as it burned was as the odour of the pink almond in spring. Others sell silver bracelets embossed all over with creamy blue turquoise stones, and anklets of brass wire fringed with little pearls, and tigers' claws set in gold, and the claws of that gilt cat, the leopard, set in gold also, and ear-rings of pierced emerald, and finger-rings of hollowed jade. From the tea-houses comes the sound of the guitar, and the opium-smokers with their white smiling faces look out at the passers-by.

"Of a truth thou shouldst have been with me. The wine-sellers elbow their way through the crowd with great black skins on their shoulders. Most of them sell the wine of Schiraz, which is as sweet as honey. They serve it in little metal cups and strew rose leaves upon it. In the market-place stand the fruitsellers, who sell all kinds of fruit: ripe figs, with their bruised purple flesh, melons, smelling of musk and yellow as topazes, citrons and rose-apples and clusters of white grapes, round red-gold oranges, and oval lemons of green gold. Once I saw an elephant go by. Its trunk was painted with vermilion and turmeric, and over its ears it had a net of crimson silk cord. It stopped opposite one of the booths and began eating the oranges, and the man only laughed. Thou canst not think how strange a people they are. When they are glad they go to the bird-sellers and buy of them a caged bird, and set it free that their joy may be greater, and when they are sad they scourge themselves with thorns that their sorrow may not grow less.

"One evening I met some negroes carrying a heavy palanquin through the bazaar. It was made of gilded bamboo, and the poles were of vermilion lacquer studded with brass peacocks. Across the windows hung thin curtains of muslin embroidered with beetles' wings and with tiny seed-pearls, and as it passed by a pale-faced Circassian looked out and smiled at me. I followed behind, and the negroes hurried their steps and scowled. But I did not care. I felt a great curiosity come over me.

"At last they stopped at a square white house. There were no windows to it, only a little door like the door of a tomb. They set down the palanquin and knocked three times with a copper hammer. An Armenian in a caftan of green leather peered through the wicket, and when he saw them he opened, and spread a carpet on the ground, and the woman stepped out. As she went in, she turned round and smiled at me again. I had never seen any one so pale.

"When the moon rose I returned to the same place and sought for the house, but it was no longer there. When I saw that, I knew who the woman was, and wherefore she had smiled at me.

"Certainly thou shouldst have been with me. On the feast of the New Moon the young Emperor came forth from his palace and went into the mosque to pray. His hair and beard were dyed with rose-leaves, and his cheeks were powdered with a fine gold dust. The palms of his feet and hands were yellow with saffron.

"At sunrise he went forth from his palace in a robe of silver, and at sunset he returned to it again in a robe of gold. The people flung themselves on the ground and hid their faces, but I would not do so. I stood by the stall of a seller of dates and waited. When the Emperor saw me, he raised his painted eyebrows and stopped. I stood quite still, and made him no obeisance. The people marvelled at my boldness, and counselled me to flee from the city. I paid no heed to them, but went and sat with the sellers of strange gods, who by reason of their craft are abominated. When I told them what I had done, each of them gave me a god and prayed me to leave them.

"That night, as I lay on a cushion in the tea-house that is in the Street of Pomegranates, the guards of the Emperor entered and led me to the palace. As I went in they closed each door behind me, and put a chain across it. Inside was a great court with an arcade running all round. The walls were of white alabaster, set here and there with blue and green tiles. The pillars were of green marble, and the pavement of a kind of peach-blossom marble. I had never seen anything like it before.

"As I passed across the court two veiled women looked down from a balcony and cursed me. The guards hastened on, and the butts of the lances rang upon the polished floor. They opened a gate of wrought ivory, and I found myself in a watered garden of seven terraces. It was planted with tulip-cups and moon-flowers, and silver-studded aloes. Like a slim reed of crystal a fountain hung in the dusky air. The cypress-trees were like burnt-out torches. From one of them a nightingale was singing.

"At the end of the garden stood a little pavilion. As we approached it two eunuchs came out to meet us. Their fat bodies swayed as they walked, and they glanced curiously at me with their yellow-lidded eyes. One of them drew aside the captain of the guard, and in a low voice whispered to him. The other kept munching scented pastilles, which he took with an affected gesture out of an oval box of lilac enamel.

"After a few moments the captain of the guard dismissed the soldiers. They went back to the palace, the eunuchs following slowly behind and plucking the sweet mulberries from the trees as they passed. Once the elder of the two turned round, and smiled at me with an evil smile.

"Then the captain of the guard motioned me towards the entrance of the pavilion. I walked on without trembling, and drawing the heavy curtain aside I entered in.

"The young Emperor was stretched on a couch of dyed lion skins, and a ger-falcon perched upon his wrist. Behind him stood a brass-turbaned Nubian, naked down to the waist, and with heavy ear-rings in his split ears. On a table by the side of the couch lay a mighty scimitar of steel.

"When the Emperor saw me he frowned, and said to me, 'What is thy name? Knowest thou not that I am Emperor of this city?' But I made him no answer.

"He pointed with his finger at the scimitar, and the Nubian seized it, and rushing forward struck at me with great violence. The blade whizzed through me, and did me no hurt. The man fell sprawling on the floor, and when he rose up his teeth chattered with terror and he hid himself behind the couch.

"The Emperor leapt to his feet, and taking a lance from a stand of arms, he threw it at me. I caught it in its flight, and brake the shaft into two pieces. He shot at me with an arrow, but I held up my hands and it stopped in mid-air. Then he drew a dagger from a belt of white leather, and stabbed the Nubian in the throat lest the slave should tell of his dishonour. The man writhed like a trampled snake, and a red foam bubbled from his lips.

"As soon as he was dead the Emperor turned to me, and when he had wiped away the bright sweat from his brow with a little napkin of purfled and purple silk, he said to me, 'Art thou a prophet, that I may not harm thee, or the son of a prophet, that I can do thee no hurt? I pray thee leave my city to-night, for while thou art in it I am no longer its lord.'

"And I answered him, 'I will go for half of thy treasure. Give me half of thy treasure, and I will go away.'

"He took me by the hand, and led me out into the garden. When the captain of the guard saw me, he wondered. When the eunuchs saw me, their knees shook and they fell upon the ground in fear.

"There is a chamber in the palace that has eight walls of red porphyry, and a brass-scaled ceiling hung with lamps. The Emperor touched one of the walls and it opened, and we passed down a corridor that was lit with many torches. In niches upon each side stood great wine-jars filled to the brim with silver pieces. When we reached the centre of the corridor the Emperor spake the word that may not be spoken, and a granite door swung back on a secret spring, and he put his hands before his face lest his eyes should be dazzled.

"Thou couldst not believe how marvellous a place it was. There were huge tortoise-shells full of pearls, and hollowed moonstones of great size piled up with red rubies. The gold was stored in coffers of elephant-hide, and the gold-dust in leather bottles. There were opals and sapphires, the former in cups of crystal, and the latter in cups of jade. Round green emeralds were ranged in order upon thin plates of ivory, and in one corner were silk bags filled, some with turquoise-stones, and others with beryls. The ivory horns were heaped with purple amethysts, and the horns of brass with chalcedonies and sards. The pillars, which were of cedar, were hung with strings of yellow lynx-stones. In the flat oval shields there were carbuncles, both wine-coloured and coloured like grass. And yet I have told thee but a tithe of what was there.

"And when the Emperor had taken away his hands from before his face he said to me: 'This is my house of treasure, and half that is in it is thine, even as I promised to thee. And I will give thee camels and camel drivers, and they shall do thy bidding and take thy share of the treasure to whatever part of the world thou desirest to go. And the thing shall be done to-night, for I would not that the Sun, who is my father, should see that there is in my city a man whom I cannot slay.'

"But I answered him, 'The gold that is here is thine, and the silver also is thine, and thine are the precious jewels and the things of price. As for me, I have no need of these. Nor shall I take aught from thee but that little ring that thou wearest on the finger of thy hand.'

"And the Emperor frowned. 'It is but a ring of lead,' he cried, 'nor has it any value. Therefore take thy half of the treasure and go from my city.'

" 'Nay,' I answered, 'but I will take nought but that leaden ring, for I know what is written within it, and for what purpose.'

"And the Emperor trembled, and besought me and said, 'Take all the treasure and go from my city. The half that is mine shall be thine also.'

"And I did a strange thing, but what I did matters not, for in a cave that is but a day's journey from this place have I hidden the Ring of Riches. It is but a day's journey from this place, and it waits for thy coming. He who has this Ring is richer than all the kings of the world. Come therefore and take it, and the world's riches shall be thine."

But the young Fisherman laughed. "Love is better than Riches," he cried, "and the little Mermaid loves me."

"Nay, but there is nothing better than Riches," said the Soul.

"Love is better," answered the young Fisherman, and he plunged into the deep, and the Soul went weeping away over the marshes.

And after the third year was over, the Soul came down to the shore of the sea, and called to the young Fisherman, and he rose out of the deep and said, "Why dost thou call to me?"

And the Soul answered, "Come nearer, that I may speak with thee, for I have seen marvellous things."

So he came nearer, and couched in the shallow water, and leaned his head upon his hand and listened.

And the Soul said to him, "In a city that I know of there is an inn that standeth by a river. I sat there with sailors who drank of two different-coloured wines, and ate bread made of barley, and little salt fish served in bay leaves with vinegar. And as we sat and made merry, there entered to us an old man bearing a leathern carpet and a lute that had two horns of amber. And when he had laid out the carpet on the floor, he struck with a quill on the wire strings of his lute, and a girl whose face was veiled ran in and began to dance before us. Her face was veiled with a veil of gauze, but her feet were naked. Naked were her feet, and they moved over the carpet like little white pigeons. Never have I seen anything so marvellous, and the city in which she dances is but a day's journey from this place."

Now when the young Fisherman heard the words of his Soul, he remembered that the little Mermaid had no feet and could not dance. And a great desire came over him, and he said to himself, "It is but a day's journey, and I can return to my love," and he laughed and stood up in the shallow water, and strode towards the shore.

And when he had reached the dry shore he laughed again, and held out his arms to his Soul. And his Soul gave a great cry of joy and ran to meet him, and entered into him, and the young Fisherman saw stretched before him upon the sand that shadow of the body that is the body of the Soul.

And his Soul said to him, "Let us not tarry, but get hence at once, for the Sea-gods are jealous, and have monsters that do their bidding."

So they made haste, and all that night they journeyed beneath the moon, and all the next day they journeyed beneath the sun, and on the evening of the day they came to a city.

And the young Fisherman said to his Soul, "Is this the city in which she dances of whom thou didst speak to me?"

And his Soul answered him, "It is not this city, but another. Nevertheless let us enter in."

So they entered in and passed through the streets, and as they passed through the Street of the Jewellers the young Fisherman saw a fair silver cup set forth in a booth. And his Soul said to him, "Take that silver cup and hide it."

So he took the cup and hid it in the fold of his tunic, and they went hurriedly out of the city.

And after that they had gone a league from the city, the young Fisherman frowned, and flung the cup away, and said to his Soul, "Why didst thou tell me to take this cup and hide it, for it was an evil thing to do?"

But his Soul answered him, "Be at peace, be at peace."

And on the evening of the second day they came to a city, and the young Fisherman said to his Soul, "Is this the city in which she dances of whom thou didst speak to me?"

And his Soul answered him, "It is not this city, but another. Nevertheless let us enter in."

So they entered in, and passed through the streets, and as they passed through the Street of the Sellers of Sandals, the young Fisherman saw a child standing by a jar of water. And his Soul said to him, "Smite that child." So he smote the child till it wept, and when he had done this they went hurriedly out of the city.

And after that they had gone a league from the city the young Fisherman grew wroth, and said to his Soul, "Why didst thou tell me to smite the child, for it was an evil thing to do?"

But his Soul answered him, "Be at peace, be at peace."

And on the evening of the third day they came to a city, and the young Fisherman said to his Soul, "Is this the city in which she dances of whom thou didst speak to me?"

And his Soul answered him, "It may be that it is in this city, therefore let us enter in."

So they entered in and passed through the streets, but nowhere could the young Fisherman find the river or the inn that stood by its side. And the people of the city looked curiously at him, and he grew afraid and said to his Soul, "Let us go hence, for she who dances with white feet is not here."

But his Soul answered, "Nay, but let us tarry, for the night is dark and there will be robbers on the way."

So he sat him down in the market-place and rested, and after a time there went by a hooded merchant who had a cloak of cloth of

Tartary, and bare a lantern of pierced horn at the end of a jointed reed. And the merchant said to him, "Why does thou sit in the market-place, seeing that the booths are closed and the bales corded?"

And the young Fisherman answered him, "I can find no inn in this city, nor have I any kinsman who might give me shelter."

"Are we not all kinsmen?" said the merchant. "And did not one God make us? Therefore come with me, for I have a guest-chamber."

So the young Fisherman rose up and followed the merchant to his house. And when he had passed through a garden of pomegranates and entered into the house, the merchant brought him rose-water in a copper dish that he might wash his hands, and ripe melons that he might quench his thirst, and set a bowl of rice and a piece of roasted kid before him.

And after that he had finished, the merchant led him to the guest-chamber, and bade him sleep and be at rest. And the young Fisherman gave him thanks, and kissed the ring that was on his hand, and flung himself down on the carpets of dyed goat's-hair. And when he had covered himself with a covering of black lamb's-wool he fell asleep.

And three hours before dawn, and while it was still night, his Soul waked him and said to him, "Rise up and go to the room of the merchant, even to the room in which he sleepeth, and slay him, and take from him his gold, for we have need of it."

And the young Fisherman rose up and crept towards the room of the merchant, and over the feet of the merchant there was lying a curved sword, and the tray by the side of the merchant held nine purses of gold. And he reached out his hand and touched the sword, and when he touched it the merchant started and awoke, and leaping up seized himself the sword and cried to the young Fisherman, "Dost thou return evil for good, and pay with the shedding of blood for the kindness that I have shown thee?"

And his Soul said to the young Fisherman, "Strike him," and he struck him so that he swooned, and he seized then the nine purses of gold, and fled hastily through the garden of pomegranates, and set his face to the star that is the star of morning.

And when they had gone a league from the city, the young

Fisherman beat his breast, and said to his Soul, "Why didst thou bid me slay the merchant and take his gold? Surely thou art evil."

But his Soul answered him, "Be at peace, be at peace."

"Nay," cried the young Fisherman, "I may not be at peace, for all that thou hast made me to do I hate. Thee also I hate, and I bid thee tell me wherefore thou hast wrought with me in this wise."

And his Soul answered him, "When thou didst send me forth into the world thou gavest me no heart, so I learned to do all these things and love them."

"What sayest thou?" murmured the young Fisherman.

"Thou knowest," answered his Soul, "thou knowest it well. Hast thou forgotten that thou gavest me no heart? I trow not. And so trouble not thyself nor me, but be at peace, for there is no pain that thou shalt not give away, nor any pleasure that thou shalt not receive."

And when the young Fisherman heard these words he trembled and said to his Soul, "Nay, but thou art evil, and hast made me forget my love, and hast tempted me with temptations, and hast set my feet in the ways of sins."

And his Soul answered him, "Thou hast not forgotten that when thou didst send me forth into the world thou gavest me no heart. Come, let us go to another city, and make merry, for we have nine purses of gold."

But the young Fisherman took the nine purses of gold, and flung them down, and trampled on them.

"Nay," he cried, "but I will have nought to do with thee, nor will I journey with thee anywhere, but even as I sent thee away before, so will I send thee away now, for thou hast wrought me no good." And he turned his back to the moon, and with the little knife that had the handle of green viper's skin he strove to cut from his feet that shadow of the body which is the body of the Soul.

Yet his Soul stirred not from him, nor paid heed to his command, but said to him, "The spell that the Witch told thee avails thee no more, for I may not leave thee, nor mayest thou drive me forth. Once in his life may a man send his Soul away, but he who receiveth back his Soul must keep it with him for ever, and this is his punishment and his reward."

And the young Fisherman grew pale and clenched his hands and cried, "She was a false Witch in that she told me not that."

"Nay," answered his Soul, "but she was true to Him she worships, and whose servant she will be ever."

And when the young Fisherman knew that he could no longer get rid of his Soul, and that it was an evil Soul, and would abide with him always, he fell upon the ground weeping bitterly.

And when it was day, the young Fisherman rose up and said to his Soul, "I will bind my hands that I may not do thy bidding, and close my lips that I may not speak thy words, and I will return to the place where she whom I love has her dwelling. Even to the sea will I return, and to the little bay where she is wont to sing, and I will call to her and tell her the evil I have done and the evil thou hast wrought on me."

And his Soul tempted him and said, "Who is thy love, that thou shouldst return to her? The world has many fairer than she is. There are the dancing-girls of Samaris who dance in the manner of all kinds of birds and beasts. Their feet are painted with henna, and in their hands they have little copper bells. They laugh while they dance, and their laughter is as clear as the laughter of water. Come with me and I will show them to thee. For what is this trouble of thine about the things of sin? Is that which is pleasant to eat not made for the eater? Is there poison in that which is sweet to drink? Trouble not thyself, but come with me to another city. There is a little city hard by in which there is a garden of tulip-trees. And there dwell in this comely garden white peacocks and peacocks that have blue breasts. Their tails when they spread them to the sun are like disks of ivory and like gilt disks. And she who feeds them dances for pleasure, and sometimes she dances on her hands and at other times she dances with her feet. Her eyes are coloured with stibium, and her nostrils are shaped like the wings of a swallow. From a hook in one of her nostrils hangs a flower that is carved out of a pearl. She laughs while she dances, and the silver rings that are about her ankles tinkle like bells of silver. And so trouble not thyself any more, but come with me to this city."

But the young Fisherman answered not his Soul, but closed his lips with the seal of silence and with a tight cord bound his hands, and journeyed back to the place from which he had come, even to the little bay where his love had been wont to sing. And ever did his Soul tempt him by the way, but he made it no answer, nor would he do any of the wickedness that it sought to make him do, so great was the power of the love that was within him.

And when he had reached the shore of the sea, he loosed the cord from his hands, and took the seal of silence from his lips, and called to the little Mermaid. But she came not to his call, though he called to her all day long and besought her.

And his Soul mocked him and said, "Surely thou hast but little joy out of thy love. Thou art as one who in time of death pours water into a broken vessel. Thou gavest away what thou hast, and nought is given to thee in return. It were better for thee to come with me, for I know where the Valley of Pleasure lies, and what things are wrought there."

But the young Fisherman answered not his Soul, but in a cleft of rock he built himself a house of wattles, and abode there for the space of a year. And every morning he called to the Mermaid, and every noon he called to her again, and at night-time he spake her name. Yet never did she rise out of the sea to meet him, nor in any place of the sea could he find her though he sought for her in the caves and in the green water, in the pools of the tide and in the wells that are at the bottom of the deep.

And ever did his Soul tempt him with evil, and whisper of terrible things. Yet did it not prevail against him, so great was the power of his love.

And after the year was over, the Soul thought within himself, "I have tempted my master with evil, and his love is stronger than I am. I will tempt him now with good, and it may be that he will come with me."

So he spake to the young Fisherman and said, "I have told thee of the joy of the world, and thou hast turned a deaf ear to me. Suffer me now to tell thee of the world's pain, and it may be that thou wilt hearken. For of a truth pain is the Lord of this world, nor is there any one who escapes from its net. There be some who lack raiment, and others who lack bread. There be widows who sit in purple, and widows who sit in rags. To and fro over the fens go the lepers, and they are cruel to each other. The beggars go up and down on the highways, and their wallets are empty. Through the streets of the cities walks Famine, and the Plague sits at their gates. Come, let us go forth and mend these things, and make them not to be. Wherefore shouldst thou tarry here calling to thy love, seeing she comes not to thy call? And what is love, that thou shouldst set this high store upon it?"

But the young Fisherman answered it nought, so great was the power of his love. And every morning he called to the Mermaid, and every noon he called to her again, and at night-time he spake her name. Yet never did she rise out of the sea to meet him, nor in any place of the sea could he find her, though he sought for her in the rivers of the sea, and in the valleys that are under the waves, in the sea that the night makes purple, and in the sea that the dawn leaves grey.

And after the second year was over, the Soul said to the young Fisherman at night-time, and as he sat in the wattled house alone, "Lo! now I have tempted thee with evil, and I have tempted thee with good, and thy love is stronger than I am. Wherefore will I tempt thee no longer, but I pray thee to suffer me to enter thy heart, that I may be one with thee even as before."

"Surely thou mayest enter," said the young Fisherman, "for in the days when with no heart thou didst go through the world thou must have much suffered."

"Alas!" cried his Soul, "I can find no place of entrance, so compassed about with love is this heart of thine."

"Yet I would that I could help thee," said the young Fisherman.

And as he spake there came a great cry of mourning from the sea, even the cry that men hear when one of the Sea-folk is dead. And the young Fisherman leapt up, and left his wattled house, and ran down to the shore. And the black waves came hurrying to the shore, bearing with them a burden that was whiter than silver. White as the surf it was, and like a flower it tossed on the waves. And the surf took it from the waves, and the foam took it from the surf, and the shore received it, and lying at his feet the young Fisherman saw the body of the little Mermaid. Dead at his feet it was lying.

Weeping as one smitten with pain he flung himself down beside it, and he kissed the cold red of the mouth, and toyed with the wet amber of the hair. He flung himself down beside it on the sand, weeping as one trembling with joy, and in his brown arms he held it to his breast. Cold were the lips, yet he kissed them. Salt was the honey of the hair, yet he tasted it with a bitter joy. He kissed the closed eyelids, and the wild spray that lay upon their cups was less salt than his tears.

And to the dead thing he made confession. Into the shells of its ears he poured the harsh wine of his tale. He put the little hands round his neck, and with his fingers he touched the thin reed of the throat. Bitter, bitter was his joy, and full of strange gladness was his pain.

The black sea came nearer, and the white foam moaned like a leper. With white claws of foam the sea grabbled at the shore. From the palace of the Sea-King came the cry of mourning again, and far out upon the sea the great Tritons blew hoarsely upon their horns.

"Flee away," said his Soul, "for ever doth the sea come nigher, and if thou tarriest it will slay thee. Flee away, for I am afraid, seeing that thy heart is closed against me by reason of the greatness of thy love. Flee away to a place of safety. Surely thou wilt not send me without a heart into another world?"

But the young Fisherman listened not to his Soul, but called on the little Mermaid and said, "Love is better than wisdom, and more precious than riches, and fairer than the feet of the daughters of men. The fires cannot destroy it, nor can the waters quench it. I called on thee at dawn, and thou didst come to my call. The moon heard thy name, yet hadst thou no heed of me. For evilly had I left thee, and to my own hurt had I wandered away. Yet ever did thy love abide with me, and ever was it strong, nor did aught prevail against it, though I have looked upon evil and looked upon good. And now that thou art dead, surely I will die with thee also."

And his Soul besought him to depart, but he would not, so great was his love. And the sea came nearer, and sought to cover him with its waves, and when he knew that the end was at hand he kissed with mad lips the cold lips of the Mermaid, and the heart that was within him brake. And as through the fullness of his love his heart did break, the Soul found an entrance and entered in, and was one with him even as before. And the sea covered the young Fisherman with its waves.

And in the morning the Priest went forth to bless the sea, for it had been troubled. And with him went the monks and the musicians, and the candle-bearers, and the swingers of censers, and a great company.

And when the Priest reached the shore he saw the young Fisherman lying drowned in the surf, and clasped in his arms was the body of the little Mermaid. And he drew back frowning, and having made the sign of the Cross, he cried aloud and said, "I will not bless the sea nor anything that is in it. Accursed be the Sea-folk, and accursed be all they who traffic with them. And as for him who for love's sake forsook God, and so lieth here with his leman slain by God's judgment, take up his body and the body of his leman, and bury them in the corner of the Field of the Fullers, and set no mark above them, nor sign of any kind, that none may know the place of their resting. For accursed were they in their lives, and accursed shall they be in their deaths also."

And the people did as he commanded them, and in the corner of the Field of the Fullers,* where no sweet herbs grew, they dug a deep pit, and laid the dead things within it.

And when the third year was over, and on a day that was a holy day, the Priest went up to the chapel, that he might show to the people the wounds of the Lord, and speak to them about the wrath of God.

And when he had robed himself with his robes, and entered in and bowed himself before the altar, he saw that the altar was covered with strange flowers that never had been seen before. Strange were they to look at, and of curious beauty, and their beauty troubled him, and their odour was sweet in his nostrils, and he felt glad, and understood not why he was glad.

And after that he had opened the tabernacle, and incensed the

* In the Bible, a field where cloth was whitened and made thicker by the use of fuller's earth, a special clay. The white altar flowers here share this purity.

monstrance that was in it, and shown the fair wafer to the people, and hid it again behind the veil of veils, he began to speak to the people, desiring to speak to them of the wrath of God. But the beauty of the white flowers troubled him, and their odour was sweet in his nostrils, and there came another word into his lips, and he spake not of the wrath of God, but of the God whose name is Love. And why he so spake, he knew not.

And when he had finished his word the people wept, and the Priest went back to his sacristy, and his eyes were full of tears. And the deacons came in and began to unrobe him, and took from him the alb and the girdle, the maniple and the stole. And he stood as one in a dream.

And after that they had unrobed him, he looked at them and said, "What are the flowers that stand on the altar, and whence do they come?"

And they answered him, "What flowers they are we cannot tell, but they come from the corner of the Fullers' Field." And the Priest trembled, and returned to his own house and prayed.

And in the morning, while it was still dawn, he went forth with the monks and the musicians, and the candle-bearers and the swingers of censers, and a great company, and came to the shore of the sea, and blessed the sea, and all the wild things that are in it. The Fauns also he blessed, and the little things that dance in the woodland, and the bright-eyed things that peer through the leaves. All the things in God's world he blessed, and the people were filled with joy and wonder. Yet never again in the corner of the Fullers' Field grew flowers of any kind, but the field remained barren even as before. Nor came the Sea-folk into the bay as they had been wont to do, for they went to another part of the sea.

THE REMARKABLE ROCKET

THE KING'S SON was going to be married, so there were general rejoicings. He had waited a whole year for his bride, and at last she had arrived. She was a Russian Princess, and had driven all the way from Finland in a sledge drawn by six reindeer. The sledge was shaped like a great golden swan, and between the swan's wings lay the little Princess herself. Her long ermine cloak reached right down to her feet, on her head was a tiny cap of silver tissue, and she was as pale as the Snow Palace in which she had always lived. So pale was she that as she drove through the streets all the people wondered. "She is like a white rose!" they cried, and they threw down flowers on her from the balconies.

At the gate of the Castle the Prince was waiting to receive her. He had dreamy violet eyes, and his hair was like fine gold. When he saw her he sank upon one knee, and kissed her hand.

"Your picture was beautiful," he murmured, "but you are more beautiful than your picture;" and the little Princess blushed.

"She was like a white rose before," said a young page to his neighbour, "but she is like a red rose now;" and the whole Court was delighted.

For the next three days everybody went about saying, "White rose, Red rose, Red rose, White rose," and the King gave orders that the Page's salary was to be doubled. As he received no salary at all this was not of much use to him, but it was considered a great honour and was duly published in the Court Gazette.

When the three days were over the marriage was celebrated. It was a magnificent ceremony, and the bride and bridegroom walked hand in hand under a canopy of purple velvet embroidered with little pearls. Then there was a State Banquet, which lasted for five hours. The Prince and Princess sat at the top of the Great Hall and drank out of a cup of clear crystal. Only true lovers could drink out of this cup, for if false lips touched it, it grew grey and dull and cloudy.

"It is quite clear that they love each other," said the little Page, "as clear as crystal!" and the King doubled his salary a second time.

"What an honour!" cried all the courtiers.

After the banquet there was to be a Ball. The bride and bridegroom were to dance the Rose-dance together, and the King had promised to play the flute. He played very badly, but no one had ever dared to tell him so, because he was the King. Indeed, he knew only two airs, and was never quite certain which one he was playing; but it made no matter, for, whatever he did, everybody cried out, "Charming! charming!"

The last item on the programme was a grand display of fireworks, to be let off exactly at midnight. The little Princess had never seen a firework in her life, so the King had given orders that the Royal Pyrotechnist should be in attendance on the day of her marriage.

"What are fireworks like?" she had asked the Prince, one morning, as she was walking on the terrace.

"They are like the Aurora Borealis," said the King, who always answered questions that were addressed to other people, "only much more natural. I prefer them to stars myself, as you always know when they are going to appear, and they are as delightful as my own flute-playing. You must certainly see them."

So at the end of the King's garden a great stand had been set up, and as soon as the Royal Pyrotechnist had put everything in its proper place, the fireworks began to talk to each other.

"The world is certainly very beautiful," cried a little Squib.* "Just look at those yellow tulips. Why! if they were real crackers they could not be lovelier. I am very glad I have travelled. Travel improves the mind wonderfully, and does away with all one's prejudices."

"The King's garden is not the world, you foolish Squib," said a big

---

* Small explosive device that may be used for rockets. In this story, Wilde personifies pyrotechnics, and rockets, like animals, become fabulous "persons."

Roman Candle; "the world is an enormous place, and it would take you three days to see it thoroughly."

"Any place you love is the world to you," exclaimed the pensive Catherine Wheel, who had been attached to an old deal box in early life, and prided herself on her broken heart; "but love is not fashionable any more, the poets have killed it. They wrote so much about it that nobody believed them, and I am not surprised. True love suffers, and is silent. I remember myself once—— But no matter now. Romance is a thing of the past."

"Nonsense!" said the Roman Candle, "Romance never dies. It is like the moon, and lives for ever. The bride and bridegroom, for instance, love each other very dearly. I heard all about them this morning from a brown-paper cartridge, who happened to be staying in the same drawer as myself, and he knew the latest Court news."

But the Catherine Wheel shook her head. "Romance is dead, Romance is dead, Romance is dead," she murmured. She was one of those people who think that, if you say the same thing over and over a great many times, it becomes truc in the end.

Suddenly, a sharp, dry cough was heard, and they all looked round.

It came from a tall, supercilious-looking Rocket, who was tied to the end of a long stick. He always coughed before he made any observations, so as to attract attention.

"Ahem! ahem!" he said, and everybody listened except the poor Catherine Wheel, who was still shaking her head, and murmuring, "Romance is dead."

"Order! order!" cried out a Cracker. He was something of a politician, and had always taken a prominent part in the local elections, so he knew the proper Parliamentary expressions to use.

"Quite dead," whispered the Catherine Wheel, and she went off to sleep.

As soon as there was perfect silence, the Rocket coughed a third time and began. He spoke with a very slow, distinct voice, as if he were dictating his memoirs, and always looked over the shoulder of the person to whom he was talking. In fact, he had a most distinguished manner.

"How fortunate it is for the King's son," he remarked, "that he is to be married on the very day on which I am to be let off! Really, if it had not been arranged beforehand, it could not have turned out better for him; but Princes are always lucky."

"Dear me!" said the little Squib, "I thought it was quite the other way, and that we were to be let off in the Prince's honour."

"It may be so with you," he answered; "indeed, I have no doubt that it is, but with me it is different. I am a very remarkable Rocket, and come of remarkable parents. My mother was the most celebrated Catherine Wheel of her day, and was renowned for her graceful dancing. When she made her great public appearance she spun round nineteen times before she went out, and each time that she did so she threw into the air seven pink stars. She was three feet and a half in diameter, and made of the very best gunpowder. My father was a Rocket like myself, and of French extraction. He flew so high that the people were afraid that he would never come down again. He did, though, for he was of a kindly disposition, and he made a most brilliant descent in a shower of golden rain. The newspapers wrote about his performance in very flattering terms. Indeed, the Court Gazette called him a triumph of Pylotechnic art."

"Pyrotechnic, Pyrotechnic, you mean," said a Bengal Light; "I know it is Pyrotechnic, for I saw it written on my own canister."

"Well, I said Pylotechnic," answered the Rocket, in a severe tone of voice, and the Bengal Light felt so crushed that he began at once to bully the little squibs, in order to show that he was still a person of some importance.

"I was saying," continued the Rocket, "I was saying—— What was I saying?"

"You were talking about yourself," replied the Roman Candle.

"Of course; I knew I was discussing some interesting subject when I was so rudely interrupted. I hate rudeness and bad manners of every kind, for I am extremely sensitive. No one in the whole world is so sensitive as I am, I am quite sure of that."

"What is a sensitive person?" said the Cracker to the Roman Candle.

"A person who, because he has corns himself, always treads on other people's toes," answered the Roman Candle in a low whisper; and the Cracker nearly exploded with laughter.

"Pray, what are you laughing at?" inquired the Rocket; "I am not laughing."

"I am laughing because I am happy," replied the Cracker.

"That is a very selfish reason," said the Rocket angrily. "What right have you to be happy? You should be thinking about others. In fact, you should be thinking about me. I am always thinking about myself, and I expect everybody else to do the same. That is what is called sympathy. It is a beautiful virtue, and I possess it in a high degree. Suppose, for instance, anything happened to me to-night, what a misfortune that would be for every one! The Prince and Princess would never be happy again, their whole married life would be spoiled; and as for the King, I know he would not get over it. Really, when I begin to reflect on the importance of my position, I am almost moved to tears."

"If you want to give pleasure to others," cried the Roman Candle, "you had better keep yourself dry."

"Certainly," exclaimed the Bengal Light, who was now in better spirits; "that is only common sense."

"Common sense, indeed!" said the Rocket indignantly; "you forget that I am very uncommon, and very remarkable. Why, anybody can have common sense, provided that they have no imagination. But I have imagination, for I never think of things as they really are; I always think of them as being quite different. As for keeping myself dry, there is evidently no one here who can at all appreciate an emotional nature. Fortunately for myself, I don't care. The only thing that sustains one through life is the consciousness of the immense inferiority of everybody else, and this is a feeling I have always cultivated. But none of you have any hearts. Here you are laughing and making merry just as if the Prince and Princess had not just been married."

"Well, really," exclaimed a small Fire-balloon, "why not? It is a most joyful occasion, and when I soar up into the air I intend to tell the stars all about it. You will see them twinkle when I talk to them about the pretty bride."

"Ah! what a trivial view of life!" said the Rocket; "but it is only what I expected. There is nothing in you; you are hollow and empty. Why, perhaps the Prince and Princess may go to live in a country where there is a deep river, and perhaps they may have one only son, a little fair-haired boy with violet eyes like the Prince himself; and perhaps some day he may go out to walk with his nurse; and perhaps the nurse may go to sleep under a great elder-tree; and perhaps the little boy may fall into the deep river and be drowned. What a terrible misfortune! Poor people, to lose their only son! It is really too dreadful! I shall never get over it."

"But they have not lost their only son," said the Roman Candle; "no misfortune has happened to them at all."

"I never said that they had," replied the Rocket; "I said that they might. If they had lost their only son there would be no use in saying any more about the matter. I hate people who cry over spilt milk. But when I think that they might lose their only son, I certainly am very much affected."

"You certainly are!" cried the Bengal Light. "In fact, you are the most affected person I ever met."

"You are the rudest person I ever met," said the Rocket, "and you cannot understand my friendship for the Prince."

"Why, you don't even know him," growled the Roman Candle.

"I never said I knew him," answered the Rocket. "I dare say that if I knew him I should not be his friend at all. It is a very dangerous thing to know one's friends."

"You had really better keep yourself dry," said the Fire-balloon. "That is the important thing."

"Very important for you, I have no doubt," answered the Rocket, "but I shall weep if I choose;" and he actually burst into real tears, which flowed down his stick like raindrops, and nearly drowned two little beetles, who were just thinking of setting up house together, and were looking for a nice dry spot to live in.

"He must have a truly romantic nature," said the Catherine Wheel, "for he weeps when there is nothing at all to weep about;" and she heaved a deep sigh and thought about the deal box.

But the Roman Candle and the Bengal Light were quite indignant, and kept saying, "Humbug! humbug!" at the top of their voices. They were extremely practical, and whenever they objected to anything they called it humbug.

Then the moon rose like a wonderful silver shield; and the stars began to shine, and a sound of music came from the palace.

The Prince and Princess were leading the dance. They danced so beautifully that the tall white lilies peeped in at the window and watched them, and the great red poppies nodded their heads and beat time.

Then ten o'clock struck, and then eleven, and then twelve, and at the last stroke of midnight every one came out on the terrace, and the King sent for the Royal Pyrotechnist.

"Let the fireworks begin," said the King; and the Royal Pyrotechnist made a low bow, and marched down to the end of the garden. He had six attendants with him, each of whom carried a lighted torch at the end of a long pole.

It was certainly a magnificent display.

Whizz! Whizz! went the Catherine Wheel, as she spun round and round. Boom! Boom! went the Roman Candle. Then the Squibs danced all over the place, and the Bengal Lights made everything look scarlet. "Good-bye," cried the Fire-balloon, as he soared away, dropping tiny blue sparks. Bang! Bang! answered the Crackers, who were enjoying themselves immensely. Every one was a great success except the Remarkable Rocket. He was so damped with crying that he could not go off at all. The best thing in him was the gunpowder, and that was so wet with tears that it was of no use. All his poor relations, to whom he would never speak, except with a sneer, shot up into the sky like wonderful golden flowers with blossoms of fire. Huzza! Huzza! cried the Court; and the little Princess laughed with pleasure.

"I suppose they are reserving me for some grand occasion," said the Rocket; "no doubt that is what it means," and he looked more supercilious than ever.

The next day the workmen came to put everything tidy. "This is evidently a deputation," said the Rocket; "I will receive them with becoming dignity:" so he put his nose in the air, and began to frown severely, as if he were thinking about some very important subject. But they took no notice of him at all till they were just going away. Then one of them caught sight of him. "Hallo!" he cried, "what a bad rocket!" and he threw him over the wall into the ditch.

"BAD ROCKET? BAD ROCKET?" he said, as he whirled through the air; "impossible! GRAND ROCKET, that is what the man said. BAD and GRAND sound very much the same, indeed they often are the same;" and he fell into the mud.

"It is not comfortable here," he remarked, "but no doubt it is some fashionable watering-place, and they have sent me away to recruit my health. My nerves are certainly very much shattered, and I require rest."

Then a little Frog, with bright jewelled eyes, and a green mottled coat, swam up to him.

"A new arrival, I see!" said the Frog. "Well, after all there is nothing like mud. Give me rainy weather and a ditch, and I am quite happy. Do you think it will be a wet afternoon? I am sure I hope so, but the sky is quite blue and cloudless. What a pity!"

"Ahem! ahem!" said the Rocket, and he began to cough.

"What a delightful voice you have!" cried the Frog. "Really it is quite like a croak, and croaking is, of course, the most musical sound in the world. You will hear our glee-club this evening. We sit in the old duck-pond close by the farmer's house, and as soon as the moon rises we begin. It is so entrancing that everybody lies awake to listen to us. In fact, it was only yesterday that I heard the farmer's wife say to her mother that she could not get a wink of sleep at night on account of us. It is most gratifying to find oneself so popular."

"Ahem! ahem!" said the Rocket angrily. He was very much annoyed that he could not get a word in.

"A delightful voice, certainly," continued the Frog; "I hope you will come over to the duck-pond. I am off to look for my daughters. I have six beautiful daughters, and I am so afraid the Pike may meet them. He is a perfect monster, and would have no hesitation in breakfasting off them. Well, good-bye; I have enjoyed our conversation very much, I assure you."

"Conversation, indeed!" said the Rocket. "You have talked the whole time yourself. That is not conversation."

"Somebody must listen," answered the Frog, "and I like to do all the talking myself. It saves time, and prevents arguments."

"But I like arguments," said the Rocket.

"I hope not," said the Frog complacently. "Arguments are extremely vulgar, for everybody in good society holds exactly the same opinions. Good-bye a second time; I see my daughters in the distance;" and the little Frog swam away.

"You are a very irritating person," said the Rocket, "and very ill-bred. I hate people who talk about themselves, as you do, when one wants to talk about oneself, as I do. It is what I call selfishness, and selfishness is a most detestable thing, especially to any one of my temperament, for I am well known for my sympathetic nature. In fact, you should take example by me; you could not possibly have a better model. Now that you have the chance you had better avail yourself of it, for I am going back to Court almost immediately. I am a great favourite at Court; in fact, the Prince and Princess were married yesterday in my honour. Of course, you know nothing of these matters, for you are a provincial."

"There is no good talking to him," said a Dragonfly, who was sitting on the top of a large brown bulrush; "no good at all, for he has gone away."

"Well, that is his loss, not mine," answered the Rocket. "I am not going to stop talking to him merely because he pays no attention. I like hearing myself talk. It is one of my greatest pleasures. I often have long conversations all by myself, and I am so clever that sometimes I don't understand a single word of what I am saying."

"Then you should certainly lecture on Philosophy," said the Dragonfly, and he spread a pair of lovely gauze wings and soared away into the sky.

"How very silly of him not to stay here!" said the Rocket. "I am sure that he has not often got such a chance of improving his mind. However, I don't care a bit. Genius like mine is sure to be appreciated some day;" and he sank down a little deeper into the mud.

After some time a large White Duck swam up to him. She had yellow legs, and webbed feet, and was considered a great beauty on account of her waddle.

"Quack, quack, quack," she said. "What a curious shape you are! May I ask were you born like that, or is it the result of an accident?"

"It is quite evident that you have always lived in the country," answered the Rocket, "otherwise you would know who I am. However,

I excuse your ignorance. It would be unfair to expect other people to be as remarkable as oneself. You will no doubt be surprised to hear that I can fly up into the sky, and come down in a shower of golden rain."

"I don't think much of that," said the Duck, "as I cannot see what use it is to any one. Now, if you could plough the fields like the ox, or draw a cart like the horse, or look after the sheep like the collie-dog, that would be something."

"My good creature," cried the Rocket in a very haughty tone of voice, "I see that you belong to the lower orders. A person of my position is never useful. We have certain accomplishments, and that is more than sufficient. I have no sympathy myself with industry of any kind, least of all with such industries as you seem to recommend. Indeed, I have always been of opinion that hard work is simply the refuge of people who have nothing whatever to do."

"Well, well," said the Duck, who was of a very peaceful disposition, and never quarrelled with any one, "everybody has different tastes. I hope, at any rate, that you are going to take up your residence here."

"Oh! dear no," cried the Rocket. "I am merely a visitor, a distinguished visitor. The fact is that I find this place rather tedious. There is neither society here, nor solitude. In fact, it is essentially suburban. I shall probably go back to Court, for I know that I am destined to make a sensation in the world."

"I had thoughts of entering public life once myself," remarked the Duck; "there are so many things that need reforming. Indeed, I took the chair at a meeting some time ago, and we passed resolutions condemning everything that we did not like. However, they did not seem to have much effect. Now I go in for domesticity, and look after my family."

"I am made for public life," said the Rocket, "and so are all my relations, even the humblest of them. Whenever we appear we excite great attention. I have not actually appeared myself, but when I do so it will be a magnificent sight. As for domesticity, it ages one rapidly, and distracts one's mind from higher things."

"Ah! the higher things of life, how fine they are!" said the Duck; "and that reminds me how hungry I feel:" and she swam away down the stream, saying, "Quack, quack, quack."

"Come back! come back!" screamed the Rocket, "I have a great deal to say to you;" but the Duck paid no attention to him. "I am glad that she has gone," he said to himself, "she has a decidedly middle-class mind;" and he sank a little deeper still into the mud, and began to think about the loneliness of genius, when suddenly two little boys in white smocks came running down the bank, with a kettle and some faggots.

"This must be the deputation," said the Rocket, and he tried to look very dignified.

"Hallo!" cried one of the boys, "look at this old stick; I wonder how it came here:" and he picked the Rocket out of the ditch.

"OLD STICK!" said the Rocket, "impossible! GOLD STICK, that is what he said. Gold Stick is very complimentary. In fact, he mistakes me for one of the Court dignitaries!"

"Let us put it into the fire!" said the other boy, "it will help to boil the kettle."

So they piled the faggots together, and put the Rocket on top, and lit the fire.

"This is magnificent," cried the Rocket, "they are going to let me off in broad daylight, so that every one can see me."

"We will go to sleep now," they said, "and when we wake up the kettle will be boiled;" and they lay down on the grass, and shut their eyes.

The Rocket was very damp, so he took a long time to burn. At last, however, the fire caught him.

"Now I am going off!" he cried, and he made himself very stiff and straight. "I know I shall go much higher than the stars, much higher than the moon, much higher than the sun. In fact, I shall go so high that——"

Fizz! Fizz! Fizz! and he went straight up into the air.

"Delightful!" he cried, "I shall go on like this for ever. What a success I am!"

But nobody saw him.

Then he began to feel a curious tingling sensation all over him.

"Now I am going to explode," he cried. "I shall set the whole world on fire, and make such a noise that nobody will talk about anything else for a whole year." And he certainly did explode. Bang! Bang! Bang! went the gunpowder. There was no doubt about it.

But nobody heard him, not even the two little boys, for they were sound asleep.

Then all that was left of him was the stick, and this fell down on the back of a Goose who was taking a walk by the side of the ditch.

"Good heavens!" cried the Goose. "It is going to rain sticks;" and she rushed into the water.

"I knew I should create a great sensation," gasped the Rocket, and he went out.

POEMS IN PROSE

THE ARTIST

One evening there came into his soul the desire to fashion an image of *The Pleasure that abideth for a Moment*. And he went forth into the world to look for bronze. For he could only think in bronze.

But all the bronze of the whole world had disappeared, nor anywhere in the whole world was there any bronze to be found, save only the bronze of the image of *The Sorrow that endureth for Ever.*

Now this image he had himself, and with his own hands, fashioned, and had set it on the tomb of the one thing he had loved in life. On the tomb of the dead thing he had most loved had he set this image of his own fashioning, that it might serve as a sign of the love of man that dieth not, and a symbol of the sorrow of man that endureth for ever. And in the whole world there was no other bronze save the bronze of this image.

And he took the image he had fashioned, and set it in a great furnace, and gave it to the fire.

And out of the bronze of the image of *The Sorrow that endureth for Ever* he fashioned an image of *The Pleasure that abideth for a Moment*.

THE DISCIPLE

When Narcissus died the pool of his pleasure changed from a cup of sweet waters into a cup of salt tears, and the Oreads came weeping through the woodland that they might sing to the pool and give it comfort.

And when they saw that the pool had changed from a cup of sweet waters into a cup of salt tears, they loosened the green tresses of their hair and cried to the pool and said, "We do not wonder that you should mourn in this manner for Narcissus, so beautiful was he."

"But was Narcissus beautiful?" said the pool.

"Who should know that better than you?" answered the Oreads.

"Us did he ever pass by, but you he sought for, and would lie on your banks and look down at you, and in the mirror of your waters he would mirror his own beauty."

And the pool answered, "But I loved Narcissus because, as he lay on my banks and looked down at me, in the mirror of his eyes I saw ever my own beauty mirrored."

THE MASTER

Now when the darkness came over the earth Joseph of Arimathea,* having lighted a torch of pinewood, passed down from the hill into the valley. For he had business in his own home.

And kneeling on the flint stones of the Valley of Desolation he saw a young man who was naked and weeping. His hair was the colour of honey, and his body was as a white flower, but he had wounded his body with thorns and on his hair had he set ashes as a crown.

And he who had great possessions said to the young man who was naked and weeping, "I do not wonder that your sorrow is so great, for surely He was a just man."

And the young man answered, "It is not for Him that I am weeping, but for myself. I too have changed water into wine, and I have healed the leper and given sight to the blind. I have walked upon the waters, and from the dwellers in the tombs I have cast out devils. I have fed the hungry in the desert where there was no food, and I have raised the dead from their narrow houses, and at my bidding, and before a great multitude of people, a barren fig-tree withered away. All things that this man has done I have done also. And yet they have not crucified me."

* According to the Gospels, he prepared Jesus' body and placed it in his own tomb after Jesus was crucified. In Arthurian legend he is said to have brought Christianity to Britain.

THE HOUSE OF JUDGMENT

And there was silence in the House of Judgment, and the Man came naked before God.

And God opened the Book of the Life of the Man.

And God said to the Man, "Thy life hath been evil, and thou hast shown cruelty to those who were in need of succour, and to those who lacked help thou hast been bitter and hard of heart. The poor called to thee and thou didst not hearken, and thine ears were closed to the cry of My afflicted. The inheritance of the fatherless thou didst take unto thyself, and thou didst send the foxes into the vineyard of thy neighbour's field. Thou didst take the bread of the children and give it to the dogs to eat, and My lepers who lived in the marshes, and were at peace and praised Me, thou didst drive forth on to the highways, and on Mine earth out of which I made thee thou didst spill innocent blood."

And the Man made answer and said, "Even so did I."

And again God opened the Book of the Life of the Man.

And God said to the Man, "Thy life hath been evil, and the Beauty I have shown thou hast sought for, and the Good I have hidden thou didst pass by. The walls of thy chamber were painted with images, and from the bed of thine abominations thou didst rise up to the sound of flutes. Thou didst build seven altars to the sins I have suffered, and didst eat of the thing that may not be eaten, and the purple of thy raiment was broidered with the three signs of shame. Thine idols were neither of gold nor of silver that endure, but of flesh that dieth. Thou didst stain their hair with perfumes and put pomegranates in their hands. Thou didst stain their feet with saffron and spread carpets before them. With antimony thou didst stain their eyelids and their bodies thou didst smear with myrrh. Thou didst bow thyself to the ground before them, and the thrones of thine idols were set in the sun. Thou didst show to the sun thy shame and to the moon thy madness."

And the Man made answer and said, "Even so did I."

And a third time God opened the Book of the Life of the Man.

And God said to the Man, "Evil hath been thy life, and with evil didst thou requite good, and with wrongdoing kindness. The hands that fed thee thou didst wound, and the breasts that gave thee suck thou didst despise. He who came to thee with water went away thirsting, and the outlawed men who hid thee in their tents at night thou didst betray before dawn. Thine enemy who spared thee thou didst snare in an ambush, and the friend who walked with thee thou didst sell for a price, and to those who brought thee Love thou didst ever give Lust in thy turn."

And the Man made answer and said, "Even so did I."

And God closed the Book of the Life of the Man, and said, "Surely I will send thee into Hell. Even into Hell will I send thee."

And the Man cried out, "Thou canst not."

And God said to the Man, "Wherefore can I not send thee to Hell, and for what reason?"

"Because in Hell have I always lived," answered the Man.

And there was silence in the House of Judgment.

And after a space God spake, and said to the Man, "Seeing that I may not send thee into Hell, surely I will send thee unto Heaven. Even unto Heaven will I send thee."

And the Man cried out, "Thou canst not."

And God said to the Man, "Wherefore can I not send thee unto Heaven, and for what reason?"

"Because never, and in no place, have I been able to imagine it," answered the Man.

And there was silence in the House of Judgment.

THE TEACHER OF WISDOM

From his childhood he had been as one filled with the perfect knowledge of God, and even while he was yet but a lad many of the saints, as well as certain holy women who dwelt in the free city of his birth, had been stirred to much wonder by the grave wisdom of his answers.

And when his parents had given him the robe and the ring of manhood he kissed them, and left them and went out into the world, that he might speak to the world about God. For there were at that time many in the world who either knew not God at all, or had but an incomplete knowledge of Him, or worshipped the false gods who dwell in groves and have no care of their worshippers.

And he set his face to the sun and journeyed, walking without sandals, as he had seen the saints walk, and carrying at his girdle a leathern wallet and a little water-bottle of burnt clay.

And as he walked along the highway he was full of the joy that comes from the perfect knowledge of God, and he sang praises unto God without ceasing; and after a time he reached a strange land in which there were many cities.

And he passed through eleven cities. And some of these cities were in valleys, and others were by the banks of great rivers, and others were set on hills. And in each city he found a disciple who loved him and followed him, and a great multitude also of people followed him from each city, and the knowledge of God spread in the whole land, and many of the rulers were converted, and the priests of the temples in which there were idols found that half of their gain was gone, and when they beat upon their drums at noon none, or but a few, came with peacocks and with offerings of flesh as had been the custom of the land before his coming.

Yet the more the people followed him, and the greater the number of his disciples, the greater became his sorrow. And he knew not why his sorrow was so great. For he spake ever about God, and out of the fulness of that perfect knowledge of God which God had Himself given to him.

And one evening he passed out of the eleventh city, which was a city of Armenia, and his disciples and a great crowd of people followed after him; and he went up on to a mountain and sat down on a rock that was on the mountain, and his disciples stood round him, and the multitude knelt in the valley.

And he bowed his head on his hands and wept, and said to his Soul, "Why is it that I am full of sorrow and fear, and that each of my disciples is as an enemy that walks in the noonday?"

And his Soul answered him and said, "God filled thee with the perfect knowledge of Himself, and thou hast given this knowledge away to others. The pearl of great price thou hast divided, and the vesture without seam thou hast parted asunder. He who giveth away wisdom robbeth himself. He is as one who giveth his treasure to a robber. Is not God wiser than thou art? Who art thou to give away the secret that God hath told thee? I was rich once, and thou hast made me poor. Once I saw God, and now thou hast hidden Him from me."

And he wept again, for he knew that his Soul spake truth to him, and that he had given to others the perfect knowledge of God, and that he was as one clinging to the skirts of God, and that his faith was leaving him by reason of the number of those who believed in him.

And he said to himself, "I will talk no more about God. He who giveth away wisdom robbeth himself."

And after the space of some hours his disciples came near him and bowed themselves to the ground and said, "Master, talk to us about God, for thou hast the perfect knowledge of God, and no man save thee hath this knowledge."

And he answered them and said, "I will talk to you about all other things that are in heaven and on earth, but about God I will not talk to you. Neither now, nor at any time, will I talk to you about God."

And they were wroth with him and said to him, "Thou hast led us into the desert that we might hearken to thee. Wilt thou send us away hungry, and the great multitude that thou hast made to follow thee?"

And he answered them and said, "I will not talk to you about God."

And the multitude murmured against him and said to him, "Thou hast led us into the desert, and hast given us no food to eat. Talk to us about God and it will suffice us."

But he answered them not a word. For he knew that if he spake to them about God he would give away his treasure.

And his disciples went away sadly, and the multitude of people returned to their own homes. And many died on the way.

And when he was alone he rose up and set his face to the moon, and journeyed for seven moons, speaking to no man nor making any answer. And when the seventh moon had waned he reached that desert which is the desert of the Great River. And having found a cavern in which a Centaur* had once dwelt, he took it for his place of dwelling, and made himself a mat of reeds on which to lie, and became a hermit. And every hour the Hermit praised God that He had suffered him to keep some knowledge of Him and of His wonderful greatness.

Now, one evening, as the Hermit was seated before the cavern in which he had made his place of dwelling, he beheld a young man of evil and beautiful face who passed by in mean apparel and with empty hands. Every evening with empty hands the young man passed by, and every morning he returned with his hands full of purple and pearls. For he was a Robber and robbed the caravans of the merchants.

And the Hermit looked at him and pitied him. But he spake not a word. For he knew that he who speaks a word loses his faith.

And one morning, as the young man returned with his hands full of purple and pearls, he stopped and frowned and stamped his foot upon the sand, and said to the Hermit: "Why do you look at me ever in this manner as I pass by? What is it that I see in your eyes? For no man has looked at me before in this manner. And the thing is a thorn and a trouble to me."

And the Hermit answered him and said, "What you see in my eyes is pity. Pity is what looks out at you from my eyes."

And the young man laughed with scorn, and cried to the Hermit in a bitter voice, and said to him, "I have purple and pearls in my hands, and you have but a mat of reeds on which to lie. What pity should you have for me? And for what reason have you this pity?"

"I have pity for you," said the Hermit, "because you have no knowledge of God."

"Is this knowledge of God a precious thing?" asked the young man, and he came close to the mouth of the cavern.

"It is more precious than all the purple and the pearls of the world," answered the Hermit.

"And have you got it?" said the young Robber, and he came closer still.

* The centaurs of Greek myth were half human (the head and torso) and half horse (the rest of the body). Chiron the Centaur was believed to be deeply wise.

"Once, indeed," answered the Hermit, "I possessed the perfect knowledge of God. But in my foolishness I parted with it, and divided it amongst others. Yet even now is such knowledge as remains to me more precious than purple or pearls."

And when the young Robber heard this he threw away the purple and the pearls that he was bearing in his hands, and drawing a sharp sword of curved steel he said to the Hermit, "Give me, forthwith, this knowledge of God that you possess, or I will surely slay you. Wherefore should I not slay him who has a treasure greater than my treasure?"

And the Hermit spread out his arms and said, "Were it not better for me to go unto the uttermost courts of God and praise Him, than to live in the world and have no knowledge of Him? Slay me if that be your desire. But I will not give away my knowledge of God."

And the young Robber knelt down and besought him, but the Hermit would not talk to him about God, nor give him his Treasure, and the young Robber rose up and said to the Hermit, "Be it as you will. As for myself, I will go to the City of the Seven Sins, that is but three days' journey from this place, and for my purple they will give me pleasure, and for my pearls they will sell me joy." And he took up the purple and the pearls and went swiftly away.

And the Hermit cried out and followed him and besought him. For the space of three days he followed the young Robber on the road and entreated him to return, nor to enter into the City of the Seven Sins.

And ever and anon the young Robber looked back at the Hermit and called to him, and said, "Will you give me this knowledge of God which is more precious than purple and pearls? If you will give me that, I will not enter the city."

And ever did the Hermit answer, "All things that I have I will give thee, save that one thing only. For that thing it is not lawful for me to give away."

And in the twilight of the third day they came nigh to the great scarlet gates of the City of the Seven Sins. And from the city there came the sound of much laughter.

And the young Robber laughed in answer, and sought to knock at the gate. And as he did so the Hermit ran forward and caught him by the skirts of his raiment, and said to him: "Stretch forth your hands, and set your arms around my neck, and put your ear close to my lips, and I will give you what remains to me of the knowledge of God." And the young Robber stopped.

And when the Hermit had given away his knowledge of God, he fell upon the ground and wept, and a great darkness hid from him the city and the young Robber, so that he saw them no more.

And as he lay there weeping he was aware of One who was standing beside him; and He who was standing beside him had feet of brass and hair like fine wool. And He raised the Hermit up, and said to him: "Before this time thou hadst the perfect knowledge of God. Now thou shalt have the perfect love of God. Wherefore art thou weeping?" And He kissed him.

POEMS

THEOCRITUS

*A Villanelle**

O singer of Persephone![†]
   In the dim meadows desolate
Dost thou remember Sicily?

Still through the ivy flits the bee
   Where Amaryllis lies in state;
O Singer of Persephone!

Simætha calls on Hecate
   And hears the wild dogs at the gate;
Dost thou remember Sicily?

Still by the light and laughing sea
   Poor Polypheme bemoans his fate;
O Singer of Persephone!

And still in boyish rivalry
   Young Daphnis challenges his mate;
Dost thou remember Sicily?

Slim Lacon keeps a goat for thee,
   For thee the jocund shepherds wait;

---

* Complex song form inherited from Provençal tradition. The nineteen lines of a villanelle contain only two line-ending sounds for rhyming. The first and third lines of the first stanza appear as alternating third lines in the next four three-line stanzas, and form a couplet at the end of the concluding quatrain.

† Mythic nymph of natural springtime rebirth, she descended, at a place in Sicily where she had been raped by Dis (also known as Pluto or Hades), to pass the winter months in the Underworld.

O Singer of Persephone!
Dost thou remember Sicily?

THE HARLOT'S HOUSE

We caught the tread of dancing feet,
We loitered down the moonlit street,
And stopped beneath the harlot's house.

Inside, above the din and fray,
We heard the loud musicians play
The "Treues Liebes Herz"* of Strauss.

Like strange mechanical grotesques,
Making fantastic arabesques,
The shadows raced across the blind.

We watched the ghostly dancers spin
To sound of horn and violin,
Like black leaves wheeling in the wind.

Like wire-pulled automatons,
Slim silhouetted skeletons
Went sidling through the slow quadrille.

They took each other by the hand,
And danced a stately saraband;
Their laughter echoed thin and shrill.

Sometimes a clockwork puppet pressed
A phantom lover to her breast,
Sometimes they seemed to try to sing.

---

* "Heart of True Love" (German); reference to a sentimental waltz tune that Wilde attributes to Johann Strauss.

Sometimes a horrible marionette
Came out, and smoked its cigarette
Upon the steps like a live thing.

Then, turning to my love, I said,
"The dead are dancing with the dead,
The dust is whirling with the dust."

But she—she heard the violin,
And left my side, and entered in:
Love passed into the house of lust.

Then suddenly the tune went false,
The dancers wearied of the waltz,
The shadows ceased to wheel and whirl.

And down the long and silent street,
The dawn, with silver-sandalled feet,
Crept like a frightened girl.

IMPRESSION DE VOYAGE*

The sea was sapphire coloured, and the sky
  Burned like a heated opal through the air;
  We hoisted sail; the wind was blowing fair
For the blue lands that to the eastward lie.
From the steep prow I marked with quickening eye
  Zakynthos, every olive grove and creek,
  Ithaca's cliff, Lycaon's snowy peak,
And all the flower-strewn hills of Arcady.
The flapping of the sail against the mast,

* This title and several that follow recall that Wilde, partly through the American painter James McNeill Whistler, was fascinated by the rise of artistic impressionism.

The ripple of the water on the side,
The ripple of girls' laughter at the stern,
The only sounds:—when 'gan the West to burn,
And a red sun upon the seas to ride.
I stood upon the soil of Greece at last!

IMPRESSION DU MATIN

The Thames nocturne* of blue and gold
Changed to a Harmony in grey:
A barge with ochre-coloured hay
Dropt from the wharf: and chill and cold

The yellow fog came creeping down
The bridges, till the houses' walls
Seemed changed to shadows and St. Paul's
Loomed like a bubble o'er the town.

Then suddenly arose the clang
Of waking life; the streets were stirred
With country waggons: and a bird
Flew to the glistening roofs and sang.

But one pale woman all alone,
The daylight kissing her wan hair,
Loitered beneath the gas lamps' flare,
With lips of flame and heart of stone.

---

* This musical term for a dreamy "night piece," like the "symphony" of the next poem's title, suggests an intense mixture of different sense data—a late Romantic synesthesia.

SYMPHONY IN YELLOW

An omnibus across the bridge
  Crawls like a yellow butterfly,
  And, here and there, a passer-by
Shows like a little restless midge.

Big barges full of yellow hay
  Are moored against the shadowy wharf,
  And, like a yellow silken scarf,
The thick fog hangs along the quay.

The yellow leaves begin to fade
  And flutter from the Temple* elms,
  And at my feet the pale green Thames
Lies like a rod of rippled jade.

IMPRESSION

Le Réveillon†

  The sky is laced with fitful red,
  The circling mists and shadows flee,
  The dawn is rising from the sea,
Like a white lady from her bed.

  And jagged brazen arrows fall
  Athwart the feathers of the night,
  And a long wave of yellow light
Breaks silently on tower and hall,

  And spreading wide across the wold,
  Wakes into flight some fluttering bird,

* Reference to the Inner and Middle Temple, two of four associations located in London at the Inns of Court, for centuries the center of English legal activity.

† The dawning of the day (French).

And all the chestnut tops are stirred,
And all the branches streaked with gold.

IMPRESSIONS

- 1 -

Le Jardin

The lily's withered chalice falls
Around its rod of dusty gold,
And from the beech-trees on the wold
The last wood-pigeon coos and calls.

The gaudy leonine sunflower
Hangs black and barren on its stalk,
And down the windy garden walk
The dead leaves scatter,—hour by hour.

Pale privet-petals white as milk
Are blown into a snowy mass:
The roses lie upon the grass
Like little shreds of crimson silk.

- 2 -

La Mer

A white mist drifts across the shrouds,
A wild moon in this wintry sky
Gleams like an angry lion's eye
Out of a mane of tawny clouds.

The muffled steersman at the wheel
Is but a shadow in the gloom;—
And in the throbbing engine-room
Leap the long rods of polished steel.

The shattered storm has left its trace
  Upon this huge and heaving dome,
  For the thin threads of yellow foam
Float on the waves like ravelled lace.

– 3 –

Le Jardin des Tuileries

This winter air* is keen and cold,
  And keen and cold this winter sun,
  But round my chair the children run
Like little things of dancing gold.

Sometimes about the painted kiosk
  The mimic soldiers strut and stride,
  Sometimes the blue-eyed brigands hide
In the bleak tangles of the bosk.

And sometimes, while the old nurse cons
  Her book, they steal across the square,
  And launch their paper navies where
Huge Triton writhes in greenish bronze.

And now in mimic flight they flee,
  And now they rush, a boisterous band—
  And, tiny hand on tiny hand,
Climb up the black and leafless tree.

Ah! cruel tree! if I were you,
  And children climbed me, for their sake
  Though it be winter I would break
Into spring blossoms white and blue!

---

* In this winter scene in the famed garden of the Tuileries Palace, located near the Louvre museum, Wilde exploits the cool formal design of a classic French urban landscape.

THE BALLAD OF READING GAOL

– 1 –

He did not wear his scarlet coat,
For blood and wine are red,
And blood and wine were on his hands
When they found him with the dead,
The poor dead woman whom he loved,
And murdered in her bed.

He walked amongst the Trial Men
In a suit of shabby grey;
A cricket cap was on his head,
And his step seemed light and gay;
But I never saw a man who looked
So wistfully at the day.

I never saw a man who looked
With such a wistful eye
Upon that little tent of blue
Which prisoners call the sky,
And at every drifting cloud that went
With sails of silver by.

I walked, with other souls in pain,
Within another ring,
And was wondering if the man had done
A great or little thing,
When a voice behind me whispered low,
"*That fellow's got to swing.*"

Dear Christ! the very prison walls
Suddenly seemed to reel,
And the sky above my head became
Like a casque of scorching steel;

And, though I was a soul in pain,
  My pain I could not feel.

I only knew what hunted thought
  Quickened his step, and why
He looked upon the garish day
  With such a wistful eye;
The man had killed the thing he loved,
  And so he had to die.

*

Yet each man kills the thing he loves,
  By each let this be heard,
Some do it with a bitter look,
  Some with a flattering word.
The coward does it with a kiss,
  The brave man with a sword!

Some kill their love when they are young,
  And some when they are old;
Some strangle with the hands of Lust,
  Some with the hands of Gold:
The kindest use a knife, because
  The dead so soon grow cold.

Some love too little, some too long,
  Some sell, and others buy;
Some do the deed with many tears,
  And some without a sigh:
For each man kills the thing he loves,
  Yet each man does not die.

He does not die a death of shame
  On a day of dark disgrace,
Nor have a noose about his neck,
  Nor a cloth upon his face,

Nor drop feet foremost through the floor
Into an empty space.

He does not sit with silent men
Who watch him night and day;
Who watch him when he tries to weep,
And when he tries to pray;
Who watch him lest himself should rob
The prison of its prey.

He does not wake at dawn to see
Dread figures throng his room,
The shivering Chaplain robed in white,
The Sheriff stern with gloom,
And the Governor all in shiny black,
With the yellow face of Doom.

He does not rise in piteous haste
To put on convict-clothes,
While some coarse-mouthed Doctor gloats, and notes
Each new and nerve-twitched pose,
Fingering a watch whose little ticks
Are like horrible hammer-blows.

He does not feel that sickening thirst
That sands one's throat, before
The hangman with his gardener's gloves
Slips through the padded door,
And binds one with three leathern thongs,
That the throat may thirst no more.

He does not bend his head to hear
The Burial Office* read,

* Traditional Anglican prayer service for a funeral.

Nor, while the terror of his soul
  Tells him he is not dead,
Cross his own coffin, as he moves
  Into the hideous shed.

He does not stare upon the air
  Through a little roof of glass:
He does not pray with lips of clay
  For his agony to pass;
Nor feel upon his shuddering cheek
  The kiss of Caiaphas.*

– 2 –

Six weeks our guardsman† walked the yard,
  In the suit of shabby grey:
His cricket cap was on his head,
  And his step seemed light and gay,
But I never saw a man who looked
  So wistfully at the day.

I never saw a man who looked
  With such a wistful eye
Upon that little tent of blue
  Which prisoners call the sky,
And at every wandering cloud that trailed
  Its ravelled fleeces by.

He did not wring his hands, as do
  Those witless men who dare
To try to rear the changeling Hope
  In the cave of black Despair:

---

* High priest who organized the plot against Christ (Matthew 26). Wilde said he meant "any priest of god who assists at the unjust and cruel punishment of man."

† For the first time in the poem, Wilde gives the rank of the prisoner. Charles Thomas Wooldridge was a trooper in the Royal Horse Guards.

He only looked upon the sun,
And drank the morning air.

He did not wring his hands nor weep,
Nor did he peek or pine,
But he drank the air as though it held
Some healthful anodyne;
With open mouth he drank the sun
As though it had been wine!

And I and all the souls in pain,
Who tramped the other ring,
Forgot if we ourselves had done
A great or little thing,
And watched with gaze of dull amaze
The man who had to swing.

And strange it was to see him pass
With a step so light and gay,
And strange it was to see him look
So wistfully at the day,
And strange it was to think that he
Had such a debt to pay.

*

For oak and elm have pleasant leaves
That in the spring-time shoot;
But grim to see is the gallows-tree,
With its adder-bitten root,
And, green or dry, a man must die
Before it bears its fruit!

The loftiest place is that seat of grace
For which all worldlings try:

But who would stand in hempen band
   Upon a scaffold high,
And through a murderer's collar take
   His last look at the sky?

It is sweet to dance to violins
   When Love and Life are fair:
To dance to flutes, to dance to lutes
   Is delicate and rare:
But it is not sweet with nimble feet
   To dance upon the air!

So with curious eyes and sick surmise
   We watched him day by day,
And wondered if each one of us
   Would end the self-same way,
For none can tell to what red Hell
   His sightless soul may stray.

At last the dead man walked no more
   Amongst the Trial Men,
And I knew that he was standing up
   In the black dock's dreadful pen,
And that never would I see his face
   In God's sweet world again.

Like two doomed ships that pass in storm
   We had crossed each other's way:
But we made no sign, we said no word,
   We had no word to say;
For we did not meet in the holy night,
   But in the shameful day.

A prison wall was round us both,
   Two outcast men we were:

The world had thrust us from its heart,
  And God from out His care:
And the iron gin that waits for Sin
  Had caught us in its snare.

– 3 –

In Debtor's Yard the stones are hard,
  And the dripping wall is high,
So it was there he took the air
  Beneath the leaden sky,
And by each side a Warder walked,
  For fear the man might die.

Or else he sat with those who watched
  His anguish night and day;
Who watched him when he rose to weep,
  And when he crouched to pray;
Who watched him lest himself should rob
  Their scaffold of its prey.

The Governor was strong upon
  The Regulations Act:
The Doctor said that Death was but
  A scientific fact:
And twice a day the Chaplain called,
  And left a little tract.

And twice a day he smoked his pipe,
  And drank his quart of beer:
His soul was resolute, and held
  No hiding-place for fear;
He often said that he was glad
  The hangman's hands were near.

But why he said so strange a thing
  No Warder dared to ask:

For he to whom a watcher's doom
   Is given as his task,
Must set a lock upon his lips,
   And make his face a mask.

Or else he might be moved, and try
   To comfort or console:
And what should Human Pity do
   Pent up in Murderers' Hole?
What word of grace in such a place
   Could help a brother's soul?

With slouch and swing around the ring
   We trod the Fools' Parade!
We did not care: we knew we were
   The Devil's Own Brigade:
And shaven head and feet of lead
   Make a merry masquerade.

We tore the tarry rope* to shreds
   With blunt and bleeding nails;
We rubbed the doors, and scrubbed the floors,
   And cleaned the shining rails:
And, rank by rank, we soaped the plank,
   And clattered with the pails.

We sewed the sacks, we broke the stones,
   We turned the dusty drill:
We banged the tins, and bawled the hymns,
   And sweated on the mill:
But in the heart of every man
   Terror was lying still.

---

* Among the hard labors Wilde performed was pulling apart old rope saturated with tar, a task that was brutally hard on the hands.

So still it lay that every day
  Crawled like a weed-clogged wave:
And we forgot the bitter lot
  That waits for fool and knave,
Till once, as we tramped in from work,
  We passed an open grave.

With yawning mouth the yellow hole
  Gaped for a living thing;
The very mud cried out for blood
  To the thirsty asphalte ring:
And we knew that ere one dawn grew fair
  Some prisoner had to swing.

Right in we went, with soul intent
  On Death and Dread and Doom:
The hangman, with his little bag,
  Went shuffling through the gloom:
And each man trembled as he crept
  Into his numbered tomb.

*

That night the empty corridors
  Were full of forms of Fear,
And up and down the iron town
  Stole feet we could not hear,
And through the bars that hide the stars
  White faces seemed to peer.

He lay as one who lies and dreams
  In a pleasant meadow-land,
The watchers watched him as he slept,
  And could not understand
How one could sleep so sweet a sleep
  With a hangman close at hand.

But there is no sleep when men must weep
Who never yet have wept:
So we—the fool, the fraud, the knave—
That endless vigil kept,
And through each brain on hands of pain
Another's terror crept.

Alas! it is a fearful thing
To feel another's guilt!
For, right within, the Sword of Sin
Pierced to its poisoned hilt,
And as molten lead were the tears we shed
For the blood we had not spilt.

The Warders with their shoes of felt
Crept by each padlocked door,
And peeped and saw, with eyes of awe,
Grey figures on the floor,
And wondered why men knelt to pray
Who never prayed before.

All through the night we knelt and prayed,
Mad mourners of a corse!
The troubled plumes of midnight were
The plumes upon a hearse:
And bitter wine upon a sponge
Was the savour of Remorse.

*

The grey cock crew, the red cock crew,
But never came the day:
And crooked shapes of Terror crouched,
In the corners where we lay:
And each evil sprite that walks by night
Before us seemed to play.

They glided past, they glided fast,
    Like travellers through a mist:
They mocked the moon in a rigadoon
    Of delicate turn and twist,
And with formal pace and loathsome grace
    The phantoms kept their tryst.

With mop and mow, we saw them go,
    Slim shadows hand in hand:
About, about, in ghostly rout
    They trod a saraband:
And the damned grotesques made arabesques,
    Like the wind upon the sand!

With the pirouettes of marionettes,
    They tripped on pointed tread:
But with flutes of Fear they filled the ear,
    As their grisly masque they led,
And loud they sang, and long they sang,
    For they sang to wake the dead.

"*Oho!*" they cried, "*The world is wide*
But fettered limbs go lame!
And once, or twice, to throw the dice
    Is a gentlemanly game,
But he does not win who plays with Sin
    In the secret House of Shame."

No things of air these antics were,
    That frolicked with such glee:
To men whose lives were held in gyves,
    And whose feet might not go free,
Ah! wounds of Christ! they were living things
    Most terrible to see.

Around, around, they waltzed and wound;
  Some wheeled in smirking pairs;
With the mincing step of a demirep
  Some sidled up the stairs:
And with subtle sneer, and fawning leer,
  Each helped us at our prayers.

The morning wind began to moan,
  But still the night went on:
Through its giant loom the web of gloom
  Crept till each thread was spun:
And, as we prayed, we grew afraid
  Of the Justice of the Sun.

The moaning wind went wandering round
  The weeping prison-wall:
Till like a wheel of turning steel
  We felt the minutes crawl:
O moaning wind! what had we done
  To have such a seneschal?

At last I saw the shadowed bars,
  Like a lattice wrought in lead,
Move right across the whitewashed wall
  That faced my three-plank bed,
And I knew that somewhere in the world
  God's dreadful dawn was red.

At six o'clock we cleaned our cells,
  At seven all was still,
But the sough and swing of a mighty wing
  The prison seemed to fill,
For the Lord of Death with icy breath
  Had entered in to kill.

He did not pass in purple pomp,
  Nor ride a moon-white steed.
Three yards of cord and a sliding board
  Are all the gallows' need:
So with rope of shame the Herald came
  To do the secret deed.

We were as men who through a fen
  Of filthy darkness grope:
We did not dare to breathe a prayer,
  Or to give our anguish scope:
Something was dead in each of us,
  And what was dead was Hope.

For Man's grim Justice goes its way,
  And will not swerve aside:
It slays the weak, it slays the strong,
  It has a deadly stride:
With iron heel it slays the strong,
  The monstrous parricide!

We waited for the stroke of eight:
  Each tongue was thick with thirst:
For the stroke of eight is the stroke of Fate
  That makes a man accursed,
And Fate will use a running noose
  For the best man and the worst.

We had no other thing to do,
  Save to wait for the sign to come:
So, like things of stone in a valley lone,
  Quiet we sat and dumb:
But each man's heart beat thick and quick,
  Like a madman on a drum!

With sudden shock the prison-clock
  Smote on the shivering air,
And from all the gaol rose up a wail
  Of impotent despair,
Like the sound that frightened marshes hear
  From some leper in his lair.

And as one sees most fearful things
  In the crystal of a dream,
We saw the greasy hempen rope
  Hooked to the blackened beam,
And heard the prayer the hangman's snare
  Strangled into a scream.

And all the woe that moved him so
  That he gave that bitter cry,
And the wild regrets, and the bloody sweats,
  None knew so well as I:
For he who lives more lives than one
  More deaths than one must die.

– 4 –

There is no chapel on the day
  On which they hang a man:
The Chaplain's heart is far too sick,
  Or his face is far too wan,
Or there is that written in his eyes
  Which none should look upon.

So they kept us close till nigh on noon,
  And then they rang the bell,
And the Warders with their jingling keys
  Opened each listening cell,
And down the iron stair we tramped,
  Each from his separate Hell.

Out into God's sweet air we went,
    But not in wonted way,
For this man's face was white with fear,
    And that man's face was grey,
And I never saw sad men who looked
    So wistfully at the day.

I never saw sad men who looked
    With such a wistful eye
Upon that little tent of blue
    We prisoners called the sky,
And at every careless cloud that passed
    In happy freedom by.

But there were those amongst us all
    Who walked with downcast head,
And knew that, had each got his due,
    They should have died instead:
He had but killed a thing that lived,
    Whilst they had killed the dead.

For he who sins a second time
    Wakes a dead soul to pain,
And draws it from its spotted shroud,
    And makes it bleed again,
And makes it bleed great gouts of blood,
    And makes it bleed in vain!

*

Like ape or clown, in monstrous garb
    With crooked arrows starred,
Silently we went round and round
    The slippery asphalte yard;
Silently we went round and round,
    And no man spoke a word.

Silently we went round and round,
And through each hollow mind
The Memory of dreadful things
Rushed like a dreadful wind,
And Horror stalked before each man,
And Terror crept behind.

*

The Warders strutted up and down,
And kept their herd of brutes,
Their uniforms were spick and span,
And they wore their Sunday suits,
But we knew the work they had been at,
By the quicklime* on their boots.

For where a grave had opened wide,
There was no grave at all:
Only a stretch of mud and sand
By the hideous prison-wall,
And a little heap of burning lime,
That the man should have his pall.

For he has a pall, this wretched man,
Such as few men can claim:
Deep down below a prison-yard,
Naked for greater shame,
He lies, with fetters on each foot,
Wrapt in a sheet of flame!

And all the while the burning lime
Eats flesh and bone away,
It eats the brittle bone by night,
And the soft flesh by day,

---

* Quicklime would dissolve the hanged man's body; no trace of him would be left in the sand.

It eats the flesh and bone by turns,
  But it eats the heart alway.

*

For three long years they will not sow
  Or root or seedling there:
For three long years the unblessed spot
  Will sterile be and bare,
And look upon the wondering sky
  With unreproachful stare.

They think a murderer's heart would taint
  Each simple seed they sow.
It is not true! God's kindly earth
  Is kindlier than men know,
And the red rose would but blow more red,
  The white rose whiter blow.

Out of his mouth a red, red rose!
  Out of his heart a white!
For who can say by what strange way,
  Christ brings His will to light,
Since the barren staff the pilgrim bore
  Bloomed in the great Pope's sight?

But neither milk-white rose nor red
  May bloom in prison-air;
The shard, the pebble, and the flint,
  Are what they give us there:
For flowers have been known to heal
  A common man's despair.

So never will wine-red rose or white,
  Petal by petal, fall
On that stretch of mud and sand that lies
  By the hideous prison-wall,

To tell the men who tramp the yard
    That God's Son died for all.

Yet though the hideous prison-wall
    Still hems him round and round,
And a spirit may not walk by night
    That is with fetters bound,
And a spirit may but weep that lies
    In such unholy ground,

He is at peace—this wretched man—
    At peace, or will be soon:
There is no thing to make him mad,
    Nor does Terror walk at noon,
For the lampless Earth in which he lies
    Has neither Sun nor Moon.

They hanged him as a beast is hanged!
    They did not even toll
A requiem that might have brought
    Rest to his startled soul,
But hurriedly they took him out,
    And hid him in a hole.

They stripped him of his canvas clothes,
    And gave him to the flies:
They mocked the swollen purple throat,
    And the stark and staring eyes:
And with laughter loud they heaped the shroud
    In which their convict lies.

The Chaplain would not kneel to pray
    By his dishonoured grave:
Nor mark it with that blessed Cross
    That Christ for sinners gave,

Because the man was one of those
   Whom Christ came down to save.

Yet all is well; he has but passed
   To Life's appointed bourne:
And alien tears will fill for him
   Pity's long-broken urn,
For his mourners will be outcast men,
   And outcasts always mourn.

– 5 –

I know not whether Laws be right,
   Or whether Laws be wrong;
All that we know who lie in gaol
   Is that the wall is strong;
And that each day is like a year,
   A year whose days are long.

But this I know, that every Law
   That men hath made for Man,
Since first Man took his brother's life,
   And the sad world began,
But straws the wheat and saves the chaff
   With a most evil fan.

This too I know—and wise it were
   If each could know the same—
That every prison that men build
   Is built with bricks of shame,
And bound with bars lest Christ should see
   How men their brothers maim.

With bars they blur the gracious moon,
   And blind the goodly sun;
And they do well to hide their Hell,
   For in it things are done

That Son of God nor son of Man
   Ever should look upon!

*

The vilest deeds like poison weeds,
   Bloom well in prison-air;
It is only what is good in Man
   That wastes and withers there:
Pale Anguish keeps the heavy gate,
   And the Warder is Despair.

For they starve the little frightened child
   Till it weeps both night and day:
And they scourge the weak, and flog the fool,
   And gibe the old and grey,
And some grow mad, and all grow bad,
   And none a word may say.

Each narrow cell in which we dwell
   Is a foul and dark latrine,
And the fetid breath of living Death
   Chokes up each grated screen,
And all, but Lust, is turned to dust
   In Humanity's machine.

The brackish water that we drink
   Creeps with a loathsome slime,
And the bitter bread they weigh in scales
   Is full of chalk and lime,
And Sleep will not lie down, but walks
   Wild-eyed, and cries to Time.

*

But though lean Hunger and green Thirst
   Like asp with adder fight,

We have little care of prison fare,
For what chills and kills outright
Is that every stone one lifts by day
Becomes one's heart by night.

With midnight always in one's heart,
And twilight in one's cell,
We turn the crank, or tear the rope,
Each in his separate Hell,
And the silence is more awful far
Than the sound of a brazen bell.

And never a human voice comes near
To speak a gentle word:
And the eye that watches through the door
Is pitiless and hard:
And by all forgot, we rot and rot,
With soul and body marred.

And thus we rust Life's iron chain
Degraded and alone:
And some men curse, and some men weep,
And some men make no moan:
But God's eternal Laws are kind
And break the heart of stone.

And every human heart that breaks,
In prison-cell or yard,
Is as that broken box that gave
Its treasure to the Lord,
And filled the unclean leper's house
With the scent of costliest nard.

Ah! happy they whose hearts can break
And peace of pardon win!

How else may man make straight his plan
  And cleanse his soul from Sin?
How else but through a broken heart
  May Lord Christ enter in?

*

And he of the swollen purple throat,
  And the stark and staring eyes,
Waits for the holy hands that took
  The Thief to Paradise;
And a broken and a contrite heart
  The Lord will not despise.

The man in red who reads the Law
  Gave him three weeks of life,
Three little weeks in which to heal
  His soul of his soul's strife,
And cleanse from every blot of blood
  The hand that held the knife.

And with tears of blood he cleansed the hand,
  The hand that held the steel:
For only blood can wipe out blood,
  And only tears can heal:
And the crimson stain that was of Cain
  Became Christ's snow-white seal.

– 6 –

In Reading gaol by Reading town
  There is a pit of shame,
And in it lies a wretched man
  Eaten by teeth of flame,
In a burning winding-sheet he lies,
  And his grave has got no name.

And there, till Christ call forth the dead,
  In silence let him lie:

No need to waste the foolish tear,
    Or heave the windy sigh:
The man had killed the thing he loved,
    And so he had to die.

And all men kill the thing they love,
    By all let this be heard,
Some do it with a bitter look,
    Some with a flattering word,
The coward does it with a kiss,
    The brave man with a sword!

LECTURES

THE ENGLISH RENAISSANCE[4]

AMONG THE MANY DEBTS which we owe to the supreme æsthetic faculty of Goethe is that he was the first to teach us to define beauty in terms the most concrete possible, to realise it, I mean, always in its special manifestations. So, in the lecture which I have the honor to deliver before you, I will not try to give you any abstract definition of beauty, any such universal formula as was sought for by the philosophy of the eighteenth century; still less to communicate to you that which in its essence is incommunicable, the virtue by which a particular picture or poem affects us with a unique or special joy; but rather to point out to you the general ideas which characterise the great English renaissance of art in this century.

The English renaissance has been described as a mere revival of the Greek modes of thought, and again as a mere revival of mediæval feeling; rather, I would say, that to these forms of the human spirit it has added whatever artistic value the intricacy and complexity and experience of modern life can give. It is from the union of Hellenism in its breadth, its sanity of purpose, its calm possession of beauty, with the adventive, the intensified individualism, the passionate colour of the romantic spirit, that springs out of the nineteenth century in England, as from the marriage of Faust and Helen of Troy sprang the beautiful Lady Euphonia. In the womb of the French revolution, and in the storm and terror of that wild time, tendencies were hidden away that the artistic renaissance bent to her own service when the time came. And that desire for perfection which lay at the base of the revolution found in a young English poet its most complete and flawless realisation. Phidias and the achievements in Greek art are foreshadowed in Homer. Dante prefigures for us the passion and colour and intensity of Italian painting. The modern love of landscape dates from Rousseau, and it is in Keats that one discerns the beginning of the artistic renaissance of England. He was the forerunner of the pre-Raphaelite school, and so of the great romantic wave of which I will speak. Speaking of the pre-Raphaelites, what are they? If you ask nine-tenths of the British public, what is the meaning of the word æsthetic, they will tell you that it is the French for affectation or the German for a dado.* If you inquire about the pre-Raphaelites, you will hear something about an eccentric lot of young men to whom a sort of divine crookedness and holy awkwardness is drawing all the chief objects of art. To know nothing about their great men is one of the necessary elements of English education.

THE ORIGIN OF THE ART REVOLUTION.

In 1847 a number of young men in London, all admirers of Keats, were in the habit of meeting together and discussing art. They had determined to revolutionise poetry and painting. To do so was to lose, in England, all their rights as citizens. They had those things which the English public never forgives—youth, power and enthusiasm. Satire paid the usual homage which mediocrity yields to genius, blinding the British public to what is noble and beautiful, but harming the artist not at all. To disagree with three-fourths of England on all points is one of the first elements of vanity, which is a deep source of consolation in all moments of spiritual doubt.

These young men called themselves pre-Raphaelites because, as opposed to the facile abstractions of Raphael they thought they had found a stronger realism of imagination, a more careful realism of technique, an individuality more intense. But of all things was it a return to Nature. Later on, there came to the old house by Black-friars Bridge, Edward Burne-Jones and William Morris, who added a more exquisite spirit of choice, a more faultless devotion to beauty, and more intense seeking for perfection. Morris felt that the close imitation of Nature was a disturbing element in imaginative art. To him we owe poetry the perfect precision of which, and the clearness of word and vision, have not been excelled in the literature of our country.

---

* Skirting board or wainscot, placed for decorative purposes along a wall.

Great eras in the history of arts have been eras not only of increased feeling, but also of new technical improvements. The revolution in modern music has been due to the invention of new instruments entirely. The artist may trace the depressed revolution of Bunthorne simply to the lack of technical means. So it has been with this romantic movement of ours. The painting of Burne-Jones shows a far more intricate wonder of design and splendour of color than English imaginative art had ever shown before. The poetry of Morris, Rossetti and Swinburne shows a sustaining consciousness of the musical value of each word which Theophile Gautier's advice* to the young poet, to read his dictionary every day as being the only book worth a poet's reading, admirably expresses. And yet, what people call the poet's inspiration has not lost its wings; but we have accustomed ourselves to count their innumerable pulsations, to estimate their limitless strength, and to govern their ungovernable freedom.

THE CHOICE OF SUBJECTS.

And now I would point out to you the operation of the artistic spirit in the choice of subject. Like the philosopher of the platonic vision, the poet is the spectator of all time and all existence. For him no form is obsolete, no subject out of date; rather, whatever of life and passion the world has known in the desert of Judea or in Arcadian valley, by the ruins of Troy or Damascus, in the crowded and hideous streets of the modern city, or by the pleasant ways of Camelot, all lies before him like an open scroll, all is still instinct with beautiful life. He will take of it what is salutary for his own spirit, choosing some facts and rejecting others, with a calm artistic control of one who is in possession of the secret of beauty. It is to no avail that the muse of poetry be called even by such a clarion note as Whitman's to migrate from Greece and Ionia and to placard "removed" and "to let" on the rocks of the snowy Parnassus. For art, to quote a noble passage of

* Theophile Gauthier (1811–1872) was a Wilde hero, especially because of his preface to his novel *Mademoiselle de Maupin*.

Mr. Swinburne's,* is very life itself and knows nothing of death. And so it comes that he who seems to stand most remote from his age is he who mirrors it best, because he has stripped life of that mist of familiarity which, as Shelley used to say, makes life obscure to us.

Whatever spiritual message an artist brings to his age, it is for us to do naught but accept his teaching. You have most of you seen probably that great masterpiece of Rubens which hangs in the gallery of Brussels, that swift and wonderful pageant of horse and rider, arrested in its most exquisite and fiery moment, when the winds are caught in crimson banner and the air is lit by the gleam of armour and the flash of plume. Well, that is joy in art, though that golden hillside be trodden by the wounded feet of Christ; and it is for the death of the Son of Man that that gorgeous cavalcade is passing.

CHANNELS THROUGH WHICH THE SOUL IS TOUCHED.

In its primary aspect a painting has no more spiritual message than an exquisite fragment of Venetian glass. The channels by which all noble and imaginative work in painting should touch the soul are not those of the truths of lives. This should be done by a certain inventive and creative handling entirely independent of anything definitely poetical in the subject, something entirely satisfying in itself, which is, as the Greeks would say, in itself an end. So the joy of poetry comes never from the subject, but from an inventive handling of rhythmical language.

THE PLACE OF CRITICISM.

What place has criticism in our culture? I think that the first duty of an art critic is to hold his tongue at all times and upon all subjects. You have listened to "Patience"† for a hundred nights, and you have

* Controversial British poet Algernon Charles Swinburne (1837–1909) was an important poetic model for Wilde.

† Gilbert and Sullivan opera satirizing Wilde and the aesthetic movement; in it he is called Reginald Bunthorne.

only heard me for one. It will make, no doubt, that satire more piquant by knowing something about the subject of it. But you must not judge of æstheticism by the satire of Mr. Gilbert, any more than you judge of the strength and splendour of sun or sea by the dust that dances in the beam or the bubble that breaks on the wave. Don't take your critic as any sure test of art. For artists, like the Greek gods, are only revealed to one another. As Emerson says somewhere, their real value and place time only can show. The true critic addresses not the artist ever, but the public. His work lies with them. Art can never have any other aim but her own perfection. I have no reverence, said Keats, for the public, or for anything in existence but the Eternal Being, the memory of great men, and the principle of beauty.

Such, then, is the spirit which I believe to be guiding and underlying our English Renaissance, a Renaissance many-sided and wonderful, promotive of strong ambitions and lofty personalities; yet for all its splendid achievements in poetry and the decorative arts, and in painting, for all the increased comeliness and grace of dress and of furniture of houses, not complete. For there can be no great sculpture without a beautiful national life, and the commercial spirit of England has killed that; no great drama without a noble national life, and the commercial spirit of England has killed that, too.

THE NOVEL AND THE DRAMA.

The novel has not killed the play, as some critics would persuade us. The romantic period of France shows that the work of Balzac and of Hugo grew up side by side together—nay, more, were complementary to each other, although neither of them saw it. The drama is the meeting place of art and life; it deals, as Mazzini said, not merely with man, but with social man, with man in relation to God and to humanity. It is the product of a period of great, national, united energy. It is impossible without a noble public, and it belongs to such ages as the age of Elizabeth, at London, Pericles, at Athens. It is part of such lofty moral and spiritual ardour as came to Greece after the defeat of the Persian fleet, and to Englishmen after the wreck of the Armada of Spain.

Shelley* felt how incomplete our movement was in this respect, and has shown in one great tragedy by what terror and pity he would have pacified our age; but in spite of the "Cenci," the drama is one of the artistic forms through which the genius of England seeks in vain an outlet and an expression.

AMERICA TO COMPLETE THE MOVEMENT.

It is rather, perhaps, to you that we would turn to complete and perfect this great movement of ours, for there is something Hellenic in your air and world, something that has a quicker breath of the joy and power of Elizabeth's England about it than our ancient civilisation can give us. For you, at least, are young; no hungry generations tread you down, and the past does not mock you with the ruins of a beauty, the secret of whose creation you have lost. That very absence of tradition which Ruskin† thought would rob your rivers of their laughter and your flowers of their light may be rather the source of your freedom and strength. To speak in literature with the perfect rectitude of the movement of animals, and the unimpeachableness of the sentiments of trees and the grass by the roadside, has been defined by one of your poets as the flawless triumph of art; it is a triumph which you above all other nations may be destined to achieve. For the voices that have their dwelling in sea and mountain are not the chosen music of liberty only. Other messages are there, if you will but listen to them—may yield you the splendour of some new imagination, the marvel of some new liberty.

If, then, this is so, and the materials for a civilisation lie all around you, what profit, you will ask me, will all this study of our poets and painters bring you? I might answer that the intellect can be engaged without a direct, didactic object, on an artistic and historical problem—that the demand of the intellect is merely to feel itself

---

* Percy Bysshe Shelley (1792–1822), the great Romantic poet, also wrote an important tragedy, *The Cenci*.

† Poet, artist, and critic John Ruskin (1819–1900) was a hero to Wilde, not only for his literary criticism, but also for his argument that society should demand serious aesthetic commitment.

alive. I think such a study will bring you something that is the knowledge of real strength in art, not that you should imitate the works of great men, but their artistic spirit.

WHERE MORALITY IS NOT IN QUESTION.

In nations, as in individuals, if the passion for creation be not accompanied by the critical, the æsthetic faculty also, it will be sure to waste its strength. It is not an increased moral sense or moral supervision that your literature needs. Indeed, one should never talk of a moral or immoral poem. Poems are either well written or badly written; that is all. Any element of morals or implied reference to a standard of good and evil in art is often a sign of a certain incompleteness of vision. All good work aims at a purely artistic effect. But as in your cities so in your literature, it is an increased sensibility to beauty that is lacking. All noble work is not national merely, but universal. Spiritual freedom your own generous lives and liberal air will give you. From us you will learn the classical restraint of form. Love art for its own sake and then all things that you need will be added to you. This devotion to beauty, and to the creation of beautiful things, is the test of all great civilisations; it is what makes the life of each citizen a sacrament and not a speculation. For beauty is the only thing that time cannot harm. Philosophies fall away like sand, creeds follow one another, but what is beautiful is a joy for all seasons, a possession for all eternity.

Wars there must be always; but I think that creating a common intellectual atmosphere might make men brothers. National hatreds are always strongest where culture is lowest. Great empires there must be as long as personal ambition and the spirit of the age are one; but art is the only empire which a nation's enemies cannot take from her. We in our Renaissance are seeking to create a sovereignty that will still be England's, when her yellow leopards have grown weary of wars, and the rose on her shield is crimsoned no more with the blood of battle. And you, too, absorbing into the heart of a great people this pervading artistic spirit, will create for yourselves such riches as you have never yet created, though your land be a network of railways, and your cities the harbours of the galleys of the world.

THE REASON OF DECORATIVE ART.

I know indeed that the divine prescience of beauty is not our inheritance. For such an informing and presiding spirit of art to shield us from all harsh and alien influences, we of the Teutonic and Saxon races must turn rather to that strained self-consciousness of the age which is the keynote of all our romantic art, and must be the source of all or nearly all our culture. I mean that intellectual curiosity of the nineteenth century which is always looking for the secret of the life that still lingers around old and bygone forms of culture. The truths of art cannot be taught. They are revealed only—revealed to natures which have made themselves receptive of all beautiful impressions by the study of and the worship of all beautiful things. Hence the enormous importance given to the decorative arts in our English Renaissance; hence all that marvel of design that comes from the hand of Edward Burne-Jones; hence all that weaving of tapestry, the staining of glass, and the beautiful working in clay and metal and wood.

THE SUNFLOWER AND THE LILY.

You have heard, I think, a few of you, of two flowers connected with the æsthetic movement in England, said (I assure you, erroneously) to be the food of some æsthetic young men. Well, let me tell you that the reason we love the lily and the sunflower, in spite of what Mr. Gilbert may tell you, is not for any vegetable fashion at all; it is because these two lovely flowers are in England the two most perfect models of design, the most naturally adapted for decorative art—the gaudy leonine beauty of the one and the precious loveliness of the other giving to the artist the most entire and perfect joy. And so with you: let there be no flower in your meadows that does not wreathe its tendrils around your pillows, no little leaf in your Titan forests that does not lend its form to design, no curving spray of wild rose or briar that does not live forever in carven arch or window of marble, no bird in your air that is not giving the iridescent wonder of its colour, the exquisite curves of its wings in flight, to make more precious the preciousness of simple adornment; for the voices that have their dwelling in sea and mountain are not the chosen music of liberty only. Other messages are there in the wonder of wind-swept heights and the majesty of silent deep—messages that, if you will listen to them, will give you the wonder of all new imagination, the treasure of all new beauty. We spend our days, each one of us, in looking for the secret of life. Well, the secret of life is in art.

DECORATIVE ART IN AMERICA

In my first lecture, I gave you something of the history of Art in England. I sought to trace the influence of the French Revolution upon its development. I said something of the song of Keats and the school of the Pre-Raphaelites. But I do not want to shelter the movement which I have called "The English Renaissance" under any palladium, however noble, or any name, however revered. The roots of it have indeed to be sought for in things that have long passed away, and not, as some suppose, in the fancy of a few young men—although I am not altogether sure that there is anything much better than the fancy of a few young men.

When I appeared before you on a previous occasion, I had seen nothing of American art save the Doric columns and Corinthian chimney-pots visible on your Broadway and Fifth Avenue. Since then I have been through your country to some fifty or sixty cities,* I think. I find what your people need is not so much high imaginative art, but that which hallows the vessels of every-day use. I suppose that the poet will sing and the artist will paint regardless whether the world praises or blames. He has his own world and is independent of his fellowmen. But the handicraftsman is dependent on your pleasure and opinion. He needs your encouragement and he must have beautiful surroundings. Your people love art, but do not sufficiently honour the handicraftsmen. Of course, those millionaires who can pillage Europe for their pleasure need have no care to encourage such; but I speak for those whose desire for beautiful things is larger than their means. I find that one great trouble all over is that your workmen are not given to noble designs. You cannot be indifferent to

* Wilde crisscrossed the United States by train, setting a relentless pace; he even had dinner at the bottom of a mine in Leadville, Colorado (see pp. 285, 287).

this, because art is not something which you can take or leave. It is a necessity of human life.

And what is the meaning of this beautiful decoration which we call art? In the first place, it means value to the workman, and it means the pleasure which he must necessarily take in making a beautiful thing. The mark of all good art is not that the thing done is done exactly or finely, for machinery may do as much, but that it is worked out with the head and the workman's heart. I cannot impress the point too frequently that beautiful and rational designs are necessary in all work. I did not imagine until I went into some of your simpler cities that there was so much bad work done. I found where I went bad wall-papers, horribly designed, and coloured carpets, and that old offender, the horse-hair sofa, whose stolid look of indifference is always so depressing. I found meaningless chandeliers and machine-made furniture, generally of rosewood, which creaked dismally under the weight of the ubiquitous interviewer. I came across the small iron stove which they always persist in decorating with machine-made ornaments, and which is as great a bore as a wet day or any other particularly dreadful institution. When unusual extravagance was indulged in it was garnished with two funeral urns.

It must always be remembered that what is well and carefully made by an honest workman after a rational design, increases in beauty and value as the years go on. The old furniture brought over by the Pilgrims two hundred years ago, which I saw in New England, is just as good and as beautiful to-day as it was when it first came here. Now, what you must do is to bring artists and handicraftsmen together. Handicraftsmen cannot live, certainly cannot thrive, without such companionship. Separate these two, and you rob art of all spiritual motive. Having done this, you must place your workman in the midst of beautiful surroundings. The artist is not dependent on the visible and the tangible. He has his visions and his dreams to feed on. But the workman must see lovely forms and beautiful forms, as he goes to his work in the morning and returns at eventide. And, in connection with this, I want to assure you that noble and beautiful designs are never the result of idle fancy or purposeless day-dreaming. They only come as the accumulation of habits of long and delightful observation. And yet such things may not be taught. Right ideas concerning them can certainly only be obtained by those who have been accustomed to rooms that are beautiful and colours that are satisfying.

Perhaps one of the most difficult things for us to do is to choose a notable and joyous dress for men. There would be more joy in life if we should accustom ourselves to use all the beautiful colours we can in fashioning our own clothes. The dress of the future, I think, will use drapery to a great extent and will abound with joyous colour. At present we have lost all nobility of dress, and in doing so, have almost annihilated the modern sculptor. And in looking around at the figures which adorn our parks, one could almost wish that we had completely killed the noble art. To see the frock coat of the drawing-room done in bronze or the double waistcoat perpetuated in marble, adds a new horror to death. But indeed, in looking through the history of costume, seeking an answer to the questions we have propounded, there is little that is either beautiful or appropriate. One of the earliest forms is the Greek drapery, which is so exquisite for young girls. And then, I think we may be pardoned a little enthusiasm over the dress of the time of Charles I, so beautiful indeed, that in spite of its invention being with the Cavaliers, it was copied by the Puritans. And the dress for the children at that time must not be passed over. It was a very golden age of the little ones. I do not think that they have ever looked so lovely as they do in the pictures of that time. The dress of the last century in England is also peculiarly gracious and graceful. There is nothing bizarre or strange about it, but it is full of harmony and beauty. In these days, when we have suffered so dreadfully from the incursions of the modern milliner, we hear ladies boast that they do not wear a dress more than once. In the old days, when the dresses were decorated with beautiful designs and worked with exquisite embroidery, ladies rather took a pride in bringing out the garment and wearing it many times and handing it down to their daughters—a process which I think would be quite appreciated by modern husbands when called upon to settle their wives' bills.

And how shall men dress? Men say they don't particularly care how they dress, and that it is little matter. I am bound to reply that I do not believe them and do not think that you do. In all my journeys through the country, the only well-dressed men that I saw—and in saying this I earnestly deprecate the polished indignation of your Fifth Avenue dandies—were the Western miners. Their wide-brimmed hats, which shaded their faces from the sun and protected them from the rain, and the cloak, which is by far the most beautiful piece of drapery ever invented, may well be dwelt on with admiration. Their high boots, too, were sensible and practical. They wore only what was comfortable and therefore beautiful. As I looked at them, I could not help thinking with regret of the time when these picturesque miners should have made their fortunes and would go East to assume again all the abominations of modern fashionable attire. Indeed, so concerned was I that I made some of them promise that when they again appeared in the more crowded scenes of Eastern civilization they would still continue to wear their lovely costume. But I don't believe they will.

Now, what America wants to-day is a school of rational design. Bad art is a great deal worse than no art at all. You must show your workmen specimens of good work, so that they may come to know what is simple and true and beautiful. To that end I would have you have a museum attached to these schools—not one of those dreadful modern institutions where there are a stuffed and very dusty giraffe and a case or two of fossils, but a place where there are gathered examples of art decoration from various periods and countries. Such a place is the South Kensington Museum in London, whereon we build greater hopes for the future than on any other one thing. There I go every Saturday night, when the Museum is opened later than usual, to see the handicraftsman, the wood-worker, the glass-blower and the worker in metals. And it is here that the man of refinement and culture comes face to face with the workman who ministers to his joy. He comes to know more of the nobility of the workman, and the workman, feeling the appreciation, comes to know more of the nobility of his work.

You have too many white walls. More colour is wanted. You should have such men as Whistler among you to teach you the beauty and joy of colour. Take Mr. Whistler's "Symphony in

White,"* which you no doubt have imagined to be something quite bizarre. It is nothing of the sort. Think of a cool grey sky, flecked here and there with white clouds, a grey ocean and three wonderfully beautiful figures robed in white, leaning over the water and dropping white flowers from their fingers. Here are no extensive intellectual scheme to trouble you and no metaphysics, of which we have had quite enough in art. But if the simple and unaided colour strikes the right keynote, the whole conception is made clear. I regard Mr. Whistler's famous "Peacock Room" as the finest thing in colour and art decoration which the world has known since Correggio painted that wonderful room in Italy where the little children are dancing on the walls. Mr. Whistler finished another room just before I came away—a breakfast room in blue and yellow. The ceiling was a light blue, the cabinetwork and furniture were of a yellow wood, the curtains at the windows were white and worked in yellow, and when the table was set for breakfast with dainty blue china, nothing can be conceived at once so simple and so joyous.

The fault which I have observed in most of your rooms is that there is apparent no definite scheme of colour. Everything is not attuned to a keynote as it should be. The apartments are crowded with pretty things which have no relation to one another. Again, your artists must decorate what is more simply useful. In your art schools I found no attempt to decorate such things as the vessels for water. I know of nothing uglier than the ordinary jug or pitcher. A museum could be filled with the different kinds of water vessels which are used in hot countries. Yet we continue to submit to the depressing jug with the handle all on one side. I do not see the wisdom of decorating dinner-plates with sunsets and soup-plates with moonlight scenes. I do not think it adds anything to the pleasure of the canvasback duck to take it out of such glories. Besides, we do not want a soup-plate whose bottom seems to vanish in the distance. One feels neither safe nor comfortable under such conditions. In fact, I did not

* James McNeill Whistler, who was born in America but lived in England, was a friend, archrival, and frequent critic of Wilde. Like Wilde, he was a proponent of art for art's sake.

find in the art schools of the country that the difference was explained between decorative and imaginative art.

The conditions of art should be simple. A great deal more depends upon the heart than the head. Appreciation of art is not secured by any elaborate scheme of learning. Art requires a good healthy atmosphere. The motives for art are still around about us as they were around about the ancients. And the subjects are also easily found by the earnest sculptor and the painter. Nothing is more picturesque and graceful than a man at work. The artist who goes to the children's playground, watches them at their sport, and sees the boy stoop to tie his shoe, will find the same themes that engaged the attention of the ancient Greeks, and such observation and the illustrations which follow will do much to correct that foolish impression that mental and physical beauty are always divorced.

To you more than perhaps to any other country, has nature been generous in furnishing material for art-workers to work in. You have marble-quarries where the stone is more beautiful in colour than the Greeks ever had for their beautiful work, and yet day after day I am confronted with the great building of some stupid man who has used the beautiful material as if it were not precious almost beyond speech. Marble should not be used save by noble workmen. There is nothing which gave me a greater sense of barrenness in travelling through the country than the entire absence of wood-carving on your houses. Wood-carving is the simplest of the decorative arts. In Switzerland the little barefooted boy beautifies the porch of his father's house with examples of skill in this direction. Why should not American boys do a great deal more and better than Swiss boys?

There is nothing to my mind more coarse in conception and more vulgar in execution than modern jewelry. This is something that can be easily corrected. Something better should be made out of the beautiful gold which is stored up in your mountain hollows and strewn along your river beds. When I was at Leadville and reflected that all the shining silver I saw coming from the mines would be made into ugly dollars, it made me sad. It should be made into something more permanent. The golden gates at Florence are as beautiful today as when Michael Angelo saw them.

We should see more of the workman than we do. We should not be content to have the salesman stand between us—the salesman, who knows nothing of what he is selling save that he is charging a great deal too much for it. And watching the workmen, will teach that most important lesson, the nobility of all rational workmanship.

I said in my last lecture that art would create a new brotherhood among men by furnishing a universal language. I said that under its beneficent influences war might pass away. Thinking this, what place can I ascribe to art in our education? If children grow up among all fair and lovely things, they will grow to love beauty and detest ugliness before they know the reason why. If you go into a house where everything is coarse, you find things chipped and broken and unsightly. Nobody exercises any care. If everything is dainty and delicate, gentleness and refinement of manner are unconsciously acquired. When I was in San Francisco I used to visit the Chinese Quarter frequently. There I used to watch a great hulking Chinese workman at his task of digging, and used to see him every day drink his tea from a little cup as delicate in texture as the petal of a flower, whereas in all the grand hotels of the land, where thousands of dollars have been lavished on great gilt mirrors and gaudy columns, I have been given my coffee or my chocolate in cups an inch and a quarter thick. I think I have deserved something nicer.

The art systems of the past have been devised by philosophers who looked upon human beings as obstructions. They have tried to educate boys' minds before they had any. How much better it would be in these early years to teach children to use their hands in the rational service of mankind! I would have a workshop attached to every school, and one hour a day given up to the teaching of simple decorative arts. It would be a golden hour to the children. And you would soon raise up a race of handicraftsmen who would transform the face of your country. I have seen only one such school in the United States, and this was in Philadelphia, and was founded by my friend Mr. Leland.* I stopped

* Folklorist, journalist, editor, publisher, and humorous writer Charles G. Leland (1824–1903) founded a school for crafts skills in Philadelphia.

there yesterday and have brought some of the work here this afternoon to show you. Here are two discs of beaten brass: the designs on them are beautiful, the workmanship is simple and the entire result is satisfactory. The work was done by a little boy twelve years old. This is a wooden bowl, decorated by a little girl of thirteen. The design is lovely, and the colouring delicate and pretty. Here you see a piece of beautiful wood-carving, accomplished by a little boy of nine. In such work as this children learn sincerity in art. They learn to abhor the liar in art—the man who paints wood to look like iron, or iron to look like stone. It is a practical school of morals. No better way is there to learn to love Nature than to understand Art. It dignifies every flower of the field. And the boy who sees the thing of beauty which a bird on the wing becomes when transferred to wood or canvas, will probably not throw the customary stone. What we want is something spiritual added to life. Nothing is so ignoble that art cannot sanctify it.

JOURNALISM

ON AMERICA

IMPRESSIONS OF AMERICA

I FEAR I CANNOT picture America as altogether an Elysium—perhaps, from the ordinary standpoint I know but little about the country.* I cannot give its latitude or longitude; I cannot compute the value of its dry goods, and I have no very close acquaintance with its politics. These are matters which may not interest you, and they certainly are not interesting to me.

The first thing that struck me on landing in America was that if the Americans are not the most well-dressed people in the world, they are the most comfortably dressed. Men are seen there with the dreadful chimney-pot hat, but there are very few hatless men; men wear the shocking swallow-tail coat, but few are to be seen with no coat at all. There is an air of comfort in the appearance of the people which is a marked contrast to that seen in this country, where, too often, people are seen in close contact with rags.

The next thing particularly noticeable is that everybody seems in a hurry to catch a train. This is a state of things which is not favourable to poetry or romance. Had Romeo or Juliet been in a constant state of anxiety about trains, or had their minds been agitated by the question of return-tickets, Shakespeare could not have given us those lovely balcony scenes which are so full of poetry and pathos.

America is the noisiest country that ever existed. One is waked up in the morning, not by the singing of the nightingale, but by the steam whistle. It is surprising that the sound practical sense of the Americans does not reduce this intolerable noise. All Art depends

* When he returned from the United States in 1883, Wilde appraised America's crude style; in this lecture he is at his casual best—never pedantic, mixing praise and satire.

upon exquisite and delicate sensibility, and such continual turmoil must ultimately be destructive of the musical faculty.

There is not so much beauty to be found in American cities as in Oxford, Cambridge, Salisbury or Winchester, where are lovely relics of a beautiful age; but still there is a good deal of beauty to be seen in them now and then, but only where the American has not attempted to create it. Where the Americans have attempted to produce beauty they have signally failed. A remarkable characteristic of the Americans is the manner in which they have applied science to modern life.

This is apparent in the most cursory stroll through New York. In England an inventor is regarded almost as a crazy man, and in too many instances invention ends in disappointment and poverty. In America an inventor is honoured, help is forthcoming, and the exercise of ingenuity, the application of science to the work of man, is there the shortest road to wealth. There is no country in the world where machinery is so lovely as in America.

I have always wished to believe that the line of strength and the line of beauty are one. That wish was realised when I contemplated American machinery. It was not until I had seen the water-works at Chicago that I realised the wonders of machinery; the rise and fall of the steel rods, the symmetrical motion of the great wheels is the most beautifully rhythmic thing I have ever seen. One is impressed in America, but not favourably impressed, by the inordinate size of everything. The country seems to try to bully one into a belief in its power by its impressive bigness.

I was disappointed with Niagara—most people must be disappointed with Niagara. Every American bride is taken there, and the sight of the stupendous waterfall must be one of the earliest, if not the keenest, disappointments in American married life. One sees it under bad conditions, very far away, the point of view not showing the splendour of the water. To appreciate it really one has to see it from underneath the fall, and to do that it is necessary to be dressed in a yellow oil-skin, which is as ugly as a mackintosh—and I hope none of you ever wears one. It is a consolation to know, however, that such an artist as Madame Bernhardt has not only worn that yellow, ugly dress, but has been photographed in it.

Perhaps the most beautiful part of America is the West, to reach which, however, involves a journey by rail of six days, racing along tied to an ugly tin-kettle of a steam engine. I found but poor consolation for this journey in the fact that the boys who infest the cars and sell everything that one can eat—or should not eat—were selling editions of my poems vilely printed on a kind of grey blotting paper, for the low price of ten cents. Calling these boys on one side I told them that though poets like to be popular they desire to be paid, and selling editions of my poems without giving me a profit is dealing a blow at literature which must have a disastrous effect on poetical aspirants. The invariable reply that they made was that they themselves made a profit out of the transaction and that was all they cared about.

It is a popular superstition that in America a visitor is invariably addressed as "Stranger." I was never once addressed as "Stranger." When I went to Texas I was called "Captain"; when I got to the centre of the country I was addressed as "Colonel," and, on arriving at the borders of Mexico, as "General." On the whole, however, "Sir," the old English method of addressing people, is the most common.

It is, perhaps, worth while to note that what many people call Americanisms are really old English expressions which have lingered in our colonies while they have been lost in our own country. Many people imagine that the term "I guess," which is so common in America, is purely an American expression, but it was used by John Locke in his work on "The Understanding," just as we now use "I think."

It is in the colonies, and not in the mother country, that the old life of the country really exists. If one wants to realise what English Puritanism is—not at its worst (when it is very bad), but at its best, and then it is not very good—I do not think one can find much of it in England, but much can be found about Boston and Massachusetts. We have got rid of it. America still preserves it, to be, I hope, a short-lived curiosity.

San Francisco is a really beautiful city. China Town, peopled by Chinese labourers, is the most artistic town I have ever come across. The people—strange, melancholy Orientals, whom many people would call common, and they are certainly very poor—have determined that they will have nothing about them that is not beautiful. In the Chinese restaurant, where these navvies meet to have supper in the evening, I found them drinking tea out of china cups as delicate as the petals of a rose-leaf, whereas at the gaudy hotels I was supplied with a delf cup an inch and a half thick. When the Chinese bill was presented it was made out on rice paper, the account being done in Indian ink as fantastically as if an artist had been etching little birds on a fan.

Salt Lake City contains only two buildings of note, the chief being the Tabernacle, which is in the shape of a soup-kettle. It is decorated by the only native artist, and he has treated religious subjects in the naive spirit of the early Florentine painters, representing people of our own day in the dress of the period side by side with people of Biblical history who are clothed in some romantic costume.

The building next in importance is called the Amelia Palace, in honour of one of Brigham Young's wives. When he died the present president of the Mormons stood up in the Tabernacle and said that it had been revealed to him that he was to have the Amelia Palace, and that on this subject there were to be no more revelations of any kind!

From Salt Lake City one travels over the great plains of Colorado and up the Rocky Mountains, on the top of which is Leadville, the richest city in the world. It has also got the reputation of being the roughest, and every man carries a revolver. I was told that if I went there they would be sure to shoot me or my travelling manager. I wrote and told them that nothing that they could do to my travelling manager would intimidate me. They are miners—men working in metals, so I lectured them on the Ethics of Art. I read them passages from the autobiography of Benvenuto Cellini and they seemed much delighted. I was reproved by my hearers for not having brought him with me. I explained that he had been dead for some little time which elicited the enquiry "Who shot him"? They afterwards took me to a dancing saloon where I saw the only rational method of art criticism I have ever come across. Over the piano was printed a notice:—

PLEASE DO NOT
SHOOT THE PIANIST.
HE IS DOING HIS BEST.

The mortality among pianists in that place is marvellous. Then they asked me to supper, and having accepted, I had to descend a mine in a rickety bucket in which it was impossible to be graceful. Having got into the heart of the mountain I had supper, the first course being whisky, the second whisky and the third whisky.

I went to the Theatre to lecture and I was informed that just before I went there two men had been seized for committing a murder, and in that theatre they had been brought on to the stage at eight o'clock in the evening, and then and there tried and executed before a crowded audience. But I found these miners very charming and not at all rough.

Among the more elderly inhabitants of the South I found a melancholy tendency to date every event of importance by the late war. "How beautiful the moon is to-night," I once remarked to a gentleman who was standing next to me. "Yes," was his reply, "but you should have seen it before the war."

So infinitesimal did I find the knowledge of Art, west of the Rocky Mountains, that an art patron—one who in his day had been a miner—actually sued the railroad company for damages because the plaster cast of Venus of Milo, which he had imported from Paris, had been delivered minus the arms. And, what is more surprising still, he gained his case and the damages.

Pennsylvania, with its rocky gorges and woodland scenery, reminded me of Switzerland. The prairie reminded me of a piece of blotting-paper.

The Spanish and French have left behind them memorials in the beauty of their names. All the cities that have beautiful names derive them from the Spanish or the French. The English people give intensely ugly names to places. One place had such an ugly name that I refused to lecture there. It was called Grigsville. Supposing I had founded a school of Art there—fancy "Early Grigsville." Imagine a School of Art teaching "Grigsville Renaissance."

As for slang I did not hear much of it, though a young lady who had changed her clothes after an afternoon dance did say that "after the heel kick she shifted her day goods."

American youths are pale and precocious, or sallow and supercilious, but American girls are pretty and charming—little oases of pretty unreasonableness in a vast desert of practical common-sense.

Every American girl is entitled to have twelve young men devoted to her. They remain her slaves and she rules them with charming nonchalance.

The men are entirely given to business; they have, as they say, their brains in front of their heads. They are also exceedingly acceptive of new ideas. Their education is practical. We base the education of children entirely on books, but we must give a child a mind before we can instruct the mind. Children have a natural antipathy to books—handicraft should be the basis of education. Boys and girls should be taught to use their hands to make something, and they would be less apt to destroy and be mischievous.

In going to America one learns that poverty is not a necessary accompaniment to civilisation. There at any rate is a country that has no trappings, no pageants and no gorgeous ceremonies. I saw only two processions—one was the Fire Brigade preceded by the Police, the other was the Police preceded by the Fire Brigade.

Every man when he gets to the age of twenty-one is allowed to vote, and thereby immediately acquires his political education. The Americans are the best politically educated people in the world. It is well worth one's while to go to a country which can teach us the beauty of the word FREEDOM and the value of the thing LIBERTY.

THE AMERICAN INVASION

A TERRIBLE DANGER IS hanging over the Americans in London. Their future, and their reputation this season, depend entirely on the success of Buffalo Bill and Mrs. Brown-Potter. The former is certain to draw; for English people are far more interested in American barbarism than they are in American civilisation. When they sight Sandy Hook, they look to their rifles and ammunition; and after dining once at Delmonico's, start off for Colorado or California, for Montana or the Yellow Stone Park. Rocky Mountains charm them more than riotous millionaires; they have been known to prefer buffaloes to Boston. Why should they not? The cities of America are inexpressibly tedious. The Bostonians take their learning too sadly; culture with them is an accomplishment rather than an atmosphere; their 'Hub,' as they call it, is the paradise of prigs. Chicago is a sort of monster-shop, full of bustle and bores. Political life at Washington is like political life in a suburban vestry. Baltimore is amusing for a week, but Philadelphia is dreadfully provincial; and though one can dine in New York, one could not dwell there. Better the Far West, with its grizzly bears and its untamed cowboys, its free, open-air life and its free, open-air manners, its boundless prairie and its boundless mendacity! This is what Buffalo Bill is going to bring to London; and we have no doubt that London will fully appreciate his show.

With regard to Mrs. Brown-Potter, as acting is no longer considered absolutely essential for success on the English stage, there is really no reason why the pretty, bright-eyed lady, who charmed us all last June by her merry laugh and her *nonchalant* ways, should not, to borrow an expression from her native language, make a big boom, and paint the town red. We sincerely hope she will; for, on the whole, the American invasion has done English society a great deal of good. American women are bright, clever, and wonderfully cosmopolitan. Their patriotic feelings are limited to an admiration for Niagara, and a regret for the Elevated Railway, and, unlike the men, they never bore us with Bunker's Hill. They take their dresses from Paris, and their manners from Piccadilly, and wear both charmingly. They have a quaint pertness, a delightful conceit, a naïve self-assertion. They insist on being paid compliments, and have almost succeeded in making Englishmen eloquent. For our aristocracy they have an ardent admiration; they adore titles, and are a permanent blow to Republican principles. In the art of amusing men they are adepts, both by nature and education, and can actually tell a story without forgetting the point—an accomplishment that is extremely rare among the women of other countries. It is true that they lack repose, and that their voices are somewhat harsh and strident when they land first at Liverpool; but after a time one gets to love these pretty whirlwinds in petticoats, that sweep so recklessly through society, and are so agitating to all duchesses who have daughters. There is something fascinating in their funny, exaggerated gestures, and their petulant way of tossing the head. Their eyes have no magic nor mystery in them, but they challenge us for combat; and when we engage, we are always worsted. Their lips seem made for laughter, and yet they never grimace. As for their voices, they soon get them into tune. Some of them have been known to acquire a fashionable drawl in two seasons; and after they have been presented to Royalty they all roll their R's as vigorously as a young equerry or an old lady-in-waiting. Still, they never really lose their accent, it keeps peeping out here and there, and when they chatter together they are like a bevy of peacocks. Nothing is more amusing than to watch two American girls greeting each other in a drawing-room or in the Row. They are like children, with their shrill *staccato* cries of wonder, their odd little exclamations. Their conversation sounds like a series of exploding crackers; they are exquisitely incoherent, and use a sort of primitive, emotional language. After five minutes they are left beautifully breathless, and look at each other, half in amusement and half in affection. If a stolid young Englishman is fortunate enough to be introduced to them, he is amazed at their extraordinary vivacity; their electric quickness of repartee; their inexhaustible store of curious catchwords. He never really understands them, for their thoughts flutter about with the sweet irresponsibility of butterflies; but he is pleased and amused, and feels as if he were in an aviary. On the whole, American girls have a wonderful charm, and, perhaps, the chief secret of their charm is that they never talk seriously, except to their dressmaker, and never think seriously, except about amusements.

They have, however, one grave fault—their mothers.

Dreary as were those old Pilgrim Fathers, who left our shores more than two centuries ago to found a New England beyond seas, the Pilgrim Mothers, who have returned to us in the nineteenth century, are drearier still. Here and there, of course, there are exceptions, but as a class they are either dull, dowdy, or dyspeptic. It is only fair to the rising generation of America to state that they are not to blame for this. Indeed, they spare no pains at all to bring up their parents properly, and to give them a suitable, if somewhat late, education. From its earliest years, every American child spends most of its time in correcting the faults of its father and mother; and no one who has had the opportunity of watching an American family on the deck of an Atlantic steamer, or in the refined seclusion of a New York boarding-house, can fail to have been struck by this characteristic of their civilisation. In America, the young are always ready to give to those who are older than themselves the full benefits of their inexperience. A boy of only eleven or twelve years of age will firmly, but kindly, point out to his father his defects of manner or temper; will never weary of warning him against extravagance, idleness, late hours, unpunctuality, and the other temptations to which the aged are so particularly exposed; and sometimes, should he fancy that he is monopolising too much of the conversation at dinner, will remind him, across the table, of the new child's adage, "Parents should be seen, not heard." Nor does any mistaken idea of kindness prevent the little American girl from censuring her mother whenever it is necessary. Often, indeed, feeling that a rebuke conveyed in the presence of others is more truly efficacious than one merely whispered in the quiet of the nursery, she will call the attention of perfect strangers to her mother's general untidiness, her want of intellectual Boston conversation, immoderate love of iced-water and green corn, stinginess in the matter of candy, ignorance of the usages of the best Baltimore society, bodily ailments, and the like. In fact, it may be truly said that no American child is ever blind to the deficiencies of its parents, no matter how much it may love them.

Yet, somehow, this educational system has not been so successful as it deserved. In many cases, no doubt, the material with which the children had to deal was crude and incapable of real development; but the fact remains that the American mother is a tedious person. The American father is better, for he is never seen in London. He passes his life entirely in Wall Street, and communicates with his family once a month by means of a telegram in cipher. The mother, however, is always with us, and, lacking the quick imitative faculty of the younger generation, remains uninteresting and provincial to the last. In spite of her, however, the American girl is always welcome. She brightens our dull dinner parties for us, and makes life go pleasantly by for a season. In the race for coronets she often carries off the prize; but once that she has gained the victory, she is generous, and forgives her English rivals everything, even their beauty. Warned by the example of her mother that American women do not grow old gracefully, she tries not to grow old at all, and often succeeds. She has exquisite feet and hands, is always *bien chaussée et bien gantée*,* and can talk brilliantly upon any subject, provided that she knows nothing about it. Her sense of humour keeps her from the tragedy of a *grande passion*,† and, as there is neither romance nor humility in her love, she makes an excellent wife. What her ultimate influence on English life will be, it is difficult to estimate at present; but there can be no doubt that of all the factors that have contributed to the social revolution of London, there are few more important, and none more delightful, than the American invasion.

---

* Well shod and well gloved (French).

† Great love (French).

THE AMERICAN MAN

One of our prettiest Duchesses enquired the other day of a distinguished traveller whether there was really such a thing as an American man, explaining, as the reason for her question, that, though she knew many fascinating American women, she had never come across any fathers, grandfathers, uncles, brothers, husbands, cousins, or, indeed, male relatives of any kind whatsoever.

The exact answer the Duchess received is not worth recording, as it took the depressing form of useful and accurate information; but there can be no doubt that the subject is an extremely interesting one, pointing, as it does, to the curious fact that, as far as society is concerned, the American invasion has been purely female in character. With the exception of the United States Minister, always a welcome personage wherever he goes, and an occasional lion from Boston or the Far West, no American man has any social existence in London. His women-folk, with their wonderful dresses, and still more wonderful dialogue, shine in our *salons*,* and delight our dinner-parties; our guardsmen are taken captive by their brilliant complexions, and our beauties made jealous by their clever wit; but the poor American man remains permanently in the background, and never rises beyond the level of the tourist. Now and then he makes an appearance in the Row, looking a somewhat strange figure in his long frock coat of glossy black cloth, and his sensible soft-felt hat; but his favourite haunt is the Strand, and the American Exchange his idea of Heaven. When he is not lounging in a rocking-chair with a cigar, he is loafing through the streets with a carpet bag, gravely taking stock of our products, and trying to understand Europe through the medium of the shop windows. He is M. Renan's *l'homme sensuel*

* Gathering, such as a literary evening (French).

moyen,* Mr. Arnold's middle-class Philistine. The telephone is his test of civilisation, and his wildest dreams of Utopia do not rise beyond elevated railways and electric bells. His chief pleasure is to get hold of some unsuspecting stranger, or some sympathetic countryman, and then to indulge in the national game of 'matching.' With a *naivete* and a nonchalance that are absolutely charming, he will gravely compare St. James' Palace to the grand central depot at Chicago, or Westminster Abbey to the Falls of Niagara. Bulk is his canon of beauty, and size his standard of excellence. To him the greatness of a country consists in the number of square miles that it contains; and he is never tired of telling the waiters at his hotel that the State of Texas is larger than France and Germany put together.

Yet, on the whole, he is happier in London than anywhere else in Europe. Here he can always make a few acquaintances, and, as a rule, can speak the language. Abroad, he is terribly at sea. He knows no one, and understands nothing, and wanders about in a melancholy manner, treating the Old World as if it were a Broadway store, and each city a counter for the sampling of shoddy goods. For him Art has no marvel, and Beauty no meaning, and the Past no message. He thinks that civilisation began with the introduction of steam, and looks with contempt upon all centuries that had no hot-water apparatuses in their houses. The ruin and decay of Time has no pathos in his eyes. He turns away from Ravenna, because the grass grows in her streets, and can see no loveliness in Verona, because there is rust on her balconies. His one desire is to get the whole of Europe into thorough repair. He is severe on the modern Romans for not covering the Colosseum with a glass roof, and utilising the building as a warehouse for dry goods. In a word, he is the Don Quixote of common sense, for he is so utilitarian that he is absolutely unpractical. As a *compagnon de voyage*† he is not desirable, for he always looks *deplacé*,‡ and feels depressed. Indeed, he would die of weariness if he were not in constant telegraphic communication with Wall Street; and the only thing that can console him for having wasted

* Man of the world; literally, average sensual man (French).

† Traveling companion (French).

‡ Out of place (French).

a day in a picture-gallery is a copy of the New York Herald or the Boston Times. Finally, having looked at everything, and seen nothing, he returns to his native land.

There he is delightful. For the strange thing about American civilisation is, that the women are most charming when they are away from their own country, the men most charming when they are at home.

At home, the American man is the best of companions, as he is the most hospitable of hosts. The young men are especially pleasant, with their bright, handsome eyes, their unwearying energy, their amusing shrewdness. They seem to get a hold on life much earlier than we do. At an age when we are still boys at Eton, or lads at Oxford, they are practising some important profession, making money in some intricate business. Real experience comes to them so much sooner than it does to us, that they are never awkward, never shy, and never say foolish things, except when they ask one how the Hudson River compares with the Rhine, or whether Brooklyn Bridge is not really more impressive than the dome of St. Paul's. Their education is quite different from ours. They know men much better than they know books, and life interests them more than literature. They have no time to study anything but the stock markets, no leisure to read anything but newspapers. Indeed, it is only the women in America who have any leisure at all; and, as a necessary result of this curious state of things, there is no doubt but that, within a century from now, the whole culture of the New World will be in petticoats. Yet, though these cute young speculators may not have culture, in the sense in which we use it, as the knowledge of the best that has been thought and said in the world, they are by no means dull. There is no such thing as a stupid American. Many Americans are horrid, vulgar, intrusive, and impertinent, just as many English people are also; but stupidity is not one of the national vices. Indeed, in America there is no opening for a fool. They expect brains even from a boot-black, and get them.

As for marriage, it is one of their most popular institutions. The American man marries early, and the American woman marries often; and they get on extremely well together. From childhood, the husband has been brought up on the most elaborate fetch-and-carry system, and his reverence for the sex has a touch of compulsory chivalry about it; while the wife exercises an absolute despotism, based upon female assertion, and tempered by womanly charm. On the whole, the great success of marriage in the States is due partly to the fact that no American man is ever idle, and partly to the fact that no American wife is considered responsible for the quality of her husband's dinners. In America, the horrors of domesticity are almost entirely unknown. There are no scenes over the soup, nor quarrels over the *entrées*, and as, by a clause inserted in every marriage settlement, the husband solemnly binds himself to use studs and not buttons for his shirts, one of the chief sources of disagreement in ordinary middle-class life is absolutely removed. The habit also of residing in hotels and boarding-houses does away with any necessity for those tedious *tête-à-têtes** that are the dream of engaged couples, and the despair of married men. Vulgarising though a *table-d'hôte*† may be, it is at least better than that eternal duologue about bills and babies to which Benedict and Beatrice so often sink, when the one has lost his wit, and the other her beauty. Even the American freedom of divorce, questionable though it undoubtedly is on many grounds, has at least the merit of bringing into marriage a new element of romantic uncertainty. When people are tied together for life they too often regard manners as a mere superfluity, and courtesy as a thing of no moment; but where the bond can be easily broken, its very fragility makes its strength, and reminds the husband that he should always try to please, and the wife that she should never cease to be charming.

As a consequence of this liberty of action, or, it may be, in spite of it, scandals are extremely rare in America, and should one occur, so paramount in society is female influence, that it is the man who is never forgiven. America is the only country in the world where Don Juan is not appreciated, and where there is sympathy for Georges Dandin.

On the whole, then, the American man at home is a very worthy person. There is just one point in which he is disappointing. American humour is a mere travellers' tale. It has no real existence. Indeed,

---

* Private conversations (French).

† Fixed-price meal (French).

so far from being humorous, the male American is the most abnormally serious creature who ever existed. He talks of Europe as being old; but it is he himself who has never been young. He knows nothing of the irresponsible light-heartedness of boyhood, of the graceful *insouciance** of animal spirits. He has always been prudent, always practical, and pays a heavy penalty for having committed no mistakes. It is only fair to admit that he can exaggerate; but even his exaggeration has a rational basis. It is not founded on wit or fancy; it does not spring from any poetic imagination; it is simply an earnest attempt on the part of language to keep pace with the enormous size of the country. It is evident that where it takes one twenty-four hours to go across a single parish, and seven days' steady railway travelling to keep a dinner engagement in another State, the ordinary resources of human speech are quite inadequate to the strain put on them, and new linguistic forms have to be invented, new methods of description resorted to. But this is nothing more than the fatal influence of geography upon adjectives; for naturally humorous the American man certainly is not. It is true that when we meet him in Europe his conversation keeps us in fits of laughter; but this is merely because his ideas are so absolutely incongruous with European surroundings. Place him in his own environment, in the midst of the civilisation that he has made for himself, and the life that is the work of his own hands, and the very same observations will fail even to excite a smile. They have sunk to the level of the commonplace truism, or the sensible remark; and what seemed a paradox when we listened to it in London, becomes a platitude when we hear it in Milwaukee.

America has never quite forgiven Europe for having been discovered somewhat earlier in history than itself. Yet how immense are its obligations to us! How enormous its debt! To gain a reputation for humour, its men have to come to London; to be famous for their *toilettes*,† its women have to shop in Paris.

Yet, though the American man may not be humorous, he is certainly

---

* Heedlessness (French).

† Fashionable attire (French).

humane. He is keenly conscious of the fact that there is a great deal of human nature in man, and tries to be pleasant to every stranger who lands on his shores. He has a healthy freedom from all antiquated prejudices, regards introductions as a foolish relic of mediæval etiquette, and makes every chance visitor feel that he is the favoured guest of a great nation. If the English girl ever met him, she would marry him; and if she married him, she would be happy. For, though he may be rough in manner, and deficient in the picturesque insincerity of romance, yet he is invariably kind and thoughtful, and has succeeded in making his own country the Paradise of Women.

This, however, is perhaps the reason why, like Eve, the women are always so anxious to get out of it.

ON ART

MR. WHISTLER'S TEN O'CLOCK

LAST NIGHT, AT PRINCE'S HALL, Mr. Whistler made his first public appearance as a lecturer on art, and spoke for more than an hour with really marvellous eloquence on the absolute uselessness of all lectures of the kind.* Mr. Whistler began his lecture with a very pretty *aria* on pre-historic history, describing how in earlier times hunter and warrior would go forth to chase and foray, while the artist sat at home making cup and bowl for their service. Rude imitations of nature they were first, like the gourd bottle, till the sense of beauty and form developed, and, in all its exquisite proportions, the first vase was fashioned. Then came a higher civilization of architecture and arm chairs, and with exquisite design, and dainty diaper, the useful things of life were made lovely; and the hunter and the warrior lay on the couch when they were tired, and, when they were thirsty, drank from the bowl, and never cared to lose the exquisite proportions of the one, or the delightful ornament of the other; and this attitude of the primitive anthropophagous Philistine formed the text of the lecture, and was the attitude which Mr. Whistler entreated his audience to adopt towards art. Remembering, no doubt, many charming invitations to wonderful private views, this fashionable assemblage seemed somewhat aghast, and not a little amused, at being told that the slightest appearance among a civilized people of any joy in beautiful things is a grave impertinence to all painters; but Mr. Whistler was relentless, and with charming ease, and much grace of manner, explained to the public that the only thing they should cultivate was ugliness, and that on their permanent stupidity rested all the hopes of art in the future.

---

* Wilde mockingly praises Whistler for touching "the secret laws of artistic creation" (p. 315).

The scene was in every way delightful; he stood there, a miniature Mephistopheles mocking the majority! he was like a brilliant surgeon lecturing to a class composed of subjects destined ultimately for dissection, and solemnly assuring them how valuable to science their maladies were, and how absolutely uninteresting the slightest symptoms of health on their part would be. In fairness to the audience, however, I must say that they seemed extremely gratified at being rid of the dreadful responsibility of admiring anything, and nothing could have exceeded their enthusiasm when they were told by Mr. Whistler that no matter how vulgar their dresses were, or how hideous their surroundings at home, still it was possible that a great painter, if there was such a thing, could, by contemplating them in the twilight, and half closing his eyes, see them under really picturesque conditions, and produce a picture which they were not to attempt to understand, much less dare to enjoy. Then there were some arrows, barbed and brilliant, shot off, with all the speed and splendour of fireworks, at the archaeologists, who spend their lives in verifying the birthplaces of nobodies, and estimate the value of a work of art by its date or its decay, at the art critics who always treat a picture as if it were a novel, and try and find out the plot; at dilettanti in general, and amateurs in particular, and (*O mea culpa!*)* at dress reformers most of all. "Did not Velásquez paint crinolines? what more do you want?"

Having thus made a holocaust of humanity, Mr. Whistler turned to Nature, and in a few moments convicted her of the Crystal Palace, Bank holidays, and a general overcrowding of detail, both in omnibuses and in landscapes; and then, in a passage of singular beauty, not unlike one that occurs in Carot's [Corot's] letters, spoke of the artistic value of dim dawns and dusks, when the mean facts of life are lost in exquisite and evanescent effects, when common things are touched with mystery and transfigured with beauty; when the warehouses become as palaces, and the tall chimneys of the factory seem like campaniles in the silver air.

* I'm to blame (Latin).

Finally, after making a strong protest against anybody but a painter judging of painting, and a pathetic appeal to the audience not to be lured by the aesthetic movement into having beautiful things about them, Mr. Whistler concluded his lecture with a pretty passage about Fusiyama on a fan, and made his bow to an audience which he had succeeded in completely fascinating by his wit, his brilliant paradoxes, and, at times, his real eloquence. Of course, with regard to the value of beautiful surroundings I differ entirely from Mr. Whistler. An artist is not an isolated fact, he is the resultant of a certain millieu [*sic*] and a certain entourage, and can no more be born of a nation that is devoid of any sense of beauty than a fig can grow from a thorn or a rose blossom from a thistle. That an artist will find beauty in ugliness, *le beau dans l'horrible*, is now a commonplace of the schools, the argot of the atelier, but I strongly deny that charming people should be condemned to live with magenta ottomans and Albert blue curtains in their rooms in order that some painter may observe the side lights on the one and the values of the other. Nor do I accept the dictum that only a painter is a judge of painting. I say that only an artist is a judge of art; there is a wide difference. As long as a painter is a painter merely, he should not be allowed to talk of anything but mediums and megilp, and on those subjects should be compelled to hold his tongue; it is only when he becomes an artist that the secret laws of artistic creation are revealed to him. For there are not many arts, but one art merely; poem, picture, and Parthenon, sonnet and statue—all are in their essence the same, and he who knows one, knows all. But the poet is the supreme artist, for he is the master of colour and of form, and the real musician besides, and is lord over all life and all arts; and so to the poet beyond all others are these mysteries known; to Edgar Allan Poe and to Baudelaire, not to Benjamin West and Paul Delaroche. However, I would not enjoy anybody else's lectures unless in a few points I disagreed with them, and Mr. Whistler's lecture last night was, like everything that he does, a masterpiece. Not merely for its clever satire and amusing jests will it be remembered, but for the pure and perfect beauty of many of its passages—passages delivered with an earnestness which seemed to amaze those who had looked on Mr. Whistler as a master of persiflage merely, and had not known him, as we do, as a master of painting also. For that he is indeed one of the very greatest masters of painting, is my opinion. And I may add that in this opinion Mr. Whistler himself entirely concurs.

THE RELATION OF DRESS TO ART. A NOTE IN BLACK AND WHITE ON MR. WHISTLER'S LECTURE

"How can you possibly paint these ugly three-cornered hats?" asked a reckless art critic once of Sir Joshua Reynolds. "I see light and shade in them," answered the artist. "*Les grands coloristes*," says Baudelaire, in a charming article on the artistic value of frock coats, "*les grands coloristes savent faire de la couleur avec un habit noir, une cravate blanche, et un fond gris*."*

"Art seeks and finds the beautiful in all times, as did her high priest Rembrandt, when he saw the picturesque grandeur of the Jews' quarter of Amsterdam, and lamented not that its inhabitants were not Greeks," were the fine and simple words used by Mr. Whistler in one of the most valuable passages of his lecture. The most valuable, that is, to the painter; for there is nothing of which the ordinary English painter more needs to be reminded than that the true artist does not wait for life to be made picturesque for him, but sees life under picturesque conditions always—under conditions, that is to say, which are at once new and delightful. But between the attitude of a painter towards the public, and the attitude of a people towards art, there is a wide difference. That, under certain conditions of light and shade, what is ugly in fact may, in its effect, become beautiful, is true; and this, indeed, is the real *modernité* of art; but these conditions are exactly what we cannot be always sure of, as we stroll down Piccadilly in the glaring vulgarity of the noonday, or lounge in the park with a

---

* The great colorists know how to create color with a black costume, a white tie, and a gray background (French).

foolish sunset as a background. Were we able to carry our *chiaroscuro** about with us, as we do our umbrellas, all would be well; but, this being impossible, I hardly think that pretty and delightful people will continue to wear a style of dress, as ugly as it is useless, and as meaningless as it is monstrous, even on the chance of such a master as Mr. Whistler is spiritualizing them into a symphony, or refining them into a mist. For the arts are made for life, and not life for the arts.

Nor do I feel quite sure that Mr. Whistler has been himself always true to the dogma he seems to lay down, that a painter should only paint the dress of his age, and of his actual surroundings; far be it from me to burden a butterfly with the heavy responsibility of its past: I have always been of opinion that consistency is the last refuge of the unimaginative: but have we not all seen, and most of us admired, a picture from his hand of exquisite English girls strolling by an opal sea in the fantastic dresses of Japan? Has not Tite-street[†] been thrilled with the tidings that the models of Chelsea were posing to the master, in peplums, for pastels?

Whatever comes from Mr. Whistler's brush is far too perfect in loveliness, to stand, or fall, by any intellectual dogmas on art, even his own: for Beauty is justified by all her children, and cares nothing for explanations; but it is impossible to look through any collection of modern pictures in London, from Burlington House to the Grosvenor Gallery, without feeling that the professional model is ruining painting, and reducing it to a condition of mere pose and *pastiche*.[‡]

Are we not all weary of him, that venerable impostor, fresh from the steps of the Piazza di Spagna,[§] who, in the leisure moments that he can spare from his customary organ, makes the round of the studios, and is waited for in Holland Park? Do we not all recognize him, when, with

---

* The use of light and shade for effect (Italian).

† Street where Wilde's house stood; he had it decorated entirely in white.

‡ Selective and incongruous borrowing from other works (French).

§ Ascending dramatically from the Piazza, Rome's celebrated Spanish Stairs were built between 1721 and 1723 to link the square to the church of the Trinità dei Monti. John Keats died in the small house at the foot of the stairs, where one can still see his room.

the gay *insouciance* of his nation, he reappears on the walls of our summer exhibitions, as everything that he is not, and as nothing that he is, glaring at us here as a patriarch of Canaan, here beaming as a brigand from the Abruzzi? Popular is he, this poor peripatetic professor of posing, with those whose joy it is to paint the posthumous portrait of the last philanthropist who, in his lifetime, had neglected to be photographed,—yet, he is the sign of the decadence, the symbol of decay.

For all costumes are caricatures. The basis of Art is not the Fancy Ball. Where there is loveliness of dress, there is no dressing up. And so, were our national attire delightful in colour, and in construction simple and sincere; were dress the expression of the loveliness that it shields, and of the swiftness and motion that it does not impede; did its lines break from the shoulder, instead of bulging from the waist; did the inverted wineglass cease to be the ideal of form: were these things brought about, as brought about they will be, then would painting be no longer an artificial reaction against the ugliness of life, but become, as it should be, the natural expression of life's beauty. Nor would painting merely, but all the other arts also, be the gainers by a change such as that which I propose; the gainers, I mean, through the increased atmosphere of Beauty by which the artists would be surrounded, and in which they would grow up. For Art is not to be taught in Academies. It is what one looks at, not what one listens to, that makes the artist. The real schools should be the streets. There is not, for instance, a single delicate line, or delightful proportion in the dress of the Greeks, which is not echoed exquisitely in their architecture. A nation arrayed in stove-pipe hats, and dress improvers, might have built the Pantechnicon, possibly, but the Parthenon, never. And, finally, there is this to be said: art, it is true, can never have any other aim but her own perfection, and, it may be, that the artist, desiring merely to contemplate and to create, is wise in not busying himself about change in others: yet wisdom is not always the best; there are times when she sinks to the level of common sense; and from the passionate folly of those, and there are many, who desire that Beauty shall be confined no longer to the *bric-à-brac* of the collector, and the dust of the museum, but shall be, as it should be, the natural and national inheritance of all,—from this noble unwisdom, I say, who knows what new loveliness shall be given to life, and, under these more exquisite conditions, what perfect artist born? *Le milieu se renouvelant, l'art se renouvelle.**

Speaking however from his own passionless pedestal, Mr. Whistler in pointing out that the power of the painter is to be found in his powers of vision, not in his cleverness of hand, has expressed a truth which needed expression, and which, coming from the lord of form and colour, cannot fail to have its influence. His lecture, the Apocrypha though it be for the people, yet remains from this time as the Bible for the painter, the masterpiece of masterpieces, the song of songs. It is true he has pronounced the panegyric of the Philistine, but I can fancy Ariel praising Caliban for a jest:† and, in that he has read the Commination Service over the critics, let all men thank him, the critics themselves indeed most of all, for he has now relieved them from the necessity of a tedious existence. Considered, again, merely as an orator, Mr. Whistler seems to me to stand almost alone. Indeed, among all our public speakers, I know but few who can combine, so felicitously as he does, the mirth and malice of Puck, with the style of the major prophets.

---

* As the world renews itself, so does art (French).

† Wilde imagines the spirit Ariel (from Shakespeare's *The Tempest*) ironically praising the monster Caliban "for a jest." Whistler cursed critics in rites called Commination Services. Commination means "denunciation."

LONDON MODELS

PROFESSIONAL MODELS ARE A purely modern invention. To the Greeks, for instance, they were quite unknown. Mr. Mahaffy,* it is true, tells us that Perikles† used to present peacocks to the great ladies of Athenian society in order to induce them to sit to his friend Pheidias, and we know that Polygnotus introduced into his picture of the Trojan women the face of Elpinike, the celebrated sister of the great Conservative leader of the day, but those *grandes dames*‡ clearly do not come under our category. As for the old masters, they undoubtedly made constant studies from their pupils and apprentices, and even their religious pictures are full of the portraits of their friends and relations, but they do not seem to have had the inestimable advantage of the existence of a class of people whose sole profession is to pose. In fact the model, in our sense of the word, is the direct creation of Academic Schools.

Every country now has its own models, except America. In New York, and even in Boston, a good model is so great a rarity that most of the artists are reduced to painting Niagara and millionaires. In Europe, however, it is different. Here we have plenty of models, and of every nationality. The Italian models are the best. The natural grace of their attitudes, as well as the wonderful picturesqueness of their colouring, makes them facile—often too facile—subjects for the painter's brush. The French models, though not so beautiful as the Italian,

---

* Rev. John Pentland Mahaffy, Wilde's early tutor in Greek, introduced Wilde to the idea of "Greek," or Platonic, love between men; he and his pupil differed over politics.

† Athenian general and statesman (c.495–429 B.C.E.) who was also a patron of the arts who commissioned and otherwise promoted the creation of monuments, statuary, and paintings.

‡ Great ladies (French).

possess a quickness of intellectual sympathy, a capacity in fact of understanding the artist, which is quite remarkable. They have also a great command over the varieties of facial expression, are peculiarly dramatic, and can chatter the *argot* of the *atelier** as cleverly as the critic of the *Gil Blas*.† The English models form a class entirely by themselves. They are not so picturesque as the Italian, nor so clever as the French, and they have absolutely no tradition, so to speak, of their order. Now and then some old veteran knocks at a studio door, and proposes to sit as Ajax defying the lightning, or as King Lear upon the blasted heath. One of them some time ago called on a popular painter who, happening at the moment to require his services, engaged him, and told him to begin by kneeling down in the attitude of prayer. "Shall I be Biblical or Shakespearean, sir?" asked the veteran. "Well—— Shakespearean," answered the artist, wondering by what subtle *nuance* of expression the model would convey the difference. "All right, sir," said the professor of posing, and he solemnly knelt down and began to wink with his left eye!‡ This class however is dying out. As a rule the model, nowadays, is a pretty girl, from about twelve to twenty-five years of age, who knows nothing about art, cares less, and is merely anxious to earn seven or eight shillings a day without much trouble. English models rarely look at a picture, and never venture on any æsthetic theories. In fact they realize very completely Mr. Whistler's idea of the function of an art-critic, for they pass no criticisms at all. They accept all schools of art with the grand catholicity of the auctioneer, and sit to a fantastic young impressionist as readily as to a learned and laborious academician. They are neither for the Whistlerites, nor against them; the quarrel between the school of facts and the school of effects touches them not; idealistic and naturalistic are words that convey no meaning to their

---

* The slang of the workshop (French).

† Picaresque novel by Alain-René Lesage (1668–1747), mentioned here as an unrefined popular work.

‡ American-born writer Henry James published a brilliant short story, "The Real Thing" (1892), in which he examined the psychological relation between the model and the subject.

ears; they merely desire that the studio shall be warm, and the lunch hot, for all charming artists give their models lunch.

As to what they are asked to do they are equally indifferent. On Monday they will don the rags of a beggar-girl for Mr. Pumper, whose pathetic pictures of modern life draw such tears from the public, and on Tuesday they will pose in a peplum for Mr. Phœbus, who thinks that all really artistic subjects are necessarily B.C. They career gaily through all centuries and through all costumes, and, like actors, are only interesting when they are not themselves. They are extremely good-natured, and very accommodating. "What do you sit for?" said a young artist to a model who had sent him in her card (all models by the way have cards and a small black bag). "Oh, for anything you like sir," said the girl; "landscape if necessary!"

Intellectually, it must be acknowledged, they are Philistines, but physically they are perfect—at least some are. Though none of them can talk Greek, many can look Greek, which to a nineteenth-century painter is naturally of great importance. If they are allowed, they chatter a great deal, but they never say anything. Their observations are the only *banalités* heard in Bohemia. However, though they cannot appreciate the artist as an artist, they are quite ready to appreciate the artist as a man. They are very sensitive to kindness, respect, and generosity. A beautiful model who had sat for two years to one of our most distinguished English painters, got engaged to a street vendor of penny ices. On her marriage the painter sent her a pretty wedding present, and received in return a nice letter of thanks with the following remarkable postscript: "Never eat the green ices!"

When they are tired a wise artist gives them a rest. Then they sit in a chair and read penny dreadfuls, till they are roused from the tragedy of literature to take their place again in the tragedy of art. A few of them smoke cigarettes. This however is regarded by the other models as showing a want of seriousness, and is not generally approved of. They are engaged by the day and by the half-day. The tariff is a shilling an hour, to which great artists usually add an omnibus fare. The two best things about them are their extraordinary prettiness, and their extreme respectability. As a class they are very well behaved, particularly those who sit for the figure, a fact which is curious or natural according to the view one takes of human nature. They usually marry well, and sometimes they marry the artist. In neither case do they ever sit again. For an artist to marry his model is as fatal as for a *gourmet* to marry his cook, the one gets no sittings, and the other gets no dinners.

On the whole the English female models are very *naïve*, very natural, and very good-humoured. The virtues which the artist values most in them are prettiness and punctuality. Every sensible model consequently keeps a diary of her engagements, and dresses neatly. The bad season is of course the summer, when the artists are out of town. However, of late years some artists have engaged their models to follow them, and the wife of one of our most charming painters has often had three or four models under her charge in the country, so that the work of her husband and his friends should not be interrupted. In France the models migrate *en masse* to the little seaport villages or forest hamlets where the painters congregate. The English models however wait patiently in London, as a rule, till the artists come back. Nearly all of them live with their parents, and help to support the house. They have every qualification for being immortalized in art except that of beautiful hands. The hands of the English model are nearly always coarse and red.

As for the male models, there is the veteran whom we have mentioned above. He has all the traditions of the grand style, and is rapidly disappearing with the school he represents. An old man who talks about Fuseli is of course unendurable, and besides patriarchs have ceased to be fashionable subjects. Then there is the true Academy model. He is usually a man of thirty, rarely good-looking, but a perfect miracle of muscles. In fact he is the apotheosis of anatomy, and is so conscious of his own splendour that he tells you of his tibia and his thorax, as if no one else had anything of the kind. Then come the Oriental models. The supply of these is limited, but there are always about a dozen in London. They are very much sought after as they can remain immobile for hours, and generally possess lovely costumes. However they have a poor opinion of English art, which they regard as something between a vulgar personality and a commonplace photograph. Next we have the Italian youth who has either come over specially to be a model, or takes to it when his organ is out of repair. He is often quite charming with his large melancholy eyes, his crisp hair, and his slim brown figure. It is true he eats garlic, but then he can stand like a faun and couch like a leopard, so he is forgiven. He is always full of pretty compliments, and has been known to have kind words of encouragement for even our greatest artists. As for the English lad of the same age he never sits at all. Apparently he does not regard the career of a model as a serious profession. In any case he is rarely if ever to be got hold of. English boys too are difficult to find. Sometimes an ex-model who has a son will curl his hair, and wash his face, and bring him the round of the studios, all soap and shininess. The young school don't like him, but the older school do, and when he appears on the walls of the Royal Academy he is called *The Infant Samuel*. Occasionally also an artist catches a couple of *gamins** in the gutter and asks them to come to his studio. The first time they always appear, but after that they don't keep their appointments. They dislike sitting still, and have a strong and perhaps natural objection to looking pathetic. Besides they are always under the impression that the artist is laughing at them. It is a sad fact, but there is no doubt that the poor are completely unconscious of their own picturesqueness. Those of them who can be induced to sit do so with the idea that the artist is merely a benevolent philanthropist who has chosen an eccentric method of distributing alms to the undeserving. Perhaps the School Board will teach the London *gamin* his own artistic value, and then they will be better models than they are now. One remarkable privilege belongs to the Academy model, that of extorting a sovereign from any newly elected Associate or R.A.† They wait at Burlington House till the announcement is made, and then race to the hapless artist's house. The one who arrives first receives the money. They have of late been much troubled at the long distances they have had to run, and they look with strong disfavour on the election of artists who live at Hampstead or at Bedford Park,

* Street urchins (French).

† Full member of the Royal Academy, from the mid-nineteenth century located at Burlington House.

for it is considered a point of honour not to employ the underground railway, omnibuses, or any artificial means of locomotion. The race is to the swift.

Besides the professional posers of the studio there are the posers of the Row, the posers at afternoon teas, the posers in politics, and the circus-posers. All four classes are delightful, but only the last class is ever really decorative. Acrobats and gymnasts can give the young painter infinite suggestions, for they bring into their art an element of swiftness, of motion, and of constant change that the studio model necessarily lacks. What is interesting in these "slaves of the ring" is that with them Beauty is an unconscious result not a conscious aim, the result in fact of the mathematical calculation of curves and distances, of absolute precision of eye, of the scientific knowledge of the equilibrium of forces, and of perfect physical training. A good acrobat is always graceful though grace is never his object; he is graceful because he does what he has to do in the best way in which it can be done—graceful because he is natural. If an ancient Greek were to come to life now, which considering the probable severity of his criticisms would be rather trying to our conceit, he would be found far oftener at the circus than at the theatre. A good circus is an oasis of Hellenism in a world that reads too much to be wise, and thinks too much to be beautiful. If it were not for the running-ground at Eton, the towing-path at Oxford, the Thames swimming baths, and the yearly circuses, humanity would forget the plastic perfection of its own form, and degenerate into a race of short-sighted professors, and spectacled *précieuses!** Not that the circus-proprietors are, as a rule, conscious of their high mission. Do they not bore us with the *haute école*, and weary us with Shakespearean clowns? Still at least they give us acrobats, and the acrobat is an artist. The mere fact that he never speaks to the audience shows how well he appreciates the great truth that the aim of art is not to reveal personality but to please. The clown may be blatant, but the acrobat is always beautiful. He is an interesting combination of the spirit of Greek sculpture with

* Artists or critics who effect a "high style" (*haute école*).

the spangles of the modern costumier. He has even had his niche in the novels of our age, and if *Manette Salomon** be the unmasking of the model, *Les Frères Zemganno*† is the apotheosis of the acrobat.

As regards the influence of the ordinary model on our English school of painting, it cannot be said that it is altogether good. It is of course an advantage for the young artist sitting in his studio to be able to isolate "a little corner of life," as the French say, from disturbing surroundings, and to study it under certain effects of light and shade. But this very isolation leads often to mere mannerism in the painter, and robs him of that broad acceptance of the general facts of life which is the very essence of art. Model-painting, in a word, while it may be the condition of art, is not by any means its aim. It is simply practice, not perfection. Its use trains the eye and the hand of the painter, its abuse produces in his work an effect of mere posing and prettiness. It is the secret of much of the artificiality of modern art, this constant posing of pretty people, and when art becomes artificial it becomes monotonous. Outside the little world of the studio, with its draperies and its *bric-à-brac*, lies the world of life with its infinite, its Shakespearian variety. We must, however[,] distinguish between the two kinds of models, those who sit for the figure and those who sit for the costume. The study of the first is always excellent, but the costume-model is becoming rather wearisome in modern pictures. It is really of very little use to dress up a London girl in Greek draperies and to paint her as a goddess. The robe may be the robe of Athens, but the face is usually the face of Brompton. Now and then, it is true, one comes across a model whose face is an exquisite anachronism, and who looks lovely and natural in the dress of any century but her own. This however is rather rare. As a rule models are absolutely *de nôtre siècle*,‡ and should be painted as such. Unfortunately they are not, and as a consequence we are shown every year a series of scenes from fancy dress balls which are called historical

---

* Novel published in 1867 by brothers Jules and Edmond de Goncourt.

† Novel published in 1879 by Edmond de Goncourt.

‡ Belonging to, or typical of, our century (French).

pictures, but are little more than mediocre representations of modern people masquerading. In France they are wiser. The French painter uses the model simply for study, for the finished picture he goes direct to life.

However we must not blame the sitters for the shortcomings of the artists. The English models are a well-behaved and hardworking class, and if they are more interested in artists than they are in art, a large section of the public is in the same condition, and most of our modern exhibitions seem to justify its choice.

ON LITERATURE

DINNERS AND DISHES

A MAN CAN LIVE for three days without bread, but no man can live for one day without poetry, was an aphorism of Baudelaire's: you can live without pictures and music, but you can't live without eating, says the author of "Dinners and Dishes:" and this latter view is no doubt the more popular. Who indeed, in these degenerate days, would hesitate between an ode and an omelette, a sonnet and a salami? Yet the position is not entirely Philistine; cookery is an art; are not its principles the subject of South Kensington lectures, and does not the Royal Academy give a banquet once a year? Besides, as the coming democracy will no doubt insist on feeding us all on penny dinners, it is well that the laws of cookery should be explained; for were the national meal burned, or badly seasoned, or served up with the wrong sauce, a dreadful revolution might follow.

Under these circumstances we strongly recommend "Dinners and Dishes" to every one: it is brief, and concise, and makes no attempts at eloquence, which is extremely fortunate. For even on ortolans who could endure oratory? It also has the advantage of not being illustrated. The subject of a work of art has of course nothing to do with its beauty, but still there is always something depressing about the coloured lithograph of a leg of mutton.

As regards the author's particular views, we entirely agree with him on the important question of macaroni. "Never," he says, "ask me to back a bill for a man who has given me a macaroni pudding." Macaroni is essentially a savoury dish, and may be served with cheese, or tomatoes, but never with sugar and milk. There are also, a useful description of how to cook risotto, a delightful dish too rarely seen in England, an excellent chapter on the different kinds of salads, which should be carefully studied by those many hostesses whose imaginations never pass beyond lettuce and beetroot, and actually a recipe for making Brussels sprouts eatable. This last is of course a masterpiece.

The real difficulty, however, that we all have to face in life, is not so much the science of cookery, as the stupidity of cooks. And in this little handbook to practical Epicureanism, the tyrant of the English kitchen is shown in her proper light. Her entire ignorance of herbs, her passion for extracts and essences, her total inability to make a soup which is anything more than a combination of pepper and gravy, her inveterate habit of sending up bread-poultices with pheasants,—all these sins, and many others, are ruthlessly unmasked by the author. Ruthlessly and rightly. For the British cook is a foolish woman, who should be turned, for her iniquities, into a pillar of that salt which she never knows how to use.

But our author is not local merely. He has been in many lands; he has eaten back-hendl at Vienna, and kulibatsch at St. Petersburg; he has had the courage to face the buffalo veal of Roumania, and to dine with a German family at one o'clock; he has serious views on the right method of cooking those famous white truffles of Turin, of which Alexandre Dumas was so fond, and, in the face of the Oriental Club, declared that Bombay curry is better than the curry of Bengal. In fact he seems to have had experience of almost every kind of meal except the "square meal" of the Americans. This he should study at once; there is a great field for the philosophic epicure in the United States. Boston beans may be dismissed at once as delusions, but soft shell crabs, terrapin, canvas-back ducks, blue fish, and the pompono of New Orleans, are all wonderful delicacies, particularly when one gets them at Delmonico's.* Indeed, the two most remarkable bits of scenery in the States are undoubtedly Delmonico's, and the Yosemité Valley, and the former place has done more to promote a good feeling between England and America than anything else has in this century.

We hope that "Wanderer" will go there soon, and add a chapter to

* The first true restaurant in the United States, it was opened by the Delmonico brothers, on William Street in New York City, in the 1830s.

"Dinners and Dishes," and that his book will have in England the influence it deserves. There are twenty ways of cooking a potato, and three hundred and sixty-five ways of cooking an egg, yet the British cook up to the present moment knows only three methods of sending up either one or the other.

TO READ, OR NOT TO READ*

As we have published so many letters advising what to read, the following advice "what not to read" from so good an authority as Mr. Oscar Wilde may be of service:—

Books, I fancy, may be conveniently divided into three classes:—†

1. Books to read, such as Cicero's Letters, Suetonius, Vasari's Lives of the Painters, the Autobiography of Benvenuto Cellini, Sir John Mandeville, Marco Polo, St. Simon's Memoirs, Mommsen, and (till we get a better one) Grote's History of Greece.

2. Books to re-read, such as Plato and Keats. In the sphere of poetry, the masters not the minstrels, in the sphere of philosophy, the seers not the *savants*.‡

3. Books not to read at all, such as Thomson's Seasons, Rogers' Italy, Paley's Evidences, all the Fathers, except St. Augustine, all John Stuart Mill, except the essay on Liberty, all Voltaire's plays without any exception, Butler's Analogy, Grant's Aristotle, Hume's England, Lewes' History of Philosophy, all argumentative books, and all books that try to prove anything. This third class is by far the most important. To tell people what to read is as a rule either useless or harmful, for the true appreciation of literature is a question of temperament not of teaching, to Parnassus there is no primer, and nothing that one can learn is ever worth learning. But to tell

* Wilde puns on Hamlet's soliloquy, implying that if you do not read, you die.

† The classification is designed to distinguish perennially "readable" classics from works of earnest pedantry, including certain treatises of the early church fathers, travel books, and histories.

‡ Learned persons (French).

people what not to read is a very different matter, and I venture to recommend it as a mission to the University Extension Scheme. Indeed, it is one that is eminently needed in this age of ours, an age which reads so much that it has no time to admire, and writes so much that it has no time to think. Whoever will select out of the chaos of our modern curricula "The Worst Hundred Books," and publish a list of them, will confer on the rising generation a real and lasting benefit.

After expressing these views I suppose that I should not offer any suggestions at all with regard to "The Best Hundred Books," but I hope that you will allow me the pleasure of being inconsistent, as I am anxious to put in a claim for a book that has been strangely omitted by most of the excellent judges who have contributed to your columns. I mean the Greek Anthology.* The beautiful poems contained in this collection seem to me to hold the same position with regard to Greek Dramatic Literature, as do the delicate little figurines of Tanagra to the Pheidian marbles, and to be quite as necessary for the complete understanding of the Greek Spirit.

I am also amazed to find that Edgar Allan Poe has been passed over. Surely this marvellous lord of rhythmic expression deserves a place? If in order to make room for him, it be necessary to elbow out some one else, I should elbow out Southey, and I think that Baudelaire might be most advantageously substituted for Keble.† No doubt, both in The Curse of Kehama and in The Christian Year there are poetical qualities of a certain kind, but absolute catholicity of taste is not without its dangers. It is only an auctioneer who should admire all schools of art.

---

* Influential collection of short poems initially compiled in the first century B.C.E. by Meleager of Gadara; new poems were as late as the tenth century C.E.

† Wilde resists including Robert Southey (1774–1843; poet laureate and author of *The Curse of Kahama*) and churchman John Keble (1792–1866; author of *The Christian Year*).

BALZAC IN ENGLISH

MANY YEARS AGO, in a number of *All the Year Round*, Charles Dickens complained that Balzac was very little read in England, and although since then the public have become more familiar with the great masterpieces of French fiction, still it may be doubted whether the "Comédie Humaine" is at all appreciated or understood by the general run of novel-readers. It is really the greatest monument that literature has produced in our century, and M. Taine* hardly exaggerates when he says that, after Shakespeare, Balzac is our most important magazine of documents on human nature. Balzac's aim, in fact, was to do for humanity what Buffon† had done for the animal creation. As the naturalist studied lions and tigers, so the novelist studied men and women. Yet he was no mere reporter. Photography and proces-verbal were not the essentials of his method. Observation gave him the facts of life, but his genius converted facts into truths, and truths into truth. He was, in a word, a marvellous combination of the artistic temperament with the scientific spirit. The latter he bequeathed to his disciples; the former was entirely his own. The distinction between such a book as M. Zola's‡ "L'Assommoir" and such a book as Balzac's "Illusions Perdues" is the distinction between unimaginative realism and imaginative reality.§ "All Balzac's characters," said Baudelaire, "are gifted with the same ardour of life that animated himself. All his fictions are as deeply

* Hippolyte Taine (1828–1893), leading French historian and critic.

† G.-L. Leclerc, comte de Buffon (1707–1788) who wrote his innovative *Natural History* in more than forty volumes, made discoveries in mathematics, and studied cosmology.

‡ Émile Zola (1840–1902) wanted novels to be "scientific" studies of society. Honoré de Balzac (1799–1850) preceded him in this; his *Human Comedy* comprises almost 100 novels and stories.

§ Wilde contrasts Zola's materialistic "realism" with the more metaphysical style of Balzac, which he calls "imaginative reality," a magical human gallery of persons.

coloured as dreams. Every mind is a weapon loaded to the muzzle with will. The very scullions have genius." He was of course accused of being immoral. Few writers who deal directly with life escape that charge. His answer to the accusation was characteristic and conclusive. "Whoever contributes his stone to the edifice of ideas," he wrote, "whoever proclaims an abuse, whoever sets his mark upon an evil to be abolished, always passes for immoral. If you are true in your portraits, if, by dint of daily and nightly toil, you succeed in writing the most difficult language in the world, the word immoral is thrown in your face." The morals of the personages of the "Comédie Humaine" are simply the morals of the world around us. They are part of the artist's subject-matter, they are not part of his method. If there be any need of censure it is to life not to literature that it should be given. Balzac, besides, is essentially universal. He sees life from every point of view. He has no preferences and no prejudices. He does not try to prove anything. He feels that the spectacle of life contains its own secret. "Il crée un monde et se tait."

And what a world it is! What a panorama of passions! What a pell-mell of men and women! It was said of Trollope that he increased the number of our acquaintances without adding to our visiting lists; but after reading the "Comédie Humaine" one begins to believe that the only real people are the people who have never existed. Lucien de Rubempré, le Père Goriot, Ursule Mirouët, Marguerite Claës, the Baron Hulot, Mdme. Marneffe, le Cousin Pons, De Marsay—all bring with them a kind of contagious illusion of life. They have a fierce vitality about them: their existence is fervent and fiery-coloured: we not merely feel for them, but we see them—they dominate our fancy and defy scepticism. A steady course of Balzac reduces our living friends to shadows, and our acquaintances to the shadows of shades. Who would care to go out to an evening party to meet Tomkins, the friend of one's boyhood, when one can sit at home with Lucien de Rubempré?* It is pleasanter to have the entrée to Balzac's society than to receive cards from all the duchesses in Mayfair.

* Main character in Balzac's *Lost Illusions* (1837).

In spite of this there are many people who have declared the "Comédie Humaine" to be indigestible. Perhaps it is, but then what about truffles? Balzac's publisher refused to be disturbed by any such criticism as that. "Indigestible, is it?" he exclaimed, with what, for a publisher, was rare good sense. "Well, I should hope so; who ever thinks of a dinner that isn't?" And our English publisher Mr. Routledge clearly agrees with M. Poulet-Malassis, as he is occupied in producing a complete translation of the "Comédie Humaine." The two volumes that at present lie before us contain "César Birotteau," that terrible tragedy of finance, "L'Illustre Gaudissart," the apotheosis of the commercial traveller, the "Duchesse de Langeais," most marvellous of modern love stories, "Le Chef-d'oeuvre Inconnu," from which Mr. Henry James took his "Madonna of the Future," and that extraordinary romance "Une Passion dans le Désert." The choice of stories is quite excellent, but the translations are very unequal, and some of them are positively bad. "L'Illustre Gaudissart," for instance, is full of the most grotesque mistakes, mistakes that would disgrace a schoolboy. "Bon conseil vaut un oeil dans la main," is translated, "Good advice is an egg in the hand!" "Ecus rebelles" is rendered "rebellious lucre," and such common expressions as "faire la barbe," "attendre la vente," "n'entendre rien," "pâlir sur une affaire," are all mistranslated. "Des bois de quoi se faire un cure-dent" is not "a few trees to slice into toothpicks," but "as much timber as would make a toothpick;" "son horloge enfermée dans une grande armoire oblongue," is not "a clock which he kept shut up in a large oblong closet," but simply a clock in a tall clock case; "journal viager" is not "an annuity," "garce" is not the same as "farce," and "dessins des Indes" are not "drawings of the Indies." On the whole, nothing can be worse than this translation, and if Mr. Routledge wishes the public to read his version of the "Comédie Humaine" he should engage translators who have some slight knowledge of French. "César Birotteau" is better, though it is not by any means free from mistakes. "To suffer under the maximum" is an absurd rendering of "subir le maximum;" "perse" is "chintz," not "Persian chintz;" "rendre le pain bénit" is not to "take the wafer;" "rivière" is hardly a "*fillet* of diamonds;" and to translate, "Son coeur avait un calus à l'endroit du loyer," by "His heart was a callus in the direction of a lease," is an insult to two languages. On the whole the best version is that of the "Duchesse de Langeais," though even this leaves much to be desired. Such a sentence as "to imitate the rough logician who marched before the Pyrrhonians *while denying his own movement*" entirely misses the point of Balzac's "imiter le rude logician qui marchait devant les pyrrhoniens, qui niaient le mouvement." We fear that Mr. Routledge's edition will not do. It is well printed, and nicely bound; but his translators do not understand French. It is a great pity, for "La Comédie Humaine" is one of the masterpieces of the age.

THE POETS AND THE PEOPLE

By One of the Latter

NEVER WAS THERE a time in our national history when there was more need than there is now for the creation of a spirit of enthusiasm among all classes of society, inspiring men and women with that social zeal and the spirit of self-sacrifice which alone can save a great people in the throes of national misfortune. Tirades of pessimism require but little intellectual effort, and the world is not much the better for them; but to inspire a people with hope and courage, to fill them with a desire after righteousness and duty, this is work that requires the combination of intelligence and feeling of the highest order. Who, in the midst of all our poverty and distress, that threatens to become intensified, will step into the breach and rouse us to the almost superhuman effort that is necessary to alter the existing state of things?

There is one class of men to whom we have a right to look for assistance, to whom the task of stirring the national conscience should be accepted with delight. When the poor are suffering from inherent faults of their own, and the greediness of capitalists, and both are in danger of suffering still more from causes over which they have but partial control, surely the hour has come when the poets should exercise their influence for good, and set fairer ideals before all than the mere love of wealth and ostentatious display on one side and the desire to appropriate wealth on the other. But we listen in vain for any inspiring ode or ballad that shall reach the hearts of the people or touch the consciences of capitalists. What do those who are designated in the columns of our newspapers as great poets bring to us in this hour of national trial, when we are so much in need of the service of a truly great poet? One* gives us a string of melancholy pessimism that has achieved no higher results than increasing the poet's fortune and drawing a magazine article from Mr. Gladstone.† Another‡ who has hitherto posed as the poet of freedom, and even licence—some would say licentiousness—when he does turn his attention to practical affairs does his best to abuse and dishearten a nation that is heroically struggling against the injustice of centuries and panting for national freedom. These things are bad enough, but what shall be said of the conduct of one who in the eyes of many is esteemed the greatest of living poets? He, at the hour when his country requires inspiration and encouragement, prostitutes his intelligence to the production of a number of unwieldy lines that to the vast majority of Englishmen are unintelligible jargon. What right has a man to the title of poet when he fails to produce music in his lines, who cannot express his thoughts in simple language that the people can understand; but, on the contrary, has so imperfect a command of his mother tongue that all the efforts of a society of intellectual pickaxes cannot discover what his words really mean? Above all, what right has a man to the title of poet who has so little sense of his duty to his fellow men as to indulge in composition of word puzzles and ear-torturing sentences when a whole people needs the assistance of every man and woman who is capable of thinking and acting? The Roman despot who played the fiddle while his city was burning might plead the ignorance of himself and his time, but Mr. Browning§ is living in the nineteenth century, and has no such excuses for banging his intellectual tin kettle

---

* Alfred, Lord Tennyson (1809–1892), a very popular English poet whose verse primarily dealt with mythological and classical themes.

† William Ewart Gladstone (1809–1898), four-time British prime minister. A Liberal Party member, he was a reformer, and not always pleasing to Queen Victoria.

‡ Algernon Charles Swinburne (1837–1909), an English poet whose controversial themes (sadomasochism and lesbianism among them) were considered decadent in his time.

§ Robert Browning (1812–1889), a major Victorian poet, is best known for writing dramatic monologues, including "My Last Duchess."

while a fourth part of his fellow-countrymen are struggling against poverty, and are weighed down by the gloomy outlook towards the future. We are assured by his admirers that he is a great thinker—yes, more, a philosopher as well as a poet. Now, England was never in greater need of such a man, and it is Mr. Browning's duty, if he has the ability, to write plain English and act the poet's true part. Let any sensible man outside the Browning Society dip into the mysterious volume of literary hocus-pocus that has recently been so solemnly reviewed, and see whether he can find a single passage likely to stir the pulses of any man or woman, create a desire to lead a higher, a holier, and a more useful life in the breast of the indifferent average citizen. The struggle to live in all parts of Western Europe, and perhaps especially England, is so fierce that we are in danger of having all that is idealistic and beautiful crushed out of us by the steam engine and the manipulations of the Stock Exchanges. We were never in greater need of good poets, and never better able than in this practical age to do without literary medicine men and mystery mongers. Is it possible that Mr. Browning can see nothing in the world around him to induce him to make an earnest endeavour to help the people out of their difficulties and to make their duty plain? He may be a man of genius so sublime that the language of the common people is inadequate to clothe his thoughts, but his right to the title of poet is not so clear as that of the humblest writer of doggerel lines in the poets' corner of a provincial newspaper, who is aiming in his own honest way to set his followers straight. The people are suffering, and are likely to suffer more; where is the poet who is the one man needful to rouse the nation to a sense of duty and inspire the people with hope?

POETRY AND PRISON

PRISON HAS HAD an admirable effect on Mr. Wilfrid Blunt as a poet.* The "Love Sonnets of Proteus," in spite of their clever Musset-like modernities, and their swift brilliant wit, were but affected or fantastic at best. They were simply the records of passing moods and moments, of which some were sad, and others sweet, and not a few shameful. Their subject was not of high or serious import. They contained much that was wilful and weak. "In Vinculis," upon the other hand, is a book that stirs one by its fine sincerity of purpose, its lofty and impassioned thought, its depth and ardour of intense feeling. "Imprisonment," says Mr. Blunt in his preface, "is a reality of discipline most useful to the modern soul, lapped as it is in physical sloth and self-indulgence. Like a sickness or a spiritual retreat it purifies and ennobles; and the soul emerges from it stronger and more self-contained." To him, certainly, it has been a mode of purification. The opening sonnets, composed in the bleak cell of Galway gaol, and written down on the flyleaves of the prisoner's prayer-book, are full of things nobly conceived and nobly uttered, and show that though Mr. Balfour may enforce "plain living" by his prison regulations, he cannot prevent "high thinking," or in any way limit or constrain the freedom of a man's soul. They are, of course, intensely personal in expression. They could not fail to be so. But the personality that they reveal has nothing petty or ignoble about it. The petulant cry of the shallow egoist, which was the chief characteristic of the "Love Sonnets of Proteus," is not to be found here. In its place we have wild grief and terrible scorn, fierce rage and flame-like passion. Such a

* Wilfrid Scawen Blunt (1840–1922) was imprisoned for his Irish separatist actions. The prisons were under the control of A. J. Balfour (1848–1930), secretary for Ireland and later prime minister. Balfour also wrote influential works on the philosophy of theism.

sonnet as the following comes out of the very fire of heart and brain:—

God knows, 'twas not with a forereasoned plan
 I left the easeful dwellings of my peace,
And sought this combat with ungodly man,
 And ceaseless still through years that do not cease
 Have warred with powers and principalities;
My natural soul, ere yet these strifes began,
 Was as a sister diligent to please
And loving all, and most the human clan.

God knows it. And He knows how the world's tears
 Touched me. And He is witness of my wrath,
How it was kindled against murderers
 Who slew for gold, and how upon their path
I met them. Since which day the world in arms
Strikes at my life with angers and alarms.

And this sonnet has all the strange strength of that despair which is but the prelude to a larger hope:—

I thought to do a deed of chivalry,
 An act of worth, which haply in her sight
Who was my mistress should recorded be
 And of the nations. And, when thus the fight
 Faltered and men once bold with faces white
Turned this and that way in excuse to flee,
 I only stood, and by the foeman's might
Was overborne and mangled cruelly.

Then crawled I to her feet, in whose clear cause
 I made this venture, and "Behold," I said,
 "How I am wounded for thee in these wars."
 But she, "Poor cripple, wouldst thou I should wed

A limbless trunk?" and laughing turned from me:
Yet she was fair, and her name "Liberty."

The sonnet beginning

A prison is a convent without God—
Poverty, Chastity, Obedience
Its precepts are:—

is very fine, and this, written just after entering the gaol, is powerful:—

Naked I came into the world of pleasure,
And naked come I to this house of pain.
Here at the gate I lay down my life's treasure,
My pride, my garments, and my name with men.
The world and I henceforth shall be as twain,
No sound of me shall pierce for good or ill
These walls of grief. Nor shall I hear the vain
Laughter and tears of those who love me still.

Within, what new life waits me? Little ease,
Cold lying, hunger, nights of wakefulness,
Harsh orders given, no voice to soothe or please,
Poor thieves for friends, for books rules meaningless;
This is the grave—nay hell. Yet, Lord of Might
Still in Thy Light my spirit shall see light.

But indeed all the sonnets are worth reading, and "The Canon of Aughrim," the longest poem in the book, is a most masterly and dramatic description of the tragic life of the Irish peasant. Literature is not much indebted to Mr. Balfour for his sophistical "Defence of Philosophic Doubt," which is one of the dullest books we know, but it must be admitted that by sending Mr. Blunt to gaol he has converted a clever rhymer into an earnest and deep-thinking poet. The narrow confines of the prison-cell seem to suit the sonnet's "scanty plot of ground," and an unjust imprisonment for a noble cause strengthens as well as deepens the nature.

Mr. Andrew Lang's "Grass of Parnassus"

Whether or not Mr. Andrew Lang* should be sent to prison, is another matter. We are inclined to think that he should not, except as a punishment for writing sonnets to Mr. Rider Haggard. His gay pleasant Muse, with her dainty if somewhat facile graces, her exquisite triviality, and her winsome irresponsible manner, would probably gain very little from such a dreary exile. When Leigh Hunt was in gaol he was allowed to console himself with a pretty wall-paper, but Mr. Balfour permits nothing but white-washed walls, and we are quite sure that Mr. Lang would find their monotony unbearable. Prison is for souls stronger than the soul revealed to us in the charming whisperings and musical echoes of the "Grass of Parnassus;" which, however, is a very fascinating little volume, in its way, and possesses many delicately-carved "ivories of speech," to borrow one of Mr. Pater's phrases. The translation of Rémy Belleau's well-known poem on April is excellent:—

April with thy gracious wiles,
   Like the smiles,
Smiles of Venus; and thy breath
Like her breath, the gods' delight,
   (From their height
They take the happy air beneath;)

It is thou that, of thy grace,
   From their place

* Andrew Lang (1844–1912), a folklorist, important translator of classical texts, and minor man of letters. Wilde puts Lang in prison for emptiness and lack of passion.

In the far-off isles dost bring
Swallows over earth and sea,
   Glad to be
Messengers of thee and Spring.

Daffodil and eglantine,
   And woodbine,
Lily, violet, and rose
Plentiful in April fair,
   To the air,
Their pretty petals to unclose.

The assonance of "their" in the last line with "air" in the line preceding is not very pleasing, and indeed the word seems otiose, but the translation as a whole is admirably done. The version of poor Henri Murger's "Old Loves" is also very good. It is a little masterpiece of felicitous rendering, and the versions from the Greek anthology show the fine taste of a true scholar and man of letters. Where Mr. Lang pipes on his own reed, we like him less, and his sonnets are deficient in any fine central motive, and really show him at his worst. But such poems as "Colinette" and "The Singing Rose" are certainly wonderfully pretty. Mr. Lang has recently been christened "the Divine Amateur," and the little book that lies before us is a good instance of how well he deserves that graceful compliment. However, this book should not have been brought out in winter. It is made for summer. On a lazy June evening no more delightful companion could be found than a poet who has the sweetest of voices and absolutely nothing to say.

THE GOSPEL ACCORDING TO WALT WHITMAN

"No one will get at my verses who insists upon viewing them as a literary performance, or as aiming mainly towards art and aestheticism. 'Leaves of Grass' has been chiefly the outcropping of my own emotional and other personal nature—an attempt from first to last to put a *Person*, a human being (myself, in the latter half of the nineteenth century, in America) freely, fully and truly on record. I could not find any similar personal record in current literature that satisfied me." In these words Walt Whitman gives us the true attitude we should adopt towards his work, having indeed a much saner view of the value and meaning of that work than either his eloquent admirers or noisy detractors can boast of possessing. His last book, "November Boughs" as he calls it, published in the winter of the old man's life, reveals to us, not indeed a soul's tragedy, for its last note is one of joy and hope and noble and unshaken faith in all that is fine and worthy of such faith, but certainly the drama of a human soul, and puts on record with a simplicity that has in it both sweetness and strength the record of his spiritual development and of the aim and motive both of the manner and the matter of his work. His strange mode of expression is shown in these pages to have been the result of deliberate and self-conscious choice. The "barbaric yawp," which he sent over "the roofs of the world" so many years ago, and which wrung from Mr. Swinburne's lips such lofty panegyric in song and such loud clamorous censure in prose, appears here in what will be to many an entirely new light. For in his very rejection of art Walt Whitman is an artist. He tried to produce a certain effect by certain means and he succeeded. There is much method in which many have termed his madness, too much method indeed some may be tempted to fancy.

In the story of his life, as he tells it to us, we find him at the age of sixteen beginning a definite and philosophical study of literature:—

> Summers and falls, I used to go off, sometimes for a week at a stretch, down in the country, or to Long Island's seashores—there in the presence of outdoor influences, I went over thoroughly the Old and New Testaments and absorb'd (probably to better advantage for me than in any library or indoor room—it makes such difference *where* you read) Shakspere, Ossian, the best translated versions I could get of Homer, Aeschylus, Sophocles, the old German Nibelungen, the ancient Hindoo poems, and one or two other masterpieces, Dante's among them. As it happen'd I read the latter mostly in an old wood. The Iliad I read first thoroughly on the peninsula of Orient, north-east end of Long Island, in a sheltered hollow of rocks and sand, with the sea on each side. (I have wondered since why I was not overwhelmed by those mighty masters. Likely because I read them, as described, in the full presence of Nature, under the sun, with the far-spreading landscapes and vistas, or the sea rolling in.)

Edgar Allan Poe's amusing bit of dogmatism that, for our occasions and for our day, there can be no such thing as a long poem, fascinated him: "The same thought had been haunting my mind before," he says, "but Poe's argument, though short, work'd the sum out and proved it to me:" and the English translation of the Bible seems to have suggested to him the possibility of a poetic form which while retaining the spirit of poetry would still be free from the trammels of rhyme and of a definite metrical system. Having thus to a certain degree settled upon what one might call the *technique* of Whitmanism, he began to brood upon the nature of that spirit that was to give life to the strange form. The central point of the poetry of the future seemed to him to be necessarily "an identical body and soul," a personality in fact, which personality he tells us frankly, "after many considerations and ponderings I deliberately settled should be myself." However for the true creation and revealing of this personality, at first only dimly felt, a new stimulus was needed. This came from the Civil War. After describing the many dreams and passions of his boyhood and early manhood he goes on to say:—

> These, however, and much more might have gone on and come to naught (almost positively would have come to naught) if a sudden, vast, terrible, direct and indirect stimulus for new and national declamatory expression had not been given to me. It is certain I say, that, although I had made a start before, only from the occurrence of the Secession War, and what it showed me as by flashes of lightning, with the emotional depths it sounded and arous'd (of course, I don't mean in my own heart only, I saw it just as plainly in others, in millions) that only from the strong flare and provocation of that war's sights and scenes the final reasons-for-being of an autochthonic and passionate song definitely came forth. I went down to the war-fields of Virginia, lived thenceforward in camp, saw great battles—and the days and nights afterwards—partook of all the fluctuations, gloom, despair, hopes again aroused, courage evoked—death readily risked—the *cause* too—along and filling those agonistic and lurid following years, the real parturition years of the henceforth homogeneous Union. Without those three or four years and the experiences they gave, "Leaves of Grass" would not now be existing.

Having thus obtained the necessary stimulus for the quickening and awakening of the personal self, some day to be endowed with universality, he sought to find new notes of song, and passing beyond the mere passion for expression—he aimed at "Suggestiveness" first. "I round and finish little, if anything; and could not, consistently with my scheme. The reader will have his or her part to do, just as much as I have had mine. I seek less to state or display any theme of thought, and more to bring you, reader, into the atmosphere of the theme or thought—there to pursue your own flight." Another "impetus word" is Comradeship, and other "word-signs" are Good Cheer, Content, and Hope. Individuality, especially, he sought for:—

> I have allowed the stress of my poems from beginning to end to bear upon American individuality and assist it—not only

> because that is a great lesson in Nature, amid all her generalizing laws, but as a counterpoise to the levelling tendencies of Democracy—and for other reasons. Defiant of ostensible literary and other conventions, I avowedly chant "the great pride of a man in himself," and permit it to be more or less a *motif* of nearly all my verse. I think this pride indispensable to an American. I think it not inconsistent with obedience, humility, deference, and self-questioning.

* * * * *

A new theme also was to be found in the relation of the sexes, conceived in a natural, simple, and healthy form, and he protests against poor Mr. William Rossetti's* attempt to Bowdlerize and expurgate his song.

> From another point of view "Leaves of Grass" is avowedly the song of Sex, and Amativeness, and even Animality—though meanings that do not usually go with these words are behind all, and will duly emerge; and all are sought to be lifted into a different light and atmosphere. Of this feature intentionally palpable in a few lines, I shall only say the espousing principle of those lines so gives breath to my whole scheme that the bulk of the pieces might as well have been left unwritten were those lines omitted. . . . Universal as are certain facts and symptoms of communities there is nothing so rare in modern conventions and poetry as their normal recognizance. Literature is always calling in the doctor for consultation and confession, and always giving evasions and swathing suppressions in place of that "heroic nudity" on which only a genuine diagnosis can be built. And in respect to editions of "Leaves of Grass" in time to come (if there should be such) I take occasion now to confirm those lines with the settled convictions and deliberate renewals of thirty years, and to hereby prohibit, as far as mine can do so, any elision of them.

* * * * *

---

* William Michael Rossetti (1829–1919), brother of Christina and Dante Gabriel Rossetti, and a founding member of the Pre-Raphaelite movement in art.

But beyond all these notes and moods and motives is the lofty spirit of a grand and free acceptance of all things that are worthy of existence. "I desired," he says, "to formulate a poem whose every thought or fact should indirectly or directly be or connive at an implicit belief in the wisdom, health, mystery, or beauty of every process, every concrete object, every human or other existence, not only consider'd from the point of view of all, but of each." His two final utterances are that really great poetry is always the result of a national spirit, and not the privilege of a polished and select few; and that the sweetest and strongest songs yet remain to be sung.

Such are the views contained in the opening essay, "A Backward Glance o'er Travel'd Roads," as he calls it: but there are many other essays in this fascinating volume, some on poets such as Burns and Lord Tennyson, for whom Walt Whitman has a profound admiration; some on old actors and singers, the elder Booth, Forrest, Alboni, and Mario being his special favourites; others on the native Indians, on the Spanish element in American nationality, on Western slang, on the poetry of the Bible, and on Abraham Lincoln. But Walt Whitman is at his best when he is analyzing his own work, and making schemes for the poetry of the future. Literature to him has a distinctly social aim. He seeks to build up the masses by "building up grand individuals." And yet literature itself must be preceded by noble forms of life. "The best literature is always the result of something far greater than itself—not the hero but the portrait of the hero. Before there can be recorded history or poem there must be the transaction." Certainly in Walt Whitman's views there is a largeness of vision, a healthy sanity, and a fine ethical purpose. He is not to be placed with the professional *littérateurs* of his country, Boston novelists, New York poets, and the like. He stands apart, and the chief value of his work is in its prophecy not in its performance. He has begun a prelude to larger themes. He is the herald to a new era. As a man he is the precursor of a fresh type. He is a factor in the heroic and spiritual evolution of the human being. If Poetry has passed him by, Philosophy will take note of him.

MR. PATER'S LAST VOLUME [*APPRECIATIONS*]

WHEN I FIRST HAD the privilege—and I count it a very high one—of meeting Mr. Walter Pater, he said to me, smiling, "Why do you always write poetry? Why do you not write prose? Prose is so much more difficult."

It was during my undergraduate days at Oxford; days of lyrical ardours and of studious sonnet-writing; days when one loved the exquisite intricacy and musical repetitions of the ballade, and the villanelle with its linked long-drawn echoes and its curious completeness; days when one solemnly sought to discover the proper temper in which a triolet should be written; delightful days, in which, I am glad to say, there was far more rhyme than reason.

I may frankly confess now that at the time I did not quite comprehend what Mr. Pater really meant; and it was not till I had carefully studied his beautiful and suggestive essays on the Renaissance that I fully realised what a wonderful self-conscious art the art of English prose-writing really is, or may be made to be. Carlyle's stormy rhetoric, Ruskin's winged and passionate eloquence, had seemed to me to spring from enthusiasm rather than from art. I don't think I knew then that even prophets correct their proofs. As for Jacobean prose, I thought it too exuberant; and Queen Anne prose appeared to me terribly bald, and irritatingly rational. But Mr. Pater's essays became to me "the golden book of spirit and sense, the holy writ of beauty." They are still this to me. It is possible, of course, that I may exaggerate about them. I certainly hope that I do; for where there is no exaggeration there is no love, and where there is no love there is no understanding. It is only about things that do not interest one, that one can give a really unbiassed opinion; and this is no doubt the reason why an unbiassed opinion is always absolutely valueless.

But I must not allow this brief notice of Mr. Pater's new volume to degenerate into an autobiography. I remember being told in America that whenever Margaret Fuller wrote an essay upon Emerson the printers had always to send out to borrow some additional capital "I's," and I feel it right to accept this transatlantic warning.

"Appreciations," in the fine Latin sense of the word, is the title given by Mr. Pater to his book, which is an exquisite collection of exquisite essays, of delicately wrought works of art—some of them being almost Greek in their purity of outline and perfection of form, others mediæval in their strangeness of colour and passionate suggestion, and all of them absolutely modern, in the true meaning of the term modernity. For he to whom the present is the only thing that is present, knows nothing of the age in which he lives. To realise the nineteenth century, one must realise every century that has preceded it, and that has contributed to its making. To know anything about oneself, one must know all about others. There must be no mood with which one cannot sympathise, no dead mode of life that one cannot make alive. The legacies of heredity may make us alter our views of moral responsibility, but they cannot but intensify our sense of the value of Criticism; for the true critic is he who bears within himself the dreams and ideas and feelings of myriad generations, and to whom no form of thought is alien, no emotional impulse obscure.

Perhaps the most interesting, and certainly the least successful, of the essays contained in the present volume is that on "Style." It is the most interesting because it is the work of one who speaks with the high authority that comes from the noble realisation of things nobly conceived. It is the least successful, because the subject is too abstract. A true artist like Mr. Pater, is most felicitous when he deals with the concrete, whose very limitations give him finer freedom, while they necessitate more intense vision. And yet what a high ideal is contained in these few pages! How good it is for us, in these days of popular education and facile journalism, to be reminded of the real scholarship that is essential to the perfect writer, who, "being a true lover of words for their own sake, a minute and constant observer of their physiognomy," will avoid what is mere rhetoric, or ostentatious ornament, or negligent misuse of terms, or ineffective surplusage, and will be known by his tact of omission, by his skilful economy of means, by his selection and self-restraint, and perhaps above all by that conscious artistic structure which is the expression of mind in style. I think I have been wrong in saying that the subject is too abstract. In Mr. Pater's hands it becomes very real to us indeed, and he shows us how, behind the perfection of a man's style, must lie the passion of a man's soul.

As one passes to the rest of the volume, one finds essays on Wordsworth and on Coleridge, on Charles Lamb and on Sir Thomas Browne, on some of Shakespeare's plays and on the English kings that Shakespeare fashioned, on Dante Rossetti, and on William Morris. As that on Wordsworth seems to be Mr. Pater's last work, so that on the singer of the "Defence of Guenevere" is certainly his earliest, or almost his earliest, and it is interesting to mark the change that has taken place in his style. This change is, perhaps, at first sight not very apparent. In 1868 we find Mr. Pater writing with the same exquisite care for words, with the same studied music, with the same temper, and something of the same mode of treatment. But, as he goes on, the architecture of the style becomes richer and more complex, the epithet more precise and intellectual. Occasionally one may be inclined to think that there is, here and there, a sentence which is somewhat long, and possibly, if one may venture to say so, a little heavy and cumbersome in movement. But if this be so, it comes from those side-issues suddenly suggested by the idea in its progress, and really revealing the idea more perfectly; or from those felicitous after-thoughts that give a fuller completeness to the central scheme, and yet convey something of the charm of chance; or from a desire to suggest the secondary shades of meaning with all their accumulating effect, and to avoid, it may be, the violence and harshness of too definite and exclusive an opinion. For in matters of art, at any rate, thought is inevitably coloured by emotion, and so is fluid rather than fixed, and, recognising its dependence upon moods and upon the passion of fine moments, will not accept the rigidity of a scientific formula or a theological dogma. The critical pleasure, too, that we receive from tracing, through what may seem the intricacies of a sentence, the working of the constructive intelligence, must not be overlooked. As soon as we have realised the design, everything appears clear and simple. After a time, these long sentences of Mr. Pater's come to have the charm of an elaborate piece of music, and the unity of such music also.

I have suggested that the essay on Wordsworth is probably the most recent bit of work contained in this volume. If one might choose between so much that is good, I should be inclined to say it is the finest also. The essay on Lamb is curiously suggestive; suggestive, indeed, of a somewhat more tragic, more sombre figure, than men have been wont to think of in connection with the author of the Essays of Elia. It is an interesting aspect under which to regard Lamb, but perhaps he himself would have had some difficulty in recognising the portrait given of him. He had, undoubtedly, great sorrows, or motives for sorrow, but he could console himself at a moment's notice for the real tragedies of life by reading any one of the Elizabethan tragedies, provided it was in a folio edition. The essay on Sir Thomas Browne is delightful, and has the strange, personal, fanciful charm of the author of the "Religio Medici;" Mr. Pater often catching the colour and accent and tone of whatever artist, or work of art, he deals with. That on Coleridge, with its insistence on the necessity of the cultivation of the relative, as opposed to the absolute spirit in philosophy and in ethics, and its high appreciation of the poet's true position in our literature, is in style and substance a very blameless work. Grace of expression, and delicate subtlety of thought and phrase, characterise the essays on Shakespeare. But the essay on Wordsworth has a spiritual beauty of its own. It appeals, not to the ordinary Wordsworthian with his uncritical temper, and his gross confusion of ethical with æsthetical problems, but rather to those who desire to separate the gold from the dross, and to reach at the true Wordsworth through the mass of tedious and prosaic work that bears his name, and that serves often to conceal him from us. The presence of an alien element in Wordsworth's art, is, of course, recognised by Mr. Pater but he touches on it merely from the psychological point of view, pointing out how this quality of higher and lower moods gives the effect in his poetry "of a power not altogether his own, or under his control"; a power which comes and goes when it wills, "so that the old fancy which made the poet's art an enthusiasm, a form of divine possession, seems almost true of him." Mr. Pater's earlier essays had their *purpurei panni*,* so eminently suitable for quotation, such as the famous passage on Monna Lisa, and that other in which Botticelli's strange conception of the Virgin is so strangely set forth. From the present volume it is difficult to select any one passage in preference to another as specially characteristic of Mr. Pater's treatment. This, however, is worth quoting at length. It contains a truth eminently useful for our age:—

> That the end of life is not action but contemplation—*being* as distinct from *doing*—a certain disposition of the mind: is, in some shape or other, the principle of all the higher morality. In poetry, in art, if you enter into their true spirit at all, you touch this principle in a measure; these, by their very sterility, are a type of beholding for the mere joy of beholding. To treat life in the spirit of art is to make life a thing in which means and ends are identified: to encourage such treatment, the true moral significance of art and poetry. Wordsworth, and other poets who have been like him in ancient or more recent times, are the masters, the experts, in this art of impassioned contemplation. Their work is not to teach lessons, or enforce rules, or even to stimulate us to noble ends, but to withdraw the thoughts for a while from the mere machinery of life, to fix them, with appropriate emotions, on the spectacle of those great facts in man's existence which no machinery affects, "on the great and universal passions of men, the most general and interesting of their occupations, and the entire world of nature"—on "the operations of the elements and the appearances of the visible universe, on storm and sunshine, on the revolutions of the seasons, on cold and heat, on loss of friends and kindred, on injuries and resentments, on gratitude and hope, on fear and sorrow." To witness this spectacle with appropriate emotions is the aim of all culture; and of these emotions poetry like Wordsworth's is a great nourisher and

* Purple passages (Latin).

> stimulant. He sees nature full of sentiment and excitement; he sees men and women as parts of nature, passionate, excited, in strange grouping and connection with the grandeur and beauty of the natural world:—images, in his own words, "of man suffering, amid awful forms and powers."

Certainly the real secret of Wordsworth has never been better expressed. After having read and re-read Mr. Pater's essay—for it requires re-reading—one returns to the poet's work with a new sense of joy and wonder, and with something of eager and impassioned expectation. And perhaps this might be roughly taken as the test or touchstone of the finest criticism.

Finally, one cannot help noticing the delicate instinct that has gone to fashion the brief epilogue that ends this delightful volume. The difference between the classical and romantic spirits in art has often, and with much over-emphasis, been discussed. But with what a light sure touch does Mr. Pater write of it. How subtle and certain are his distinctions! If imaginative prose be really special art of this century, Mr. Pater must rank amongst our century's most characteristic artists. In certain things he stands almost alone. The age has produced wonderful prose styles, turbid with individualism, and violent with excess of rhetoric. But in Mr. Pater, as in Cardinal Newman,* we find the union of personality with perfection. He has no rival in his own sphere, and he has escaped disciples. And this, not because he has not been imitated, but because in art so fine as his there is something that, in its essence, is inimitable.

---

* John Henry Cardinal Newman (1801–1890), an eminent convert to Catholicism, wrote *Essay in Aid of a Grammar of Assent* and *The Idea of a University*.

ESSAYS

THE DECAY OF LYING

An Observation

A Dialogue.
Persons: Cyril and Vivian.
Scene: the library of a country house in Nottinghamshire.

CYRIL (*coming in through the open window from the terrace*). My dear Vivian, don't coop yourself up all day in the library. It is a perfectly lovely afternoon. The air is exquisite. There is a mist upon the woods, like the purple bloom upon a plum. Let us go and lie on the grass, and smoke cigarettes, and enjoy Nature.

VIVIAN. Enjoy Nature! I am glad to say that I have entirely lost that faculty. People tell us that Art makes us love Nature more than we loved her before; that it reveals her secrets to us; and that after a careful study of Corot and Constable we see things in her that had escaped our observation. My own experience is that the more we study Art, the less we care for Nature. What Art really reveals to us is Nature's lack of design, her curious crudities, her extraordinary monotony, her absolutely unfinished condition. Nature has good intentions, of course, but, as Aristotle once said, she cannot carry them out. When I look at a landscape I cannot help seeing all its defects. It is fortunate for us, however, that Nature is so imperfect, as otherwise we should have had no art at all. Art is our spirited protest, our gallant attempt to teach Nature her proper place. As for the infinite variety of Nature, that is a pure myth. It is not to be found in Nature herself. It resides in the imagination, or fancy, or cultivated blindness of the man who looks at her.

CYRIL. Well, you need not look at the landscape. You can lie on the grass and smoke and talk.

VIVIAN. But Nature is so uncomfortable. Grass is hard and lumpy and damp, and full of dreadful black insects. Why, even Morris'*

* William Morris (1834–1896) was one of the founders of the English arts and crafts movement.

poorest workman could make you a more comfortable seat than the whole of Nature can. Nature pales before the furniture of "the street which from Oxford has borrowed its name," as the poet you love so much once vilely phrased it. I don't complain. If Nature had been comfortable, mankind would never have invented architecture, and I prefer houses to the open air. In a house we all feel of the proper proportions. Everything is subordinated to us, fashioned for our use and our pleasure. Egotism itself, which is so necessary to a proper sense of human dignity, is entirely the result of indoor life. Out of doors one becomes abstract and impersonal. One's individuality absolutely leaves one. And then Nature is so indifferent, so unappreciative. Whenever I am walking in the park here, I always feel that I am no more to her than the cattle that browse on the slope, or the burdock that blooms in the ditch. Nothing is more evident than that Nature hates Mind. Thinking is the most unhealthy thing in the world, and people die of it just as they die of any other disease. Fortunately, in England at any rate, thought is not catching. Our splendid physique as a people is entirely due to our national stupidity. I only hope we shall be able to keep this great historic bulwark of our happiness for many years to come; but I am afraid that we are beginning to be over-educated; at least everybody who is incapable of learning has taken to teaching—that is really what our enthusiasm for education has come to. In the meantime, you had better go back to your wearisome uncomfortable Nature, and leave me to correct my proofs.

CYRIL. Writing an article! That is not very consistent after what you have just said.

VIVIAN. Who wants to be consistent? The dullard and the doctrinaire, the tedious people who carry out their principles to the bitter end of action, to the *reductio ad absurdum** of practice. Not I. Like Emerson, I write over the door of my library the word "Whim." Besides, my article is really a most salutary and valuable warning. If it is attended to, there may be a new Renaissance of Art.

CYRIL. What is the subject?

* Carrying something to an absurd extreme (Latin).

VIVIAN. I intend to call it "The Decay of Lying: A Protest."

CYRIL. Lying! I should have thought that our politicians kept up that habit.

VIVIAN. I assure you that they do not. They never rise beyond the level of misrepresentation, and actually condescend to prove, to discuss, to argue. How different from the temper of the true liar, with his frank, fearless statements, his superb irresponsibility, his healthy, natural disdain of proof of any kind! After all, what is a fine lie? Simply that which is its own evidence. If a man is sufficiently unimaginative to produce evidence in support of a lie, he might just as well speak the truth at once. No, the politicians won't do. Something may, perhaps, be urged on behalf of the Bar. The mantle of the Sophist has fallen on its members. Their feigned ardours and unreal rhetoric are delightful. They can make the worse appear the better cause, as though they were fresh from Leontine schools, and have been known to wrest from reluctant juries triumphant verdicts of acquittal for their clients, even when those clients, as often happens, were clearly and unmistakeably innocent. But they are briefed by the prosaic, and are not ashamed to appeal to precedent. In spite of their endeavors, the truth will out. Newspapers, even, have degenerated. They may now be absolutely relied upon. One feels it as one wades through their columns. It is always the unreadable that occurs. I am afraid that there is not much to be said in favour of either the lawyer or the journalist. Besides, what I am pleading for is Lying in art. Shall I read you what I have written? It might do you a great deal of good.

CYRIL. Certainly, if you give me a cigarette. Thanks. By the way, what magazine do you intend it for?

VIVIAN. For the *Retrospective Review*. I think I told you that the elect had revived it.

CYRIL. Whom do you mean by "the elect"?

VIVIAN. Oh, The Tired Hedonists of course. It is a club to which I belong. We are supposed to wear faded roses in our button-holes when we meet, and to have a sort of cult for Domitian. I am afraid you are not eligible. You are too fond of simple pleasures.

CYRIL. I should be black-balled on the ground of animal spirits, I suppose?

VIVIAN. Probably. Besides, you are a little too old. We don't admit anybody who is of the usual age.

CYRIL. Well, I should fancy you are all a good deal bored with each other.

VIVIAN. We are. That is one of the objects of the club. Now, if you promise not to interrupt too often, I will read you my article.

CYRIL. You will find me all attention.

VIVIAN (*reading in a very clear, musical voice*). "THE DECAY OF LYING: A PROTEST.—One of the chief causes that can be assigned for the curiously commonplace character of most of the literature of our age is undoubtedly the decay of Lying as an art, a science, and a social pleasure. The ancient historians gave us delightful fiction in the form of fact; the modern novelist presents us with dull facts under the guise of fiction. The Blue-Book* is rapidly becoming his ideal both for method and manner. He has his tedious *'document humain,'* his miserable little *'coin de la création,'* into which he peers with his microscope. He is to be found at the Librairie Nationale, or at the British Museum, shamelessly reading up his subject. He has not even the courage of other people's ideas, but insists on going directly to life for everything, and ultimately, between encyclopædias and personal experience, he comes to the ground, having drawn his types from the family circle or from the weekly washerwoman, and having acquired an amount of useful information from which never, even in his most meditative moments, can he thoroughly free himself.

"The loss that results to literature in general from this false ideal of our time can hardly be overestimated. People have a careless way of talking about a 'born liar,' just as they talk about a 'born poet.' But in both cases they are wrong. Lying and poetry are arts—arts, as Plato saw, not unconnected with each other—and they require the most careful study, the most disinterested devotion. Indeed, they have their technique, just as the more material arts of painting aud sculpture

---

* Official government report in which facts created an illusion of a *document humain* ("human document" [French]) centered on a narrow *coin de la création* ("corner of creation").

have, their subtle secrets of form and colour, their craft-mysteries, their deliberate artistic methods. As one knows the poet by his fine music, so one can recognize the liar by his rich rhythmic utterance, and in neither case will the casual inspiration of the moment suffice. Here, as elsewhere, practice must precede perfection. But in modern days while the fashion of writing poetry has become far too common, and should, if possible, be discouraged, the fashion of lying has almost fallen into disrepute. Many a young man starts in life with a natural gift for exaggeration which, if nurtured in congenial and sympathetic surroundings, or by the imitation of the best models, might grow into something really great and wonderful. But, as a rule, he comes to nothing. He either falls into careless habits of accuracy——"

CYRIL. My dear fellow!

VIVIAN. Please don't interrupt in the middle of a sentence. "He either falls into careless habits of accuracy, or takes to frequenting the society of the aged and the well-informed. Both things are equally fatal to his imagination, as indeed they would be fatal to the imagination of anybody, and in a short time he develops a morbid and unhealthy faculty of truth-telling, begins to verify all statements made in his presence, has no hesitation in contradicting people who are much younger than himself, and often ends by writing novels which are so like life that no one can possibly believe in their probability. This is no isolated instance that we are giving. It is simply one example out of many; and if something cannot be done to check, or at least to modify, our monstrous worship of facts, Art will become sterile, and Beauty will pass away from the land.

"Even Mr. Robert Louis Stevenson,* that delightful master of delicate and fanciful prose, is tainted with this modern vice, for we know positively no other name for it. There is such a thing as robbing a story of its reality by trying to make it too true, and *The Black Arrow* is so inartistic as not to contain a single anachronism to boast of, while the transformation of Dr. Jekyll reads dangerously like an experiment out

---

* In this paragraph, Wilde lists notable English and French novelists who had succumbed to a viciously prosaic fashion of realism. Vivian calls it "vulgarising" (p. 370).

of the *Lancet*. As for Mr. Rider Haggard, who really has, or had once, the makings of a perfectly magnificent liar, he is now so afraid of being suspected of genius that when he does tell us anything marvellous, he feels bound to invent a personal reminiscence, and to put it into a footnote as a kind of cowardly corroboration. Nor are our other novelists much better. Mr. Henry James writes fiction as if it were a painful duty, and wastes upon mean motives and imperceptible 'points of view' his neat literary style, his felicitous phrases, his swift and caustic satire. Mr. Hall Caine, it is true, aims at the grandiose, but then he writes at the top of his voice. He is so loud that one cannot hear what he says. Mr. James Payn is an adept in the art of concealing what is not worth finding. He hunts down the obvious with the enthusiasm of a short-sighted detective. As one turns over the pages, the suspense of the author becomes almost unbearable. The horses of Mr. William Black's phaeton do not soar towards the sun. They merely frighten the sky at evening into violent chromolithographic effects. On seeing them approach, the peasants take refuge in dialect. Mrs. Oliphant prattles pleasantly about curates, lawn-tennis parties, domesticity, and other wearisome things. Mr. Marion Crawford has immolated himself upon the altar of local colour. He is like the lady in the French comedy who keeps talking about 'le beau ciel d'Italie.' Besides, he has fallen into a bad habit of uttering moral platitudes. He is always telling us that to be good is to be good, and that to be bad is to be wicked. At times he is almost edifying. *Robert Elsmere* is of course a masterpiece—a masterpiece of the 'genre ennuyeux,' the one form of literature that the English people seem to thoroughly enjoy. A thoughtful young friend of ours once told us that it reminded him of the sort of conversation that goes on at a meat tea in the house of a serious Nonconformist family, and we can quite believe it. Indeed it is only in England that such a book could be produced. England is the home of lost ideas. As for that great and daily increasing school of novelists for whom the sun always rises in the East-End, the only thing that can be said about them is that they find life crude, and leave it raw.

"In France, though nothing so deliberately tedious as *Robert Elsmere* has been produced, things are not much better. M. Guy de Maupassant, with his keen mordant irony and his hard vivid style, strips life of the few poor rags that still cover her, and shows us foul sore and festering wound. He writes lurid little tragedies in which everybody is ridiculous; bitter comedies at which one cannot laugh for very tears. M. Zola, true to the lofty principle that he lays down in one of his pronunciamentos on literature, 'L'homme de génie n'a jamais d'esprit,' is determined to show that, if he has not got genius, he can at least be dull. And how well he succeeds! He is not without power. Indeed at times, as in *Germinal*, there is something almost epic in his work. But his work is entirely wrong from beginning to end, and wrong not on the ground of morals, but on the ground of art. From any ethical standpoint it is just what it should be. The author is perfectly truthful, and describes things exactly as they happen. What more can any moralist desire? We have no sympathy at all with the moral indignation of our time against M. Zola. It is simply the indignation of Tartuffe on being exposed. But from the standpoint of art, what can be said in favour of the author of *L'Assommoir, Nana*, and *Pot-Bouille?* Nothing. Mr. Ruskin once described the characters in George Eliot's novels as being like the sweepings of a Pentonville omnibus, but M. Zola's characters are much worse. They have their dreary vices, and their drearier virtues. The record of their lives is absolutely without interest. Who cares what happens to them? In literature we require distinction, charm, beauty, and imaginative power. We don't want to be harrowed and disgusted with an account of the doings of the lower orders. M. Daudet is better. He has wit, a light touch, and an amusing style. But he has lately committed literary suicide. Nobody can possibly care for Delobelle with his 'Il faut lutter pour l'art,' or for Valmajour with his eternal refrain about the nightingale, or for the poet in *Jack* with his 'mots cruels,' now that we have learned from *Vingt Ans de ma Vie littéraire* that these characters were taken directly from life. To us they seem to have suddenly lost all their vitality, all the few qualities they ever possessed. The only real people are the people who never existed, and if a novelist is base enough to go to life for his personages he should at least pretend that they are creations, and not boast of them as copies. The justification of a character in a novel is not that other persons are what they are, but that the author is what he is. Otherwise the novel is not a work of art. As for M. Paul Bourget, the master of the *roman psychologique*,* he commits the error of imagining that the men and women of modern life are capable of being infinitely analysed for an innumerable series of chapters. In point of fact what is interesting about people in good society—and M. Bourget rarely moves out of the Faubourg St. Germain, except to come to London,—is the mask that each one of them wears, not the reality that lies behind the mask. It is a humiliating confession, but we are all of us made out of the same stuff. In Falstaff there is something of Hamlet, in Hamlet there is not a little of Falstaff. The fat knight has his moods of melancholy, and the young prince his moments of coarse humour. Where we differ from each other is purely in accidentals: in dress, manner, tone of voice, religious opinions, personal appearance, tricks of habit, and the like. The more one analyses people, the more all reasons for analysis disappear. Sooner or later one comes to that dreadful universal thing called human nature. Indeed, as any one who has ever worked among the poor knows only too well, the brotherhood of man is no mere poet's dream, it is a most depressing and humiliating reality; and if a writer insists upon analysing the upper classes, he might just as well write of match-girls and costermongers at once." However, my dear Cyril, I will not detain you any further just here. I quite admit that modern novels have many good points. All I insist on is that, as a class, they are quite unreadable.

CYRIL. That is certainly a very grave qualification, but I must say that I think you are rather unfair in some of your strictures. I like *The Deemster*, and *The Daughter of Heth*, and *Le Disciple*, and *Mr. Isaacs*, and as for *Robert Elsmere* I am quite devoted to it. Not that I can look upon it as a serious work. As a statement of the problems that confront the earnest Christian it is ridiculous and antiquated. It is simply Arnold's *Literature and Dogma* with the literature left out. It is as much behind the age as Paley's *Evidences*, or Colenso's method of Biblical exegesis. Nor could anything be less impressive than the unfortunate hero gravely heralding a dawn that rose long ago, and so completely missing its true

* Psychological novel (French).

significance that he proposes to carry on the business of the old firm under the new name. On the other hand, it contains several clever caricatures, and a heap of delightful quotations, and Green's philosophy very pleasantly sugars the somewhat bitter pill of the author's fiction. I also cannot help expressing my surprise that you have said nothing about the two novelists whom you are always reading, Balzac and George Meredith. Surely they are realists, both of them?

VIVIAN. Ah! Meredith! Who can define him? His style is chaos illumined by flashes of lightning. As a writer he has mastered everything except language: as a novelist he can do everything, except tell a story: as an artist he is everything, except articulate. Somebody in Shakespeare—Touchstone, I think—talks about a man who is always breaking his shins over his own wit, and it seems to me that this might serve as the basis for a criticism of Meredith's method. But whatever he is, he is not a realist. Or rather I would say that he is a child of realism who is not on speaking terms with his father. By deliberate choice he has made himself a romanticist. He has refused to bow the knee to Baal, and after all, even if the man's fine spirit did not revolt against the noisy assertions of realism, his style would be quite sufficient of itself to keep life at a respectful distance. By its means he has planted round his garden a hedge full of thorns, and red with wonderful roses. As for Balzac, he was a most remarkable combination of the artistic temperament with the scientific spirit. The latter he bequeathed to his disciples: the former was entirely his own. The difference between such a book as M. Zola's *L'Assommoir* and Balzac's *Illusions Perdues* is the difference between unimaginative realism and imaginative reality. "All Balzac's characters," said Baudelaire, "are gifted with the same ardour of life that animated himself. All his fictions are as deeply coloured as dreams. Each mind is a weapon loaded to the muzzle with will. The very scullions have genius." A steady course of Balzac reduces our living friends to shadows, and our acquaintances to the shadows of shades. His characters have a kind of fervent fiery-coloured existence. They dominate us, and defy scepticism. One of the greatest tragedies of my life is the death of Lucien de Rubempré. It is a grief from which I have never been able to completely rid myself. It haunts me in my moments of pleasure. I remember it when I laugh. But Balzac is no more a realist than Holbein was. He created life, he did not copy it. I admit, however, that he set far too high a value on modernity of form, and that, consequently, there is no book of his that, as an artistic masterpiece, can rank with *Salammbô* or *Esmond*, or *The Cloister and the Hearth*, or the *Vicomte de Bragelonne*.

CYRIL. Do you object to modernity of form, then?

VIVIAN. Yes. It is a huge price to pay for a very poor result. Pure modernity of form is always somewhat vulgarising. It cannot help being so. The public imagine that, because they are interested in their immediate surroundings, Art should be interested in them also, and should take them as her subject-matter. But the mere fact that they are interested in these things makes them unsuitable subjects for Art. The only beautiful things, as somebody once said, are the things that do not concern us. As long as a thing is useful or necessary to us, or affects us in any way, either for pain or for pleasure, or appeals strongly to our sympathies, or is a vital part of the environment in which we live, it is outside the proper sphere of art. To art's subject-matter we should be more or less indifferent. We should, at any rate, have no preferences, no prejudices, no partisan feeling of any kind. It is exactly because Hecuba is nothing to us that her sorrows are such an admirable motive for a tragedy. I do not know anything in the whole history of literature sadder than the artistic career of Charles Reade. He wrote one beautiful book, *The Cloister and the Hearth*, a book as much above *Romola* as *Romola* is above *Daniel Deronda*,* and wasted the rest of his life in a foolish attempt to be modern, to draw public attention to the state of our convict prisons, and the management of our private lunatic asylums. Charles Dickens was depressing enough in all conscience when he tried to arouse our sympathy for the victims of the poor-law administration; but Charles Reade, an artist, a scholar, a man with a true sense of beauty, raging and roaring over the abuses of contemporary life like a common pamphleteer or a sensational journalist, is really a sight for the angels to weep over. Believe me, my dear

* Historically detailed novels of George Eliot, published in 1863 and 1877, respectively; they are less powerful than her *Middlemarch* (1872).

Cyril, modernity of form and modernity of subject-matter are entirely and absolutely wrong. We have mistaken the common livery of the age for the vesture of the Muses, and spend our days in the sordid streets and hideous suburbs of our vile cities when we should be out on the hillside with Apollo. Certainly we are a degraded race, and have sold our birthright for a mess of facts.

CYRIL. There is something in what you say, and there is no doubt that whatever amusement we may find in reading a purely modern novel, we have rarely any artistic pleasure in re-reading it. And this is perhaps the best rough test of what is literature and what is not. If one cannot enjoy reading a book over and over again, there is no use reading it at all. But what do you say about the return to Life and Nature? This is the panacea that is always being recommended to us.

VIVIAN. I will read you what I say on that subject. The passage comes later on in the article, but I may as well give it to you now:—

"The popular cry of our time is 'Let us return to Life and Nature; they will recreate Art for us, and send the red blood coursing through her veins; they will shoe her feet with swiftness and make her hand strong.' But, alas! we are mistaken in our amiable and well-meaning efforts. Nature is always behind the age. And as for Life, she is the solvent that breaks up Art, the enemy that lays waste her house."

CYRIL. What do you mean by saying that Nature is always behind the age?

VIVIAN. Well, perhaps that is rather cryptic. What I mean is this. If we take Nature to mean natural simple instinct as opposed to self-conscious culture, the work produced under this influence is always old-fashioned, antiquated, and out of date. One touch of Nature may make the whole world kin, but two touches of Nature will destroy any work of Art. If, on the other hand, we regard Nature as the collection of phenomena external to man, people only discover in her what they bring to her. She has no suggestions of her own. Wordsworth went to the lakes, but he was never a lake poet. He found in stones the sermons he had already hidden there. He went moralizing about the district, but his good work was produced when he returned, not to Nature but to poetry. Poetry gave him "Laodamia," and the fine sonnets, and the great Ode, such as it is. Nature gave him "Martha Ray" and "Peter Bell," and the address to Mr. Wilkinson's spade.

CYRIL. I think that view might be questioned. I am rather inclined to believe in the "impulse from a vernal wood," though of course the artistic value of such an impulse depends entirely on the kind of temperament that receives it, so that the return to Nature would come to mean simply the advance to a great personality. You would agree with that, I fancy. However, proceed with your article.

VIVIAN (*reading*). "Art begins with abstract decoration with purely imaginative and pleasurable work dealing with what is unreal and non-existent. This is the first stage. Then Life becomes fascinated with this new wonder, and asks to be admitted into the charmed circle. Art takes life as part of her rough material, recreates it, and refashions it in fresh forms, is absolutely indifferent to fact, invents, imagines, dreams, and keeps between herself and reality the impenetrable barrier of beautiful style, of decorative or ideal treatment. The third stage is when Life gets the upper hand, and drives Art out into the wilderness. This is the true decadence, and it is from this that we are now suffering.

"Take the case of the English drama. At first in the hands of the monks Dramatic Art was abstract, decorative, and mythological. Then she enlisted Life in her service, and using some of life's external forms, she created an entirely new race of beings, whose sorrows were more terrible than any sorrow man has ever felt, whose joys were keener than lover's joys, who had the rage of the Titans and the calm of the gods, who had monstrous and marvellous sins, monstrous and marvellous virtues. To them she gave a language different from that of actual use, a language full of resonant music and sweet rhythm, made stately by solemn cadence, or made delicate by fanciful rhyme, jewelled with wonderful words, and enriched with lofty diction. She clothed her children in strange raiment and gave them masks, and at her bidding the antique world rose from its marble tomb. A new Cæsar stalked through the streets of risen Rome, and with purple sail and flute-led oars another Cleopatra passed up the river to Antioch. Old myth and legend and dream took shape and substance. History was entirely re-written, and there was hardly one of the dramatists who did not recognize that the object of Art is not simple truth but complex beauty. In this they were perfectly right. Art itself is really a form of exaggeration; and selection, which is the very spirit of art, is nothing more than an intensified mode of over-emphasis.

"But Life soon shattered the perfection of the form. Even in Shakespeare we can see the beginning of the end. It shows itself by the gradual breaking up of the blank-verse in the later plays, by the predominance given to prose, and by the over-importance assigned to characterisation. The passages in Shakespeare—and they are many—where the language is uncouth, vulgar, exaggerated, fantastic, obscene even, are entirely due to Life calling for an echo of her own voice, and rejecting the intervention of beautiful style, through which alone should Life be suffered to find expression. Shakespeare is not by any means a flawless artist. He is too fond of going directly to life, and borrowing life's natural utterance. He forgets that when Art surrenders her imaginative medium she surrenders everything. Goethe says, somewhere—

> In der Beschränkung zeigt sich erst der Meister,

'It is in working within limits that the master reveals himself,' and the limitation, the very condition of any art is style. However, we need not linger any longer over Shakespeare's realism. *The Tempest* is the most perfect of palinodes. All that we desired to point out was, that the magnificent work of the Elizabethan and Jacobean artists contained within itself the seeds of its own dissolution, and that, if it drew some of its strength from using life as rough material, it drew all its weakness from using life as an artistic method. As the inevitable result of this substitution of an imitative for a creative medium, this surrender of an imaginative form, we have the modern English melodrama. The characters in these plays talk on the stage exactly as they would talk off it; they have neither aspirations nor aspirates; they are taken directly from life and reproduce its vulgarity down to the smallest detail; they present the gait, manner, costume, and accent of real people; they would pass unnoticed in a third-class railway carriage. And yet how wearisome the plays are! They do not succeed in producing even that impression of reality at which they aim, and which is their only reason for existing. As a method, realism is a complete failure.

"What is true about drama and the novel is no less true about those arts that we call decorative arts. The whole history of these arts in Europe is the record of the struggle between Orientalism, with its frank rejection of imitation, its love of artistic convention, its dislike to the actual representation of any object in Nature, and our own imitative spirit. Wherever the former has been paramount, as in Byzantium, Sicily, and Spain, by actual contact, or in the rest of Europe by the influence of the Crusades, we have had beautiful and imaginative work in which the visible things of life are transmuted into artistic conventions, and the things that Life has not are invented and fashioned for her delight. But wherever we have returned to Life and Nature, our work has always become vulgar, common, and uninteresting. Modern tapestry, with its aërial effects, its elaborate perspective, its broad expanses of waste sky, its faithful and laborious realism, has no beauty whatsoever. The pictorial glass of Germany is absolutely detestable. We are beginning to weave possible carpets in England, but only because we have returned to the method and spirit of the East. Our rugs and carpets of twenty years ago, with their solemn depressing truths, their inane worship of Nature, their sordid reproductions of visible objects, have become, even to the Philistine, a source of laughter. A cultured Mahomedan once remarked to us, 'You Christians are so occupied in misinterpreting the fourth commandment that you have never thought of making an artistic application of the second.' He was perfectly right, and the whole truth of the matter is this: The proper school to learn art in is not Life but Art."

And now let me read you a passage which seems to me to settle the question very completely.

"It was not always thus. We need not say anything about the poets, for they, with the unfortunate exception of Mr. Wordsworth, have been really faithful to their high mission, and are universally recognized as being absolutely unreliable. But in the works of Herodotus,* who, in spite of the shallow and ungenerous attempts

* Wilde mentions the writings of Herodotus (c.484–414 B.C.E.), the "father of history," first in a long series of famed historical works, from Suetonius to Carlyle.

of modern sciolists to verify his history, may justly be called the 'Father of Lies'; in the published speeches of Cicero and the biographies of Suetonius; in Tacitus at his best; in Pliny's *Natural History*; in Hanno's *Periplus*; in all the early chronicles; in the Lives of the Saints; in Froissart and Sir Thomas Mallory; in the travels of Marco Polo; in Olaus Magnus, and Aldrovandus, and Conrad Lycosthenes, with his magnificent *Prodigiorum et Ostentorum Chronicon*; in the autobiography of Benvenuto Cellini; in the memoirs of Casanuova; in Defoe's *History of the Plague*; in Boswell's *Life of Johnson*; in Napoleon's despatches, and in the works of our own Carlyle, whose *French Revolution* is one of the most fascinating historical novels ever written, facts are either kept in their proper subordinate position, or else entirely excluded on the general ground of dulness. Now, everything is changed. Facts are not merely finding a footing-place in history, but they are usurping the domain of Fancy, and have invaded the kingdom of Romance. Their chilling touch is over everything. They are vulgarising mankind. The crude commercialism of America, its materialising spirit, its indifference to the poetical side of things, and its lack of imagination and of high unattainable ideals, are entirely due to that country having adopted for its national hero a man, who according to his own confession, was incapable of telling a lie, and it is not too much to say that the story of George Washington and the cherry-tree has done more harm, and in a shorter space of time, than any other moral tale in the whole of literature."

CYRIL. My dear boy!

VIVIAN. I assure you it is the case, and the amusing part of the whole thing is that the story of the cherry-tree is an absolute myth. However, you must not think that I am too despondent about the artistic future either of America or of our own country. Listen to this:—

"That some change will take place before this century has drawn to its close we have no doubt whatsoever. Bored by the tedious and improving conversation of those who have neither the wit to exaggerate nor the genius to romance, tired of the intelligent person whose reminiscences are always based upon memory, whose statements are invariably limited by probability, who is at any time liable to be corroborated by the merest Philistine who happens to be present, Society sooner or later must return to its lost leader, the cultured and fascinating liar. Who he was who first, without ever having gone out to the rude chase, told the wondering cavemen at sunset how he had dragged the Megatherium from the purple darkness of its jasper cave, or slain the Mammoth in single combat and brought back its gilded tusks, we cannot tell, and not one of our modern anthropologists, for all their much-boasted science, has had the ordinary courage to tell us. Whatever was his name or race, he certainly was the true founder of social intercourse. For the aim of the liar is simply to charm, to delight, to give pleasure. He is the very basis of civilized society, and without him a dinner party, even at the mansions of the great, is as dull as a lecture at the Royal Society, or a debate at the Incorporated Authors, or one of Mr. Burnand's farcical comedies.

"Nor will he be welcomed by society alone. Art, breaking from the prison-house of realism, will run to greet him, and will kiss his false, beautiful lips, knowing that he alone is in possession of the great secret of all her manifestations, the secret that Truth is entirely and absolutely a matter of style; while Life—poor, probable, uninteresting human life—tired of repeating herself for the benefit of Mr. Herbert Spencer,* scientific historians, and the compilers of statistics in general, will follow meekly after him, and try to produce, in her own simple and untutored way, some of the marvels of which he talks.

"No doubt there will always be critics who, like a certain writer in the *Saturday Review*, will gravely censure the teller of fairy tales for his defective knowledge of natural history, who will measure imaginative work by their own lack of any imaginative faculty, and will hold up their inkstained hands in horror if some honest gentleman, who has never been farther than the yew-trees of his own garden, pens a fascinating book of travels like Sir John Mandeville, or, like great Raleigh, writes a whole history of the world, without knowing anything whatsoever about the past. To excuse themselves they will

---

* Herbert Spencer (1820–1903), philosophic proponent of Social Darwinism and coiner of the phrase "survival of the fittest."

try and shelter under the shield of him who made Prospero the magician, and gave him Caliban and Ariel as his servants, who heard the Tritons blowing their horns round the coral reefs of the Enchanted Isle, and the fairies singing to each other in a wood near Athens, who led the phantom kings in dim procession across the misty Scottish heath, and hid Hecate in a cave with the weird sisters. They will call upon Shakespeare—they always do—and will quote that hackneyed passage about Art holding the mirror up to Nature, forgetting that this unfortunate aphorism is deliberately said by Hamlet in order to convince the bystanders of his absolute insanity in all art-matters."

CYRIL. Ahem! Another cigarette, please.

VIVIAN. My dear fellow, whatever you may say, it is merely a dramatic utterance, and no more represents Shakespeare's real views upon art than the speeches of Iago represent his real views upon morals. But let me get to the end of the passage:

"Art finds her own perfection within, and not outside of, herself. She is not to be judged by any external standard of resemblance. She is a veil, rather than a mirror. She has flowers that no forests know of, birds that no woodland possesses. She makes and unmakes many worlds, and can draw the moon from heaven with a scarlet thread. Hers are the 'forms more real than living man,' and hers the great archetypes of which things that have existence are but unfinished copies. Nature has, in her eyes, no laws, no uniformity. She can work miracles at her will, and when she calls monsters from the deep they come. She can bid the almond tree blossom in winter, and send the snow upon the ripe cornfield. At her word the frost lays its silver finger on the burning mouth of June, and the winged lions creep out from the hollows of the Lydian hills. The dryads peer from the thicket as she passes by, and the brown fauns smile strangely at her when she comes near them. She has hawk-faced gods that worship her, and the centaurs gallop at her side."

CYRIL. I like that. I can see it. Is that the end?

VIVIAN. No. There is one more passage, but it is purely practical. It simply suggests some methods by which we could revive this lost art of Lying.

CYRIL. Well, before you read it to me, I should like to ask you a question. What do you mean by saying that life, "poor, probable, uninteresting human life," will try to reproduce the marvels of art? I can quite understand your objection to art being treated as a mirror. You think it would reduce genius to the position of a cracked looking-glass. But you don't mean to say that you seriously believe that Life imitates Art, that Life in fact is the mirror, and Art the reality?

VIVIAN. Certainly I do. Paradox though it may seem—and paradoxes are always dangerous things—it is none the less true that Life imitates art far more than Art imitates life. We have all seen in our own day in England how a certain curious and fascinating type of beauty, invented and emphasised by two imaginative painters, has so influenced Life that whenever one goes to a private view or to an artistic salon one sees, here the mystic eyes of Rossetti's dream, the long ivory throat, the strange square-cut jaw, the loosened shadowy hair that he so ardently loved, there the sweet maidenhood of "The Golden Stair," the blossom-like mouth and weary loveliness of the "Laus Amoris," the passion-pale face of Andromeda, the thin hands and lithe beauty of the Vivien in "Merlin's Dream." And it has always been so. A great artist invents a type, and Life tries to copy it, to reproduce it in a popular form, like an enterprising publisher. Neither Holbein nor Vandyck found in England what they have given us. They brought their types with them, and Life with her keen imitative faculty set herself to supply the master with models. The Greeks, with their quick artistic instinct, understood this, and set in the bride's chamber the statue of Hermes or of Apollo, that she might bear children as lovely as the works of art that she looked at in her rapture or her pain. They knew that Life gains from Art not merely spirituality, depth of thought and feeling, soul-turmoil or soul-peace, but that she can form herself on the very lines and colours of art, and can reproduce the dignity of Pheidias as well as the grace of Praxiteles. Hence came their objection to realism. They disliked it on purely social grounds. They felt that it inevitably makes people ugly, and they were perfectly right. We try to improve the conditions of the race by means of good air, free sunlight, wholesome water, and hideous bare buildings for the better housing of the lower orders. But these things merely produce health, they do not produce beauty. For this, Art is required, and the true disciples of the great artist are not his studio-imitators, but those who become like his works of art, be they plastic as in the Greek days, or pictorial as in modern times; in a word, Life is Art's best, Art's only pupil.

As it is with the visible arts, so it is with literature. The most obvious and the vulgarest form in which this is shown is in the case of the silly boys who, after reading the adventures of Jack Sheppard or Dick Turpin,* pillage the stalls of unfortunate apple-women, break into sweet-shops at night, and alarm old gentlemen who are returning home from the city by leaping out on them in suburban lanes, with black masks and unloaded revolvers. This interesting phenomenon, which always occurs after the appearance of a new edition of either of the books I have alluded to, is usually attributed to the influence of literature on the imagination. But this is a mistake. The imagination is essentially creative and always seeks for a new form. The boy-burglar is simply the inevitable result of life's imitative instinct. He is Fact, occupied as Fact usually is, with trying to reproduce Fiction, and what we see in him is repeated on an extended scale throughout the whole of life. Schopenhauer has analysed the pessimism that characterises modern thought, but Hamlet invented it. The world has become sad because a puppet was once melancholy. The Nihilist,† that strange martyr who has no faith, who goes to the stake without enthusiasm, and dies for what he does not believe in, is a purely literary product. He was invented by Tourgénieff, and completed by Dostoieffski. Robespierre‡ came out of the pages of Rousseau as surely as the People's Palace rose out of the *débris* of a novel. Literature always anticipates life. It does not copy it, but moulds it to its purpose. The nineteenth century, as we know it, is largely an invention of Balzac. Our Luciens de Rubempré, our Rastignacs, and

---

* Famous highwaymen.

† Wilde's play *Vera* (1882) deals with political nihilism, which is also an important theme in Russian novels, including those of Ivan Turgenev (1818–1883) and Fyodor Dostoevsky (1821–1881).

‡ French Revolutionary leader Maximilien de Robespierre (1758–1794) was a disciple of French philosopher and novelist Jean-Jacques Rousseau (1712–1778).

De Marsays made their first appearance on the stage of the *Comédie Humaine*. We are merely carrying out, with footnotes and unnecessary additions, the whim or fancy or creative vision of a great novelist. I once asked a lady, who knew Thackeray intimately, whether he had had any model for Becky Sharp.* She told me that Becky was an invention, but that the idea of the character had been partly suggested by a governess who lived in the neighbourhood of Kensington Square, and was the companion of a very selfish and rich old woman. I inquired what became of the governess, and she replied that, oddly enough, some years after the appearance of *Vanity Fair*, she ran away with the nephew of the lady with whom she was living, and for a short time made a great splash in society, quite in Mrs. Rawdon Crawley's style, and entirely by Mrs. Rawdon Crawley's methods. Ultimately she came to grief, disappeared to the Continent, and used to be occasionally seen at Monte Carlo and other gambling places. The noble gentleman from whom the same great sentimentalist drew Colonel Newcome died, a few months after *The Newcomes* had reached a fourth edition, with the word "Adsum" on his lips. Shortly after Mr. Stevenson published his curious psychological story of transformation, a friend of mine, called Mr. Hyde, was in the north of London, and being anxious to get to a railway station, took what he thought would be a short cut, lost his way, and found himself in a network of mean, evil-looking streets. Feeling rather nervous he began to walk extremely fast, when suddenly out of an archway ran a child right between his legs. It fell on the pavement, he tripped over it, and trampled upon it. Being of course very much frightened and a little hurt, it began to scream, and in a few seconds the whole street was full of rough people who came pouring out of the houses like ants. They surrounded him, and asked him his name. He was just about to give it when he suddenly remembered the opening incident in Mr. Stevenson's story. He was so filled with horror at having realized in his

---

* Ironically "sharp" anti-heroine of *Vanity Fair: A Novel without a Hero*, by William Makepeace Thackeray (1811–1863); Mrs. Rawdon Crawley appears in the same novel.

own person that terrible and well written scene, and at having done accidently, though in fact, what the Mr. Hyde of fiction had done with deliberate intent, that he ran away as hard as he could go. He was, however, very closely followed, and finally he took refuge in a surgery, the door of which happened to be open, where he explained to a young assistant, who happened to be there, exactly what had occurred. The humanitarian crowd were induced to go away on his giving them a small sum of money, and as soon as the coast was clear he left. As he passed out, the name on the brass door-plate of the surgery caught his eye. It was "Jekyll." At least it should have been.

Here the imitation, as far as it went, was of course accidental. In the following case the imitation was self-conscious. In the year 1879, just after I had left Oxford, I met at a reception at the house of one of the Foreign Ministers a woman of very curious exotic beauty. We became great friends, and were constantly together. And yet what interested most in her was not her beauty, but her character, her entire vagueness of character. She seemed to have no personality at all, but simply the possibility of many types. Sometimes she would give herself up entirely to art, turn her drawing-room into a studio, and spend two or three days a week at picture-galleries or museums. Then she would take to attending race-meetings, wear the most horsey clothes, and talk about nothing but betting. She abandoned religion for mesmerism, mesmerism for politics, and politics for the melodramatic excitements of philanthropy. In fact, she was a kind of Proteus, and as much a failure in all her transformations as was that wondrous sea-god when Odysseus laid hold of him. One day a serial began in one of the French magazines. At that time I used to read serial stories, and I well remember the shock of surprise I felt when I came to the description of the heroine. She was so like my friend that I brought her the magazine, and she recognized herself in it immediately, and seemed fascinated by the resemblance. I should tell you, by the way, that the story was translated from some dead Russian writer, so that the author had not taken his type from my friend. Well, to put the matter briefly, some months afterwards I was in Venice, and finding the magazine in the reading-room of the hotel, I took it up casually to see what had become of the heroine. It was a most piteous tale, as the girl had ended by running away with a man absolutely inferior to her, not merely in social station, but in character and intellect also. I wrote to my friend that evening about my views on John Bellini,* and the admirable ices at Florio's, and the artistic value of gondolas, but added a postscript to the effect that her double in the story had behaved in a very silly manner. I don't know why I added that, but I remember I had a sort of dread over me that she might do the same thing. Before my letter had reached her, she had run away with a man who deserted her in six months. I saw her in 1884 in Paris, where she was living with her mother, and I asked her whether the story had had anything to do with her action. She told me that she had felt an absolutely irresistible impulse to follow the heroine step by step in her strange and fatal progress, and that it was with a feeling of real terror that she had looked forward to the last few chapters of the story. When they appeared, it seemed to her that she was compelled to reproduce them in life, and she did so. It was a most clear example of this imitative instinct of which I was speaking, and an extremely tragic one.

However, I do not wish to dwell any further upon individual instances. Personal experience is a most vicious and limited circle. All that I desire to point out is the general principle that Life imitates Art far more than Art imitates Life, and I feel sure that if you think seriously about it you will find that it is true. Life holds the mirror up to Art, and either reproduces some strange type imagined by painter or sculptor, or realizes in fact what has been dreamed in fiction. Scientifically speaking, the basis of life—the energy of life, as Aristotle would call it—is simply the desire for expression, and Art is always presenting various forms through which this expression can be attained. Life seizes on them and uses them, even if they be to her own hurt. Young men have committed suicide because Rolla did so, have died by their own hand because by his own hand Werther died.†

---

* Italian Renaissance painter Giovanni Bellini (c.1430–1516), master of richly decorative coloristic effects, came from a Venetian family of painters.

† In Johann Wolfgang von Goethe's novel *The Sorrows of Young Werther* (1774), Werther commits suicide, influenced by romantic fables—again, life imitates art.

Think of what we owe to the imitation of Christ, of what we owe to the imitation of Cæsar.

CYRIL. The theory is certainly a very curious one, but to make it complete you must show that Nature, no less than Life, is an imitation of Art. Are you prepared to prove that?

VIVIAN. My dear fellow, I am prepared to prove anything.

CYRIL. Nature follows the landscape painter then, and takes her effects from him?

VIVIAN. Certainly. Where, if not from the Impressionists, do we get those wonderful brown fogs that come creeping down our streets, blurring the gas-lamps and changing the houses into monstrous shadows? To whom, if not to them and their master, do we owe the lovely silver mists that brood over our river, and turn to faint forms of fading grace curved bridge and swaying barge? The extraordinary change that has taken place in the climate of London during the last ten years is entirely due to this particular school of Art. You smile. Consider the matter from a scientific or a metaphysical point of view, and you will find that I am right. For what is Nature? Nature is no great mother who has borne us. She is our creation. It is in our brain that she quickens to life. Things are because we see them, and what we see, and how we see it, depends on the Arts that have influenced us. To look at a thing is very different from seeing a thing. One does not see anything until one sees its beauty. Then, and then only, does it come into existence. At present, people see fogs, not because there are fogs, but because poets and painters have taught them the mysterious loveliness of such effects. There may have been fogs for centuries in London. I dare say there were. But no one saw them, and so we do not know anything about them. They did not exist till Art had invented them. Now, it must be admitted, fogs are carried to excess. They have become the mere mannerism of a clique, and the exaggerated realism of their method gives dull people bronchitis. Where the cultured catch an effect, the uncultured catch cold. And so, let us be humane, and invite Art to turn her wonderful eyes elsewhere. She has done so already, indeed. That white quivering sunlight that one sees now in France, with its strange blotches of mauve, and its restless violet shadows, is her latest fancy, and, on the whole, Nature reproduces it quite admirably.

Where she used to give us Corots and Daubignys, she gives us now exquisite Monets and entrancing Pisaros. Indeed there are moments, rare, it is true, but still to be observed from time to time, when Nature becomes absolutely modern. Of course she is not always to be relied upon. The fact is that she is in this unfortunate position. Art creates an incomparable and unique effect, and, having done so, passes on to other things. Nature, upon the other hand, forgetting that imitation can be made the sincerest form of insult, keeps on repeating this effect until we all become absolutely wearied of it. Nobody of any real culture, for instance, ever talks now-a-days about the beauty of a sunset. Sunsets are quite old-fashioned. They belong to the time when Turner was the last note in art. To admire them is a distinct sign of provincialism of temperament. Upon the other hand they go on. Yesterday evening Mrs. Arundel insisted on my going to the window, and looking at the glorious sky, as she called it. Of course I had to look at it. She is one of those absurdly pretty Philistines, to whom one can deny nothing. And what was it? It was simply a very second-rate Turner, a Turner of a bad period,* with all the painter's worst faults exaggerated and overemphasized. Of course, I am quite ready to admit that Life very often commits the same error. She produces her false Renés and her sham Vautrins, just as Nature gives us, on one day a doubtful Cuyp, and on another a more than questionable Rousseau. Still, Nature irritates one more when she does things of that kind. It seems so stupid, so obvious, so unnecessary. A false Vautrin might be delightful. A doubtful Cuyp is unbearable. However, I don't want to be too hard on Nature. I wish the Channel, especially at Hastings, did not look quite so often like a Henry Moore, grey pearl with yellow lights, but then, when Art is more varied, Nature will, no doubt, be more varied also. That she imitates Art, I don't think even her worst enemy would deny now. It

* In the passage that follows, Wilde links painting (J.M.W. Turner, Aelbert Cuyp, and, later, Katsushika Hokusai) with literature (François-René de Chateaubriand's character René and Balzac's Vautrin), a mixture that often colors his theories.

is the one thing that keeps her in touch with civilized man. But have I proved my theory to your satisfaction?

CYRIL. You have proved it to my dissatisfaction, which is better. But even admitting this strange imitative instinct in Life and Nature, surely you would acknowledge that Art expresses the temper of its age, the spirit of its time, the moral and social conditions that surround it, and under whose influence it is produced.

VIVIAN. Certainly not! Art never expresses anything but itself. This is the principle of my new æsthetics; and it is this, more than that vital connection between form and substance, on which Mr. Pater dwells, that makes music the type of all the arts. Of course, nations and individuals, with that healthy natural vanity which is the secret of existence, are always under the impression that it is of them that the Muses are talking, always trying to find in the calm dignity of imaginative art some mirror of their own turbid passions, always forgetting that the singer of life is not Apollo, but Marsyas. Remote from reality, and with her eyes turned away from the shadows of the cave, Art reveals her own perfection, and the wondering crowd that watches the opening of the marvellous, many-petalled rose fancies that it is its own history that is being told to it, its own spirit that is finding expression in a new form. But it is not so. The highest art rejects the burden of the human spirit, and gains more from a new medium or a fresh material than she does from any enthusiasm for art, or from any lofty passion, or from any great awakening of the human consciousness. She develops purely on her own lines. She is not symbolic of any age. It is the ages that are her symbols.

Even those who hold that Art is representative of time and place and people, cannot help admitting that the more imitative an art is, the less it represents to us the spirit of its age. The evil faces of the Roman emperors look out at us from the foul porphyry and spotted jasper in which the realistic artists of the day delighted to work, and we fancy that in those cruel lips and heavy sensual jaws we can find the secret of the ruin of the Empire. But it was not so. The vices of Tiberius could not destroy that supreme civilization, any more than the virtues of the Antonines could save it. It fell for other, for less interesting reasons. The sibyls and prophets of the Sistine may indeed serve to interpret for some that new birth of the emancipated spirit that we call the Renaissance; but what do the drunken boors and brawling peasants of Dutch art tell us about the great soul of Holland? The more abstract, the more ideal an art is, the more it reveals to us the temper of its age. If we wish to understand a nation by means of its art, let us look at its architecture or its music.

CYRIL. I quite agree with you there. The spirit of an age may be best expressed in the abstract ideal arts, for the spirit itself is abstract and ideal. Upon the other hand, for the visible aspect of an age, for its look, as the phrase goes, we must of course go to the arts of imitation.

VIVIAN. I don't think so. After all, what the imitative arts really give us are merely the various styles of particular artists, or of certain schools of artists. Surely you don't imagine that the people of the Middle Ages bore any resemblance at all to the figures on mediæval stained glass, or in mediæval stone and wood carving, or on mediæval metal-work, or tapestries, or illuminated MSS. They were probably very ordinary-looking people, with nothing grotesque, or remarkable, or fantastic in their appearance. The Middle Ages, as we know them in art, are simply a definite form of style, and there is no reason at all why an artist with this style should not be produced in the nineteenth century. No great artist ever sees things as they really are. If he did, he would cease to be an artist. Take an example from our own day. I know that you are fond of Japanese things. Now, do you really imagine that the Jappanese people, as they are presented to us in art, have any existence? If you do, you have never understood Japanese art at all. The Japanese people are the deliberate self-conscious creation of certain individual artists. If you set a picture by Hokusai, or Hokkei, or any of the great native painters, beside a real Japanese gentleman or lady, you will see that there is not the slightest resemblance between them. The actual people who live in Japan are not unlike the general run of English people; that is to say, they are extremely commonplace, and have nothing curious or extraordinary about them. In fact the whole of Japan is a pure invention. There is no such country, there are no such people. One of our most charming painters went recently to the Land of the Chrysanthemum in the foolish hope of seeing the Japanese. All he saw, all he had the chance of painting, were a few lanterns and some fans. He was quite unable to discover the inhabitants, as his delightful exhibition at Messrs. Dowdeswell's Gallery showed only too well. He did not know that the Japanese people are, as I have said, simply a mode of style, an exquisite fancy of art. And so, if you desire to see a Japanese effect, you will not behave like a tourist and go to Tokio. On the contrary, you will stay at home, and steep yourself in the work of certain Japanese artists, and then, when you have absorbed the spirit of their style, and caught their imaginative manner of vision, you will go some afternoon and sit in the Park or stroll down Piccadilly, and if you cannot see an absolutely Japanese effect there, you will not see it anywhere. Or, to return again to the past, take as another instance the ancient Greeks. Do you think that Greek art ever tells us what the Greek people were like? Do you believe that the Athenian women were like the stately dignified figures of the Parthenon frieze,* or like those marvellous goddesses who sat in the triangular pediments of the same building? If you judge from the art, they certainly were so. But read an authority, like Aristophanes† for instance. You will find that the Athenian ladies laced tightly, wore high-heeled shoes, dyed their hair yellow, painted and rouged their faces, and were exactly like any silly fashionable or fallen creature of our own day. The fact is that we look back on the ages entirely through the medium of Art, and Art, very fortunately, has never once told us the truth.

CYRIL. But modern portraits by English painters, what of them? Surely they are like the people they pretend to represent?

VIVIAN. Quite so. They are so like them that a hundred years from now no one will believe in them. The only portraits in which one believes are portraits where there is very little of the sitter, and a very great deal of the artist. Holbein's drawings of the men and women of his time impress us with a sense of their absolute reality. But this is

---

* A famous bas-relief sculpture from ancient Greece, the frieze was partially removed to England by Lord Elgin and exhibited in the British Museum as part of the Elgin Marbles.

† Fifth-century comic dramatist (c.450–388 B.C.E.), author of *Lysistrata* and other plays in which women of Athens played the central roles.

simply because Holbein compelled life to accept his conditions, to restrain itself within his limitations, to reproduce his type, and to appear as he wished it to appear. It is style that makes us believe in a thing—nothing but style. Most of our modern portrait painters are doomed to absolute oblivion. They never paint what they see. They paint what the public sees, and the public never sees anything.

CYRIL. Well, after that I think I should like to hear the end of your article.

VIVIAN. With pleasure. Whether it will do any good I really cannot say. Ours is certainly the dullest and most prosaic century possible. Why, even Sleep has played us false, and has closed up the gates of ivory, and opened the gates of horn. The dreams of the great middle classes of this country, as recorded in Mr. Myers's two bulky volumes on the subject and in the Transactions of the Psychical Society,* are the most depressing things that I have ever read. There is not even a fine nightmare among them. They are commonplace, sordid, and tedious. As for the Church I cannot conceive anything better for the culture of a country than the presence in it of a body of men whose duty it is to believe in the supernatural, to perform daily miracles, and to keep alive that mythopœic faculty which is so essential for the imagination. But in the English Church a man succeeds, not through his capacity for belief, but through his capacity for disbelief. Ours is the only Church where the sceptic stands at the altar, and where St. Thomas is regarded as the ideal apostle. Many a worthy clergyman, who passes his life in admirable works of kindly charity, lives and dies unnoticed and unknown; but it is sufficient for some shallow uneducated pass-man out of either University to get up in his pulpit and express his doubts about Noah's ark, or Balaam's ass, or Jonah and the whale, for half of London to flock to hear him, and to sit openmouthed in rapt admiration at his superb intellect. The growth of common sense in the English Church is a thing very much to be regretted. It is really

* Frederic William Henry Myers (1843–1901) was the leading Victorian researcher into paranormal experiences, contributing books and many articles to "psychical" speculation.

a degrading concession to a low form of realism. It is silly, too. It springs from an entire ignorance of psychology. Man can believe the impossible, but man can never believe the improbable. However, I must read the end of my article:—

"What we have to do, what at any rate it is our duty to do, is to revive this old art of Lying. Much of course may be done, in the way of educating the public, by amateurs in the domestic circle, at literary lunches, and at afternoon teas. But this is merely the light and graceful side of lying, such as was probably heard at Cretan dinner parties.* There are many other forms. Lying for the sake of gaining some immediate personal advantage, for instance—lying with a moral purpose, as it is usually called—though of late it has been rather looked down upon, was extremely popular with the antique world. Athena laughs when Odysseus tells her 'his words of sly devising,' as Mr. William Morris phrases it, and the glory of mendacity illumines the pale brow of the stainless hero of Euripidean tragedy, and sets among the noble women of the past the young bride of one of Horace's most exquisite odes. Later on, what at first had been merely a natural instinct was elevated into a self-conscious science. Elaborate rules were laid down for the guidance of mankind, and an important school of literature grew up round the subject. Indeed, when one remembers the excellent philosophical treaties of Sanchez† on the whole question, one cannot help regretting that no one has ever thought of publishing a cheap and condensed edition of the works of that great casuist. A short primer, 'When to Lie and How,' if brought out in an attractive and not too expensive a form, would no doubt command a large scale, and would prove of real practical service to many earnest and deep-thinking people. Lying for the sake of the improvement of the young, which is the basis of home education, still lingers amongst us, and its advantages are so admirably set forth in the early books of Plato's

---

* Wilde alludes to the "Cretan liar paradox." Epimenides, a Cretan, says: "All Cretans are liars." If true, the statement is false; if false, it is true—a very deep paradox, which logicians simply call "The Liar."

† Wilde is referring to the *Treatise on the Noble and Lofty Science of Ignorance* (1581), by Francisco Sánchez (1550–1623).

Republic that it is unnecessary to dwell upon them here. It is a mode of lying for which all good mothers have peculiar capabilities, but it is capable of still further development, and has been sadly overlooked by the School Board. Lying for the sake of a monthly salary is of course well known in Fleet Street, and the profession of a political leader-writer is not without its advantages. But it is said to be a somewhat dull occupation, and it certainly does not lead to much beyond a kind of ostentatious obscurity. The only form of lying that is absolutely beyond reproach is Lying for its own sake, and the highest development of this is, as we have already pointed out, Lying in Art. Just as those who do not love Plato more than Truth cannot pass beyond the threshold of the Academe, so those who do not love Beauty more than Truth never know the inmost shrine of Art. The solid stolid British intellect lies in the desert sands like the Sphinx in Flaubert's marvellous tale,* and fantasy, *La Chimère*, dances round it, and calls to it with her false, flute-toned voice. It may not hear her now, but surely some day, when we are all bored to death with the commonplace character of modern fiction, it will hearken to her and try to borrow her wings.

"And when that day dawns, or sunset reddens, how joyous we shall all be! Facts will be regarded as discreditable, Truth will be found mourning over her fetters, and Romance, with her temper of wonder, will return to the land. The very aspect of the world will change to our startled eyes. Out of the sea will rise Behemoth and Leviathan, and sail round the high-pooped galleys, as they do on the delightful maps of those ages when books on geography were actually readable. Dragons will wander about the waste places, and the phœnix will soar from her nest of fire into the air. We shall lay our hands upon the basilisk, and see the jewel in the toad's head. Champing his gilded oats, the Hippogriff will stand in our stalls, and over our heads will float the Blue Bird singing of beautiful and impossible things, of things that are lovely

---

* Gustave Flaubert's *The Temptation of St. Anthony* (1874), a fantastic, chimerical, and grotesque fable, was of immense importance to Wilde's literary development as a fabulist.

and that never happen, of things that are not and that should be. But before this comes to pass we must cultivate the lost art of Lying."

CYRIL. Then we must certainly cultivate it at once. But in order to avoid making any error I want you to tell me briefly the doctrines of the new æsthetics.

VIVIAN. Briefly, then, they are these. Art never expresses anything but itself. It has an independent life, just as Thought has, and develops purely on its own lines. It is not necessarily realistic in an age of realism, nor spiritual in an age of faith. So far from being the creation of its time, it is usually in direct opposition to it, and the only history that it preserves for us is the history of its own progress. Sometimes it returns upon its footsteps, and revives some antique form, as happened in the archaistic movement of late Greek Art, and in the pre-Raphaelite movement of our own day. At other times it entirely anticipates its age, and produces in one century work that it takes another century to understand, to appreciate, and to enjoy. In no case does it reproduce its age. To pass from the art of a time to the time itself is the great mistake that all historians commit.

The second doctrine is this. All bad art comes from returning to Life and Nature, and elevating them into ideals. Life and Nature may sometimes be used as part of Art's rough material, but before they are of any real service to art they must be translated into artistic conventions. The moment Art surrenders its imaginative medium it surrenders everything. As a method Realism is a complete failure, and the two things that every artist should avoid are modernity of form and modernity of subject-matter. To us, who live in the nineteenth century, any century is a suitable subject for art except our own. The only beautiful things are the things that do not concern us. It is, to have the pleasure of quoting myself, exactly because Hecuba is nothing to us that her sorrows are so suitable a motive for a tragedy. Besides, it is only the modern that ever becomes old-fashioned. M. Zola sits down to give us a picture of the Second Empire. Who cares for the Second Empire now? It is out of date. Life goes faster than Realism, but Romanticism is always in front of Life.

The third doctrine is that Life imitates Art far more than Art imitates Life. This results not merely from Life's imitative instinct, but from the fact that the self-conscious aim of Life is to find expression, and that Art offers it certain beautiful forms through which it may realize that energy. It is a theory that has never been put forward before, but it is extremely fruitful, and throws an entirely new light upon the history of Art.

It follows, as a corollary from this, that external Nature also imitates Art. The only effects that she can show us are effects that we have already seen through poetry, or in paintings. This is the secret of Nature's charm, as well as the explanation of Nature's weakness.

The final revelation is that Lying, the telling of beautiful untrue things, is the proper aim of Art. But of this I think I have spoken at sufficient length. And now let us go out on the terrace, where "droops the milk-white peacock like a ghost," while the evening star "washes the dusk with silver." At twilight nature becomes a wonderfully suggestive effect, and is not without loveliness, though perhaps its chief use is to illustrate quotations from the poets. Come! We have talked long enough.

THE CRITIC AS ARTIST

With some remarks upon the importance of doing nothing

A Dialogue. Part I.
Persons: Gilbert and Ernest.
Scene: the library of a house in Piccadilly, overlooking the Green Park.

GILBERT (*at the Piano*). My dear Ernest, what are you laughing at?

ERNEST (*looking up*). At a capital story that I have just come across in this volume of Reminiscences that I have found on your table.

GILBERT. What is the book? Ah! I see. I have not read it yet. Is it good?

ERNEST. Well, while you have been playing, I have been turning over the pages with some amusement, though, as a rule, I dislike modern memoirs. They are generally written by people who have either entirely lost their memories, or have never done anything worth remembering; which, however, is, no doubt, the true explanation of their popularity, as the English public always feels perfectly at its ease when a mediocrity is talking to it.

GILBERT. Yes: the public is wonderfully tolerant. It forgives everything except genius. But I must confess that I like all memoirs. I like them for their form, just as much as for their matter. In literature mere egotism is delightful. It is what fascinates us in the letters of personalities so different as Cicero and Balzac, Flaubert and Berlioz, Byron and Madame de Sévigné. Whenever we come across it, and, strangely enough, it is rather rare, we cannot but welcome it, and do not easily forget it. Humanity will always love Rousseau for having confessed his sins, not to a priest, but to the world, and the couchant nymphs that Cellini* wrought in bronze for the castle of King Francis, the green

* Benvenuto Cellini (1500–1571), renowned Italian sculptor and jeweler; his autobiography identified his artworks with murders he claimed to have committed.

and gold Perseus, even, that in the open Loggia at Florence shows the moon the dead terror that once turned life to stone, have not given it more pleasure than has that autobiography in which the supreme scoundrel of the Renaissance relates the story of his splendour and his shame. The opinions, the character, the achievements of the man, matter very little. He may be a sceptic like the gentle Sieur de Montaigne, or a saint like the bitter son of Monica,* but when he tells his own secrets he can always charm our ears to listening and our lips to silence. The mode of thought that Cardinal Newman represented—if that can be called a mode of thought which seeks to solve intellectual problems by a denial of the supremacy of the intellect—may not, cannot, I think, survive. But the world will never weary of watching that troubled soul in its progress from darkness to darkness. The lonely church at Littlemore, where "the breath of the morning is damp, and worshippers are few," will always be dear to it, and whenever men see the yellow snapdragon blossoming on the wall of Trinity they will think of that gracious undergraduate who saw in the flower's sure recurrence a prophecy that he would abide for ever with the Benign Mother of his days—a prophecy that Faith, in her wisdom or her folly, suffered not to be fulfilled. Yes; autobiography is irresistible. Poor, silly, conceited Mr. Secretary Pepys† has chattered his way into the circle of the Immortals, and, conscious that indiscretion is the better part of valour, bustles about among them in that "shaggy purple gown with gold buttons and looped lace" which he is so fond of describing to us, perfectly at his ease, and prattling, to his own and our infinite pleasure, of the Indian blue petticoat that he bought for his wife, of the "good hog's harslet," and the "pleasant French fricassee of veal" that he loved to eat, of his game of bowls with Will Joyce, and his "gadding after beauties," and his reciting of *Hamlet* on a Sunday, and his playing of the viol on week days, and other wicked or trivial things. Even in actual life egotism is not

* Saint Augustine (354–430 C.E.); Monica had a great influence on the development of her son's spirituality, as revealed in his *Confessions*.

† Samuel Pepys (1633–1703), author of the most famous English private diary; he was secretary of the Admiralty.

without its attractions. When people talk to us about others they are usually dull. When they talk to us about themselves they are nearly always interesting, and if one could shut them up, when they become wearisome, as easily as one can shut up a book of which one has grown wearied, they would be perfect absolutely.

ERNEST. There is much virtue in that If, as Touchstone would say. But do you seriously propose that every man should become his own Boswell? What would become of our industrious compilers of Lives and Recollections in that case?

GILBERT. What has become of them? They are the pest of the age, nothing more and nothing less. Every great man nowadays has his disciples, and it is always Judas who writes the biography.

ERNEST. My dear fellow!

GILBERT. I am afraid it is true. Formerly we used to canonize our heroes. The modern method is to vulgarise them. Cheap editions of great books may be delightful, but cheap editions of great men are absolutely detestable.

ERNEST. May I ask, Gilbert, to whom you allude?

GILBERT. Oh! to all our second-rate *litterateurs*. We are overrun by a set of people who, when poet or painter passes away, arrive at the house along with the undertaker, and forget that their one duty is to behave as mutes. But we won't talk about them. They are the mere body-snatchers of literature. The dust is given to one, and the ashes to another, and the soul is out of their reach. And now, let me play Chopin to you, or Dvorák? Shall I play you a fantasy by Dvorák? He writes passionate, curiously-coloured things.

ERNEST. No; I don't want music at present. It is far too indefinite. Besides, I took the Baroness Bernstein down to dinner last night, and, though absolutely charming in every other respect, she insisted on discussing music as if it were actually written in the German language. Now, whatever music sounds like, I am glad to say that it does not sound in the smallest degree like German. There are forms of patriotism that are really quite degrading. No; Gilbert, don't play any more. Turn round and talk to me. Talk to me till the white-horned day comes into the room. There is something in your voice that is wonderful.

GILBERT (*rising from the piano*). I am not in a mood for talking to-night. How horrid of you to smile? I really am not. Where are the cigarettes? Thanks. How exquisite these single daffodils are! They seem to be made of amber and cool ivory. They are like Greek things of the best period. What was the story in the confessions of the remorseful Academician that made you laugh? Tell it to me. After playing Chopin, I feel as if I had been weeping over sins that I had never committed, and mourning over tragedies that were not my own. Music always seems to me to produce that effect. It creates for one a past of which one has been ignorant, and fills one with a sense of sorrows that have been hidden from one's tears. I can fancy a man who had led a perfectly commonplace life, hearing by chance some curious piece of music, and suddenly discovering that his soul, without his being conscious of it, had passed through terrible experiences, and known fearful joys, or wild romantic loves, or great renunciations. And so, tell me this story, Ernest. I want to be amused.

ERNEST. Oh! I don't know that it is of any importance. But I thought it a really admirable illustration of the true value of ordinary art-criticism. It seems that a lady once gravely asked the remorseful Academician, as you call him, if his celebrated picture of "A Spring-Day at Whiteley's," or "Waiting for the Last Omnibus," or some subject of that kind, was all painted by hand?

GILBERT. And was it?

ERNEST. You are quite incorrigible. But, seriously speaking, what is the use of art-criticism? Why cannot the artist be left alone, to create a new world if he wishes it, or, if not, to shadow forth the world which we already know, and of which, I fancy, we would each one of us be wearied if Art, with her fine spirit of choice and delicate instinct of selection, did not, as it were, purify it for us, and give to it a momentary perfection. It seems to me that the imagination spreads, or should spread, a solitude around it, and works best in silence and in isolation. Why should the artist be troubled by the shrill clamour of criticism? Why should those who cannot create take upon themselves to estimate the value of creative work? What can they know about it? If a man's work is easy to understand, an explanation is unnecessary. . . .

Gilbert. And if his work is incomprehensible, an explanation is wicked.

Ernest. I did not say that.

Gilbert. Ah! but you should have. Nowadays, we have so few mysteries left to us that we cannot afford to part with one of them. The members of the Browning Society,* like the theologians of the Broad Church Party, or the authors of Mr. Walter Scott's Great Writers' Series, seem to me to spend their time in trying to explain their divinity away. Where one had hoped that Browning was a mystic, they have sought to show that he was simply inarticulate. Where one had fancied that he had something to conceal, they have proved that he had but little to reveal. But I speak merely of his incoherent work. Taken as a whole, the man was great. He did not belong to the Olympians, and had all the incompleteness of the Titan. He did not survey, and it was but rarely that he could sing. His work is marred by struggle, violence and effort, and he passed not from emotion to form, but from thought to chaos. Still, he was great. He has been called a thinker, and was certainly a man who was always thinking, and always thinking aloud; but it was not thought that fascinated him, but rather the processes by which thought moves. It was the machine he loved, not what the machine makes. The method by which the fool arrives at his folly was as dear to him as the ultimate wisdom of the wise. So much, indeed, did the subtle mechanism of mind fascinate him that he despised language, or looked upon it as an incomplete instrument of expression. Rhyme, that exquisite echo which in the Muse's hollow hill creates and answers its own voice; rhyme, which in the hands of the real artist becomes not merely a material element of metrical beauty, but a spiritual element of thought and passion also, waking a new mood, it may be, or stirring a fresh train of ideas, or opening by mere sweetness and suggestion of sound some golden door at which the Imagination itself had knocked in vain;

---

* Founded in 1881, the society, with numerous branches in Britain and the United States, was earnestly dedicated to "explicating" and hence, in Wilde's view, increasing the obscurity of the writing of Robert Browning (1812–1889).

rhyme, which can turn man's utterance to the speech of gods; rhyme, the one chord we have added to the Greek lyre, became in Robert Browning's hands a grotesque, misshapen thing, which at times made him masquerade in poetry as a low comedian, and ride Pegasus too often with his tongue in his cheek. There are moments when he wounds us by monstrous music. Nay, if he can only get his music by breaking the strings of his lute, he breaks them, and they snap in discord, and no Athenian tettix, making melody from tremulous wings, lights on the ivory horn to make the movement perfect, or the interval less harsh. Yet, he was great: and though he turned language into ignoble clay, he made from it men and women that live. He is the most Shakespearian creature since Shakespeare. If Shakespeare could sing with myriad lips, Browning could stammer through a thousand mouths. Even now, as I am speaking, and speaking not against him but for him, there glides through the room the pageant of his persons. There, creeps Fra Lippo Lippi with his cheeks still burning from some girl's hot kiss. There, stands dread Saul with the lordly male-sapphires gleaming in his turban. Mildred Tresham is there, and the Spanish monk, yellow with hatred, and Blougram, and Ben Ezra, and the Bishop of St. Praxed's. The spawn of Setebos gibbers in the corner, and Sebald, hearing Pippa pass by, looks on Ottima's haggard face, and loathes her and his own sin, and himself. Pale as the white satin of his doublet, the melancholy king watches with dreamy treacherous eyes too loyal Strafford pass forth to his doom, and Andrea shudders as he hears the cousins whistle in the garden, and bids his perfect wife go down. Yes, Browning was great. And as what will he be remembered? As a poet? Ah, not as a poet! He will be remembered as a writer of fiction, as the most supreme writer of fiction, it may be, that we have ever had. His sense of dramatic situation was unrivalled, and, if he could not answer his own problems, he could at least put problems forth, and what more should an artist do? Considered from the point of view of a creator of character he ranks next to him who made Hamlet. Had he been articulate, he might have sat beside him. The only man who can touch the hem of his garment is George Meredith. Meredith is a prose Browning, and so is Browning. He used poetry as a medium for writing in prose.

ERNEST. There is something in what you say, but there is not everything in what you say. In many points you are unjust.

GILBERT. It is difficult not to be unjust to what one loves. But let us return to the particular point at issue. What was it that you said?

ERNEST. Simply this: that in the best days of art there were no art-critics.

GILBERT. I seem to have heard that observation before, Ernest. It has all the vitality of error and all the tediousness of an old friend.

ERNEST. It is true. Yes: there is no use your tossing your head in that petulant manner. It is quite true. In the best days of art there were no art-critics. The sculptor hewed from the marble block the great white-limbed Hermes that slept within it. The waxers and gilders of images gave tone and texture to the statue, and the world, when it saw it, worshipped and was dumb. He poured the glowing bronze into the mould of sand, and the river of red metal cooled into noble curves and took the impress of the body of a god. With enamel or polished jewels he gave sight to the sightless eyes. The hyacinth-like curls grew crisp beneath his graver. And when, in some dim frescoed fane, or pillared sunlit portico, the child of Leto stood upon his pedestal, those who passed by, ἁβρῶς βαίνοντες διὰ λαμπρο τάτου αἰθέρος,* became conscious of a new influence that had come across their lives, and dreamily, or with a sense of strange and quickening joy, went to their homes or daily labour, or wandered, it may be, through the city gates to that nymph-haunted meadow where young Phædrus† bathed his feet, and, lying there on the soft grass, beneath the tall wind-whispering planes and flowering *agnus castus*, began to think of the wonder of beauty, and grew silent with unaccustomed awe. In those days the artist was free. From the river valley he took the fine clay in his fingers, and with a little tool of wood or bone, fashioned it into forms so exquisite that the people

* Apollo, the Greek god of poetry, whose music (like the Athenians named in this section) "passed gaily in that brightest air." The line, much favored by Wilde, is from Euripides' *Medea* (431 B.C.E.).

† Handsome youth in Plato's dialogue of that name. Enthused, Ernest sings an extended anthem to the beauty and erotic divinity of an idealized Greek world.

gave them to the dead as their playthings, and we find them still in the dusty tombs on the yellow hillside by Tanagra, with the faint gold and the fading crimson still lingering about hair and lips and raiment. On a wall of fresh plaster, stained with bright sandyx or mixed with milk and saffron, he pictured one who trod with tired feet the purple white-starred fields of asphodel, one 'in whose eyelids lay the whole of the Trojan War,' Polyxena, the daughter of Priam; or figured Odysseus, the wise and cunning, bound by tight cords to the mast-step, that he might listen without hurt to the singing of the Sirens, or wandering by the clear river of Acheron, where the ghosts of fishes flitted over the pebbly bed; or showed the Persian in trews and mitre flying before the Greek at Marathon, or the galleys clashing their beaks of brass in the little Salaminian bay. He drew with silver-point and charcoal upon parchment and prepared cedar. Upon ivory and rose-coloured terra-cotta he painted with wax, making the wax fluid with juice of olives, and with heated irons making it firm. Panel and marble and linen canvas became wonderful as his brush swept across them; and life seeing her own image, was still, and dared not speak. All life, indeed, was his, from the merchants seated in the market-place to the cloaked shepherd lying on the hill; from the nymph hidden in the laurels and the faun that pipes at noon, to the king whom, in long green-curtained litter, slaves bore upon oil-bright shoulders, and fanned with peacock fans. Men and women, with pleasure or sorrow in their faces, passed before him. He watched them, and their secret became his. Through form and colour he re-created a world.

All subtle arts belonged to him also. He held the gem against the revolving disk, and the amethyst became the purple couch for Adonis, and across the veined sardonyx sped Artemis with her hounds. He beat out the gold into roses, and strung them together for necklace or armlet. He beat out the gold into wreaths for the conqueror's helmet, or into palmates for the Tyrian robe, or into masks for the royal dead. On the back of the silver mirror he graved Thetis borne by her Nereids, or love-sick Phædra with her nurse, or Persephone, weary of memory, putting poppies in her hair. The potter sat in his shed, and, flower-like from the silent wheel, the vase rose up beneath his hands. He decorated the base and stem and ears with pattern of dainty olive-leaf, or foliated acanthus, or curved and crested wave. Then in black or red he painted lads wrestling, or in the race: knights in full armour, with strange heraldic shields and curious visors, leaning from shell-shaped chariot over rearing steeds: the gods seated at the feast or working their miracles: the heroes in their victory or in their pain. Sometimes he would etch in thin vermilion lines upon a ground of white the languid bridegroom and his bride, with Eros hovering round them—an Eros like one of Donatello's angels, a little laughing thing with gilded or with azure wings. On the curved side he would write the name of his friend. ΚΑΛΟΣ ΑΛΚΙΒΙΑΔΗΣ or ΚΑΛΟΣ ΧΑΡΜΙΔΗΣ tells us the story of his days. Again, on the rim of the wide flat cup he would draw the stag browsing, or the lion at rest, as his fancy willed it. From the tiny perfume-bottle laughed Aphrodite at her toilet, and, with barelimbed Mænads in his train, Dionysus danced round the wine-jar on naked must-stained feet, while, satyr-like, the old Silenus sprawled upon the bloated skins, or shook that magic spear which was tipped with a fretted fir-cone, and wreathed with dark ivy. And no one came to trouble the artist at his work. No irresponsible chatter disturbed him. He was not worried by opinions. By the Ilyssus, says Arnold somewhere, there was no Higginbotham. By the Ilyssus, my dear Gilbert, there were no silly art-congresses, bringing provincialism to the provinces and teaching the mediocrity how to mouth. By the Ilyssus there were no tedious magazines about art, in which the industrious prattle of what they do not understand. On the reed-grown banks of that little stream strutted no ridiculous journalism monopolizing the seat of judgment when it should be apologizing in the dock. The Greeks had no art-critics.

GILBERT. Ernest, you are quite delightful, but your views are terribly unsound. I am afraid that you have been listening to the conversation of someone older than yourself. That is always a dangerous thing to do, and if you allow it to degenerate into a habit, you will find it absolutely fatal to any intellectual development. As for modern journalism, it is not my business to defend it. It justifies its own existence by the great Darwinian principle of the survival of the vulgarest. I have merely to do with literature.

ERNEST. But what is the difference between literature and journalism?

GILBERT. Oh! journalism is unreadable, and literature is not read. That is all. But with regard to your statement that the Greeks had no art-critics, I assure you that is quite absurd. It would be more just to say that the Greeks were a nation of art-critics.

ERNEST. Really?

GILBERT. Yes, a nation of art-critics. But I don't wish to destroy the delightfully unreal picture that you have drawn of the relation of the Hellenic artist to the intellectual spirit of his age. To give an accurate description of what has never occurred is not merely the proper occupation of the historian, but the inalienable privilege of any man of parts and culture. Still less do I desire to talk learnedly. Learned conversation is either the affectation of the ignorant or the profession of the mentally unemployed. And, as for what is called improving conversation, that is merely the foolish method by which the still more foolish philanthropist feebly tries to disarm the just rancour of the criminal classes. No: let me play to you some mad scarlet thing by Dvorák. The pallid figures on the tapestry are smiling at us, and the heavy eyelids of my bronze Narcissus are folded in sleep. Don't let us discuss anything solemnly. I am but too conscious of the fact that we are born in an age when only the dull are treated seriously, and I live in terror of not being misunderstood. Don't degrade me into the position of giving you useful information. Education is an admirable thing, but it is well to remember from time to time that nothing that is worth knowing can be taught. Through the parted curtains of the window I see the moon like a clipped piece of silver. Like gilded bees the stars cluster round her. The sky is a hard hollow sapphire. Let us go out into the night. Thought is wonderful, but adventure is more wonderful still. Who knows but we may meet Prince Florizel of Bohemia, and hear the fair Cuban tell us that she is not what she seems?

ERNEST. You are horribly wilful. I insist on your discussing this matter with me. You have said that the Greeks were a nation of art-critics. What art-criticism have they left us?

GILBERT. My dear Ernest, even if not a single fragment of art-criticism had come down to us from Hellenic or Hellenistic days, it would be none the less true that the Greeks were a nation of art-critics, and that they invented the criticism of art just as they invented the criticism of everything else. For, after all, what is our primary debt to the Greeks? Simply the critical spirit. And, this spirit, which they exercised on questions of religion and science, of ethics and metaphysics, of politics and education, they exercised on questions of art also, and, indeed, of the two supreme and highest arts, they have left us the most flawless system of criticism that the world has ever seen.

ERNEST. But what are the two supreme and highest arts?

GILBERT. Life and Literature, life and the perfect expression of life. The principles of the former, as laid down by the Greeks, we may not realize in an age so marred by false ideals of our own. The principles of the latter, as they laid them down, are, in many cases, so subtle that we can hardly understand them. Recognizing that the most perfect art is that which most fully mirrors man in all his infinite variety, they elaborated the criticism of language, considered in the light of the mere material of that art, to a point to which we, with our accentual system of reasonable or emotional emphasis, can barely if at all attain; studying, for instance, the metrical movements of a prose as scientifically as a modern musician studies harmony and counterpoint, and, I need hardly say, with much keener æsthetic instinct. In this they were right, as they were right in all things. Since the introduction of printing, and the fatal development of the habit of reading amongst the middle and lower classes of this country, there has been a tendency in literature to appeal more and more to the eye, and less and less to the ear which is really the sense which, from the standpoint of pure art, it should seek to please, and by whose canons of pleasure it should abide always. Even the work of Mr. Pater, who is, on the whole, the most perfect master of English prose now creating amongst us, is often far more like a piece of mosaic than a passage in music, and seems, here and there, to lack the true rhythmical life of words and the fine freedom and richness of effect that such rhythmical life produces. We, in fact, have made writing a definite mode of composition, and have treated it as a form of elaborate design. The Greeks, upon the other hand, regarded writing simply as a method of chronicling. Their test was always the spoken word in its musical and metrical relations. The voice was the medium, and the ear the critic. I have sometimes thought that the story of Homer's blindness might be really an artistic myth, created in critical days, and serving to remind us, not merely that the great poet is always a seer, seeing less with the eyes of the body than he does with the eyes of the soul, but that he is a true singer also, building his song out of music, repeating each line over and over again to himself till he has caught the secret of its melody, chaunting in darkness the words that are winged with light. Certainly, whether this be so or not, it was to his blindness, as an occasion if not as a cause, that England's great poet owed much of the majestic movement and sonorous splendour of his later verse. When Milton could no longer write, he began to sing. Who would match the measures of *Comus** with the measures of *Samson Agonistes*, or of *Paradise Lost* or *Regained?* When Milton became blind he composed, as everyone should compose, with the voice purely, and so the pipe or reed of earlier days became that mighty many-stopped organ whose rich reverberant music has all the stateliness of Homeric verse, if it seeks not to have its swiftness, and is the one imperishable inheritance of English literature, sweeping through all the ages, because above them, and abiding with us ever, being immortal in its form. Yes: writing has done much harm to writers. We must return to the voice. That must be our test, and perhaps then we shall be able to appreciate some of the subleties of Greek art-criticism.

As it now is, we cannot do so. Sometimes, when I have written a piece of prose that I have been modest enough to consider absolutely free from fault, a dreadful thought comes over me that I may have been guilty of the immoral effeminacy of using trochaic and tribrachic movements, a crime for which a learned critic of the Augustan age censures with most just severity the brilliant if somewhat paradoxical Hegesias. I grow cold when I think of it, and wonder to myself if the admirable ethical effect of the prose of that charming writer, who

* This early court masque by John Milton, first performed in 1634, lacks the grand style of his later works.

once in a spirit of reckless generosity towards the uncultivated portion of our community proclaimed the monstrous doctrine that conduct is three-fourths of life, will not some day be entirely annihilated by the discovery that the pæons have been wrongly placed.

ERNEST. Ah! now you are flippant.

GILBERT. Who would not be flippant when he is gravely told that the Greeks had no art-critics? I can understand it being said that the constructive genius of the Greeks lost itself in criticism, but not that the race to whom we owe the critical spirit did not criticise. You will not ask me to give you a survey of Greek art criticism from Plato to Plotinus. The night is too lovely for that, and the moon, if she heard us, would put more ashes on her face than are there already. But think merely of one perfect little work of æsthetic criticism, Aristotle's *Treatise on Poetry*. It is not perfect in form, for it is badly written, consisting perhaps of notes jotted down for an art lecture, or of isolated fragments destined for some larger book, but in temper and treatment it is perfect absolutely. The ethical effect of art, its importance to culture, and its place in the formation of character, had been done once for all by Plato; but here we have art treated, not from the moral, but from the purely æsthetic point of view. Plato had, of course, dealt with many definitely artistic subjects, such as the importance of unity in a work of art, the necessity for tone and harmony, the æsthetic value of appearances, the relation of the visible arts to the external world, and the relation of fiction to fact. He first perhaps stirred in the soul of man that desire which we have not yet satisfied, the desire to know the connection between Beauty and Truth, and the place of Beauty in the moral and intellectual order of the Kosmos. The problems of idealism and realism, as he sets them forth, may seem to many to be somewhat barren of results in the metaphysical sphere of abstract being in which he places them, but transfer them to the sphere of art, and you will find that they are still vital and full of meaning. It may be that it is as a critic of Beauty that Plato is destined to live, and by altering the name of the sphere of his speculation we shall find a new philosophy. But Aristotle, like Goethe, deals with art primarily in its concrete manifestations, taking Tragedy, for instance, and investigating the material it uses, which is language, its subject-matter, which is life, the method by which it works, which is action, the conditions under which it reveals itself, which are those of theatric presentation, its logical structure, which is plot, and its final æsthetic appeal, which is to the sense of beauty realized through the passions of pity and awe. That purification and spiritualizing of the nature which he calls *κάθαρσις** is, as Goethe saw, essentially æsthetic, and is not moral, as Lessing fancied. Concerning himself primarily with the impression that the work of art produces, Aristotle sets himself to analyse that impression, to investigate its source, to see how it is engendered. As a physiologist and psychologist, he knows that the health of a function resides in energy. To have a capacity for a passion and not to realize it, is to make oneself incomplete and limited. The mimic spectacle of life that Tragedy affords cleanses the bosom of much 'perilous stuff,' and by presenting high and worthy objects for the exercise of the emotions purifies and spiritualizes the man; nay, not merely does it spiritualize him, but it initiates him also into noble feelings of which he might else have known nothing, the word *κάθαρσις* having, it has sometimes seemed to me, a definite allusion to the rite of initiation, if indeed that be not, as I am occasionally tempted to fancy, its true and only meaning here. This is of course a mere outline of the book. But you see what a perfect piece of æsthetic criticism it is. Who indeed but a Greek could have analysed art so well? After reading it, one does not wonder any longer that Alexandria devoted itself so largely to art-criticism, and that we find the artistic temperaments of the day investigating every question of style and manner, discussing the great Academic schools of painting, for instance, such as the school of Sicyon, that sought to preserve the dignified traditions of the antique mode, or the realistic and impressionist schools, that aimed at reproducing actual life, or the elements of ideality in portraiture, or the artistic value of the epic form in an age so modern as theirs, or the proper subject-matter for the artist. Indeed, I fear that the inartistic temperaments of the day busied themselves also in matters of literature and art, for the accusations of

---

* Catharsis, the purgation of fear and pity, described by Aristotle's *Poetics* as the chief effect and purpose of tragedy.

plagiarism were endless, and such accusations proceed either from the thin colourless lips of impotence, or from the grotesque mouths of those who, possessing nothing of their own, fancy that they can gain a reputation for wealth by crying out that they have been robbed. And I assure you, my dear Ernest, that the Greeks chattered about painters quite as much as people do nowadays, and had their private views, and shilling exhibitions, and Arts and Crafts guilds, and Pre-Raphaelite movements, and movements towards realism, and lectured about art, and wrote essays on art, and produced their art-historians, and their archæologists, and all the rest of it. Why, even the theatrical managers of travelling companies brought their dramatic critics with them when they went on tour, and paid them very handsome salaries for writing laudatory notices. Whatever, in fact, is modern in our life we owe to the Greeks. Whatever is an anachronism is due to mediævalism. It is the Greeks who have given us the whole system of art-criticism, and how fine their critical instinct was, may be seen from the fact that the material they criticised with most care was, as I have already said, language. For the material that painter or sculptor uses is meagre in comparison with that of words. Words have not merely music as sweet as that of viol and lute, colour as rich and vivid as any that makes lovely for us the canvas of the Venetian or the Spaniard, and plastic form no less sure and certain than that which reveals itself in marble or in bronze, but thought and passion and spirituality are theirs also, are theirs indeed alone. If the Greeks had criticised nothing but language, they would still have been the great art-critics of the world. To know the principles of the highest art, is to know the principles of the arts.

But I see that the moon is hiding behind a sulphur-coloured cloud. Out of a tawny mane of drift she gleams like a lion's eye. She is afraid that I will talk to you of Lucian and Longinus, of Quinctilian and Dionysius, of Pliny and Fronto and Pausanias,* of all those who in the antique world wrote or lectured upon art-matters. She need not be afraid. I am tired of my expedition into the dim, dull abyss of facts.

* Ancient authors who wrote, among other things, about poetics and rhetoric.

There is nothing left for me now but the divine *μονόχρονος ἡδονή** of another cigarette. Cigarettes have at least the charm of leaving one unsatisfied.

ERNEST. Try one of mine. They are rather good. I get them direct from Cairo. The only use of our *attachés* is that they supply their friends with excellent tobacco. And as the moon has hidden herself, let us talk a little longer. I am quite ready to admit that I was wrong in what I said about the Greeks. They were, as you have pointed out, a nation of art-critics. I acknowledge it, and feel a little sorry for them. For the creative faculty is higher than the critical. There is really no comparison between them.

GILBERT. The antithesis between them is entirely arbitrary. Without the critical faculty, there is no artistic creation at all, worthy of the name. You spoke a little while ago of that fine spirit of choice and delicate instinct of selection by which the artist realizes life for us, and gives to it a momentary perfection. Well, that spirit of choice, that subtle tact of omission, is really the critical faculty in one of its most characteristic moods, and no one who does not possess this critical faculty can create anything at all in art. Arnold's definition of literature as a criticism of life, was not very felicitous in form, but it showed how keenly he recognized the importance of the critical element in all creative work.

ERNEST. I should have said that great artists worked unconsciously, that they were "wiser than they knew," as, I think, Emerson remarks somewhere.

GILBERT. It is really not so, Ernest. All fine imaginative work is self-conscious and deliberate. No poet sings because he must sing. At least, no great poet does. A great poet sings because he chooses to sing. It is so now, and it has always been so. We are sometimes apt to think that the voices that sounded at the dawn of poetry were simpler, fresher, and more natural than ours, and that the world which the early poets

---

* Pleasure lasting only a moment; ideally intense pleasure, occurring when the "hard gem-like flame" described by Walter Pater in his *Renaissance* yields the highest truth.

looked at, and through which they walked, had a kind of poetical quality of its own, and almost without changing could pass into song. The snow lies thick now upon Olympus, and its steep scarped sides are bleak and barren, but once, we fancy, the white feet of the Muses brushed the dew from the anemones in the morning, and at evening came Apollo to sing to the shepherds in the vale. But in this we are merely lending to other ages what we desire, or think we desire, for our own. Our historical sense is at fault. Every century that produces poetry is, so far, an artificial century, and the work that seems to us to be the most natural and simple product of its time is always the result of the most self-conscious effort. Believe me, Ernest, there is no fine art without self-consciousness, and self-consciousness and the critical spirit are one.

ERNEST. I see what you mean, and there is much in it. But surely you would admit that the great poems of the early world, the primitive, anonymous collective poems, were the result of the imagination of races, rather than of the imagination of individuals?

GILBERT. Not when they became poetry. Not when they received a beautiful form. For there is no art where there is no style, and no style where there is no unity, and unity is of the individual. No doubt Homer had old ballads and stories to deal with, as Shakespeare had chronicles and plays and novels from which to work, but they were merely his rough material. He took them, and shaped them into song. They become his, because he made them lovely. They were built out of music,

> And so not built at all,
> And therefore built for ever.*

The longer one studies life and literature, the more strongly one feels that behind everything that is wonderful stands the individual, and that it is not the moment that makes the man, but the man who creates the age. Indeed, I am inclined to think that each myth and

---

* An allusion to the building of Camelot; the lines are from *Idylls of the King*, by Alfred, Lord Tennyson (1809–1892).

legend that seems to us to spring out of the wonder, or terror, or fancy of tribe and nation, was in its origin the invention of one single mind. The curiously limited number of the myths seems to me to point to this conclusion. But we must not go off into questions of comparative mythology. We must keep to criticism. And what I want to point out is this. An age that has no criticism is either an age in which art is immobile, hieratic, and confined to the reproduction of formal types, or an age that possesses no art at all. There have been critical ages that have not been creative, in the ordinary sense of the word, ages in which the spirit of man has sought to set in order the treasures of his treasure-house, to separate the gold from the silver, and the silver from the lead, to count over the jewels, and to give names to the pearls. But there has never been a creative age that has not been critical also. For it is the critical faculty that invents fresh forms. The tendency of creation is to repeat itself. It is to the critical instinct that we owe each new school that springs up, each new mould that art finds ready to its hand. There is really not a single form that art now uses that does not come to us from the critical spirit of Alexandria, where these forms were either stereotyped, or invented, or made perfect. I say Alexandria, not merely because it was there that the Greek spirit became most self-conscious, and indeed ultimately expired in scepticism and theology, but because it was to that city, and not to Athens, that Rome turned for her models, and it was through the survival, such as it was, of the Latin language that culture lived at all. When, at the Renaissance, Greek literature dawned upon Europe, the soil had been in some measure prepared for it. But, to get rid of the details of history, which are always wearisome and usually inaccurate, let us say generally, that the forms of art have been due to the Greek critical spirit. To it we owe the epic, the lyric, the entire drama in every one of its developments, including burlesque, the idyll, the romantic novel, the novel of adventure, the essay, the dialogue, the oration, the lecture, for which perhaps we should not forgive them, and the epigram, in all the wide meaning of that word. In fact, we owe it everything, except the sonnet, to which, however, some curious parallels of thought-movement may be traced in the Anthology, American journalism, to which no parallel can be found anywhere and the ballad in sham Scotch dialect, which one of our most industrious writers has recently proposed should be made the basis for a final and unanimous effort on the part of our second-rate poets to make themselves really romantic. Each new school, as it appears, cries out against criticism, but it is to the critical faculty in man that it owes its origin. The mere creative instinct does not innovate, but reproduces.

ERNEST. You have been talking of criticism as an essential part of the creative spirit, and I now fully accept your theory. But what of criticism outside creation? I have a foolish habit of reading periodicals, and it seems to me that most modern criticism is perfectly valueless.

GILBERT. So is most modern creative work also. Mediocrity weighing mediocrity in the balance, and incompetence applauding its brother—that is the spectacle which the artistic activity of England affords us from time to time. And yet, I feel I am a little unfair in this matter. As a rule, the critics—I speak, of course, of the higher class, of those in fact who write for the sixpenny papers—are far more cultured than the people whose work they are called upon to review. This is, indeed, only what one would expect, for criticism demands infinitely more cultivation than creation does.

ERNEST. Really?

GILBERT. Certainly. Anybody can write a three-volumed novel. It merely requires a complete ignorance of both life and literature. The difficulty that I should fancy the reviewer feels is the difficulty of sustaining any standard. Where there is no style a standard must be impossible. The poor reviewers are apparently reduced to be the reporters of the police-court of literature, the chroniclers of the doings of the habitual criminals of art. It is sometimes said of them that they do not read all through the works they are called upon to criticise. They do not. Or at least they should not. If they did so, they would become confirmed misanthropes, or if I may borrow a phrase from one of the pretty Newnham graduates,* confirmed womanthropes for the rest of

* Graduates of Newnham, the women's college at Cambridge University, established in 1871.

their lives. Nor is it necessary. To know the vintage and quality of a wine one need not drink the whole cask. It must be perfectly easy in half an hour to say whether a book is worth anything or worth nothing. Ten minutes are really sufficient, if one has the instinct for form. Who wants to wade through a dull volume? One tastes it, and that is quite enough—more than enough, I should imagine. I am aware that there are many honest workers in painting as well as in literature who object to criticism entirely. They are quite right. Their work stands in no intellectual relation to their age. It brings us no new element of pleasure. It suggests no fresh departure of thought, or passion, or beauty. It should not be spoken of. It should be left to the oblivion that it deserves.

Ernest. But, my dear fellow—excuse me for interrupting you—you seem to me to be allowing your passion for criticism to lead you a great deal too far. For, after all, even you must admit that it is much more difficult to do a thing than to talk about it.

Gilbert. More difficult to do a thing than to talk about it? Not at all. That is a gross popular error. It is very much more difficult to talk about a thing than to do it. In the sphere of actual life that is of course obvious. Anybody can make history. Only a great man can write it. There is no mode of action, no form of emotion, that we do not share with the lower animals. It is only by language that we rise above them, or above each other—by language, which is the parent, and not the child, of thought. Action, indeed, is always easy, and when presented to us in its most aggravated, because most continuous form, which I take to be that of real industry, becomes simply the refuge of people who have nothing whatsoever to do. No, Ernest, don't talk about action. It is a blind thing dependent on external influences, and moved by an impulse of whose nature it is unconscious. It is a thing incomplete in its essence, because limited by accident, and ignorant of its direction, being always at variance with its aim. Its basis is the lack of imagination. It is the last resource of those who know not how to dream.

Ernest. Gilbert, you treat the world as if it were a crystal ball. You hold it in your hand, and reverse it to please a wilful fancy. You do nothing but rewrite history.

GILBERT. The one duty we owe to history is to rewrite it. That is not the least of the tasks in store for the critical spirit. When we have fully discovered the scientific laws that govern life, we shall realize that the one person who has more illusions than the dreamer is the man of action. He, indeed, knows neither the origin of his deeds nor their results. From the field in which he thought that he had sown thorns, we have gathered our vintage, and the fig-tree that he planted for our pleasure is as barren as the thistle, and more bitter. It is because Humanity has never known where it was going that it has been able to find its way.

ERNEST. You think, then, that in the sphere of action a conscious aim is a delusion?

GILBERT. It is worse than a delusion. If we lived long enough to see the results of our actions it may be that those who call themselves good would be sickened with a dull remorse, and those whom the world calls evil stirred by a noble joy. Each little thing that we do passes into the great machine of life which may grind our virtues to powder and make them worthless, or transform our sins into elements of a new civilization, more marvellous and more splendid than any that has gone before. But men are the slaves of words. They rage against Materialism, as they call it, forgetting that there has been no material improvement that has not spiritualized the world, and that there have been few, if any, spiritual awakenings that have not wasted the world's faculties in barren hopes, and fruitless aspirations, and empty or trammelling creeds. What is termed Sin is an essential element of progress. Without it the world would stagnate, or grow old, or become colourless. By its curiosity, Sin increases the experience of the race. Through its intensified assertion of individualism, it saves us from monotony of type. In its rejection of the current notions about morality, it is one with the higher ethics. And as for the virtues! What are the virtues? Nature, M. Renan* tells us,

---

* Author of the famed *Life of Jesus*, Ernest Renan (1823–1892) was a skeptic; later in this sentence Wilde refers to the pure Lucrece, heroine of Shakespeare's poem *The Rape of Lucrece*.

cares little about chastity, and it may be that it is to the shame of the Magdalen, and not to their own purity, that the Lucretias of modern life owe their freedom from stain. Charity, as even those of whose religion it makes a formal part have been compelled to acknowledge, creates a multitude of evils. The mere existence of conscience, that faculty of which people prate so much nowadays, and are so ignorantly proud, is a sign of our imperfect development. It must be merged in instinct before we become fine. Self-denial is simply a method by which man arrests his progress, and self-sacrifice a survival of the mutilation of the savage, part of that old worship of pain which is so terrible a factor in the history of the world, and which even now makes its victims day by day, and has its altars in the land. Virtues! Who knows what the virtues are? Not you. Not I. Not anyone. It is well for our vanity that we slay the criminal, for if we suffered him to live he might show us what we had gained by his crime. It is well for his peace that the saint goes to his martyrdom. He is spared the sight of the horror of his harvest.

ERNEST. Gilbert, you sound too harsh a note. Let us go back to the more gracious fields of literature. What was it you said? That it was more difficult to talk about a thing than to do it?

GILBERT (*after a pause*). Yes: I believe I ventured upon that simple truth. Surely you see now that I am right? When man acts he is a puppet. When he describes he is a poet. The whole secret lies in that. It was easy enough on the sandy plains by windy Ilion to send the notched arrow from the painted bow, or to hurl against the shield of hide and flame-like brass the long ash-handled spear. It was easy for the adulterous queen to spread the Tyrian carpets for her lord, and then, as he lay couched in the marble bath, to throw over his head the purple net, and call to her smooth-faced lover to stab through the meshes at the heart that should have broken at Aulis. For Antigone even, with Death waiting for her as her bridegroom, it was easy to pass through the tainted air at noon, and climb the hill, and strew with kindly earth the wretched naked corse that had no tomb. But what of those who wrote about these things? What of those who gave them reality, and made them live for ever? Are they not greater than the men and women they sing of? "Hector that sweet knight is dead," and Lucian tells us how in the dim underworld Menippus saw the bleaching skull of Helen, and marvelled that it was for so grim a favour that all those horned ships were launched, those beautiful mailed men laid low, those towered cities brought to dust. Yet, every day the swan-like daughter of Leda comes out on the battlements, and looks down at the tide of war. The greybeards wonder at her loveliness, and she stands by the side of the king. In his chamber of stained ivory lies her leman. He is polishing his dainty armour, and combing the scarlet plume. With squire and page, her husband passes from tent to tent. She can see his bright hair, and hears, or fancies that she hears, that clear cold voice. In the courtyard below, the son of Priam is buckling on his brazen cuirass. The white arms of Andromache are around his neck. He sets his helmet on the ground, lest their babe should be frightened. Behind the embroidered curtains of his pavilion sits Achilles, in perfumed raiment, while in harness of gilt and silver the friend of his soul arrays himself to go forth to the fight. From a curiously carven chest that his mother Thetis had brought to his ship-side, the Lord of the Myrmidons takes out that mystic chalice that the lip of man had never touched, and cleanses it with brimstone, and with fresh water cools it, and, having washed his hands, fills with black wine its burnished hollow, and spills the thick grape-blood upon the ground in honour of Him whom at Dodona barefooted prophets worshipped, and prays to Him, and knows not that he prays in vain, and that by the hands of two knights from Troy, Panthous' son, Euphorbus, whose love-locks were looped with gold, and the Priamid, the lion-hearted, Patroklus, the comrade of comrades, must meet his doom. Phantoms, are they? Heroes of mist and mountain? Shadows in a song? No: they are real. Action! What is action? It dies at the moment of its energy. It is a base concession to fact. The world is made by the singer for the dreamer.

Ernest. While you talk it seems to me to be so.

Gilbert. It is so in truth. On the mouldering citadel of Troy lies the lizard like a thing of green bronze. The owl has built her nest in the palace of Priam. Over the empty plain wander shepherd and goatherd with their flocks, and where, on the wine-surfaced, oily sea, *οἶνοψ πόντος*, as Homer calls it, copper-prowed and streaked with vermilion, the great galleys of the Danaoi came in their gleaming crescent; the lonely tunny-fisher sits in his little boat and watches the bobbing corks of his net. Yet, every morning the doors of the city are thrown open, and on foot, or in horse-drawn chariot, the warriors go forth to battle, and mock their enemies from behind their iron masks. All day long the fight rages, and when night comes the torches gleam by the tents, and the cresset burns in the hall. Those who live in marble or on painted panel, know of life but a single exquisite instant, eternal indeed in its beauty, but limited to one note of passion or one mood of calm. Those whom the poet makes live have their myriad emotions of joy and terror, of courage and despair, of pleasure and of suffering. The seasons come and go in glad or saddening pageant, and with winged or leaden feet the years pass by before them. They have their youth and their manhood, they are children, and they grow old. It is always dawn for St. Helena, as Veronese* saw her at the window. Through the still morning air the angels bring her the symbol of God's pain. The cool breezes of the morning lift the gilt threads from her brow. On that little hill by the city of Florence, where the lovers of Giorgione are lying, it is always the solstice of noon, of noon made so languorous by summer suns that hardly can the slim naked girl dip into the marble tank the round bubble of clear glass, and the long fingers of the lute-player rest idly upon the chords. It is twilight always for the dancing nymphs whom Corot set free among the silver poplars of France. In eternal twilight they move, those frail diaphanous figures, whose tremulous white feet seem not to touch the dew-drenched grass they tread on. But those who walk in epos, drama, or romance, see through the labouring months the young moons wax and wane, and watch the night from evening unto morning star, and from sunrise unto sun-setting can note the shifting day with all its gold and shadow. For them, as for us, the flowers bloom and wither, and the Earth, that Green-tressed

* Gilbert is recalling three memorably atmospheric works: Paolo Veronese's *Vision of St. Helen*, Giorgione's *Fete Champetre*, and Jean-Baptiste Corot's *Dance of the Nymphs*.

Goddess as Coleridge calls her, alters her raiment for their pleasure. The statue is concentrated to one moment of perfection. The image stained upon the canvas possesses no spiritual element of growth or change. If they know nothing of death, it is because they know little of life, for the secrets of life and death belong to those, and those only, whom the sequence of time affects, and who possess not merely the present but the future, and can rise or fall from a past of glory or of shame. Movement, that problem of the visible arts, can be truly realized by Literature alone. It is Literature that shows us the body in its swiftness and the soul in its unrest.

ERNEST. Yes; I see now what you mean. But, surely, the higher you place the creative artist, the lower must the critic rank.

GILBERT. Why so?

ERNEST. Because the best that he can give us will be but an echo of rich music, a dim shadow of clear-outlined form. It may, indeed, be that life is chaos, as you tell me that it is; that its martyrdoms are mean and its heroisms ignoble; and that it is the function of Literature to create, from the rough material of actual existence, a new world that will be more marvellous, more enduring, and more true than the world that common eyes look upon, and through which common natures seek to realize their perfection. But surely, if this new world has been made by the spirit and touch of a great artist, it will be a thing so complete and perfect that there will be nothing left for the critic to do. I quite understand now, and indeed admit most readily, that it is far more difficult to talk about a thing than to do it. But it seems to me that this sound and sensible maxim, which is really extremely soothing to one's feelings, and should be adopted as its motto by every Academy of Literature all over the world, applies only to the relations that exist between Art and Life, and not to any relations that there may be between Art and Criticism.

GILBERT. But, surely, Criticism is itself an art. And just as artistic creation implies the working of the critical faculty, and, indeed, without it cannot be said to exist at all, so Criticism is really creative in the highest sense of the word. Criticism is, in fact, both creative and independent.

ERNEST. Independent?

GILBERT. Yes; independent. Criticism is no more to be judged by any low standard of imitation or resemblance than is the work of poet or sculptor. The critic occupies the same relation to the work of art that he criticises as the artist does to the visible world of form and colour, or the unseen world of passion and of thought. He does not even require for the perfection of his art the finest materials. Anything will serve his purpose. And just as out of the sordid and sentimental amours of the silly wife of a small country doctor in the squalid village of Yonville-l'Abbaye, near Rouen, Gustave Flaubert was able to create a classic, and make a masterpiece of style, so, from subjects of little or of no importance, such as the pictures in this year's Royal Academy, or in any year's Royal Academy for that matter, Mr. Lewis Morris's poems, M. Ohnet's novels, or the plays of Mr. Henry Arthur Jones, the true critic can, if it be his pleasure so to direct or waste his faculty of contemplation, produce work that will be flawless in beauty and instinct with intellectual subtlety. Why not? Dulness is always an irresistible temptation for brilliancy, and stupidity is the permanent *Bestia Trionfans** that calls wisdom from its cave. To an artist so creative as the critic, what does subject-matter signify? No more and no less than it does to the novelist and the painter. Like them, he can find his motives everywhere. Treatment is the test. There is nothing that has not in it suggestion or challenge.

ERNEST. But is Criticism really a creative art?

GILBERT. Why should it not be? It works with materials, and puts them into a form that is at once new and delightful. What more can one say of poetry? Indeed, I would call criticism a creation within a creation. For just as the great artists, from Homer and Æschylus, down to Shakespeare and Keats, did not go directly to life for their subject-matter, but sought for it in myth, and legend and ancient tale, so the critic deals with materials that others have, as it were, purified for him, and to which imaginative form and colour have been already added. Nay, more, I would say that the highest Criticism, being the purest form of personal impression, is in its way more creative than

* Triumphant beast (Italian).

creation, as it has least reference to any standard external to itself, and is, in fact, its own reason for existing, and, as the Greeks would put it, in itself, and to itself, an end. Certainly, it is never trammelled by any shackles of verisimilitude. No ignoble considerations of probability, that cowardly concession to the tedious repetitions of domestic or public life, affect it ever. One may appeal from fiction unto fact. But from the soul there is no appeal.

ERNEST. From the soul?

GILBERT. Yes, from the soul. That is what the highest criticism really is, the record of one's own soul. It is more fascinating than history, as it is concerned simply with oneself. It is more delightful than philosophy, as its subject is concrete and not abstract, real and not vague. It is the only civilized form of autobiography, as it deals not with the events, but with the thoughts of one's life; not with life's physical accidents of deed or circumstance, but with the spiritual moods and imaginative passions of the mind. I am always amused by the silly vanity of those writers and artists of our day who seem to imagine that the primary function of the critic is to chatter about their second-rate work. The best that one can say of most modern creative art is that it is just a little less vulgar than reality, and so the critic, with his fine sense of distinction and sure instinct of delicate refinements, will prefer to look into the silver mirror or through the woven veil, and will turn his eyes away from the chaos and clamour of actual existence, though the mirror be tarnished and the veil be torn. His sole aim is to chronicle his own impressions. It is for him that pictures are painted, books written, and marble hewn into form.

ERNEST. I seem to have heard another theory of Criticism.

GILBERT. Yes: it has been said by one whose gracious memory we all revere, and the music of whose pipe once lured Proserpina from her Sicilian fields, and made those white feet stir, and not in vain, the Cumnor cowslips, that the proper aim of Criticism is to see the object as in itself it really is. But this is a very serious error, and takes no cognizance of Criticism's most perfect form, which is in its essence purely subjective, and seeks to reveal its own secret and not the secret of another. For the highest Criticism deals with art not as expressive but as impressive purely.

ERNEST. But is that really so?

GILBERT. Of course it is. Who cares whether Mr. Ruskin's views on Turner are sound or not? What does it matter? That mighty and majestic prose of his, so fervid and so fiery-coloured in its noble eloquence, so rich in its elaborate symphonic music, so sure and certain, at its best, in subtle choice of word and epithet, is at least as great a work of art as any of those wonderful sunsets that bleach or rot on their corrupted canvases in England's Gallery; greater indeed, one is apt to think at times, not merely because its equal beauty is more enduring, but on account of the fuller variety of its appeal, soul speaking to soul in those long-cadenced lines, not through form and colour alone, though through these, indeed, completely and without loss, but with intellectual and emotional utterance, with lofty passion and with loftier thought, with imaginative insight, and with poetic aim; greater, I always think, even as Literature is the greater art. Who, again, cares whether Mr. Pater has put into the portrait of Monna Lisa something that Lionardo never dreamed of? The painter may have been merely the slave of an archaic smile, as some have fancied, but whenever I pass into the cool galleries of the Palace of the Louvre, and stand before that strange figure "set in its marble chair in that cirque of fantastic rocks, as in some faint light under sea," I murmur to myself, "She is older than the rocks among which she sits; like the vampire, she has been dead many times, and learned the secrets of the grave; and has been a diver in deep seas, and keeps their fallen day about her; and trafficked for strange webs with Eastern merchants; and, as Leda, was the mother of Helen of Troy, and, as St. Anne, the mother of Mary; and all this has been to her but as the sound of lyres and flutes, and lives only in the delicacy with which it has moulded the changing lineaments, and tinged the eyelids and the hands." And I say to my friend, "The presence that thus so strangely rose beside the waters is expressive of what in the ways of a thousand years man had come to desire;" and he answers me, "Hers is the head upon which all 'the ends of the world are come,' and the eyelids are a little weary."

And so the picture becomes more wonderful to us than it really is, and reveals to us a secret of which, in truth, it knows nothing, and the music of the mystical prose is as sweet in our ears as was that flute-player's music that lent to the lips of La Gioconda those subtle and poisonous curves. Do you ask me what Lionardo would have said had anyone told him of this picture that "all the thoughts and experience of the world had etched and moulded there in that which they had of power to refine and make expressive the outward form, the animalism of Greece, the lust of Rome, the reverie of the Middle Age with its spiritual ambition and imaginative loves, the return of the Pagan world, the sins of the Borgias?" He would probably have answered that he had contemplated none of these things, but had concerned himself simply with certain arrangements of lines and masses, and with new and curious colour-harmonies of blue and green. And it is for this very reason that the criticism which I have quoted is criticism of the highest kind. It treats the work of art simply as a starting-point for a new creation. It does not confine itself—let us at least suppose so for the moment—to discovering the real intention of the artist and accepting that as final. And in this it is right, for the meaning of any beautiful created thing is, at least, as much in the soul of him who looks at it, as it was in his soul who wrought it. Nay, it is rather the beholder who lends to the beautiful thing its myriad meanings, and makes it marvellous for us, and sets it in some new relation to the age, so that it becomes a vital portion of our lives, and a symbol of what we pray for, or perhaps of what, having prayed for, we fear that we may receive. The longer I study, Ernest, the more clearly I see that the beauty of the visible arts is, as the beauty of music, impressive primarily, and that it may be marred, and indeed often is so, by any excess of intellectual intention on the part of the artist. For when the work is finished it has, as it were, an independent life of its own, and may deliver a message far other than that which was put into its lips to say. Sometimes, when I listen to the overture to *Tannhäuser*, I seem indeed to see that comely knight treading delicately on the flower-strewn grass, and to hear the voice of Venus calling to him from the caverned hill. But at other times it speaks to me of a thousand different things, of myself, it may be, and my own life, or of the lives of others whom one has loved and grown weary of loving, or of the passions that man has known, or of the passions that man has not known, and so has sought for. To-night it may fill one with that ΕΡΩΣ ΤΩΝ ΑΔΤΝΑΤΩΝ, that *Amour de l'Impossible*,* which falls like a madness on many who think they live securely and out of reach of harm, so that they sicken suddenly with the poison of unlimited desire, and, in the infinite pursuit of what they may not obtain, grow faint and swoon or stumble. To-morrow, like the music of which Aristotle and Plato tell us, the noble Dorian music of the Greek, it may perform the office of a physician, and give us an anodyne against pain, and heal the spirit that is wounded, and "bring the soul into harmony with all right things." And what is true about music is true about all the arts. Beauty has as many meanings as man has moods. Beauty is the symbol of symbols. Beauty reveals everything, because it expresses nothing. When it shows us itself, it shows us the whole fiery-coloured world.

ERNEST. But is such work as you have talked about really criticism?

GILBERT. It is the highest Criticism, for it criticises not merely the individual work of art, but Beauty itself, and fills with wonder a form which the artist may have left void, or not understood, or understood incompletely.

ERNEST. The highest Criticism, then, is more creative than creation, and the primary aim of the critic is to see the object as in itself it really is not; that is your theory, I believe?

GILBERT. Yes, that is my theory. To the critic the work of art is simply a suggestion for a new work of his own, that need not necessarily bear any obvious resemblance to the thing it criticises. The one characteristic of a beautiful form is that one can put into it whatever one wishes, and see in it whatever one chooses to see; and the Beauty, that gives to creation its universal and æsthetic element, makes the critic a creator in his turn, and whispers of a thousand different things which were not present in the mind of him who carved the statue or painted the panel or graved the gem.

It is sometimes said by those who understand neither the nature of the highest Criticism nor the charm of the highest Art, that the pictures that the critic loves most to write about are those that belong to

* Love of the impossible (French).

the anecdotage of painting, and that deal with scenes taken out of literature or history. But this is not so. Indeed, pictures of this kind are far too intelligible. As a class, they rank with illustrations, and even considered from this point of view are failures, as they do not stir the imagination, but set definite bounds to it. For the domain of the painter is, as I suggested before, widely different from that of the poet. To the latter belongs life in its full and absolute entirety; not merely the beauty that men look at, but the beauty that men listen to also; not merely the momentary grace of form or the transient gladness of colour, but the whole sphere of feeling, the perfect cycle of thought. The painter is so far limited that it is only through the mask of the body that he can show us the mystery of the soul; only through conventional images that he can handle ideas; only through its physical equivalents that he can deal with psychology. And how inadequately does he do it then, asking us to accept the torn turban of the Moor for the noble rage of Othello, or a dotard in a storm for the wild madness of Lear! Yet it seems as if nothing could stop him. Most of our elderly English painters spend their wicked and wasted lives in poaching upon the domain of the poets, marring their motives by clumsy treatment, and striving to render, by visible form or colour, the marvel of what is invisible, the splendour of what is not seen. Their pictures are, as a natural consequence, insufferably tedious. They have degraded the visible arts into the obvious arts, and the one thing not worth looking at is the obvious. I do not say that poet and painter may not treat of the same subject. They have always done so, and will always do so. But while the poet can be pictorial or not, as he chooses, the painter must be pictorial always. For a painter is limited, not to what he sees in nature, but to what upon canvas may be seen.

And so, my dear Ernest, pictures of this kind will not really fascinate the critic. He will turn from them to such works as make him brood and dream and fancy, to works that possess the subtle quality of suggestion, and seem to tell one that even from them there is an escape into a wider world. It is sometimes said that the tragedy of an artist's life is that he cannot realize his ideal. But the true tragedy that dogs the steps of most artists is that they realize their ideal too absolutely. For, when the ideal is realized, it is robbed of its wonder and its mystery, and becomes simply a new starting-point for an ideal that is other than itself. This is the reason why music is the perfect type of art. Music can never reveal its ultimate secret. This, also, is the explanation of the value of limitations in art. The sculptor gladly surrenders imitative colour, and the painter the actual dimensions of form, because by such renunciations they are able to avoid too definite a presentation of the Real, which would be mere imitation, and too definite a realization of the Ideal, which would be too purely intellectual. It is through its very incompleteness that Art becomes complete in beauty, and so addresses itself, not to the faculty of recognition nor to the faculty of reason, but to the æsthetic sense alone, which, while accepting both reason and recognition as stages of apprehension, subordinates them both to a pure synthetic impression of the work of art as a whole, and, taking whatever alien emotional elements the work may possess, uses their very complexity as a means by which a richer unity may be added to the ultimate impression itself. You see, then, how it is that the æsthetic critic rejects those obvious modes of art that have but one message to deliver, and having delivered it become dumb and sterile, and seeks rather for such modes as suggest reverie and mood, and by their imaginative beauty make all interpretations true and no interpretation final. Some resemblance, no doubt, the creative work of the critic will have to the work that has stirred him to creation, but it will be such resemblance as exists, not between Nature and the mirror that the painter of landscape or figure may be supposed to hold up to her, but between Nature and the work of the decorative artist. Just as on the flowerless carpets of Persia, tulip and rose blossom indeed and are lovely to look on, though they are not reproduced in visible shape or line; just as the pearl and purple of the sea-shell is echoed in the church of St. Mark at Venice; just as the vaulted ceiling of the wondrous chapel of Ravenna is made gorgeous by the gold and green and sapphire of the peacock's tail, though the birds of Juno fly not across it; so the critic reproduces the work that he criticises in a mode that is never imitative, and part of whose charm may really consist in the rejection of resemblance, and shows us in this way not merely the meaning but also the mystery of Beauty, and, by transforming each art into literature, solves once for all the problem of Art's unity.

But I see it is time for supper. After we have discussed some Chambertin and a few ortolans, we will pass on to the question of the critic considered in the light of the interpreter.

ERNEST. Ah! you admit, then, that the critic may occasionally be allowed to see the object as in itself it really is.

GILBERT. I am not quite sure. Perhaps I may admit it after supper. There is a subtle influence in supper.

THE CRITIC AS ARTIST

With some remarks upon the importance of discussing everything

A Dialogue. Part II.
Persons: the same.
Scene: the same.

ERNEST. The ortolans were delightful, and the Chambertin perfect. And now let us return to the point at issue.

GILBERT. Ah! don't let us do that. Conversation should touch everything, but should concentrate itself on nothing. Let us talk about *Moral Indignation, its Cause and Cure*, a subject on which I think of writing: or about *The Survival of Thersites*, as shown by the English comic papers; or about any topic that may turn up.

ERNEST. No: I want to discuss the critic and criticism. You have told me that the highest criticism deals with art, not as expressive, but as impressive purely, and is consequently both creative and independent, is in fact an art by itself, occupying the same relation to creative work that creative work does to the visible world of form and colour, or the unseen world of passion and of thought. Well, now tell me, will not the critic be sometimes a real interpreter?

GILBERT. Yes; the critic will be an interpreter, if he chooses. He can pass from his synthetic impression of the work of art as a whole, to an analysis or exposition of the work itself, and in this lower sphere, as I hold it to be, there are many delightful things to be said and done. Yet his object will not always be to explain the work of art. He may seek rather to deepen its mystery, to raise round it, and round its maker, that mist of wonder which is dear to both gods and worshippers alike. Ordinary people are "terribly at ease in Zion." They propose to walk arm in arm with the poets, and have a glib ignorant way of saying "Why should we read what is written about Shakespeare and Milton? We can read the plays and the poems. That is enough." But an appreciation of Milton is, as the late Rector of Lincoln* remarked once, the reward of consummate scholarship. And he who desires to understand Shakespeare truly must understand the relations in which Shakespeare stood to the Renaissance and the Reformation, to the age of Elizabeth and the age of James; he must be familiar with the history of the struggle for supremacy between the old classical forms and the new spirit of romance, between the school of Sidney, and Daniel, and Jonson, and the school of Marlowe and Marlowe's greater son; he must know the materials that were at Shakespeare's disposal, and the method in which he used them, and the conditions of theatric presentation in the sixteenth and seventeenth century, their limitations and their opportunities for freedom, and the literary criticism of Shakespeare's day, its aims and modes and canons; he must study the English language in its progress, and blank or rhymed verse in its various developments; he must study the Greek drama, and the connection between the art of the creator of the Agamemnon and the art of the creator of Macbeth; in a word, he must be able to bind Elizabethan London to the Athens of Pericles, and to learn Shakespeare's true position in the history of European drama and the drama of the world. The critic will certainly be an interpreter, but he will not treat Art as a riddling Sphinx, whose shallow secret may be guessed and revealed by one whose feet are wounded and who knows not his name. Rather, he will look upon Art as a goddess whose mystery it is his province to intensify, and whose majesty his privilege to make more marvellous in the eyes of men.

And here, Ernest, this strange thing happens. The critic will indeed be an interpreter, but he will not be an interpreter in the sense of one who simply repeats in another form a message that has been put into his lips to say. For, just as it is only by contact with the art of foreign nations that the art of a country gains that individual and separate life that we call nationality, so, by curious inversion, it is only by intensifying his own personality that the critic can interpret the personality

---

* Mark Pattison (1813–1884), master or rector of Lincoln College, Oxford, wrote on John Milton's life.

and work of others, and the more strongly this personality enters into the interpretation the more real the interpretation becomes, the more satisfying, the more convincing, and the more true.

ERNEST. I would have said that personality would have been a disturbing element.

GILBERT. No; it is an element of revelation. If you wish to understand others you must intensify your own individualism.

ERNEST. What, then, is the result?

GILBERT. I will tell you, and perhaps I can tell you best by definite example. It seems to me that, while the literary critic stands of course first, as having the wider range, and larger vision, and nobler material, each of the arts has a critic, as it were, assigned to it. The actor is a critic of the drama. He shows the poet's work under new conditions, and by a method special to himself. He takes the written word, and action, gesture, and voice become the media of revelation. The singer, or the player on lute and viol, is the critic of music. The etcher of a picture robs the painting of its fair colours, but shows us by the use of a new material its true colour-quality, its tones and values, and the relations of its masses, and so is, in his way, a critic of it, for the critic is he who exhibits to us a work of art in a form different from that of the work itself, and the employment of a new material is a critical as well as a creative element. Sculpture, too, has its critic, who may be either the carver of a gem, as he was in Greek days, or some painter like Mantegna, who sought to reproduce on canvas the beauty of plastic line and the symphonic dignity of processional bas-relief. And in the case of all these creative critics of art it is evident that personality is an absolute essential for any real interpretation. When Rubinstein* plays to us the *Sonata Appassionata* of Beethoven, he gives us not merely Beethoven, but also himself, and so gives us Beethoven absolutely—Beethoven reinterpreted through a rich artistic nature, and made vivid and wonderful to us by a new and intense personality. When a great actor plays Shakespeare we have the same experience. His own individuality becomes a vital part

* Russian virtuoso pianist and composer Anton Rubinstein (1829–1894).

of the interpretation. People sometimes say that actors give us their own Hamlets, and not Shakespeare's; and this fallacy—for it is a fallacy—is, I regret to say, repeated by that charming and graceful writer who has lately deserted the turmoil of literature for the peace of the House of Commons, I mean the author of *Obiter Dicta*. In point of fact, there is no such thing as Shakespeare's Hamlet. If Hamlet has something of the definiteness of a work of art, he has also all the obscurity that belongs to life. There are as many Hamlets as there are melancholies.

ERNEST. As many Hamlets as there are melancholies?

GILBERT. Yes: and as art springs from personality, so it is only to personality that it can be revealed, and from the meeting of the two comes right interpretative criticism.

ERNEST. The critic, then, considered as the interpreter, will give no less than he receives, and lend as much as he borrows?

GILBERT. He will be always showing us the work of art in some new relation to our age. He will always be reminding us that great works of art are living things—are, in fact, the only things that live. So much, indeed, will he feel this, that I am certain that, as civilization progresses and we become more highly organized, the elect spirits of each age, the critical and cultured spirits, will grow less and less interested in actual life, and *will seek to gain their impressions almost entirely from what Art has touched*. For Life is terribly deficient in form. Its catastrophes happen in the wrong way and to the wrong people. There is a grotesque horror about its comedies, and its tragedies seem to culminate in farce. One is always wounded when one approaches it. Things last either too long, or not long enough.

ERNEST. Poor life! Poor human life! Are you not even touched by the tears that the Roman poet tells us are part of its essence?

GILBERT. Too quickly touched by them, I fear. For when one looks back upon the life that was so vivid in its emotional intensity, and filled with such fervent moments of ecstasy or of joy, it all seems to be a dream and an illusion. What are the unreal things, but the passions that once burned one like fire? What are the incredible things, but the things that one has faithfully believed? What are the improbable things? The things that one has done oneself. No, Ernest; life cheats us with shadows, like a puppet-master. We ask it for pleasure. It gives it to us, with bitterness and disappointment in its train. We come across some noble grief that we think will lend the purple dignity of tragedy to our days, but it passes away from us, and things less noble take its place, and on some grey windy dawn, or odorous eve of silence and of silver, we find ourselves looking with callous wonder, or dull heart of stone, at the trees of gold-flecked hair that we had once so wildly worshipped and so madly kissed.

ERNEST. Life then is a failure?

GILBERT. From the artistic point of view, certainly. And the chief thing that makes life a failure from this artistic point of view is the thing that lends to life its sordid security, the fact that one can never repeat exactly the same emotion. How different it is in the world of Art! On a shelf of the bookcase behind you stands the *Divine Comedy*, and I know that, if I open it at a certain place, I shall be filled with a fierce hatred of some one who has never wronged me, or stirred by a great love for some one whom I shall never see. There is no mood or passion that Art cannot give us, and those of us who have discovered her secret can settle beforehand what our experiences are going to be. We can say to ourselves, "To-morrow, at dawn, we shall walk with grave Virgil through the valley of the shadow of death," and lo! the dawn finds us in the obscure wood, and the Mantuan stands by our side. We pass through the gate of the legend fatal to hope, and with pity or with joy behold the horror of another world. The hypocrites go by, with their painted faces and their cowls of gilded lead. Out of the ceaseless winds that drive them, the carnal look at us, and we watch the heretic rending his flesh, and the glutton lashed by the rain. We break the withered branches from the tree in the grove of the Harpies, and each dull-hued poisonous twig bleeds with red blood before us, and cries aloud with bitter cries. Out of a horn of fire Odysseus speaks to us, and when from his sepulchre of flame the great Ghibelline rises, the pride that triumphs over the torture of that bed becomes ours for a moment. Through the dim purple air fly those who have stained the world with the beauty of their sin, and in the pit of loathsome disease, dropsy-stricken and swollen of body into the semblance of a monstrous lute, lies Adamo di Brescia,* the coiner of false coin. He bids us listen to his misery; we stop, and with dry and gaping lips he tells us how he dreams day and night of the brooks of clear water that in cool dewy channels gush down the green Casentine hills. Sinon, the false Greek of Troy, mocks at him. He smites him in the face and they wrangle. We are fascinated by their shame, and loiter, till Virgil chides us and leads us away to that city turreted by giants where great Nimrod blows his horn. Terrible things are in store for us, and we go to meet them in Dante's raiment and with Dante's heart.† We traverse the marshes of the Styx, and Argenti swims to the boat through the slimy waves. He calls to us, and we reject him. When we hear the voice of his agony we are glad, and Virgil praises us for the bitterness of our scorn. We tread upon the cold crystal of Cocytus, in which traitors stick like straws in glass. Our foot strikes against the head of Bocca. He will not tell us his name, and we tear the hair in handfuls from the screaming skull. Alberigo prays us to break the ice upon his face that he may weep a little. We pledge our word to him, and when he has uttered his dolorous tale we deny the word that we have spoken, and pass from him; such cruelty being courtesy indeed, for who more base than he who has mercy for the condemned of God? In the jaws of Lucifer we see the man who sold Christ, and in the jaws of Lucifer the men who slew Cæsar. We tremble, and come forth to rebehold the stars.

In the land of Purgation the air is freer, and the holy mountain rises into the pure light of day. There is peace for us, and for those who for a season abide in it there is some peace also, though, pale from the poison of the Maremma, Madonna Pia passes before us, and

---

* A coiner or counterfeiter—see canto 30 of *The Inferno* of Dante's *Divine Comedy*. Wilde retells this section of the fourteenth-century *Comedy* as a dreamlike mingling of history and ideal vision.

† As so often with Wilde's "voices," Gilbert here launches into impassioned declamation. This summoning of literary and historical names is not so much critical as rhetorical, designed to support an ultimate aesthetic vision based on Dante's final vision: "the Love that moves the sun and all the stars" (p. 433).

Ismene, with the sorrow of earth still lingering about her, is there. Soul after soul makes us share in some repentance or some joy. He whom the mourning of his widow taught to drink the sweet wormwood of pain, tells us of Nella praying in her lonely bed, and we learn from the mouth of Buonconte how a single tear may save a dying sinner from the fiend. Sordello, that noble and disdainful Lombard, eyes us from afar like a couchant lion. When he learns that Virgil is one of Mantua's citizens, he falls upon his neck, and when he learns that he is the singer of Rome he falls before his feet. In that valley whose grass and flowers are fairer than cleft emerald and Indian wood, and brighter than scarlet and silver, they are singing who in the world were kings; but the lips of Rudolph of Hapsburg do not move to the music of the others, and Philip of France beats his breast and Henry of England sits alone. On and on we go, climbing the marvellous stair, and the stars become larger than their wont, and the song of the kings grows faint, and at length we reach the seven trees of gold and the garden of the Earthly Paradise. In a griffin-drawn chariot appears one whose brows are bound with olive, who is veiled in white, and mantled in green, and robed in a vesture that is coloured like live fire. The ancient flame wakes within us. Our blood quickens through terrible pulses. We recognize her. It is Beatrice, the woman we have worshipped. The ice congealed about our heart melts. Wild tears of anguish break from us, and we bow our forehead to the ground, for we know that we have sinned. When we have done penance, and are purified, and have drunk of the fountain of Lethe and bathed in the fountain of Eunoe, the mistress of our soul raises us to the Paradise of Heaven. Out of that eternal pearl, the moon, the face of Piccarda Donati leans to us. Her beauty troubles us for a moment, and when, like a thing that falls through water, she passes away, we gaze after her with wistful eyes. The sweet planet of Venus is full of lovers. Cunizza, the sister of Ezzelin, the lady of Sordello's heart, is there, and Folco, the passionate singer of Provence, who in sorrow for Azalais forsook the world, and the Canaanitish harlot whose soul was the first that Christ redeemed. Joachim of Flora stands in the sun, and, in the sun, Aquinas recounts the story of St. Francis and Bonaventure the story of St. Dominic. Through the burning rubies of Mars, Cacciaguida approaches. He tells us of the arrow that is shot from the bow of exile, and how salt tastes the bread of another, and how steep are the stairs in the house of a stranger. In Saturn the souls sing not, and even she who guides us dare not smile. On a ladder of gold the flames rise and fall. At last, we see the pageant of the Mystical Rose. Beatrice fixes her eyes upon the face of God to turn them not again. The beatific vision is granted to us; we know the Love that moves the sun and all the stars.

Yes, we can put the earth back six hundred courses and make ourselves one with the great Florentine, kneel at the same altar with him, and share his rapture and his scorn. And if we grow tired of an antique time, and desire to realize our own age in all its weariness and sin, are there not books that can make us live more in one single hour than life can make us live in a score of shameful years? Close to your hand lies a little volume, bound in some Nile-green skin that has been powdered with gilded nenuphars and smoothed with hard ivory. It is the book that Gautier loved, it is Baudelaire's masterpiece. Open it at that sad madrigal that begins

> "Que m'importe que tu sois sage?
> Sois belle! et sois triste!"*

and you will find yourself worshipping sorrow as you have never worshipped joy. Pass on to the poem on the man who tortures himself, let its subtle music steal into your brain and colour your thoughts, and you will become for a moment what he was who wrote it; nay, not for a moment only, but for many barren moonlit nights and sunless sterile days will a despair that is not your own make its dwelling within you, and the misery of another gnaw your heart away. Read the whole book, suffer it to tell even one of its secrets to your soul, and your soul will grow eager to know more, and will feed upon poisonous honey, and seek to repent of strange crimes of which it is guiltless, and to make atonement for terrible pleasures that it has never known. And then, when you are tired of these flowers of evil,

* What does it matter that you are wise? / Be beautiful! And be sad! (French).

turn to the flowers that grow in the garden of Perdita,* and in their dew-drenched chalices cool your fevered brow, and let their loveliness heal and restore your soul; or wake from his forgotten tomb the sweet Syrian, Meleager, and bid the lover of Heliodore make you music, for he too has flowers in his song, red pomegranate-blossoms, and irises that smell of myrrh, ringed daffodils and dark-blue hyacinths, and marjoram and crinkled ox-eyes. Dear to him was the perfume of the bean-field at evening, and dear to him the odorous eared-spikenard that grew on the Syrian hills, and the fresh green thyme, the wine-cup's charm. The feet of his love as she walked in the garden were like lilies set upon lilies. Softer than sleep-laden poppy petals were her lips, softer than violets and as scented. The flame-like crocus sprang from the grass to look at her. For her the slim narcissus stored the cool rain; and for her the anemones forgot the Sicilian winds that wooed them. And neither crocus, nor anemone, nor narcissus was as fair as she was.

It is a strange thing, this transference of emotion. We sicken with the same maladies as the poets, and the singer lends us his pain. Dead lips have their message for us, and hearts that have fallen to dust can communicate their joy. We run to kiss the bleeding mouth of Fantine, and we follow Manon Lescaut† over the whole world. Ours is the love-madness of the Tyrian, and the terror of Orestes‡ is ours also. There is no passion that we cannot feel, no pleasure that we may not gratify, and we can choose the time of our initiation and the time of our freedom also. Life! Life! Don't let us go to life for our fulfilment or our experience. It is a thing narrowed by circumstances, incoherent in its utterance, and without that fine correspondence of form and spirit which is the only thing that can satisfy the artistic and critical temperament. It

* The heroine of *The Winter's Tale*, she is a princess raised as a shepherdess.

† In *Manon Lescaut* (1731), a novel by Antoine François Prévost (the Abbé Prévost), Manon ends her life as a deserted and miserable exile in Louisiana; she dies in the desert, after a long and desperate romantic love affair.

‡ Orestes avenges his mother, Clytemnestra's, murder of his father, Agamemnon, by killing her and her lover, Aegisthus, but then he is possessed by the Furies, who drive him mad.

makes us pay too high a price for its wares, and we purchase the meanest of its secrets at a cost that is monstrous and infinite.

ERNEST. Must we go, then, to Art for everything?

GILBERT. For everything. Because Art does not hurt us. The tears that we shed at a play are a type of the exquisite sterile emotions that it is the function of Art to awaken. We weep, but we are not wounded. We grieve, but our grief is not bitter. In the actual life of man, sorrow, as Spinoza says somewhere, is a passage to a lesser perfection. But the sorrow with which Art fills us both purifies and initiates, if I may quote once more from the great art-critic of the Greeks. It is through Art, and through Art only, that we can realize our perfection; through Art, and through Art only, that we can shield ourselves from the sordid perils of actual existence. This results not merely from the fact that nothing that one can imagine is worth doing, and that one can imagine everything, but from the subtle law that emotional forces, like the forces of the physical sphere, are limited in extent and energy. One can feel so much, and no more. And how can it matter with what pleasure life tries to tempt one, or with what pain it seeks to maim and mar one's soul, if in the spectacle of the lives of those who have never existed one has found the true secret of joy, and wept away one's tears over their deaths who, like Cordelia and the daughter of Brabantio,* can never die?

ERNEST. Stop a moment. It seems to me that in everything that you have said there is something radically immoral.

GILBERT. All art is immoral.

ERNEST. All art?

GILBERT. Yes. For emotion for the sake of emotion is the aim of art, and emotion for the sake of action is the aim of life, and of that practical organization of life that we call society. Society, which is the beginning and basis of morals, exists simply for the concentration of human energy, and in order to ensure its own continuance and healthy stability it demands, and no doubt rightly demands, of each of

---

* Cordelia is the youngest daughter of the king in Shakespeare's *King Lear*; Desdemona is Brabantio's daughter in Shakespeare's *Othello*.

its citizens that he should contribute some form of productive labour to the common weal, and toil and travail that the day's work may be done. Society often forgives the criminal; it never forgives the dreamer. The beautiful sterile emotions that art excites in us, are hateful in its eyes, and so completely are people dominated by the tyranny of this dreadful social ideal that they are always coming shamelessly up to one at Private Views and other places that are open to the general public, and saying in a loud stentorian voice, "What are you doing?" whereas "What are you thinking?" is the only question that any single civilized being should ever be allowed to whisper to another. They mean well, no doubt, these honest beaming folk. Perhaps that is the reason why they are so excessively tedious. But some one should teach them that while, in the opinion of society, Contemplation is the gravest sin of which any citizen can be guilty, in the opinion of the highest culture it is the proper occupation of man.

ERNEST. Contemplation?

GILBERT. Contemplation. I said to you some time ago that it was far more difficult to talk about a thing than to do it. Let me say to you now that to do nothing at all is the most difficult thing in the world, the most difficult and the most intellectual. To Plato, with his passion for wisdom, this was the noblest form of energy. To Aristotle, with his passion for knowledge, this was the noblest form of energy also. It was to this that the passion for holiness led the saint and the mystic of medieval days.

ERNEST. We exist, then, to do nothing?

GILBERT. It is to do nothing that the elect exist. Action is limited and relative. Unlimited and absolute is the vision of him who sits at ease and watches, who walks in loneliness and dreams. But we who are born at the close of this wonderful age, are at once too cultured and too critical, too intellectually subtle and too curious of exquisite pleasures, to accept any speculations about life in exchange for life itself. To us the *citta divina** is colourless, and the *fruitio Dei*† without

---

* Heavenly city (Italian).

† Scholastic term for "the enjoyment of God." Wilde had copied this phrase into his undergraduate Oxford copybook.

meaning. Metaphysics do not satisfy our temperaments, and religious ecstasy is out of date. The world through which the Academic philosopher becomes "the spectator of all time and of all existence" is not really an ideal world, but simply a world of abstract ideas. When we enter it, we starve amidst the chill mathematics of thought. The courts of the city of God are not open to us now. Its gates are guarded by Ignorance, and to pass them we have to surrender all that in our nature is most divine. It is enough that our fathers believed. They have exhausted the faith-faculty of the species. Their legacy to us is the scepticism of which they were afraid. Had they put it into words, it might not live within us as thought. No, Ernest, no. We cannot go back to the saint. There is far more to be learned from the sinner. We cannot go back to the philosopher, and the mystic leads us astray. Who, as Mr. Pater suggests somewhere, would exchange the curve of a single rose-leaf for that formless intangible Being which Plato rates so high? What to us is the Illumination of Philo, the Abyss of Eckhart, the Vision of Böhme, the monstrous Heaven itself that was revealed to Swedenborg's* blinded eyes? Such things are less than the yellow trumpet of one daffodil of the field, far less than the meanest of the visible arts; for, just as Nature is matter struggling into mind, so Art is mind expressing itself under the conditions of matter, and thus, even in the lowliest of her manifestations, she speaks to both sense and soul alike. To the æsthetic temperament the vague is always repellent. The Greeks were a nation of artists, because they were spared the sense of the infinite. Like Aristotle, like Goethe after he had read Kant, we desire the concrete, and nothing but the concrete can satisfy us.

ERNEST. What then do you propose?

GILBERT. It seems to me that with the development of the critical spirit we shall be able to realize, not merely our own lives, but the collective life of the race, and so to make ourselves absolutely modern,

---

* Wilde cites several mystical thinkers from antiquity to the modern period. Ralph Waldo Emerson was especially concerned with the thought of Swedish scientist, philosopher and Christian mystic Emanuel Swedenborg (1688–1772).

in the true meaning of the word modernity. For he to whom the present is the only thing that is present, knows nothing of the age in which he lives. To realize the nineteenth century, one must realize every century that has preceded it and that has contributed to its making. To know anything about oneself, one must know all about others. There must be no mood with which one cannot sympathize, no dead mode of life that one cannot make alive. Is this impossible? I think not. By revealing to us the absolute mechanism of all action, and so freeing us from the self-imposed and trammelling burden of moral responsibility, the scientific principle of Heredity has become, as it were, the warrant for the contemplative life. It has shown us that we are never less free than when we try to act. It has hemmed us round with the nets of the hunter, and written upon the wall the prophecy of our doom. We may not watch it, for it is within us. We may not see it, save in a mirror that mirrors the soul. It is Nemesis without her mask. It is the last of the Fates, and the most terrible. It is the only one of the Gods whose real name we know.

And yet, while in thc sphere of practical and external life it has robbed energy of its freedom and activity of its choice, in the subjective sphere, where the soul is at work, it comes to us, this terrible shadow, with many gifts in its hands, gifts of strange temperaments and subtle susceptibilities, gifts of wild ardours and chill moods of indifference, complex multiform gifts of thoughts that are at variance with each other, and passions that war against themselves. And so, it is not our own life that we live, but the lives of the dead, and the soul that dwells within us is no single spiritual entity, making us personal and individual, created for our service, and entering into us for our joy. It is something that has dwelt in fearful places, and in ancient sepulchres has made its abode. It is sick with many maladies, and has memories of curious sins. It is wiser than we are, and its wisdom is bitter. It fills us with impossible desires, and makes us follow what we know we cannot gain. One thing, however, Ernest, it can do for us. It can lead us away from surroundings whose beauty is dimmed to us by the mist of familiarity, or whose ignoble ugliness and sordid claims are marring the perfection of our development. It can help us to leave the age in which we were born, and to pass into other ages, and find ourselves not exiled from their air.

It can teach us how to escape from our experience, and to realize the experiences of those who are greater than we are. The pain of Leopardi crying out against life becomes our pain. Theocritus blows on his pipe, and we laugh with the lips of nymph and shepherd. In the wolfskin of Pierre Vidal we flee before the hounds, and in the armour of Lancelot we ride from the bower of the Queen. We have whispered the secret of our love beneath the cowl of Abelard, and in the stained raiment of Villon have put our shame into song. We can see the dawn through Shelley's eyes, and when we wander with Endymion the Moon grows amorous of our youth. Ours is the anguish of Atys, and ours the weak rage and noble sorrows of the Dane. Do you think that it is the imagination that enables us to live these countless lives? Yes: it is the imagination; and the imagination is the result of heredity. It is simply concentrated race-experience.

ERNEST. But where in this is the function of the critical spirit?

GILBERT. The culture that this transmission of racial experiences makes possible can be made perfect by the critical spirit alone, and indeed may be said to be one with it. For who is the true critic but he who bears within himself the dreams, and ideas, and feelings of myriad generations, and to whom no form of thought is alien, no emotional impulse obscure? And who the true man of culture, if not he who by fine scholarship and fastidious rejection has made instinct self-conscious and intelligent, and can separate the work that has distinction from the work that has it not, and so by contact and comparison makes himself master of the secrets of style and school, and understands their meanings, and listens to their voices, and develops that spirit of disinterested curiosity which is the real root, as it is the real flower, of the intellectual life, and thus attains to intellectual clarity, and, having learned "the best that is known and thought in the world," lives—it is not fanciful to say so—with those who are the Immortals.

Yes, Ernest: the contemplative life, the life that has for its aim not *doing* but *being*, and not *being* merely, but *becoming*—that is what the critical spirit can give us. The gods live thus: either brooding over their own perfection, as Aristotle tells us, or, as Epicurus fancied, watching with the calm eyes of the spectator the tragi-comedy of the world that they have made. We, too, might live like them, and set ourselves to witness with appropriate emotions the varied scenes that man and nature afford. We might make ourselves spiritual by detaching ourselves from action, and become perfect by the rejection of energy. It has often seemed to me that Browning felt something of this. Shakespeare hurls Hamlet into active life, and makes him realize his mission by effort. Browning might have given us a Hamlet who would have realized his mission by thought. Incident and event were to him unreal or unmeaning. He made the soul the protagonist of life's tragedy, and looked on action as the one undramatic element of a play. To us, at any rate, the ΒΙΟΣ ΘΕΩΡΗΤΙΚΟΣ* is the true ideal. From the high tower of Thought we can look out at the world. Calm, and self-centred, and complete, the æsthetic critic contemplates life, and no arrow drawn at a venture can pierce between the joints of his harness. He at least is safe. He has discovered how to live.

Is such a mode of life immoral? Yes: all the arts are immoral, except those baser forms of sensual or didactic art that seek to excite to action of evil or of good. For action of every kind belongs to the sphere of ethics. The aim of art is simply to create a mood. Is such a mode of life unpractical? Ah! it is not so easy to be unpractical as the ignorant Philistine imagines. It were well for England if it were so. There is no country in the world so much in need of unpractical people as this country of ours. With us, Thought is degraded by its constant association with practice. Who that moves in the stress and turmoil of actual existence, noisy politician, or brawling social reformer, or poor narrow-minded priest blinded by the sufferings of that unimportant section of the community among whom he has cast his lot, can seriously claim to be able to form a disinterested intellectual judgment about any one thing? Each of the professions means a prejudice. The necessity for a career forces every one to take sides. We live in the age of the overworked, and the undereducated; the age in which people are so industrious that they become absolutely stupid. And, harsh though it may sound, I cannot help saying that such

* The life of the mind, or of theory (Greek).

people deserve their doom. The sure way of knowing nothing about life is to try to make oneself useful.

ERNEST. A charming doctrine, Gilbert.

GILBERT. I am not sure about that, but it has at least the minor merit of being true. That the desire to do good to others produces a plentiful crop of prigs is the least of the evils of which it is the cause. The prig is a very interesting psychological study, and though of all poses a moral pose is the most offensive, still to have a pose at all is something. It is a formal recognition of the importance of treating life from a definite and reasoned standpoint. That Humanitarian Sympathy wars against Nature, by securing the survival of the failure, may make the man of science loathe its facile virtues. The political economist may cry out against it for putting the improvident on the same level as the provident, and so robbing life of the strongest, because most sordid, incentive to industry. But, in the eyes of the thinker, the real harm that emotional sympathy does is that it limits knowledge, and so prevents us from solving any single social problem. We are trying at present to stave off the coming crisis, the coming revolution as my friends the Fabianists call it, by means of doles and alms. Well, when the revolution or crisis arrives, we shall be powerless because we shall know nothing. And so, Ernest, let us not be deceived. England will never be civilized till she has added Utopia to her dominions. There is more than one of her colonies that she might with advantage surrender for so fair a land. What we want are unpractical people who see beyond the moment, and think beyond the day. Those who try to lead the people can only do so by following the mob. It is through the voice of one crying in the wilderness that the ways of the gods must be prepared.

But perhaps you think that in beholding for the mere joy of beholding, and contemplating for the sake of contemplation, there is something that is egotistic. If you think so, do not say so. It takes a thoroughly selfish age, like our own, to deify self-sacrifice. It takes a thoroughly grasping age, such as that in which we live, to set above the fine intellectual virtues, those shallow and emotional virtues that are an immediate practical benefit to itself. They miss their aim, too, these philanthropists and sentimentalists of our day, who are always chattering to one about one's duty to one's neighbour. For the development of the race depends on the development of the individual, and where self-culture has ceased to be the ideal, the intellectual standard is instantly lowered, and, often, ultimately lost. If you meet at dinner a man who has spent his life in educating himself—a rare type in our time, I admit, but still one occasionally to be met with—you rise from table richer, and conscious that a high ideal has for a moment touched and sanctified your days. But oh! my dear Ernest, to sit next a man who has spent his life in trying to educate others! What a dreadful experience that is! How appalling is that ignorance which is the inevitable result of the fatal habit of imparting opinions! How limited in range the creature's mind proves to be! How it wearies us, and must weary himself, with its endless repetitions and sickly reiteration! How lacking it is in any element of intellectual growth! In what a vicious circle it always moves!

ERNEST. You speak with strange feeling, Gilbert. Have you had this dreadful experience, as you call it, lately?

GILBERT. Few of us escape it. People say that the schoolmaster is abroad. I wish to goodness he were. But the type of which, after all, he is only one, and certainly the least important, of the representatives, seems to me to be really dominating our lives; and just as the philanthropist is the nuisance of the ethical sphere, so the nuisance of the intellectual sphere is the man who is so occupied in trying to educate others, that he has never had any time to educate himself. No, Ernest, self-culture is the true ideal of man. Goethe saw it, and the immediate debt that we owe to Goethe is greater than the debt we owe to any man since Greek days. The Greeks saw it, and have left us, as their legacy to modern thought, the conception of the contemplative life as well as the critical method by which alone can that life be truly realized. It was the one thing that made the Renaissance great, and gave us Humanism. It is the one thing that could make our own age great also; for the real weakness of England lies, not in incomplete armaments or unfortified coasts, not in the poverty that creeps through sunless lanes, or the drunkenness that brawls in loathsome courts, but simply in the fact that her ideals are emotional and not intellectual.

I do not deny that the intellectual ideal is difficult of attainment, still less that it is, and perhaps will be for years to come, unpopular with the crowd. It is so easy for people to have sympathy with suffering. It is so difficult for them to have sympathy with thought. Indeed, so little do ordinary people understand what thought really is, that they seem to imagine that, when they have said that a theory is dangerous, they have pronounced its condemnation, whereas it is only such theories that have any true intellectual value. An idea that is not dangerous is unworthy of being called an idea at all.

ERNEST. Gilbert, you bewilder me. You have told me that all art is, in its essence, immoral. Are you going to tell me now that all thought is, in its essence, dangerous?

GILBERT. Yes, in the practical sphere it is so. The security of society lies in custom and unconscious instinct, and the basis of the stability of society, as a healthy organism, is the complete absence of any intelligence amongst its members. The great majority of people being fully aware of this, rank themselves naturally on the side of that splendid system that elevates them to the dignity of machines, and rage so wildly against the intrusion of the intellectual faculty into any question that concerns life, that one is tempted to define man as a rational animal who always loses his temper when he is called upon to act in accordance with the dictates of reason. But let us turn from the practical sphere, and say no more about the wicked philanthropists, who, indeed, may well be left to the mercy of the almond-eyed sage of the Yellow River, Chuang Tsŭ the wise, who has proved that such well-meaning and offensive busy-bodies have destroyed the simple and spontaneous virtue that there is in man. They are a wearisome topic, and I am anxious to get back to the sphere in which criticism is free.

ERNEST. The sphere of the intellect?

GILBERT. Yes. You remember that I spoke of the critic as being in his own way as creative as the artist, whose work, indeed, may be merely of value in so far as it gives to the critic a suggestion for some new mood of thought and feeling which he can realize with equal, or perhaps greater, distinction of form, and, through the use of a fresh medium of expression, make differently beautiful and more perfect. Well, you seemed to me to be a little sceptical about the theory. But perhaps I wronged you?

Ernest. I am not really sceptical about it, but I must admit that I feel very strongly that such work as you describe the critic producing—and creative such work must undoubtedly be admitted to be—is, of necessity, purely subjective, whereas the greatest work is objective always, objective and impersonal.

Gilbert. The difference between objective and subjective work is one of external form merely. It is accidental, not essential. All artistic creation is absolutely subjective. The very landscape that Corot looked at was, as he said himself, but a mood of his own mind; and those great figures of Greek or English drama that seem to us to possess an actual existence of their own, apart from the poets who shaped and fashioned them, are, in their ultimate analysis, simply the poets themselves, not as they thought they were, but as they thought they were not; and by such thinking came in strange manner, though but for a moment, really so to be. For out of ourselves we can never pass, nor can there be in creation what in the creator was not. Nay, I would say that the more objective a creation appears to be, the more subjective it really is. Shakespeare might have met Rosencrantz and Guildenstern in the white streets of London, or seen the serving-men of rival houses bite their thumbs at each other in the open square; but Hamlet came out of his soul, and Romeo out of his passion. They were elements of his nature to which he gave visible form, impulses that stirred so strongly within him that he had, as it were perforce, to suffer them to realize their energy, not on the lower plane of actual life, where they would have been trammelled and constrained and so made imperfect, but on that imaginative plane of art where Love can indeed find in Death its rich fulfilment, where one can stab the eavesdropper behind the arras, and wrestle in a new-made grave, and make a guilty king drink his own hurt, and see one's father's spirit, beneath the glimpses of the moon, stalking in complete steel from misty wall to wall. Action being limited would have left Shakespeare unsatisfied and unexpressed; and, just as it is because he did nothing that he has been able to achieve everything, so it is because he never speaks to us of himself in his plays that his plays reveal him to us absolutely, and show us his true nature and temperament far more completely than do those strange and exquisite sonnets, even, in which he bares to crystal eyes the secret closet of his heart. Yes, the objective form is the most subjective in matter. Man is least himself when he talks in his own person. Give him a mask, and he will tell you the truth.

ERNEST. The critic, then, being limited to the subjective form, will necessarily be less able to fully express himself than the artist, who has always at his disposal the forms that are impersonal and objective.

GILBERT. Not necessarily, and certainly not at all if he recognizes that each mode of criticism is, in its highest development, simply a mood, and that we are never more true to ourselves than when we are inconsistent. The æsthetic critic, constant only to the principle of beauty in all things, will ever be looking for fresh impressions, winning from the various schools the secret of their charm, bowing, it may be, before foreign altars, or smiling, if it be his fancy, at strange new gods. What other people call one's past has, no doubt, everything to do with them, but has absolutely nothing to do with oneself. The man who regards his past is a man who deserves to have no future to look forward to. When one has found expression for a mood, one has done with it. You laugh; but believe me it is so. Yesterday it was Realism that charmed one. One gained from it that *nouveau frisson** which it was its aim to produce. One analyzed it, explained it, and wearied of it. At sunset came the *Luministe* in painting, and the *Symboliste* in poetry, and the spirit of mediævalism, that spirit which belongs not to time but to temperament, woke suddenly in wounded Russia, and stirred us for a moment by the terrible fascination of pain. To-day the cry is for Romance, and already the leaves are tremulous in the valley, and on the purple hill-tops walks Beauty with slim gilded feet. The old modes of creation linger, of course. The artists reproduce either themselves or each other, with wearisome iteration. But Criticism is always moving on, and the critic is always developing.

Nor, again, is the critic really limited to the subjective form of expression. The method of the drama is his, as well as the method of the epos. He may use dialogue, as he did who set Milton talking to

* New thrill (French).

Marvel on the nature of comedy and tragedy, and made Sidney and Lord Brooke discourse on letters beneath the Penshurst oaks;* or adopt narration, as Mr. Pater is fond of doing, each of whose Imaginary Portraits—is not that the title of the book?—presents to us, under the fanciful guise of fiction, some fine and exquisite piece of criticism, one on the painter Watteau, another on the philosophy of Spinoza, a third on the Pagan elements of the early Renaissance, and the last, and in some respects the most suggestive, on the source of that Aufklärung, that enlightening which dawned on Germany in the last century, and to which our own culture owes so great a debt. Dialogue, certainly, that wonderful literary form which, from Plato to Lucian, and from Lucian to Giordano Bruno, and from Bruno to that grand old Pagan in whom Carlyle took such delight, the creative critics of the world have always employed, can never lose for the thinker its attraction as a mode of expression. By its means he can both reveal and conceal himself, and give form to every fancy, and reality to every mood. By its means he can exhibit the object from each point of view, and show it to us in the round, as a sculptor shows us things, gaining in this manner all the richness and reality of effect that comes from those side issues that are suddenly suggested by the central idea in its progress, and really illumine the idea more completely, or from those felicitous after-thoughts that give a fuller completeness to the central scheme, and yet convey something of the delicate charm of chance.

Ernest. By its means, too, he can invent an imaginary antagonist, and convert him when he chooses by some absurdly sophistical argument.

Gilbert. Ah! it is so easy to convert others. It is so difficult to convert oneself. To arrive at what one really believes, one must speak through lips different from one's own. To know the truth one must imagine myriads of falsehoods. For what is Truth? In matters of religion, it is simply the opinion that has survived. In matters of science, it is the ultimate sensation. In matters of art, it is one's last mood.

---

* Wilde is alluding to Walter Savage Landor (1775–1864), poet and author of *Imaginary Conversations*.

And you see now, Ernest, that the critic has at his disposal as many objective forms of expression as the artist has. Ruskin put his criticism into imaginative prose, and is superb in his changes and contradictions; and Browning put his into blank verse, and made painter and poet yield us their secret; and M. Renan uses dialogue, and Mr. Pater fiction, and Rossetti translated into sonnet-music the colour of Giorgione and the design of Ingres, and his own design and colour also, feeling, with the instinct of one who had many modes of utterance, that the ultimate art is literature, and the finest and fullest medium that of words.

ERNEST. Well, now that you have settled that the critic has at his disposal all objective forms, I wish you would tell me what are the qualities that should characterize the true critic.

GILBERT. What would you say they were?

ERNEST. Well, I should say that a critic should above all things be fair.

GILBERT. Ah! not fair. A critic cannot be fair in the ordinary sense of the word. It is only about things that do not interest one that one can give a really unbiassed opinion, which is no doubt the reason why an unbiassed opinion is always absolutely valueless. The man who sees both sides of a question, is a man who sees absolutely nothing at all. Art is a passion, and, in matters of art, Thought is inevitably coloured by emotion, and so is fluid rather than fixed, and, depending upon fine moods and exquisite moments, cannot be narrowed into the rigidity of a scientific formula or a theological dogma. It is to the soul that Art speaks, and the soul may be made the prisoner of the mind as well as of the body. One should, of course, have no prejudices; but, as a great Frenchman remarked a hundred years ago, it is one's business in such matters to have preferences, and when one has preferences one ceases to be fair. It is only an auctioneer who can equally and impartially admire all schools of Art. No: fairness is not one of the qualities of the true critic. It is not even a condition of criticism. Each form of Art with which we come in contact dominates us for the moment to the exclusion of every other form. We must surrender ourselves absolutely to the work in question, whatever it may be, if we wish to gain its secret. For the time, we must think of nothing else, can think of nothing else, indeed.

ERNEST. The true critic will be rational, at any rate, will he not?

GILBERT. Rational? There are two ways of disliking art, Ernest. One is to dislike it. The other, to like it rationally. For Art, as Plato saw, and not without regret, creates in listener and spectator a form of divine madness. It does not spring from inspiration, but it makes others inspired. Reason is not the faculty to which it appeals. If one loves Art at all, one must love it beyond all other things in the world, and against such love, the reason, if one listened to it, would cry out. There is nothing sane about the worship of beauty. It is too splendid to be sane. Those of whose lives it forms the dominant note will always seem to the world to be pure visionaries.

ERNEST. Well, at least, the critic will be sincere.

GILBERT. A little sincerity is a dangerous thing, and a great deal of it is absolutely fatal. The true critic will, indeed, always be sincere in his devotion to the principle of beauty, but he will seek for beauty in every age and in each school, and will never suffer himself to be limited to any settled custom of thought, or stereotyped mode of looking at things. He will realize himself in many forms, and by a thousand different ways, and will ever be curious of new sensations and fresh points of view. Through constant change, and through constant change alone, he will find his true unity. He will not consent to be the slave of his own opinions. For what is mind but motion in the intellectual sphere? The essence of thought, as the essence of life, is growth. You must not be frightened by words, Ernest. What people call insincerity is simply a method by which we can multiply our personalities.

ERNEST. I am afraid I have not been fortunate in my suggestions.

GILBERT. Of the three qualifications you mentioned, two, sincerity and fairness, were, if not actually moral, at least on the borderland of morals, and the first condition of criticism is that the critic should be able to recognize that the sphere of Art and the sphere of Ethics are absolutely distinct and separate. When they are confused, Chaos has come again. They are too often confused in England now, and though our modern Puritans cannot destroy a beautiful thing, yet, by means of their extraordinary prurience, they can almost taint beauty for a moment. It is chiefly, I regret to say, through journalism that such people find expression. I regret it because there is much to be said in favour of modern journalism. By giving us the opinions of the uneducated, it keeps us in touch with the ignorance of the community. By carefully chronicling the current events of contemporary life, it shows us of what very little importance such events really are. By invariably discussing the unnecessary, it makes us understand what things are requisite for culture, and what are not. But it should not allow poor Tartuffe* to write articles upon modern art. When it does this it stultifies itself. And yet Tartuffe's articles, and Chadband's notes do this good, at least. They serve to show how extremely limited is the area over which ethics, and ethical considerations, can claim to exercise influence. Science is out of the reach of morals, for her eyes are fixed upon eternal truths. Art is out of the reach of morals, for her eyes are fixed upon things beautiful and immortal and ever-changing. To morals belong the lower and less intellectual spheres. However, let these mouthing Puritans pass; they have their comic side. Who can help laughing when an ordinary journalist seriously proposes to limit the subject-matter at the disposal of the artist? Some limitation might well, and will soon, I hope, be placed upon some of our newspapers and newspaper writers. For they give us the bald, sordid, disgusting facts of life. They chronicle, with degrading avidity, the sins of the second-rate, and with the conscientiousness of the illiterate give us accurate and prosaic details of the doings of people of absolutely no interest whatsoever. But the artist, who accepts the facts of life, and yet transforms them into shapes of beauty, and makes them vehicles of pity or of awe, and shows their colour-element, and their wonder, and their true ethical import also, and builds out of them a world more real than reality itself, and of loftier and more noble import—who shall set limits to him? Not the apostles of that new Journalism which is but the old vulgarity "writ large." Not the apostles of that new Puritanism, which is but the whine of the hypocrite, and is both writ and spoken badly. The mere suggestion is ridiculous. Let us leave these wicked people,

---

* The greatest of dramatic hypocrites; the falsely pious subject of Molière's play *Tartuffe*, performed at the court of Louis XIV in 1664.

and proceed to the discussion of the artistic qualifications necessary for the true critic.

Ernest. And what are they? Tell me yourself.

Gilbert. Temperament is the primary requisite for the critic—a temperament exquisitely susceptible to beauty, and to the various impressions that beauty gives us. Under what conditions, and by what means, this temperament is engendered in race or individual, we will not discuss at present. It is sufficient to note that it exists, and that there is in us a beauty-sense, separate from the other senses and above them, separate from the reason and of nobler import, separate from the soul and of equal value—a sense that leads some to create, and others, the finer spirits as I think, to contemplate merely. But to be purified and made perfect, this sense requires some form of exquisite environment. Without this it starves, or is dulled. You remember that lovely passage in which Plato describes how a young Greek should be educated, and with what insistence he dwells upon the importance of surroundings, telling us how the lad is to be brought up in the midst of fair sights and sounds, so that the beauty of material things may prepare his soul for the reception of the beauty that is spiritual. Insensibly, and without knowing the reason why, he is to develop that real love of beauty which, as Plato is never weary of reminding us, is the true aim of education. By slow degrees there is to be engendered in him such a temperament as will lead him naturally and simply to choose the good in preference to the bad, and, rejecting what is vulgar and discordant, to follow by fine instinctive taste all that possesses grace and charm and loveliness. Ultimately, in its due course, this taste is to become critical and self-conscious, but at first it is to exist purely as a cultivated instinct, and "he who has received this true culture of the inner man will with clear and certain vision perceive the omissions and faults in art or nature, and with a taste that cannot err, while he praises, and finds his pleasure in what is good, and receives it into his soul, and so becomes good and noble, he will rightly blame and hate the bad, now in the days of his youth, even before he is able to know the reason why:" and so, when, later on, the critical and self-conscious spirit develops in him, he "will recognize and salute it as a friend with whom his education has made him long familiar." I need hardly say, Ernest, how far we in England have fallen short of this ideal, and I can imagine the smile that would illuminate the glossy face of the Philistine if one ventured to suggest to him that the true aim of education was the love of beauty, and that the methods by which education should work were the development of temperament, the cultivation of taste, and the creation of the critical spirit.

Yet, even for us, there is left some loveliness of environment, and the dulness of tutors and professors matters very little when one can loiter in the grey cloisters at Magdalen, and listen to some flute-like voice singing in Waynfleete's chapel, or lie in the green meadow, among the strange snake-spotted fritillaries, and watch the sunburnt noon smite to a finer gold the tower's gilded vanes, or wander up the Christ Church staircase beneath the vaulted ceiling's shadowy fans, or pass through the sculptured gateway of Laud's building in the College of St. John. Nor is it merely at Oxford, or Cambridge, that the sense of beauty can be formed and trained and perfected. All over England there is a Renaissance of the decorative Arts. Ugliness has had its day. Even in the houses of the rich there is taste, and the houses of those who are not rich have been made gracious and comely and sweet to live in. Caliban, poor noisy Caliban, thinks that when he has ceased to make mows at a thing, the thing ceases to exist. But if he mocks no longer, it is because he has been met with mockery, swifter and keener than his own, and for a moment has been bitterly schooled into that silence which should seal for ever his uncouth distorted lips. What has been done up to now, has been chiefly in the clearing of the way. It is always more difficult to destroy than it is to create, and when what one has to destroy is vulgarity and stupidity, the task of destruction needs not merely courage but also contempt. Yet it seems to me to have been, in a measure, done. We have got rid of what was bad. We have now to make what is beautiful. And though the mission of the æsthetic movement is to lure people to contemplate, not to lead them to create, yet, as the creative instinct is strong in the Celt, and it is the Celt who leads in art, there is no reason why in future years this strange Renaissance should not become almost as mighty in its way as was that new birth of Art that woke many centuries ago in the cities of Italy.

Certainly, for the cultivation of temperament, we must turn to the decorative arts: to the arts that touch us, not to the arts that teach us. Modern pictures are, no doubt, delightful to look at. At least, some of them are. But they are quite impossible to live with; they are too clever, too assertive, too intellectual. Their meaning is too obvious, and their method too clearly defined. One exhausts what they have to say in a very short time, and then they become as tedious as one's relations. I am very fond of the work of many of the Impressionist painters of Paris and London. Subtlety and distinction have not yet left the school. Some of their arrangements and harmonies serve to remind one of the unapproachable beauty of Gautier's immortal *Symphonie en Blanc Majeur*, that flawless masterpiece of colour and music which may have suggested the type as well as the titles of many of their best pictures. For a class that welcomes the incompetent with sympathetic eagerness, and that confuses the bizarre with the beautiful, and vulgarity with truth, they are extremely accomplished. They can do etchings that have the brilliancy of epigrams, pastels that are as fascinating as paradoxes, and as for their portraits, whatever the commonplace may say against them, no one can deny that they possess that unique and wonderful charm which belongs to works of pure fiction. But even the Impressionists, earnest and industrious as they are, will not do. I like them. Their white keynote, with its variations in lilac, was an era in colour. Though the moment does not make the man, the moment certainly makes the Impressionist, and for the moment in art, and the "moment's monument" as Rossetti phrased it, what may not be said? They are suggestive also. If they have not opened the eyes of the blind, they have at least given great encouragement to the short-sighted, and while their leaders may have all the inexperience of old age, their young men are far too wise to be ever sensible. Yet they will insist on treating painting as if it were a mode of autobiography invented for the use of the illiterate, and are always prating to us on their coarse gritty canvases of their unnecessary selves and their unnecessary opinions, and spoiling by a vulgar over-emphasis that fine contempt of nature which is the best and only modest thing about them. One tires, at the end, of the work of individuals whose individuality is always noisy, and generally uninteresting. There is far more to be said in favour of that newer school at Paris, the *Archaicistes*, as they call themselves, who, refusing to leave the artist entirely at the mercy of the weather, do not find the ideal of art in mere atmospheric effect, but seek rather for the imaginative beauty of design and the loveliness of fair colour, and rejecting the tedious realism of those who merely paint what they see, try to see something worth seeing, and to see it not merely with actual and physical vision, but with that nobler vision of the soul which is as far wider in spiritual scope as it is far more splendid in artistic purpose. They, at any rate, work under those decorative conditions that each art requires for its perfection, and have sufficient æsthetic instinct to regret those sordid and stupid limitations of absolute modernity of form which have proved the ruin of so many of the Impressionists. Still, the art that is frankly decorative is the art to live with. It is, of all visible arts, the one art that creates in us both mood and temperament. Mere colour, unspoiled by meaning, and unallied with definite form, can speak to the soul in a thousand different ways. The harmony that resides in the delicate proportions of lines and masses becomes mirrored in the mind. The repetitions of pattern give us rest. The marvels of design stir the imagination. In the mere loveliness of the materials employed there are latent elements of culture. Nor is this all. By its deliberate rejection of Nature as the ideal of beauty, as well as of the imitative method of the ordinary painter, decorative art not merely prepares the soul for the reception of true imaginative work, but develops in it that sense of form which is the basis of creative no less than of critical achievement. For the real artist is he who proceeds, not from feeling to form, but from form to thought and passion. He does not first conceive an idea, and then say to himself, "I will put my idea into a complex metre of fourteen lines," but, realizing the beauty of the sonnet-scheme, he conceives certain modes of music and methods of rhyme, and the mere form suggests what is to fill it and make it intellectually and emotionally complete. From time to time the world cries out against some charming artistic poet, because, to use its hackneyed and silly phrase, he has "nothing to say." But if he had something to say, he would probably say it, and the result would be tedious. It is just because he has no new message, that he can do beautiful work.

He gains his inspiration from form, and from form purely, as an artist should. A real passion would ruin him. Whatever actually occurs is spoiled for art. All bad poetry springs from genuine feeling. To be natural is to be obvious, and to be obvious is to be inartistic.

ERNEST. I wonder do you really believe what you say.

GILBERT. Why should you wonder? It is not merely in art that the body is the soul. In every sphere of life Form is the beginning of things. The rhythmic harmonious gestures of dancing convey, Plato tells us, both rhythm and harmony into the mind. Forms are the food of faith, cried Newman in one of those great moments of sincerity that made us admire and know the man. He was right, though he may not have known how terribly right he was. The Creeds are believed, not because they are rational, but because they are repeated. Yes: Form is everything. It is the secret of life. Find expression for a sorrow, and it will become dear to you. Find expression for a joy, and you intensify its ecstasy. Do you wish to love? Use Love's Litany, and the words will create the yearning from which the world fancies that they spring. Have you a grief that corrodes your heart? Steep yourself in the language of grief, learn its utterance from Prince Hamlet and Queen Constance, and you will find that mere expression is a mode of consolation, and that Form, which is the birth of passion, is also the death of pain. And so, to return to the sphere of Art, it is Form that creates not merely the critical temperament, but also the æsthetic instinct, that unerring instinct that reveals to one all things under their conditions of beauty. Start with the worship of form, and there is no secret in art that will not be revealed to you, and remember that in criticism, as in creation, temperament is everything, and that it is, not by the time of their production, but by the temperaments to which they appeal, that the schools of art should be historically grouped.

ERNEST. Your theory of education is delightful. But what influence will your critic, brought up in these exquisite surroundings, possess? Do you really think that any artist is ever affected by criticism?

GILBERT. The influence of the critic will be the mere fact of his own existence. He will represent the flawless type. In him the culture of the century will see itself realized. You must not ask of him to have any aim other than the perfecting of himself. The demand of the intellect, as has been well said, is simply to feel itself alive. The critic may, indeed, desire to exercise influence; but, if so, he will concern himself not with the individual, but with the age, which he will seek to wake into consciousness, and to make responsive, creating in it new desires and appetites, and lending it his larger vision and his nobler moods. The actual art of to-day will occupy him less than the art of to-morrow, far less than the art of yesterday, and as for this or that person at present toiling away, what do the industrious matter? They do their best, no doubt, and consequently we get the worst from them. It is always with the best intentions that the worst work is done. And besides, my dear Ernest, when a man reaches the age of forty, or becomes a Royal Academician, or is elected a member of the Athenæum Club, or is recognized as a popular novelist, whose books are in great demand at suburban railway stations, one may have the amusement of exposing him, but one cannot have the pleasure of reforming him. And this is, I dare say, very fortunate for him; for I have no doubt that reformation is a much more painful process than punishment, is indeed punishment in its most aggravated and moral form—a fact which accounts for our entire failure as a community to reclaim that interesting phenomenon who is called the confirmed criminal.

ERNEST. But may it not be that the poet is the best judge of poetry, and the painter of painting? Each art must appeal primarily to the artist who works in it. His judgment will surely be the most valuable?

GILBERT. The appeal of all art is simply to the artistic temperament. Art does not address herself to the specialist. Her claim is that she is universal, and that in all her manifestations she is one. Indeed, so far from its being true that the artist is the best judge of art, a really great artist can never judge of other people's work at all, and can hardly, in fact, judge of his own. That very concentration of vision that makes a man an artist, limits by its sheer intensity his faculty of fine appreciation. The energy of creation hurries him blindly on to his own goal. The wheels of his chariot raise the dust as a cloud around him. The gods are hidden from each other. They can recognize their worshippers. That is all.

ERNEST. You say that a great artist cannot recognize the beauty of work different from his own.

GILBERT. It is impossible for him to do so. Wordsworth saw in *Endymion* merely a pretty piece of Paganism, and Shelley, with his dislike of actuality, was deaf to Wordsworth's message, being repelled by its form, and Byron, that great passionate human incomplete creature, could appreciate neither the poet of the cloud nor the poet of the lake, and the wonder of Keats was hidden from him. The realism of Euripides was hateful to Sophokles. Those droppings of warm tears had no music for him. Milton, with his sense of the grand style, could not understand the method of Shakespeare, any more than could Sir Joshua the method of Gainsborough.* Bad artists always admire each other's work. They call it being large-minded and free from prejudice. But a truly great artist cannot conceive of life being shown, or beauty fashioned, under any conditions other than those that he has selected. Creation employs all its critical faculty within its own sphere. It may not use it in the sphere that belongs to others. It is exactly because a man cannot do a thing that he is the proper judge of it.

ERNEST. Do you really mean that?

GILBERT. Yes, for creation limits, while contemplation widens, the vision.

ERNEST. But what about technique? Surely each art has its separate technique?

GILBERT. Certainly: each art has its grammar and its materials. There is no mystery about either, and the incompetent can always be correct. But, while the laws upon which Art rests may be fixed and certain, to find their true realization they must be touched by the imagination into such beauty that they will seem an exception, each one of them. Technique is really personality. That is the reason why the artist cannot teach it, why the pupil cannot learn it, and why the æsthetic critic can understand it. To the great poet, there is only one

* Sir Joshua Reynolds and Thomas Gainsborough, two of the greatest eighteenth-century English painters.

method of music—his own. To the great painter, there is only one manner of painting—that which he himself employs. The æsthetic critic, and the æsthetic critic alone, can appreciate all forms and modes. It is to him that Art makes her appeal.

ERNEST. Well, I think I have put all my questions to you. And now I must admit—

GILBERT. Ah! don't say that you agree with me. When people agree with me I always feel that I must be wrong.

ERNEST. In that case I certainly won't tell you whether I agree with you or not. But I will put another question. You have explained to me that criticism is a creative art. What future has it?

GILBERT. It is to criticism that the future belongs. The subject-matter at the disposal of creation becomes every day more limited in extent and variety. Providence and Mr. Walter Besant have exhausted the obvious. If creation is to last at all, it can only do so on the condition of becoming far more critical than it is at present. The old roads and dusty highways have been traversed too often. Their charm has been worn away by plodding feet, and they have lost that element of novelty or surprise which is so essential for romance. He who would stir us now by fiction must either give us an entirely new background, or reveal to us the soul of man in its innermost workings. The first is for the moment being done for us by Mr. Rudyard Kipling. As one turns over the pages of his *Plain Tales from the Hills*, one feels as if one were seated under a palm-tree reading life by superb flashes of vulgarity. The bright colours of the bazaars dazzle one's eyes. The jaded, second-rate Anglo-Indians are in exquisite incongruity with their surroundings. The mere lack of style in the story-teller gives an odd journalistic realism to what he tells us. From the point of view of literature Mr. Kipling is a genius who drops his aspirates. From the point of view of life, he is a reporter who knows vulgarity better than any one has ever known it. Dickens knew its clothes and its comedy. Mr. Kipling knows its essence and its seriousness. He is our first authority on the second-rate, and has seen marvellous things through keyholes, and his backgrounds are real works of art. As for the second condition, we have had Browning, and Meredith is with us. But there is still much to be done in the sphere of introspection. People sometimes say that fiction is getting too morbid. As far as psychology is concerned, it has never been morbid enough. We have merely touched the surface of the soul, that is all. In one single ivory cell of the brain there are stored away things more marvellous and more terrible than even they have dreamed of, who, like the author of *Le Rouge et le Noir,** have sought to track the soul into its most secret places, and to make life confess its dearest sins. Still, there is a limit even to the number of untried backgrounds, and it is possible that a further development of the habit of introspection may prove fatal to that creative faculty to which it seeks to supply fresh material. I myself am inclined to think that creation is doomed. It springs from too primitive, too natural an impulse. However this may be, it is certain that the subject-matter at the disposal of creation is always diminishing, while the subject-matter of criticism increases daily. There are always new attitudes for the mind, and new points of view. The duty of imposing form upon chaos does not grow less as the world advances. There was never a time when Criticism was more needed than it is now. It is only by its means that Humanity can become conscious of the point at which it has arrived.

Hours ago, Ernest, you asked me the use of Criticism. You might just as well have asked me the use of thought. It is Criticism, as Arnold points out, that creates the intellectual atmosphere of the age. It is Criticism, as I hope to point out myself some day, that makes the mind a fine instrument. We, in our educational system, have burdened the memory with a load of unconnected facts, and laboriously striven to impart our laboriously-acquired knowledge. We teach people how to remember, we never teach them how to grow. It has never occurred to us to try and develop in the mind a more subtle quality of apprehension and discernment. The Greeks did this, and when we come in contact with the Greek critical intellect, we cannot but be conscious that, while our subject-matter is in every respect larger and more varied than theirs, theirs is the only method by which this subject-matter can be interpreted. England has done one

* French writer Henri Beyle, author of *The Red and the Black* (1830), published his novels under the pseudonym Stendhal.

thing; it has invented and established Public Opinion, which is an attempt to organize the ignorance of the community, and to elevate it to the dignity of physical force. But Wisdom has always been hidden from it. Considered as an instrument of thought, the English mind is coarse and undeveloped. The only thing that can purify it is the growth of the critical instinct.

It is Criticism, again, that, by concentration, makes culture possible. It takes the cumbersome mass of creative work, and distils it into a finer essence. Who that desires to retain any sense of form could struggle through the monstrous multitudinous books that the world has produced, books in which thought stammers or ignorance brawls? The thread that is to guide us across the wearisome labyrinth is in the hands of Criticism. Nay more, where there is no record, and history is either lost or was never written, Criticism can recreate the past for us from the very smallest fragment of language or art, just as surely as the man of science can from some tiny bone, or the mere impress of a foot upon a rock, recreate for us the winged dragon or Titan lizard that once made the earth shake beneath its tread, can call Behemoth out of his cave, and make Leviathan swim once more across the startled sea. Prehistoric history belongs to the philological and archæological critic. It is to him that the origins of things are revealed. The self-conscious deposits of an age are nearly always misleading. Through philological criticism alone we know more of the centuries of which no actual record has been preserved, than we do of the centuries that have left us their scrolls. It can do for us what can be done neither by physics nor metaphysics. It can give us the exact science of mind in the process of becoming. It can do for us what History cannot do. It can tell us what man thought before he learned how to write. You have asked me about the influence of Criticism. I think I have answered that question already; but there is this also to be said. It is Criticism that makes us cosmopolitan. The Manchester school* tried to make men

---

* Nineteenth-century movement that espoused theories of free trade and laissez-faire economics, linked to such political analysts of industrial capitalism as Richard Cobden and John Bright.

realize the brotherhood of humanity, by pointing out the commercial advantages of peace. It sought to degrade the wonderful world into a common market-place for the buyer and the seller. It addressed itself to the lowest instincts, and it failed. War followed upon war, and the tradesman's creed did not prevent France and Germany from clashing together in blood-stained battle. There are others of our own day who seek to appeal to mere emotional sympathies, or to the shallow dogmas of some vague system of abstract ethics. They have their Peace Societies, so dear to the sentimentalists, and their proposals for unarmed International Arbitration, so popular among those who have never read history. But mere emotional sympathy will not do. It is too variable, and too closely connected with the passions; and a board of arbitrators who, for the general welfare of the race, are to be deprived of the power of putting their decisions into execution, will not be of much avail. There is only one thing worse than Injustice, and that is Justice without her sword in her hand. When Right is not Might, it is Evil.

No: the emotions will not make us cosmopolitan, any more than the greed for gain could do so. It is only by the cultivation of the habit of intellectual criticism that we shall be able to rise superior to race prejudices. Goethe—you will not misunderstand what I say—was a German of the Germans. He loved his country—no man more so. Its people were dear to him; and he led them. Yet, when the iron hoof of Napoleon trampled upon vineyard and cornfield, his lips were silent. "How can one write songs of hatred without hating?" he said to Eckerman,* "and how could I, to whom culture and barbarism are alone of importance, hate a nation which is among the most cultivated of the earth, and to which I owe so great a part of my own cultivation?" This note, sounded in the modern world by Goethe first, will become, I think, the starting point for the cosmopolitanism of the future. Criticism will annihilate race-prejudices, by insisting upon the unity of the human mind in the variety of its forms. If we

* Many of Goethe's most interesting remarks on life and literature are preserved in conversations with Johann Eckermann, recorded between 1823 and 1832.

are tempted to make war upon another nation, we shall remember that we are seeking to destroy an element of our own culture, and possibly its most important element. As long as war is regarded as wicked, it will always have its fascination. When it is looked upon as vulgar, it will cease to be popular. The change will, of course, be slow, and people will not be conscious of it. They will not say "We will not war against France because her prose is perfect," but because the prose of France is perfect, they will not hate the land. Intellectual criticism will bind Europe together in bonds far closer than those that can be forged by shopman or sentimentalist. It will give us the peace that springs from understanding.

Nor is this all. It is Criticism that, recognizing no position as final, and refusing to bind itself by the shallow shibboleths of any sect or school, creates that serene philosophic temper which loves truth for its own sake, and loves it not the less because it knows it to be unattainable. How little we have of this temper in England, and how much we need it! The English mind is always in a rage. The intellect of the race is wasted in the sordid and stupid quarrels of second-rate politicians or third-rate theologians. It was reserved for a man of science to show us the supreme example of that "sweet reasonableness" of which Arnold spoke so wisely, and alas! to so little effect. The author of the *Origin of Species* had, at any rate, the philosophic temper. If one contemplates the ordinary pulpits and platforms of England, one can but feel the contempt of Julian, or the indifference of Montaigne. We are dominated by the fanatic, whose worst vice is his sincerity. Anything approaching to the free play of the mind is practically unknown amongst us. People cry out against the sinner, yet it is not the sinful, but the stupid, who are our shame. There is no sin except stupidity.

ERNEST. Ah! what an antinomian you are!

GILBERT. The artistic critic, like the mystic, is an antinomian always. To be good, according to the vulgar standard of goodness, is obviously quite easy. It merely requires a certain amount of sordid terror, a certain lack of imaginative thought, and a certain low passion for middle-class respectability. Æsthetics are higher than ethics. They belong to a more spiritual sphere. To discern the beauty of a thing is the finest point to which we can arrive. Even a colour-sense is more important, in the development of the individual, than a sense of right and wrong. Æsthetics, in fact, are to Ethics in the sphere of conscious civilization, what, in the sphere of the external world, sexual is to natural selection. Ethics, like natural selection, make existence possible. Æsthetics, like sexual selection, make life lovely and wonderful, fill it with new forms, and give it progress, and variety and change. And when we reach the true culture that is our aim, we attain to that perfection of which the saints have dreamed, the perfection of those to whom sin is impossible, not because they make the renunciations of the ascetic, but because they can do everything they wish without hurt to the soul, and can wish for nothing that can do the soul harm, the soul being an entity so divine that it is able to transform into elements of a richer experience, or a finer susceptibility, or a newer mode of thought, acts or passions that with the common would be commonplace, or with the uneducated ignoble, or with the shameful vile. Is this dangerous? Yes; it is dangerous—all ideas, as I told you, are so. But the night wearies, and the light flickers in the lamp. One more thing I cannot help saying to you. You have spoken against Criticism as being a sterile thing. The nineteenth century is a turning point in history simply on account of the work of two men, Darwin and Renan, the one the critic of the Book of Nature, the other the critic of the books of God. Not to recognize this is to miss the meaning of one of the most important eras in the progress of the world. Creation is always behind the age. It is Criticism that leads us. The Critical Spirit and the World-Spirit are one.

Ernest. And he who is in possession of this spirit or whom this spirit possesses, will, I suppose, do nothing?

Gilbert. Like the Persephone of whom Landor tells us, the sweet pensive Persephone around whose white feet the asphodel and amaranth are blooming, he will sit contented "in that deep, motionless, quiet which mortals pity, and which the gods enjoy." He will look out upon the world and know its secret. By contact with divine things, he will become divine. His will be the perfect life, and his only.

Ernest. You have told me many strange things tonight, Gilbert. You have told me that it is more difficult to talk about a thing than to do it, and that to do nothing at all is the most difficult thing in the world; you have told me that all Art is immoral, and all thought dangerous; that criticism is more creative than creation, and that the highest criticism is that which reveals in the work of Art what the artist had not put there; that it is exactly because a man cannot do a thing that he is the proper judge of it; and that the true critic is unfair, insincere, not rational. My friend, you are a dreamer.

GILBERT. Yes: I am a dreamer. For a dreamer is one who can only find his way by moonlight, and his punishment is that he sees the dawn before the rest of the world.

ERNEST. His punishment?

GILBERT. And his reward. But see, it is dawn already. Draw back the curtains and open the windows wide. How cool the morning air is! Piccadilly lies at our feet like a long riband of silver. A faint purple mist hangs over the Park, and the shadows of the white houses are purple. It is too late to sleep. Let us go down to Covent Garden and look at the roses. Come! I am tired of thought.

THE TRUTH OF MASKS

A note on illusion

In many of the somewhat violent attacks that have recently been made on that splendour of mounting which now characterizes our Shakespearian revivals in England, it seems to have been tacitly assumed by the critics that Shakespeare himself was more or less indifferent to the costume of his actors, and that, could he see Mrs. Langtry's* production of *Antony and Cleopatra,* he would probably say that the play, and the play only, is the thing, and that everything else is leather and prunella. While, as regards any historical accuracy in dress, Lord Lytton,† in an article in the *Nineteenth Century,* has laid it down as a dogma of art that archæology is entirely out of place in the presentation of any of Shakespeare's plays, and the attempt to introduce it one of the stupidest pedantries of an age of prigs.

Lord Lytton's position I shall examine later on; but, as regards the theory that Shakespeare did not busy himself much about the costume-wardrobe of his theatre, anybody who cares to study Shakespeare's method will see that there is absolutely no dramatist of the French, English, or Athenian stage who relies so much for his illusionist effects on the dress of his actors as Shakespeare does himself.

Knowing how the artistic temperament is always fascinated by beauty of costume, he constantly introduces into his plays masques and dances, purely for the sake of the pleasure which they give the eye; and we have still his stage-directions for the three great processions in

---

* Wilde admired the beauty and dramatic skill of British actress Lily Langtry (1853–1929); she was known for her love affairs, including a liaison with the Prince of Wales.

† Edward Robert Bulwer-Lytton (1831–1891). In an 1884 article he attacked E. W. Godwin, who decorated Wilde's home.

*Henry the Eighth,** directions which are characterized by the most extraordinary elaborateness of detail down to the collars of S.S.† and the pearls in Anne Boleyn's hair. Indeed it would be quite easy for a modern manager to reproduce these pageants absolutely as Shakespeare had them designed; and so accurate were they that one of the Court officials of the time, writing an account of the last performance of the play at the Globe Theatre to a friend, actually complains of their realistic character, notably of the production on the stage of the Knights of the Garter in the robes and insignia of the order, as being calculated to bring ridicule on the real ceremonies; much in the same spirit in which the French Government, some time ago, prohibited that delightful actor, M. Christian, from appearing in uniform, on the plea that it was prejudicial to the glory of the army that a colonel should be caricatured. And elsewhere the gorgeousness of apparel which distinguished the English stage under Shakespeare's influence was attacked by the contemporary critics, not as a rule, however, on the grounds of the democratic tendencies of realism, but usually on those moral grounds which are always the last refuge of people who have no sense of beauty.

The point, however, which I wish to emphasize is, not that Shakespeare appreciated the value of lovely costumes in adding picturesqueness to poetry, but that he saw how important costume is as a means of producing certain dramatic effects. Many of his plays, such as *Measure for Measure, Twelfth Night, The Two Gentlemen of Verona, All's Well that Ends Well, Cymbeline*, and others, depend for their illusion on the character of the various dresses worn by the hero or the heroine; the delightful scene in *Henry the Sixth,* on the modern miracles of healing by faith, loses all its point unless Gloster is in black and scarlet; and the *dénoûment* of the *Merry Wives of Windsor* hinges on the

* One of Shakespeare's last plays. The roof of the Globe Theater caught fire during one performance after real cannons were fired on stage, and the theater burned down.

† Heraldic S-marks on the livery collars (heavy gold chains) worn by nobles to show loyalty to the House of Lancaster. For an example, see Hans Holbein's portrait of Sir Thomas More.

colour of Anne Page's gown. As for the uses Shakespeare makes of disguises the instance[s] are almost numberless. Posthumus hides his passion under a peasant's garb, and Edgar his pride beneath an idiot's rags; Portia wears the apparel of a lawyer, and Rosalind, is attired, in "all points as a man"; the cloak-bag of Pisanio changes Imogen to the youth Fidele; Jessica flees from her father's house in boy's dress, and Julia ties up her yellow hair in fantastic love-knots, and dons hose and doublet; Henry the Eighth woos his lady as a shepherd, and Romeo his as a pilgrim; Prince Hal and Poins appear first as footpads in buckram suits, and then in white aprons and leather jerkins as the waiters in a tavern: and as for Falstaff, does he not come on as a highwayman, as an old woman, as Herne the Hunter, and as the clothes going to the laundry?

Nor are the examples of the employment of costume as a mode of intensifying dramatic situation less numerous. After slaughter of Duncan, Macbeth appears in his night-gown as if aroused from sleep; Timon ends in rags the play he had begun in splendour; Richard flatters the London citizens in a suit of mean and shabby armour, and, as soon as he has stepped in blood to the throne, marches through the streets in crown and George and Garter; the climax of the *Tempest* is reached when Prospero, throwing off his enchanter's robes, sends Ariel for his hat and rapier, and reveals himself as the great Italian Duke; the very Ghost in *Hamlet* changes his mystical apparel to produce different effects; and as for Juliet, a modern playwright would probably have lain her out in her shroud, and made the scene a scene of horror merely, but Shakespeare arrays her in rich and gorgeous raiment, whose loveliness makes the vault "a feasting presence full of light," turns the tomb into a bridal chamber, and gives the cue and motive for Romeo's speech of the triumph of Beauty over Death.

Even small details of dress, such as the colour of a majordomo's stockings, the pattern on a wife's handkerchief, the sleeve of a young soldier, and a fashionable woman's bonnets, become in Shakespeare's hands points of actual dramatic importance, and by some of them the action of the play in question is conditioned absolutely. Many other dramatists have availed themselves of costume as a method of expressing directly to the audience the character of a person on his entrance, though hardly so brilliantly as Shakespeare has done in the case of the dandy Parolles, whose dress, by the way, only an archæologist can understand; the fun of a master and servant exchanging coats in presence of the audience, of shipwrecked sailors squabbling over the division of a lot of fine clothes, and of a tinker dressed up like a duke while he is in his cups, may be regarded as part of that great career which costume has always played in comedy from the time of Aristophanes down to Mr. Gilbert; but nobody from the mere details of apparel and adornment has ever drawn such irony of contrast, such immediate and tragic effect, such pity and such pathos, as Shakespeare himself. Armed cap-à-pié, the dead King stalks on the battlements of Elsinore because all is not right with Denmark; Shylock's Jewish gaberdine is part of the stigma under which that wounded and embittered nature writhes; Arthur begging for his life can think of no better plea than the handkerchief he had given Hubert—

> Have you the heart? when your head did but ache,
> I knit my handkerchief about your brows,
> (The best I had, a princess wrought it me)
> And I did never ask it you again.

and Orlando's blood-stained napkin strikes the first sombre note in that exquisite woodland idyll, and shows us the depth of feeling that underlies Rosalind's fanciful wit and wilful jesting.

> Last night 'twas on my arm; I kissed it;
> I hope it be not gone to tell my lord
> That I kiss aught but he.

says Imogen, jesting on the loss of the bracelet which was already on its way to Rome to rob her of her husband's faith; the little Prince passing to the Tower plays with the dagger in his uncle's girdle; Duncan sends a ring to Lady Macbeth on the night of his own murder, and the ring of Portia turns the tragedy of the merchant into a wife's comedy. The great rebel York dies with paper crown on his head; Hamlet's black suit is a kind of colour-motive in the piece, like the mourning of the Chimène in the *Cid*; and the climax of Antony's speech is the production of Cæsar's cloak:—

> I remember
> The first time ever Cæsar put it on.
> 'Twas on a summer's evening, in his tent,
> The day he overcame the Nervii:—
> Look, in this place ran Cassius' dagger through:
> See what a rent the envious Casca made:
> Through this the well-beloved Brutus stabbed. . . .
> Kind souls, what, weep you when you but behold
> Our Cæsar's vesture wounded?

The flowers which Ophelia carries with her in her madness are as pathetic as the violets that blossom on a grave; the effect of Lear's wandering on the heath is intensified beyond words by his fantastic attire; and when Cloten, stung by the taunt of that simile which his sister draws from her husband's raiment, arrays himself in that husband's very garb to work upon her the deed of shame, we feel that there is nothing in the whole of modern French realism, nothing even in *Thérèse Raquin,** that masterpiece of horror, which for terrible and tragic significance can compare with this strange scene in *Cymbeline*.

In the actual dialogue also some of the most vivid passages are those suggested by costume. Rosalind's

> Dost thou think, though I am caparisoned like a man, I have a doublet and hose in my disposition?

Constance's

---

* Novel (1867) by Émile Zola in which Thérèse and Laurent, her lover, conspire to murder Thérèse's husband; guilt-ridden, they are driven to suicide.

Grief fills the place up of my absent child,
Stuffs out his vacant garments with his form;

and the quick sharp cry of Elizabeth—

Ah! cut my lace asunder!

are only a few of the many examples one might quote. One of the finest effects I have ever seen on the stage was Salvini, in the last act of *Lear*, tearing the plume from Kent's cap and applying it to Cordelia's lips when he came to the line,

This feather stirs; she lives!

Mr. Booth, whose Lear had many noble qualities of passion, plucked, I remember, some fur from his archæologically-incorrect ermine for the same business; but Salvini's was the finer effect of the two, as well as the truer. And those who saw Mr. Irving in the last act of *Richard the Third* have not, I am sure, forgotten how much the agony and terror of his dream was intensified, by contrast, through the calm and quiet that preceded it, and the delivery of such lines as

What, is my beaver easier than it was?
And all my armour laid into my tent?
Look that my staves be sound and not too heavy—

lines which had a double meaning for the audience, remembering the last words which Richard's mother called after him as he was marching to Bosworth:—

Therefore take with thee my most grievous curse,
Which in the day of battle tire thee more
Than all the complete armour that thou wear'st.

As regards the resources which Shakespeare had at his disposal, it is to be remarked that, while he more than once complains of the smallness of the stage on which he has to produce big historical plays, and of the want of scenery which obliges him to cut out many effective open-air incidents, he always writes as a dramatist who had at his disposal a most elaborate theatrical wardrobe, and who could rely on the actors taking pains about their make-up. Even now it is difficult to produce such a play as the *Comedy of Errors*; and to the picturesque accident of Miss Ellen Terry's brother resembling herself we owe the opportunity of seeing *Twelfth Night* adequately performed. Indeed, to put any play of Shakespeare's on the stage, absolutely as he himself wished it to be done, requires the services of a good property-man, a clever wig-maker, a costumier with a sense of colour and a knowledge of textures, a master of the methods of making up, a fencing-master, a dancing-master, and an artist to personally direct the whole production. For he is most careful to tell us the dress and appearance of each character. "Racine abhorre la réalité," says Auguste Vacquerie* somewhere; "il ne daigne pas s'occuper de son costume. Si l'on s'en rapportait aux indications du poète, Agamemnon serait vêtu d'un sceptre et Achille d'une épée."† But with Shakespeare it is very different. He gives us directions about the costumes of Perdita, Florizel, Autolycus, the Witches of *Macbeth,* and the apothecary in *Romeo and Juliet,* several elaborate descriptions of his fat knight, and a detailed account of the extraordinary garb in which Petruchio is to be married. Rosalind, he tells us, is tall, and is to carry a spear and a little dagger; Celia is smaller, and is to paint her face brown so as to look sunburnt. The children who play at fairies in Windsor Forest are to be dressed in white and green—a compliment, by the way, to Queen Elizabeth, whose favourite colours they were—and in white, with green garlands and gilded vizors, the angels are to come to Katharine in Kimbolton. Bottom is in homespun, Lysander is distinguished from Oberon by his wearing an Athenian dress, and Launce has holes in his boots. The Duchess of Gloucester stands in a white sheet with

* Auguste Vacquerie (1819–1895), French journalist and man of letters.

† Racine abhors reality. He disdains any interest in costume. If one followed the suggestions of the poet, Agamemnon would be dressed in scepter only, and Achilles in merely a sword.

her husband in mourning beside her. The motley of the Fool, the scarlet of the Cardinal, and the French lilies broidered on the English coats, are all made occasion for jest or taunt in the dialogue. We know the patterns on the Dauphin's armour and the Pucelle's sword, the crest on Warwick's helmet and the colour of Bardolph's nose. Portia has golden hair, Phœbe is black-haired, Orlando has chestnut curls, and Sir Andrew Aguecheek's hair hangs like flax on a distaff, and won't curl at all. Some of the characters are stout, some lean, some straight, some hunchbacked, some fair, some dark, and some are to blacken their faces. Lear has a white beard, Hamlet's father a grizzled, and Benedict is to shave his in the course of the play. Indeed, on the subject of stage beards Shakespeare is quite elaborate; tells us of the many different colours in use, and gives a hint to actors to always see that their own are properly tied on. There is a dance of reapers in rye-straw hats, and of rustics in hairy coats like satyrs; a masque of Amazons, a masque of Russians, and a classical masque; several immortal scenes over a weaver in an ass's head, a riot over the colour of a coat which it takes the Lord Mayor of London to quell, and a scene between an infuriated husband and his wife's milliner about the slashing of a sleeve.

As for the metaphors Shakespeare draws from dress, and the aphorisms he makes on it, his hits at the costume of his age, particularly at the ridiculous size of the ladies' bonnets, and the many descriptions of the *mundus muliebris,** from the song of Autolycus in the *Winter's Tale* down to the account of the Duchess of Milan's gown in *Much Ado About Nothing,* they are far too numerous to quote; though it may be worth while to remind people that the whole of the Philosophy of Clothes is to be found in Lear's scene with Edgar—a passage which has the advantage of brevity and style over the grotesque wisdom and somewhat mouthing metaphysics of *Sartor Resartus*.† But I think that from what I have already said it is quite clear that Shakespeare was

* Feminine world (Latin).

† In this satire of philosophy, published in book form in 1838, essayist and historian Thomas Carlyle sees all social behaviors as matters of external appearance and costume.

very much interested in costume. I do not mean in that shallow sense by which it has been concluded from his knowledge of deeds and daffodils that he was the Blackstone and Paxton of the Elizabethan age; but that he saw that costume could be made at once impressive of a certain effect on the audience and expressive of certain types of character, and is one of the essential factors of the means which a true illusionist has at his disposal. Indeed to him the deformed figure of Richard was of as much value as Juliet's loveliness; he sets the serge of the radical beside the silks of the lord, and sees the stage effects to be got from each: he has as much delight in Caliban as he has in Ariel, in rags as he has in cloth of gold, and recognizes the artistic beauty of ugliness.

The difficulty Ducis felt about translating *Othello* in consequence of the importance given to such a vulgar thing as a handkerchief, and his attempt to soften its grossness by making the Moor reiterate "Le bandeau! le bandeau!"* may be taken as an example of the difference between *la tragédie philosophique*† and the drama of real life; and the introduction for the first time of the word *mouchoir*‡ at the Théâtre Français was an era in that romantic-realistic movement of which Hugo is the father and M. Zola the *enfant terrible,*§ just as the classicism of the earlier part of the century was emphasized by Talma's refusal to play Greek heroes any longer in a powdered periwig—one of the many instances, by the way, of that desire for archæological accuracy in dress which has distinguished the great actors of our age.

In criticising the importance given to money in *La Comédie Humaine,* Théophile Gautier says that Balzac may claim to have invented a new hero in fiction, *le héros métallique*.¶ Of Shakespeare it may be said that he was the first to see the dramatic value of doublets, and that a climax may depend on a crinoline.

---

* The scarf (French).

† Philosophical tragedy (French).

‡ Handkerchief (French).

§ Literally, dreadful child (French); someone who causes damage or disruption with rash or imprudent actions.

¶ Literally, the metallic hero (French).

The burning of the Globe Theatre—an event due, by the way, to the results of the passion for illusion that distinguished Shakespeare's stage-management—has unfortunately robbed us of many important documents; but in the inventory, still in existence, of the costume-wardrobe of a London theatre in Shakespeare's time, there are mentioned particular costumes for cardinals, shepherds, kings, clowns, friars, and fools; green coats for Robin Hood's men, and a green gown for Maid Marian; a white and gold doublet for Henry the Fifth, and a robe for Longshanks; besides surplices, copes, damask gowns, gowns of cloth of gold and of cloth of silver, taffeta gowns, calico gowns, velvet coats, satin coats, frieze coats, jerkins of yellow leather and black leather, red suits, grey suits, French Pierrot suits, a robe "for to goo invisibell," which seems inexpensive at 3*l.* 10*s.*, and four incomparable fardingales—all of which show a desire to give every character an appropriate dress. There are also entries of Spanish, Moorish and Danish costumes, of helmets, lances, painted shields, imperial crowns, and papal tiaras, as well as of costumes for Turkish Janissaries, Roman Senators, and all the gods and goddesses of Olympus, which evidence a good deal of archæological research on the part of the manager of the theatre. It is true that there is a mention of a bodice for Eve, but probably the *donnée** of the play was after the Fall.

Indeed, anybody who cares to examine the age of Shakespeare will see that archæology was one of its special characteristics. After that revival of the classical forms of architecture which was one of the notes of the Renaissance, and the printing at Venice and elsewhere of the masterpieces of Greek and Latin literature, had come naturally an interest in the ornamentation and costume of the antique world. Nor was it for the learning that they could acquire, but rather for the loveliness that they might create, that the artists studied these things. The curious objects that were being constantly brought to light by excavations were not left to moulder in a museum, for the contemplation of a callous curator, and the *ennui* of a policeman bored by the absence

* Set of assumptions on which a work is based (French).

of crime. They were used as motives for the production of a new art, which was to be not beautiful merely, but also strange.

Infessura tells us that in 1485 some workmen digging on the Appian Way came across an old Roman sarcophagus inscribed with the name "Julia, daughter of Claudius." On opening the coffer they found within its marble womb the body of a beautiful girl of about fifteen years of age, preserved by the embalmer's skill from corruption and the decay of time. Her eyes were half open, her hair rippled round her in crisp curling gold, and from her lips and cheek the bloom of maidenhood had not yet departed. Borne back to the Capitol, she became at once the centre of a new cult, and from all parts of the city crowded pilgrims to worship at the wonderful shrine till the Pope fearing lest those who had found the secret of beauty in a Pagan tomb might forget what secrets Judæa's rough and rock-hewn sepulchre contained, had the body conveyed away by night, and in secret buried. Legend though it may be, yet the story is none the less valuable as showing us the attitude of the Renaissance towards the antique world. Archæology to them was not a mere science for the antiquarian; it was a means by which they could touch the dry dust of antiquity into the very breath and beauty of life, and fill with the new wine of romanticism forms that else had been old and outworn. From the pulpit of Niccola Pisano down to Mantegna's "Triumph of Cæsar," and the service Cellini designed for King Francis, the influence of this spirit can be traced; nor was it confined merely to the immobile arts—the arts of arrested movement—but its influence was to be seen also in the great Græco-Roman masques which were the constant amusement of the gay courts of the time, and in the public pomps and processions with which the citizens of big commercial towns were wont to greet the princes that chanced to visit them; pageants, by the way, which were considered so important that large prints were made of them and published—a fact which is a proof of the general interest at the time in matters of such kind.

And this use of archæology in shows, so far from being a bit of priggish pedantry, is in every way legitimate and beautiful. For the stage is not merely the meeting place of all the arts, but is also the return of art to life. Sometimes in an archæological novel the use of strange and obsolete terms seems to hide the reality beneath the learning, and I dare say that many of the readers of *Notre Dame de Paris** have been much puzzled over the meaning of such expressions as *la casaque à mahoitres, les voulgiers, le gallimard taché d'encre, les craaquiniers*, and the like; but with the stage how different it is! The ancient world wakes from its sleep, and history moves as a pageant before our eyes, without obliging us to have recourse to a dictionary or an encyclopædia for the perfection of our enjoyment. Indeed, there is not the slightest necessity that the public should know the authorities for the mounting of any piece. From such materials, for instance, as the disk of Theodosius, materials with which the majority of people are probably not very familiar, Mr. E. W. Godwin, one of the most artistic spirits of this century in England, created the marvellous loveliness of the first act of *Claudian,* and showed us the life of Byzantium in the fourth century, not by a dreary lecture and a set of grimy casts, not by a novel which requires a glossary to explain it, but by the visible presentation before us of all the glory of that great town. And while the costumes were true to the smallest points of colour and design, yet the details were not assigned that abnormal importance which they must necessarily be given in a piecemeal lecture, but were subordinated to the rules of lofty composition and the unity of artistic effect. Mr. Symonds, speaking of that great picture of Mantegna's, now in Hampton Court, says that the artist has converted an antiquarian motive into a theme for melodies of line. The same could have been said with equal justice of Mr. Godwin's scene. Only the foolish called it pedantry only those who would neither look nor listen spoke of the passion of the play being killed by its paint. It was in reality a scene not merely perfect in its picturesqueness, but absolutely dramatic also, getting rid of any necessity for tedious descriptions, and showing us, by the colour and character of Claudian's dress, and the dress of his attendants, the whole nature

---

* Victor Hugo's historical novel (1831; better known in English as *The Hunchback of Notre Dame*) makes much use of archaic expressions. Wilde argues that art alone can make such archeology significant, as he now shows.

and life of the man, from what school of philosophy he affected, down to what horses he backed on the turf.

And indeed archæology is only really delightful when transfused into some form of art. I have no desire to underrate the services of laborious scholars, but I feel that the use Keats made of Lemprière's Dictionary is of far more value to us than Professor Max Müller's treatment of the same mythology as a disease of language. Better *Endymion* than any theory, however sound, or, as in the present instance, unsound, of an epidemic among adjectives! And who does not feel that the chief glory of Piranesi's book on Vases is that it gave Keats the suggestion for his 'Ode on a Grecian Urn'? Art, and art only, can make archæology beautiful; and the theatric art can use it most directly and most vividly, for it can combine in one exquisite presentation the illusion of actual life with the wonder of the unreal world. But the sixteenth century was not merely the age of Vitruvius; it was the age of Vecellio also. Every nation seems suddenly to have become interested in the dress of its neighbours. Europe began to investigate its own clothes, and the amount of books published on national costumes is quite extraordinary. At the beginning of the century the *Nuremberg Chronicle,* with its two thousand illustrations, reached its fifth edition, and before the century was over seventeen editions were published of Munster's *Cosmography*. Besides these two books there were also the works of Michael Colyns, of Hans Weigel, of Amman, and of Vecellio himself, all of them well illustrated, some of the drawings in Vecellio being probably from the hand of Titian.

Nor was it merely from books and treatises that they acquired their knowledge. The development of the habit of foreign travel, the increased commercial intercourse between countries, and the frequency of diplomatic missions, gives every nation many opportunities of studying the various forms of contemporary dress. After the departure from England, for instance, of the ambassadors from the Czar, the Sultan and the Prince of Morocco, Henry the Eighth and his friends gave several masques in the strange attire of their visitors. Later on London saw, perhaps too often, the sombre splendour of the Spanish Court, and to Elizabeth came envoys from all lands, whose dress, Shakespeare tells us, had an important influence on English costume.

And the interest was not confined merely to classical dress, or the dress of foreign nations; there was also a good deal of research, amongst theatrical people especially, into the ancient costume of England itself: and when Shakespeare, in the prologue to one of his plays, expresses his regret at being unable to produce helmets of the period, he is speaking as an Elizabethan manager and not merely as an Elizabethan poet. At Cambridge, for instance, during his day, a play of *Richard the Third* was performed, in which the actors were attired in real dresses of the time, procured from the great collection of historical costume in the Tower, which was always open to the inspection of managers, and sometimes placed at their disposal. And I cannot help thinking that this performance must have been far more artistic, as regards costume, than Garrick's mounting of Shakespeare's own play on the subject, in which he himself appeared in a nondescript fancy dress, and everybody else in the costume of the time of George the Third, Richmond especially being much admired in the uniform of a young guardsman.

For what is the use to the stage of that archæology which has so strangely terrified the critics, but that it, and it alone, can give us the architecture and apparel suitable to the time in which the action of the play passes? It enables us to see a Greek dressed like a Greek, and an Italian like an Italian; to enjoy the arcades of Venice and the balconies of Verona; and, if the play deals with any of the great eras in our country's history, to contemplate the age in its proper attire, and the king in his habit as he lived. And I wonder, by the way, what Lord Lytton would have said some time ago, at the Princess's Theatre, had the curtain risen on his father's Brutus reclining in a Queen Anne chair, attired in a flowing wig and a flowered dressing-gown, a costume which in the last century was considered peculiarly appropriate to an antique Roman! For in those halcyon days of the drama no archæology troubled the stage, or distressed the critics, and our inartistic grandfathers sat peaceably in a stifling atmosphere of anachronisms, and beheld with the calm complacency of the age of prose an Iachimo in powder and patches, a Lear in lace ruffles, and a Lady Macbeth in a large crinoline. I can understand archæology being attacked on the ground of its excessive realism, but to attack it as pedantic seems to be very much beside the mark. However, to attack it for any reason is foolish; one might just as well speak disrespectfully of the equator. For archæology, being a science, is neither good nor bad, but a fact simply. Its value depends entirely on how it is used, and only an artist can use it. We look to the archæologist for the materials, to the artist for the method.

In designing the scenery and costumes for any of Shakespeare's plays, the first thing the artist has to settle is the best date for the drama. This should be determined by the general spirit of the play, more than by any actual historical references which may occur in it. Most *Hamlets* I have seen were placed far too early. *Hamlet* is essentially a scholar of the Revival of Learning; and if the allusion to the recent invasion of England by the Danes puts it back to the ninth century, the use of foils brings it down much later. Once, however, that the date has been fixed, then the archæologist is to supply us with the facts which the artist is to convert into effects.

It has been said that the anachronisms in the plays themselves show us that Shakespeare was indifferent to historical accuracy, and a great deal of capital has been made out of Hector's indiscreet quotation from Aristotle. Upon the other hand, the anachronisms are really few in number, and not very important, and, had Shakespeare's attention been drawn to them by a brother artist, he would probably have corrected them. For, though they can hardly be called blemishes, they are certainly not the great beauties of his work; or, at least, if they are, their anachronistic charm cannot be emphasized unless the play is accurately mounted according to its proper date. In looking at Shakespeare's plays as a whole, however, what is really remarkable is their extraordinary fidelity as regards his personages and his plots. Many of his *dramatis personæ* are people who had actually existed, and some of them might have been seen in real life by a portion of his audience. Indeed the most violent attack that was made on Shakespeare in his time was for his supposed caricature of Lord Cobham. As for his plots, Shakespeare constantly draws them either from authentic history, or from the old ballads and traditions which served as history to the Elizabethan public, and which even now no scientific historian would dismiss as absolutely untrue. And not merely did he select fact instead of fancy as the basis of much of his imaginative work, but he always gives to each play the general character, the social atmosphere in a word, of the age in question. Stupidity he recognizes as being one of the permanent characteristics of all European civilizations; so he sees no difference between a London mob of his own day and a Roman mob of Pagan days, between a silly watchman in Messina and a silly Justice of the Peace in Windsor. But when he deals with higher characters, with those exceptions of each age which are so fine that they become its types, he gives them absolutely the stamp and seal of their time. Virgilia is one of those Roman wives on whose tomb was written "Domi mansit, lanam fecit,"* as surely as Juliet is the romantic girl of the Renaissance. He is even true to the characteristics of race. Hamlet has all the imagination and irresolution of the Northern nations, and the Princess Katharine is as entirely French as the heroine of *Divorçons*. Harry the Fifth is a pure Englishman, and Othello a true Moor.

Again when Shakespeare treats of the history of England from the fourteenth to the sixteenth centuries, it is wonderful how careful he is to have his facts perfectly right—indeed he follows Holinshed with curious fidelity. The incessant wars between France and England are described with extraordinary accuracy down to the names of the besieged towns, the ports of landing and embarkation, the sites and dates of the battles, the title of the commanders on each side, and the lists of the killed and wounded. And as regards the Civil Wars of the Roses we have many elaborate genealogies of the seven sons of Edward the Third; the claims of the rival Houses of York and Lancaster to the throne are discussed at length; and if the English aristocracy will not read Shakespeare as a poet, they should certainly read him as a sort of early Peerage. There is hardly a single title in the Upper House, with the exception of course of the uninteresting titles assumed by the law lords, which does not appear in Shakespeare along with many details of family history, creditable and discreditable. Indeed if it be really necessary that the School Board children should know all about the Wars

* She stayed at home and made cloth (Latin).

of the Roses, they could learn their lessons just as well out of Shakespeare as out of shilling primers, and learn them, I need not say, far more pleasurably. Even in Shakespeare's own day this use of his plays was recognized. "The historical plays teach history to those who cannot read it in the chronicles," says Heywood in a tract about the stage, and yet I am sure that sixteenth-century chronicles were much more delightful reading than nineteenth-century primers are.

Of course the æsthetic value of Shakespeare's plays does not, in the slightest degree, depend on their facts, but on the Truth, and Truth is independent of facts always, inventing or selecting them at pleasure. But still Shakespeare's use of facts is a most interesting part of his method of work, and shows us his attitude towards the stage, and his relations to the great art of illusion. Indeed he would have been very much surprised at anyone classing his plays with "fairy tales," as Lord Lytton does; for one of his aims was to create for England a national historical drama, which should deal with incidents with which the public was well acquainted, and with heroes that lived in the memory of a people. Patriotism, I need hardly say, is not a necessary quality of art; but it means, for the artist the substitution of a universal for an individual feeling, and for the public the presentation of a work of art in a most attractive and popular form. It is worth noticing that Shakespeare's first and last successes were both historical plays.

It may be asked what has this to do with Shakespeare's attitude towards costume. I answer that a dramatist who laid such stress on historical accuracy of fact would have welcomed historical accuracy of costume as a most important adjunct to his illusionist method. And I have no hesitation in saying that he did so. The reference to helmets of the period in the prologue to *Henry the Fifth* may be considered fanciful, though Shakespeare must have often seen

The very casque
That did affright the air at Agincourt,

where it still hangs in the dusky gloom of Westminster Abbey, along with the saddle of that "imp of fame," and the dinted shield with its torn blue velvet lining and its tarnished lilies of gold; but the use of military tabards in *Henry the Sixth* is a bit of pure archæology, as they were not worn in the sixteenth century; and the King's own tabard, I may mention, was still suspended over his tomb in St. George's Chapel, Windsor, in Shakespeare's day. For, up to the time of the unfortunate triumph of the Philistines in 1645,* the chapels and cathedrals of England were the great national museums of archæology, and in them was kept the armour and attire of the heroes of English history. A good deal was of course preserved in the Tower, and even in Elizabeth's day tourists were brought there to see such curious relics of the past as Charles Brandon's huge lance, which is still, I believe, the admiration of our country visitors; but the cathedrals and churches were, as a rule, selected as the most suitable shrines for reception of the historic antiquities. Canterbury can still show us the helm of the Black Prince. Westminster the robes of our kings, and in old St. Paul's the very banner that had waved on Bosworth field was hung up by Richmond himself.

In fact, everywhere that Shakespeare turned in London, he saw the apparel and appurtenances of past ages, and it is impossible to doubt that he made use of his opportunities. The employment of lance and shield, for instance, in actual warfare, which is so frequent in his plays, is drawn from archæology, and not from the military accoutrements of his day; and his general use of armour in battle was not a characteristic of his age, a time when it was rapidly disappearing before firearms. Again, the crest on Warwick's helmet, of which such a point is made in *Henry the Sixth,* is absolutely correct in a fifteenth-century play when crests were generally worn, but would not have been so in a play of Shakespeare's own time, when feathers and plumes had taken their place—a fashion which, as he tells us in *Henry the Eighth,* was borrowed from France. For the historical plays, then, we may be sure that archaæology was employed, and as for the others I feel certain it was the case also. The appearance of Jupiter on his eagle, thunderbolt in hand, of Juno with her peacocks,

* Oliver Cromwell's defeat of the royal forces of King Charles I, at the Battle of Naseby. Wilde regards Puritans as prime enemies of art, and hence Philistines.

and of Iris with her many-coloured bow; the Amazon masque and the masque of the Five Worthies, may all be regarded as archæological; and the vision which Posthumus sees in prison of Sicilius Leonatus—"an old man, attired like a warrior, leading an ancient matron"—is clearly so. Of the "Athenian dress" by which Lysander is distinguished from Oberon I have already spoken; but one of the most marked instances is in the case of the dress of Coriolanus, for which Shakespeare goes directly to Plutarch. That historian, in his Life of the great Roman, tells us of the oak-wreath with which Caius Marcius was crowned, and of the curious kind of dress in which, according to ancient fashion, he had to canvass his electors; and on both of these points he enters into long disquisitions, investigating the origin and meaning of the old customs. Shakespeare, in the spirit of the true artist, accepts the facts of the antiquarian and converts them into dramatic and picturesque effects: indeed the gown of humility, the "woolvish gown," as Shakespeare calls it, is the central note of the play. There are other cases I might quote, but this one is quite sufficient for my purpose; and it is evident from it at any rate that, in mounting a play in the accurate costume of the time, according to the best authorities, we are carrying out Shakespeare's own wishes and method.

Even if it were not so, there is no more reason that we should continue any imperfections which may be supposed to have characterized Shakespeare's stage-mounting than that we should have Juliet played by a young man, or give up the advantage of changeable scenery. A great work of dramatic art should not merely be made expressive of modern passion by means of the actor, but should be presented to us in the form most suitable to the modern spirit. Racine produced his Roman plays in Louis-Quatorze dress on a stage crowded with spectators; but we require different conditions for the enjoyment of his art. Perfect accuracy of detail, for the sake of perfect illusion, is necessary for us. What we have to see is that the details are not allowed to usurp the principal place. They must be subordinate always to the general motive of the play. But subordination in art does not mean disregard of truth; it means conversion of fact into effect, and assigning to each detail its proper relative value.

> Les petits détails d'histoire et de vie domestique (says Hugo) doivent être scrupuleusement étudiés et reproduits par le poète, mais uniquement comme des moyens d'accroître la réalité de l'ensemble, et de faire pénétrer jusque dans les coins les plus obscurs de l'œuvre cette vie générale et puissante au milieu de laquelle les personnages sont plus vrais, et les catastrophes, par conséquent, plus poignantes. Tout doit être subordonné à ce but. L'Homme sur le premier plan, le reste au fond.*

The passage is interesting as coming from the first great French dramatist who employed archæology on the stage, and whose plays, though absolutely correct in detail, are known to all for their passion, not for their pedantry—for their life, not for their learning. It is true that he has made certain concessions in the case of the employment of curious or strange expressions. Ruy Blas talks of M. de Priego as "sujet du roi" instead of "noble du roi," and Angelo Malipieri speaks of "la croix rouge" instead of "la croix de gueules." But they are concessions made to the public, or rather to a section of it. "J'en offre ici toutes mes excuses aux spectateurs intelligents," he says in a note to one of the plays; "espérons qu'un jour un seigneur vénitien pourra dire tout bonnement sans péril son blason sur le théâtre. C'est un

* The small details of history and domestic life [says Hugo] must be scrupulously studied and reproduced by the poet, but only as a means of building up an ensemble reality, illuminating the darkest corners of the work with this powerful general view, at the center of which persons are more real, and catastrophes therefore more poignant. Everything must be subordinated to this end. Man in the foreground, all the rest in the background (French).

† Wilde, commenting on the need for proper display in costume, quotes Hugo again: "I can only offer my excuses to intelligent spectators. Let's hope that one day a Venetian nobleman will not hesitate to display his coat of arms in the theater. That progress will surely come" (French).

progrès qui viendra."[†] And, though the description of the crest is not couched in accurate language, still the crest itself was accurately right. It may, of course, be said that the public do not notice these things; upon the other hand, it should be remembered that Art has no other aim but her own perfection, and proceeds simply by her own laws, and that the play which Hamlet describes as being caviare to the general is a play he highly praises. Besides, in England, at any rate, the public have undergone a transformation; there is far more appreciation of beauty now than there was a few years ago; and though they may not be familiar with the authorities and archæological data for what is shown to them, still they enjoy whatever loveliness they look at. And this is the important thing. Better to take pleasure in a rose than to put its root under a microscope. Archæological accuracy is merely a condition of illusionist stage effect; it is not its quality. And Lord Lytton's proposal that the dresses should merely be beautiful without being accurate is founded on a misapprehension of the nature of costume, and of its value on the stage. This value is twofold, picturesque and dramatic; the former depends on the colour of the dress, the latter on its design and character. But so interwoven are the two that, whenever in our own day historical accuracy has been disregarded, and the various dresses in a play taken from different ages, the result has been that the stage has been turned into that chaos of costume, that caricature of the centuries, the Fancy Dress Ball, to the entire ruin of all dramatic and picturesque effect. For the dresses of one age do not artistically harmonize with the dresses of another; and, as far as dramatic value goes, to confuse the costumes is to confuse the play. Costume is a growth, an evolution, and a most important, perhaps the most important, sign of the manners, customs, and mode of life of each century. The Puritan dislike of colour, adornment, and grace in apparel was part of the great revolt of the middle classes against Beauty in the seventeenth century. A historian who disregarded it would give us a most inaccurate picture of the time, and a dramatist who did not avail himself of it would miss a most vital element in producing an illusionist effect. The effeminacy of dress that characterized the reign of Richard the Second was a constant theme of contemporary authors. Shakespeare, writing two hundred years after, makes the King's fondness for gay apparel and foreign fashions a point in the play, from John of Gaunt's reproaches down to Richard's own speech in the third act on his disposition from the throne. And that Shakespeare examined Richard's tomb in Westminster Abbey seems to me certain from York's speech:—

> See, see, King Richard doth himself appear,
> As doth the blushing discontented sun
> From out the fiery portal of the east,
> When he perceives the envious clouds are bent
> To dim his glory.

For we can still discern on the King's robe his favourite badge—the sun issuing from a cloud. In fact, in every age the social conditions are so exemplified in costume, that to produce a sixteenth-century play in fourteenth-century attire, or *vice versâ,* would make the performance seem unreal because untrue. And, valuable as beauty of effect on the stage is, the highest beauty is not merely comparable with absolute accuracy of detail, but really dependent on it. To invent an entirely new costume is almost impossible except in burlesque or extravaganza, and as for combining the dress of different centuries into one, the experiment would be dangerous, and Shakespeare's opinion of the artistic value of such a medley may be gathered from his incessant satire of the Elizabethan dandies for imagining that they were well dressed because they got their doublets in Italy, their hats in Germany, and their hose in France. And it should be noted that the most lovely scenes that have been produced on our stage have been those that have been characterized by perfect accuracy, such as Mr. and Mrs. Bancroft's eighteenth-century revivals at the Haymarket, Mr. Irving's superb production of *Much Ado About Nothing,* and Mr. Barrett's *Claudian*. Besides, and this is perhaps the most complete answer to Lord Lytton's theory, it must be remembered that neither in costume nor in dialogue is beauty the dramatist's primary aim at all. The true dramatist aims first at what is characteristic, and no more desires that all his personages should be beautifully attired than he desires that they should all have beautiful natures or speak beautiful

English. The true dramatist, in fact, shows us life under the conditions of art, not art in the form of life. The Greek dress was the loveliest dress the world has ever seen, and the English dress of the last century one of the most monstrous; yet we cannot costume a play by Sheridan as we would costume a play by Sophokles. For, as Polonius says in his excellent lecture, a lecture to which I am glad to have the opportunity of expressing my obligations, one of the first qualities of apparel is its expressiveness. And the affected style of dress in the last century was the natural characteristic of a society of affected manners and affected conversation—a characteristic which the realistic dramatist will highly value down to the smallest detail of accuracy, and the materials for which he can only get from archæology.

But it is not enough that a dress should be accurate; it must be also appropriate to the stature and appearance of the actor, and to his supposed condition, as well as to his necessary action in the play. In Mr. Hare's production of *As You Like It* at the St. James's Theatre, for instance, the whole point of Orlando's complaint that he is brought up like a peasant, and not like a gentleman, was spoiled by the gorgeousness of his dress, and the splendid apparel worn by the banished Duke and his friends was quite out of place. Mr. Lewis Wingfield's explanation that the sumptuary laws of the period necessitated their doing so, is, I am afraid, hardly sufficient. Outlaws, lurking in a forest and living by the chase, are not very likely to care much about ordinances of dress. They were probably attired like Robin Hood's men, to whom, indeed, they are compared in the course of the play. And that their dress was not that of wealthy noblemen may be seen by Orlando's words when he breaks in upon them. He mistakes them for robbers, and is amazed to find that they answer him in courteous and gentle terms. Lady Archibald Campbell's production, under Mr. E. W. Godwin's direction, of the same play in Coombe Wood was, as regards mounting, far more artistic. At least it seemed so to me. The Duke and his companions were dressed in serge tunics, leathern jerkins, high boots, and gauntlets, and wore bycocket hats and hoods. And as they were playing in a real forest, they found, I am sure, their dresses extremely convenient. To every character in the play was given a perfectly appropriate attire, and the brown and green of their costumes harmonized exquisitely with the ferns through which they wandered, the trees beneath which they lay, and the lovely English landscape that surrounded the Pastoral Players. The perfect naturalness of the scene was due to the absolute accuracy and appropriateness of everything that was worn. Nor could archæology have been put to a severer test, or come out of it more triumphantly. The whole production showed once for all that, unless a dress is archæologically correct, and artistically appropriate, it always looks unreal, unnatural, and theatrical in the sense of artificial.

Nor, again, is it enough that there should be accurate and appropriate costumes of beautiful colours; there must be also beauty of colour on the stage as a whole, and as long as the background is painted by one artist, and the foreground figures independently designed by another, there is the danger of a want of harmony in the scene as a picture. For each scene the colour-scheme should be settled as absolutely as for the decoration of a room, and the textures which it is proposed to use should be mixed and re-mixed in every possible combination, and what is discordant removed. Then, as regards the particular kinds of colours, the stage is often made too glaring, partly through the excessive use of hot, violent reds, and partly through the costumes looking too new. Shabbiness, which in modern life is merely the tendency of the lower orders towards tone, is not without its artistic value, and modern colours are often much improved by being a little faded. Blue also is too frequently used: it is not merely a dangerous colour to wear by gaslight, but it is really difficult in England to get a thoroughly good blue. The fine Chinese blue, which we all so much admire, takes two years to dye, and the English public will not wait so long for a colour. Peacock blue, of course, has been employed on the stage, notably at the Lyceum, with great advantage; but all attempts at a good light blue, or good dark blue, which I have seen have been failures. The value of black is hardly appreciated; it was used effectively by Mr. Irving in *Hamlet* as the central note of a composition, but as a tone-giving neutral its importance is not recognized. And this is curious, considering the general colour of the dress of a century in which, as

Baudelaire says, "Nous célébrons tous quelque enterrement."* The archæologist of the future will probably point to this age as a time when the beauty of black was understood; but I hardly think that, as regards stage-mounting or house decoration, it really is. Its decorative value is, of course, the same as that of white or gold; it can separate and harmonize colours. In modern plays the black frock coat of the hero becomes important in itself, and should be given a suitable background. But it rarely is. Indeed the only good background for a play in modern dress which I have ever seen was the dark grey and cream-white scene of the first act of the *Princesse Georges* in Mrs. Langtry's production. As a rule, the hero is smothered in *bric-à-brac* and palm trees, lost in the gilded abyss of Louis Quatorze furniture, or reduced to a mere midge in the midst of marqueterie; whereas the background should always be kept as a background, and colour subordinated to effect. This, of course, can only be done when there is one single mind directing the whole production. The facts of art are diverse, but the essence of artistic effect is unity. Monarchy, Anarchy, and Republicanism may contend for the government of nations; but a theatre should be in the power of a cultured despot. There may be division of labour, but there must be no division of mind. Whoever understands the costume of an age understands of necessity its architecture and its surroundings also, and it is easy to see from the chairs of a century whether it was a century of crinolines or not. In fact, in art there is no specialism, and a really artistic production should bear the impress of one master, and one master only, who not merely should design and arrange everything, but should have complete control over the way in which each dress is to be worn.

Mademoiselle Mars, in the first production of *Hernani*, absolutely refused to call her lover *"Mon Lion!"*† unless she was allowed to wear a little fashionable *toque*‡ then much in vogue on the Boulevards; and many young ladies on our own stage insist to the present day on

---

* We are each of us attending some funeral or other (French).

† My lion! (French).

‡ Hat (French).

wearing stiff starched petticoats under Greek dresses, to the entire ruin of all delicacy of line and fold; but these wicked things should not be allowed. And there should be far more dress rehearsals than there are now. Actors such as Mr. Forbes-Robertson, Mr. Conway, Mr. George Alexander, and others, not to mention older artists, can move with ease and elegance in the attire of any century; but there are not a few who seem dreadfully embarrassed about their hands if they have no side pockets, and who always wear their dresses as if they were costumes. Costumes, of course, they are to the designer; but dresses they should be to those that wear them. And it is time that a stop should be put to the idea, very prevalent on the stage, that the Greeks and Romans always went about bare-headed in the open air—a mistake the Elizabethan managers did not fall into, for they gave hoods as well as gowns to their Roman senators.

More dress rehearsals would also be of value in explaining to the actors that there is a form of gesture and movement that is not merely appropriate to each style of dress, but really conditioned by it. The extravagant use of the arms in the eighteenth century, for instance, was the necessary result of the large hoop, and the solemn dignity of Burleigh owed as much to his ruff as to his reason. Besides, until an actor is at home in his dress, he is not at home in his part.

Of the value of beautiful costume in creating an artistic temperament in the audience, and producing that joy in beauty for beauty's sake without which the great masterpieces of art can never be understood, I will not here speak; though it is worth while to notice how Shakespeare appreciated that side of the question in the production of his tragedies, acting them always by artificial light, and in a theatre hung with black; but what I have tried to point out is that archæology is not a pedantic method, but a method of artistic illusion, and that costume is a means of displaying character without description, and of producing dramatic situations and dramatic effects. And I think it is a pity that so many critics should have set themselves to attack one of the most important movements on the modern stage before that movement has at all reached its proper perfection. That it will do so, however, I feel as certain as that we shall require from our dramatic critics in the future higher qualifications than that they can remember Macready or have seen Benjamin Webster: we shall require of them indeed, that they cultivate a sense of beauty. *Pour être plus difficile, la tâche n'en est que plus glorieuse.** And if they will not encourage, at least they must not oppose, a movement of which Shakespeare of all dramatists would have most approved, for it has the illusion of truth for its method, and the illusion of beauty for its result. Not that I agree with everything that I have said in this essay. There is much with which I entirely disagree. The essay simply represents an artistic standpoint, and in æsthetic criticism attitude is everything. For in art there is no such thing as a universal truth. A Truth in art is that whose contradictory is also true. And just as it is only in art-criticism, and through it, that we can apprehend the Platonic theory of ideas, so it is only in art-criticism, and through it, that we can realize Hegel's system of contraries. The truths of metaphysics are the truths of masks.

---

* The harder the task, the greater the reward (French).

THE SOUL OF MAN UNDER SOCIALISM

THE CHIEF ADVANTAGE that would result from the establishment of Socialism[5] is, undoubtedly, the fact that Socialism would relieve us from that sordid necessity of living for others which, in the present condition of things, presses so hardly upon almost everybody. In fact, scarcely anyone at all escapes.

Now and then, in the course of the century, a great man of science, like Darwin; a great poet, like Keats; a fine critical spirit, like M. Renan; a supreme artist, like Flaubert, has been able to isolate himself, to keep himself out of reach of the clamorous claims of others, to stand "under the shelter of the wall," as Plato puts it, and so to realise the perfection of what was in him, to his own incomparable gain, and to the incomparable and lasting gain of the whole world. These, however, are exceptions. The majority of people spoil their lives by an unhealthy and exaggerated altruism—are forced, indeed, so to spoil them. They find themselves surrounded by hideous poverty, by hideous ugliness, by hideous starvation. It is inevitable that they should be strongly moved by all this. The emotions of man are stirred more quickly than man's intelligence; and, as I pointed out some time ago in an article on the function of criticism, it is much more easy to have sympathy with suffering than it is to have sympathy with thought. Accordingly, with admirable though misdirected intentions, they very seriously and very sentimentally set themselves to the task of remedying the evils that they see. But their remedies do not cure the disease: they merely prolong it. Indeed, their remedies are part of the disease.

They try to solve the problem of poverty, for instance, by keeping the poor alive or, in the case of a very advanced school, by amusing the poor.

But this is not a solution: it is an aggravation of the difficulty. *The proper aim is to try and reconstruct society on such a basis that poverty will be impossible*. And the altruistic virtues have really prevented the carrying out of this aim. Just as the worst slave-owners were those who were kind to their slaves, and so prevented the horror of the system being realised by those who suffered from it, and understood by those who contemplated it, so, in the present state of things in England, the people who do most harm are the people who try to do most good; and at last we have had the spectacle of men who have really studied the problem and know the life—educated men who live in the East-end—coming forward and imploring the community to restrain its altruistic impulses of charity, benevolence, and the like. They do so on the ground that such charity degrades and demoralizes. They are perfectly right. Charity creates a multitude of sins.

There is also this to be said. It is immoral to use private property in order to alleviate the horrible evils that result from the institution of private property. It is both immoral and unfair.

Under Socialism all this will, of course, be altered. There will be no people living in fetid dens and fetid rags, and bringing up unhealthy, hunger-pinched children in the midst of impossible and absolutely repulsive surroundings. The security of society will not depend, as it does now, on the state of the weather. If a frost comes we shall not have a hundred thousand men out of work, tramping about the streets in a state of disgusting misery, or whining to their neighbours for alms, or crowding round the doors of loathsome shelters to try and secure a hunch of bread and a night's unclean lodging. Each member of the society will share in the general prosperity and happiness of the society, and if a frost comes no one will practically be anything the worse.

Upon the other hand, *Socialism itself will be of value simply because it will lead to Individualism*.

Socialism, Communism, or whatever one chooses to call it, by converting private property into public wealth, and substituting co-operation for competition, will restore society to its proper condition of a thoroughly healthy organism, and insure the material well-being of each member of the community. It will, in fact, give Life its proper basis and its proper environment. But for the full development of Life to its highest mode of perfection, something more is needed. What is needed is Individualism. If the Socialism is Authoritarian; if there are Governments armed with economic power as they are now with political power; if, in a word, we are to have Industrial Tyrannies, then the last state of man will be worse than the first. At present, in consequence of the existence of private property, a great many people are enabled to develop a certain very limited amount of Individualism. They are either under no necessity to work for their living, or are enabled to choose the sphere of activity that is really congenial to them, and gives them pleasure. These are the poets, the philosophers, the men of science, the men of culture—in a word, the real men, the men who have realised themselves, and in whom all Humanity gains a partial realisation. Upon the other hand, there are a great many people who, having no private property of their own, and being always on the brink of sheer starvation, are compelled to do the work of beasts of burden, to do work that is quite uncongenial to them, and to which they are forced by the peremptory, unreasonable, degrading Tyranny of want. These are the poor, and amongst them there is no grace of manner, or charm of speech, or civilization, or culture, or refinement in pleasures, or joy of life. From their collective force Humanity gains much in material prosperity. But it is only the material result that it gains, and the man who is poor is in himself absolutely of no importance. He is merely the infinitesimal atom of a force that, so far from regarding him, crushes him: indeed, prefers him crushed, as in that case he is far more obedient.

Of course, it might be said that the Individualism generated under conditions of private property is not always, or even as a rule, of a fine or wonderful type, and that the poor, if they have not culture and charm, have still many virtues. Both these statements would be quite true. The possession of private property is very often extremely demoralising, and that is, of course, one of the reasons why Socialism wants to get rid of the institution. In fact, property is really a nuisance. Some years ago people went about the country saying that property has duties. They said it so often and so tediously that, at last, the church has begun to say it. One hears it now from every pulpit. It is perfectly true. Property not merely has duties, but has so many duties that its possession to any large extent is a bore. It involves endless claims upon one, endless attention to business, endless bother. If property had simply pleasures, we could stand it; but its duties make it unbearable. In the interest of the rich we must get rid of it. The virtues of the poor may be readily admitted, and are much to be regretted. We are often told that the poor are grateful for charity. Some of them are, no doubt, *but the best amongst the poor are never grateful*. They are ungrateful, discontented, disobedient, and rebellious. They are quite right to be so. Charity they feel to be a ridiculously inadequate mode of partial restitution, or a sentimental dole, usually accompanied by some impertinent attempt on the part of the sentimentalist to tyrannize over their private lives. Why should they be grateful for the crumbs that fall from the rich man's table? They should be seated at the board, and are beginning to know it. As for being discontented, a man who would not be discontented with such surroundings and such a low mode of life would be a perfect brute. Disobedience, in the eyes of any one who has read history, is man's original virtue. It is through disobedience that progress has been made, through disobedience and through rebellion. Sometimes the poor are praised for being thrifty. But to recommend thrift to the poor is both grotesque and insulting. It is like advising a man who is starving to eat less. For a town or country labourer to practise thrift would be absolutely immoral. Man should not be ready to show that he can live like a badly-fed animal. He should decline to live like that, and should either steal or go on the rates, which is considered by many to be a form of stealing. As for begging, it is safer to beg than to take, but it is finer to take than to beg. No: a poor man who is ungrateful, unthrifty, discontented, and rebellious is probably a real personality, and has much in him. He is at any rate a healthy protest. As for the virtuous poor, one can pity them, of course, but one cannot possibly admire them. They have made private terms with the enemy, and sold their birthright for very bad pottage. They must also be extraordinarily stupid. I can quite understand a man accepting laws that protect private property, and admit of its accumulation, as long as he himself is able under those conditions to realise some form of beautiful and intellectual life. But it is almost incredible to me how a man whose life is marred and made hideous by such laws can possibly acquiesce in their continuance.

However, the explanation is not really difficult to find. It is simply this. Misery and poverty are so absolutely degrading, and exercise such a paralysing effect over the nature of men, that no class is ever really conscious of its own suffering. They have to be told of it by other people, and they often entirely disbelieve them. What is said by great employers of labour against agitators is unquestionably true. Agitators are a set of interfering, meddling people, who come down to some perfectly contented class of the community, and sow the seeds of discontent amongst them. That is the reason why agitators are so absolutely necessary. Without them, in our incomplete state, there would be no advance towards civilization. Slavery was put down in America, not in consequence of any action on the part of the slaves, or even any express desire on their part that they should be free. It was put down entirely through the grossly illegal conduct of certain agitators in Boston and elsewhere, who were not slaves themselves, nor owners of slaves, nor had anything to do with the question really. It was, undoubtedly, the Abolitionists who set the torch alight, who began the whole thing. And it is curious to note that from the slaves themselves they received, not merely very little assistance, but hardly any sympathy even; and when at the close of the war the slaves found themselves free, found themselves indeed so absolutely free that they were free to starve, many of them bitterly regretted the new state of things. To the thinker, the most tragic fact in the whole of the French Revolution is not that Marie Antoinette was killed for being a queen, but that the starved peasant of the Vendee voluntarily went out to die for the hideous cause of feudalism.

It is clear, then, that no Authoritarian Socialism will do. For while under the present system a very large number of people can lead lives of a certain amount of freedom and expression and happiness, under an industrial-barrack system, or a system of economic tyranny, nobody would be able to have any such freedom at all. It is to be regretted that a portion of our community should be practically in slavery, but to propose to solve the problem by enslaving the entire community is childish. Every man must be left quite free to choose his own work. No form of compulsion must be exercised over him. If there is, his work will not be good for him, will not be good in itself, and will not be good for others. And by work I simply mean activity of any kind.

I hardly think that any Socialist, nowadays, would seriously propose that an inspector should call every morning at each house to see that each citizen rose up and did manual labour for eight hours. Humanity has got beyond that stage, and reserves such a form of life for the people whom, in a very arbitrary manner, it chooses to call criminals. But I confess that many of the socialistic views that I have come across seem to me to be tainted with ideas of authority, if not of actual compulsion. Of course authority and compulsion are out of the question. All association must be quite voluntary. *It is only in voluntary associations that man is fine.*

But it may be asked how Individualism, which is now more or less dependent on the existence of private property for its development, will benefit by the abolition of such private property. The answer is very simple. It is true that, under existing conditions, a few men who have had private means of their own, such as Byron, Shelley, Browning, Victor Hugo, Baudelaire, and others, have been able to realise their personality more or less completely. Not one of these men ever did a single day's work for hire. They were relieved from poverty. They had an immense advantage. The question is whether it would be for the good of Individualism that such an advantage should be taken away. Let us suppose that it is taken away. What happens then to Individualism? How will it benefit?

It will benefit in this way. Under the new conditions Individualism will be far freer, far finer, and far more intensified than it is now. I am not talking of the great imaginatively-realised individualism of such poets as I have mentioned, but of the great actual Individualism latent and potential in mankind generally. For the recognition of private property has really harmed Individualism, and obscured it, by confusing a man with what he possesses. It has led Individualism entirely astray. It has made gain not growth its aim. So that man thought that the important thing was to have, and did not know that the important thing is to be. *The true perfection of man lies, not in what man has, but in what man is.* Private property has crushed true Individualism, and set up an Individualism that is false. It has debarred one part of the community from being individual by starving them. It has debarred the other part of the community from being individual by putting them on the wrong road, and encumbering them. Indeed, so completely has man's personality been absorbed by his possessions that the English law has always treated offences against a man's property with far more severity than offences against his person, and property is still the test of complete citizenship. The industry necessary for the making of money is also very demoralising. In a community like ours, where property confers immense distinction, social position, honour, respect, titles, and other pleasant things of the kind, man, being naturally ambitious, makes it his aim to accumulate this property, and goes on wearily and tediously accumulating it long after he has got far more than he wants, or can use, or enjoy, or perhaps even know of. Man will kill himself by over-work in order to secure property, and really, considering the enormous advantages that property brings, one is hardly surprised. One's regret is that society should be constructed on such a basis that man has been forced into a groove in which he cannot freely develop what is wonderful, and fascinating, and delightful in him—in which, in fact, he misses the true pleasure and joy of living. He is also, under existing conditions, very insecure. An enormously wealthy merchant may be—often is—at every moment of his life at the mercy of things that are not under his control. If the wind blows an extra point or so, or the weather suddenly changes, or some trivial thing happens, his ship may go down, his speculations may go wrong, and he finds himself a poor man, with his social position quite gone. Now, nothing should be able to harm a man except himself. Nothing should be able to rob a man at all. What a man really has, is what is in him. What is outside of him should be a matter of no importance.

With the abolition of private property, then, we shall have true beautiful, healthy Individualism. Nobody will waste his life in accumulating things, and the symbols for things. One will live. To live is the rarest thing in the world. Most people exist, that is all.

It is a question whether we have ever seen the full expression of a personality, except on the imaginative plane of art. In action, we never have. Cæsar, says Mommsen,* was the complete and perfect man. But how tragically insecure was Cæsar! Wherever there is a man who exercises authority, there is a man who resists authority. Cæsar was very perfect, but his perfection travelled by too dangerous a road. Marcus Aurelius was the perfect man, says Renan. Yes; the great emperor was a perfect man. But how intolerable were the endless claims upon him! He staggered under the burden of the empire. He was conscious how inadequate one man was to bear the weight of that Titan and too vast orb. What I mean by a perfect man is one who develops under perfect conditions; one who is not wounded, or worried, or maimed, or in danger. *Most personalities have been obliged to be rebels. Half their strength has been wasted in friction*. Byron's personality, for instance, was terribly wasted in its battle with the stupidity, and hypocrisy, and Philistinism of the English. Such battles do not always intensify strength: they often exaggerate weakness. Byron was never able to give us what he might have given us. Shelley escaped better. Like Byron, he got out of England as soon as possible. But he was not so well known. If the English had had any idea of what a great poet he really was, they would have fallen on him with tooth and nail, and made his life as unbearable to him as they possibly could. But he was not a remarkable figure in society, and consequently he escaped, to a certain degree. Still, even in Shelley the note of rebellion is sometimes too strong. The note of the perfect personality is not rebellion, but peace.

It will be a marvellous thing—the true personality of man—when we see it. It will grow naturally and simply, flower-like, or as a tree grows. It will not be at discord. It will never argue or dispute. It will not prove things. It will know everything. And yet it will not busy itself about knowledge. It will have wisdom. Its value will not be measured by material things. It will have nothing. And yet it will have everything, and whatever one takes from it, it will still have, so rich will it be. It will not be always meddling with others, or asking them to be like itself. It will love them because they

* German scholar Theodore Mommsen (1817–1903) wrote the *History of Rome*, which Wilde valued highly; he asked for it particularly when he was imprisoned.

will be different. And yet while it will not meddle with others it will help all, as a beautiful thing helps us, by being what it is. The personality of man will be very wonderful. It will be as wonderful as the personality of a child.

In its development it will be assisted by Christianity, if men desire that; but if men do not desire that, it will develop none the less surely. For it will not worry itself about the past, nor care whether things happened or did not happen. Nor will it admit any laws but its own laws; nor any authority but its own authority. Yet it will love those who sought to intensify it, and speak often of them. And of these Christ was one.

"Know Thyself" was written over the portal of the antique world. Over the portal of the new world, "Be thyself" shall be written. And the message of Christ to man was simply "Be thyself." That is the secret of Christ.

When Jesus talks about the poor he simply means personalities, just as when he talks about the rich he simply means people who have not developed their personalities. Jesus moved in a community that allowed the accumulation of private property just as ours does, and the gospel that he preached was not that in such a community it is an advantage for a man to live on scanty, unwholesome food, to wear ragged, unwholesome clothes, to sleep in horrid, unwholesome dwellings, and a disadvantage for a man to live under healthy, pleasant, and decent conditions. Such a view would have been wrong there and then, and would of course be still more wrong now and in England; for as man moves northwards the material necessities of life become of more vital importance, and our society is infinitely more complex, and displays far greater extremes of luxury and pauperism than any society of the antique world. What Jesus meant, was this. He said to man, "You have a wonderful personality. Develop it. Be yourself. Don't imagine that your perfection lies in accumulating or possessing external things. *Your perfection is inside of you.* If only you could realise that, you would not want to be rich. Ordinary riches can be stolen from a man. Real riches cannot. In the treasury-house of your soul, there are infinitely precious things, that may not be taken from you. And so, try to so shape your life that external things will not harm you. And try also to get rid of personal property. It involves sordid preoccupation, endless industry, continual wrong. Personal property hinders Individualism at every step." It is to be noted that Jesus never says that impoverished people are necessarily good, or wealthy people necessarily bad. That would not have been true. Wealthy people are, as a class, better than impoverished people, more moral, more intellectual, more well-behaved. *There is only one class in the community that thinks more about money than the rich, and that is the poor*. The poor can think of nothing else. That is the misery of being poor. What Jesus does say is that man reaches his perfection, not through what he has, not even through what he does, but entirely through what he is. And so the wealthy young man who comes to Jesus is represented as a thoroughly good citizen, who has broken none of the laws of his state, none of the commandments of his religion. He is quite respectable, in the ordinary sense of that extraordinary word. Jesus says to him, "You should give up private property. It hinders you from realising your perfection. It is a drag within you, and not outside of you, that you will find what you really are, and what you really want." To his own friends he says the same thing. He tells them to be themselves, and not to be always worrying about other things. What do other things matter? Man is complete in himself. When they go into the world, the world will disagree with them. That is inevitable. The world hates Individualism. But this is not to trouble them. They are to be calm and self-centred. If a man takes their cloak, they are to give him their coat, just to show that material things are of no importance. If people abuse them, they are not to answer back. What does it signify? The things people say of a man do not alter a man. He is what he is. Public opinion is of no value whatsoever. Even if people employ actual violence, they are not to be violent in turn. That would be to fall to the same low level. After all, even in prison, a man can be quite free. His soul can be free. His personality can be untroubled. He can be at peace. And, above all things, they are not to interfere with other people or judge them in any way. Personality is a very mysterious thing. A man cannot always be estimated by what he does. He may keep the law, and yet be worthless. He may break the law, and yet be fine. He may be bad, without ever doing anything bad. He may commit a sin against society, and yet realise through that sin his true perfection.

There was a woman who was taken in adultery. We are not told the history of her love, but that love must have been very great; for Jesus said that her sins were forgiven her, not because she repented, but because her love was so intense and wonderful. Later on, a short time before his death, as he sat at a feast, the woman came in and poured costly perfumes on his hair. His friends tried to interfere with her, and said that it was an extravagance, and that the money that the perfume cost should have been expended on charitable relief of people in want, or something of that kind. Jesus did not accept that view. He pointed out that the material needs of Man were great and very permanent, but that the spiritual needs of Man were greater still, and that in one divine moment, and by selecting its own mode of expression, a personality might make itself perfect. The world worships the woman, even now, as a saint.

Yes; there are suggestive things in Individualism. Socialism annihilates family life, for instance. With the abolition of private property, marriage in its present form must disappear. This is part of the programme. Individualism accepts this and makes it fine. It converts the abolition of legal restraint into a form of freedom that will help the full development of personality, and make the love of man and woman more wonderful, more beautiful, and more ennobling. Jesus knew this. He rejected the claims of family life, although they existed in his day and community in a very marked form. "Who is my mother? Who are my brothers?" he said, when he was told that they wished to speak to him. When one of his followers asked leave to go and bury his father, "Let the dead bury the dead," was his terrible answer. He would allow no claim whatsoever to be made on personality.

And so he who would lead a Christ-like life is he who is perfectly and absolutely himself. He may be a great poet, or a great man of science; or a young student at a University, or one who watches sheep upon a moor; or a maker of dramas, like Shakespeare, or a thinker about God, like Spinoza; or a child who plays in a garden, or a fisherman who throws his nets into the sea. It does not matter what he is, as long as he realises the perfection of the soul that is within him.

All imitation in morals and in life is wrong. Through the streets of Jerusalem at the present day crawls one who is mad and carries a wooden cross on his shoulders. He is a symbol of the lives that are marred by imitation. Father Damien* was Christ-like when he went out to live with the lepers, because in such service he realised fully what was best in him. But he was not more Christ-like than Wagner, when he realised his soul in music; or than Shelley, when he realised his soul in song. There is no one type for man. There are as many perfections as their are imperfect men. And while to the claims of charity a man may yield and yet be free, to the claims of conformity no man may yield and remain free at all.

Individualism, then, is what through Socialism we are to attain to. As a natural result the State must give up all idea of government. It must give it up because, as a wise man once said many centuries before Christ, there is such a thing as leaving mankind alone; there is no such thing as governing mankind. *All modes of government are failures.* Despotism is unjust to everybody, including the despot, who was probably made for better things. Oligarchies are unjust to the many, and ochlocracies are unjust to the few. High hopes were once formed of democracy; but democracy means simply the bludgeoning of the people by the people for the people. It has been found out. I must say that it was high time, for all authority is quite degrading. It degrades those who exercise it, and degrades those over whom it is exercised. When it is violently, grossly, and cruelly used, it produces a good effect, by creating, or at any rate bringing out, the spirit of revolt and individualism that is to kill it. When it is used with a certain amount of kindness, and accompanied by prizes and rewards, it is dreadfully demoralizing. People, in that case, are less conscious of the horrible pressure that is being put on them, and so go through their lives in a sort of coarse comfort, like petted animals, without ever realising that they are probably thinking other people's thoughts, living by other people's standards, wearing practically what one may call other

---

* A Catholic priest, Damien (1840–1889) ministered over many years to the lepers exiled from Hawaii to the island of Molokay, where he himself died of leprosy.

people's second-hand clothes, and never being themselves for a single moment. "He who would be free," says a fine thinker, "must not conform." And authority, by bribing people to conform, produces a very gross kind of over-fed barbarism amongst us.

With authority, punishment will pass away. This will be a great gain—a gain, in fact, of incalculable value. As one reads history, not in the expurgated editions written for schoolboys and passmen, but in the original authorities of each time, one is absolutely sickened, not by the crimes that the wicked have committed, but by the punishments that the good have inflicted; *and a community is infinitely more brutalised by the habitual employment of punishment, than it is by the occasional occurrence of crime*. It obviously follows that the more punishment is inflicted the more crime is produced, and most modern legislation has clearly recognised this, and has made it its task to diminish punishment as far as it thinks it can. Wherever it has really diminished it, the results have always been extremely good. The less punishment, the less crime. When there is not punishment at all, crime will either cease to exist, or if it occurs, will be treated by physicians as a very distressing form of dementia, to be cured by care and kindness. For what are called criminals nowadays are not criminals at all. Starvation, and not sin, is the parent of modern crime. That indeed is the reason why our criminals are, as a class, so absolutely uninteresting from any psychological point of view. They are not marvellous Macbeths and terrible Vautrins. They are merely what ordinary, respectable, commonplace people would be if they had not got enough to eat. When private property is abolished there will be no necessity for crime, no demand for it; it will cease to exist. Of course all crimes are not crimes against property, though such are the crimes that the English law, valuing what a man has more than what a man is, punishes with the harshest and most horrible severity, if we except the crime of murder, and regard death as worse than penal servitude, a point on which our criminals, I believe, disagree. But though a crime may not be against property, it may spring from the misery and rage and depression produced by our wrong system of property-holding, and so, when that system is abolished, will disappear. When each member of the community has sufficient for his wants, and is not interfered with by his neighbour, it will not be an object of any interest to him to interfere with anyone else. Jealousy, which is an extraordinary source of crime in modern life, is an emotion closely bound up with our conceptions of property, and under Socialism and Individualism will die out. It is remarkable that in communistic tribes jealousy is entirely unknown.

Now as the State is not to govern, it may be asked what the State is to do. The State is to be a voluntary association that will organize labour, and be the manufacturer and distributor of necessary commodities. *The State is to make what is useful. The individual is to make what is beautiful*. And as I have mentioned the word labour, I cannot help saying that a great deal of nonsense is being written and talked nowadays about the dignity of manual labour. There is nothing necessarily dignified about manual labour at all, and most of it is absolutely degrading. It is mentally and morally injurious to man to do anything in which he does not find pleasure, and many forms of labour are quite pleasureless activities, and should be regarded as such. To sweep a slushy crossing for eight hours on a day when the east wind is blowing is a disgusting occupation. To sweep it with mental, moral, or physical dignity seems to me to be impossible. To sweep it with joy would be appalling. Man is made for something better than disturbing dirt. All work of that kind should be done by a machine.

And I have no doubt that it will be so. Up to the present, man has been, to a certain extent, the slave of machinery, and there is something tragic in the fact that as soon as man had invented a machine to do his work he began to starve. This, however, is, of course, the result of our property system and our system of competition. One man owns a machine which does the work of five hundred men. Five hundred men are, in consequence, thrown out of employment, and having no work to do, become hungry and take to thieving. The one man secures the produce of the machine and keeps it, and has five hundred times as much as he should have, and probably, which is of much more importance, a great deal more than he really wants. Were that machine the property of all, every one would benefit by it. It would be an immense advantage to the community. All unintellectual labour, all monotonous, dull labour, all labour that deals with dreadful things, and involves unpleasant conditions, must be done by machinery. Machinery must work for us in coal mines, and do all sanitary services, and be the stoker of steamers, and clean the streets, and run messages on wet days, and do anything that is tedious or distressing. *At present machinery competes against man. Under proper conditions machinery will serve man*. There is no doubt at all that this is the future of machinery, and just as trees grow while the country gentleman is asleep, so while Humanity will be amusing itself, or enjoying cultivated leisure—which, and not labour, is the aim of man—or making beautiful things, or reading beautiful things, or simply contemplating the world with admiration and delight, machinery will be doing all the necessary and unpleasant work. The fact is, that civilization requires slaves. The Greeks were quite right there. Unless there are slaves to do the ugly, horrible, uninteresting work, culture and contemplation become almost impossible. Human slavery is wrong, insecure, and demoralising. On mechanical slavery, on the slavery of the machine, the future of the world depends. And when scientific men are no longer called upon to go down to a depressing East-end and distribute bad cocoa and worse blankets to starving people, they will have delightful leisure in which to devise wonderful and marvellous things for their own joy and the joy of everyone else. There will be great storages of force for every city, and for every house if required, and this force man will convert into heat, light, or motion, according to his needs. Is this Utopian? A map of the world that does not include Utopia is not worth even glancing at, for it leaves out the one country at which Humanity is always landing. And when Humanity lands there, it looks out, and, seeing a better country, sets sail. Progress is the realisation of Utopias.

Now, I have said that the community by means of organization of machinery will supply the useful things, and that the beautiful things will be made by the individual. This is not merely necessary, but it is the only possible way by which we can get either the one or the other. An individual who has to make things for the use of others, and with reference to their wants and their wishes, does not work with interest, and consequently cannot put into his work what is best in him. Upon the other hand, whenever a community or a powerful section of a community, or a government of any kind, attempts to dictate to the artist what he is to do, Art either entirely vanishes, or becomes stereotyped, or degenerates into a low and ignoble form of craft. *A work of art is the unique result of a unique temperament. Its beauty comes from the fact that the author is what he is. It has nothing to do with the fact that other people want what they want.* Indeed, the moment that an artist takes notice of what other people want, and tries to supply the demand, he ceases to be an artist, and becomes a dull or an amusing craftsman, an honest or a dishonest tradesman. He has no further claim to be considered as an artist. *Art is the most intense mode of individualism that the world has known.* I am inclined to say that it is the only real mode of individualism that the world has known. Crime, which, under certain conditions, may seem to have created individualism, must take cognizance of other people and interfere with them. It belongs to the sphere of action. But alone, without any reference to his neighbours, without any interference, the artist can fashion a beautiful thing; and if he does not do it solely for his own pleasure, he is not an artist at all.

And it is to be noted that it is the fact that Art is this intense form of individualism that makes the public try to exercise over it an authority that is as immoral as it is ridiculous, and as corrupting as it is contemptible. It is not quite their fault. The public has always, and in every age, been badly brought up. They are continually asking Art to be popular, to please their want of taste, to flatter their absurd vanity, to tell them what they have been told before, to show them what they ought to be tired of seeing, to amuse them when they feel heavy after eating too much, and to distract their thoughts when they are wearied of their own stupidity. *Now Art should never try to be popular. The public should try to make itself artistic.* There is a very wide difference. If a man of science were told that the results of his experiments, and the conclusions that he arrived at, should be of such a character that they would not upset the received popular notions on the subject, or disturb popular prejudice, or hurt the sensibilities of people who knew nothing about science; if a philosopher were told that he had a perfect right to speculate in the highest spheres of thought, provided that he arrived at the same conclusions as were held by those who had never thought in any sphere at all—well, nowadays the man of science and the philosopher would be considerably amused. Yet it is really a very few years since both philosophy and science were subjected to brutal popular control, to authority in fact—the authority of either the general ignorance of the community, or the terror and greed for power of an ecclesiastical or governmental class. Of course, we have to a very great extent got rid of any attempt on the part of the community, or the Church, or the Government, to interfere with the individualism of speculative thought, but the attempt to interfere with the individualism of imaginative art still lingers. In fact, it does more than linger: it is aggressive, offensive, and brutalizing.

In England, the arts that have escaped best are the arts in which the public take no interest. Poetry is an instance of what I mean. We have been able to have fine poetry in England because the public do not read it, and consequently do not influence it. The public like to insult poets because they are individual, but once they have insulted them they leave them alone. In the case of the novel and the drama, arts in which the public does take an interest, the result of the exercise of popular authority has been absolutely ridiculous. No country produces such badly written fiction, such tedious, common work in the novel-form, such silly, vulgar plays as in England. It must necessarily be so. The popular standard is of such a character that no artist can get to it. It is at once too easy and too difficult to be a popular novelist. It is too easy, because the requirements of the public as far as plot, style, psychology, treatment of life, and treatment of literature are concerned are within the reach of the very meanest capacity and the most uncultivated mind. It is too difficult, because to meet such requirements the artist would have to do violence to his temperament, would have to write not for the artistic joy of writing, but for the amusement of half-educated people, and so would have to suppress his individualism, forget his culture, annihilate his style, and surrender everything that is valuable in him. In the case of the drama, things are a little better: the theatre-going public like the obvious, it is true, but they do not like the tedious; and burlesque and farcical comedy, the two most popular forms, are distinct forms of art. Delightful work may be produced under burlesque and farcical conditions, and in work of this kind the artist in England is allowed very great freedom. It is when one comes to the higher forms of the drama that the result of popular control is seen. The one thing that the public dislike is novelty. Any attempt to extend the subject-matter of art is extremely distasteful to the public; and yet the vitality and progress of art depend in a large measure on the continual extension of subject-matter. The public dislike novelty because they are afraid of it. It represents to them a mode of Individualism, an assertion on the part of the artist that he selects his own subject, and treats it as he chooses. The public are quite right in their attitude. Art is Individualism, and Individualism is a disturbing and disintegrating force. Therein lies its immense value. For what it seeks to disturb is monotony of type, slavery of custom, tyranny of habit, and the reduction of man to the level of a machine. In Art, the public accept what has been, because they cannot alter it, not because they appreciate it. They swallow their classics whole, and never taste them. They endure them as the inevitable, and, as they cannot mar them, they mouth about them. Strangely enough, or not strangely, according to one's own views, this acceptance of the classics does a great deal of harm. The uncritical admiration of the Bible and Shakespeare in England is an instance of what I mean. With regard to the Bible, considerations of ecclesiastical authority enter into the matter, so that I need not dwell upon the point.

But in the case of Shakespeare it is quite obvious that the public really see neither the beauties nor the defects of his plays. If they saw the beauties, they would not object to the development of the drama; and if they saw the defects, they would not object to the development of the drama either. *The fact is, the public makes use of the classics of a country as a means of checking the progress of Art*. They degrade the classics into authorities. They use them as bludgeons for preventing the free expression of Beauty in new forms. They are always asking a writer why he does not write like somebody else, or a painter why he does not paint like somebody else, quite oblivious of the fact that if either of them did anything of the kind he would cease to be an artist. A fresh mode of Beauty is absolutely distasteful to them, and whenever it appears they get so angry and bewildered that they always use two stupid expressions—one is that the work of art is grossly unintelligible; the other, that the work of art is grossly immoral. What they mean by these words seems to me to be this. When they say a work is grossly unintelligible, they mean that the artist has said or made a beautiful thing that is new; when they describe a work as grossly immoral, they mean that the artist has said or made a beautiful thing that is true. The former expression has reference to style; the latter to subject matter. But they probably use the words very vaguely, as an ordinary mob will use ready-made paving-stones. *There is not a single real poet or prose-writer of this century, for instance, on whom the British public have not solemnly conferred diplomas of immorality*, and these diplomas practically take the place, with us, of what in France is the formal recognition of an Academy of Letters, and fortunately make the establishment of such an institution quite unnecessary in England. Of course the public are very reckless in their use of the word. That they should have called Wordsworth an immoral poet, was only to be expected. Wordsworth was a poet. But that they should have called Charles Kingsley* an immoral novelist is extraordinary. Kingsley's prose was not of a very fine quality. Still, there is the word, and they use it as best they can. An artist is, of course, not disturbed by it. The true artist is a man who believes absolutely in himself, because he is absolutely himself. But I can fancy that if an artist produced a work of art in England that immediately on its appearance was recognised by the public, through their medium, which is the public press, as a work that was quite intelligible and highly moral, he would begin to seriously question whether in its creation he had really been himself at all, and consequently whether the work was not quite unworthy of him, and either of a thoroughly second-rate order, or of no artistic value whatsoever.

Perhaps, however, I have wronged the public in limiting them to such words as "immoral," "unintelligible," "exotic," and "unhealthy."

* The early novels of Anglican minister Charles Kingsley (1819–1875) exposing poverty infuriated church authorities, and he was forbidden to preach in London.

There is one other word that they use. That word is "morbid." They do not use it often. The meaning of the word is so simple that they are not afraid of using it. Still, they use it sometimes, and, now and then, one comes across it in popular newspapers. It is, of course, a ridiculous word to apply to a work of art. For what is morbidity but a mood of emotion or a mode of thought that one cannot express? The public are all morbid, because the public can never find expression for anything. *The artist is never morbid. He expresses everything*. He stands outside his subject, and through its medium produces incomparable and artistic effects. To call an artist morbid because he deals with morbidity as his subject matter is as silly as if one called Shakespeare mad because he wrote *King Lear*.

On the whole, an artist in England gains something by being attacked. His individuality is intensified. He becomes more completely himself. Of course the attacks are very gross, very impertinent, and very contemptible. But then no artist expects grace from the vulgar mind, or style from the suburban intellect. Vulgarity and stupidity are two very vivid facts in modern life. One regrets them, naturally. But there they are. They are subjects for study, like everything else. And it is only fair to state, with regard to modern journalists, that they always apologise to one in private for what they have written against one in public.

Within the last few years two other adjectives, it may be mentioned, have been added to the very limited vocabulary of art-abuse that is at the disposal of the public. One is the word "unhealthy," the other is the word "exotic." The latter merely expresses the rage of the momentary mushroom against the immortal, entrancing, and exquisitely-lovely orchid. It is a tribute, but a tribute of no importance. The word "unhealthy," however, admits of analysis. It is a rather interesting word. In fact, it is so interesting that the people who use it do not know what it means.

What does it mean? What is a healthy, or an unhealthy work of art? All terms that one applies to a work of art, provided that one applies them rationally, have reference to either its style or its subject, or to both together. From the point of view of style, a healthy work of art is one whose style recognises the beauty of the material it employs, be that material one of words or of bronze, of colour or of ivory, and uses that beauty as a factor in producing the æsthetic effect. From the point of view of subject, a healthy work of art is one the choice whose subject is conditioned by the temperament of the artist, and comes directly out of it. In fine, a healthy work of art is one that has both perfection and personality. Of course, form and substance cannot be separated in a work of art; they are always one. But for purposes of analysis, and setting the wholeness of æsthetic impression aside for a moment, we can intellectually so separate them. An unhealthy work of art, on the other hand, is a work whose style is obvious, old-fashioned, and common, and whose subject is deliberately chosen, not because the artist has any pleasure in it, but because he thinks that the public will pay him for it. *In fact, the popular novel that the public calls healthy is always a thoroughly unhealthy production; and what the public call an unhealthy novel is always a beautiful and healthy work of art.*

I need hardly say that I am not, for a single moment, complaining that the public and the public press misuse these words. I do not see how, with their lack of comprehension of what Art is, they could possibly use them in the proper sense. I am merely pointing out the misuse; and as for the origin of the misuse and the meaning that lies behind it all, the explanation is very simple. It comes from the barbarous conception of authority. It comes from the natural inability of a community corrupted by authority to understand or appreciate Individualism. In a word, it comes from that monstrous and ignorant thing that is called Public Opinion, which bad and well-meaning as it is when it tries to control action, is infamous and of evil meaning when it tries to control Thought or Art.

Indeed, there is much more to be said in favour of the physical force of the public than there is in favour of the public's opinion. The former may be fine. The latter must be foolish. It is often said that force is no argument. That, however, entirely depends on what one wants to prove. Many of the most important problems of the last few centuries, such as the continuance of personal government in England, or of feudalism in France, have been solved entirely by means of physical force. The very violence of a revolution may make the public grand and splendid for a moment. It was a fatal day when the public discovered that the pen is mightier than the paving-stone, and can be made as offensive as the brickbat. They at once sought for the journalist, found him, developed him; and made him their industrious and well-paid servant. It is greatly to be regretted, for both their sakes. Behind the barricade there may be much that is noble and heroic. But what is there behind the leading-article but prejudice, stupidity, cant, and twaddle? And when these four are joined together they make a terrible force, and constitute the new authority.

In old days men had the rack. Now they have the press. That is an improvement certainly. But still it is very bad, and wrong, and demoralising. Somebody—was it Burke?—called journalism the fourth estate.* That was true at the time, no doubt. But at the present moment it really is the only estate. It has eaten up the other three. The Lords Temporal say nothing, the Lords Spiritual have nothing to say, and the House of Commons has nothing to say and says it. We are dominated by Journalism. In America the President reigns for four years, and Journalism governs for ever and ever. Fortunately in America journalism has carried its authority to the grossest and most brutal extreme. As a natural consequence it has begun to create a spirit of revolt. People are amused by it, or disgusted by it, according to their temperaments. But it is no longer the real force it was. It is not seriously treated. In England, Journalism, not, except in a few well-known instances, having been carried to such excesses of brutality, is still a great factor, a really remarkable power. The tyranny that it proposes to exercise over people's private lives seems to me to be quite extraordinary. *The fact is, that the public have an insatiable curiosity to know everything, except what is worth knowing.* Journalism, conscious of this, and having tradesmanlike habits, supplies their demands. In centuries before ours the public nailed the ears of journalists to the pump. That was quite hideous. In this century journalists have nailed their own ears to the keyhole. That is much worse. And what aggravates the mischief is

* The traditional three estates were the church, the nobility, and the commoners, to which political theorist Edmund Burke (or so historian Thomas Carlyle thought) added the idea of a fourth estate, the press.

that the journalists who are most to blame are not the amusing journalists who write for what are called Society papers. The harm is done by the serious, thoughtful, earnest journalists, who solemnly, as they are doing at present, will drag before the eyes of the public some incident in the private life of a great statesman, of a man who is a leader of political thought as he is a creator of political force, and invite the public to discuss the incident, to exercise authority in the matter, to give their views, and not merely to give their views, but to carry them into action, to dictate to the man upon all other points, to dictate to his party, to dictate to his country, in fact to make themselves ridiculous, offensive, and harmful. The private lives of men and women should not be told to the public. The public have nothing to do with them at all. In France they manage these things better. There they do not allow the details of the trials that take place in the divorce courts to be published for the amusement or criticism of the public. All that the public are allowed to know is that the divorce has taken place and was granted on petition of one or other or both of the married parties concerned. In France, in fact, they limit the journalist, and allow the artist almost perfect freedom. *Here we allow absolute freedom to the journalist, and entirely limit the artist.* English public opinion, that is to say, tries to constrain and impede and warp the man who makes things that are beautiful in effect, and compels the journalist to retail things that are ugly, or disgusting, or revolting in fact, so that we have the most serious journalists in the world, and the most indecent newspapers. It is no exaggeration to talk of compulsion. There are possibly some journalists who take a real pleasure in publishing horrible things, or who, being poor, look to scandals as forming a sort of permanent basis for an income. But there are other journalists, I feel certain, men of education and cultivation, who really dislike publishing these things, who know that it is wrong to do so, and only do it because the unhealthy conditions under which their occupation is carried on oblige them to supply the public with what the public wants, and to compete with other journalists in making that supply as full and satisfying to the gross popular appetite as possible. It is a very degrading position for any body of educated men to be placed in, and I have no doubt that most of them feel it acutely.

However, let us leave what is really a very sordid side of the subject, and return to the question of popular control in the matter of Art, by which I mean Public Opinion dictating to the artist the form which he is to use, the mode in which he is to use it, and the materials with which he is to work. I have pointed out that the arts which have escaped best in England are the arts in which the public have not been interested. They are, however, interested in the drama, and as a certain advance has been made in the drama within the last ten or fifteen years, it is important to point out that this advance is entirely due to a few individual artists refusing to accept the popular want of taste as their standard, and refusing to regard Art as a mere matter of demand and supply. With his marvellous and vivid personality, with a style that has really a true colour-element in it, with his extraordinary power, not over mere mimicry but over imaginative and intellectual creation, Mr. Irving,* had his sole object been to give the public what they wanted, could have produced the commonest plays in the commonest manner, and made as much success and money as a man could possibly desire. But his object was not that. His object was to realise his own perfection as an artist, under certain conditions, and in certain forms of Art. At first he appealed to the few: now he has educated the many. He has created in the public both taste and temperament. The public appreciate his artistic success immensely. I often wonder, however, whether the public understand that that success is entirely due to the fact that he did not accept their standard, but realised his own. With their standard the Lyceum would have been a sort of second-rate booth, as some of the popular theatres in London are at present. Whether they understand it or not the fact however remains, that taste and temperament have, to a certain extent, been created in the public, and that the public is capable of developing these qualities. The problem then is, why do not the public become more civilised? They have the capacity. What stops them?

---

* Henry Irving (1838–1905), actor and impresario. His productions at London's Lyceum Theatre were notable for shrewd direction, high fashion design, and brilliant display.

The thing that stops them, it must be said again, is their desire to exercise authority over the artist and over works of art. To certain theatres, such as the Lyceum and the Haymarket, the public seem to come in a proper mood. In both of these theatres there have been individual artists, who have succeeded in creating in their audiences—and every theatre in London has its own audience—the temperament to which Art appeals. And what is that temperament? It is the temperament of receptivity. That is all.

If a man approaches a work of art with any desire to exercise authority over it and the artist, he approaches it in such a spirit that he cannot receive any artistic impression from it at all. *The work of art is to dominate the spectator: the spectator is not to dominate the work of art.* The spectator is to be receptive. He is to be the violin on which the master is to play. And the more completely he can suppress his own silly views, his own foolish prejudices, his own absurd ideas of what Art should be or should not be, the more likely he is to understand and appreciate the work of art in question. This is, of course, quite obvious in the case of the vulgar theatre-going public of English men and women. But it is equally true of what are called educated people. For an educated person's ideas of Art are drawn naturally from what Art has been, whereas the new work of art is beautiful by being what Art has never been; and to measure it by the standard of the past is to measure it by a standard on the rejection of which its real perfection depends. A temperament capable of receiving, through an imaginative medium, and under imaginative conditions, new and beautiful impressions is the only temperament that can appreciate a work of art. And true as this is in the case of the appreciation of sculpture and painting, it is still more true of the appreciation of such arts as the drama. For a picture and a statue are not at war with Time. They take no count of its succession. In one moment their unity may be apprehended. In the case of literature it is different. Time must be traversed before the unity of effect is realised. And so, in the drama, there may occur in the first act of the play something whose real artistic value may not be evident to the spectator till the third or fourth act is reached. Is the silly fellow to get angry and call out, and disturb the play, and annoy the artists? No. The honest man is to sit quietly, and know the delightful emotions of wonder, curiosity, and suspense. He is not to go to the play to lose a vulgar temper. He is to go to the play to realise an artistic temperament. He is to go to the play to gain an artistic temperament. He is not the arbiter of the work of art. He is one who is admitted to contemplate the work of art, and, if the work be fine, to forget in its contemplation all the egotism that mars him—the egotism of his ignorance, or the egotism of his information. This point about the drama is hardly, I think, sufficiently recognised. I can quite understand that were *Macbeth* produced for the first time before a modern London audience, many of the people present would strongly and vigorously object to the introduction of the witches in the first act, with their grotesque phrases and their ridiculous words. But when the play is over one realises that the laughter of the witches in *Macbeth* is as terrible as the laughter of madness in *Lear*, more terrible than the laughter of Iago in the tragedy of the Moor. No spectator of art needs a more perfect mood of receptivity than the spectator of a play. The moment he seeks to exercise authority he becomes the avowed enemy of Art and of himself. Art does not mind. It is he who suffers.

With the novel it is the same thing. Popular authority and the recognition of popular authority are fatal. Thackeray's *Esmond* is a beautiful work of art because he wrote it to please himself. In his other novels, in *Pendennis*, in *Philip*, in *Vanity Fair* even, at times, he is too conscious of the public, and spoils his work by appealing directly to the sympathies of the public, or by directly mocking at them. *A true artist takes no notice whatever of the public. The public are to him non-existent.* He has no poppied or honeyed cakes through which to give the monster sleep or sustenance. He leaves that to the popular novelist. One incomparable novelist we have now in England, Mr. George Meredith. There are better artists in France, but France has no one whose view of life is so large, so varied, so imaginatively true. There are tellers of stories in Russia who have a more vivid sense of what pain in fiction may be. But to him belongs philosophy in fiction. His people not merely live, but they live in thought. One can see them from myriad points of view. They are suggestive. There is soul in them and around them. They are interpretative and symbolic. And he who made them, those wonderful quickly-moving figures, made them for his own pleasure, and has never asked the public what they wanted, has never cared to know what they wanted, has never allowed the public to dictate to him or influence him in any way, but has gone on intensifying his own personality, and producing his own individual work. At first none came to him. That did not matter. Then the few came to him. That did not change him. The many have come now. He is still the same. He is an incomparable novelist.

With the decorative arts it is not different. The public clung with really pathetic tenacity to what I believe were the direct traditions of the Great Exhibition of international vulgarity, traditions that were so appalling that the houses in which people lived were only fit for blind people to live in. Beautiful things began to be made, beautiful colours came from the dyer's hand, beautiful patterns from the artist's brain, and the use of beautiful things and their value and importance were set forth. The public were really very indignant. They lost their temper. They said silly things. No one minded. No one was a whit the worse. No one accepted the authority of public opinion. And now it is almost impossible to enter any modern house without seeing some recognition of good taste, some recognition of the value of lovely surroundings, some sign of appreciation of beauty. In fact, people's houses are, as a rule, quite charming nowadays. People have been to a very great extent civilised. It is only fair to state, however, that the extraordinary success of the revolution in house-decoration and furniture and the like has not really been due to the majority of the public developing a very fine taste in such matters. It has been chiefly due to the fact that the craftsmen of things so appreciated the pleasure of making what was beautiful, and woke to such a vivid consciousness of the hideousness and vulgarity of what the public had previously wanted, that they simply starved the public out. It would be quite impossible at the present moment to furnish a room as rooms were furnished a few years ago, without going for everything to an auction of second-hand furniture from some third-rate lodging-house. The things are no longer made. However they may object to it, people must nowadays have something charming in their surroundings. Fortunately for them, their assumption of authority in these art-matters came to entire grief.

It is evident, then, that all authority in such things is bad. People sometimes inquire what form of government is most suitable for an artist to live under. To this question there is only one answer. *The form of government that is most suitable to the artist is no government at all.* Authority over him and his art is ridiculous. It has been stated that under despotisms artists have produced lovely work. This is not quite so. Artists have visited despots, not as subjects to be tyrannized over, but as wandering wonder-makers, as fascinating vagrant personalities, to be entertained and charmed and suffered to be at peace, and allowed to create. There is this to be said in favour of the despot, that he, being an individual, may have culture, while the mob, being a monster, has none. One who is an Emperor and King may stoop down to pick up a brush for a painter, but when the democracy stoops down it is merely to throw mud. And yet the democracy have not so far to stoop as the emperor. In fact, when they want to throw mud they have not to stoop at all. But there is no necessity to separate the monarch from the mob; all authority is equally bad.

There are three kinds of despots. There is the despot who tyrannizes over the body. There is the despot who tyrannizes over the soul. There is the despot who tyrannizes over soul and body alike. The first is called the Prince. The second is called the Pope. The third is called the People. The Prince may be cultivated. Many Princes have been. Yet in the Prince there is danger. One thinks of Dante at the bitter feast in Verona,* of Tasso in Ferrara's madman's cell.† It is better for the artist not to live with Princes. The Pope may be cultivated. Many Popes have been; the bad Popes have been. The bad Popes loved Beauty, almost as passionately, nay, with as much passion as the good

---

* In exile from Florence in the early 1300s, Dante went to Verona, where it is said he was badly treated by his host, Cangrande della Scala.

† The great Renaissance poet Torquato Tasso (1544–1595) was imprisoned by the Duke of Ferrara, and went mad from his isolation.

Popes hated Thought. To the wickedness of the Papacy humanity owes much. The goodness of the Papacy owes a terrible debt to humanity. Yet, though the Vatican has kept the rhetoric of its thunders and lost the rod of its lightning, it is better for the artist not to live with Popes. It was a Pope who said of Cellini to a conclave of Cardinals that common laws and common authority were not made for men such as he; but it was a Pope who thrust Cellini* into prison, and kept him there till he sickened with rage, and created unreal visions for himself, and saw the gilded sun enter his room, and grew so enamoured of it that he sought to escape, and crept out from tower to tower, and falling through dizzy air at dawn, maimed himself, and was by a vine-dresser covered with vine leaves, and carried in a cart to one who, loving beautiful things, had care of him. There is danger in Popes. And as for the People, what of them and their authority? Perhaps of them and their authority one has spoken enough. Their authority is a thing blind, deaf, hideous, grotesque, tragic, amusing, serious and obscene. It is impossible for the artist to live with the People. All despots bribe. The people bribe and brutalize. Who told them to exercise authority? They were made to live, to listen, and to love. Someone has done them a great wrong. They have marred themselves by imitation of their inferiors. They have taken the sceptre of the Prince. How should they use it? They have taken the triple tiara of the Pope. How should they carry its burden? They are as a clown whose heart is broken. They are as a priest whose soul is not yet born. Let all who love Beauty pity them. Though they themselves love not Beauty, yet let them pity themselves. Who taught them the trick of tyranny?

There are many other things that one might point out. One might point out how the Renaissance was great, because it sought to solve no social problem, and busied itself not about such things, but suffered the individual to develop freely, beautifully, and naturally, and

---

* Renowned autobiographer, jeweler, sculptor, and sexual adventurer Benvenuto Cellini (1500–1571) was imprisoned in Rome, escaped, was recaptured, and was freed.

so had great and individual artists, and great and individual men. One might point out how Louis XIV., by creating the modern state, destroyed the individualism of the artist, and made things monstrous in their monotony of repetition, and contemptible in their conformity to rule, and destroyed throughout all France all those fine freedoms of expression that had made tradition new in beauty, and new modes one with antique form. But the past is of no importance. The present is of no importance. It is with the future that we have to deal. For the past is what man should not have been. The present is what man ought not to be. The future is what artists are.

It will, of course, be said that such a scheme as is set forth here is quite unpractical, and goes against human nature. This is perfectly true. It is unpractical, and it goes against human nature. This is why it is worth carrying out, and that is why one proposes it. For what is a practical scheme? *A practical scheme is either a scheme that is already in existence, or a scheme that could be carried out under existing conditions.* But it is exactly the existing conditions that one objects to; and any scheme that could accept these conditions is wrong and foolish. The conditions will be done away with, and human nature will change. The only thing that one really knows about human nature is that it changes. Change is the one quality we can predicate of it. The systems that fail are those that rely on the permanency of human nature, and not on its growth and development. The error of Louis XIV. was that he thought human nature would always be the same. The result of his error was the French Revolution. It was an admirable result. All the results of the mistakes of governments are quite admirable.

It is to be noted also that Individualism does not come to man with any sickly cant about duty, which merely means doing what other people want because they want it; or any hideous cant about self-sacrifice, which is merely a survival of savage mutilation. *In fact, it does not come to man with any claims upon him at all. It comes naturally and inevitably out of man.* It is the point to which all development tends. It is the differentiation to which all organisms grow. It is the perfection that is inherent in every mode of life, and towards which every mode of life quickens. And so Individualism exercises no compulsion over man. On the contrary it says to man that he should suffer no compulsion to be exercised over him. It does not try to force people to be good. It knows that people are good when they are let alone. Man will develop Individualism out of himself. Man is now so developing Individualism. To ask whether Individualism is practical is like asking whether Evolution is practical. *Evolution is the law of life, and there is no evolution except towards Individualism.* Where this tendency is not expressed, it is a case of artificially-arrested growth, or of disease, or of death.

Individualism will also be unselfish and unaffected. It has been pointed out that one of the results of the extraordinary tyranny of authority is that words are absolutely distorted from their proper and simple meaning, and are used to express the obverse of their right signification. What is true about Art is true about Life. A man is called affected, now-a-days, if he dresses as he likes to dress. But in doing that he is acting in a perfectly natural manner. Affectation, in such matters, consists in dressing according to the views of one's neighbour, whose views, as they are the views of the majority, will probably be extremely stupid. Or a man is called selfish if he lives in the manner that seems to him most suitable for the full realisation of his own personality; if, in fact, the primary aim of his life is self-development. But this is the way in which everyone should live. *Selfishness is not living as one wishes to live, it is asking others to live as one wishes to live.* And unselfishness is letting other people's lives alone, not interfering with them. Selfishness always aims at creating around it an absolute uniformity of type. Unselfishness recognizes infinite variety of type as a delightful thing, accepts it, acquiesces in it, enjoys it. It is not selfish to think for oneself. A man who does not think for himself does not think at all. It is grossly selfish to require of one's neighbour that he should think in the same way, and hold the same opinions. Why should he? If he can think, he will probably think differently. If he cannot think, it is monstrous to require thought of any kind from him. A red rose is not selfish because it wants to be a red rose. It would be horribly selfish if it wanted all the other flowers in the garden to be both red and roses. Under Individualism people will be quite natural and absolutely unselfish, and will know the meanings of the words, and realise them in their free, beautiful lives. Nor will men be egotistic as they are now. For the egotist is he who makes claims upon others, and the Individualist will not desire to do that. It will not give him pleasure. When man has realised Individualism, he will also realise sympathy and exercise it freely and spontaneously. Up to the present man has hardly cultivated sympathy at all. He has merely sympathy with pain, and sympathy with pain is not the highest form of sympathy. *All sympathy is fine, but sympathy with suffering is the least fine mode.* It is tainted with egotism. It is apt to become morbid. There is in it a certain element of terror for our own safety. We become afraid that we ourselves might be as the leper or as the blind, and that no man would have care of us. It is curiously limiting, too. One should sympathise with the entirety of life, not with life's sores and maladies merely, but with life's joy and beauty and energy and health and freedom. The wider sympathy is, of course, the more difficult. It requires more unselfishness. Anybody can sympathise with the sufferings of a friend, but it requires a very fine nature—it requires, in fact, the nature of a true Individualist—to sympathise with a friend's success. In the modern stress of competition and struggle for place, such sympathy is naturally rare, and is also very much stifled by the immoral ideal of uniformity of type and conformity to rule which is so prevalent everywhere, and is perhaps most obnoxious in England.

Sympathy with pain there will, of course, always be. It is one of the first instincts of man. The animals which are individual, the higher animals that is to say, share it with us. But it must be remembered that while sympathy with joy intensifies the sum of joy in the world, sympathy with pain does not really diminish the amount of pain. It may make man better able to endure evil, but the evil remains. Sympathy with consumption does not cure consumption; that is what Science does. And when Socialism has solved the problem of poverty, and Science solved the problem of disease, the area of the sentimentalists will be lessened, and the sympathy of man will be large, healthy, and spontaneous. Man will have joy in the contemplation of the joyous lives of others.

For it is through joy that the Individualism of the future will develop itself. *Christ made no attempt to reconstruct society, and consequently the Individualism that he preached to man could be realised only through pain or in solitude.* The ideals that we owe to Christ are the ideals of the man who abandons society entirely, or of the man who resists society absolutely. But man is naturally social. Even the Thebaid became peopled at last. And though the cenobite realises his personality, it is often an impoverished personality that he so realises. Upon the other hand, the terrible truth that pain is a mode through which man may realise himself exercised a wonderful fascination over the world. Shallow speakers and shallow thinkers in pulpits and on platforms often talk about the world's worship of pleasure, and whine against it. But it is rarely in the world's history that its ideal has been one of joy and beauty. The worship of pain has far more often dominated the world. Mediævalism, with its saints and martyrs, its love of self-torture, its wild passion for wounding itself, its gashing with knives, and its whipping with rods—Mediævalism is real Christianity, and the mediæval Christ is the real Christ. When the Renaissance dawned upon the world, and brought with it the new ideals of the beauty of life and the joy of living, men could not understand Christ. Even Art shows us that. The painters of the Renaissance drew Christ as a little boy playing with another boy in a palace or a garden, or lying back in his mother's arms, smiling at her, or at a flower, or at a bright bird; or as a noble stately figure moving nobly through the world; or as a wonderful figure rising in a sort of ecstasy from death to life. Even when they drew him crucified they drew him as a beautiful God on whom evil men had inflicted suffering. But he did not preoccupy them much. What delighted them was to paint the men and women whom they admired, and to show the loveliness of this lovely earth. They painted many religious pictures—in fact, they painted far too many, and the monotony of type and motive is wearisome, and was bad for art. It was the result of the authority of the public in art-matters, and is to be deplored. But their soul was not in the subject. Raphael was a great artist when he painted his portrait of the Pope. When he painted his Madonnas and infant Christs, he is not a great artist at all. Christ had no message for the Renaissance, which was wonderful because it brought an ideal at variance with his, and to find the presentation of the real Christ we must go to mediæval art. There he is one maimed and marred; one who is not comely to look on, because Beauty is a joy; one who is not in fair raiment, because that may be a joy also: he is a beggar who has a marvellous soul; he is a leper whose soul is divine; he needs neither property nor health; he is a God realising his perfection through pain.

The evolution of man is slow. The injustice of man is great. It was necessary that pain should be put forward as a mode of self-realisation. Even now, in some places in the world, the message of Christ is necessary. No one who lived in modern Russia could possibly realise his perfection except by pain. A few Russian artists have realised themselves in Art, in a fiction that is mediæval in character, because its dominant note is the realisation of men through suffering. But for those who are not artists, and to whom there is no mode of life but the actual life of fact, pain is the only door to perfection. A Russian who lives happily under the present system of government in Russia must either believe that man has no soul, or that, if he has, it is not worth developing. A Nihilist who rejects all authority, because he knows authority to be evil, and who welcomes all pain, because through that he realises his personality, is a real Christian. To him the Christian ideal is a true thing.

And yet, Christ did not revolt against authority. He accepted the imperial authority of the Roman Empire and paid tribute. He endured the ecclesiastical authority of the Jewish Church, and would not repel its violence by any violence of his own. He had, as I said before, no scheme for the reconstruction of society. But the modern world has schemes. It proposes to do away with poverty and the suffering that it entails. It desires to get rid of pain, and the suffering that pain entails. It trusts to Socialism and to Science as its methods. What it aims at is an Individualism expressing itself through joy. This Individualism will be larger, fuller, lovelier than any Individualism has ever been. Pain is not the ultimate mode of perfection. It is merely provisional and a protest. It has reference to wrong, unhealthy, unjust surroundings. When the wrong, and the disease, and the injustice are removed, it will have no further place. It will have done its work. It was a great work, but it is almost over. Its sphere lessens every day.

Nor will man miss it. *For what man has sought for is, indeed, neither pain nor pleasure, but simply Life.* Man has sought to live intensely, fully, perfectly. When he can do so without exercising restraint on others, or suffering it ever, and his activities are all pleasurable to him, he will be saner, healthier, more civilized, more himself. Pleasure is Nature's test, her sign of approval. When man is happy, he is in harmony with himself and his environment. The new Individualism, for whose service Socialism, whether it wills it or not, is working, will be perfect harmony. It will be what the Greeks sought for, but could not, except in Thought, realise completely, because they had slaves, and fed them; it will be what the Renaissance sought for, but could not realise completely except in Art, because they had slaves, and starved them. It will be complete, and through it each man will attain to his perfection. The new Individualism is the new Hellenism.

APHORISMS

A FEW MAXIMS FOR THE INSTRUCTION OF THE OVER-EDUCATED

Education is an admirable thing. But it is well to remember from time to time that nothing that is worth knowing can be taught.

Public opinion exists only where there are no ideas.

The English are always degrading truths into facts. When a truth becomes a fact it loses all its intellectual value.

It is a very sad thing that nowadays there is so little useless information.

The only link between Literature and the Drama left to us in England at the present moment is the bill of the play.

In old days books were written by men of letters and read by the public. Nowadays books are written by the public and read by nobody.

Most women are so artificial that they have no sense of Art. Most men are so natural that they have no sense of Beauty.

Friendship is far more tragic than love. It lasts longer.

What is abnormal in Life stands in normal relations to Art. It is the only thing in Life that stands in normal relations to Art.

A subject that is beautiful in itself gives no suggestion to the artist. It lacks imperfection.

The only thing that the artist cannot see is the obvious. The only thing that the public can see is the obvious. The result is the Criticism of the Journalist.

Art is the only serious thing in the world. And the artist is the only person who is never serious.

To be really mediæval one should have no body. To be really modern one should have no soul. To be really Greek one should have no clothes.

Dandyism is the assertion of the absolute modernity of Beauty.

The only thing that can console one for being poor is extravagance. The only thing that can console one for being rich is economy.

One should never listen. To listen is a sign of indifference to one's hearers.

Even the disciple has his uses. He stands behind one's throne, and at the moment of one's triumph whispers in one's ear that, after all, one is immortal.

The criminal classes are so close to us that even the policeman can see them. They are so far away from us that only the poet can understand them.

Those whom the gods love grow young.

PHRASES AND PHILOSOPHIES FOR THE USE OF THE YOUNG*

The first duty in life is to be as artificial as possible.

What the second duty is no one has as yet discovered.

Wickedness is a myth invented by good people to account for the curious attractiveness of others.

If the poor only had profiles there would be no difficulty in solving the problem of poverty.

Those who see any difference between soul and body have neither.

A really well-made buttonhole is the only link between Art and Nature.

Religions die when they are proved to be true. Science is the record of dead religions.

The well-bred contradict other people. The wise contradict themselves.

Nothing that actually occurs is of the smallest importance.

Dullness is the coming of age of seriousness.

In all unimportant matters, style, not sincerity, is the essential. In all important matters, style, not sincerity, is the essential.

If one tells the truth, one is sure, sooner or later, to be found out.

---

* At the request of Lord Alfred Douglas, Wilde sent these aphorisms, some known from other works, to the undergraduate magazine *The Chameleon*, which published them in December 1894.

Pleasure is the only thing one should live for. Nothing ages like happiness.

It is only by not paying one's bills that one can hope to live in the memory of the commercial classes.

No crime is vulgar, but all vulgarity is crime. Vulgarity is the conduct of others.

Only the shallow know themselves.

Time is waste of money.

One should always be a little improbable.

There is a fatality about all good resolutions. They are invariably made too soon.

The only way to atone for being occasionally a little overdressed is by being always absolutely over-educated.

To be premature is to be perfect.

Any preoccupation with ideas of what is right or wrong in conduct shows an arrested intellectual development.

Ambition is the last refuge of the failure.

A truth ceases to be true when more than one person believes in it.

In examinations the foolish ask questions that the wise cannot answer.

Greek dress was in its essence inartistic. Nothing should reveal the body but the body.

One should either be a work of art, or wear a work of art.

It is only the superficial qualities that last. Man's deeper nature is soon found out.

Industry is the root of all ugliness.

The ages live in history through their anachronisms.

It is only the gods who taste of death. Apollo has passed away, but

Hyacinth, whom men say he slew, lives on. Nero and Narcissus are always with us.

The old believe everything: the middle-aged suspect everything: the young know everything.

The condition of perfection is idleness: the aim of perfection is youth.

Only the great masters of style ever succeed in being obscure.

There is something tragic about the enormous number of young men there are in England at the present moment who start life with perfect profiles, and end by adopting some useful profession.

To love oneself is the beginning of a life-long romance.

PREFACE TO *THE PICTURE OF DORIAN GRAY*

The artist is the creator of beautiful things.

To reveal art and conceal the artist is art's aim.

The critic is he who can translate into another manner or a new material his impression of beautiful things.

The highest as the lowest form of criticism is a mode of autobiography.

Those who find ugly meanings in beautiful things are corrupt without being charming. This is a fault.

Those who find beautiful meanings in beautiful things are the cultivated. For these there is hope.

They are the elect to whom beautiful things mean only Beauty.

There is no such thing as a moral or an immoral book. Books are well written, or badly written. That is all.

The nineteenth century dislike of Realism is the rage of Caliban seeing his own face in a glass.

The nineteenth century dislike of Romanticism is the rage of Caliban not seeing his own face in a glass.

The moral life of man forms part of the subject-matter of the artist, but the morality of art consists in the perfect use of an imperfect medium.

No artist desires to prove anything. Even things that are true can be proved.

No artist has ethical sympathies. An ethical sympathy in an artist is an unpardonable mannerism of style.

No artist is ever morbid. The artist can express everything.

Thought and language are to the artist instruments of an art.

Vice and virtue are to the artist materials for an art.

From the point of view of form, the type of all the arts is the art of the musician. From the point of view of feeling, the actor's craft is the type.

All art is at once surface and symbol.

Those who go beneath the surface do so at their peril.

Those who read the symbol do so at their peril.

It is the spectator, and not life, that art really mirrors.

Diversity of opinion about a work of art shows that the work is new, complex, and vital.

When critics disagree the artist is in accord with himself.

We can forgive a man for making a useful thing as long as he does not admire it. The only excuse for making a useless thing is that one admires it intensely.

All art is quite useless.

THE IMPORTANCE OF BEING EARNEST

A TRIVIAL COMEDY FOR SERIOUS PEOPLE

[Three-Act Version]

CHARACTERS

John Worthing, J.P.

Algernon Moncrieff

Rev. Canon Chasuble, D.D.

Merriman *(Butler)*

Miss Prism *(Governess)*

Lane *(Manservant)*

Lady Bracknell

hon. Gwendolen Fairfax

Cecily Cardew

THE SCENES OF THE PLAY

Act I. Algernon Moncrieff's Flat in Half-Moon Street, W.

Act II. The Garden at the Manor House, Woolton.

Act III. Drawing-Room of the Manor House, Woolton.

Time.—The Present. Place.—London.

ACT I

SCENE.—*Morning-room in* ALGERNON'S *flat in Half-Moon Street. The room is luxuriously and artistically furnished. The sound of a piano is heard in the adjoining room.* (LANE *is arranging afternoon tea on the table, and after the music has ceased,* ALGERNON *enters.*)

ALGERNON. Did you hear what I was playing, Lane?

LANE. I didn't think it polite to listen, sir.

ALGERNON. I'm sorry for that, for your sake. I don't play accurately—anyone can play accurately—but I play with wonderful expression. As far as the piano is concerned, sentiment is my forte. I keep science for Life.

LANE. Yes, sir.

ALGERNON. And, speaking of the science of Life, have you got the cucumber sandwiches cut for Lady Bracknell?

LANE. Yes, sir. (*Hands them on a salver.*)

ALGERNON (*inspects them, takes two, and sits down on the sofa*). Oh! . . . by the way, Lane, I see from your book that on Thursday night, when Lord Shoreman and Mr. Worthing were dining with me, eight bottles of champagne are entered as having been consumed.

LANE. Yes, sir; eight bottles and a pint.

ALGERNON. Why is it that at a bachelor's establishment the servants invariably drink the champagne? I ask merely for information.

LANE. I attribute it to the superior quality of the wine, sir. I have often observed that in married households the champagne is rarely of a first-rate brand.

ALGERNON. Good Heavens! Is marriage so demoralizing as that?

LANE. I believe it *is* a very pleasant state, sir. I have had very little experience of it myself up to the present. I have only been married once. That was in consequence of a misunderstanding between myself and a young woman.

ALGERNON (*languidly*). I don't know that I am much interested in your family life, Lane.

LANE. No, sir; it is not a very interesting subject. I never think of it myself.

ALGERNON. Very natural, I am sure. That will do, Lane, thank you.

LANE. Thank you, sir. (LANE *goes out*.)

ALGERNON. Lane's views on marriage seem somewhat lax. Really, if the lower orders don't set us a good example, what on earth is the use of them? They seem, as a class, to have absolutely no sense of moral responsibility.

(*Enter* LANE.)

LANE. Mr. Ernest Worthing.

(*Enter* JACK. LANE *goes out*.)

ALGERNON. How are you, my dear Ernest? What brings you up to town?

JACK. Oh, pleasure, pleasure! What else should bring one anywhere? Eating as usual, I see, Algy!

ALGERNON (*stiffly*). I believe it is customary in good society to take some slight refreshment at five o'clock. Where have you been since last Thursday?

JACK (*sitting down on the sofa*). In the country.

ALGERNON. What on earth do you do there?

JACK (*pulling off his gloves*). When one is in town one amuses oneself. When one is in the country one amuses other people. It is excessively boring.

ALGERNON. And who are the people you amuse?

JACK (*airily*). Oh, neighbours, neighbours.

ALGERNON. Got nice neighbours in your part of Shropshire?

JACK. Perfectly horrid! Never speak to one of them.

ALGERNON. How immensely you must amuse them! (*Goes over and takes sandwich*.) By the way, Shropshire is your county, is it not?

JACK. Eh? Shropshire? Yes, of course. Hallo! Why all these cups?

Why cucumber sandwiches? Why such reckless extravagance in one so young? Who is coming to tea?

ALGERNON. Oh! merely Aunt Augusta and Gwendolen.

JACK. How perfectly delightful!

ALGERNON. Yes, that is all very well; but I am afraid Aunt Augusta won't quite approve of your being here.

JACK. May I ask why?

ALGERNON. My dear fellow, the way you flirt with Gwendolen is perfectly disgraceful. It is almost as bad as the way Gwendolen flirts with you.

JACK. I am in love with Gwendolen. I have come up to town expressly to propose to her.

ALGERNON. I thought you had come up for pleasure? . . . I call that business.

JACK. How utterly unromantic you are!

ALGERNON. I really don't see anything romantic in proposing. It is very romantic to be in love. But there is nothing romantic about a definite proposal. Why, one may be accepted. One usually is, I believe. Then the excitement is all over. The very essence of romance is uncertainty. If ever I get married, I'll certainly try to forget the fact.

JACK. I have no doubt about that, dear Algy. The Divorce Court was specially invented for people whose memories are so curiously constituted.

ALGERNON. Oh! there is no use speculating on that subject. Divorces are made in Heaven——(JACK *puts out his hand to take a sandwich.* ALGERNON *at once interferes.*) Please don't touch the cucumber sandwiches. They are ordered specially for Aunt Augusta. (*Takes one and eats it.*)

JACK. Well, you have been eating them all the time.

ALGERNON. That is quite a different matter. She is my aunt. (*Takes plate from below.*) Have some bread and butter. The bread and butter is for Gwendolen. Gwendolen is devoted to bread and butter.

JACK (*advancing to table and helping himself*). And very good bread and butter it is, too.

ALGERNON. Well, my dear fellow, you need not eat as if you were going to eat it all. You behave as if you were married to her already. You are not married to her already, and I don't think you ever will be.

JACK. Why on earth do you say that?

ALGERNON. Well, in the first place girls never marry the men they flirt with. Girls don't think it right.

JACK. Oh, that is nonsense!

ALGERNON. It isn't. It is a great truth. It accounts for the extraordinary number of bachelors that one sees all over the place. In the second place, I don't give my consent.

JACK. Your consent!

ALGERNON. My dear fellow, Gwendolen is my first cousin. And before I allow you to marry her, you will have to clear up the whole question of Cecily. (*Rings bell.*)

JACK. Cecily! What on earth do you mean? What do you mean, Algy, by Cecily? I don't know anyone of the name of Cecily.

(*Enter* LANE.)

ALGERNON. Bring me that cigarette case Mr. Worthing left in the smoking-room the last time he dined here.

LANE. Yes, sir. (LANE *goes out.*)

JACK. Do you mean to say you have had my cigarette case all this time? I wish to goodness you had let me know. I have been writing frantic letters to Scotland Yard about it. I was very nearly offering a large reward.

ALGERNON. Well, I wish you would offer one. I happen to be more than usually hard up.

JACK. There is no good offering a large reward now that the thing is found.

(*Enter* LANE *with the cigarette case on a salver.* ALGERNON *takes it at once.* LANE *goes out.*)

ALGERNON. I think that is rather mean of you, Ernest, I must say. (*Opens case and examines it.*) However, it makes no matter, for, now that I look at the inscription, I find that the thing isn't yours after all.

JACK. Of course it's mine. (*Moving to him.*) You have seen me with it a hundred times, and you have no right whatsoever to read what is written inside. It is a very ungentlemanly thing to read a private cigarette case.

ALGERNON. Oh! it is absurd to have a hard-and-fast rule about what one should read and what one shouldn't. More than half of modern culture depends on what one shouldn't read.

JACK. I am quite aware of the fact, and I don't propose to discuss modern culture. It isn't the sort of thing one should talk of in private. I simply want my cigarette case back.

ALGERNON. Yes; but this isn't your cigarette case. This cigarette case is a present from someone of the name of Cecily, and you said you didn't know anyone of that name.

JACK. Well, if you want to know, Cecily happens to be my aunt.

ALGERNON. Your aunt!

JACK. Yes. Charming old lady she is, too. Lives at Tunbridge Wells. Just give it back to me, Algy.

ALGERNON (*retreating to back of sofa*). But why does she call herself little Cecily if she is your aunt and lives at Tunbridge Wells? (*Reading.*) "From little Cecily with her fondest love."

JACK (*moving to sofa and kneeling upon it*). My dear fellow, what on earth is there in that? Some aunts are tall, some aunts are not tall. That is a matter that surely an aunt may be allowed to decide for herself. You seem to think that every aunt should be exactly like your aunt! That is absurd! For Heaven's sake give me back my cigarette case. (*Follows* ALGERNON *round the room.*)

ALGERNON. Yes. But why does your aunt call you her uncle? "From little Cecily, with her fondest love to her dear Uncle Jack." There is no objection, I admit, to an aunt being a small aunt, but why an aunt, no matter what her size may be, should call her own nephew her uncle, I can't quite make out. Besides, your name isn't Jack at all; it is Ernest.

JACK. It isn't Ernest; it's Jack.

ALGERNON. You have always told me it was Ernest. I have introduced you to everyone as Ernest. You answer to the name of Ernest. You look as if your name was Ernest. You are the most ernest looking person I ever saw in my life. It is perfectly absurd your saying that your name isn't Ernest. It's on your cards. Here is one of them. (*Taking it from case.*) "Mr. Ernest Worthing, B 4, The Albany." I'll keep this as a proof your name is Ernest if ever you attempt to deny it to me, or to Gwendolen, or to anyone else. (*Puts the card in his pocket.*)

JACK. Well, my name is Ernest in town and Jack in the country, and the cigarette case was given to me in the country.

ALGERNON. Yes, but that does not account for the fact that your small Aunt Cecily, who lives at Tunbridge Wells, calls you her dear uncle. Come, old boy, you had much better have the thing out at once.

JACK. My dear Algy, you talk exactly as if you were a dentist. It is very vulgar to talk like a dentist when one isn't a dentist. It produces a false impression.

ALGERNON. Well, that is exactly what dentists always do. Now, go on! Tell me the whole thing. I may mention that I have always suspected you of being a confirmed and secret Bunburyist; and I am quite sure of it now.

JACK. Bunburyist? What on earth do you mean by a Bunburyist?

ALGERNON. I'll reveal to you the meaning of that incomparable expression as soon as you are kind enough to inform me why you are Ernest in town and Jack in the country.

JACK. Well, produce my cigarette case first.

ALGERNON. Here it is. (*Hands cigarette case.*) Now produce your explanation, and pray make it improbable. (*Sits on sofa.*)

JACK. My dear fellow, there is nothing improbable about my explanation at all. In fact it's perfectly ordinary. Old Mr. Thomas Cardew, who adopted me when I was a little boy, made me in his will guardian to his granddaughter, Miss Cecily Cardew. Cecily, who addresses me as her uncle from motives of respect that you could not possibly appreciate, lives at my place in the country under the charge of her admirable governess, Miss Prism.

ALGERNON. Where is that place in the country, by the way?

JACK. That is nothing to you, dear boy. You are not going to be invited. . . . I may tell you candidly that the place is not in Shropshire.

ALGERNON. I suspected that, my dear fellow! I have Bunburyed all over Shropshire on two separate occasions. Now, go on. Why are you Ernest in town and Jack in the country?

JACK. My dear Algy, I don't know whether you will be able to understand my real motives. You are hardly serious enough. When one is placed in the position of guardian, one has to adopt a very high moral tone on all subjects. It's one's duty to do so. And as a high moral tone can hardly be said to conduce very much to either one's health or one's happiness, in order to get up to town I have always pretended to have a younger brother of the name of Ernest, who lives in the Albany, and gets into the most dreadful scrapes. That, my dear Algy, is the whole truth pure and simple.

ALGERNON. The truth is rarely pure and never simple. Modern life would be very tedious if it were either, and modern literature a complete impossibility!

JACK. That wouldn't be at all a bad thing.

ALGERNON. Literary criticism is not your forte, my dear fellow. Don't try it. You should leave that to people who haven't been at a University. They do it so well in the daily papers. What you really are is a Bunburyist. I was quite right in saying you were a Bunburyist. You are one of the most advanced Bunburyists I know.

JACK. What on earth do you mean?

ALGERNON. You have invented a very useful younger brother called Ernest, in order that you may be able to come up to town as often as you like. I have invented an invaluable permanent invalid called Bunbury, in order that I may be able to go down into the country whenever I choose. Bunbury is perfectly invaluable. If it wasn't for Bunbury's extraordinary bad health, for instance, I wouldn't be able to dine with you at Willis's to-night, for I have been really engaged to Aunt Augusta for more than a week.

JACK. I haven't asked you to dine with me anywhere tonight.

ALGERNON. I know. You are absolutely careless about sending out invitations. It is very foolish of you. Nothing annoys people so much as not receiving invitations.

JACK. You had much better dine with your Aunt Augusta.

ALGERNON. I haven't the smallest intention of doing anything of the kind. To begin with, I dined there on Monday, and once a week is quite enough to dine with one's own relatives. In the second place, whenever I do dine there I am always treated as a member of the family, and sent down with either no woman at all, or two. In the third place, I know perfectly well whom she will place me next to, tonight. She will place me next Mary Farquhar, who always flirts with her own husband across the dinner-table. That is not very pleasant. Indeed, it is not even decent . . . and that sort of thing is enormously on the increase. The amount of women in London who flirt with their own husbands is perfectly scandalous. It looks so bad. It is simply washing one's clean linen in public. Besides, now that I know you to be a confirmed Bunburyist I naturally want to talk to you about Bunburying. I want to tell you the rules.

JACK. I'm not a Bunburyist at all. If Gwendolen accepts me, I am going to kill my brother, indeed I think I'll kill him in any case. Cecily is a little too much interested in him. It is rather a bore. So I am going to get rid of Ernest. And I strongly advise you to do the same with Mr. . . . with your invalid friend who has the absurd name.

ALGERNON. Nothing will induce me to part with Bunbury, and if you ever get married, which seems to me extremely problematic, you will be very glad to know Bunbury. A man who marries without knowing Bunbury has a very tedious time of it.

JACK. That is nonsense. If I marry a charming girl like Gwendolen, and she is the only girl I ever saw in my life that I would marry, I certainly won't want to know Bunbury.

ALGERNON. Then your wife will. You don't seem to realize, that in married life three is company and two is none.

JACK (*sententiously*). That, my dear young friend, is the theory that the corrupt French Drama has been propounding for the last fifty years.

ALGERNON. Yes; and that the happy English home has proved in half the time.

JACK. For heaven's sake, don't try to be cynical. It's perfectly easy to be cynical.

ALGERNON. My dear fellow, it isn't easy to be anything now-a-days. There's such a lot of beastly competition about. (*The sound of an electric bell is heard.*) Ah! that must be Aunt Augusta. Only relatives, or creditors, ever ring in that Wagnerian manner. Now, if I get her out of the way for ten minutes, so that you can have an opportunity for proposing to Gwendolen, may I dine with you to-night at Willis's?

JACK. I suppose so if you want to.

ALGERNON. Yes, but you must be serious about it. I hate people who are not serious about meals. It is so shallow of them.

(*Enter* LANE.)

LANE. Lady Bracknell and Miss Fairfax. (ALGERNON *goes forward to meet them. Enter* LADY BRACKNELL *and* GWENDOLEN.)

LADY BRACKNELL. Good afternoon, dear Algernon, I hope you are behaving very well.

ALGERNON. I'm feeling very well, Aunt Augusta.

LADY BRACKNELL. That's not quite the same thing. In fact the two things rarely go together. (*Sees* JACK *and bows to him with icy coldness.*)

ALGERNON (*to* GWENDOLEN). Dear me, you are smart!

GWENDOLEN. I am always smart! Aren't I, Mr. Worthing?

JACK. You're quite perfect, Miss Fairfax.

GWENDOLEN. Oh! I hope I am not that. It would leave no room for developments, and I intend to develop in *many directions*. (GWENDOLEN *and* JACK *sit down together in the corner*.)

LADY BRACKNELL. I'm sorry if we are a little late, Algernon, but I was obliged to call on dear Lady Harbury. I hadn't been there since her poor husband's death. I never saw a woman so altered; she looks quite twenty years younger. And now I'll have a cup of tea, and one of those nice cucumber sandwiches you promised me.

ALGERNON. Certainly, Aunt Augusta. (*Goes over to tea-table*.)

LADY BRACKNELL. Won't you come and sit here, Gwendolen?

GWENDOLEN. Thanks, mamma, I'm quite comfortable where I am.

ALGERNON (*picking up empty plate in horror*). Good heavens! Lane! Why are there no cucumber sandwiches? I ordered them specially.

LANE (*gravely*). There were no cucumbers in the market this morning, sir. I went down twice.

ALGERNON. No cucumbers!

LANE. No, sir. Not even for ready money.

ALGERNON. That will do, Lane, thank you.

LANE. Thank you sir. (*Goes out.*)

ALGERNON. I am greatly distressed, Aunt Augusta, about there being no cucumbers, not even for ready money.

LADY BRACKNELL. It really makes no matter, Algernon. I had some crumpets with Lady Harbury, who seems to me to be living entirely for pleasure now.

ALGERNON. I hear her hair has turned quite gold from grief.

LADY BRACKNELL. It certainly has changed its colour. From what cause I, of course, cannot say. (ALGERNON *crosses and hands tea.*) Thank you. I've quite a treat for you to-night, Algernon. I am going to send you down with Mary Farquhar. She is such a nice woman, and so attentive to her husband. It's delightful to watch them.

ALGERNON. I am afraid, Aunt Augusta, I shall have to give up the pleasure of dining with you to-night after all.

LADY BRACKNELL (*frowning*). I hope not, Algernon. It would put my table completely out. Your uncle would have to dine upstairs. Fortunately he is accustomed to that.

ALGERNON. It is a great bore, and, I need hardly say, a terrible disappointment to me, but the fact is I have just had a telegram to say that my poor friend Bunbury is very ill again. (*Exchanges glances with* JACK.) They seem to think I should be with him.

LADY BRACKNELL. It is very strange. This Mr. Bunbury seems to suffer from curiously bad health.

ALGERNON. Yes; poor Bunbury is a dreadful invalid.

LADY BRACKNELL. Well, I must say, Algernon, that I think it is high time that Mr. Bunbury made up his mind whether he was going to live or to die. This shilly-shallying with the question is absurd.

Nor do I in any way approve of the modern sympathy with invalids. I consider it morbid. Illness of any kind is hardly a thing to be encouraged in others. Health is the primary duty of life. I am always telling that to your poor uncle, but he never seems to take much notice . . . as far as any improvement in his ailments goes. I should be much obliged if you would ask Mr. Bunbury, from me, to be kind enough not to have a relapse on Saturday, for I rely on you to arrange my music for me. It is my last reception and one wants something that will encourage conversation, particularly at the end of the season when everyone has practically said whatever they had to say, which, in most cases, was probably not much.

ALGERNON. I'll speak to Bunbury, Aunt Augusta, if he is still conscious, and I think I can promise you he'll be all right by Saturday. You see, if one plays good music, people don't listen, and if one plays bad music people don't talk. But I'll run over the programme I've drawn out, if you will kindly come into the next room for a moment.

LADY BRACKNELL. Thank you, Algernon. It is very thoughtful of you. (*Rising, and following* ALGERNON.) I'm sure the programme will be delightful, after a few expurgations. French songs I cannot possibly allow. People always seem to think that they are improper, and either look shocked, which is vulgar, or laugh, which is worse. But German sounds a thoroughly respectable language, and indeed, I believe is so. Gwendolen, you will accompany me.

GWENDOLEN. Certainly, mamma. (LADY BRACKNELL *and* ALGERNON *go into the music-room,* GWENDOLEN *remains behind.*)

JACK. Charming day it has been, Miss Fairfax.

GWENDOLEN. Pray don't talk to me about the weather, Mr. Worthing. Whenever people talk to me about the weather, I always feel quite certain that they mean something else. And that makes me so nervous.

JACK. I do mean something else.

GWENDOLEN. I thought so. In fact, I am never wrong.

JACK. And I would like to be allowed to take advantage of Lady Bracknell's temporary absence . . .

GWENDOLEN. I would certainly advise you to do so. Mamma has a way of coming back suddenly into a room that I have often had to speak to her about.

JACK (*nervously*). Miss Fairfax, ever since I met you I have admired you more than any girl . . . I have ever met since . . . I met you.

GWENDOLEN. Yes, I am quite aware of the fact. And I often wish that in public, at any rate, you had been more demonstrative. For me you have always had an irresistible fascination. Even before I met you I was far from indifferent to you. (JACK *looks at her in amazement.*) We live, as I hope you know, Mr. Worthing, in an age of ideals. The fact is constantly mentioned in the more expensive monthly magazines, and has reached the provincial pulpits I am told: and my ideal has always been to love some one of the name of Ernest. There is something in that name that inspires absolute confidence. The moment Algernon first mentioned to me that he had a friend called Ernest, I knew I was destined to love you.

JACK. You really love me, Gwendolen?

GWENDOLEN. Passionately!

JACK. Darling! You don't know how happy you've made me.

GWENDOLEN. My own Ernest!

JACK. But you don't really mean to say that you couldn't love me if my name wasn't Ernest?

GWENDOLEN. But your name is Ernest.

JACK. Yes, I know it is. But supposing it was something else? Do you mean to say you couldn't love me then?

GWENDOLEN (*glibly*). Ah! that is clearly a metaphysical speculation, and like most metaphysical speculations has very little reference at all to the actual facts of real life, as we know them.

JACK. Personally, darling, to speak quite candidly, I don't much care about the name of Ernest . . . I don't think that name suits me at all.

GWENDOLEN. It suits you perfectly. It is a divine name. It has a music of its own. It produces vibrations.

JACK. Well, really, Gwendolen, I must say that I think there are lots of other much nicer names. I think, Jack, for instance, a charming name.

GWENDOLEN. Jack? . . . No, there is very little music in the name Jack, if any at all, indeed. It does not thrill. It produces absolutely no vibration. . . . I have known several Jacks, and they all, without exception, were more than usually plain. Besides, Jack is a notorious domesticity for John! And I pity any woman who is married to a man called John. She would probably never be allowed to know the entrancing pleasure of a single moment's solitude. The only really safe name is Ernest.

JACK. Gwendolen, I must get christened at once—I mean we must get married at once. There is no time to be lost.

GWENDOLEN. Married, Mr. Worthing?

JACK (*astounded*). Well . . . surely. You know that I love you, and you led me to believe, Miss Fairfax, that you were not absolutely indifferent to me.

GWENDOLEN. I adore you. But you haven't proposed to me yet. Nothing has been said at all about marriage. The subject has not even been touched on.

JACK. Well . . . may I propose to you now?

GWENDOLEN. I think it would be an admirable opportunity. And to spare you any possible disappointment, Mr. Worthing, I think it only fair to tell you quite frankly beforehand that I am fully determined to accept you.

JACK. Gwendolen!

GWENDOLEN. Yes, Mr. Worthing, what have you got to say to me?

JACK. You know what I have got to say to you.

GWENDOLEN. Yes, but you don't say it.

JACK. Gwendolen, will you marry me? (*Goes on his knees.*)

GWENDOLEN. Of course I will, darling. How long you have been about it! I am afraid you have had very little experience in how to propose.

JACK. My own one, I have never loved anyone in the world but you.

GWENDOLEN. Yes, but men often propose for practice. I know my brother Gerald does. All my girl-friends tell me so. What wonderfully blue eyes you have, Ernest! They are quite, quite blue. I hope you will always look at me just like that, especially when there are other people present.

(*Enter* LADY BRACKNELL.)

LADY BRACKNELL. Mr. Worthing! Rise, sir, from this semi-recumbent posture. It is most indecorous.

GWENDOLEN. Mamma! (*He tries to rise; she restrains him.*) I must beg you to retire. This is no place for you. Besides, Mr. Worthing has not quite finished yet.

LADY BRACKNELL. Finished what, may I ask?

GWENDOLEN. I am engaged to Mr. Worthing, mamma. (*They rise together.*)

LADY BRACKNELL. Pardon me, you are not engaged to anyone. When you do become engaged to some one, I, or your father, should his health permit him, will inform you of the fact. An engagement should come on a young girl as a surprise, pleasant or unpleasant, as the case may be. It is hardly a matter that she could be allowed to arrange for herself. . . . And now I have a few questions to put to you, Mr. Worthing. While I am making these inquiries, you, Gwendolen, will wait for me below in the carriage.

GWENDOLEN (*reproachfully*). Mamma!

LADY BRACKNELL. In the carriage, Gwendolen! (GWENDOLEN *goes to the door. She and* JACK *blow kisses to each other behind* LADY BRACKNELL'S *back.* LADY BRACKNELL *looks vaguely about as if she could not understand what the noise was. Finally turns round.*) Gwendolen, the carriage!

GWENDOLEN. Yes, mamma. (*Goes out, looking back at* JACK.)

LADY BRACKNELL (*sitting down*). You can take a seat, Mr. Worthing. (*Looks in her pocket for notebook and pencil.*)

JACK. Thank you, Lady Bracknell, I prefer standing.

LADY BRACKNELL (*pencil and notebook in hand*). I feel bound to tell you that you are not down on my list of eligible young men, although I have the same list as the dear Duchess of Bolton has. We work together, in fact. However, I am quite ready to enter your name, should your answers be what a really affectionate mother requires. Do you smoke?

JACK. Well, yes, I must admit I smoke.

LADY BRACKNELL. I am glad to hear it. A man should always have an occupation of some kind. There are far too many idle men in London as it is. How old are you?

JACK. Twenty-nine.

LADY BRACKNELL. A very good age to be married at. I have always been of opinion that a man who desires to get married should know either everything or nothing. Which do you know?

JACK (*after some hesitation*). I know nothing, Lady Bracknell.

LADY BRACKNELL. I am pleased to hear it. I do not approve of anything that tampers with natural ignorance. Ignorance is like a delicate exotic fruit; touch it and the bloom is gone. The whole theory of modern education is radically unsound. Fortunately in England, at any rate, education produces no effect whatsoever. If it did, it would prove a serious danger to the upper classes, and probably lead to acts of violence in Grosvenor Square. What is your income?

JACK. Between seven and eight thousand a year.

LADY BRACKNELL (*makes a note in her book*). In land, or in investments?

JACK. In investments, chiefly.

LADY BRACKNELL. That is satisfactory. What between the duties expected of one during one's life-time, and the duties exacted from one after one's death, land has ceased to be either a profit or a pleasure. It gives one position, and prevents one from keeping it up. That's all that can be said about land.

JACK. I have a country house with some land, of course, attached to it, about fifteen hundred acres, I believe; but I don't depend on that for my real income. In fact, as far as I can make out, the poachers are the only people who make anything out of it.

LADY BRACKNELL. A country house! How many bedrooms? Well, that point can be cleared up afterwards. You have a town house, I hope? A girl with a simple, unspoiled nature, like Gwendolen, could hardly be expected to reside in the country.

JACK. Well, I own a house in Belgrave Square, but it is let by the year to Lady Bloxham. Of course, I can get it back whenever I like, at six months' notice.

LADY BRACKNELL. Lady Bloxham? I don't know her.

JACK. Oh, she goes about very little. She is a lady considerably advanced in years.

LADY BRACKNELL. Ah, now-a-days that is no guarantee of respectability of character. What number in Belgrave Square?

JACK. 149.

LADY BRACKNELL (*shaking her head*). The unfashionable side. I thought there was something. However, that could easily be altered.

JACK. Do you mean the fashion, or the side?

LADY BRACKNELL (*sternly*). Both, if necessary, I presume. What are your politics?

JACK. Well, I am afraid I really have none. I am a Liberal Unionist.

LADY BRACKNELL. Oh, they count as Tories. They dine with us. Or come in the evening, at any rate. Now to minor matters. Are your parents living?

JACK. I have lost both my parents.

LADY BRACKNELL. Both? . . . That seems like carelessness. Who was your father? He was evidently a man of some wealth. Was he born in what the Radical papers call the purple of commerce, or did he rise from the ranks of the aristocracy?

JACK. I am afraid I really don't know. The fact is, Lady Bracknell, I said I had lost my parents. It would be nearer the truth to say that my parents seem to have lost me . . . I don't actually know who I am by birth. I was . . . well, I was found.

LADY BRACKNELL. Found!

JACK. The late Mr. Thomas Cardew, an old gentleman of a very charitable and kindly disposition, found me, and gave me the name of Worthing, because he happened to have a first-class ticket for Worthing in his pocket at the time. Worthing is a place in Sussex. It is a seaside resort.

LADY BRACKNELL. Where did the charitable gentleman who had a first-class ticket for this seaside resort find you?

JACK (*gravely*). In a hand-bag.

LADY BRACKNELL. A hand-bag?

JACK (*very seriously*). Yes, Lady Bracknell. I was in a hand-bag—a somewhat large, black leather hand-bag, with handles to it—an ordinary hand-bag in fact.

LADY BRACKNELL. In what locality did Mr. James, or Thomas, Cardew come across this ordinary hand-bag?

JACK. In the cloak-room at Victoria Station. It was given to him in mistake for his own.

LADY BRACKNELL. The cloak-room at Victoria Station?

JACK. Yes. The Brighton line.

LADY BRACKNELL. The line is immaterial. Mr. Worthing, I confess I feel somewhat bewildered by what you have just told me. To be born, or at any rate bred, in a hand-bag, whether it had handles or not, seems to me to display a contempt for the ordinary decencies of family life that remind one of the worst excesses of the French Revolution. And I presume you know what that unfortunate movement led to? As for the particular locality in which the hand-bag was found, a cloak-room at a railway station might serve to conceal a social indiscretion—has probably, indeed, been used for the purpose before now—but it could hardly be regarded as an assured basis for a recognized position in good society.

JACK. May I ask you then what you would advise me to do? I need hardly say I would do anything in the world to ensure Gwendolen's happiness.

LADY BRACKNELL. I would strongly advise you, Mr. Worthing, to try and acquire some relations as soon as possible, and to make a definite effort to produce at any rate one parent, of either sex, before the season is quite over.

JACK. Well, I don't see how I could possibly manage to do that. I can produce the hand-bag at any moment. It is in my dressing-room at home. I really think that should satisfy you, Lady Bracknell.

LADY BRACKNELL. Me, sir! What has it to do with me? You can hardly imagine that I and Lord Bracknell would dream of allowing our only daughter—a girl brought up with the utmost care—to marry into a cloak-room, and form an alliance with a parcel? Good morning, Mr. Worthing! (LADY BRACKNELL *sweeps out in majestic indignation*.)

JACK. Good morning! (ALGERNON, *from the other room, strikes up the Wedding March.* JACK *looks perfectly furious, and goes to the door.*) For goodness' sake don't play that ghastly tune, Algy! How idiotic you are! (*The music stops, and* ALGERNON *enters cheerily.*)

ALGERNON. Didn't it go off all right, old boy? You don't mean to say Gwendolen refused you? I know it is a way she has. She is always refusing people. I think it is most ill-natured of her.

JACK. Oh, Gwendolen is as right as a trivet. As far as she is concerned, we are engaged. Her mother is perfectly unbearable. Never met such a Gorgon . . . I don't really know what a Gorgon is like, but I am quite sure that Lady Bracknell is one. In any case, she is a monster, without being a myth, which is rather unfair. . . . I beg your pardon, Algy, I suppose I shouldn't talk about your own aunt in that way before you.

ALGERNON. My dear boy, I love hearing my relations abused. It is the only thing that makes me put up with them at all. Relations are simply a tedious pack of people, who haven't got the remotest knowledge of how to live, nor the smallest instinct about when to die.

JACK. Oh, that is nonsense!

ALGERNON. It isn't!

JACK. Well, I won't argue about the matter. You always want to argue about things.

ALGERNON. That is exactly what things were originally made for.

JACK. Upon my word, if I thought that, I'd shoot myself . . . (*A pause.*) You don't think there is any chance of Gwendolen becoming like her mother in about a hundred and fifty years, do you, Algy?

ALGERNON. All women become like their mothers. That is their tragedy. No man does. That's his.

JACK. Is that clever?

ALGERNON. It is perfectly phrased! and quite as true as any observation in civilized life should be.

JACK. I am sick to death of cleverness. Everybody is clever nowa-days. You can't go anywhere without meeting clever people. The thing has become an absolute public nuisance. I wish to goodness we had a few fools left.

ALGERNON. We have.

JACK. I should extremely like to meet them. What do they talk about?

ALGERNON. The fools? Oh! about the clever people, of course.

JACK. What fools!

ALGERNON. By the way, did you tell Gwendolen the truth about your being Ernest in town, and Jack in the country?

JACK (*in a very patronising manner*). My dear fellow, the truth isn't quite the sort of thing one tells to a nice, sweet, refined girl. What extraordinary ideas you have about the way to behave to a woman!

ALGERNON. The only way to behave to a woman is to make love to her, if she is pretty, and to someone else if she is plain.

JACK. Oh, that is nonsense.

ALGERNON. What about your brother? What about the profligate Ernest?

JACK. Oh, before the end of the week I shall have got rid of him. I'll say he died in Paris of apoplexy. Lots of people die of apoplexy, quite suddenly, don't they?

ALGERNON. Yes, but it's hereditary, my dear fellow. It's a sort of thing that runs in families. You had much better say a severe chill.

JACK. You are sure a severe chill isn't hereditary, or anything of that kind?

ALGERNON. Of course it isn't!

JACK. Very well, then. My poor brother Ernest is carried off suddenly in Paris, by a severe chill. That gets rid of him.

ALGERNON. But I thought you said that . . . Miss Cardew was a little too much interested in your poor brother Ernest? Won't she feel his loss a good deal?

JACK. Oh, that is all right. Cecily is not a silly, romantic girl, I am glad to say. She has got a capital appetite, goes for long walks, and pays no attention at all to her lessons.

ALGERNON. I would rather like to see Cecily.

JACK. I will take very good care you never do. She is excessively pretty, and she is only just eighteen.

ALGERNON. Have you told Gwendolen yet that you have an excessively pretty ward who is only just eighteen?

JACK. Oh! one doesn't blurt these things out to people. Cecily and Gwendolen are perfectly certain to be extremely great friends. I'll bet you anything you like that half an hour after they have met, they will be calling each other sister.

ALGERNON. Women only do that when they have called each other a lot of other things first. Now, my dear boy, if we want to get a good table at Willis's, we really must go and dress. Do you know it is nearly seven?

JACK (*irritably*). Oh! it always is nearly seven.

ALGERNON. Well, I'm hungry.

JACK. I never knew you when you weren't. . . .

ALGERNON. What shall we do after dinner? Go to a theatre?

JACK. Oh, no! I loathe listening.

ALGERNON. Well, let us go to the Club?

JACK. Oh, no! I hate talking.

ALGERNON. Well, we might trot round to the Empire at ten?

JACK. Oh, no! can't bear looking at things. It is so silly.

ALGERNON. Well, what shall we do?

JACK. Nothing!

ALGERNON. It is awfully hard work doing nothing. However, I don't mind hard work where there is no definite object of any kind.

(*Enter* LANE.)

LANE. Miss Fairfax.

(*Enter* GWENDOLEN. LANE *goes out*.)

ALGERNON. Gwendolen, upon my word!

GWENDOLEN. Algy, kindly turn your back. I have something very particular to say to Mr. Worthing.

ALGERNON. Really, Gwendolen, I don't think I can allow this at all.

GWENDOLEN. Algy, you always adopt a strictly immoral attitude towards life. You are not quite old enough to do that. (ALGERNON *retires to the fireplace*.)

JACK. My own darling!

GWENDOLEN. Ernest, we may never be married. From the expression on mamma's face I fear we never shall. Few parents now-a-days pay any regard to what their children say to them. The old-fashioned respect for the young is fast dying out. Whatever influence I ever had over mamma, I lost at the age of three. But although she may prevent us from becoming man and wife, and I may marry someone else, and marry often, nothing that she can possibly do can alter my eternal devotion to you.

JACK. Dear Gwendolen.

GWENDOLEN. The story of your romantic origin, as related to me by mamma, with unpleasing comments, has naturally stirred the deeper fibers of my nature. Your Christian name has an irresistible fascination. The simplicity of your character makes you exquisitely incomprehensible to me. Your town address at the Albany I have. What is your address in the country?

JACK. The Manor House, Woolton, Hertfordshire. (ALGERNON, *who has been carefully listening, smiles to himself, and writes the address on his shirt-cuff. Then picks up the Railway Guide.*)

GWENDOLEN. There is a good postal service, I suppose? It may be necessary to do something desperate. That, of course, will require serious consideration. I will communicate with you daily.

JACK. My own one!

GWENDOLEN. How long do you remain in town?

JACK. Till Monday.

GWENDOLEN. Good! Algy, you may turn round now.

ALGERNON. Thanks, I've turned round already.

GWENDOLEN. You may also ring the bell.

JACK. You will let me see you to your carriage, my own darling?

GWENDOLEN. Certainly.

JACK (*to* LANE, *who now enters*). I will see Miss Fairfax out.

LANE. Yes, sir. (JACK *and* GWENDOLEN *go off.* LANE *presents several letters on a salver to* ALGERNON. *It is to be surmised that they are bills, as* ALGERNON, *after looking at the envelopes, tears them up.*)

ALGERNON. A glass of sherry, Lane.

LANE. Yes, sir.

ALGERNON. To-morrow, Lane, I'm going Bunburying.

LANE. Yes, sir.

ALGERNON. I shall probably not be back till Monday. You can put up my dress clothes, my smoking jacket, and all the Bunbury suits . . .

LANE. Yes, sir. (*Handing sherry.*)

ALGERNON. I hope to-morrow will be a fine day, Lane.

LANE. It never is, sir.

ALGERNON. Lane, you're a perfect pessimist.

LANE. I do my best to give satisfaction, sir.

(*Enter* JACK. LANE *goes off.*)

JACK. There's a sensible, intellectual girl! the only girl I ever cared for in my life. (ALGERNON *is laughing immoderately.*) What on earth are you so amused at?

ALGERNON. Oh, I'm a little anxious about poor Bunbury, that's all.

JACK. If you don't take care, your friend Bunbury will get you into a serious scrape some day.

ALGERNON. I love scrapes. They are the only things that are never serious.

JACK. Oh, that's nonsense, Algy. You never talk anything but nonsense.

ALGERNON. Nobody ever does. (JACK *looks indignantly at him, and leaves the room.* ALGERNON *lights a cigarette, reads his shirt-cuff and smiles.*)

ACT II

SCENE.—*Garden at the Manor House. A flight of gray stone steps leads up to the house. The garden, an old-fashioned one, full of roses. Time of year, July. Basket chairs, and a table covered with books are set under a large yew tree.*

(MISS PRISM *discovered seated at the table.* CECILY *is at the back watering flowers.*)

MISS PRISM (*calling*). Cecily, Cecily! Surely such a utilitarian occupation as the watering of flowers is rather Moulton's duty than yours? Especially at a moment when intellectual pleasures await you. Your German grammar is on the table. Pray open it at page fifteen. We will repeat yesterday's lesson.

CECILY (*coming over very slowly*). But I don't like German. It isn't at all a becoming language. I know perfectly well that I look quite plain after my German lesson.

MISS PRISM. Child, you know how anxious your guardian is that you should improve yourself in every way. He laid particular stress on your German, as he was leaving for town yesterday. Indeed, he always lays stress on your German when he is leaving for town.

CECILY. Dear Uncle Jack is so very serious! Sometimes he is so serious that I think he cannot be quite well.

MISS PRISM (*drawing herself up*). Your guardian enjoys the best of health, and his gravity of demeanour is especially to be commended in one so comparatively young as he is. I know no one who has a higher sense of duty and responsibility.

CECILY. I suppose that is why he often looks a little bored when we three are together.

MISS PRISM. Cecily! I am surprised at you. Mr. Worthing has many troubles in his life. Idle merriment and triviality would be out of place in his conversation. You must remember his constant anxiety about that unfortunate young man, his brother.

CECILY. I wish Uncle Jack would allow the unfortunate young man, his brother, to come down here sometimes. We might have a good influence over him, Miss Prism. I am sure you certainly would. You know German, and geology, and things of that kind influence a man very much. (CECILY *begins to write in her diary.*)

MISS PRISM (*shaking her head*). I do not think that even I could produce any effect on a character that, according to his own brother's admission, is irretrievably weak and vacillating. Indeed, I am not sure that I would desire to reclaim him. I am not in favour of this modern mania for turning bad people into good people at a moment's notice. As a man sows so let him reap. You must put away your diary, Cecily. I really don't see why you should keep a diary at all.

CECILY. I keep a diary in order to enter the wonderful secrets of my life. If I didn't write them down I should probably forget all about them.

MISS PRISM. Memory, my dear Cecily, is the diary that we all carry about with us.

CECILY. Yes, but it usually chronicles the things that have never happened, and couldn't possibly have happened. I believe that Memory is responsible for nearly all the three-volume novels that Mudie sends us.

MISS PRISM. Do not speak slightingly of the three-volume novel, Cecily. I wrote one myself in earlier days.

CECILY. Did you really, Miss Prism? How wonderfully clever you are! I hope it did not end happily? I don't like novels that end happily. They depress me so much.

MISS PRISM. The good ended happily, and the bad unhappily. That is what Fiction means.

CECILY. I suppose so. But it seems very unfair. And was your novel ever published?

MISS PRISM. Alas! no. The manuscript unfortunately was abandoned. I use the word in the sense of lost or mislaid. To your work, child, these speculations are profitless.

CECILY (*smiling*). But I see dear Dr. Chasuble coming up through the garden.

MISS PRISM (*rising and advancing*). Dr. Chasuble! This is indeed a pleasure.

(*Enter* CANON CHASUBLE.)

CHASUBLE. And how are we this morning? Miss Prism, you are, I trust, well?

CECILY. Miss Prism has just been complaining of a slight headache. I think it would do her so much good to have a short stroll with you in the park, Dr. Chasuble.

MISS PRISM. Cecily, I have not mentioned anything about a headache.

CECILY. No, dear Miss Prism, I know that, but I felt instinctively that you had a headache. Indeed I was thinking about that, and not about my German lesson, when the Rector came in.

CHASUBLE. I hope, Cecily, you are not inattentive.

CECILY. Oh, I am afraid I am.

CHASUBLE. That is strange. Were I fortunate enough to be Miss Prism's pupil, I would hang upon her lips. (MISS PRISM *glares.*) I spoke metaphorically.—My metaphor was drawn from bees. Ahem! Mr. Worthing, I suppose, has not returned from town yet?

MISS PRISM. We do not expect him till Monday afternoon.

CHASUBLE. Ah, yes, he usually likes to spend his Sunday in London. He is not one of those whose sole aim is enjoyment, as by all accounts, that unfortunate young man, his brother, seems to be. But I must not disturb Egeria and her pupil any longer.

MISS PRISM. Egeria? My name is Lætitia, Doctor.

CHASUBLE (*bowing*). A classical allusion merely, drawn from the Pagan authors. I shall see you both no doubt at Evensong.

MISS PRISM. I think, dear Doctor, I will have a stroll with you. I find I have a headache after all, and a walk might do it good.

CHASUBLE. With pleasure, Miss Prism, with pleasure. We might go as far as the schools and back.

MISS PRISM. That would be delightful. Cecily, you will read your

Political Economy in my absence. The chapter on the Fall of the Rupee you may omit. It is somewhat too sensational. Even these metallic problems have their melodramatic side.

(*Goes down the garden with* DR. CHASUBLE.)

CECILY (*picks up books and throws them back on table*). Horrid Political Economy! Horrid Geography! Horrid, horrid German!

(*Enter* MERRIMAN *with a card on a salver.*)

MERRIMAN. Mr. Ernest Worthing has just driven over from the station. He has brought his luggage with him.

CECILY (*takes the card and reads it*). "Mr. Ernest Worthing, B 4 The Albany, W." Uncle Jack's brother! Did you tell him Mr. Worthing was in town?

MERRIMAN. Yes, Miss. He seemed very much disappointed. I mentioned that you and Miss Prism were in the garden. He said he was anxious to speak to you privately for a moment.

CECILY. Ask Mr. Ernest Worthing to come here. I suppose you had better talk to the housekeeper about a room for him.

MERRIMAN. Yes, Miss. (MERRIMAN *goes off.*)

CECILY. I have never met any really wicked person before. I feel rather frightened. I am so afraid he will look just like everyone else.

(*Enter* ALGERNON, *very gay and debonair.*)

He does!

ALGERNON (*raising his hat*). You are my little cousin Cecily, I'm sure.

CECILY. You are under some strange mistake. I am not little. In fact, I am more than usually tall for my age. (ALGERNON *is rather taken aback.*) But I am your cousin Cecily. You, I see from your card, are Uncle Jack's brother, my cousin Ernest, my wicked cousin Ernest.

ALGERNON. Oh! I am not really wicked at all, cousin Cecily. You mustn't think that I am wicked.

CECILY. If you are not, then you have certainly been deceiving us all in a very inexcusable manner. I hope you have not been leading a double life, pretending to be wicked and being really good all the time. That would be hypocrisy.

ALGERNON (*looks at her in amazement*). Oh! of course I have been rather reckless.

CECILY. I am glad to hear it.

ALGERNON. In fact, now you mention the subject, I have been very bad in my own small way.

CECILY. I don't think you should be so proud of that, though I am sure it must have been very pleasant.

ALGERNON. It is much pleasanter being here with you.

CECILY. I can't understand how you are here at all. Uncle Jack won't be back till Monday afternoon.

ALGERNON. That is a great disappointment. I am obliged to go up by the first train on Monday morning. I have a business appointment that I am anxious . . . to miss.

CECILY. Couldn't you miss it anywhere but in London?

ALGERNON. No; the appointment is in London.

CECILY. Well, I know, of course, how important it is not to keep a business engagement, if one wants to retain any sense of the beauty of life, but still I think you had better wait till Uncle Jack arrives. I know he wants to speak to you about your emigrating.

ALGERNON. About my what?

CECILY. Your emigrating. He has gone up to buy your outfit.

ALGERNON. I certainly wouldn't let Jack buy my outfit. He has no taste in neckties at all.

CECILY. I don't think you will require neckties. Uncle Jack is sending you to Australia.

ALGERNON. Australia! I'd sooner die.

CECILY. Well, he said at dinner on Wednesday night, that you would have to choose between this world, the next world, and Australia.

ALGERNON. Oh, well! The accounts I have received of Australia and the next world, are not particularly encouraging. This world is good enough for me, cousin Cecily.

CECILY. Yes, but are you good enough for it?

ALGERNON. I'm afraid I'm not that. That is why I want you to reform me. You might make that your mission, if you don't mind, cousin Cecily.

CECILY. I'm afraid I've not time, this afternoon.

ALGERNON. Well, would you mind my reforming myself this afternoon?

CECILY. That is rather Quixotic of you. But I think you should try.

ALGERNON. I will. I feel better already.

CECILY. You are looking a little worse.

ALGERNON. That is because I am hungry.

CECILY. How thoughtless of me. I should have remembered that when one is going to lead an entirely new life, one requires regular and wholesome meals. Won't you come in?

ALGERNON. Thank you. Might I have a button-hole first? I never have any appetite unless I have a button-hole first.

CECILY. A Maréchal Niel? (*Picks up scissors.*)

ALGERNON. No, I'd sooner have a pink rose.

CECILY. Why? (*Cuts a flower.*)

ALGERNON. Because you are like a pink rose, cousin Cecily.

CECILY. I don't think it can be right for you to talk to me like that. Miss Prism never says such things to me.

ALGERNON. Then Miss Prism is a short-sighted old lady. (CECILY *puts the rose in his button-hole.*) You are the prettiest girl I ever saw.

CECILY. Miss Prism says that all good looks are a snare.

ALGERNON. They are a snare that every sensible man would like to be caught in.

CECILY. Oh! I don't think I would care to catch a sensible man. I shouldn't know what to talk to him about.

(*They pass into the house.* MISS PRISM *and* DR. CHASUBLE *return.*)

MISS PRISM. You are too much alone, dear Dr. Chasuble. You should get married. A misanthrope I can understand—a womanthrope, never!

CHASUBLE (*with a scholar's shudder*). Believe me, I do not deserve so neologistic a phrase. The precept as well as the practice of the Primitive Church was distinctly against matrimony.

MISS PRISM (*sententiously*). That is obviously the reason why the

Primitive Church has not lasted up to the present day. And you do not seem to realize, dear Doctor, that by persistently remaining single, a man converts himself into a permanent public temptation. Men should be careful; this very celibacy leads weaker vessels astray.

CHASUBLE. But is a man not equally attractive when married?

MISS PRISM. No married man is ever attractive except to his wife.

CHASUBLE. And often, I've been told, not even to her.

MISS PRISM. That depends on the intellectual sympathies of the woman. Maturity can always be depended on. Ripeness can be trusted. Young women are green. (DR. CHASUBLE *starts.*) I spoke horticulturally. My metaphor was drawn from fruits. But where is Cecily?

CHASUBLE. Perhaps she followed us to the schools.

(*Enter* JACK *slowly from the back of the garden. He is dressed in the deepest mourning, with crepe hatband and black gloves.*)

MISS PRISM. Mr. Worthing!

CHASUBLE. Mr. Worthing?

MISS PRISM. This is indeed a surprise. We did not look for you till Monday afternoon.

JACK (*shakes* MISS PRISM'S *hand in a tragic manner*). I have returned sooner than I expected. Dr. Chasuble, I hope you are well?

CHASUBLE. Dear Mr. Worthing, I trust this garb of woe does not betoken some terrible calamity?

JACK. My brother.

MISS PRISM. More shameful debts and extravagance?

CHASUBLE. Still leading his life of pleasure?

JACK (*shaking his head*). Dead!

CHASUBLE. Your brother Ernest dead?

JACK. Quite dead.

MISS PRISM. What a lesson for him! I trust he will profit by it.

CHASUBLE. Mr. Worthing, I offer you my sincere condolence. You have at least the consolation of knowing that you were always the most generous and forgiving of brothers.

JACK. Poor Ernest! He had many faults, but it is a sad, sad blow.

CHASUBLE. Very sad indeed. Were you with him at the end?

JACK. No. He died abroad; in Paris, in fact. I had a telegram last night from the manager of the Grand Hotel.

CHASUBLE. Was the cause of death mentioned?

JACK. A severe chill, it seems.

MISS PRISM. As a man sows, so shall he reap.

CHASUBLE (*raising his hand*). Charity, dear Miss Prism, charity! None of us are perfect. I myself am peculiarly susceptible to draughts. Will the interment take place here?

JACK. No. He seems to have expressed a desire to be buried in Paris.

CHASUBLE. In Paris! (*Shakes his head.*) I fear that hardly points to any very serious state of mind at the last. You would no doubt wish me to make some slight allusion to this tragic domestic affliction next Sunday. (JACK *presses his hand convulsively.*) My sermon on the meaning of the manna in the wilderness can be adapted to almost any occasion, joyful, or, as in the present case, distressing. (*All sigh.*) I have preached it at harvest celebrations, christenings, confirmations, on days of humiliation and festal days. The last time I delivered it was in the Cathedral, as a charity sermon on behalf of the Society for the Prevention of Discontentment among the Upper Orders. The Bishop, who was present, was much struck by some of the analogies I drew.

JACK. Ah, that reminds me, you mentioned christenings I think, Dr. Chasuble? I suppose you know how to christen all right? (DR. CHASUBLE *looks astounded.*) I mean, of course, you are continually christening, aren't you?

MISS PRISM. It is, I regret to say, one of the Rector's most constant duties in this parish. I have often spoken to the poorer classes on the subject. But they don't seem to know what thrift is.

CHASUBLE. But is there any particular infant in whom you are interested, Mr. Worthing? Your brother was, I believe, unmarried, was he not?

JACK. Oh, yes.

MISS PRISM (*bitterly*). People who live entirely for pleasure usually are.

JACK. But it is not for any child, dear Doctor. I am very fond of children. No! the fact is, I would like to be christened myself, this afternoon, if you have nothing better to do.

CHASUBLE. But surely, Mr. Worthing, you have been christened already?

JACK. I don't remember anything about it.

CHASUBLE. But have you any grave doubts on the subject?

JACK. I certainly intend to have. Of course, I don't know if the thing would bother you in any way, or if you think I am a little too old now.

CHASUBLE. Not at all. The sprinkling, and, indeed, the immersion of adults is a perfectly canonical practice.

JACK. Immersion!

CHASUBLE. You need have no apprehensions. Sprinkling is all that is necessary, or indeed I think advisable. Our weather is so changeable. At what hour would you wish the ceremony performed?

JACK. Oh, I might trot around about five if that would suit you.

CHASUBLE. Perfectly, perfectly! In fact I have two similar ceremonies to perform at that time. A case of twins that occurred recently in one of the outlying cottages on your own estate. Poor Jenkins the carter, a most hard-working man.

JACK. Oh! I don't see much fun in being christened along with other babies. It would be childish. Would half-past five do?

CHASUBLE. Admirably! Admirably! (*Takes out watch.*) And now, dear Mr. Worthing, I will not intrude any longer into a house of sorrow. I would merely beg you not to be too much bowed down by grief. What seem to us bitter trials at the moment are often blessings in disguise.

MISS PRISM. This seems to me a blessing of an extremely obvious kind.

(*Enter* CECILY *from the house.*)

CECILY. Uncle Jack! Oh, I am pleased to see you back. But what horrid clothes you have on! Do go and change them.

MISS PRISM. Cecily!

CHASUBLE. My child! my child! (CECILY *goes towards* JACK; *he kisses her brow in a melancholy manner.*)

CECILY. What is the matter, Uncle Jack? Do look happy! You look as if you had a toothache and I have such a surprise for you. Who do you think is in the dining-room? Your brother!

JACK. Who?

CECILY. Your brother Ernest. He arrived about half an hour ago.

JACK. What nonsense! I haven't got a brother.

CECILY. Oh, don't say that. However badly he may have behaved to you in the past he is still your brother. You couldn't be so heartless as to disown him. I'll tell him to come out. And you will shake hands with him, won't you, Uncle Jack? (*Runs back into the house.*)

CHASUBLE. There are very joyful tidings.

MISS PRISM. After we had all been resigned to his loss, his sudden return seems to me peculiarly distressing.

JACK. My brother is in the dining-room? I don't know what it all means. I think it is perfectly absurd.

(*Enter* ALGERNON *and* CECILY *hand in hand.*
They come slowly up to JACK.)

JACK. Good heavens! (*Motions* ALGERNON *away.*)

ALGERNON. Brother John, I have come down from town to tell you that I am very sorry for all the trouble I have given you, and that I intend to lead a better life in the future. (JACK *glares at him and does not take his hand.*)

CECILY. Uncle Jack, you are not going to refuse your own brother's hand.

JACK. Nothing will induce me to take his hand. I think his coming down here disgraceful. He knows perfectly well why.

CECILY. Uncle Jack, do be nice. There is good in everyone. Ernest has just been telling me about his poor invalid friend, Mr. Bunbury, whom he goes to visit so often. And surely there must be much good in one who is kind to an invalid, and leaves the pleasures of London to sit by a bed of pain.

JACK. Oh, he has been talking about Bunbury, has he?

CECILY. Yes, he has told me all about poor Mr. Bunbury, and his terrible state of health.

JACK. Bunbury! Well, I won't have him talk to you about Bunbury or about anything else. It is enough to drive one perfectly frantic.

ALGERNON. Of course I admit that the faults were all on my side. But I must say that I think that Brother John's coldness to me is peculiarly painful. I expected a more enthusiastic welcome, especially considering it is the first time I have come here.

CECILY. Uncle Jack, if you don't shake hands with Ernest I will never forgive you.

JACK. Never forgive me?

CECILY. Never, never, never!

JACK. Well, this is the last time I shall ever do it. (*Shakes hands with* ALGERNON *and glares.*)

CHASUBLE. It's pleasant, is it not, to see so perfect a reconciliation? I think we might leave the two brothers together.

MISS PRISM. Cecily, you will come with us.

CECILY. Certainly, Miss Prism. My little task of reconciliation is over.

CHASUBLE. You have done a beautiful action to-day, dear child.

MISS PRISM. We must not be premature in our judgments.

CECILY. I feel very happy. (*They all go off.*)

JACK. You young scoundrel, Algy, you must get out of this place as soon as possible. I don't allow any Bunburying here.

(*Enter* MERRIMAN.)

MERRIMAN. I have put Mr. Ernest's things in the room next to yours, sir. I suppose that is all right?

JACK. What?

MERRIMAN. Mr. Ernest's luggage, sir. I have unpacked it and put it in the room next to your own.

JACK. His luggage?

MERRIMAN. Yes, sir. Three portmanteaus, a dressing-case, two hatboxes, and a large luncheon-basket.

ALGERNON. I am afraid I can't stay more than a week this time.

JACK. Merriman, order the dog-cart at once. Mr. Ernest has been suddenly called back to town.

MERRIMAN. Yes, sir. (*Goes back into the house.*)

ALGERNON. What a fearful liar you are, Jack. I have not been called back to town at all.

JACK. Yes, you have.

ALGERNON. I haven't heard anyone call me.

JACK. Your duty as a gentleman calls you back.

ALGERNON. My duty as a gentleman has never interfered with my pleasures in the smallest degree.

JACK. I can quite understand that.

ALGERNON. Well, Cecily is a darling.

JACK. You are not to talk of Miss Cardew like that. I don't like it.

ALGERNON. Well, I don't like your clothes. You look perfectly ridiculous in them. Why on earth don't you go up and change? It is perfectly childish to be in deep mourning for a man who is actually staying for a whole week with you in your house as a guest. I call it grotesque.

JACK. You are certainly not staying with me for a whole week as a guest or anything else. You have got to leave . . . by the four-five train.

ALGERNON. I certainly won't leave you so long as you are in mourning. It would be most unfriendly. If I were in mourning you would stay with me, I suppose. I should think it very unkind if you didn't.

JACK. Well, will you go if I change my clothes?

ALGERNON. Yes, if you are not too long. I never saw anybody take so long to dress, and with such little result.

JACK. Well, at any rate, that is better than being always over-dressed as you are.

ALGERNON. If I am occasionally a little over-dressed, I make up for it by being always immensely over-educated.

JACK. Your vanity is ridiculous, your conduct an outrage, and your presence in my garden utterly absurd. However, you have got to catch the four-five, and I hope you will have a pleasant journey back to town. This Bunburying, as you call it, has not been a great success for you. (*Goes into the house.*)

ALGERNON. I think it has been a great success. I'm in love with

Cecily, and that is everything. (*Enter* CECILY *at the back of the garden. She picks up the can and begins to water the flowers.*) But I must see her before I go, and make arrangements for another Bunbury. Ah, there she is.

CECILY. Oh, I merely came back to water the roses. I thought you were with Uncle Jack.

ALGERNON. He's gone to order the dog-cart for me.

CECILY. Oh, is he going to take you for a nice drive?

ALGERNON. He's going to send me away.

CECILY. Then have we got to part?

ALGERNON. I am afraid so. It's a very painful parting.

CECILY. It is always painful to part from people whom one has known for a very brief space of time. The absence of old friends one can endure with equanimity. But even a momentary separation from anyone to whom one has just been introduced is almost unbearable.

ALGERNON. Thank you.

(*Enter* MERRIMAN.)

MERRIMAN. The dog-cart is at the door, sir. (ALGERNON *looking appealingly at* CECILY.)

CECILY. It can wait, Merriman . . . for . . . five minutes.

MERRIMAN. Yes, miss. (*Exit* MERRIMAN.)

ALGERNON. I hope, Cecily, I shall not offend you if I state quite frankly and openly that you seem to me to be in every way the visible personification of absolute perfection.

CECILY. I think your frankness does you great credit, Ernest. If you will allow me I will copy your remarks into my diary. (*Goes over to table and begins writing in diary.*)

ALGERNON. Do you really keep a diary? I'd give any thing to look at it. May I?

CECILY. Oh, no. (*Puts her hand over it.*) You see, it is simply a very young girl's record of her own thoughts and impressions, and consequently meant for publication. When it appears in volume form I hope you will order a copy. But pray, Ernest, don't stop. I delight in taking down from dictation. I have reached "absolute perfection." You can go on. I am quite ready for more.

ALGERNON (*somewhat taken aback*). Ahem! Ahem!

CECILY. Oh, don't cough, Ernest. When one is dictating one should speak fluently and not cough. Besides, I don't know how to spell a cough. (*Writes as* ALGERNON *speaks.*)

ALGERNON (*speaking very rapidly*). Cecily, ever since I first looked upon your wonderful and incomparable beauty, I have dared to love you wildly, passionately, devotedly, hopelessly.

CECILY. I don't think that you should tell me that you love me wildly, passionately, devotedly, hopelessly. Hopelessly doesn't seem to make much sense, does it?

ALGERNON. Cecily!

(*Enter* MERRIMAN.)

MERRIMAN. The dog-cart is waiting, sir.

ALGERNON. Tell it to come round next week, at the same hour.

MERRIMAN (*looks at* CECILY, *who makes no sign*). Yes, sir.

(MERRIMAN *retires.*)

CECILY. Uncle Jack would be very much annoyed if he knew you were staying on till next week, at the same hour.

ALGERNON. Oh, I don't care about Jack. I don't care for anybody in the whole world but you. I love you, Cecily. You will marry me, won't you?

CECILY. You silly you! Of course. Why, we have been engaged for the last three months.

ALGERNON. For the last three months?

CECILY. Yes, it will be exactly three months on Thursday.

ALGERNON. But how did we become engaged?

CECILY. Well, ever since dear Uncle Jack first confessed to us that he had a younger brother who was very wicked and bad, you of course have formed the chief topic of conversation between myself and Miss Prism. And of course a man who is much talked about is always very attractive. One feels there must be something in him after all. I daresay it was foolish of me, but I fell in love with you, Ernest.

ALGERNON. Darling! And when was the engagement actually settled?

CECILY. On the 14th of February last. Worn out by your entire ignorance of my existence, I determined to end the matter one way or the other, and after a long struggle with myself I accepted you under this dear old tree here. The next day I bought this little ring in your name, and this is the little bangle with the true lovers' knot I promised you always to wear.

ALGERNON. Did I give you this? It's very pretty, isn't it?

CECILY. Yes, you've wonderfully good taste, Ernest. It's the excuse I've always given for your leading such a bad life. And this is the box in which I keep all your dear letters. (*Kneels at table, opens box, and produces letters tied up with blue ribbon*.)

ALGERNON. My letters! But my own sweet Cecily, I have never written you any letters.

CECILY. You need hardly remind me of that, Ernest. I remember only too well that I was forced to write your letters for you. I wrote always three times a week, and sometimes oftener.

ALGERNON. Oh, do let me read them, Cecily?

CECILY. Oh, I couldn't possibly. They would make you far too conceited. (*Replaces box*.) The three you wrote me after I had broken off the engagement are so beautiful, and so badly spelled, that even now I can hardly read them without crying a little.

ALGERNON. But was our engagement ever broken off?

CECILY. Of course it was. On the 22nd of last March. You can see the entry if you like. (*Shows diary*.) "Today I broke off my engagement with Ernest. I feel it is better to do so. The weather still continues charming."

ALGERNON. But why on earth did you break it off? What had I done? I had done nothing at all, Cecily. I am very much hurt indeed to hear you broke it off. Particularly when the weather was so charming.

CECILY. It would hardly have been a really serious engagement if it hadn't been broken off at least once. But I forgave you before the week was out.

ALGERNON (*crossing to her, and kneeling*). What a perfect angel you are, Cecily.

CECILY. You dear romantic boy. (*He kisses her, she puts her fingers through his hair.*) I hope your hair curls naturally, does it?

ALGERNON. Yes, darling, with a little help from others.

CECILY. I am so glad.

ALGERNON. You'll never break off our engagement again, Cecily?

CECILY. I don't think I could break it off now that I have actually met you. Besides, of course, there is the question of your name.

ALGERNON. Yes, of course. (*Nervously.*)

CECILY. You must not laugh at me, darling, but it had always been a girlish dream of mine to love some one whose name was Ernest. (ALGERNON *rises*, CECILY *also*.) There is something in that name that seems to inspire absolute confidence. I pity any poor married woman whose husband is not called Ernest.

ALGERNON. But, my dear child, do you mean to say you could not love me if I had some other name?

CECILY. But what name?

ALGERNON. Oh, any name you like—Algernon, for instance. . . .

CECILY. But I don't like the name of Algernon.

ALGERNON. Well, my own dear, sweet, loving little darling, I really can't see why you should object to the name of Algernon. It is not at all a bad name. In fact, it is rather an aristocratic name. Half of the chaps who get into the Bankruptcy Court are called Algernon. But seriously, Cecily . . . (*Moving to her*) . . . if my name was Algy, couldn't you love me?

CECILY (*rising*). I might respect you, Ernest, I might admire your character, but I fear that I should not be able to give you my undivided attention.

ALGERNON. Ahem! Cecily! (*Picking up hat.*) Your Rector here is, I suppose, thoroughly experienced in the practice of all the rites and ceremonials of the church?

CECILY. Oh, yes. Dr. Chasuble is a most learned man. He has never written a single book, so you can imagine how much he knows.

ALGERNON. I must see him at once on a most important christening—I mean on most important business.

CECILY. Oh!

ALGERNON. I sha'n't be away more than half an hour.

CECILY. Considering that we have been engaged since February the 14th, and that I only met you to-day for the first time, I think it is rather hard that you should leave me for so long a period as half an hour. Couldn't you make it twenty minutes?

ALGERNON. I'll be back in no time. (*Kisses her and rushes down the garden.*)

CECILY. What an impetuous boy he is. I like his hair so much. I must enter his proposal in my diary.

(*Enter* MERRIMAN.)

MERRIMAN. A Miss Fairfax has just called to see Mr. Worthing. On very important business, Miss Fairfax states.

CECILY. Isn't Mr. Worthing in his library?

MERRIMAN. Mr. Worthing went over in the direction of the Rectory some time ago.

CECILY. Pray ask the lady to come out here; Mr. Worthing is sure to be back soon. And you can bring tea.

MERRIMAN. Yes, miss. (*Goes out.*)

CECILY. Miss Fairfax! I suppose one of the many good elderly women who are associated with Uncle Jack in some of his philanthropic work in London. I don't quite like women who are interested in philanthropic work. I think it is so forward of them.

(*Enter* MERRIMAN.)

MERRIMAN. Miss Fairfax.

(*Enter* GWENDOLEN. *Exit* MERRIMAN.)

CECILY (*advancing to meet her*). Pray let me introduce myself to you. My name is Cecily Cardew.

GWENDOLEN. Cecily Cardew? (*Moving to her and shaking hands.*) What a very sweet name! Something tells me that we are going to be great friends. I like you already more than I can say. My first impressions of people are never wrong.

CECILY. How nice of you to like me so much after we have known each other such a comparatively short time. Pray sit down.

GWENDOLEN (*still standing up*). I may call you Cecily, may I not?

CECILY. With pleasure!

GWENDOLEN. And you will always call me Gwendolen, won't you?

CECILY. If you wish.

GWENDOLEN. Then that is all quite settled, is it not?

CECILY. I hope so. (*A pause. They both sit down together.*)

GWENDOLEN. Perhaps this might be a favourable opportunity for my mentioning who I am. My father is Lord Bracknell. You have never heard of papa, I suppose?

CECILY. I don't think so.

GWENDOLEN. Outside the family circle, papa, I am glad to say, is entirely unknown. I think that is quite as it should be. The home seems to me to be the proper sphere for the man. And certainly once a man begins to neglect his domestic duties he becomes painfully effeminate, does he not? And I don't like that. It makes men so very attractive. Cecily, mamma, whose views on education are remarkably strict, has brought me up to be extremely short-sighted; it is part of her system; so do you mind my looking at you through my glasses?

CECILY. Oh, not at all, Gwendolen. I am very fond of being looked at.

GWENDOLEN (*after examining* CECILY *carefully through a lorgnette*). You are here on a short visit, I suppose.

CECILY. Oh, no, I live here.

GWENDOLEN (*severely*). Really? Your mother, no doubt, or some female relative of advanced years, resides here also?

CECILY. Oh, no. I have no mother, nor, in fact, any relations.

GWENDOLEN. Indeed?

CECILY. My dear guardian, with the assistance of Miss Prism, has the arduous task of looking after me.

GWENDOLEN. Your guardian?

CECILY. Yes, I am Mr. Worthing's ward.

GWENDOLEN. Oh! It is strange he never mentioned to me that he had a ward. How secretive of him! He grows more interesting hourly. I am not sure, however, that the news inspires me with feelings of unmixed delight. (*Rising and going to her.*) I am very fond of you, Cecily; I have liked you ever since I met you. But I am bound to state that now that I know that you are Mr. Worthing's ward, I cannot help expressing a wish you were—well, just a little older than you seem to be—and not quite so very alluring in appearance. In fact, if I may speak candidly—

CECILY. Pray do! I think that whenever one has anything unpleasant to say, one should always be quite candid.

GWENDOLEN. Well, to speak with perfect candour, Cecily, I wish that you were fully forty-two, and more than usually plain for your age. Ernest has a strong upright nature. He is the very soul of truth and honour. Disloyalty would be as impossible to him as deception. But even men of the noblest possible moral character are extremely susceptible to the influence of the physical charms of others. Modern, no less than Ancient History, supplies us with many most painful examples of what I refer to. If it were not so, indeed, History would be quite unreadable.

CECILY. I beg your pardon, Gwendolen, did you say Ernest?

GWENDOLEN. Yes.

CECILY. Oh, but it is not Mr. Ernest Worthing who is my guardian. It is his brother—his elder brother.

GWENDOLEN (*sitting down again*). Ernest never mentioned to me that he had a brother.

CECILY. I am sorry to say they have not been on good terms for a long time.

GWENDOLEN. Ah! that accounts for it. And now that I think of it I have never heard any man mention his brother. The subject seems distasteful to most men. Cecily, you have lifted a load from my mind. I was growing almost anxious. It would have been terrible if any cloud had come across a friendship like ours, would it not? Of course you are quite, quite sure that it is not Mr. Ernest Worthing who is your guardian?

CECILY. Quite sure. (*A pause.*) In fact, I am going to be his.

GWENDOLEN (*enquiringly*). I beg your pardon?

CECILY (*rather shy and confidingly*). Dearest Gwendolen, there is no reason why I should make a secret of it to you. Our little county newspaper is sure to chronicle the fact next week. Mr. Ernest Worthing and I are engaged to be married.

GWENDOLEN (*quite politely, rising*). My darling Cecily, I think there must be some slight error. Mr. Ernest Worthing is engaged to me. The announcement will appear in the *Morning Post* on Saturday at the latest.

CECILY (*very politely, rising*). I am afraid you must be under some misconception. Ernest proposed to me exactly ten minutes ago. (*Shows diary.*)

GWENDOLEN (*examines diary through her lorgnette carefully*). It is certainly very curious, for he asked me to be his wife yesterday afternoon at 5.30. If you would care to verify the incident, pray do so. (*Produces diary of her own.*) I never travel without my diary. One should always have something sensational to read in the train. I am so sorry, dear Cecily, if it is any disappointment to you, but I am afraid *I* have the prior claim.

CECILY. It would distress me more than I can tell you, dear Gwendolen, if it caused you any mental or physical anguish, but I feel bound to point out that since Ernest proposed to you he clearly has changed his mind.

GWENDOLEN (*meditatively*). If the poor fellow has been entrapped into any foolish promise I shall consider it my duty to rescue him at once, and with a firm hand.

CECILY (*thoughtfully and sadly*). Whatever unfortunate entanglement my dear boy may have got into, I will never reproach him with it after we are married.

GWENDOLEN. Do you allude to me, Miss Cardew, as an entanglement? You are presumptuous. On an occasion of this kind it becomes more than a moral duty to speak one's mind. It becomes a pleasure.

CECILY. Do you suggest, Miss Fairfax, that I entrapped Ernest into an engagement? How dare you? This is no time for wearing the shallow mask of manners. When I see a spade I call it a spade.

GWENDOLEN (*satirically*). I am glad to say that I have never seen a spade. It is obvious that our social spheres have been widely different.

(*Enter* MERRIMAN, *followed by the footman. He carries a salver, table-cloth, and plate-stand.* CECILY *is about to retort. The presence of the servants exercises a restraining influence, under which both girls chafe.*)

MERRIMAN. Shall I lay tea here as usual, miss?

CECILY (*sternly, in a calm voice*). Yes, as usual. (MERRIMAN *begins to clear and lay cloth. A long pause.* CECILY *and* GWENDOLYN *glare at each other.*)

GWENDOLEN. Are there many interesting walks in the vicinity, Miss Cardew?

CECILY. Oh, yes, a great many. From the top of one of the hills quite close one can see five counties.

GWENDOLEN. Five counties! I don't think I should like that. I hate crowds.

CECILY (*sweetly*). I suppose that is why you live in town? (GWENDOLEN *bites her lip, and beats her foot nervously with her parasol.*)

GWENDOLEN (*looking round*). Quite a well-kept garden this is, Miss Cardew.

CECILY. So glad you like it, Miss Fairfax.

GWENDOLEN. I had no idea there were any flowers in the country.

CECILY. Oh, flowers are as common here, Miss Fairfax, as people are in London.

GWENDOLEN. Personally I cannot understand how anybody manages to exist in the country, if anybody who is anybody does. The country always bores me to death.

CECILY. Ah! This is what the newspapers call agricultural depression, is it not? I believe the aristocracy are suffering very much from it just at present. It is almost an epidemic amongst them, I have been told. May I offer you some tea, Miss Fairfax?

GWENDOLEN (*with elaborate politeness*). Thank you. (*Aside.*) Detestable girl! But I require tea!

CECILY (*sweetly*). Sugar?

GWENDOLEN (*superciliously*). No, thank you. Sugar is not fashionable any more. (CECILY *looks angrily at her, takes up the tongs and puts four lumps of sugar into the cup.*)

CECILY (*severely*). Cake or bread and butter?

GWENDOLEN (*in a bored manner*). Bread and butter, please. Cake is rarely seen at the best houses nowadays.

CECILY (*cuts a very large slice of cake, and puts it on the tray*). Hand that to Miss Fairfax. (MERRIMAN *does so, and goes out with footman.* GWENDOLEN *drinks the tea and makes a grimace. Puts down cup at once, reaches out her hand to the bread and butter, looks at it, and finds it is cake. Rises in indignation.*)

GWENDOLEN. You have filled my tea with lumps of sugar, and though I asked most distinctly for bread and butter, you have given me cake. I am known for the gentleness of my disposition, and the extraordinary sweetness of my nature, but I warn you, Miss Cardew, you may go too far.

CECILY (*rising*). To save my poor, innocent, trusting boy from the machinations of any other girl there are no lengths to which I would not go.

GWENDOLEN. From the moment I saw you I distrusted you. I felt that you were false and deceitful. I am never deceived in such matters. My first impressions of people are invariably right.

CECILY. It seems to me, Miss Fairfax, that I am trespassing on your valuable time. No doubt you have many other calls of a similar character to make in the neighbourhood.

(*Enter* JACK.)

GWENDOLEN (*catching sight of him*). Ernest! My own Ernest!

JACK. Gwendolen! Darling! (*Offers to kiss her.*)

GWENDOLEN (*drawing back*). A moment! May I ask if you are engaged to be married to this young lady? (*Points to* CECILY.)

JACK (*laughing*). To dear little Cecily! Of course not! What could have put such an idea into your pretty little head?

GWENDOLEN. Thank you. You may. (*Offers her cheek.*)

CECILY (*very sweetly*). I knew there must be some misunderstanding, Miss Fairfax. The gentleman whose arm is at present around your waist is my dear guardian, Mr. John Worthing.

GWENDOLEN. I beg your pardon?

CECILY. This is Uncle Jack.

GWENDOLEN (*receding*). Jack! Oh!

(*Enter* ALGERNON.)

CECILY. Here is Ernest.

ALGERNON (*goes straight over to* CECILY *without noticing anyone else*). My own love! (*Offers to kiss her.*)

CECILY (*drawing back*). A moment, Ernest! May I ask you—are you engaged to be married to this young lady?

ALGERNON (*looking round*). To what young lady? Good heavens! Gwendolen!

CECILY. Yes, to good heavens, Gwendolen, I mean to Gwendolen.

ALGERNON (*laughing*). Of course not! What could have put such an idea into your pretty little head?

CECILY. Thank you. (*Presenting her cheek to be kissed.*) You may. (ALGERNON *kisses her.*)

GWENDOLEN. I felt there was some slight error, Miss Cardew. The gentleman who is now embracing you is my cousin, Mr. Algernon Moncrieff.

CECILY (*breaking away from* ALGERNON). ALGERNON Moncrieff! Oh! (*The two girls move towards each other and put their arms round each other's waists as if for protection.*)

CECILY. Are you called Algernon?

ALGERNON. I cannot deny it.

CECILY. Oh!

GWENDOLEN. Is your name really John?

JACK (*standing rather proudly*). I could deny it if I liked. I could deny anything if I liked. But my name certainly is John. It has been John for years.

CECILY (*to* GWENDOLEN). A gross deception has been practised on both of us.

GWENDOLEN. My poor wounded Cecily!

CECILY. My sweet, wronged Gwendolen!

GWENDOLEN (*slowing and seriously*). You will call me sister, will you not? (*They embrace.* JACK *and* ALGERNON *groan and walk up and down.*)

CECILY (*rather brightly*). There is just one question I would like to be allowed to ask my guardian.

GWENDOLEN. An admirable idea! Mr. Worthing, there is just one question I would like to be permitted to put to you. Where is your brother Ernest? We are both engaged to be married to your brother Ernest, so it is a matter of some importance to us to know where your brother Ernest is at present.

JACK (*slowly and hesitatingly*). Gwendolen—Cecily—it is very painful for me to be forced to speak the truth. It is the first time in my life that I have ever been reduced to such a painful position, and I am really quite inexperienced in doing anything of the kind. However I will tell you quite frankly that I have no brother Ernest. I have no brother at all. I never had a brother in my life, and I certainly have not the smallest intention of ever having one in the future.

CECILY (*surprised*). No brother at all?

JACK (*cheerily*). None!

GWENDOLEN (*severely*). Had you never a brother of any kind?

JACK (*pleasantly*). Never. Not even of any kind.

GWENDOLEN. I am afraid it is quite clear, Cecily, that neither of us is engaged to be married to anyone.

CECILY. It is not a very pleasant position for a young girl suddenly to find herself in. Is it?

GWENDOLEN. Let us go into the house. They will hardly venture to come after us there.

CECILY. No, men are so cowardly, aren't they? (*They retire into the house with scornful looks.*)

JACK. This ghastly state of things is what you call Bunburying, I suppose?

ALGERNON. Yes, and a perfectly wonderful Bunbury it is. The most wonderful Bunbury I have ever had in my life.

JACK. Well, you've no right whatsoever to Bunbury here.

ALGERNON. That is absurd. One has a right to Bunbury anywhere one chooses. Every serious Bunburyist knows that.

JACK. Serious Bunburyist! Good heavens!

ALGERNON. Well, one must be serious about something, if one wants to have any amusement in life. I happen to be serious about Bunburying. What on earth you are serious about I haven't got the remotest idea. About everything, I should fancy. You have such an absolutely trivial nature.

JACK. Well, the only small satisfaction I have in the whole of this wretched business is that your friend Bunbury is quite exploded. You won't be able to run down to the country quite so often as you used to do, dear Algy. And a very good thing, too.

ALGERNON. Your brother is a little off colour, isn't he, dear Jack? You won't be able to disappear to London quite so frequently as your wicked custom was. And not a bad thing, either.

JACK. As for your conduct towards Miss Cardew, I must say that your taking in a sweet, simple, innocent girl like that is quite inexcusable. To say nothing of the fact that she is my ward.

ALGERNON. I can see no possible defence at all for your deceiving a brilliant, clever, thoroughly experienced young lady like Miss Fairfax. To say nothing of the fact that she is my cousin.

JACK. I wanted to be engaged to Gwendolen, that is all. I love her.

ALGERNON. Well, I simply wanted to be engaged to Cecily. I adore her.

JACK. There is certainly no chance of your marrying Miss Cardew.

ALGERNON. I don't think there is much likelihood, Jack, of you and Miss Fairfax being united.

JACK. Well, that is no business of yours.

ALGERNON. If it was my business, I wouldn't talk about it. (*Begins to eat muffins.*) It is very vulgar to talk about one's business. Only people like stock-brokers do that, and then merely at dinner parties.

JACK. How you can sit there, calmly eating muffins, when we are in this horrible trouble, I can't make out. You seem to me to be perfectly heartless.

ALGERNON. Well, I can't eat muffins in an agitated manner. The butter would probably get on my cuffs. One should always eat muffins quite calmly. It is the only way to eat them.

JACK. I say it's perfectly heartless your eating muffins at all, under the circumstances.

ALGERNON. When I am in trouble, eating is the only thing that consoles me. Indeed, when I am in really great trouble, as anyone who knows me intimately will tell you, I refuse everything except food and drink. At the present moment I am eating muffins because I am unhappy. Besides, I am particularly fond of muffins. (*Rising.*)

JACK (*rising*). Well, that is no reason why you should eat them all in that greedy way. (*Takes muffin from* ALGERNON.)

ALGERNON (*offering tea-cake*). I wish you would have tea-cake instead. I don't like tea-cake.

JACK. Good heavens! I suppose a man may eat his own muffins in his own garden.

ALGERNON. But you have just said it was perfectly heartless to eat muffins.

JACK. I said it was perfectly heartless of you, under the circumstances. That is a very different thing.

ALGERNON. That may be. But the muffins are the same. (*He seizes the muffin dish from* JACK.)

JACK. Algy, I wish to goodness you would go.

ALGERNON. You can't possibly ask me to go without having some dinner. It's absurd. I never go without my dinner. No one ever does, except vegetarians and people like that. Besides I have just made arrangements with Dr. Chasuble to be christened at a quarter to six under the name of Ernest.

JACK. My dear fellow, the sooner you give up that nonsense the better. I made arrangements this morning with Chasuble to be christened myself at 5.30, and I naturally will take the name of Ernest. Gwendolen would wish it. We can't both be christened Ernest. It's absurd. Besides, I have a perfect right to be christened if I like.

There is no evidence at all that I ever have been christened by anybody. I should think it extremely probable I never was, and so does Dr. Chasuble. It is entirely different in your case. You have been christened already.

ALGERNON. Yes, but I have not been christened for years.

JACK. Yes, but you have been christened. That is the important thing.

ALGERNON. Quite so. So I know my constitution can stand it. If you are not quite sure about your ever having been christened, I must say I think it rather dangerous your venturing on it now. It might make you very unwell. You can hardly have forgotten that some-one very closely connected with you was very nearly carried off this week in Paris by a severe chill.

JACK. Yes, but you said yourself that a severe chill was not hereditary.

ALGERNON. It usedn't to be, I know—but I daresay it is now. Science is always making wonderful improvements in things.

JACK (*picking up the muffin-dish*). Oh, that is nonsense; you are always talking nonsense.

ALGERNON. Jack, you are at the muffins again! I wish you wouldn't. There are only two left. (*Takes them.*) I told you I was particularly fond of muffins.

JACK. But I hate tea-cake.

ALGERNON. Why on earth then do you allow tea-cake to be served up for your guests? What ideas you have of hospitality!

JACK. Algernon! I have already told you to go. I don't want you here. Why don't you go?

ALGERNON. I haven't quite finished my tea yet, and there is still one muffin left. (JACK *groans, and sinks into a chair.* ALGERNON *still continues eating.*)

CURTAIN

ACT III

SCENE.—*Morning-room at the Manor House.* GWENDOLEN *and* CECILY *are at the window, looking out into the garden.*

GWENDOLEN. The fact that they did not follow us at once into the house, as anyone else would have done, seems to me to show that they have some sense of shame left.

CECILY. They have been eating muffins. That looks like repentance.

GWENDOLEN (*after a pause*). They don't seem to notice us at all. Couldn't you cough?

GWENDOLEN. They're looking at us. What effrontery!

CECILY. They're approaching. That's very forward of them.

GWENDOLEN. Let us preserve a dignified silence.

CECILY. Certainly, it's the only thing to do now.

(*Enter* JACK, *followed by* ALGERNON. *They whistle some dreadful popular air from a British opera.*)

GWENDOLEN. This dignified silence seems to produce an unpleasant effect.

CECILY. A most distasteful one.

GWENDOLEN. But we will not be the first to speak.

CECILY. Certainly not.

GWENDOLEN. Mr. Worthing, I have something very particular to ask you. Much depends on your reply.

CECILY. Gwendolen, your common sense is invaluable. Mr. Moncrieff, kindly answer me the following question. Why did you pretend to be my guardian's brother?

ALGERNON. In order that I might have an opportunity of meeting you.

CECILY (*to* GWENDOLEN). That certainly seems a satisfactory explanation, does it not?

GWENDOLEN. Yes, dear, if you can believe him.

CECILY. I don't. But that does not affect the wonderful beauty of his answer.

GWENDOLEN. True. In matters of grave importance, style, not sincerity, is the vital thing. Mr. Worthing, what explanation can you offer to me for pretending to have a brother? Was it in order that you might have an opportunity of coming up to town to see me as often as possible?

JACK. Can you doubt it, Miss Fairfax?

GWENDOLEN. I have the gravest doubts upon the subject. But I intend to crush them. This is not the moment for German scepticism. (*Moving to* CECILY.) Their explanations appear to be quite satisfactory, especially Mr. Worthing's. That seems to me to have the stamp of truth upon it.

CECILY. I am more than content with what Mr. Moncrieff said. His voice alone inspires one with absolute credulity.

GWENDOLEN. Then you think we should forgive them?

CECILY. Yes. I mean no.

GWENDOLEN. True! I had forgotten. There are principles at stake that one cannot surrender. Which of us should tell them? The task is not a pleasant one.

CECILY. Could we not both speak at the same time?

GWENDOLEN. An excellent idea! I nearly always speak at the same time as other people. Will you take the time from me?

CECILY. Certainly. (GWENDOLEN *beats time with uplifted finger*.)

GWENDOLEN *and* CECILY (*speaking together*). Your Christian names are still an insuperable barrier. That is all!

JACK *and* ALGERNON (*speaking together*). Our Christian names! Is that all? But we are going to be christened this afternoon.

GWENDOLEN (*to* JACK). For my sake you are prepared to do this terrible thing?

JACK. I am.

CECILY (*to* ALGERNON). To please me you are ready to face this fearful ordeal?

ALGERNON. I am!

GWENDOLEN. How absurd to talk of the equality of the sexes!

Where questions of self-sacrifice are concerned, men are infinitely beyond us.

JACK. We are. (*Clasps hands with* ALGERNON.)

CECILY. They have moments of physical courage of which we women know absolutely nothing.

GWENDOLEN (*to* JACK). Darling!

ALGERNON (*to* CECILY). Darling! (*They fall into each other's arms.*)

(*Enter* MERRIMAN. *When he enters he coughs loudly, seeing the situation.*)

MERRIMAN. Ahem! Ahem! Lady Bracknell!

JACK. Good heavens!

(*Enter* LADY BRACKNELL. *The couples separate in alarm. Exit* MERRIMAN.)

LADY BRACKNELL. Gwendolen! What does this mean?

GWENDOLEN. Merely that I am engaged to be married to Mr. Worthing, Mamma.

LADY BRACKNELL. Come here. Sit down. Sit down immediately. Hesitation of any kind is a sign of mental decay in the young, of physical weakness in the old. (*Turns to* JACK.) Apprised, sir, of my daughter's sudden flight by her trusty maid, whose confidence I purchased by means of a small coin, I followed her at once by a luggage train. Her unhappy father is, I am glad to say, under the impression that she is attending a more than usually lengthy lecture by the University Extension Scheme on the Influence of a Permanent Income on Thought. I do not propose to undeceive him. Indeed I have never undeceived him on any question. I would consider it wrong. But of course, you will clearly understand that all communication between yourself and my daughter must cease immediately from this moment. On this point, as indeed on all points, I am firm.

JACK. I am engaged to be married to Gwendolen, Lady Bracknell!

LADY BRACKNELL. You are nothing of the kind, sir. And now, as regards Algernon! . . . Algernon!

ALGERNON. Yes, Aunt Augusta.

LADY BRACKNELL. May I ask if it is in this house that your invalid friend Mr. Bunbury resides?

ALGERNON (*stammering*). Oh no! Bunbury doesn't live here. Bunbury is somewhere else at present. In fact, Bunbury is dead.

LADY BRACKNELL. Dead! When did Mr. Bunbury die? His death must have been extremely sudden.

ALGERNON (*airily*). Oh, I killed Bunbury this afternoon. I mean poor Bunbury died this afternoon.

LADY BRACKNELL. What did he die of?

ALGERNON. Bunbury? Oh, he was quite exploded.

LADY BRACKNELL. Exploded! Was he the victim of a revolutionary outrage? I was not aware that Mr. Bunbury was interested in social legislation. If so, he is well punished for his morbidity.

ALGERNON. My dear Aunt Augusta, I mean he was found out! The doctors found out that Bunbury could not live, that is what I mean—so Bunbury died.

LADY BRACKNELL. He seems to have had great confidence in the opinion of his physicians. I am glad, however, that he made up his mind at the last to some definite course of action, and acted under proper medical advice. And now that we have finally got rid of this Mr. Bunbury, may I ask, Mr. Worthing, who is that young person whose hand my nephew Algernon is now holding in what seems to me a peculiarly unnecessary manner?

JACK. That lady is Miss Cecily Cardew, my ward. (LADY BRACKNELL *bows coldly to* CECILY.)

ALGERNON. I am engaged to be married to Cecily, Aunt Augusta.

LADY BRACKNELL. I beg your pardon?

CECILY. Mr. Moncrieff and I are engaged to be married, Lady Bracknell.

LADY BRACKNELL (*with a shiver, crossing to the sofa and sitting down*). I do not know whether there is anything peculiarly exciting in the air of this particular part of Hertfordshire, but the number of engagements that go on seems to me considerably above the proper average that statistics have laid down for our guidance. I think some preliminary enquiry on my part would not be out of place. Mr. Worthing, is Miss Cardew at all connected with any of the larger railway stations in London? I merely desire information. Until yesterday I had no idea that there were any families or persons whose origin was a Terminus. (JACK *looks perfectly furious, but restrains himself.*)

JACK (*in a clear, cold voice*). Miss Cardew is the granddaughter of the late Mr. Thomas Cardew of 149, Belgrave Square, S.W.; Gervase Park, Dorking, Surrey; and the Sporran, Fifeshire, N.B.

LADY BRACKNELL. That sounds not unsatisfactory. Three addresses always inspire confidence, even in tradesmen. But what proof have I of their authenticity?

JACK. I have carefully preserved the Court Guide of the period. They are open to your inspection, Lady Bracknell.

LADY BRACKNELL (*grimly*). I have known strange errors in that publication.

JACK. Miss Cardew's family solicitors are Messrs. Markby, Markby, and Markby.

LADY BRACKNELL. Markby, Markby, and Markby? A firm of the very highest position in their profession. Indeed I am told that one of the Mr. Markbys is occasionally to be seen at dinner parties. So far I am satisfied.

JACK (*very irritably*). How extremely kind of you, Lady Bracknell! I have also in my possession, you will be pleased to hear, certificates of Miss Cardew's birth, baptism, whooping cough, registration, vaccination, confirmation, and the measles; both the German and the English variety.

LADY BRACKNELL. Ah! A life crowded with incident, I see; though perhaps somewhat too exciting for a young girl. I am not myself in favor of premature experiences. (*Rises, looks at her watch.*) Gwendolen! the time approaches for our departure. We have not a moment to lose. As a matter of form, Mr. Worthing, I had better ask you if Miss Cardew has any little fortune?

JACK. Oh, about a hundred and thirty thousand pounds in the Funds. That is all. Good-bye, Lady Bracknell. So pleased to have seen you.

LADY BRACKNELL (*sitting down again*). A moment, Mr. Worthing.

A hundred and thirty thousand pounds! And in the Funds! Miss Cardew seems to me a most attractive young lady, now that I look at her. Few girls of the present day have any really solid qualities, any of the qualities that last, and improve with time. We live, I regret to say, in an age of surfaces. (*To* CECILY.) Come over here, dear. (CECILY *goes across.*) Pretty child! your dress is sadly simple, and your hair seems almost as Nature might have left it. But we can soon alter all that. A thoroughly experienced French maid produces a really marvellous result in a very brief space of time. I remember recommending one to young Lady Lancing, and after three months her own husband did not know her.

JACK (*aside*). And after six months nobody knew her.

LADY BRACKNELL (*glares at* JACK *for a few moments. Then bends, with a practised smile, to* CECILY). Kindly turn round, sweet child. (CECILY *turns completely round.*) No, the side view is what I want. (CECILY *presents her profile.*) Yes, quite as I expected. There are distinct social possibilities in your profile. The two weak points in our age are its want of principle and its want of profile. The chin a little higher, dear. Style largely depends on the way the chin is worn. They are worn very high, just at present. Algernon!

ALGERNON. Yes, Aunt Augusta!

LADY BRACKNELL. There are distinct social possibilities in Miss Cardew's profile.

ALGERNON. Cecily is the sweetest, dearest, prettiest girl in the whole world. And I don't care twopence about social possibilities.

LADY BRACKNELL. Never speak disrespectfully of society, Algernon. Only people who can't get into it do that. (*To* CECILY.) Dear child, of course you know that Algernon has nothing but his debts to depend upon. But I do not approve of mercenary marriages. When I married Lord Bracknell I had no fortune of any kind. But I never dreamed for a moment of allowing that to stand in my way. Well, I suppose I must give my consent.

ALGERNON. Thank you, Aunt Augusta.

LADY BRACKNELL. Cecily, you may kiss me!

CECILY (*kisses her*). Thank you, Lady Bracknell.

LADY BRACKNELL. You may also address me as Aunt Augusta for the future.

CECILY. Thank you, Aunt Augusta.

LADY BRACKNELL. The marriage, I think, had better take place quite soon.

ALGERNON. Thank you, Aunt Augusta.

CECILY. Thank you, Aunt Augusta.

LADY BRACKNELL. To speak frankly, I am not in favour of long engagements. They give people the opportunity of finding out each other's character before marriage, which I think is never advisable.

JACK. I beg your pardon for interrupting you, Lady Bracknell, but this engagement is quite out of the question. I am Miss Cardew's guardian, and she cannot marry without my consent until she comes of age. That consent I absolutely decline to give.

LADY BRACKNELL. Upon what grounds, may I ask? Algernon is an extremely, I may almost say an ostentatiously, eligible young man. He has nothing, but he looks everything. What more can one desire?

JACK. It pains me very much to have to speak frankly to you, Lady Bracknell, about your nephew, but the fact is that I do not approve at all of his moral character. I suspect him of being untruthful. (ALGERNON *and* CECILY *look at him in indignant amazement.*)

LADY BRACKNELL. Untruthful! My nephew Algernon? Impossible! He is an Oxonian.

JACK. I fear there can be no possible doubt about the matter. This afternoon, during my temporary absence in London on an important question of romance, he obtained admission to my house by means of the false pretence of being my brother. Under an assumed name he drank, I've just been informed by my butler, an entire pint bottle of my Perrier-Jouet, Brut, '89; a wine I was specially reserving for myself. Continuing his disgraceful deception, he succeeded in the course of the afternoon in alienating the affections of my only ward. He subsequently stayed to tea, and devoured every single muffin. And what makes his conduct all the more heartless is, that he was perfectly well aware from the first that I have no brother, that I never had a brother, and that

I don't intend to have a brother, not even of any kind. I distinctly told him so myself yesterday afternoon.

LADY BRACKNELL. Ahem! Mr. Worthing, after careful consideration I have decided entirely to overlook my nephew's conduct to you.

JACK. That is very generous of you, Lady Bracknell. My own decision, however, is unalterable. I decline to give my consent.

LADY BRACKNELL (*to* CECILY). Come here, sweet child. (CECILY *goes over*.) How old are you, dear?

CECILY. Well, I am really only eighteen, but I always admit to twenty when I go to evening parties.

LADY BRACKNELL. You are perfectly right in making some slight alteration. Indeed, no woman should ever be quite accurate about her age. It looks so calculating. . . . (*In meditative manner*.) Eighteen, but admitting to twenty at evening parties. Well, it will not be very long before you are of age and free from the restraints of tutelage. So I don't think your guardian's consent is, after all, a matter of any importance.

JACK. Pray excuse me, Lady Bracknell, for interrupting you again, but it is only fair to tell you that according to the terms of her grandfather's will Miss Cardew does not come legally of age till she is thirty-five.

LADY BRACKNELL. That does not seem to me to be a grave objection. Thirty-five is a very attractive age. London society is full of women of the very highest birth who have, of their own free choice, remained thirty-five for years. Lady Dumbleton is an instance in point. To my own knowledge she had been thirty-five ever since she arrived at the age of forty, which was many years ago now. I see no reason why our dear Cecily should not be even still more attractive at the age you mention than she is at present. There will be a large accumulation of property.

CECILY. Algy, could you wait for me till I was thirty-five?

ALGERNON. Of course I could, Cecily. You know I could.

CECILY. Yes, I felt it instinctively, but I couldn't wait all that time. I hate waiting even five minutes for anybody. It always makes me rather cross. I am not punctual myself, I know, but I do like punctuality in others, and waiting, even to be married, is quite out of the question.

ALGERNON. Then what is to be done, Cecily?

CECILY. I don't know, Mr. Moncrieff.

LADY BRACKNELL. My dear Mr. Worthing, as Miss Cardew states positively that she cannot wait till she is thirty-five—a remark which I am bound to say seems to me to show a somewhat impatient nature—I would beg of you to reconsider your decision.

JACK. But my dear Lady Bracknell, the matter is entirely in your own hands. The moment you consent to my marriage with Gwendolen, I will most gladly allow your nephew to form an alliance with my ward.

LADY BRACKNELL (*rising and drawing herself up*). You must be quite aware that what you propose is out of the question.

JACK. Then a passionate celibacy is all that any of us can look forward to.

LADY BRACKNELL. That is not the destiny I propose for Gwendolen. Algernon, of course, can choose for himself. (*Pulls out her watch.*) Come, dear, (GWENDOLEN *rises*) we have already missed five, if not six, trains. To miss any more might expose us to comment on the platform.

(*Enter* DR. CHASUBLE.)

CHASUBLE. Everything is quite ready for the christenings.

LADY BRACKNELL. The christenings, sir! Is not that somewhat premature?

CHASUBLE (*looking rather puzzled, and pointing to* JACK *and* ALGERNON). Both these gentlemen have expressed a desire for immediate baptism.

LADY BRACKNELL. At their age? The idea is grotesque and irreligious! Algernon, I forbid you to be baptised. I will not hear of such excesses. Lord Bracknell would be highly displeased if he learned that that was the way in which you wasted your time and money.

CHASUBLE. Am I to understand then that there are to be no christenings at all this afternoon?

JACK. I don't think that, as things are now, it would be of much practical value to either of us, Dr. Chasuble.

CHASUBLE. I am grieved to hear such sentiments from you, Mr. Worthing. They savour of the heretical views of the Anabaptists, views that I have completely refuted in four of my unpublished sermons. However, as your present mood seems to be one peculiarly secular, I will return to the church at once. Indeed, I have just been informed by the pew-opener that for the last hour and a half Miss Prism has been waiting for me in the vestry.

LADY BRACKNELL (*starting*). Miss Prism! Did I hear you mention a Miss Prism?

CHASUBLE. Yes, Lady Bracknell. I am on my way to join her.

LADY BRACKNELL. Pray allow me to detain you for a moment. This matter may prove to be one of vital importance to Lord Bracknell and myself. Is this Miss Prism a female of repellent aspect, remotely connected with education?

CHASUBLE (*somewhat indignantly*). She is the most cultivated of ladies, and the very picture of respectability.

LADY BRACKNELL. It is obviously the same person. May I ask what position she holds in your household?

CHASUBLE (*severely*). I am a celibate, madam.

JACK (*interposing*). Miss Prism, Lady Bracknell, has been for the last three years Miss Cardew's esteemed governesss and valued companion.

LADY BRACKNELL. In spite of what I hear of her, I must see her at once. Let her be sent for.

CHASUBLE (*looking off*). She approaches; she is nigh.

(*Enter* MISS PRISM *hurriedly*.)

MISS PRISM. I was told you expected me in the vestry, dear Canon. I have been waiting for you there for an hour and three-quarters. (*Catches sight of* LADY BRACKNELL, *who has fixed her with a stony glare*. MISS PRISM *grows pale and quails. She looks anxiously round as if desirous to escape*.)

LADY BRACKNELL (*in a severe, judicial voice*). Prism! (MISS PRISM *bows her head in shame.*) Come here, Prism! (MISS PRISM *approaches in a humble manner.*) Where is that baby? (*General consternation. The Canon starts back in horror.* ALGERNON *and* JACK *pretend to be anxious to shield* CECILY *and* GWENDOLEN *from hearing the details of a terrible public scandal.*) Twenty-eight years ago, Prism, you left Lord Bracknell's house, Number 104, Upper Grosvenor Street, in charge of a perambulator that contained a baby, of the male sex. You never returned. A few weeks later, through the elaborate investigations of the Metropolitan police, the perambulator was discovered at midnight, standing by itself in a remote corner of Bayswater. It contained the manuscript of a three-volume novel of more than usually revolting sentimentality. (MISS PRISM *starts in involuntary indignation.*) But the baby was not there! (*Everyone looks at* MISS PRISM.) Prism, where is that baby? (*A pause.*)

MISS PRISM. Lady Bracknell, I admit with shame that I do not know. I only wish I did. The plain facts of the case are these. On the morning of the day you mention, a day that is forever branded on my memory, I prepared as usual to take the baby out in its perambulator. I had also with me a somewhat old but capacious hand-bag in which I had intended to place the manuscript of a work of fiction that I had written during my few unoccupied hours. In a moment of mental abstraction, for which I never can forgive myself, I deposited the manuscript in the bassinette, and placed the baby in the hand-bag.

JACK (*who had been listening attentively*). But where did you deposit the hand-bag?

MISS PRISM. Do not ask me, Mr. Worthing.

JACK. Miss Prism, this is a matter of no small importance to me. I insist on knowing where you deposited the hand-bag that contained that infant.

MISS PRISM. I left it in the cloak-room of one of the larger railway stations in London.

JACK. What railway station?

MISS PRISM (*quite crushed*). Victoria. The Brighton line. (*Sinks into a chair.*)

JACK. I must retire to my room for a moment. Gwendolen, wait here for me.

GWENDOLEN. If you are not too long, I will wait here for you all my life.

(*Exit* JACK *in great excitement.*)

CHASUBLE. What do you think this means, Lady Bracknell?

LADY BRACKNELL. I dare not even suspect, Dr. Chasuble. I need hardly tell you that in families of high position strange coincidences are not supposed to occur. They are hardly considered the thing. (*Noises heard overhead as if someone was throwing trunks about. Everybody looks up.*)

CECILY. Uncle Jack seems strangely agitated.

CHASUBLE. Your guardian has a very emotional nature.

LADY BRACKNELL. This noise is extremely unpleasant. It sounds as if he was having an argument. I dislike arguments of any kind. They are always vulgar, and often convincing.

CHASUBLE (*looking up*). It has stopped now. (*The noise is redoubled.*)

LADY BRACKNELL. I wish he would arrive at some conclusion.

GWENDOLEN. The suspense is terrible. I hope it will last.

(*Enter* JACK *with a hand-bag of black leather in his hand.*)

JACK (*rushing over to* MISS PRISM). Is this the hand-bag, Miss Prism? Examine it carefully before you speak. The happiness of more than one life depends on your answers.

MISS PRISM (*calmly*). It seems to be mine. Yes, here is the injury it received through the upsetting of a Gower Street omnibus in younger and happier days. Here is the stain on the lining caused by the explosion of a temperance beverage, an incident that occurred at Leamington. And here, on the lock, are my initials. I had forgotten that in an extravagant mood I had had them placed there. The bag is undoubtedly mine. I am delighted to have it so unexpectedly restored to me. It has been a great inconvenience being without it all these years.

JACK (*in a pathetic voice*). Miss Prism, more is retored to you than this hand-bag. I was the baby you placed in it.

MISS PRISM (*amazed*). You?

JACK (*embracing her*). Yes . . . mother!

MISS PRISM (*recoiling in indignant astonishment*). Mr. Worthing! I am unmarried!

JACK. Unmarried! I do not deny that is a serious blow. But after all, who has the right to cast a stone against one who has suffered? Cannot repentance wipe out an act of folly? Why should there be one law for men and another for women? Mother, I forgive you. (*Tries to embrace her again.*)

MISS PRISM (*still more indignant*). Mr. Worthing, there is some error. (*Pointing to* LADY BRACKNELL.) There is the lady who can tell you who you really are.

JACK (*after a pause*). Lady Bracknell, I hate to seem inquisitive, but would you kindly inform me who I am?

LADY BRACKNELL. I am afraid that the news I have to give you will not altogether please you. You are the son of my poor sister, Mrs. Moncrieff, and consequently Algernon's elder brother.

JACK. Algy's elder brother! Then I have a brother after all. I knew I had a brother! I always said I had a brother! Cecily,—how could you have ever doubted that I had a brother? (*Seizes hold of* ALGERNON.) Dr. Chasuble, my unfortunate brother. Miss Prism, my unfortunate brother. Gwendolen, my unfortunate brother. Algy, you young scoundrel, you will have to treat me with more respect in the future. You have never behaved to me like a brother in all your life.

ALGERNON. Well, not till to-day, old boy, I admit. I did my best, however, though I was out of practice. (*Shakes hands.*)

GWENDOLEN (*to* JACK). My own! But what own are you? What is your Christian name, now that you have become someone else?

JACK. Good heavens! . . . I had quite forgotten that point. Your decision on the subject of my name is irrevocable, I suppose?

GWENDOLEN. I never change, except in my affections.

CECILY. What a noble nature you have, Gwendolen!

JACK. Then the question had better be cleared up at once. Aunt

Augusta, a moment. At the time when Miss Prism left me in the hand-bag, had I been christened already?

LADY BRACKNELL. Every luxury that money could buy, including christening, had been lavished on you by your fond and doting parents.

JACK. Then I was christened! That is settled. Now, what name was I given? Let me know the worst.

LADY BRACKNELL. Being the eldest son you were naturally christened after your father.

JACK (*irritably*). Yes, but what was my father's Christian name?

LADY BRACKNELL (*meditatively*). I cannot at the present moment recall what the General's Christian name was. But I have no doubt he had one. He was eccentric, I admit. But only in later years. And that was the result of the Indian climate, and marriage, and indigestion, and other things of that kind.

JACK. Algy! Can't you recollect what our father's Christian name was?

ALGERNON. My dear boy, we were never even on speaking terms. He died before I was a year old.

JACK. His name would appear in the Army Lists of the period, I suppose, Aunt Augusta?

LADY BRACKNELL. The general was essentially a man of peace, except in his domestic life. But I have no doubt his name would appear in any military directory.

JACK. The Army Lists of the last forty years are here. These delightful records should have been my constant study. (*Rushes to bookcase and tears the books out.*) M. Generals . . . Mallham, Maxbohm, Magley, what ghastly names they have—Markby, Migsby, Mobbs, Moncrieff! Lieutenant 1840, Captain, Lieutenant-Colonel, Colonel, General 1869, Christian names, Ernest John. (*Puts book very quietly down and speaks quite calmly.*) I always told you, Gwendolen, my name was Ernest, didn't I? Well, it is Ernest after all, I mean it naturally is Ernest.

LADY BRACKNELL. Yes, I remember the General was called Ernest. I knew I had some particular reason for disliking the name.

GWENDOLEN. Ernest! My own Ernest! I felt from the first that you could have no other name!

JACK. Gwendolen, it is a terrible thing for a man to find out suddenly that all his life he has been speaking nothing but the truth. Can you forgive me?

GWENDOLEN. I can. For I feel sure that you are sure to change.

JACK. My own one!

CHASUBLE (*to* Miss Prism). Lætitia! (*Embraces her.*)

MISS PRISM (*enthusiastically*). Frederick! At last!

ALGERNON. Cecily! (*Embraces her.*) At last!

JACK. Gwendolen! (*Embraces her.*) At last!

LADY BRACKNELL. My nephew, you seem to be displaying signs of triviality.

JACK. On the contrary, Aunt Augusta, I've now realized for the first time in my life the vital Importance of Being Earnest.

TABLEAU

CURTAIN

ENDNOTES

1. (p. 5) *Macpherson, Ireland, and Chatterton:* In the Pre-Romantic period James Macpherson (1736–1796), William Ireland (1777–1835), and Thomas Chatterton (1752–1770) created the "forged" poetical works of actual poets like Shakespeare (Ireland), imaginary figures like the Celtic bard Ossian (Macpherson), and the medieval song-writer Rowley (Chatterton). These pretended original works were all significant for Romantic poetry, not least because they cast doubt on the dubious belief that humans can "own ideas" which in turn become their intellectual property, and hence possible unwitting causes of their own forgery. The authors named all belong to, or pretend to belong to, a period when most poetry was oral and aural and traditional in its spirit and its production. Wilde notes them in order to raise subtle questions about authentication which arise when we speak of any author's "original" works—that is, when we try to fix the sense in which an invented imaginary work is held to be "true" or "truthful" in its fictive dreams. Here, as elsewhere, Wilde inherits the romantic view of art.
2. (p. 12) *any publisher of the time:* Throughout the ensuing passage Wilde suggests several historical barriers against learning or fixing the identity of persons known by mere initials, such as "Mr. W. H.," chiefly because modern historians lack the social details of an early period. By mentioning actual persons like Lord Buckhurst, Fitton, Vernon, Hathaway, Willobie, Drayton, Davies, and others, the "Portrait" changes the direction of its narrative—away from the notorious literary puzzle of "Mr. W. H.," a famous bibliographic publishing riddle, toward another mystery, one that really interests Wilde. This central enigma is the Platonic question of inspiration, since Wilde's imagined Willie Hewes, whose portrait may or not be authentic, becomes a magically inspiring

presence both for Shakespeare and for its discoverer, Cyril Graham. Finally all parties to the narrative begin to share in a metaphysical question, raised often by Shakespeare himself, whether we humans are not in fact living a dream existence. If so, then history itself is a fiction. The known poets Michael Drayton and Sir John Davies then become "unreal," though we can "verify" their existence in the *Dictionary of National Biography*.

3. (p. 46) *Robin Armin:* As he does throughout the "portrait," Wilde here builds a composite picture gallery of linked names in which the aim is not so much to show particular cases as to convey the general probability that there were numerous young and beautiful boy-actors who might just as well be called "Willie Hewes." He uses particular names to create the merest illusion of proof, to be sure, but the names of the plays and court-masques of playwrights like Ben Jonson (1572–1637) and Philip Massinger (1583–1640) conspire to suggest why connoisseurs of theater believed that women could not perform women's roles with the same grace and power as could these adolescent male actors. Fearful Puritan attitudes rebelled against the gender-changing illusion, and Wilde in turn, like other artists, felt free to attack Puritan "uncouth morals and ignoble minds." Sir Philip Sidney wrote his great *Defence of Poesie* (1579–1580) precisely to show that Puritan attacks—like those of Stephen Gosson, William Prynne, and Francis Lenton, mentioned below, when they fulminated against poetry and the stage—were expressions of aesthetic fear. Among them, Prynne suffered a cruel penalty, for in the 1630s he was pilloried and had both ears cut off. Let no one say that literature is mere verbiage.

4. (p. 273) *The English Renaissance:* Wilde was accustomed to improvising his public lectures, which he had already practiced while lecturing in Britain, but when he arrived in New York, famously declaring his genius, he nevertheless seems to have hesitated over what to include in his first public appearance. Finally, during his first week on American shores, he wrote out a lecture on the English Renaissance and its modern significance, had the lecture typed, and delivered it to a capacity crowd in Chickering

Hall on January 9, 1882. Over the course of his lecturing marathon he was to use this text many times, often shortening it to fit the occasion. Eventually he decided to add two other speeches to his repertory—"The House Beautiful" and "The Decorative Arts."

Despite massive press coverage and much obsessive public fascination with Wilde's dandified costume and his authority in matters of fashion, the Renaissance oration remained central to his tour. According to Robert Ross, his close friend and his 1908 editor, the talk exists in at least four versions, of which the one reprinted in this edition is not the longest. Nevertheless, our reprint gives the full flavor of Wilde's Renaissance enthusiasms and his noble, at times ironic, casually amusing, and always entertaining way of introducing and amplifying an important historical subject.

5. (p. 491) *Socialism:* Wilde initially presents his case for "socialism" as an antidote for the Victorian pretense of "charitable deeds," which flatter the donor's conscience while doing nothing substantial to remedy the causes of jobless poverty. Like certain Marxists of a later date, he suggests that such philanthropy is not only a travesty of Christian generosity but also is politically flawed by its fundamental contradictions. The essay makes a political plea for a method of truly shared wealth, for a true "common wealth." But Wilde, as always, must be read in the terms of his theory of Art, in which we find him calling poets, philosophers, and scientists "the real men," owing to their basic independence, their "individualism."

The reader should therefore take this essay as a brief treatise on the individual as creative being, since those real men are real because they "have realized themselves," and in them "all Humanity gains a partial realization." Such utopian words and thought will be seen to carry Wilde beyond political theory, as enunciated by Herbert Spencer's "social Darwinism" or by any other extended versions of Darwinian principles. These ideas had long fascinated the poet—he had noted in his college notebooks that Darwin was a chief modern philosophical truth-bearer, to whom all serious thinkers must now pay heed. Making this philosophical case, Wilde's *Soul of Man* adduces the Socratic maxim "Know Thyself," which leads Wilde to the wisdom of Marcus Aurelius, to the great English Romantic poets, and finally to the spiritual teachings of Jesus. He imagines the socialist view of a just world much as if he were what is called a "primitive" Christian, a Christian acting before St. Paul's organization of the faith, and certainly before the later ecclesiastical ordering of Christianity as a "religion."

Critical to all such "political" discussions is their spirit, and in this vein the essay focuses on the common public fear of novelty, specifically as represented by artists, since "Art is Individualism," while "Individualism is a disturbing and disintegrating force." To overcome this fear is the task of Wildean socialism, and success in this attempt will minister to the soul of man. The poet seems to be punning on one of his given names, even as he reminds his reader of real working and living conditions.

The reader will therefore need to recall that Wilde had always recognized and spoken of the vicious reality and causes of poverty, especially in the Victorian city, be it Dublin or London. He recognized and knew facts of the tragic fury of Chicago's 1886 Haymarket Riots, and of riots and retributions equally evil in Britain. As a man of the world and a journalist, he had always studied the wide-ranging conditions of culture, from the bottom levels up to the top. Hence his essay may be taken as an interpretive gloss on more purely literary and artistic essays, such as "The Decay of Lying." By linking a political theory, however loosely defined, to the spiritual life of mankind, the essay carries pragmatic thought to the highest level, reminding us that to read Wilde is to read utopian hope into the most distressing ironies of honest social perceptions. Like other utopian thinkers, Wilde expresses his hope that artistic imagination will lead us all to imagine better future conditions, equally shared by all. One senses that Wilde, at this stage of his career, is attempting to weave the aesthetic pursuit of beauty and balance into the cloth Darwin wove as the main principle of his *Origin of Species:* "Evolution is the law of life, and there is no evolution except towards

Individualism." We are to imagine that whatever Art is, it must rise to the philosophic status of a paradigm as grand as Darwinian theory itself.

At the same time, this essay signals to the reader that Wilde is a strange combination of spiritual thinker and pragmatic observer. One comes away from the essay thinking that he wants himself, and us, to do good deeds in the world. If Bertrand Russell the agnostic could later argue the case for "a free man's worship," so Wilde in this essay argues the case for the individual artist's worship—or, as Franz Kafka would say, he argues for writing as a form of prayer.

ORIGINAL PUBLICATION INFORMATION

The Portrait of Mr. W. H., p. 5: This expanded version was originally published in 1921. An early version was first published in *Blackwood's Edinburgh Magazine* (July 1889).

Lord Arthur Savile's Crime, p. 79: First published in serial form in the *Court and Society Review* (May 1887) and subtitled "A Study of Cheiromancy." Printed here is the slightly revised version from *Lord Arthur Savile's Crime and Other Stories* (1891).

The Model Millionaire, p. 113: First published in *The World* (June 22, 1887) and reprinted in *Lord Arthur Savile's Crime and Other Stories* (1891).

The Canterville Ghost, p. 119: First published in the *Court and Society Review* (March 2, 1887) and reprinted in *Lord Arthur Savile's Crime and Other Stories* (1891).

The Young King, p. 148: First published in *Lady's Pictorial* (December 1888) and reprinted in *A House of Pomegranates* (1891).

The Birthday of the Infanta, p. 162: First published in *Paris Illustré* (March 30, 1889), in both French and English, and reprinted in *A House of Pomegranates* (1891).

The Fisherman and His Soul, p. 181: First published in *A House of Pomegranates* (1891).

The Remarkable Rocket, p. 214: First published in *The Happy Prince and Other Tales* (1888).

The Artist, p. 229: First published in *Poems in Prose* in the *Fortnightly Review* (July 1894).

The Disciple, p. 229: First published in the *Spirit Lamp* (June 6, 1893) and reprinted, with revisions, in *Poems in Prose* in the *Fortnightly Review* (July 1894).

The Master, p. 230: First published in *Poems in Prose* in the *Fortnightly Review* (July 1894).

The House of Judgment, p. 231: First published in the *Spirit Lamp* (February 17, 1893) and reprinted, with revisions, in *Poems in Prose* in the *Fortnightly Review* (July 1894).

The Teacher of Wisdom, p. 232: First published in *Poems in Prose* in the *Fortnightly Review* (July 1894).

Theocritus, p. 241: First published in *Poems* (1881).

The Harlot's House, p. 242: First published in the *Dramatic Review* (April 11, 1885).

Impression de Voyage, p. 243: First published in *Waifs and Strays* (March 1880). A slightly revised version titled *Impression du Voyage* appeared in *Poems* (1881). The poem reverted to its original title in *Poems* (1882).

Impression du Matin, p. 244: First published as *Impression de Matin* in *The World* (March 2, 1881). Printed here is the revised version from *Poems* (1881).

Symphony in Yellow, p. 245: First published in the *Centennial Magazine* (February 5, 1889).

Impression: Le Réveillon, p. 245: First published in *Poems* (1881), this poem is the revised second stanza of "Lotus Leaves," which first appeared in the *Irish Monthly* (February, 1887).

Impressions: [1] Le Jardin, [2] La Mer, [3] Le Jardin des Tuileries, p. 246: [1] First published in *Our Continent* (February 15, 1882). [2] First published in *Our Continent* (February 15, 1882). [3] First published in *In a Good Cause* (1885).

The Ballad of Reading Gaol, p. 248: First published in 1898 under the pseudonym C.3.3., which was Wilde's prisoner number. Printed here is the revised edition, which appeared the same year.

The English Renaissance, p. 273: First delivered in New York City on January 9, 1882. Text from *The Works of Oscar Wilde: Poems in Prose*, Sunflower Edition (New York: Lamb Publishers: 1909).

Decorative Art in America, p. 282: First delivered in New York

City on May 11, 1882. Text from *Decorative Art in America*, edited by Richard Butler Glaenzer (New York, 1906).

Impressions of America, p. 295: Lecture given by Wilde following his return from the United States in 1883. Text from *Impressions of America*, edited by Stuart Mason (London, 1912).

The American Invasion, p. 301: From the *Court and Society Review* (March 23, 1887). Unsigned.

The American Man, p. 305: From the *Court and Society Review* (April 13, 1887). Unsigned.

Mr. Whistler's Ten O'Clock, p. 313: From the *Pall Mall Gazette* (February 21, 1885).

The Relation of Dress to Art, p. 317: From the *Pall Mall Gazette* (February 28, 1885).

London Models, p. 321: From the *English Illustrated Magazine* (January 1889).

Dinners and Dishes, p. 331: Review of *Dinners and Dishes*, by an author using the pseudonym "Wanderer." From the *Pall Mall Gazette* (March 7, 1885). Unsigned.

To Read, or Not to Read, p. 334: From the *Pall Mall Gazette* (February 8, 1886).

Balzac in English, p. 336: Review of Honoré de Balzac's *The Duchesse de Langeais, and Other Stories*. From the *Pall Mall Gazette* (September 13, 1886). Unsigned.

The Poets and the People, p. 340: From the *Pall Mall Gazette* (February 17, 1887). Unsigned.

Poetry and Prison, p. 343: Review of *In Vinculis*, by Wilfrid Scawen Blunt, and *Grass of Parnassus*, by Andrew Lang. From the *Pall Mall Gazette* (January 3, 1889). Unsigned.

The Gospel According to Walt Whitman, p. 348: Review of Walt Whitman's "November Boughs," a late addition to his *Leaves of Grass*. From the *Pall Mall Gazette* (January 25, 1889). Unsigned.

Mr. Pater's Last Volume [Appreciations], p. 353: From *The Speaker* (March 22, 1890).

The Decay of Lying, p. 361: From *Intentions* (1891). Previously appeared in an earlier version in *The Nineteenth Century* (January 1889).

The Critic as Artist, Part I, p. 393: From *Intentions* (1891). Previously appeared in an earlier version in *The Nineteenth Century* (July 1890).

The Critic as Artist, Part II, p. 426: From *Intentions* (1891). Previously appeared in an earlier version in *The Nineteenth Century* (September 1890).

The Truth of Masks, p. 464: From *Intentions* (1891). Previously appeared in an earlier version in *The Nineteenth Century* (May 1885).

The Soul of Man under Socialism, p. 491: From the *Fortnightly Review* (February 1891). Reprinted as *The Soul of Man* (1895).

A Few Maxims for the Instruction of the Over-Educated, p. 529: From the *Saturday Review* (November 17, 1894). Unsigned.

Phrases and Philosophies for the Use of the Young, p. 531: From *The Chameleon* (December 1894).

Preface to *The Picture of Dorian Gray*, p. 534: First published in Philadelphia in *Lippincott's Monthly Magazine* (July 20, 1890, pp. 3–100). First published in England in the *Fortnightly Review* (March 1891). Printed here is the slightly revised version that was added as a preface to the novel upon its publication as a single volume in 1891.

The Importance of Being Earnest, p. 537: The play was originally written in four acts and was first performed in 1895. This text is the later three-act play that combines the original acts II and III.

INSPIRED BY OSCAR WILDE

THE TRIALS OF OSCAR WILDE

The centennial of Oscar Wilde's tragic trials and conviction on charges of "gross indecency" gave rise to a rash of works dedicated to telling the story of the brilliant novelist and playwright, whose career was so suddenly cut short. Two historical approaches to Wilde's trials were published: *The Trials of Oscar Wilde: Deviance, Morality, and Late-Victorian Society*, by Michael S. Foldy (1997), followed by *Oscar Wilde's Last Stand: Decadence, Conspiracy, and the Most Outrageous Trial of the Century* (1998), by Philip Hoare. In 1997 *Wilde*, a film based on Richard Ellmann's 1988 biography *Oscar Wilde*, premiered, with Stephen Fry perfectly cast as the notorious Dubliner; this biopic, directed by Brian Gilbert, unlike earlier films such as 1960's *The Trials of Oscar Wilde*, provides a panoramic portrait of Wilde's life.

Perhaps the most appropriate tribute to Wilde was the proliferation, in the late 1990s, of plays dedicated to his memory. Thomas Kilroy's *The Secret Fall of Constance Wilde* (1997) deals with Wilde's often unnoticed wife and the mother of his two children. *The Judas Kiss* (1998), written by David Hare, develops the twin themes of love and betrayal as it focuses on Wilde and his lover Lord Alfred Douglas. In *Gross Indecency: The Three Trials of Oscar Wilde* (1997), playwright Moisés Kaufman weaves together court transcripts and Wilde's writing and quotations.

THE IMPORTANCE OF BEING EARNEST ON SCREEN

Three years after their 1999 film adaptation of Wilde's *An Ideal Husband*, director Oliver Parker and actor Rupert Everett teamed up again to make the charmingly droll *The Importance of Being Earnest*. In the 2002 film, Everett plays Algy, and Colin Firth (*Pride and Prejudice*) plays his cohort Jack Worthing. Parker's film flaunts a variety of London settings that surface in flashback and fantasy sequences (of questionable success). The film's sumptuousness often trumps the power of Wilde's language, painting a world in which characters seem to recite quotations rather than speak. The production is saved by superior acting, however, in particular by Judi Dench as the imperious Lady Bracknell and Reese Witherspoon as insipid Cecily Cardew.

An earlier and notable screen incarnation of *The Importance of Being Earnest*, in 1952, was adapted and directed by Anthony Asquith (*Pygmalion*). Sir Michael Redgrave steals the show as Jack Worthing; Michael Denison breathes sardonic charm into Algernon; the fierce Margaret Rutherford plays Miss Prism with intelligence; and Dame Edith Evans plays Lady Bracknell in what is probably that character's most famous portrayal (Evans had played the icy Bracknell onstage countless times prior to the film). Asquith's adaptation does not take the play far from its theatrical roots; indeed, a Technicolor red curtain opening and closing on the stage emphasizes them. Primacy is given to the lines themselves, which are rarely interrupted by fancy camera tricks and distracting interiors. An interesting note: Asquith, a gay man, was the son of British home secretary and, later, prime minister Herbert Asquith. It was the elder Asquith who ordered Wilde's arrest, which in turn led to his conviction on charges of "gross indecency" and his subsequent imprisonment.

COMMENTS & QUESTIONS

In this section, we aim to provide the reader with an array of perspectives on the text, as well as questions that challenge those perspectives. The commentary has been culled from sources as diverse as comments contemporaneous with the work, literary criticism of later generations, and appreciations written throughout the work's history. Following the commentary, a series of questions seeks to filter the writings in The Collected Oscar Wilde *through a variety of points of view and bring about a richer understanding of these enduring works.*

COMMENTS

Arthur Symons

Mr. Wilde is much too brilliant to be ever believed; he is much too witty to be ever taken seriously. A passion for caprice, a whimsical Irish temperament, a love of art for art's sake—it is in qualities such as these that we find the origin of the beautiful farce of æstheticism, the exquisite echoes of the *Poems*, the subtle decadence of *Dorian Gray*, and the paradoxical truths, the perverted common sense, of the *Intentions*. Mr. Wilde, with a most reasonable hatred of the *bourgeois* seriousness of dull people, has always taken refuge from the commonplace in irony. Intentionally or not—scarcely without intention—he has gained a reputation for frivolity which does injustice to a writer who has at least always been serious in the reality of his devotion to art. The better part of his new book [*Intentions*] is simply a plea for the dignity, an argument for the supremacy, of imaginative art.

—from an unsigned review in the *Speaker* (July 4, 1891)

W. B. Yeats

Here now is Mr. Oscar Wilde, who does not care what strange opinions he defends or what time-honoured virtue he makes laughter of, provided he does it cleverly. Many were injured by the escapades of the rakes and duellists, but no man is likely to be the worse for Mr. Wilde's shower of paradox. We are not likely to poison any one because he writes with appreciation of Wainwright—art critic and poisoner—nor have I heard that there has been any increased mortality among deans because the good young hero of his last book tries to blow up one with an infernal machine; but upon the other hand we are likely enough to gain something of brightness and refinement from the deft and witty pages in which he sets forth these matters.

"Beer, bible, and the seven deadly virtues have made England what she is," wrote Mr. Wilde once; and a part of the Nemesis that has fallen upon her is a complete inability to understand anything he says. *We* should not find him so unintelligible—for much about him is Irish of the Irish. I see in his life and works an extravagant Celtic crusade against Anglo-Saxon stupidity. "I labour under a perpetual fear of not being misunderstood," he wrote, a short time since, and from behind this barrier of misunderstanding he peppers John Bull with his pea-shooter of wit, content to know there are some few who laugh with him.

—from *United Ireland* (September 26, 1891)

Max Beerbohm

Except Ruskin in his prime, no modern writer has achieved through prose the limpid and lyrical effects that were achieved by Oscar Wilde. One does not seem to be reading a written thing. The words sing. There is nothing of that formality, that hard and cunning precision, which marks so much of the prose that we admire, and rightly admire. The meaning is artificial, but the expression is always magically natural and beautiful. The simple words seem to grow together like wild flowers. In his use of rhyme and metre, Oscar Wilde was academic—never at all decadent, by the way, as one critic has suggested. But the prose of the *Intentions*, and of his plays, and of his fairy-stories, was perfect in its lively and unstudied grace.

—from *Vanity Fair* (March 2, 1905)

G. K. Chesterton

Now Wilde often uttered remarks which he must have known to be literally valueless. Shaw may be high or low, but he never talks down to the audience. Wilde did talk down, sometimes very far down.

Wilde and his school professed to stand as solitary artistic souls apart from the public. They professed to scorn the middle class, and declared that the artist must not work for the bourgeois. The truth is that no artist so really great ever worked so much for the bourgeois as Oscar Wilde. No man, so capable of thinking about truth and beauty, ever thought so constantly about his own effect on the middle classes. He studied the Surbiton school-mistress with exquisite attention, and knew exactly how to shock and how to please her. Mr. Shaw often gets above her in seraphic indignation, and often below her in sterile and materialistic explanations. He disgusts her with new truths or he bores her with old truths; but they are always living truths to Bernard Shaw. Wilde knew how to say the precise thing which, whether true or false, is irresistible. As, for example, 'I can resist anything but temptation.'

But he sometimes sank lower, sank into the lowest gorges and chasms of Surbiton. One might go through his swift and sparkling plays with a red and blue pencil marking two kinds of epigrams; the real epigram which he wrote to please his own wild intellect, and the sham epigram which he wrote to thrill the very tamest part of our tame civilization. This is what I mean by saying that he was strictly a charlatan—among other things. He descended below himself to be on top of others. He became purposely stupider than Oscar Wilde that he might seem cleverer than the nearest curate. He lowered himself to superiority; he stooped to conquer.

One might easily take examples of the phrase meant to lightly touch the truth and the phrase meant only to bluff the bourgeoisie.

For instance, in *A Woman of No Importance*, he makes his chief philosopher say that all thought is immoral, being essentially destructive; 'Nothing survives being thought of.' That is nonsense, but nonsense of the nobler sort; there is an idea in it. It is, like most professedly modern ideas, a death-dealing idea not a life-giving one; but it is an idea. There is truly a sense in which all definition is deletion. Turn a few pages of the same play and you will find somebody asking, 'What is an immoral woman?' The philosopher answers, 'The kind of woman a man never gets tired of.' Now that is not nonsense, but rather rubbish. It is without value of any sort or kind. It is not symbolically true; it is not fantastically true; it is not true at all.

Anyone with the mildest knowledge of the world knows that nobody can be such a consuming bore as a certain kind of immoral woman. That vice never tires men, might be a tenable and entertaining lie; that the individual instrument of vice never tires them is not, even as a lie, tenable enough to be entertaining. Here the great wit was playing the cheap dandy to the incredibly innocent; as much as if he had put on paper cuffs and collars. He is simply shocking a tame curate; and he must be rather a specially tame curate even to be shocked. This irritating duplication of real brilliancy with snobbish bluff runs through all his three comedies. 'Life is much too important to be taken seriously'; that is the true humorist. 'Man can believe the impossible, but man can never believe the improbable'; that is said by a fine philosopher. 'Nothing is so fatal to a personality as the keeping of promises, unless it be telling the truth'; that is said by a tried quack. 'A man can be happy with any woman so long as he does not love her'; that is wild truth. 'Good intentions are invariably ungrammatical'; that is tame trash.

—from the *Daily News* (October 19, 1909)

James Joyce

The truth is that Wilde, far from being a perverted monster who sprang in some inexplicable way from the civilization of modern England, is the logical and inescapable product of the Anglo-Saxon college and university system, with its secrecy and restrictions. . . .

And here is the pulse of Wilde's art—sin. He deceived himself into believing that he was the bearer of good news of neo-paganism to an enslaved people. His own characteristic qualities, the qualities, perhaps, of his race—wit, generosity, and a sexless intellect—he placed at the service of a theory of beauty which, according to him, was to bring back the Golden Age and the joy of the world's youth. But if some truth adheres to his subjective interpretations of Aristotle, to his restless thought that proceeds by sophisms and not by syllogisms, to his assimilations of other natures, alien to his own, as the delinquent is to the humble, it is the inherent truth in the soul of Catholicism: that man cannot arrive at the divine heart except through that sense of separation and loss called sin.

—from *Il Piccolo della Sera* (March 24, 1909)

Richard Le Galienne

The writings of Oscar Wilde, brilliant and even beautiful as they are, are but the marginalia, so to say, of a strikingly fantastic personality.

—from *The Works of Oscar Wilde* (1909)

Arthur Ransome

Wilde preserved, even in those of his writings that cost him most dearly, a feeling of recreation. His books are those of a wonderfully gifted and accomplished man who is an author only in his moments of leisure. Only one comparison is possible, and that is with Horace Walpole; but Wilde's was infinitely the richer intellect. Walpole is weighted by his distinction. Wilde wears his like a flower. Walpole is without breadth, or depth, and equals only as a gossip Wilde's enchanting freedom as a juggler with ideas. Wilde was indolent and knew it. Indolence was, perhaps, the only sin that stared him in the face as he lay dying, for it was the only one that he had committed with a bad conscience. It had lessened his achievement, and left its marks on what he had done. Even in his best work he is sometimes ready to secure an effect too easily. "Meredith is a prose Browning, and so is Browning," may be regarded as an example of such effects.

Much of his work fails; much of it has faded, but *Intentions*, *The Sphinx*, *The Ballad of Reading Gaol*, *Salomé*, *The Importance of Being Earnest*, one or two of the fairy tales, and *De Profundis*, are surely enough with which to challenge the attention of posterity.

These things were the toys of a critical spirit, of a critic as artist, of a critic who took up first one and then another form of art, and played with it almost idly, one and then another form of thought, and gave it wings for the pleasure of seeing it in the light; of a man of action with the eyes of a child; of a man of contemplation curious of all the secrets of life, not only of those that serve an end; of a virtuoso with a distaste for the obvious and a delight in disguising subtlety behind a mask of the very obvious that he disliked. His love for the delicate and the rare brought him into the power of things that are vulgar and coarse. His attempt to weave his life as a tapestry clothed him in a soiled and unbeautiful reality. Even this he was able to subdue. *Nihil tetigit quod non ornavit.* He touched nothing that he did not decorate. He touched nothing that he did not turn into a decoration.

—from *Oscar Wilde: A Critical Study* (1912)

Edward Shanks

[Wilde] was not an originator, he was, much as he would have disliked the designation, a populariser. He summarised in his work what was then called *fin de siècle* art, and made it easy for the great public to understand. Almost every aspect of the movement was there. The sensualism of Baudelaire and his hinting at strange vices, Gautier's disinterested immoral adoration of things, hard, bright, and sharp-edged, Verlaine's religiosity—all these with dashes of Satanism and cruelty and just so much of the doctrines of Ruskin and Morris as could be made to fit in with the rest without too startling an incongruity. One might almost say that Wilde was not so much a writer as a museum.

—from the *London Mercury* (July 1924)

QUESTIONS

1. Wilde established himself as an arbiter of style, and above all he reproached mediocrity—"the English public always feels perfectly at ease when a mediocrity is talking to it"—yet we might ask how a democratic society can rise above such mediocrity and still remain democratic. Was Wilde an elitist? Is art necessarily elitist, like professional sports?

2. The great Irish poet William Butler Yeats tells us that for Wilde there was a direct line between boredom—including boring behavior and lack of imagination—and "the seven deadly virtues." Is it possible that Wilde wanted to reveal that virtue, as commonly understood, is only a hypocritical veil thrown over the dishonest or shameful things we humans actually do?

3. According to Beerbohm, Wilde mostly wrote his poems in an academic and conventional style. *The Ballad of Reading Gaol* adopts traditional ballad meter, somewhat like S. T. Coleridge's *Rime of the Ancient Mariner*. Can one make the case that the terrifying story of an execution in Wilde's *Ballad* required the poet to neutralize our fear by using ancient rhymes and rhythms?

4. While G. K. Chesterton praises much of Wilde's epigrammatic wit, he also attacks him for playing down to audiences, thus demeaning his gift. But is it fair to ask an entertainer, who writes for a living, to deny the groundlings their unsophisticated pleasures? Is there a hypocritical vein in Wilde's wit?

5. If we follow Richard le Galienne, we may think that a poet's work is the direct mirror of his life. Is this a useful biographical approach for reading Wilde? How would this relate to Wilde's Irish heritage?

6. "The Decay of Lying" is about the decay of truth-telling in Victorian times. If to be a hypocrite is a full-time job, is it possible that Wilde's satire throughout his plays and criticism is intended less to expose personal errors of judgment than to expose the cynical exploitation of unchallenged political, economic, and religious power?

FOR FURTHER READING

WRITINGS OF OSCAR WILDE

The Artist as Critic: Critical Writings of Oscar Wilde. Edited by Richard Ellmann. New York: Random House, 1969.

The Complete Letters of Oscar Wilde. Edited by Merlin Holland and Rupert Hart-Davis. New York: Henry Holt, 2000.

The Complete Shorter Fiction. Edited by Isobel Murray. Oxford: Oxford University Press, 1979.

Complete Works of Oscar Wilde. Edited by Vyvyan Holland. London: Collins, 1966.

The Definitive Four-Act Version of "The Importance of Being Earnest." Edited by Ruth Berggren. New York: Vanguard, 1987.

The Importance of Being Earnest. Edited by Russell Jackson. New Mermaid Series. New York: W. W. Norton, 1980.

The Importance of Being Earnest and Four Other Plays. Edited by Kenneth Krauss. New York: Barnes and Noble Classics, 2003.

Selected Journalism. Edited by Anya Clayworth. Oxford: Oxford University Press, 2004.

WORKS RELATED TO WILDE'S LIFE AND WRITING

Beckson, Karl, ed. *Oscar Wilde: The Critical Heritage.* London: Routledge and Kegan Paul, 1970.

Bloom, Harold, ed. *Oscar Wilde.* Modern Critical Views. New York: Chelsea House, 1985.

Brown, Julia Prewitt. *Cosmopolitan Criticism: Oscar Wilde's Philosophy of Art.* Charlottesville: University Press of Virginia, 1997.

Calloway, Stephen. "Wilde and the Dandyism of the Senses," in *The Cambridge Companion to Oscar Wilde*, edited by Peter Raby. Cambridge: Cambridge University Press, 1997, pp. 34–54.

Danson, Lawrence. *Wilde's Intentions: The Artist in His Criticism.* Oxford: Clarendon Press, 1997.

Douglas, Lord Alfred. *The Autobiography of Lord Alfred Douglas.* London: Martin Secker, 1929.

Dowling, Linda. *The Vulgarization of Art: The Victorians and Aesthetic Democracy.* Charlottesville: University Press of Virginia, 1996.

———, ed. *The Soul of Man under Socialism and Selected Critical Prose*, by Oscar Wilde. With a critical introduction and explanatory notes. London: Penguin Books, 2001.

Ellmann, Richard. *Oscar Wilde.* New York: Alfred A. Knopf, 1988.

Eltis, Sos. *Revising Wilde: Society and Subversion in the Plays of Oscar Wilde.* Oxford: Clarendon Press, 1996.

Fletcher, Ian, and John Stokes. "Oscar Wilde," in *Anglo-Irish Literature: A Review of Research*, edited by Richard J. Finneran. New York: Modern Language Association of America, 1976.

———. "Oscar Wilde." In *Recent Research on Anglo-Irish Writers*, edited by Richard J. Finneran. New York: Modern Language Association of America, 1983.

Frye, Northrop. *The Secular Scripture: A Study of the Structure of Romance.* Cambridge, MA: Harvard University Press, 1976.

Gagnier, Regenia. *Idylls of the Marketplace: Oscar Wilde and the Victorian Public.* Stanford, CA: Stanford University Press, 1986.

Gide, André. *Oscar Wilde.* Translated by Bernard Frechtman. New York: Philosophical Library, 1949.

Hall, N. John. *Max Beerbohm: A Kind of a Life.* New Haven, CT: Yale University Press, 2002.

Holland, Merlin, ed. *The Real Trial of Oscar Wilde: The First Uncensored Transcript of the Trial of Oscar Wilde vs. John Douglas, Marquess of Queensberry, 1895.* With introduction and commentary. Foreword by John Mortimer. New York: HarperCollins, 2003.

Holland, Vyvyan. *Son of Oscar Wilde.* 1954. Foreword by Merlin Holland. New York: Oxford University Press, 1988.

Hollander, Elizabeth. "Oscar Wilde," in *Encyclopedia of Aesthetics*, edited by Michael Kelly. New York: Oxford University Press, 1998, vol. 4, pp. 447–453.

Hyde, H. Montgomery. *Lord Alfred Douglas: A Biography.* New York: Dodd, Mead, 1985.

———. *Carson.* London: Heinemann, 1953.

Kiberd, Declan. "Oscar Wilde: The Resurgence of Lying," in *The Cambridge Companion to Oscar Wilde*, pp. 276–294.

Marcus, Steven. *The Other Victorians: A Study of Sexuality and Pornography in Mid-Nineteenth-Century England.* 1966. New York: Meridian, 1974.

Martin, R. B. *The Triumph of Wit: A Study of Victorian Comic Theory.* Oxford: Clarendon Press, 1974.

McCormack, Jerusha, ed. *Wilde the Irishman.* New Haven, CT: Yale University Press, 1998.

Norman, Marc, and Tom Stoppard. *Shakespeare in Love: A Screenplay.* New York: Hyperion, 1998.

Pater, Walter. *Plato and Platonism.* 1893. Edited by Martin Golding. New York: Barnes and Noble Books, 2005.

———. *The Renaissance: Studies in Art and Poetry.* Edited by D. L. Hill. Berkeley: University of California Press, 1980. (Hill includes the Conclusion, which had been dropped from the 1877 reprint of the 1873 edition, originally titled *Studies in the History of the Renaissance*.)

Pearson, Hesketh. *The Life of Oscar Wilde.* London: Methuen, 1954.

Raby, Peter. *Oscar Wilde.* New York: Cambridge University Press, 1988.

———, ed. *The Cambridge Companion to Oscar Wilde.* Cambridge: Cambridge University Press, 1997.

Sainsbury, R. M. *Paradoxes.* Cambridge: Cambridge University Press, 1988.

Schoenbaum, S. *Shakespeare's Lives.* Oxford: Clarendon Press, 1970.

Smith, Phillip E., and Michael S. Helfand, eds. *Oscar Wilde's Oxford Notebooks: A Portrait of Mind in the Making.* Oxford: Oxford University Press, 1989.

Stokes, John. *Oscar Wilde: Myths, Miracles, and Imitations.* Cambridge: Cambridge University Press, 1996.

Stoppard, Tom. *The Invention of Love.* New York: Grove Press, 1998.

Symons, Arthur. *A Study of Oscar Wilde.* London: Charles Sawyer, 1930.

White, Terence de Vere. *The Parents of Oscar Wilde: Sir William and Lady Wilde.* London: Hodder and Stoughton, 1967.

Jude the Obscure	Thomas Hardy	1-59308-035-2	$8.95
The Jungle	Upton Sinclair	1-59308-118-9	$9.95
The Last of the Mohicans	James Fenimore Cooper	1-59308-137-5	$9.95
Les Liaisons Dangereuses	Pierre Choderlos de Laclos	1-59308-240-1	$9.95
Little Women	Louisa May Alcott	1-59308-108-1	$7.95
Lost Illusions	Honoré de Balzac	1-59308-315-7	$11.95
Main Street	Sinclair Lewis	1-59308-386-6	$10.95
Mansfield Park	Jane Austen	1-59308-154-5	$6.95
The Metamorphosis and Other Stories	Franz Kafka	1-59308-029-8	$9.95
Moby-Dick	Herman Melville	1-59308-018-2	$11.95
My Ántonia	Willa Cather	1-59308-202-9	$6.95
Narrative of Sojourner Truth		1-59308-293-2	$7.95
The Odyssey	Homer	1-59308-009-3	$9.95
Oliver Twist	Charles Dickens	1-59308-206-1	$6.95
The Origin of Species	Charles Darwin	1-59308-077-8	$10.95
Paradise Lost	John Milton	1-59308-095-6	$9.95
Persuasion	Jane Austen	1-59308-130-8	$5.95
The Picture of Dorian Gray	Oscar Wilde	1-59308-025-5	$6.95
A Portrait of the Artist as a Young Man and Dubliners	James Joyce	1-59308-031-X	$8.95
Pride and Prejudice	Jane Austen	1-59308-201-0	$6.95
The Prince and Other Writings	Niccolò Machiavelli	1-59308-060-3	$5.95
The Red Badge of Courage and Selected Short Fiction	Stephen Crane	1-59308-119-7	$6.95
Republic	Plato	1-59308-097-2	$8.95
Robinson Crusoe	Daniel Defoe	1-59308-360-2	$6.95
The Scarlet Letter	Nathaniel Hawthorne	1-59308-207-X	$6.95
The Secret Agent	Joseph Conrad	1-59308-305-X	$8.95
Selected Stories of O. Henry		1-59308-042-5	$9.95
Sense and Sensibility	Jane Austen	1-59308-125-1	$5.95
Siddhartha	Hermann Hesse	1-59308-379-3	$8.95
The Souls of Black Folk	W. E. B. Du Bois	1-59308-014-X	$8.95
The Strange Case of Dr. Jekyll and Mr. Hyde and Other Stories	Robert Louis Stevenson	1-59308-131-6	$6.95
A Tale of Two Cities	Charles Dickens	1-59308-138-3	$6.95
Three Theban Plays	Sophocles	1-59308-235-5	$8.95
Thus Spoke Zarathustra	Friedrich Nietzsche	1-59308-278-9	$9.95
The Time Machine and The Invisible Man	H. G. Wells	1-59308-388-2	$7.95
Treasure Island	Robert Louis Stevenson	1-59308-247-9	$6.95
The Turn of the Screw, The Aspern Papers and Two Stories	Henry James	1-59308-043-3	$5.95
Uncle Tom's Cabin	Harriet Beecher Stowe	1-59308-121-9	$7.95
Vanity Fair	William Makepeace Thackeray	1-59308-071-9	$8.95
Walden and Civil Disobedience	Henry David Thoreau	1-59308-208-8	$8.95
The War of the Worlds	H. G. Wells	1-59308-362-9	$6.95
Ward No. 6 and Other Stories	Anton Chekhov	1-59308-003-4	$8.95
Wuthering Heights	Emily Brontë	1-59308-128-6	$5.95